CRIMSON SCIMITAR

Attack on America 2001-2027
Including the Official Proceedings of the
Capture and Trial of Osama bin Laden

"...the awakening epic novel of our times"

S.P. GROGAN

CRIMSON SCIMITAR

Attack on America 2001-2027
Including the Official Proceedings of the
Capture and Trial of Osama bin Laden

Addison & Highsmith

Addison & Highsmith Publishers

Las Vegas ◊ Chicago ◊ Palm Beach

Published in the United States of America by
Histria Books
7181 N. Hualapai Way, Ste. 130-86
Las Vegas, NV 89166 USA
HistriaBooks.com

Addison & Highsmith is an imprint of Histria Books. Titles published under the imprints of Histria Books are distributed worldwide.

All rights reserved. No part of this book may be reprinted or reproduced or utilized in any form or by any electronic, mechanical or other means, now known or hereafter invented, including photocopying and recording, or in any information storage or retrieval system, without the permission in writing from the Publisher.

This is a work of historical fiction. The story within has been based partly on actual events, previously written accounts, personal interviews, and news articles, with substantiation from newly-released U.S. documents gained through the Freedom of Information Act. For the most part names, characters, places, and incidents are used in a fictional manner, as are certain public figures. Any character resemblance to actual persons, living or dead, or events and locales is entirely coincidental except for existing news stories, actual events, and subjective views of history.

Library of Congress Control Number: 2023937878

ISBN 978-1-59211-331-6 (hardcover)
ISBN 978-1-59211-345-3 (eBook)

Copyright © 2023 by S.P. Grogan

"No act of terror can match the strength or the character of our country… nothing can ever break us."

Remarks from President Barack Obama at the dedication of the *National September 11 Memorial and Museum,* May 14, 2014

"It should not take another tragedy to unite our country."

9/11 name reader at annual remembrance ceremony September 11, 2022

Dedicated to the innocent victims of unholy perversity

Twin Towers on 9/11

REEL ONE

EPISODE ONE — Prologue

Scene 1: On That Day, Where Were They?
Setting: September 11, 2001, New York, Chicago, Jalalabad

Booker Langston, defense attorney

He was angry with her. Not really. His Tuesday schedule went into flux with his fiancée's casual request (non-negotiable demand) for a mutual shopping appointment before his afternoon court session, where he was set to deliver his closing argument, defending the accused.

Judy said it would be a quick decision on her final choice of the wedding gown design. But he knew women. Maybe he didn't. He did know that he was in love with investment banker/trader Judith Yu, her brilliance of mind, her beauty, the warmth of her smile, and her malleable body. The perfect cultural match: 3rd generation Chinese, she a math whiz, to merge by wedding vows to a 2nd generation African, his family political refugees, the elite of the previous regime, from a civil war in Liberia. Now, totally Americanized, successful though not yet rich, 'Bookie' was gaining a rep as a savvy defender of the legally entangled downtrodden of New York City. Complacent in his happiness within this work day, he had agreed to meet her in the lobby of the World Trade Center, North Tower. She would ride the elevator down from her currency exchange executive position in the financial trading office of Cantleigh & Fitzpatrick on the 103rd Floor. He checked his watch. 8:40 am. He picked up his pace, grinning. This time he would be early. Surprise her. He had flowers in his hand, a small bouquet.

The shadow of an aircraft momentarily darkened his steps. A grumbling scream filled the skies above his head, and then....

Hugh Fox, inventor/entrepreneur

He typed one word into his Tablet PC electronic notepad (re-purposed by his tinkering), *'Lunch, Wild Blue, late breakfast, after loan closes. They pay.'* To this engagement, he now added, *'Decline.'* The Wild Blue restaurant was part of the restaurant *Windows of the World* in the North Tower. More intimate for private business dealings, this smaller venue had the best views from the southern tip of Manhattan Island. Hugh Fox knew he would not be hungry, nor would he attend. Instead, he must rush back to his factory garret to complete another prototype. More so, he did not wish to be scrutinized too closely.

To make this loan, he had lied, or rather 'misdirected,' downplaying his involvement in his own loan funding. The Montblanc ink pen they had offered for initialing and signing the 35-page loan document would be their gift for the borrower. They, the bankers, looked as such, all formal uppity, suit uniforms of charcoal Emporio Armani, while his attorney, immaculate in pin-stripe Ermenegildo Zegna. Of course, the bankers would believe his attorney was the corporate borrower, for he had that money stuffiness look about him. It came from stratospheric legal billing, like today. Hugh could only afford to pay him two hours of contract work for agreeing to this prank charade.

Still the kid, wary of grown-ups, Hugh Fox did not yet feel comfortable around power, like the control of the purse, like bankers. Of the steep interest, an exorbitant 7.5% on new customer borrowed funds he would pay back to them; he prayed this would be the last time he would be dependent on debt. They would not appreciate his subterfuge. But risk takers take risks. This was to be his first formal corporate loan. Not much. $400,000. Still a great deal for any financial transaction of a boot-strapped, start-up technology firm in early fall of 2001.

When the loan documents were brought out, his attorney had asked for a private room for him and his 'aide' to discuss and sign the papers. The bankers had no problem with this; after all, the grey-haired attorney smiled respectability in his request. They paid the young man little attention in his tan khaki slacks and thin black tie with a white shirt (frayed at the sleeves), yet Hugh Fox was the true corporation at the table. He was the idea generator, the inventor, the scrounger of sophisticated second-hand motherboards, scrubber of floppies.

The bankers, with offices in the Deutsch Bank Building on Liberty Street, next to the World Trade Center complex, understood collateral risk, and they now had a lien on all his 'research equipment' including lockbox loan repayment on account receivables from his four sales contracts. He had accepted that he would make a deal with the devil to bring his products to market. As part of his ruse, his attorney had introduced him as the law office's runner, who would take the signed papers back to the law firm while the attorney would stay to handle the wire transfer details.

Everyone was in synch; both men exited the side office with the transactional legal mumbo-jumbo signed. The bankers then signed their pages, and all was concluded within 15 minutes. Acting in his toady courier role, Hugh exited carrying the papers under his arm; the attorney stayed to chat, pocketing the $200 Montblanc pen for himself for services rendered.

Crimson Scimitar

Hugh had done it. A little fakery, not fraudulent, but the bankers would not have loaned the funds to a 19-year-old kid, who some called an 'erratic genius,' where others colored him as wild and driven, tinged with unpredictability. The bankers were under the impression that the product he was developing and marketing was 'transistor type' because one of the contracts he had signed was with Radio Shack, giving comfort for a relationship with a major retail corporation and thus credence to an asset valuation to support the collateral. He told no one his prototype, ready for his small shop assembly line, was, in fact, going to be a video game of his own design for easy play on the industry's sixth generation of video game consoles, involving MMORPG (massively multiplayer online role-playing games). The Radio Shack sales contract was of little interest to Hugh; he was merely supplying tooled computer circuitry for how-to-kits, knocked off from a Japanese company for ready cash. As he had envisioned, the 'home run,' the 'pay dirt,' lay in video games for the masses. That was the future.

Like all those with a belief in themselves and their ideas, Hugh had hocked all his development and tooling equipment. Of the assets on his balance sheet, one line item he had excluded was for his three patents, the most valuable of all. These he controlled with fierceness, his future coin of the realm. One U.S. patent, granted in 1989 (when he was in high school!) for a system that he, with an advanced course for an accelerated MIT diploma, a degree at the age of 19, just completed, had prototyped his design bearing similarities closely mimicking the revolutionary Sega Dreamcast. By his own tweaks, there were enough variances to be awarded a 'new' allowed patent. He had engineered a 100 Kbps modem and his own modification of the PlanetWeb browser, moving from LAN networks to a more advanced player system for the improving internet. He called this system, *Skilleo*, betting that what he had researched was what the player market might want. A second patent, a 'method of play,' created by computer input, offered a social survey taken by the player of their thoughts that then would be imposed into a game character which would play the game as the player's doppelganger. Early A.I. The final patent, approved yet as a concept test program, would put the player's mind itself directly into video gameplay. Early Virtual Reality meets Sci-Fi futurism.

At this point in today's journey, he took no chance of street mugging interference or taxi mishaps and placed his signed loan papers into a large pre-stamped envelope taken from his back pocket. Though his attorney and the bank would have signed copies of the lending documents, he would take no chances of misadventure and deposited his future into the mail chute next to the building's bank of elevators. The U.S. Post office, he accepted, was the one institution that could perform reasonably well with first-class handling.

Hugh Fox felt, no, knew that with this lending capital, he could now succeed. He was in a buoyant mood. Then, just as his finger hit the elevator's down button, he looked out the hall window to see American Airlines Flight 11 hit the North Tower.

Shock — loss of momentary comprehension, a sudden horror realized. His mind clicked in. *Flee.* He avoided the elevator and took the stairs, ten flights down, skipping steps two at a time. He exited, out of breath, finding himself on the street in an unreal world of falling debris, glass fragment rain, the smell of burning jet fuel, and the detritus from 1,000 office desks. With little thought, he joined the growing melee of those believing stampeding and distancing from the tragedy was the best course of action.

His speed took him down Liberty Street; he cut over to Cortland and finally stopped running at the corner of Dey Street and Broadway. Stopping, sweating, catching his breath, admitting that his jumbled mind of fictional battle scenarios and designing ungodly creatures were overwhelmed by his morbid curiosity about the fire and smoke on the still quite visible landmark of the World Trade Center. It came to him perhaps to loiter somewhat, to bear witness (?), accepting that he was part of current headlines unfolding.

Transfixed, he was staring up at the conflagration when United Airlines Flight 175 hit the South Tower. His mind focused. This was an attack. Had to be. He witnessed a body falling from on high, then another. He had to do something, anything to help.

Samantha Carlisle, fashion designer

A hole-in-the-wall office, on the second floor, in the Garment District. The name on the glass kept simple. S. Carlisle, Creative Fashions. Sam, as she was known to amiable friends, Sammie to her family, wasn't satisfied with the moniker for a future fashion trademark. She would scribble out words, match, and juggle, but nothing screamed, 'famous apparel stylist works here.' Sam was smart, smart-alecky, with a natural dose of ambition. One had to be bold, if not brash, if not outlandish, to succeed in this world of couture glam.

Eve, one of her two seamstresses, arriving late, rushed in, slurring out her sentences.

"A plane hit the World Tower. And not a small plane, a big jet. You can see the smoke from the street." So, all three of them did just that. Sam, Eve, and Madeline, the other seamstress and the occasional part-time bookkeeper. She saw others were straying outside, glancing, peering down to the end of the island. And yes, black smoke appeared from not just one but both towers. *'How could one plane set both buildings on fire?'* thought Sam, now hearing the emergency sirens from all directions heading towards the 'accident.'

"Let's go, girls," Sam felt they had the broad picture, and the office television would have on-the-spot coverage, and quickly the news made all too apparent the reality of what had happened and what was happening. On TV, they were saying the words, 'terrorist attack.' Unbelievable. Madeline started to cry; Eve chewed on her fingernails.

The shop's 9:30 appointment had not appeared.

"The streets are going to be a nightmare jam," moaned Madeline, who lived over in Brooklyn, with a sad expression.

Sam, as boss, got the subtle suggestion.

"You're right; no one is going to be coming in today. You both scram out of here and get home safely before they do something crazy and shut down the island and close the bridges." Sam slept in her office, in a store room converted to a one-bedroom apartment. Life in the city was expensive for the twenty-eight-ish sole business shop owner, hopeful for a future, someday soon-to-be the famous fashionista with her own salon, showroom, and more importantly, The Brand — when she discovered it.

The collapsing dual towers cemented their concern and quiet panic. Both seamstress employees rushed out, slight comfort in being together, unsure of what to do but make their way to some form of safety, which they hoped were their apartments and crowded families, full of hugs.

Samantha Carlisle, with one eye glued to the TV, fixated on commentators and the multiple scenes reminding her of what Dante's Inferno must be like. She gathered up and shoved her color-inked designs for the wedding dress into a file folder marked 'Yu-Langston Wedding.' She draped a plastic covering over the fabrics she was going to suggest to Judith Yu today with her fiancé in tow. She accepted that under the circumstances, no one would be paying social or business calls on this terrible day.

She turned her attention back to the television. Good God, *it is* Dante's Hell, as she saw 'ghosts' coming out of a tsunami cloud of grey ash. Her eyes focused on two men, stumbling toward the camera, neither one recognizable, even to what ethnicity they might be. Leaning, holding each other up, strangers clinging. Aloud, to no one, shaking her head, she mourned, "Everyone is grey confusion, like amnesiac ghosts." Then thinking as a fashion designer might, seeing the perspective of all people now running. "No ethnics; no discerning tribes, no stuffy cliques, no Benetton colors of culture. The world has gone drab." No one was around to hear what she later called her epiphany. She threw in a couple of curse words to emphasize a world gone crazy. And then, thinking more, she gained direction, *"I will use a grey-black fabric background with minimalist color slashes, walking art of a chained political statement, of starkness representing sadness personified. Disturbed Valentino embraces nihilist Versace."* And Samantha Carlisle began to sketch, ignoring the wail of distant sirens.

Hugh Fox and Booker Langston, survivors

Hugh had found his calling. Never with cash on him, he had earlier that morning borrowed some crisp, large denomination bills to buy his first suit from his attorney to be repaid from loan proceeds. Yet who needed a suit at times like these? Instead, he bought the entire stock of bottled water from a small bodega and began passing them out to frightened people running away in their fear-stoked marathon and later to the police and firefighters arriving in a blaring cacophony of uncertainty. The rescuers knew they would need lots of hydration this day, for they would have to go in and go up to reach survivors.

Hugh did not comprehend that he was in the best position to see the marshaling of rescue efforts to enter the buildings. All civilians were being sent away from the scene, but helpful water boys seemed to have the approval to remain.

He glanced up to see a tall black man in a business suit running towards him and past in anguished panic. Near him, the first line of a police barrier stopped the man with a cautioning upraised hand and warning. Hugh could hear the shouted exchange.

"My fiancée is inside the North Tower. I need to get to her!" It was a demand laced with hysteria.

"Only first responders beyond here." The cop's own tribulations cut no slack or sympathy.

"No, you must hear this. I think I can reach her." He pulled out his cell phone and turned on the recording, thumbing it to loud. Hugh leaned in to listen.

A woman's voice, the man's fiancée, screamed in crying anguish,

"Bookie, Bookie, what's going on? We can't find an exit; there is smoke all over one side of the building. Someone said a plane hit the building. Bookie, what am I going to do? I love you. Some of us will try all the stairs; the smoke is getting bad. I love you, Bookie." Nothing more. The anguished black man looked at the police officer. The uniform just shrugged. "I'm sorry. They're sending in fire battalions now, helping with the evacuation. Please don't get any closer. There is nothing you can do. Please move back."

The man turned, downcast, devastated. Hugh shoved a bottle of water toward him. "Is your name, Bookie?" He had to break the man's concentration on something he could do nothing about.

The man repeated his name, disconnected, "Bookie?" Then he looked at Hugh, began to reach for the bottled water, then, as if for the first time, realized he held a crumpled bouquet of flowers. He threw them down, took the water proffered, guzzled it all, and nodded grimly, "Booker, my name's Booker." Aware of his surroundings, Booker walked away towards safety, and Hugh could see the man's expression, not disconsolation, not anger, but sad determination.

"Oh-oh," said Hugh, then distracted, finding himself passing out more water as fast as he could. The rush coming and going was at its apex. Within a half hour, all bottles gone, he looked around, wondering what else he might do, when he saw half a block away, the executive named Booker skirting an unattended barricade next to a fire truck. He was now without his jacket, his sleeves rolled up, looking more a part of the scene. '*What the — ?*' thought Hugh, noticing the man heading toward the North Tower, now a flaming and smoking torch. Not good, and not knowing why or the reasoning for what he suddenly did, he took off running. Perhaps he had to stop that man from entering a building on fire. That's the least he could do, bring rationalization to a hopeless task, maybe save one person on this deadly day.

They were both climbing over rubble, dodging fire equipment unlimbered, rescuers running towards the danger. Desperation drove Booker; adrenalin charged Hugh Fox, who eventually caught up, grabbed the man by the arm and spun him around.

"You can't go in there!" he shouted, not sure he had the right to make such a demand. "The fire up there needs to be first controlled; let the fire departments reach her. After that, it's a waiting game. Maybe she is already coming down another stairway. What if you miss her going up, and she coming down? What's she going to say if you get hurt? She's coming to you. Just wait here. We'll know soon enough." With that rush of words, he stared at the man. He noticed tears running down Booker's face, streaked by the floating dust.

Booker had been in his own world, a reality that all possible ways of being a hero to Judy were available to him, and then some stranger, a kid, yelled out at him to think practically. Like an attorney. Evidence. Facts. He slowed his mad rush, almost ready to plunge inside, to push aside the rescuers, most suited up with masks, and axes, trying to string water hoses.

"I'll wait; I won't leave her."

"Okay, we will wait. Together."

Booker looked at the young man, gauging why he was taking a risk for him. There was an understanding.

The 'kid' spoke. 'My name's Hugh. Hugh Fox. I just borrowed money from a bank. It's a known fact bankers will not let their clients get hurt before the scheduled repayment."

Booker stared at this ridiculous statement, spoken within a tempest of carnage and rescuer hope. He looked to the door, waiting to see a familiar face exit.

Not looking at Fox, he answered, "Booker Langston. My fiancée, Judith Yu. We are planning an early spring wedding." His voice was stunned.

Just then, they heard, within seconds, two sounds, not sirens, not from the rescue teams shouting commands. The crash of a beam to the ground, coming from on high; Hugh thought it might be not façade decoration but looked like an outside column supporting truss.

And inside the lobby, somewhere a 'crack,' the source undefined. Hugh glanced to the inside at one of the major steel supporting buttresses. He saw it bending ever so slightly. Stress-to stress-fracture. "Oh, shit." His liberal arts engineering studies came to him. This building

14 S.P. Grogan

was not going to fall over. It was going to pancake, collapse in on itself. "Oh, shit, shit. We have to go. Leave now, no time." He grabbed Booker's arm and started pulling him down the hill of refuse.

"No, no, I'm not going to leave her."

"She may already have left the building." Hugh lied; he was good at that, telling convincing fibs.

Booker was an emotional wreck. He had no anchor, no firm belief that would have kept him riveted to one spot, so he allowed Hugh to lead him along, the kid's firm grip on his shirt. He would wait for her further away. But then, at 9:59 a.m., the South Tower collapsed. Booker and Hugh ran like hell, like their lives depended upon it, as rightly so, staying alive requiring such action.

At 10:28 am, the North Tower followed, imploding. Within that short time, Hugh and Booker had been running like crazed madmen, seeing over their shoulders a rushing, suffocating curtain, chasing them, overcoming all within its path, embracing them in thick particulates of destroyed buildings and tissue fragments of human bodies.

That day, 2,764 people were killed, currency trading employee Judith Yu among them.

Barack Obama, Illinois State Senator

For his part, he remembered it beginning as probably an 'unremarkable day.' He was driving on Lake Shore Drive on his way to a required yet probably tedious Illinois Legislative Committee Meeting on Administrative Policy. The radio's music channel switched to 'Breaking News,' and he first learned of a plane crash into one of the World Trade Center buildings in New York. By the time he arrived at his meeting, it had been canceled, and people were milling outside, many of them staring at Chicago's Sears Tower, wondering, as he put it later, *'Would this building go from workplace to target'*? He drove to his law firm, where he worked at his holding place day job, and found everyone huddled in the basement conference room. The second plane had hit, and he joined his partners with exchanged stares, now saying aloud to no one but for a posterity of sorts, *"All the misery and evil in the world has brought a black cloud blocking the sun."*

After a while of repetitive commentators, with the same horrific visuals but little information on the how and why, Barack left for home. He had night duty. Sasha had just been born, and to give Michele a needed respite, he was on feeding and burping patrol, multitasking, and at the same time, watching the television. Television that went beyond its rightful purpose as news delivery. Like the rest of the American population that September day, now late at night, Barack's screen staring quickly zombied him into another internally wounded citizen.

Barack, the politician, had to consider the ramifications. Accepting that the national grief would be pervasive, the calls for immediate revenge. But, beyond the gut calls for firing squad justice, perhaps the following days and months might hold unsought latent opportunities. Barack, after all, was an elected politician; his credentials as a community activist saw him elected in 1996 for the 13th District, Chicago's South Side. Honing his skills, using his associate professor voice, that of deep timbre to educate, loud enunciation to reach the farthest corners of a lecture hall, he thought he was ready. Not yet, but as part of the learning process of living within machine politics in the trenches, in 2000, he lost a political race for the U.S. Congress. A year later, learning from his failed battle to reach Washington, he had to weigh his public political response carefully to what his constituent base expected of him to what they now called *9/11*. His response, crafted and loftier: "I have no empathy for terrorists." A short pause as if something profound was forthcoming. "We must realize the pain they created was from poverty and ignorance. It is up to us to lift the despair from these regions."

Several months later, State Senator Obama was having lunch with his go-to media consultant. The purpose — discussing where to, what next — all clichés appropriate: a finger to the wind or testing the [lake] waters. The question asked, cautiously, 'What was the climate like for a run at the U.S. Senate?'

"Not good," replied the consultant. "You have a major hurdle to overcome." His advisor tapped the morning newspaper on the luncheon table. A grainy black-and-white Associated Press photograph of an angry turbaned and bearded man stared back at them, the man now identified as the 'alleged' leader of the terrorist attack: Sheik Osama bin Laden of the radical revolutionary *al Qaeda*, referred to in the same sentence as *Islamic Jihadists*. One and the same.

They both nodded to what that meant. His strange name of Barack, his African lineage of 'Obama' that easily rhymes with 'Osama' and a middle name with Mid East connotations, 'Hussein.' The whispering, the wink-wink suggestion of a tie to 'Mohammed,' his name would be disastrous in the current climate where 'Remember the Alamo,' 'Remember the Maine,' and 'Remember Pearl Harbor' seemed all rolled into one shouted cry, 'Avenge 9/11!' With all political parties speaking with tenuous unity.

The consultant opined. "The time's not right. They either get this guy or new events move him off the front page. Barack, you must be patient. Give it time."

Barack did not like 'hurdles' or bumps in the road to deflect his goals. He passed the luncheon check over to the consultant, smiled, and thanked him for his advice. He would wait, but not for long.

16 S.P. Grogan

Three years later, in 2004, he made his move and was elected to the U.S. Senate. He followed the John F. Kenney model: 'Don't make controversial waves, low profile, and get the hell out of the Senate.' He knew where he was going, and it was not to be a long-serving U.S. Senator like the black Republican Edward Burke. Even if a member of that august chamber, he would not long be one of fifty.

Still, it leads one to wonder, that day with his media advisor, both discussing strategic moves to consider, at the luncheon's end, did State Senator Obama himself tap that face on the newspaper's front page, thumping hard with a stabbing finger, forming a resolution known only to him?

There were one too many Osama-Obama and Hussein-Mohammed connections on the world stage. And did he pledge to himself: *'I will be the last man standing?'*

Osama bin Mohammed bin Awad bin Laden, Pan-Islamic al-Qaeda leader

He had called his mother the night before. "You might not be able to reach me for some time." She asked no questions. They had a pleasant visit about her life, his wives, and children. "No, they will not be coming with me for a month or so." His mother did not ask why. He ended the call, both of them exchanging endearing goodbyes. Neither said they loved the other. That was not a ritual done in the bin Laden tribal clan. Yet, the call placed him in a good mood, as did other events yet to be.

Wearing no watch, he asked his bodyguard what time it was. Where they were, it was Tuesday evening, 6 pm in Jalalabad, Pakistan. He calculated that it was around 8 am in New York City. Osama bin Laden, also known as Usama bin Laden, an unknown to most of the Western world, had few concerns, and the news at this moment was more good than bad. The good news was, he had heard nothing of the attack being aborted. So, his fellow tactician, Khalid Sheik Mohammed's first concept outline, had become the blueprint for this multi-faceted launch. A bold move and all Khalid's idea. Bin Laden could accept letting someone else take the credit. But you could not rest on your laurels when fighting the Great Satan. A battle well done can be called a small victory; only many battles fought lead to a great victory. New planning would be required for the next attack, and Osama bin Laden had his own idea of what might come next, and he had brought with him plenty of writing materials to sketch his thoughts.

"It is time to go," he touched his driver's shoulder. They always traveled at night in two SUVs, and this trip with a truck laden with weapons and ammunition. Ironically, in other events happening a world away, his armed followers, his 'revolutionary army' always had to worry about the 'death-from-the-skies,' ship-to-land missile attacks or U.S. aircraft laser bombs [Military Predator drones were first used in October 2001 (see below), and CIA targeted drones were not used until February 2002].

He knew success would bring a response. It was time to go out and find a safe house with his most loyal supporters. The small convoy was leaving Jalalabad on the way to Spin Ghar Range (Pashto: 'White Mountains'), a natural mountain frontier border between Pakistan and Afghanistan. His later plans, not yet set, might, if circumstances dictated, require a move to the more secluded and remote hide-outs in the Tora Bora region of Afghanistan. Let his Taliban brothers form a shield of armed protection. Soon enough, they would know why he had sought them out, to be hidden among the various tribes.

Everything that would be said about him, he would shrug off. All of the accusations and shouting were mere propaganda noise to him. He had done nothing except to right perceived wrongs. If he were to admit to any of their accusations, he would deny all or only speak out to foment new soldiers to his banners, to the caliphate he would create, lead, and rule with a sharp-honed sword.

A bloody scimitar.

He leaned back in the bumping vehicle, his head resting, and was soon asleep. All was well with his world.

[The American government, with the almost unanimous approval of their citizens, would indeed respond less than a month later, on October 7th 2001 ('Operation Enduring Freedom') with CIA agents and Special Forces, dependent on anti-Taliban allies and the accuracy of U.S. Air Force's laser-dropped munitions and the Navy's Tomahawk sea-based cruise missiles. Not an invasion at that time but a surgical strike. One of their strategic targets to be removed was head Taliban leader Mullah Omar. Tracked and located, military high command infighting bungled a Predator drone strike. It failed; an empty truck destroyed, and Mullah Omar and the senior Taliban leadership fled, some even jumping out of windows, all escaping. The irony was that the Taliban knew nothing of what would happen in New York City and elsewhere on September 11th. They were bad people, certainly, but not the ones who unleashed the whirlwind of avenging might. Source: '*The Story of America's First Drone Strike*,' by Chris Woods, *Atlantic* Magazine, May 30, 2015]

Ten Years Later

EPISODE TWO — Two Versions of December 2010

Scene 1: Lost Goal.
Setting: December 2010, Afghanistan

There is the old war movie cliché that if your buddy sharing the foxhole with you shows you his worn photo of his wife and baby from back home, then he or both of you are doomed to the sniper's bullet or the falling mortar round.

E-4 rated Shawn Pacheco of Navy SEAL Team Four hadn't gone that far in believing he had jinxed his buddies, but in his platoon, the night before the mission, he felt the odd man out, uncomfortable, sensing they looked at him with unspoken expressions of disdain.

Everyone knew of his earlier Skype telephone call with Janet, his fiancée, making wedding plans; she waiting for him in Cleveland, Ohio. In the mess tent, he had boasted of his optimism about love and honeymooning, of going home soon, just like in a war movie. Fated. You just don't talk that shit before a mission. And now....

There were feather-stepped shuffles across the light snow. They were stalking their quarry, or so they thought. No words were exchanged; it was all hand signals as they approached the cave, its gray-etched outline over the eastern mountains in the Pachir Wa Agam District of Nangarhar Province. In another half hour, they would not need their night vision goggles, so the push was on to move quickly, silently, and with stealth. Pacheco, a member of the elite SEAL Team Four, was proud to be part of the unit, expecting greater recognition when his paperwork was approved for a new status as an expert in explosives. He assumed this was why they put him on point, further fieldwork, that from his knowledge, they expected him to spot nuances in the landscape — disturbances that might be telltale signs of planted IEDs.

This mission was to engage Taliban or al-Qaeda combatants thought to be situated in or near this cave location in hopes that a high-valued target might be present.

Though his squad said little while prepping, their hopes buoyed, and there were little exchanges of ribbing and joking. They wished that any target might be the Big Guy himself, Osama bin Laden, or even his second-in-command, the Doctor, al-Zawahiri, so they could go home, away from this damn cold country. And Shawn, back to Ohio and to Janet, his promised bride.

The cave, with its small squat entrance, was shallow, with little depth — and empty. Its litter showed habitation from at least two months ago. It was bad intel, more usual than not these days if you got your information, pried the scuttlebutt from hesitant local villagers. Anxiety waned, and fingers on triggers relaxed, but only slightly. Several team members were pissed and cursed at limestone walls, one SEAL even shouting, looking for an echo response: "Where the fuck are you, Osama?" It was less about the mission's failure than about a lack of action, which cemented a SEAL Team's honed training into the élan expected of them.

In single file, they backtracked down the narrow trail, hearing distant choppers returning to the LZ for embarkation. Tensions eased more. The first arc of sunlight hit distant mountaintops, and daylight, like melting butter, moved down toward the valley below. When the trail opened up, Pacheco's best friend, Reyes Montoya, gave him a friendly nudge to the side and moved to the front of the small column. 'Let's pick up the pace,' he said with a kidding laugh.

On a switchback turn, Montoya spotted an old juice can sticking out of the snow.

Probably recalling his high school soccer days, he made a move at playing, rushing the net with the winning kick. It was a mental mistake and a fatal one because what looked benign in this godforsaken land never was.

A thin wire attached to the juice can tripped the detonator on the PMA-2 mine. 'Goal, he scores,' whispered Montoya. It was loud enough that Pacheco knew in that second what was about to occur. He could do nothing but turn his head and accept the blast.

When he awoke in the base hospital, he discovered he had been concussed, bruised, and had scattered wounds stitched up. Fit for duty in a week, they told him. He still had all his limbs, though, and he felt himself damn lucky. The doctors later told him that the flecks of bone and gristle removed from his neck and hands had been Montoya's.

To SEAL Team Four, blame could not be affixed without collective guilt about a stupid mistake by a dead friend, and it wasn't a mistake since SEAL members did not make such errors in judgment. Except maybe guilt on Pacheco, who should have maintained point position instead of Montoya. Would he have done the same, would he have kicked the juice can, or would he have been more cautious, he wondered? The latter, he knew, but it mattered little.

To his comrades, Shawn, they groused, had failed in his assignment to watch out for all of them, steer them away from booby traps, and take the explosion himself if it had come to that. He came out of the hospital to find himself a Jonah and a pariah, shunned. Personal grief made him accept his fellow SEAL members' silent accusations, and he began to believe he had killed Montoya himself.

And perhaps it was he who should have died instead of his friend? Physically he recovered quickly, but the mental damage ate at his conscience like a cancer. He did not talk to Janet for a week, and when he did, the conversation seemed one-sided, stilted. Talk of pre-wedding parties had lost its allure.

Scene 2: Putting on the Ritz.
Setting: New York City, December 2010

"Should not creativity be used for a higher moral purpose?"

She zapped him, tore into his mindset, just at the climax where Starfighter Hugh Fox began, at the 20th Level, destroying the headquarters of MegaToth Command and Control. The woman's voice had brought him from the galactic unworldly back to the familiar reality of a chattering cocktail crowd.

He dropped his cosmic beam weapon away from the movie theater-sized flat screen and turned to the crowd of the imbibing inquisitive, all well-heeled and attired formally for the charity event evening. His avatar, looking like Hugh Fox himself and programmed by his company, Skilleo Games Technology, to offer human-styled expressive emotions, turned to say 'What the — ?' but not finishing the surprise of abandonment, it was blasted instead into jellied gore by one of the thousand MegaToth NucleoDisseminators the game master had thus far defeated. "You are history," came the programmed voice as gameplay went into stasis, waiting for the Starfighter game player to reboot.

Hugh's eyes turned to his audience, seeking out his presumed critic. Those in the small group surrounding him were not fans but consumers, the parents of fans who had so far made "MegaToth Doomslayer V" the top-selling electronic game of the last holiday season and winner of this year's *Achievement Interactive Awards*. He was here tonight, at an uppity charity event, where he would offer a lucky bidder, at the celebrity auction following dinner, the right to put their name, character, and personality into his next Skilleo game as the evil OverLord. Among gamesters, this would be on par with Marvel Comics creating an action hero based on one's own image. He expected frenzied bidding that night by indulgent parents who were pressured by their precocious children to purchase a rare and personalized piece of the Hugh Fox Skilleo Empire.

Hugh spotted her in the crowd. She dressed stylishly in expensive and tasteful clothes, and she was quite attractive — for an older woman, maybe near thirty-plus years old, he guessed. 34-36 range. He found most of the society crowd much older than his twenty-nine and still growing age.

She seemed alone.

He passed his weapon baton to J-Q, his PA, personal assistant, and highly-paid gofer. J-Q, ultimate in loyalty to his boss, was nicknamed 'J' after the Men in Black movie character and 'Q' for James Bond's weapons supplier. He worked mainly for the fun of hanging around a corporate atmosphere that was based on imaginary realms that offered unknown, mind-boggling surprises.

When J-Q picked up the weapon and resumed the demonstration, the computer game downloaded all of J-Q's stored play habit information based on fingerprint recognition and his hand grip's strength pressure. The game began anew with J-Q's avatar fighting MegaToths at Level 7. Only Hugh Fox, two lab engineers, and three walled-in game junkies scattered around the world had ever played Level 20, *Ender's Game Platform* as it was called by those joy-stick pilgrims who, with admiration and reverence, seek the ultimate video game high.

Hugh ignored those who pointed him out in low whispers and didn't care that by tomorrow's editions, the tabloids would describe his blue jeans and black corduroy tux jacket with no tie as his usual, slovenly nerd image. He was quite comfortable with himself, and as a gentleman might, he guided the woman away from the game he had fantasized, nurtured, and brought into being with the support of his 1,600 loyal employees and fellow thrill geekers.

"You say I am not using my creative juices properly?"

"No, one can certainly see that genius must have its outlets, and it certainly seems you have found your calling." Her voice trilled lightly, easily melting into mild laughter.

With a slight shrug of his shoulders, he replied, "I'm no genius." He truly believed that, though his intelligence and success suggested otherwise.

"Not according to how *The Journal* and *Forbes* and all the business writers go on about you. Founded Skilleo at 17, your first billion dollars in sales by 21. Privately owned, you and only a few venture capital firms, which I might add, makes you master of your domain. I just wonder if you could do more with your creative spirit to help, you know, mankind."

Even though she was smiling, Hugh felt he was being lectured. The implication seemed to be that he was still a young man of potential but one handicapped by immaturity. His feathers bristled.

"I am here tonight for a worthy cause," he said seriously. "My company does have a foundation that contributes generously. Its primary focus is challenge grants and scholarships for science and math education in the public schools." He had his litany down pat.

"Yes, but Mr. Fox," she replied and leaned in. Her perfume enhanced her closeness; his brain computed an orange scent, and his vision snapped the outlines of a shapely body within a sleek black dress. He studied her face and expression; freckles, a deep purple eye shadow drawing out fathomless aquamarine eyes, and a singular skin color, an actual and natural tan, not dark, but from the outside, the real world. He was intrigued. Not that old, he decided, as she continued, "I do not find fault in your corporate benevolence. But are you maximizing all of that talent within? You have made money, yes, but are you sure you could not do more? Instead of other people using your money for the greater good, you and your ideas could directly solve a problem of worldly magnitude. Self-satisfaction in its purest form."

It was one of those moments, a long pause during which silent communication was in process, intense yet undefined. She placed her hand on his arm — not electricity or a tingle, but… then someone called out, and she turned, her touch drifting away.

"Samantha. There you are." An elegant gentleman, Armani-tuxed and coiffed in a weathered commodore look, with a slight gray sanding to his thick hair, appeared with an extra glass of champagne, which he handed over. "Thought I'd lost you."

"I wandered over to see Mr. Fox's display," she told him. "It's quite exceptional — if one is into destroying NucleoDisseminators." She smiled at him, a disarming tease. Hugh put a look of surprise on his face, brightened that this lady knew the details of his game. She introduced the gentleman, and Hugh filed away his name, somewhere unimportant, after noting that Samantha called the man her "escort for the evening" in a kind, solicitous fashion so as not to offend. It left a lot unsaid, he thought. The man was not a boyfriend, or she would not have said "escort," nor was he a fiancé — though she would make a great trophy wife at this sort of event, he thought, recognizing his callousness towards the high and mighty stuffed shirts.

The power couple, 'Samantha' and what's-his-name, graciously excused themselves and went to find their assigned table as the non-profit festivities of the hotel-catered meal were beginning. He, himself, sat with an assortment of Fortune 100 CEOs and their spouses, where talk weaved and flowed over government intrusion into business by taxes and burdensome oversight, putted into fabled golf games, and niggling complaints on nightmare remodels of second and third homes on the ski slopes or at the beach.

Hugh smiled and indulged the genial table conversations, mostly as a listener since the others did not know on what level and on what subject they could easily discourse with him. Whether awkward silence to his youth or his balance sheet, he did not care, one way or the other.

After the salad plates were removed, and while waiting for the entrée, he glanced through the evening's program, and there she was.

Samantha Carlisle. Of course! *That* Samantha, the one known to the world for SammyC Fashions, well branded for her spritzy clothing lines. One of her couture lines was called *Provac,* short for 'provocative.' Every teen girl, those adolescent caterpillars morphing into coquettish butterflies, had a closet rack dedicated to SammyC labels. Mature women seeking to imply naughty ways through their fashion wore Jimmie Chu and Gucci accessories but dazzled in SammyC's *Kling* for night-on-the-town/next-morning outfits.

He did not know this firsthand, introverted bachelor that he was, wedded only to the design table and computer screen. He knew it because of his speed-scanning of news sources to stay on pace with youth marketing and tracking the fickleness of cultural fads as they might eventually arise in one of his games.

Tonight, his curiosity did one better. He pulled out his personalized handheld, the walkabout computer designed by his engineers to be larger than an iPhone but less intrusive than an iPad, to be something inoffensive but expected of any multi-tasked executive, especially someone like himself who was known as the Gadgets Guy. He put on his WiFi earplug, and as the dinner buzzed around him like a distant hum, he pulled up a Google-Nexus search. As his finger scrolled across a sentence, it was translated into vocalized speech in his ear and automatically archived in a file for future reference. As he smiled and exchanged comments with his dinner companions, he was also being educated.

In minutes, Hugh knew her bio and all her public secrets.

According to SEC filings, Samantha Carlisle could boast of having achieved multimillionaire status in her own right. At the height of a rebounding stock market, she had sold her fashion house to an Italian public conglomerate for $400 million in cash and stock.

That information counterbalanced his insecurities about why she had made a play for him at the party. She hadn't. As an unattached, now wealthy woman, she did not need him (or any man) for her bliss and financial security. Burned in past surface encounters with women who wanted his credit card and not his heart, he realized their meeting showed her true character: She was merely being friendly, engaging in banter, and with that, he found parity with Ms. Carlisle.

He found her a fresh, kindred spirit.

The evening's ceremony launched into speeches calling for financial action and underwriting of the new cause célèbre, Lyme disease in children, and touting generosity for the upcoming auction with a two-page list of special high-end glamorous bid items from personally prepared dinners for ten by a top Michelin-starred chef to yacht cruises off the Bahamas or front row seats and backstage visit at the latest Broadway hit.

Hugh read that Samantha Carlisle was offering her own donation to the non-profit:

A Ten-Day African Photographic Safari, including a personal tour of the SammyC Save

Our Wildlife Refuge in Kenya. It was all-inclusive, featuring catered meals and private jet access — hers — and the private tour would be hosted by the refuge's namesake.

Interesting, he thought. His capsulated research had revealed that she was active in many charities. There was social column chatter about her attendance at highbrow functions where she was seen with various male escorts, no female sidekicks. Then it hit him, and he replayed their brief conversation, beginning with her opening line: "Should not creativity be used for a higher moral purpose?"

That was it. She was not talking about him; she was talking about herself. At the pinnacle of what everyone else would laud as success, Samantha Carlisle was probably bored, not necessarily with the functions and responsibilities of daily fashion design or charity boards, but because she lacked a true-life purpose. Was the African animal refuge her discovered and ultimate good deed? No, he decided; she was still searching for that pizzazz of significance.

Just like him. The ever-elusive next thrill.

At the appropriate time, he raised his hand and outbid everyone else. At the back of the room, J-Q made a note in his PDA: *SammyC's Save Our Wildlife Refuge — ask date, plan trip* — and later, at the auction settlement desk, J-Q wrote a Skilleo Foundation check to the charity for $150,000, the highest of all the bid items that evening. Hugh Fox never carried cash or credit cards.

EPISODE THREE — Creative Styles

Scene 1: Inspiration Amuck
Setting: Silicon Valley, California January 2011

End of the day. Hugh Fox let the sweat run from his gritting face, a feel-good sense of accomplishment. He punched in a higher setting on the treadmill: *Climb the Mountain* mode.

After their respective assistants had compared calendars, the photo safari tour to Africa had been set for two weeks hence, and Hugh, returning to California and his corporate campus, felt himself needing to take stock of his physical condition. He did not think this trip would be strenuous; nevertheless, he wanted to upgrade his cardio and have his bodily fluids balanced to take the African heat and offset the required infusion of medical immunizations. Even his corporation's in-house insurance section and his private doctor made provisions for possible scenarios of travel emergencies, from kidnappings to Ebola infections.

Today, in the Skilleo company gym, an optional job benefit, fellow employees groaned and grunted at their own health maintenance programs. Running in place allowed Hugh's mind to wander, checking off priorities, thinking on multi-dimensional levels, still falling back to his social introduction to Samantha Carlisle. He was not so much attracted to her, or so he told himself, as haunted by the thread of that lingering conversation. Had he indeed given his all to a goal beneficial to others? Her words nagged. He felt them thrown back on him like a challenge.

Yes, he could up the dollars of his foundation gifts, but where? Bill and Melinda already had world health covered. Most movie stars publicized their own importance to a specific charity or went out of their way to adopt an underprivileged waif. Didn't Brangelina have a baker's dozen of little critters? Not for him. He already spent too much of his life in the daily grind of trying to guess what was in the buying minds of a young audience, the finicky — the never satisfied. The Rockefeller and Ford Foundations were too staid and, he had to admit, not the public relations he might want to display. No flashy press release. Good deeds by a Games Guy downplayed still paid positive dividends, but boasting was not in his DNA.

Whatever extra effort he could afford, he didn't want to be seen as a me-too sort of grandstander. Most of his corporate giving was generous but under the radar, a package of gifts to United Way-type 501(c)(3) charities. Even Jerry's Kids (now sans Jerry) received a donation, though not during telethon season. His corporate giving philosophy mirrored his personality; a shyness to his presence.

Gaining attention was not his norm, except as an adjunct to promoting his games sales. He would leave headline-grabbing to Virgin's Branson and realtor Donald Trump's televised *The Apprentice* (going into Season 11). As for start-up wealth, he had heard of this Bezos guy who was making a splash in online shopping but did not think he was worthy of an internet search. As he climbed to the treadmill's first plateau, he watched the multiple television screens before him, their sound muted: sports, market, and business news. Such silence, the seeing but not hearing, compartmentalized his mood: he was good at what he did, which was turning creative thinking into popular game design. How that skill could be put to a specific use — as this woman, acting as a catalyst, or maybe a 'muse' called "for the benefit of mankind?"

A news feature caught his attention, and he turned up the sound. A law firm was being chastised for placing newspaper ads seeking to represent 9/11 victims regarding the disbursement of monies by the federal government's *Victim Benefit Relief Fund.* The ad used stock footage of a fireman, placing him before a grainy image of the aftermath of the Twin Tower destruction.

The fire helmet was photo-shopped out and placed in his hands instead some sort of marketing plaque. Tacky. It had since been learned that the fireman had not been at the World Trade Center that tragic day, nor had he even been a fireman yet on that historic date.

The television's talking head critics were yelling at the insensitivity of the ambulance-chasing shysters. They shouted that 9/11 should never be forgotten, should never be commercialized in any way. 9/11, they said, should always be a wake-up call for the innocent, a reminder that there are very evil people in the world who have no compassion and will kill

26 S.P. Grogan

anyone to achieve their aims, one specific goal being the fall and destruction of the United States.

September 11, 2001. The terrorist attacks on Washington, D.C., and New York City and a burning, cratered field in Pennsylvania impacted the psyche of American citizens and changed their way of living forever. Hugh admitted to himself that he had not thought about that tragedy in a long time, though he had been at the site on that violent day. He remembered the day he had consoled a man about the loss of his fiancée's life, a friendship out of pain, each occasionally tracking the other's career. Hugh gave into these thoughts: *I wonder how Booker liked his move to California? Nearly eight years ago. Did the change of heart from defense to district attorney, to the dark side, one with a vendetta to put all bad guys away, soothe his tormented soul? The man was infected with the revenge bug, not yet cured by obliterating the original crime from the face of the earth.* Hugh concluded, "Bookie is a good man, half possessed to right society's ills." Hugh shrugged, sad that he could not think of an antidote to cure his friend, to just find a new life of happiness. Abject gloom is not a lifestyle.

As the televised news item ended, he agreed with an interviewed survivor, who bemoaned that we all should be reminded we are still under attack and that complacency is this country's greatest weakness.

He felt his running pace picking up. Weren't they building a memorial in New York?

Maybe his foundation could be useful in some way. He went one step further. Had they caught all the perpetrators of this evil? Hadn't he heard that they were prosecuting some of the 9/11 plotters in a military court? Weren't some condemned to the secret not-so-secret Guantanamo prison? But that didn't include all of them, right? No, it didn't. Not all of the alleged masterminds had been brought to justice. He turned to J-Q, who was off to the side and on his back, grunting 60 pounds of weights hoisted above his head. Hugh called out to his aide,

"Have they ever caught — what's his name, that bin Laden guy?"

Scene 2: A Partnership of Surprises
Setting: Aberdare National Park, Kenya February 2011

"That's a growl I'm hearing? Out there, close by?"

"Yes, and sounds like it's getting closer," murmured Samantha, not moving. She sipped her unfiltered 2006 Chardonnay, personally bottled for her by the de Wetshof Estate winery of South Africa.

If she were not going to look concerned, Hugh would act accordingly, and his face slipped into an ambivalent mask.

They sat on the veranda of a treehouse overlooking the watering hole, the luxurious private hotel hundreds of yards behind them, near the crest of a hill. The serving staff had cleared their dinner plates and properly absented themselves. Now the deep heart of Africa, the darkness of the savannah night, lay outside the ring of spotlights which allowed both of them, Hugh Fox in curious excitement, to watch wildebeests, hyenas, giraffes, and antelopes trek to the muddy watering hole for an evening drink.

Predators were soon approaching, so he was told. Hugh pulled his camera to his side, ready for another telescopic masterpiece, knowing he would have to remodel a room in his house with a Dark Continent motif using the results of his weeklong Bwana adventure.

It had been an exciting trip; everything he could have asked for. His lovely guide was the best part of the tour, and he felt their personalities mesh. They were two intelligent people always interested in learning more about the world around them, about each other. *Copacetic*, that was a good word. Tomorrow would be the tour of the Refuge and the animal hospital she founded, and then back to civilization.

Perhaps the moment was right — with the dinner afterglow and the nocturnal noises sounding like a jungle meditation tape, though real. Why not?

"I have an idea I am pursuing and would welcome your opinion."

She curled up in her canvas chair.

"I wouldn't be good at analyzing a video game concept," Samantha replied, wine glass in hand, "unless you wished me to advise you on color coordination or the interior design of space stations. But you have me here, or rather, I have you here; the night is young, and I am quite lucid. Pray, go on. I appreciate mind stimulation in any form."

They exchanged comfortable smiles. On previous nights, their dinner conversations had been enlightening, refreshing. They learned they were two intellectuals who could maintain discourses without seeming condescending to the other. Friendly banter.

Hugh Fox dove in.

"Excluding natural disasters that we have no control over, what is the greatest threat to our civilization?"

"If this were a set-up for the unanswerable, I would plead ignorance. But knowing you, I would guess 'nuclear misadventure' would definitely impact everyone in the world and threaten the existence of human civilization. Chernobyl, and more recently, Japan. Radiation, once loose, is impossible to stick back in the genie bottle."

"True. Now, if I rephrased the question: '*Who* would be the greatest threat?'"

Sipping her wine and mulling over her thoughts, she answered,

28   S.P. Grogan

"Rogue governments. Dictators out of control, though most seem contained, or at least only interested in their own backyards."

"Nine-eleven. The attack on the U.S. by Islamic fundamentalists — what does that conjure in your mind?" he asked.

"Definitely out of control, blinded-by-religion fanaticism. They spout, 'No one can go to heaven except me and mine; everyone else is consigned to damnable hellfire.'"

"And you are correct at your first guess. Did you know that these al-Qaeda operatives originally targeted nuclear power plants on the East Coast? Later they changed their targets to symbols of America: the Trade Center, the Pentagon, and the last presumed to be Congress, the U.S. Capitol. The targets were only changed because the terrorist leaders could not guarantee where on a nuclear plant would be the most sensitive point to hit to do maximum damage by crashing a plane into."

"But didn't I read that the U.S. is prosecuting the conspirators, the masterminds in 9/11, by holding military trials at Guantanamo? I read that in the *Times* on my way to the Fashion section."

"Mere appendages of a multi-headed snake, but not the head itself."

"Hugh, what are *you* thinking? I have the feeling your mind is several steps ahead of anyone else's."

He looked straight at her. "I am going to capture Osama bin Laden, the titular head of al Qaeda, the directing force behind the 9/11 attacks."

"The U.S. has tried, as have the CIA and other government security forces. Isn't he hiding in a cave somewhere?"

"Governments have tried, yes, but they've not succeeded. From personal experience, I have more faith in the power of private enterprise. I believe I could put together a team, supported with the latest technology and energized with the right motivation."

"Motivated to capture and bring evil to justice?" He expected to see her laugh at him, but she did not. Instead, she continued, "You might not realize it, but there is a coincidence here. I founded my company in New York City, and it was fledgling and struggling back in 2001. Cherisee Fortier worked in the loft studios next to mine, and I could draw on her expertise as a bargain hunter to locate quality fabrics for me. Her two young nieces were in town from Iowa that day, and she took them to an early lunch at the Windows of the World restaurant on top of the World Trade Center. I can't tell you all our anguish and heartache.

"I think of Cherisee, smart as a whip. In the middle of that tragedy, she would have shepherded her two nieces towards the rooftop, believing helicopters would save them — and, from what I've read, finding the doors bolted shut. No escape, no hope." Samantha's voice cracked, and tears welled.

Hugh felt her story made the point, and his telling his own on-site experience that day would have added nothing to what he said next. "I can assure you my goal in capturing him is only for noble reasons, and that is the first step I am going to concentrate on."

"And what if you, or your group with the military's support, find him? What next?"

He found it interesting she did not belittle his idea, call it a wild goose chase, or give him one of those funny tart looks skeptical superficial women do.

"Well, I'm thinking of that as a Phase 2 problem. Let me achieve Phase 1 first. Let me show you something." He pulled out his ever-present, pencil-thin, hand-held computer and punched a few buttons.

He nodded at it. "I got an insider to get me this before its release and had my crew cut out superfluous background plotting."

He moved to sit next to her, and she leaned into his shoulder and placed her hand on his thigh — to steady her balance, he presumed. He played the short version of "Grandmother Mary's Gift" from the *King's Retribution* bounty hunter reality television show and produced by Five Aces Studioz. When it was over, he beamed as might a student who knew he had all the answers and would breeze through his SAT exams with high scores, as he, indeed, did in high school, entering college a year early.

Samantha Carlisle searched the young man's features, trying to delve deep into his makeup, her eyes curious about what she accepted as intense energy unbundling. His excitement seemed contagious — stimulation for others to latch onto.

"You are very serious. And you are going to what, hire these actors. For…?"

"As my paid mercenary team. They would be the nucleus of what I am calling on paper my "Hunter-Capture Team." They have spent two years, or seasons, as they say, 18 televised shows altogether, analyzing the workings of criminals and figuring out how to locate and capture crooks. A terrorist is just a crook with a political megaphone and a bomb. I will supplement them with funds and the support of my brightest tech gurus. I can make them more efficient and — ."

His fast talk and enthusiasm were interrupted by a sharp, guttural scream, followed by a lingering banshee cry that sounded like a baby in distress. It was close, near the watering hole.

"That's not the cry of a big cat hunting," said Samantha. "That's pain." She arose and went to a large flat suitcase off to the side of the expansive deck. She took out a leather case and, from that, a long rifle. She started putting the barrel and stock together efficiently, and at the barrel end, she inserted a lethal-looking arrow stub, needle-thin with a feather attached.

"My god," was Hugh's response.

"Pneu-Dart X Caliber rifle. It can put 1 to 10 ccs of knock-out drugs into an animal from a great distance."

Samantha walked to the railing with the rifle under her arm. Calling into a walkie-talkie, she picked up from a tabletop, speaking the patois of an African language — it was somewhat of an English pidgin, so far as Hugh could determine — she directed the listener to be prepared with a holding box. At the balcony railing, they strained their eyes into the darkness. Another scream had them both looking to the left of the water hole. The last of the animals, two miniature gazelles, bolted from their drinking place and disappeared.

"Suspicious critter, circling. Not looking for dinner but definitely needing to get to the water." Out of a backpack, she pulled a large, scope-like object bearing irregular optics; one end larger than the other.

She intrigued him with her sudden metamorphous from the anthropologist Jane Goodall to the white huntress Calamity Jane. It was somewhat sexy with its connotations of impassioned violence: hunter facing prey. It was like what he had been thinking about all along but had not yet visualized, what was missing as he jelled his ideas into cohesion — the passion of the hunt. He watched her add the device to the rifle. Yes, she was a hunter.

"Sniper Scope?"

"It's something of my own invention — an adaptation of a golf course range finder, but with night vision capabilities. One of the problems animal naturalists have in capturing animals with sedatives is gauging the right combination of ketamine and medetomidine in a ten cc dart.

"Too much and they die, but too little and they run off, sick and vulnerable to carnivores. So, what I do when I am sighting the rifle is have the scope data chip determine what type of animal and its weight and make an immediate dosage calculation to remix in the dart if necessary. And then I can put the animal to sleep safely and quickly."

"There it is," cried Hugh, excited. "It's a leopard. It's limping."

"Actually, a cheetah. And look at its side. See that blood? The cat wants to roll in the mud and cover the wound, but that's not a gash. It's not a tusk or clawing wound. It looks like a bullet hole. It went in the side, most likely hit the ribs, and then out the hip. Damn poachers!"

She brought the rifle to bear, sighted it, made an adjustment, let out her breath, stilled, and fired. The bright feather appeared on the flank of the cheetah, and the animal screamed in new pain. It bared its fangs, stood a moment, wavered, and then slowly crouched to the ground, and in a minute, it rolled to its side.

From nowhere, a group of workers appeared, pushing a large box. One checked the animal's vital signs, and soon the creature was loaded and carted off.

"You will see our new patient tomorrow."

"I am impressed; a woman who puts her rifle where her convictions are."

"Poachers are driving African animals to extinction," she explained. "We try to stop them and repopulate species in zoos, but zoos are not a natural environment to maintain the wild instincts. Whether it's due to poverty or revolutions, local poachers sneak in here to kill for pelts to wrap a fashionable woman. I never use fur in my designs.

"Then there are the poachers of horn and tusk used for illegal aphrodisiacs, which, of course, are like snake oil liniment. Superstition and totally unproven."

"Would you say the extinction of the world's nature deserves to be prevented?" he asked.

"Of course." She broke down the rifle and laid it aside.

"You can see my point, then, of tracking down evil. My focus is only on one evil person. Capture him, and the morale and strength of the entire beast is depleted. I believe there might be a chance for success by bringing new perspectives to bear on the hunt. Using that analogy, what I want is to design a specialized and modified rifle by using new technology, so to speak, to track down the human prey."

She picked up her wine glass, and he refilled it. Her drink was to calm rushed adrenaline, her thrill of pulling the trigger, the power of release; yes, of the hunt, the capture without killing.

She stared, her eyes locked into his, and raised her glass.

"I salute you, Hugh. You have set, as you said, a noble quest. More power to you, but it lacks one important asset."

"It does?" His mind raced; he thought he had allowed for all contingencies.

"It's missing my presence. I intend to join you. The killers of innocents first and animal slaughterers next. Helping you will be a progression with my own goals in mind."

"Sam, this could be dangerous."

"Yes, it could be," she said. "We shouldn't waste time. Let's go and talk more about your plans."

"Go?"

"To the hotel, my suite. If we are to be fellow travelers, I want to learn more about the man behind the idea." She gave him a slow, warm kiss, letting her fingers trace his face.

Hugh followed, giving no response except curious acquiescence.

By James Wolcott, *Vanity Fair*, December 2009

The influence of Reality TV has been insidious and pervasive. It has ruined television, and by ruining television, it has ruined America.... In the voyeurism of Reality TV, the viewer's passivity is kept intact, pampered and massaged, and force-fed Chicken McNuggets of carefully edited snippets that permit them to sit in easy judgment and feel superior, watching familiar strangers make fools of themselves. Reality TV looks in only one direction: down....

EPISODE FOUR — The World is a Stage

Scene 1: The Actors
Setting: The previous December 2010, São Paulo, Brazil

From the balcony, Carlita 'Callie' Cardoza watched her computer screen, which featured five small boxes in the matrix showing live camera feeds. CAM ONE, the videographer, was aimed at the front of the deluxe apartment complex. CAM TWO, another camera-carrying staffer, peered across the street, scanning light auto and pedestrian traffic. CAM THREE was at the airport, on standby, prepared for their arrival if everything went right. It was a big "if." Cameras Four and Five were head cams in ball caps, one inside the van down the street on the driver's head and the other inside an apartment on the ground level, waiting for the appropriate rushed exit. Callie did not know their first names, only by job function: CAM ONE, CAM TWO, CAM THREE. Celebrities like herself, too focused on the set, avoided most buddy-buddy familiarity.

"Heads up," she spoke into her headset's microphone. "Lights just went out in the penthouse. He's on the move. Everyone alert." She slammed closed her laptop, threw it into her backpack, swung it to her shoulder, tore off down the hall, and took the staircase in bounds.

She had previously timed her exit. She had 20 seconds before the Target would reach the ground floor and exit the elevator.

On the street, giving a few huffs from her sprint, she positioned herself across from the two guards at the front door. The men picked up on her presence, noted her fine form, and began some undercurrent of smutty dialogue between them. *Good*, she thought; *they are distracted*. She glanced up the street and saw the black van, with the detachable 'Floristas' sign on its side, begin its slow acceleration crawl.

"Here he comes," she said into her ear bud mike. "One guard."

Timing made a blur of the snatch.

The Target and his bodyguard exited the front door, nodded to the guards on either side and turned to walk down the street. Callie knew, from his habits, that he was heading to his favorite nightclub. *Not tonight or thereafter*, she thought.

Following right behind the Target, coming out from the dummy apartment they had rented weeks earlier, Colonel Richard 'Storm' King smiled at the armed doormen, then brought his hands from his pockets and zapped them both with 5 million volts from his two Streetwise Blackout stun guns. Next, he re-pocketed the stun guns and whipped out two black bags. He jerked the bags over the men's heads as they spasmed on the ground and pulled the plastic tie cuffs so they locked tight to the neck. There were breathing holes, but even if the guards could pull their weapons, they could not see what to shoot. It was King's invention for tactical advantage.

In the same few seconds, the side door of the onrushing black van flew open, and another stun gun shot out electrical wires as the bodyguard standing next to the Target turned to see what the commotion was at the apartment entrance. As he fell, a large muscular man jumped from the van, collared the Target, and tossed him like a sack of garbage into the van.

The bodyguard, better trained than the rent-a-cop door guards, was pulling his revolver just as Callie stepped on his wrist. She wrenched the weapon from his hand and drew another black bag over the man's head. She was covered by King, who had taken down the apartment guard duo and had now drawn a semi-automatic Walther P99. Both Cardoza and King jumped into the van, yanking the door shut as the vehicle burned rubber, squealing away from the curb, dodging late-night traffic on its way to Sao Paulo's Guarulhos International Airport.

A stationary mini-cam and microphone inside the van picked up Callie, and one of the ball cap cams gave a close-up.

To the Target, she said, "Welcome, Mr. Pettigrew, to your worst nightmare," and then administered the hypodermic, with its cocktail solution of chloral hydrate and haloperidol.

"Night-night," said King, "you motherfucker." The guys in the editing department would later bleep out the expletive.

Back at the room where moments ago Callie had watched the apartment, a man stood wearing his own headset communicator. He watched the three head-bagged men writhing on the ground in neuron pain. He saw the black van speed away with the Target. "Cut," said the director. "That's a wrap on this end

Scene 2: Script Edit Reality
Setting: Burbank, California January 2011

INTEROFFICE MEMO: Private and Confidential

34   S.P. Grogan

(*Summary of Final Script: Route from Production to Edit Department — Work from my notes*)

Show: King's Retribution

Season Two Final Episode: *Grandma Mary's Gift*

Opening Scene: Colonel King and his second-in-command, 'Callie' Cardoza, arrive at the Midwest home of Mary Branch, a widow in her mid-60s. Exterior shot shows a quiet, unassuming neighborhood of mature trees, clean yards, and blooming gardens.

Interior: Mary's living room is maintained with family photos [close-up of deceased husband photo], collectible china bells, and glass paperweights [close up].

Talent: Mary explains that she invested $55,000 of her husband's insurance money into the Peregrine Fund after her stockbroker sent a prospectus saying that this investment would provide the best return for her during her lifetime and then act as a tax-free estate gift to her two grandchildren. When the fund stopped paying interest, she called, only to discover that the fund manager, touted Wall Street biz whiz Matthew Pettigrew, had looted all the funds' assets under his control and fled the country, disappearing with more than $85 million.

VOICEOVER: Hundreds of investors were robbed, and Grandma Mary lost everything she had invested. Her home's mortgage was at risk — the house she'd lived in for more than 40 years [She is crying at this point; CUT to Callie, who looks teary-eyed] and which she wanted to leave as a legacy for her grandchildren.

[Trademark King voice, holding Mary's hand: "Mr. Pettigrew will face the King's Retribution."]

SHOW LOGO — flaming arrow flying into Pettigrew's target face] [dub music] <<Break>>

Scene: Collage of bits and news snippets, narrated by King. History of Pettigrew, his fund, and the theft of fund assets. Typical Ponzi scheme. As the house of cards falls, he flees the U.S. to hide out and enjoy his spoils.

Scene: Office of New York City Prosecutor's Office, Securities Division. Meeting with Storm, Callie, and a Federal Bureau of Investigation prosecutor and agent. Also in attendance, New York District Attorney Cotton Matther V. [Make sure you close up that cemented frown of his and that smarmy suit Cotton wears with his bowtie — Man's running for some higher office next year. We give him face-time; he'll be good to us.]

Meeting highlights [cut and paste]: Charges are filed, and Pettigrew is wanted. FBI believes he is in South America, there's one clue pointing to Brazil, but Brazil has no fast extradition policy. [Again, make sure you get prominent head-nodding from the D.A. — he expects this]

Agent bemoans how long it would take to get Pettigrew back to the States; even longer if he has high-priced attorneys. The prosecutor mentions there is a $1 million award for his capture and return for prosecution.

[CUT TO: Callie] "This is our sort of case."

Usual disclaimer: Warning from FBI agent not to take action into one's own hands. That Pettigrew could have bodyguards and be dangerous.

[CUT TO: Storm smiling at Callie]

<<BREAK>>

Scene: Flying Squad Headquarters. Back and forth shots [STORM RECOMMENDS PICKING UP SEQUENCE SPEED]. Callie on computer tracking last payment Pettigrew made to his attorney before services terminated. From mid-town, First Federal. Show criminal's timeline.

Show payment made after Pettigrew left country. Callie fakes out bank with a verification notice.

Funds wired from bank in São Paulo, Brazil.

Storm, with Clayton and Bennie, discusses travel itinerary and extraction method. Callie shows off snatch equipment. Callie and Bennie will be point team to locate Pettigrew (TARGET) in São Paulo, Brazil.

[STORM SAYS MAKE POINT OF NEEDLE IN HAYSTACK. THIS IS 6th LARGEST POPULATED CITY IN WORLD, 11 MILLION.]

<<BREAK >>

SCENE: Pick up archival film on São Paulo: airplane landing, city view, etc.

Shot of street, patch in fast graphics, cut-aways of Target apartment house. We have grainy footage of Pettigrew (TARGET) walking the street with bodyguard

[CUT: back to old photo; his hair is now dyed, and he has a beard].

Hotel Room: Strategy Session — Three Days — show anxious faces, plenty of them. Callie will use the bank ploy, say there is a problem with Pettigrew's wire account, and can he come in personally and re-sign forms. [PUT IN VERBAL FIGHT BETWEEN CALLIE AND STORM.

ONCE AGAIN, SHE WANTS FIELD ACTION AND NOT ALWAYS TO BE ON LOGISTICS]

Scramble. New information, TARGET tip now going to night club. Bank out.

SCENE: Grab off the street. Van used. Tased bodyguard — black bag to all including apartment door guards [Setting up cameras was harder on this than last; used FIVE locations.

CAMERA ONE, roving: Three head caps on Storm, Callie, and Bennie. CAMERA TWO, stationary. If we missed the right spot for the grab, the whole thing would have been blown, and we'd have had to use post-event junk.]

Street: [STORM SAYS SHOW HE AND CLAYTON CHECKING GUNS — THAT'S A NEW ONE. USUALLY, IT'S TASERS, AND ONLY CLAYTON WITH LOW-LOAD SHOTGUN — BUT DO IT]

Fast action takedown. (Storm is the man — great action shots). Van driving away.

<<BREAK>>

WRAP: Jet landing NYC, closed limo to Halls of Justice, use the prisoner hand-over with DA Cotton Matther... police taking Pettigrew away, handcuffs visible. (We invited news channels to shoot it all; use some of their footage as source).

FINAL SCENE: Grandma Mary's house. Storm hands her a check for $55,000, hugs all around.

Find it, but she does say, 'What a wonderful gift.' <<END>>

(Source: $55,000 as usual from our production fund while we wait for reward payment. Probably will take the other Peregrine Fund investors years to get their monies back. Jeez, don't the viewers know we wouldn't have even used the Grandmommy segment if we had not first apprehended Pettigrew?!

As Storm says, 'no glory for failure.' By the way, be forewarned, a first: Storm wants to view the post edit. Has a bug up his ass; guess he wants to give this show a little goosing. Hope it's not a new Stormin' Norm. Don't forget, wrap party next week. Like to see rough cut by then. Producers want an early copy for some promo or something —

Confidential, do not distribute — Hope this helps us for next season's renewal. Remember, we have two projects floating, six months out in research. In May or June, another snatch and grab to film for the pipeline. Hope it's not the last. Ciao. — b/a

Scene 3: Season Wrap Party
Setting: Late night, Sky Bar at Mondrian Hotel, West Hollywood, February 2011

The private party bounced and weaved, and even with a Gestapo-like bouncer at the door, the terrace was sprinkled with crashers and wannabes, interspersed with front office executives of the Five Aces Studioz production company and their guests. Not the A-List; it was more of a B-gathering, gentrified enough to have a few paparazzi hanging out downstairs, their cameras poised. Just in case, Lindsay (drunk and wearing a monitoring bracelet) or Lady Gaga (naked but painted in Day-Glo colors) dropped by.

Callie stood near the bar, a glass of champagne in her hand as a defense mechanism, warding off groupie handshakes and hugs from the front office personnel. "Great year for *King's Retribution*," they all seemed to say while snarfing down the production company's complimentary cocktails and buffet canapés. She replied stiffly, accepting their congratulations with a forced smile, listening to advice given by people who knew nothing about how the show could be made better, and blathering reminiscences of certain shows that seemed to stand out, or so she was informed.

The staff crew visited among themselves in whispers, on a downer bender; the next season was unannounced, and they were worried about their futures. The two cameras, CAM ONE and CAM TWO, were present, as usual, and in operating mode. The contracts they had signed meant that at all public functions and on set, they had to be unobtrusively filming, so video film of the stars was candid, not showing actors playing to the camera. CAM TWO was stationary, to the side of the entry door, most certainly focused, Callie supposed, on Storm's grand celebrity entrance. CAM ONE wandered the crowd fringes, picking up snatch shots; perhaps for a future documentary in the making, or maybe a requiem, or planning for the sales pitch deck to be used later for syndication.

"You gonna get drunk and slug someone?" This came from the show's on-camera muscle, Clayton Briggs. He took the empty glass from her hand and replaced it with more bubbly.

"He hasn't arrived, and I am sober, dammit."

"Hey, it's not that he has all the control. Scriptwriters and production suits have put our little pegs in the holes." He stood over her, looking down. Clayton, an ex-NFL linebacker, was Storm's shadow when the grabs were made, more pushing and shoving than fists flying.

After two years in close proximity, Storm and Callie knew Clayton's secrets, even the one his former wife had been unaware of during eight years of a turbulent marriage. Callie saw him glance over above the imbibing, giggling young women on the bar couch who thought his stares were for them. His eyes fell instead on the thin young man nattily dressed in Polo garb. Quick smiles about the in-joke flashed between the men. In Hollywood, career positioning for second banana hunks required remaining in the closet.

"Your agent has you booked off-season?" asked Clayton. The strong man had a good side business himself, appearing in television ads for a national chain of health clubs.

"Nothing lucrative per se. A guest appearance on *Ellen* prior to the Grandmother Mary episode." She chugged at the champagne. "Storm will do Leno."

"That's it?"

"Negotiating for a mobile phone app commercial. Guess I'm just not in the league of Paris, Snookie, or a Kardashian yet." Callie enjoyed her minor stardom and wished for more recognition but did not begrudge the heightened world of other television stars in reality world entertainment, the ones who pulled down $5-10 million a year from someone else writing their tell-all fashion and health hint books and hosting raucous birthday parties at Vegas night club venues. There was a public demand for the unique to amuse people during their daily drudge, in these days when they could create stars out of even pawnshop employees. *King's Retribution* seemed more respectable than the outlandish or trite formulas, with *Retribution's* audience Nielsen ratings in proximity to *Cops* and *48 Hours,* and it definitely ranked higher than storage war auctions and car repo shows.

Reviewers had niched this television action show as one entertainment critic wrote: "*King's Retribution* is where bounty hunters meet U.S. Marshalls, tinged with Mission Impossible tech, spiced up with a little A-Team humor thrown in." These days, Callie found no humor in her employment at all.

Growing applause drew their attention. Colonel (Ret.) David 'Storm' King, star of the reality television show "*King's Retribution,*" made his entrance, hitting invisible cue spots, shaking hands and accepting praise for a season well done. He worked the room, a consummate politician knowing whose ego needed to be stroked. Though to Callie, Storm's ego always came first.

His walk of fame brought him to Callie; her expression set strong, heat emanating, ember tinder to the powder keg. He ignored her temper with a forehead kiss and, in turn, was ignored by her; she looked away.

"You aren't going to make a scene here tonight? A few low-life paparazzi are stalking the sidewalks outside, eager for your flare-up." He talked through his bared teeth, so his face seemed locked in a grin.

"There will be plenty of time to make my sentiments known. Of course, you know them already."

"They are not going to replace Clayton, or even Bennie, the wheelman, with you. Strength is required, and you know it. Give yourself credit — you're designated as the Beauty-with-Brains-Babe. Everyone admits to that. Once an army colonel, I now play the director general of ops. And *you are a co-star,* somewhat. Can you ask for more than that?" He threw a few beguiling nods to passing fans.

Callie seethed.

"I have worked hard, and I could do more. You know that. I'm an ex-policewoman. I have the creds."

"Yes, my dear, but a policewoman, even if once the head of the computer section of the San Diego Police Department, does not make you a ball buster for hand-to-hand fisticuffs with criminals."

"I didn't do too bad with the bodyguard in Brazil. And I've stayed in shape, even on that one episode where I ran the FBI field course at Quantico. I held my own."

"Indeed." He gave her a leering tug to his eyebrow. "And am I to assume I will see more of that tonight? Exertion, that is?"

"Is there a choice? Just don't show up at my place drunk. And I am not in the mood for you to bring along some stray bimbo for a three-way."

"Tonight is a celebration, and tipsy might be an acceptable outcome. Besides, the Five Aces Studioz front office a-holes set you and me up with a business luncheon tomorrow. I need my special relaxation program in order to bring my A-game." He gave her that Storm smolder look, a mixture of desire and testosterone.

He did have animalism. After the show's debut season, their star pairing, her Spanish ancestry's hot blood, and his insecurities, which required constant propping up of his manliness, drew them together, collided more like it, two moths sucked into the candle of rutting passion. What they both knew, though did not admit, was that at this juncture in their careers, they needed and used each other for stability, to keep out all that was bad in the Hollywood-Burbank scene; the temptations and leeches that could drag down their ministardom by the wrong interview or an ill-timed photo.

Not ready to admit she was at a dead-end in their relationship, she capitulated with gruffness. "Don't be too late." And star and co-star went their separate ways in the continued frenzy of the wrap party.

Scene 4: A Woeful Ballad
Setting: Los Angeles, California

King stood naked before the window that flung the entire lights of the city of L.A. at him.

Mixed within the lights, his reflection stood out and bounced back from a soft glow emanating from the bathroom. He couldn't sleep. Callie could and was nestled under the covers, deep in another world of peace. *Good for her*, he thought.

His mind buzzed from alcohol and the ramifications of his recent memo to the post-production editor. King usually did not exercise his contract clause for overseeing final editing, but in this case, there was justification, known only to him. He prayed that the television crew and, later, the viewing public did not understand the crises as he did.

The season finale was in the can, following the proven storyline formula of a successful hunt and capture of the bad guy. This Pettigrew creep. King needed to subtly direct the editor to tweak and add revised cliffhanger flourishes at each commercial break. Maybe no one else saw it like he did, nor felt the mellow vibes he felt while shooting the last bit of location footage. The spark and magic the show had in the earlier episodes was not evident, and the tight-paced action did not match up to the military-style precision of execution he sought in each script.

His on-camera cast members, the "Flying Squad," each with their own expertise, seemed lethargic now, merely marching to the repetitive cadence of the first two successful seasons. Not having grit in your stomach nor the fervor to live each dangerous moment in a war zone would leave you a mangled corpse on the battlefield, and in the reality TV world, the results were similar, as in fatal, with show cancellation being the deadly bullet.

They could blame the inattentiveness on the uncertainty and the undertone of gossip in the last few weeks: Would *King's Retribution* be picked up for a third season? Cast and crew members were updating their curriculum vitae, just in case, and scanning *The Hollywood Reporter* and *Variety* for job opportunities in the more current reality shows with their hip, scatological, sex-texting voyeurism. Where was the next *Housewives Of* …? The next Jersey den of sin tableaux? All Reality TV was manufactured to whore before the gods of commercial revenue, anointed by audience-measured ratings. And, King would admit, but only to himself, he was among those tarnished zealots. He could not afford a cancellation or career setback. The paycheck was too good.

When the last season episode aired in a month, viewers probably wouldn't see the lifelessness, the plodding. Instead, the audience would view the standard formula, the hunt and capture and would certainly applaud this particular outcome. *King's Retribution* succeeded by appealing to a wide range of demographics. Women viewers, and many gay men, tuned in, hoping, as they had come to expect, that Storm King would somehow, for whatever reason, be able to take his shirt off and flex his well-toned abs and muscles, whether he was lighting an explosive fuse or swimming in shark-infested waters. Note: muscle man Clayton Briggs was never allowed to compete with a naked chest.

Demographics showed that straight men in the 16-30 age group enjoyed the macho aspect though most of the dangerous work, except for the actual grabbing of the culprits, was staged by the Special Effects coordinator, Hiram Abbas, but it was not all fakery. Storm had the talent on his resume, including the U.S. Army's Silver Star. True hero status did not hurt the rep.

As Season Two filming ended, athletic moves before the cameras were not coming easily to King. He increased his morning exercise regimen to rid himself of creaking knee pops. Pain pills and a few bracer cocktails masked the aches in his lower back, where micro shrapnel fragments lay dangerously close to his spine. Certified healthy by the production company's doctor, he was good for a few more years of gung-ho acting. His pained swagger made him look fierce, with the intensity of a rogue killer, and the audience, caught up in the chase and catch, forgot that the show had never killed a fugitive.

Maybe, he mused, that was a negative for the violence-acclimated media masses — the lack of blood spatter. Most injuries to the apprehension team were the fault of missteps and bad luck, nothing too serious. Leave the jackass moves to cretins. Meticulous planning; that was the key. Avoid risks.

The future dogged King's thoughts. The television show, in the right time slot, had its loyal fan base and should be picked up by the network, but King feared fatal stagnancy, and this doubt made a soldier vulnerable. There needed to be an infusion of new ideas — some brainstorming to make everyone take notice.

These were his thoughts as King gargled the last of his warm scotch. He glanced at the sleeping Callie, unsure of where they were heading. Too many uncertainties. And then there was this lunch tomorrow. He didn't even know whom they were meeting with or what sort of game face he should wear. Certainly, fake optimism would have to be plastered onto the expected King caricature, not as a soldier but as a media star. That was a role he could handle well.

Scene 5: A New Script
Setting: Los Angeles, California, February 2011

Smoldering, a slow, angry fire burning inside left Callie hot flashing. She was mad at King for being an insensitive jerk, for dumping her at the wrap party and later coming to her drunk, the sex more groping and pawing. She could analyze all that and see the man insecure about being a star or, with all the young starlet sex, no reason for him to offer commitment. Easy for him to wake to see a new face each week, and then when remorse sets in, run back to her as the only stable force in his life.

What galled her even more was that now he sat across from her, nibbling on bruschetta, giving off no warmth, no charm, no indications that she was someone special. Men!

Dammit, it was really her own fault, she conceded. Her needs were screwed up, and avoiding "Shallow Hal" types putting the moves on her drove her into a self-imposed cloister, rationalizing acceptance of the man sitting across from her, the star of *King's Retribution*, was the safe bet for the moment.

The scheduled luncheon meeting found them both at the Asian fusion restaurant *Katsuya* on Hollywood Boulevard, where they were surrounded by the movers-and-shakers crowd. She was not privy to the topic of the meeting and despised blind agendas. She had just been told to show up, a star required to make a showing, the luncheon blessed by the heads of Five Aces Studioz, their production company. Five Aces owned and produced King's reality show, as well as a couple of mediocre sitcoms. Several years back, they'd had a string of hit, low-budget slasher movies, reruns on late-night cable, where Callie feared her own career might be headed.

"I'll ask the writers to enlarge your part next season," said King. It was his tactless way of asking forgiveness.

She was having none of the bullshit. "That's how the fight started, you may recall. I don't need my role as the show's 'Hooters Computer Tactician' expanded. I want to do action field work, so if you're sincere about helping my career, redesign me as a Lady Rambo."

"You saw how the Pettigrew grab went down. That bodyguard could have shot me. What would you have done if he pulled a gun on you?"

"Shot him in the leg. And, as you'll recall, I did help disarm the asshole."

It wasn't what King wanted to hear. She was Rambo, alright, very much like Sly's movie character: off-kilter, the loner. He did not come out and tell Callie, though she certainly had guessed, that the show's producers had hired her because of her curvaceous body, her pixy-tease face.

She was typecast as a Sandra Bullock Spanish-Mexican actress, and her sexual salsa allure was a balance for Retribution's masculinity. *Too bad she smoldered as much off-screen as on-screen*, thought King, dismissing her concerns as he wondered who the studio was sending over for them to schmooze.

Callie arched her back like a spitting she-cat, looking around the table for the messiest thing to throw in his face if needed. Sushi seemed to be the fare of choice, but she stopped as a stretch limousine pulled up in front of *Katsuya* and paparazzi positioned their camera cannons. A staged arrival, which was not unusual in Tinseltown, where restaurants like *The Ivy*, *Bazzar* or *Michael Mina's XIV* were the places to be seen and caught unaware (yeah, right). Most diners turned their heads, wondering who would alight from the opening limo.

The buzz began.

"Hugh Fox and Samantha Carlisle," Callie whispered aloud more for her own benefit than King's. Stars can be star-struck, and though a television personality where she had her own public recognition, she accepted she was not on any 'A' List. "People Magazine reported they are an item. Quite close for the last two weeks, I read."

"I see you're into deep literature."

"This from a man who quotes Rush Limbaugh as the gospel?" She watched as the beautiful and extremely nouveau riche couple gave directions to their assistants. Their mutual bodyguard, a hefty, broad-shouldered wrestler-type in a sports coat, moved unobtrusively into nearby shadows.

"I wonder what they're doing here?" Callie had spoken too soon.

"Colonel King and Miss Cardoza," beamed Hugh Fox, walking their way and extending his hand. His other hand rested gently on Samantha Carlisle's back. Touching tenderly, Callie noted; not so much guiding.

Rising to meet them, both Callie and Storm reacted to this honor with mild shock, soaking in the people-watchers near their table and themselves wondering what was going on.

After cordial greetings were exchanged, the lunch menu was perused, and food orders — rock shrimp tempura and miso-marinated black cod — were placed. Awkward silence infused the high-profile foursome. *Nothing left to do but get down to the business at hand*, thought King with a Scotch neat in his bloodstream, and being an ex-military aggressor, he took the lead.

"I had no idea the show's producers wanted us to meet with you. Wish I had been forewarned," he remarked.

"I am a recent fan," Samantha told him, smiling at both TV personalities. "In fact, in the last two weeks, I have studied all your episodes. Miss Cardoza, I think you have hidden talents."

Callie could not help but beam and shot a quick glance at King that said, 'See? Told you so.'

"I wonder how you go about selecting your show's topics, your quarry?" Hugh gave off an aura of sincere curiosity, and King felt it his duty to illuminate his honored hosts, assuming one of them would pick up the check.

"Well, the producers have a research team that scours newspapers, gets tip reports from prosecutors' offices, or even from bail bondsmen who handle high-priority cases. With our show's popularity, sometimes there are anonymous contacts to our office with a lead or a storyline to pursue."

"What comes next?" asked Samantha, showing her interest but also studying Colonel King with an apprising intensity. Callie, his co-star, knew how much the *King's Retribution* star loved being the center of attention.

"They start a priority system, using the information they have so far. Who's on the run, and where might they be hiding? Then our writers have a bull session with Research and see which story is best to develop. Several of our story projects are two years out."

"And when you do select a target, you seem to catch the criminal."

"Teamwork we can be proud of." King gave a nodding kudos to Callie, trying to mend fences. Callie hoped these mega-rich people realized that many shows were scrubbed, either because the crook was caught or because the bad guy went to ground without a single clue to give direction. Much of the show's camera work never saw the light of day.

The luncheon courses started, and between bites, Hugh and Samantha tag-teamed with questions about the show and its personnel to the point that Callie realized something was in play.

These two multi-millionaires knew too much, and their questions were not naïve. On the contrary, they were confirming what they already knew.

"I notice that the networks, and nearly all cable channels, have one or more of their own reality shows," said Samantha. Further, she commented, "I read somewhere that COPS, on Fox, debuted in 1989, won the 1993 American Television Award for best reality show, and it is still tops in its time slot. Fans seem to really get into reality crime-police shows like *King's Retribution*." Callie kicked at King under the table, but the flattery smothered his senses over her shin-pain warning.

Hugh Fox asked, "Do you see reality shows like yours fostering stereotypes about criminals? Most are minorities, aren't they?"

"I have read those editorials," answered King, "but we're different. We go after criminals who are business savvy and who think they can get away with it. Most of our criminals are Anglo, whereas pure cop shows, like *48 Hours*, are inner city and have a higher percentage of urban minorities. We would go after any fugitive, though."

"I find some reality shows demeaning," said Samantha. "They speak to our lower base values. They're all about television executives going for ratings. And they exploit the participants' hunger for attention and their eagerness to publicly parade any lack of moral integrity.

"Why can't a show aim for a greater moral target, try to benefit mankind?"

Callie saw Fox hide a chuckle as he put a piece of sushi into his mouth.

King felt he had to defend his livelihood. "I agree there are shows aimed at a young audience and pandering to sexual stupidity, but again, look at *King's Retribution*. People, audiences, want to see good prevail. That has always been my — our — objective."

All four of them left the truth unsaid: Ratings were the measurement to gain paying advertisers, the lifeblood of all public media platforms.

Hugh Fox looked at Samantha Carlisle with a smile that acknowledged silent agreement.

"What if we had an idea for a story?" asked Hugh. "Someone to pursue and capture; would that interest you?"

Colonel King finally saw the trap. He had accepted the compliments as his due, when in truth, he concluded, he was being set up to read a fledgling, wannabe author's script. He maintained his graciousness, though, rocking back in his chair, a little more suspect. Callie gave him a subtle, 'You're on your own, buster' look.

"The show's producers would be open to any great plot line," responded King, always the soldier-statesman. "Especially from you, of course. But they make the final decisions." He spoke quickly, correcting an error relating to his ego. "Naturally, my opinion is heard when I see any of our action elements missing. And the prize, the evildoer, must have the panache to catch the audience's attention and draw them in from crime to capture."

Callie saw Hugh Fox beam. It was a surprising trait; child-like, a kid on Christmas morning. His looks, she decided, leaned toward cute, boyish. He was an adult youngster having fun, not someone wearing a masculine mask like Storm King.

"I'm glad to hear you say that," said Hugh. "Indeed, I have an evil fugitive in mind. And the research required and qualified apprehension team not only fits well with your television show, but we both have decided you are the people to bring it about."

Callie had a feeling of foreboding and sensed trouble.

"Who is this felon you're after?" King asked heatedly, disregarding who their luncheon guests were. "Some ex-employee who defrauded you?" His voice got a little bit sarcastic. "I don't think we can create a solid hour around an executive's personal vendetta."

Hugh paused a good ten seconds before answering.

"Osama bin Laden."

"What?"

"Who, rather," corrected Samantha. "Osama bin Laden, the terrorist war criminal."

"Bin Laden." King scoffed and laughed. "The U.S. Government, with all its spy and satellite tools, has not even gotten close since they botched up his capture in the Tora Bora Mountains of Afghanistan. That was the last known sighting. Some say he's dead."

"And he may be which would be glad news for the world. However, my initial research indicates that he is still alive. But the question is: if you were given an infusion of logistical support, additional funding, and enough research personnel to accomplish an intense investigation about his location, would you undertake to search for, and if possible, capture Osama bin Laden?"

King began a silent staring contest around the table as his mind clicked. Fast comprehension, like a military field decision, data in, assessment risk — yet, when it came to an answer, he felt he would go no farther than lip service, and he knew he could fake interest. His 10-second decision took in television viewer statistics. Maybe *King's Retribution* could build the storyline's intrigue over a two-show segment and generate a media circus with *History Channel* flair. Touting the chasing of a terrorist as a season opener, even if they didn't catch him, would guarantee high ratings and a third season. But he also saw the downside. A program like this, attempting to capture a world-famous terrorist, he believed, would certainly fail to reach its objective and perhaps end in ridicule, like when the mustached hypester-journalist Geraldo opened mobster Capone's safe only to discover it empty. Yes, that captured a large viewer audience, but Geraldo had come off as a cliché for sensationalist and poor investigative journalism. So, King prudently took a neutral course. Don't offend the money.

"Yes, I would be interested. But I don't see the producers going along. They like safe formats, outcomes assured, and all packaged up sweetly."

"I don't think you have to worry about your production company being in opposition," Samantha said. She was all business, folding her napkin on her plate as if the meeting were at an end. "Hugh and I bought Five Aces Studioz last week. We're your new bosses. And we want you to capture Osama bin Laden."

REEL TWO

Headline from *Washington Times* — December 23, 2010

Osama bin Laden is Dead

Is bin Laden dead or alive? Nobody seems to know for sure, or if anybody does, he isn't saying.

The White House's Afghanistan-Pakistan Review this month didn't even mention him despite an ongoing, decade-long manhunt.... Al-Qaeda wants America and the world to believe bin Laden is alive. His image is a specter of the horrors of September 11, helping build public support for everything from troop surges a globe away to warrantless wiretaps. But the image of bin Laden is getting moldy, and there's little reason for his ghost to scare anyone anymore. If al-Qaeda wants America to believe bin Laden is alive, it should put up or shut up.

[Column written by Robert Weiner, former Clinton White House spokesman]

EPISODE FIVE — Strength Lies Not In Defense

Scene: Al-Qaeda at Home
Setting: Somewhere in Northwestern Pakistan Mid-March 2011

"And that is the last of your reports?"

"Yes, beloved Sheik. Well, there is an odd one. It should be dismissed for its silliness, but it does pertain to you."

"Irrelevance to you or the Council may, to me, have importance."

"Various media outlets report they are mobilizing another team to find you."

"For six years, we have been safe here. Corrupt governments cannot smite we who are righteous to a just cause; again, as all others, they will fail." His puffed bravado was for show.

"As you say, but they are not government agents. It is an American television show."

"What?"

"From Hollywood."

"Khalaf, that is insufferable. Allah watch over us from such decadent gnats. You were right; think no more of what is doomed. Let our plan proceed. After all these years, we have heard from the Scientist. The time is coming. Go to al-Awlaki and tell him to awaken the Professor

48   S.P. Grogan

from his long slumber. When all is in place, I shall authorize, and only by my command, the launching of *Crimson Scimitar.*"

"Yes, sire. Once again, an assured victory to the Faithful."

"Indeed. When we shall succeed with *Scimitar*, and that day is near, then the world will have television worth watching. Allah be praised I hear no more of such cow dung."

With a nod of his esteemed leader's head, the man known simply as Khalaf was dismissed.

From his sitting position, he leaned over and bowed reverently. Then he rose and, with homage, kissed the older man on the cheek, noticing the tiredness in his Sheik's taut face.

Watching Khalaf depart, sipping on water to ease his throat, bin Laden had to ruminate on all past jihadist enthusiasts who had come to his banner. A torn fluttering banner to this date, perhaps not so to the future. He could look back to understand that since 2004 al-Qaeda had been reduced to a disorganized organization in name only. Yes, there had been attacks on the 'unfaithful' but not by al-Qaeda's supreme direction, nor the approval of bin Laden, who still had to praise those 'martyrs' publicly. It was as if al-Qaeda operated independent franchises, most now run by those making decisions to their own local political ideological whims. Certainly, they were not listening to the pronouncements leaking out from bin Laden's undisclosed location, where he was trying to shift these mosquito bites to a more encompassing scourge. America was the true enemy, the one to focus on; to drive them out of the Middle East would bring the rise of the Emirate. He had to admit that in recent years, since 2008, he'd had difficulty with the messaging.

First came President Obama's decision in 2008 to launch more missile and Predator drone attacks against his leadership cadre, which had indeed been successful and had forced bin Laden to create a strategy of *kumun*, basically 'hide yourselves.' And one cannot effectively create a public groundswell of support if the followers can't find the leaders.

Next, and more recently, the rise of the Arab Spring in December 2010. He admitted to senior leaders that he was caught off guard by the public demonstrations and the demand for regime change. He was truly unprepared for stepping up and being seen as a leader of the masses. And so, his singular thinking came to be: an attack on America would mean the resurgence of the 'new and improved' al-Qaeda. He knew 9/11 had not achieved the goals of U.S. forces' withdrawal, quite the contrary. He needed a grandiose scheme to impact how Americans lived and visibly demonstrate their comfort of living could and would be impaired. To that focus, he was an excellent planner, a master of ideas, mind to paper, to create shock-and-awe events, tempered towards the implementation of success with secrecy and paranoia.

Two attack plans were in motion. First, a young zealot, Younis al-Mauritani, a member of the North African jihadi group al-Murabirun, had made a favorable impression on bin Laden and the senior leadership group when Younis was sent as an envoy to North Waziristan. What bin Laden liked about Younis was his fervor demanding al-Qaeda launch offensive actions sooner than later and on the world stage. It did not hurt his standing; he revered bin Laden.

Communications soon developed between them, and a concept was born, based partly on the success of the *U.S.S. Cole* attack in Yemen; the new idea was bin Laden's, but Younis was honored to be appointed 'project manager.' The plan: multi-strikes against the world's maritime oil tankers, those capable of carrying more than 1 million barrels of crude oil. With 700 tankers on the seas, destroying even 10% of them would shake up the world markets and economically impact the United States, dependent on foreign sourcing in the last decades. Hurt them before they could achieve self-sufficiency and not need the Middle East reserves, which would be a blow to one of the main base tenets of bin Laden's antipathy against the Great Satan.

By September 2010, bin Laden had funded €200,000 to Younis to begin planning the attack on ocean tank carrier operations, but when Younis suggested these attacks be coordinated with the other planned American attacks, bin Laden said, no, two separate attacks were better to improve the chances that one would succeed to maximize their goals.

What bin Laden was really counting on was *Crimson Scimitar*, the most developed of his plans, its germination beginning as far back as 2002 with the Mombassa attacks and 2004 Madrid train attacks, all of which were laid at the feet of al-Qaeda, but neither had been sanctioned by al-Qaeda leadership. This lack of operational control, forcing them to publicly laud these deadly achievements, definitely chafed the al Qaeda leader. Bin Laden even became shrill and, in one of his communications, said attacks should be made on those U.S. States that voted for George W. Bush, the re-election then occurring. Faced with structural disarray and becoming a pariah among Muslim countries like Iran, Pakistan, and even Iraq, bin Laden began internal efforts to revitalize al-Qaeda, starting with new leadership, a new, younger generation, and those with a rabid commitment to the Cause.

The arrival of the university-educated Egyptian jihadist, Khalaf, who was born Maulawi Abd al-Khaliq, came about by a circuitous route dealing with a serious thorn in Osama bin Laden's life at that time: turmoil at the hidden family enclave in Abbottabad, Pakistan.

Little known to the outside world, during the last many years, bin Laden was being held 'hostage,' more pressured than physical, in several ways; one with Iran and the other force being brought by his bodyguards who had been protecting him for over nine years. Long story short, in Iran, this was hostage blackmail. With many al-Qaeda families fleeing from the invasion of Afghanistan by a U.S.-led coalition, the jihadists fled with their families to Pakistan and several groups to Iran.

Understanding the Mideast requires a non-confusing simplified scorecard: al Qaeda (known also as *Qaedat-al-Jihad*) was composed of Sunni Islamic extremists, who find the Shia

50   S.P. Grogan

Muslims of Iraq, Pakistan, and Afghanistan to be apostates. Tenuous peace marred by occasional blood feuds existed over the eons between these two religions, and as of recent, Iran 'captured' and imprisoned many al-Qaeda fighters, the implication being: 'if you attack us or our mosques, your people will remain with us and suffer extreme privation.' Bin Laden had sons in Iranian prisons, his wives and children were forced to live under 'house arrest.' He wanted to get them freed and bring them to live with him.

His other issue was with his two bodyguards, Ibrahim and Abrar, who did not want their protection to be overwhelmed by added family members, for by this date, March 2011, sixteen individuals were living in the compound; and these two *guards* believed they could not control more arrivals, could not protect the al-Qaeda leader, and verbally refused him the right to bring in those members who had escaped Iran. In this Spring of 2011, Family versus Cause was coming to an internal face-off. The bodyguards threatened to quit, but bin Laden hastily persuaded them to stay until June 1st, 2011. He needed time. Secretly, Osama bin Laden was looking to replace the bodyguards and had begun a search for those who would meet his strict requirements: intelligent, brave, and who understood his vision of the Cause. On the original shortlist was Khalaf. More academic than a gun-wielding Bedouin type, Khalaf had impressed bin Laden with the young man's voracious appetite for book reading and critical Islamic thinking. In the late-night discussions that followed, Khalaf found himself an operational planner to an idea of bin Laden's, coincidently formed by Khalaf's hunger for books. During his visits, the young man appeared in the compound as the always traveling Senior Courier, hinted to be a distant cousin by blood; while structuring the details Osama bin Laden, as tactician, saw them. Over a four-month period, *Crimson Scimitar* came into being. As the end of March approached, the plans had moved to 'Standby,' awaiting the 'Launch' signal from the Supreme Leader. Bin Laden hesitated; sooner would work, but an attack on the 9/11 anniversary would generate a more politically and media-driven impact.

Osama bin Laden watching Khalaf exit, nodded approvingly and thought highly of the boy's scholastic ability. In Emir bin Laden's growing judgment, and after Younis's field success, he would elevate Younis to full status within the Leadership and, if proven worthy, Khalaf, still too young and unseasoned, could move into the vacant spot as deputy to the Legal Committee. Certainly not bodyguard material, as he discovered Khalaf had never even fired a weapon.

It would not be an understatement to say that in late March of 2011, Osama bin Laden had a full plate of activities before him, but were these too many spinning plates to juggle?

And, by his growing confidence, al-Qaeda was again destined for new glories. Who could trifle with a decadent American television show or whatever? Bin Laden made a note to see if any of these *King's Retribution* programs, as Khalaf told him, were out on VHS.

Scene 2: The Compound
Setting: Abbottabad, Pakistan

Khalaf left the large room on the third floor and went down the stairs past the second floor, where he stayed overnight on occasion for reasons of both exhaustion and safety. The second floor was the Media Center, but a certain hide-away sleeping niche had been created behind a desk in the side wall for Khalaf's minimal needs and as his solitary reading space.

He walked out into the hard-packed dirt compound of the ground level, filled with running children and women at domestic work. A tethered milk cow grazed upon a small hay pile. His emotions were mixed. His meeting with his mentor and leader, Sheik Osama bin Laden, had gone extremely well. It was his fourth meeting since being elevated to primary contact between the leader of al-Qaeda and the Supreme Council, who, on rubber-stamped consensus, then forwarded its leader's commands to the jihadist network. Khalaf's position as a special courier required him to make a physical appearance before the other ruling members of the Council, all of them secreted throughout various countries, his messages designed to avoid any chance of telecommunication eavesdropping. He accepted the truth of his posting, for such travel occurred when grandiose plans were in play. If he was caught or placed in a compromising position, it was understood that death must come swiftly from his own hand.

Recently his thoughts were jumbled and caused by his ambition, which he acknowledged to himself, this knowing desire that he wished to achieve more. Gratified, yes: he had been singled out for his past success in infiltrating the Muslim Brotherhood in Cairo, creating a small cadre of followers who, though swearing fidelity to a conservative strain of Islam, all secretly swore a blood oath to the Caliphate of al-Qaeda, a true belief in the coming new power in the region, superior to all current weak governments in the Middle East. Their mantra was eons old: *Death to all unbelievers.* Sheik Osama bin Laden was destined by Allah to be the first Emir, and Khalaf challenged himself, eager in his determination to one day be sitting next to the holy throne.

He watched a goat being brought into the compound. Life around him seemed pastoral, although Khalaf thought this place of high walls seemed more prison than refuge. Osama's son, the one called Khalid, stepped to his side.

"Where is he sending you this time?"

"Yemen. To speak to our brothers al-Wahishi and al-Awlaki." Khalaf did not trust the cleric, Anwar al-Awlaki. He was suspicious of everything from the West, and al-Awlaki came from America, born and raised. But bin Laden seemed to trust the young spokesperson of al-Qaeda, and Khalaf acquiesced to his supreme commander. Still....

"Will the 'Sword of the Just' be there?"

"Yes, I expect so. This is a major meeting concerning our activities in the West." Saif al-Adel, known as the 'Sword of the Just,' had been appointed November 2010, by Khalid's father as the "new commander to spearhead al-Qaeda's offensive of operations in the West," so stated an English-language New Delhi newspaper.

"It must be nice to see the world," said Khalid, his eyes observing the cloudless sky. "I would like to see Paris sometime. Photographs in magazines are quite elegant. Did you bring us any new books or magazines?"

"One book only, sad to say." Khalaf knew they all suffered from various forms of cloistered stress. He smiled at the 22-year-old, expressing encouragement to the son of his leader, perhaps someday an heir-apparent — although another son, Hamza bin Laden, a year younger, had the reputation and name of 'Crown Prince of Terror.' Khalaf understood that one must make many friends to have a few worthy allies.

"Your books have been quite helpful, have they not?"

"Yes," said Khalaf, believing that bin Laden's son did not know how much these books had come to assist the cause. "Read them again, for they will improve your reading of English."

"The tongue of dogs," laughed Khalid. They watched as one of the women slit the bleating goat's throat while another caught its flowing blood in a cooking pot. The woman holding the red-drenched knife looked up. She smiled at Khalaf and went back to her work, slitting the goat's belly. From his recent visits, Khalaf had been accepted as a distant cousin to the Sheik. It was not true, yet it gave him stature in an Arabic world based on tribes held taut by the strict Koran code of family obedience and blood honor.

"Ahmed," Khalaf called out. A man, looking disheveled, as if he had just arisen from sleep, approached. He smelled of sweat and greasy food, but then Khalaf considered the whole compound ripe with nefarious odors, stale and, at the same time, pungent like old garbage not yet discarded.

He held out his hand. "From the Emir. He wants it sent out today; now, if you could."

Khalaf's voice was determined as if to set the pecking order — that he was not a mere runner but a higher-up. The other man took the small thumb-sized flash drive that was their method of conveying messages to the outside world.

Ibrahim Saeed Ahmed and his brother, Abu Ahmed al-Kuwaiti, were couriers who made trips to local coffee shops and connected via the Internet with others across the globe in the al-Qaeda network. It was simple and effective against the risks. Khalaf glanced up, more of a twitch in his afterthought. The Americans, NATO, had too many eyes in the sky. Were they, he wondered, at this moment, spying on him?

Scene 3: The Watchers
Setting: Abbottabad, Pakistan

Indeed, they were watching, but they were in a whitewashed building only four hundred yards away. On its second floor, two men, dark-skinned with beards, were taking turns at observation, one watching from the shadows with binoculars, the other resting on an iron-framed bed, its rumpled mattress decades old. A Nikon camera with a telescopic scope lay on the table next to him.

"The gate is opening." The man adjusted his 10x42mm Swarovski Optik binoculars and focused.

The other man grabbed the camera and moved quickly to his post.

Half of the large green gate door had swung open.

A gray-bearded man with hunched shoulders walked out carrying gardening tools and a ragged sack in the other hand.

"Their occasional gardener. The local weed whacker." Both men spoke English with Middle Eastern accents. Eyes went back to the opened gate. "Wait. Here comes Scooter."

Abu Ahmed exited on an aged Vespa, its exhaust smoking. For their records, he was known as 'PI #1' [*Person of Interest*]. At times, for longer drives, he also drove the compound's only vehicle, a never-washed cream-colored SUV that the watchers could identify by a white rhino image on the back spare-tire cover.

"Wish we could follow him," the photographer said, clicking digital pics of Abu. He turned his view back to the closing gate, saw no one else, and noted that the gardener had disappeared around a corner of the compound, perhaps towards the fields that lay beyond.

"Can't blow our cover. Just log occurrence, date, and time," said the man with the binoculars, scanning the high walls and the surrounding land. Nothing out of the ordinary, everything as usual, including the butchering of the goat in the corner of the compound.

"Someone else up the food chain will tell us what we are doing here."

"Do we even know who or what we are looking at?"

"No idea. But someone thinks ho-hum Pakistani suburban life is worth cataloging. And we informed them of that one occupant we rarely see, our 'Tall Man,' (dubbed by the higher-ups as 'The Pacer') as being of interest."

"You have to admit it's strange that a group of hired help has run of the place."

"Pakistani squatters, my guess." They returned to their routine, one observing and the other lying on the bed, resting.

54 S.P. Grogan

Shouldering his field implements of hoe and rake, Khalaf maintained his disguise for the half-mile walk past the potato fields to his predetermined niche between two large houses, unseen from the roadway. Leaning the gardening tools against the wall, he stripped off his robe, tugged away his false grey beard, then rifled through the sack and emerged from the shadows a captain in the Pakistan military. It was a logical choice because of the proximity of their compound to the Pakistan Military Academy in Kakul. This disguise would have few questioning him, his forged papers leaving no doubt about his reassignment and posting down to Karachi.

What set him apart, and gave him a no-nonsense need for saluted response, is that he wore the green ribbon of Sitarae-Jurat (Star of Courage), the third-highest military award in the country. Any authority to challenge him would be awed by his seething contempt at their bothering a hero. It was enough aloofness to get him to the airport in Islamabad, where his next disguise would turn him into the traveling computer salesman for IBM Egypt. Two flight stops, and he would be in Yemen for his meeting with al-Qaida leadership in the Arabian Peninsula. Khalaf would deliver the message on *Crimson Scimitar* that bin Laden said to stand ready, activation to soon follow.

More importantly, Khalaf wanted to have a one-on-one with Naser Al-Wahishi and, better still, with al-Adel to build up support for him joining the *Scimitar* campaign in what he knew would be al-Qaida's greatest triumph against the United States since the attack one decade ago that forced Osama bin Laden into hiding…in plain sight.

And Khalaf knew his day of proving himself was fast approaching. Secreted upon him, he held the thumb drive with the innocuous letter that had been coded: *Crimson Scimitar is activated.* Only a select few would receive the message to be conveyed by word-of-mouth to even fewer: the Sleepers, buried deep within an unsuspecting populace.

Scene 4: The Professor Meets the Enforcer
Setting: Las Vegas, Nevada, March 2011

Halibut with a mango avocado salsa sounded enticing, a treat that even his kids might appreciate from their old man. In recent years, he had become quite the gourmet, addicted to experimenting off the foodie websites and television food networks. Tonight, fish sounded right for a healthy menu. As he pushed his grocery cart down the aisle of the gourmet market, he stopped to pick up a bottle of northern California virgin olive oil for a light brushing on the fish that he would grill outside. What else? Mixed spring greens sounded good, with a Balsamic vinegar dressing. Only the best for Marcie and the kids. Thinking of his children reminded him that it was another hour before he needed to arrive at the soccer field and pick up the youngest for the drive home.

He did not see the dark-haired man with the ponytail approach, also pushing a grocery cart, staring at shelves as if seeking a hidden food item. As they slowly passed each other, the man leaned over and whispered, "On the day of victory, no one is tired." In Arabic!

The family man, the cook, and chauffeur of children froze at those words of a distant memory. He turned in shock that was tinged with fear, aware that the world as he knew it had just changed.

The stranger spoke again, a smiling casual tone. "Do you mind, that jar of pickles behind you, the sweet gherkins, could you hand it to me? ... Professor Rogers."

The Professor noted that the stranger peered from beneath a ball cap bearing the number 51 of the local baseball farm team. The man was clean-shaven, with light olive skin that could pass for a suntan, and seemed like an ordinary shopper unless one looked closely, as the Professor did. The ball cap pulled down, scraggly raven-dark and greased hair poking out, hid what he finally realized was the oddity. The man's right ear was missing. Barely visible, half covered by his hair, a nub of flesh with a dark hole, like an enlarged but deformed belly button. The stranger spoke again, an unknown accent barely discernible. "And do you have something to say to me?"

Hesitation first, then, as if by a mute who had just found his lost voice, scratchy and strained, came the English response: "Days will show what we were ignorant of; and news will come that you have not sent." He paused, glanced both ways to be assured of being alone in the shopping aisle with this man, the messenger, knowing he was about to reveal a deep mystery.

In Arabic, he whispered, "In the name of Allah, the Benevolent, the Merciful."

"Very good, Professor." The smile seemed innocent as between friends, but the stranger's severe tone showed otherwise. "Had you not said those words, I would have had to kill you on the spot, and your Marcie would be a grieving widow unless I decided to visit your home tonight and slit her throat and those of your children. Too messy, I have found, and what with all that new carpeting in your bedrooms."

The Professor felt the blood drain from his face, both with mortified fear for his family but more because of knowing the truth. James Rogers, the Professor, was not the man others in this community knew. Long before his wife and children, before the house in the Las Vegas Henderson suburbs, his soul had gone over to a darker cause.

"What do you want of me?"

"Are you prepared? Are they ready?"

"Yes, but they will be as surprised as I am. Such a day seemed like it would never come."

56   S.P. Grogan

The man sneered and leaned close, venom coming from his lips. "You are fated to play your part. Prepare your people. Look for a man who calls himself a scientist, perhaps within the next month or within several months. He will say the word, 'Scimitar.' You will learn more from him. I will return with your supplies. If you have any issue, however minor, that might put our plan at risk, contact me immediately. Here is a telephone number. Memorize it. Let it ring five times, then hang up. I will contact you and see what can be done about your problem.

"Goodbye, Professor." With a casual air, the messenger sauntered to the end of the aisle, abandoned his cart, and disappeared around the corner.

For the longest time, the Professor could not move. Memories flooded back, bitter-tasting ones. His stomach soured, and his heart went cold.

Scene 5: A Distant Memory Recalled
Setting: Ten years earlier, Las Vegas, Nevada, June 2001

The Report of the National Commission on Terrorist Attacks Upon the United States would give the specific date as of June 29th, 2001. The Professor remembered that night quite clearly, especially the meeting place, a strip club called Olympic Gardens. A young, idealistic jihadist back then, mostly due to brazen thoughts forged by a personal history demanding his private revenge, he sought contact with like minds and had a passion for action. In his recruitment during his Middle East tour in the early 1990s, they allowed him to sidestep the training camps to preserve anonymity, and he became known, only to Osama bin Laden and the Supreme Council, as *The Professor*. This code name was bestowed because, at that time, in his early career, he struggled as a low-paid teaching assistant in the International Affairs department at the University of Nevada-Las Vegas, UNLV.

He could have arranged the meeting for their motel room at the EconoLodge on Las Vegas Boulevard. But no, they were being careful, and later, on national news after the attacks, he understood why. All four men were tightly wound, which was visible only by eye-darting paranoia, and skittish towards an assignment of which they told him nothing and dropped no hints. He admired their minimal speech of caution, seeing them as they were, True Believers, Defenders of the Faith, unquestioning soldiers, focused and absorbed by details towards the execution of the plan. For two days, disguised as awed tourists, they cruised Sin City, ridiculing all they saw as being the heart of the Great Satan. Or so they told him.

Dance music blared while women in negligee costumes circulated, pitching their wares of 20-dollar lap dances or, for that extra something, the hands-on more in the back VIP room. The music covered their conversation. Three of the men kept the women from approaching too closely by the subterfuge of pretending to be enamored by enhanced breasts, leering at the pandering pasty, perfumed beauties, the men liberal in paying the harlots to press against their crotches with swaying friction. The Professor noticed, by the men's sarcastic smiles, that they did not mind suggestive banter with the strippers and, in fact, enjoyed testing in conversation the cover stories they were using while traveling the United States.

"Are you committed?" their leader asked into the Professor's ear.

"My parents died in Lebanon by Israeli warplanes, planes made in the U.S., dropping U.S. manufactured bombs." It was not quite a true story, but his hatred for the foreign policy politics of his adopted homeland was real and surged from deeply buried aggravations.

"Can the heat of your anger remain fired years from now when you are called to your destiny?"

"I pledged with my dripping blood to Allah, to the brotherhood of al-Qaeda. There is no turning back."

"You may rejoice that we will first strike a magnificent blow, and you may watch with pride as this government run by drunken cowboys quakes and quivers in fear. That will be the beginning of their undoing, and then later, and I do not know the details, your task may be even greater. But you must wait and control your desire for revenge.

"Patience must be your ardent wife. Someday the call will come."

"I am ready. What must I do?"

"You must create three cells of four members each, no cell to know of the other, all to live quiet lives until they are called upon. And best that they look more like you, faceless, indescribable as to country of origin, rather than like us, like Saudi exchange students with limited visas."

"It will be done."

"Consider several years, if not longer. Beyond that, I know nothing more, except when from a stranger you hear the words in Arabic, 'On the day of victory no one is tired.'"

He handed over a scrap of paper. "Memorize this and respond to your messenger."

The Professor repeated the code words with deep emotion, his eyes closed as if he had heard a command from heaven, and when he recovered his senses, the young men were gone, and he was left, jostled in the midst of parading flesh, to pay their bar tab. Maybe one lap dance would not hurt, he considered, a reward for the distinction they had tendered and how they must value him. Eyeing an attractive blonde who wiggled his way, he pulled out $40. *My pledge is sacrosanct,* he thought in affirmation, feeling himself harden. *Playing with her breasts will not compromise my assignment.*

From the date of the strip club meeting, only two months remained before 9/11 and the burning, imploding towers, the Pentagon, and the lonely Pennsylvania field. Those men, those heroes he had met, did change the world, but the Professor did not think such change was to the benefit of his people or his faith. Transgressions continued. The Unfaithful still occupied his people's land. His own call to duty would not arrive until more than ten years later, to this day, when this severe Messenger of Allah in the supermarket had awoken his other self. Success or failure, the implied message had been delivered: be prepared to succeed or die. He breathed deeply and finished his shopping. Yes, fish tonight. If he hurried, perhaps he still had time to watch his son's soccer game.

Scene Six: The Night Stroll of Contemplation
Setting: Late March, The Compound house, Abbottabad, Pakistan

Well past midnight, the Watcher saw the gate open, recognized one of the men, a Pakistani 'squatter,' they still believed, and saw the man walk out, someone shutting the gate behind him. What had recently added to make the occupants of the house more suspicious was what the man did next. He took his time looking down each side of the road, looked across the street at the several homes, not seeing he was being spied upon from the shadows of the second floor of one of the residences, where a room had been rented out.

Known as PI#3 (Person of Interest), when the man seemed satisfied that nothing about the empty roadway and the surrounding quiet homes might cause concern, he, as his custom, lit a cigarette and walked down the road. The Watcher let him disappear into the darkness. If on schedule, PI #3 would return in approximately an hour, knock on the gate, be let in, and the large house would be silent until early morning when the women rose to tend to the meals and the children. The Watcher went to the small desk, trying not to wake his companion, nearby snoring lightly. A book was opened, and under pinpoint illumination, a notation was made, the occurrence logged, date and time. PI#3's return would be likewise noted. All seemed routine. But the two Watchers, and those that came to relieve them every two days, were curious, and requests had come lately from their superiors to hurry up their identification of the residents.

Everything they saw seemed pretty standard hum-drum, except that they all agreed, as did those at CIA headquarters in Langley, Virginia, across from Washington, D.C., it had been too normal, too routine, and that suggested 'organization.' Last week, they had identified one of the men, PI#2, as a known al-Qaeda courier who lived there, and there was this 'tall man' in the courtyard once spotted by their surveillance drone, used rarely. Slim evidence. Nevertheless, these patchwork facts were being brought together. Wild guesswork was given more weight, probably by an Agency analyst, probably bored, who wanted something, anything to add some excitement — who wrote in the front-page margin during his last week's

Crimson Scimitar

review of the Watchers and their filed report. *Is He Here?* Those three words launched events based on vague conjecture.

PI#3, bodyguard Ibrahim, unseen by the Watchers, made his usual circuit, walking a quarter of a mile to a path that cut through a field, which then brought him in a circle to the back of the house, all the while his head swinging side to side, looking for signs of the odd. The pistol in the waistband of his sirwal made him feel uncomfortable in the way he walked, his worn balghas treading each step, careful not to trip.

At the back of the house, after one last furtive check of his surroundings, he began to uncover piled brush, then discarded broken crates, an old rug with worn holes — all covering, concealing…a cellar door in the ground. He knocked and heard a knock below returned; the snap of a lock, and as the wooden trapdoor moved, Ibrahim helped to pull it up, and Osama bin Laden made his way up the steep stairs grasping handholds as he came up into the cool night air.

Would it not be reasonable to believe that a house with one large front gate, and a smaller side gate, might also have some sort of back entrance, an escape route? That the house itself might have some hidey-holes built into rooms of a house the owner arising from the cellar had designed himself, ignoring various building permits as required in the submitted architectural plans.

Bin Laden was dressed in casual mufti, his white garments, dishdasha, replaced with a deep brown costume of sorts. No turban, his hair hung down. No one would recognize him, except he was slightly taller than Ibrahim. But at that hour, no one was to be seen, though, in the distance, muffled night noises floated over the rooftops from the town square, a few cars and trucks revved and gears changed on the two-lane highway over a mile away.

Osama bin Laden made his own sweep of his surroundings, and then both men took off on a ritual walk, not far, more like four or five circuits, in the back fields, so his legs would limber up, and he could shake out the kinks in his back from lying around watching too much television, and old videos. The titular head of the world's most dangerous terrorist organization, so thought those of the Western World, had what they might call 'cabin fever.' In his thoughts, since they never talked aloud, Osama bin Laden was seriously considering moving to a more friendly country, somewhere safe to hide and protect himself and his large family, when reunited, and doing so before his *Crimson Scimitar* attack was launched. His thinking this night was on domestic matters; hiring a new obedient staff of guards around him and having his entire extended family within reach of his embrace. As he walked in the darkness, guided by a sliver of moonlight, and with his bodyguard at his side, he mulled, *"Next month, I will put in motion a house-hunting search to another country. I have been here too long. One must not become careless."*

EPISODE SIX — Planning is Everything

Scene 1: The Talent Hunt
Setting: Late March, downtown Los Angeles

Hugh Fox entered quietly, sliding into a seat at the back of the courtroom. The trial in progress. Los Angeles Assistant District Attorney Booker Langston addressing the witness on the stand, his witness.

"Let's talk about the robbery again. It is your written statement...The State's exhibit 12-C...that on the day of the robbery where store owner Trang Lin was slain, it was your testimony that you were in the car waiting for your buddy, Mr. Jasperson, to exit, believing he was just buying cigarettes. That is what you told the arresting detectives, and that is what you are telling the court and jury here today?"

"Yeah, I had no idea what Jasp, Mr. Jasperson, was going to do." The witness's name was Rafael Gomez. It was noticed that Langston never gave him the courtesy of calling him 'Mr. Gomez.'

"And that is why you are testifying today that you were not part of any robbery. And that when the police showed up by chance, you and Mr. Jasperson jumped from the car [it had been established earlier that the car had been stolen], and both ran until apprehended a couple of blocks away, the alleged murder weapon found in a direct line between you two and the store, but you said Mr. Jasperson, and he alone entered and shot the proprietor, Mr. Lin. Correct?

"Yeah, I only ran because I saw Jasp had the gun, news to me, and I wanted no part of whatever he had done."

"No further questions at this time."

The jury saw Langston's furrowed hard face as he retreated to his seat, and they might have inferred that his grimace was for satisfaction at the testimony, or jaw-set of repulsion, as if being near the State's key witness, his witness, the man was not without sin. That this alleged criminal, regardless of trying to save his own skin, had agreed to 'snitch' for a lesser sentence.

From Fox's perspective, as he watched the public defender grill the State's witness, he was surprised to see she was holding her own, seeking to poke holes in the witness's testimony. Jasperson's appointed attorney went by, as she was addressed by the court, 'Miss Eberhardt' or 'Counselor' at other times. Fox, as he studied the give-and-take, realized that defense attorney Eberhardt was trapped in an awkward dichotomy of physical appearance. With Bookie, there was no doubt; he was black as the heart of equatorial Africa's darkness. Where Miss Eberhardt was light mocha in color, mixed enough that she might win points if jurors were prejudicial to a client's representation, meaning white to white view, or that she must be black to black jurors.

And as Fox analyzed the players, it was apparent that Miss Eberhardt, to be part of the club, had downplayed her wardrobe into a serious player in court; dark grey skirt, dark blue blouse, long black hair in some artful bun, but in her face, even with dismissive expressions as she questioned Jasperson's once-friend, Gomez, perhaps where beauty might be a handicap, her face was 'child-like,' very attractive, but still baby-faced enough that it might be a detriment. She seemed an attorney pushing hard, too obviously seeking to be taken seriously.

Still, she scored a few points. Had not Gomez received a lesser sentence for his testimony for the prosecution? Yes, as he testified, he was innocent, but a few years he would accept the proffered 'accessory' charge versus the main charge against Jasperson of felony murder. She tried to get him to admit he was the shooter, but he denied that and stuck to his story. Just the driver, no more. When she got to him, defendant Gomez gave off mean stares and shook his head with negative vehemence so that the judge warned him about being too demonstrative.

Hugh saw that his friend Langston seemed detached, not following the defense's legalistic jabs against Gomez, "betraying his *former* best 'buddy,' Jasp, to save himself." Langston missed a creditable chance to throw out an objection, but the distracted prosecutor flipped through, it seemed, exhibit photos of the crime scene. Revisiting a particular set of images.

In a moment, ADA Booker Langston rose and interrupted the defense's cross-examination.

"If it pleases Your Honor, I apologize to you and the jury, but I would request a sidebar without the jury's presence."

The judge gave a few seconds thought, but Langston's reputation barred few questions of those within the Halls of Justice. The judge gave the proper address to the jury not to talk amongst themselves, and they were led out by the court bailiff. The sheriff's deputy carted witness Gomez, handcuffed once more, into a side annex.

When all was quiet, the judge directed himself back to the prosecutor.

"Mr. Langston?"

"Your Honor, when the State made its case against Mr. Jasperson, the detectives and the District Attorney's office based their decision to file against him on the basis of the evidence, and that we had one witness who gave sworn testimony that defendant Jasperson pulled the trigger. Mr. Gomez was offered a lesser sentence, but on the condition that his sworn plea to the lesser charges affidavit held the truth as to what actually happened. Today, I find we may have partially erred in relying on Mr. Gomez."

The defense, Miss Eberhardt, unsure of where this was going, assumed that she should say something profound and jumped in. "If the prosecution says there was malfeasance in their rush to judgment, I demand a mistrial."

Both judge and prosecutor looked to Counsel Eberhardt. The prosecution certainly would re-file any charges dismissed today, but Harriet wanted a win, sweet victory, against the best prosecutor in the city.

Langston smiled a tut-tut dismissal at her on behalf of the judge and himself.

"If I may, Your Honor." He went to his desk and picked up several crime scene photos.

"Your Honor, these photos were entered into evidence. They were used by the prosecution to show where the suspect's getaway car was abandoned. It is my understanding that the car, untouched, was hauled off to impound and searched, but as I see photos of both before and after the search here, I believe the car was left in the abandoned condition, exactly as it was first brought in."

"And what does all this have to do with the price of bread?" admonished the judge. "I hope we are arriving at a conclusion."

"Yes, Your Honor. Look at this series of photos of the car, photos taken at the scene, and then ones taken after the car search at the police auto garage." He handed photos to the judge, who stared at them, and handed them over to Miss Eberhardt, who likewise glanced through them, but with an expression of confusion.

"Your Honor, the car seats," explained Langston.

The defense stared, then gave the photos back to the judge, who likewise squinted at the detail.

"Yes," inquired the judge, "What am I supposed to see?"

"The girth of the suspects. Mr. Gomez is heavyset, Mr. Jasperson is the beanpole, Mutt & Jeff differences. Yet the car seats inform us where they actually sat, which is directly opposite to what Gomez testified, that he was the car's driver, waiting on his buddy. The way the car seats are set, only Jasperson could have easily fit into the driver's side, not Gomez. It leads one to believe, and we admit the defense probably would have eventually seen this discrepancy (he threw her a sympathetic smile that she took as demeaning condescension), that Gomez as the passenger and Jasperson as the getaway driver is a more logical conclusion.

"But before our capable colleague continues with her request, let me forestall that by saying the prosecution, from now on, on any redirect, will be treating Mr. Gomez as a hostile witness, and we will re-file tomorrow that Gomez violated his agreement, and further, I will be filing first-degree murder charges against Gomez."

"Then my client is innocent?" Eberhardt asked, confused. Had she indeed won for her client?

"Not in the least. As you are well aware, under California law, in the commission of a crime where there is a death, those participating can be held accountable. It will be my position that Gomez and Jasperson are both guilty of felony murder, regardless of any argument on who pulled the trigger. As I am sure, Judge, you will draw to the jury's attention when the verdict instructions are read into the record."

The judge, accepting Prosecutor Langston's request as reasonable, ruled to dismiss the court for the day, so he could await and review the prosecution's newly filed charges before deciding if a new trial was called for. By law, a new trial would be mandatory. Miss Eberhardt returned to the Public Defender's office, unsure what had happened. Was her case in a better position, or were two alleged killers going for the same fall? She had to ask for separate trials to keep Gomez from tainting any defense for Jasperson. Still, less befuddlement as introspection grimace, she should have caught the nuances of the car seats. She had prep to do on what her new strategy might be, definitely on placing the gun into Gomez's hands and seeking a sympathetic juror on 'reasonable doubt.' She felt she might have the edge to win one for her team. She turned to leave, noticing the young man in the last row slip out among the exiting crowd. Was that....? No couldn't be. Why would a mega-biz wheel be here slumming with the lowlifes? Booker, putting papers into his briefcase, had not noticed his friend silently come and go and did not realize that Hugh Fox had been on a talent hunt, a star search.

Scene 2: The Pitch
Setting: Grand Central Market, Los Angeles

Seeking to place another brick in the wall.

The call came out of the blue, and they agreed to meet for lunch.

Fox launched the discussion topic.

"Whatever happened to that one case I read about a couple of months back, the two gang-bangers who killed a store clerk. Some controversy to that?"

Booker Langston was surprised that Hugh read anything but business and technology media, especially the stuff in daily newsprint, from stuff made from trees. Oh, yeah, he does the internet.

"About ten cases ago. They were both convicted of murder, though the killer got life without parole, the getaway driver has a chance for parole in 10-15 years."

"The driver involved in a homicide got less of a sentence?"

"I thought I had them both on the greater charge, but he had a great defense attorney, kept niggling me down on details, that gained empathy with the jury, to throw her a bone, I guess." Booker could have believed that she gained an advantage, but she was a capable attorney; he could grant her that without blowing too much smoke up....

"Why are you asking? My trial work provides a new entertainment platform for you?"

Their brunch, downtown L.A, at a new place, *Eggslut* in the Grand Central Market. They had to stand waiting for a table, but the food made the wait worth it. Their conversation was general, the usual entry points: weather, health matters (none), and what was happening in their separate worlds. Booker unattached, Hugh at the beginning of dating someone more than once. More general than specific. By mid-meal, Hugh had his diagnosis.

Finally, answering Booker's question. "I have been checking into you, reading clippings, talking to people. Nothing too invasive but to confirm what's wrong with you."

"And that is?"

"You are bored."

"I disagree. Fighting crime by putting away scum has its moments."

"But you are on a circular track, ambition burned out, no hunger for upward mobility. Plain to see. I know the signs well. I border on a 'Thomas Crown' complex myself.

"The movie?"

"So successful, one might seek other diversions, even criminal ones, to find refreshing entertainment. But don't worry, you won't see me in court, with you across the aisle. Not quite yet." Hugh coughed out a laugh like he knew an inside joke. "But I can see the signs in you. The lost spark."

The attorney put down his knife and fork to consider this conversation they were having and not necessarily disagreeing with his friend's assumptions.

"And, if so, what do I do? Go to the beach, paint seascapes? Swim in the ocean where there are real sharks, not the land ones I deal with daily?"

"You would die if you chose an activity that did not stimulate your juices to right wrongs."

Booker stared at his friend. He knew the young man was wealthy beyond several small countries' economies combined, but he always found the essence of Hugh Fox was, though a case of mild eccentricity, the guy was actually shy, down-to-earth, no snob attitude, no 'greater than thou.' Like a Midwestern hick with an 'aw shucks' frame of mind. Of course, sharp, that part of the brain which saw solutions through several depths of chaff complexities. And to the lawyer, who himself could construct legally brilliant arguments, the young man who had come calling, who would pick up the check, even when not an expensive lunch, had an agenda.

"And do you have something in mind to cure me of institutional funk?"

"Requires a leave of absence. A sabbatical. Quite a bit, in fact. Maybe three to six months."

"Eight years of vacation time stored up." The unsaid said. Now out in the open that Booker had been considering possible changes.

"Do you have a problem if I pick up all costs to underwrite a project, a portion of it you will be in charge of?"

"I think the past balance sheet is in your favor. You did pave the way for me to make a transitional jump from New York to Los Angeles. I was in a little bit of a stupefied haze during those years."

"Alcohol-induced grief only caused a short-term absence of your talent. Once we cleaned you up, your intensity impressed everyone in the legal circles."

"Yeah, you can call in a few markers, if reasonable, and if you are paying for whatever you're pitching, I say that salves any guilt I might be afraid of feeling. I assume this 'project' is going to be one of the Fox spectacular undertakings. Am I to do patent law? Or defend you against some sexual multi-orgy trap you wish to escape?

"I want you to oversee a mock trial." Booker gave Hugh a stare of surprise.

"Like a law school might put on with graduate students?"

"A little bit more formal. Let's say it's more like reality television, like a show trial, let's say."

"Like Judge Judy TV?"

"More show trial fancy than that, higher entertainment values, and, yes, televised. Probably pay-per-view format and before a live audience. Who knows, maybe an 800 call-in number to express who's winning at each session. That sort of pure snazzy show production."

"I don't know. Sounds like tawdry Perry Mason, legal sleaze. And you know I am not a public sort like that. My confidence was once damaged and still is not totally repaired."

"But everyone sees a man dedicated to justice when you perform in the courtroom; I can testify if I must that you are healed. That Miss Defense Attorney I once saw in court with you, she certainly recognizes talent, probably worships you from afar."

"Harriet 'Harry' Eberhardt is smart as a whip herself. She will do fine, just needs a little more court experience."

"You will not disagree that every court appearance before a jury is supposedly a calculated performance, a prepared act. Throw evidence into the mix, add spontaneity, proffer doubt, and that's what makes a television show like 'Law & Order' and subsequent franchise spin-offs successful.

66   S.P. Grogan

"What I am offering will be a challenge. I am just now putting my idea into a game plan. Lots of pieces still to fit in."

"You say a 'game plan'?"

"Perhaps the wrong wording. I'm serious, quite serious. I know the victims. I just need to catch the 'alleged perpetrator.'

"Catch?"

Hugh laughed. "Isn't that crazy? I know the crime, the victims; I just don't have the criminal in custody."

Langston was a little bewildered.

"You mean, if this is television, you haven't cast the bad guy?"

"Something like that. In the script, the bad guy, as you call him, has all the evidence stacked against him, the people are against him, he definitely comes across by his 'alleged deeds' as being evil.

"I will give you all the funds to put together the set, the trial event. It has to be done just in a certain way, and I have my reasons for that. And, since it is reality TV, you appear in a courtroom that is televised. You've been in trials that are taped. Just act your natural self. And I want you to participate."

"And I am to be the calculating and hated prosecutor who wars against the brilliant defense attorney, nursing his loss in the end with pained stoicism?"

"Something like that. But I want you to be the defense attorney. I want you to save this guy from being executed. After all, in your early days, before life went to shit, you were the best in New York. You bested the District Attorney and his office all the time. This script is made for you, in that ironic sort of twist."

Booker knew Hugh was in his Save-the-World mode, that he would do what he set out to do. He should be honored to be asked. Did he want to catch the comet and go along for the ride? Maybe he did need a diversion in his life. What life?

"And you want me to go from real-life prosecutor to show trial defense attorney and become the hero and save the client? Your script must be a doozy?"

"Something like that. But you should know how it may come to be: I think your client is guilty. But if I am to be surprised at the verdict, you may be the one who can win."

"Why not?" Booker Langston really did not have much happening in his life, nothing that was exciting. Why not, indeed.

"Great. However, before you defend, I just need to catch the bad guy." They both laughed, Booker not understanding the truth in the joke. It was a doozy — something like that.

Scene 3: Return to the Fray
Setting: March 2011, Bagram Airbase, Afghanistan

He saluted. His SEAL commander opened a file in front of him. Shawn remained at attention and realized there was another man in the small office.

"How are you healing, Pacheco?"

"Fine, sir. Ready to go back active."

"Good." His commander glanced into a file folder. "Records indicate you finished your SO [Special Warfare Operations] Training. Your skill set, I see, is explosives. High marks. Know your stuff, sailor?"

His commander gave him a throw-off smile. It was an inside joke. SEALS were of the Navy, Delta Force, the Army. The officer closed the file.

Shawn did not like where this was going and was unsure of his response; nevertheless, he straightened his backbone even further, tightened his stomach, and pushed out his chest.

"Yes, sir. I feel I am quite qualified at anything those terrorists throw at us or bury on the roadways." He did not mean to say all that. The words surged beyond his usual control.

From the other man seated off to the side, "The leader of your platoon says you took it very hard when you lost a friend in the field?" Shawn, caught off guard, froze for a second as bad memories of brilliant flashes in his face resurfaced.

The man added, "Losing someone that close can cloud your decision-making. A booby trap going off can make a SEAL over-cautious the next time."

Pacheco now understood. The other man was a Navy shrink. They had flown in a psychiatrist specifically to sideline him and take him out of the action. No way. His answer had to be to their psyche, not his. He had to hide his torn feelings and erase Montoya's smile, which came to him most nights in his dreams as a haunting image.

"A SEAL has to go on. He can't compromise his training or put those around him at risk. Sir, it is sad to lose anyone. But the job is foremost."

"And you think you can perform your duties and be the explosives expert you were trained to be?"

"Yes, sir!"

"That's what I thought too. A few scrapes can't stop a SEAL." The commander reached inside his drawer and handed over a small black insignia patch. It was a SO badge, an anchor crossed horizontally by a trident and diagonally by a flintlock pistol.

Pacheco could not hold back a smile. Finally, all the concentrated work, the long hours, had paid off.

68   S.P. Grogan

"Don't thank me too soon. You're not going to be sewing that on quite yet. I've just signed papers to transfer you."

"Sir?" Suddenly, bile stood in his throat. Did his fellow SEAL team members not want him around? Was there a conspiracy to trade him off? Stateside perhaps?

"It's an official request order. You are going over to SEAL Team Six. One of their ordinance SOs came down with appendicitis. Bad luck for him, and they require backup. That's you. Six is being called up and is training on an operation. I have no details.

"Does that suit you?"

He wasn't being asked for input. At least it sounded temporary — out on loan, a fill-in job, and then they might send him back. A team was a team. Four was not Six, and he knew he would be treated as an outsider until he showed his stuff. But it was no different from the vibes he was getting around here.

"I'm ready, sir."

"Pack it. You're going to a special camp Six is setting up. Leaving tomorrow at 0900. Orders are outside and cut for you. Dismissed."

Pacheco saluted and departed.

The commander looked to the Navy doctor, waiting for an opinion.

"What can I tell you? He's combat-stressed, but aren't all those kids? Does he have a breaking point? Is he at it? Yes, and maybe, but it's buried deep. I couldn't see anything from looking at him. His medicals show me nothing. And as for all this 'black cat jinx crap' coming out of his unit, that's what it is. Pure bull shit."

"Everything else about Pacheco is top-rated. I don't want to lose a good SEAL."

"He won't be productive, nor will his comrades, if they're all looking over their shoulders at him. Yeah, the transfer might solve most of the problems, providing the Six operation is nothing too explosive, pardon the pun."

Scene 4: Our Doubts are the Real Traitors
Setting: Late March, Yemen, at a village north of the city of Sayyan

It was his second trip in the last two months, and Khalaf had not made this entire trip to watch an execution.

From the moment he landed in Sana'a, Yemen's capital, he found himself in a war zone, surrounded by citizens teetering on civil war. His escort guide met him at the airport and then deposited Khalaf into a rusted bus filled with people going in his planned direction. Soldiers in military trucks rushed down streets, and the closer he got to the city's edge, the more armed men were in civilian clothes. All along his route, he heard scattered gunfire.

Precautions were essential, and there was safety in feigning innocence. Everyone was nervous about what group, government or anti-government, might erect roadblocks and randomly rob or shoot the passengers, or both. During the three-hour trip, with its many stops to load and unload passengers, the bus baked from the heat to the point that interior shade was no help. Nor did the desert breeze make a difference, with its light dusting as the bus growled along.

The roadway leaving the capital was surreal, with refugees trudging along pushing carts or driving overburdened cars and trucks, making their way on both sides of the road heading in both directions — into the city, toward the safety of government forces, and out into the desert towns, seeking safe harbor among the revolutionary tribes. Near the coast, al-Qaeda maintained strength and vied to be a major player. Because of this, the meeting had been scheduled in the opposite direction, away from any disputing factions.

For this journey, Khalaf styled himself as a relief aid worker, wearing a red crescent armband, a variation of the West's Red Cross. He would not hide in traditional garb. He wore jeans, covered loosely by a short-sleeved, white cotton shirt, and secreted in his waistband a German-made Heckler & Koch, a P2000 9 mm, a lighter pistol nevertheless quite deadly. His disguise was designed to confuse any questioner, who would not easily guess which side he belonged to. If any rifle pointed their way, he and his guide, a young Yemeni boy barely 10, would take control of the bus and shoot and kill whoever impeded their journey. Firing away would be only in facing death since he had never trained on the pistol he had been given by the boy.

He abhorred this method of crowded, bumpy transportation. His presence deserved more consideration: he was a diplomat at the behest of bin Laden, with important messages.

And, as he felt, they would try to put him in his place at the end of his arduous trip; he did not like to be "invited" to stand under the broiling sun, waiting for the prisoner to be led out.

Shahin orchestrated this show, which was undoubtedly timed for Khalaf's benefit. The men had met several times since 2005, and always it was as if they were competitors in one-upmanship games, suggestive, though never anything overt. It was merely role-playing, strutting.

Khalaf had bin Laden's confidence. Shahin basked in recognition from the Supreme Council.

By bearing witness, the inference was obvious — he must carry back to their leader in

Pakistan, the fervor shown by the Islamic fighters in Yemen, unwavering to Jihad. Narrow-faced, with a pointed, reddish-black beard, Shahin, the hawk for al-Awkari, motioned to his men.

They dragged a beaten man out of a mud-plastered building and threw him in front of a crumbling wall. The prisoner was black-skinned and not of Arabic origin. Khalaf could hear the man's wails, certainly crying out his innocence and mumbling shouted prayers. The men surrounded this unfortunate, laughing at his discomfort, and it was apparent to Khalaf they could not understand what the man was saying. They slung their weapons carelessly, smoking cigarettes as they glanced at the offender on the ground. He did not cower but writhed in pained lamentations from a broken leg and arm.

"You have been found guilty against Islam. You are a spy!" shouted Shahin.

The man muttered indecipherable incantations, certainly reciting his prayers.

"Accept your fate."

The man began to stutter out words of anguished woe, and Khalaf realized he recognized the words but held his tongue to silence. To intercede would be to invite confrontation and an awkward showdown with meaningless consequences. Khalaf had more important goals to accomplish, which were more valuable than a stranger's destined doom.

Shahin called to the small boy who had been Khalaf's guide to the meeting.

"Taeal huna warith wamushahida" ["Come here, my heir and watch."] The boy left his mother's side and moved closer into the wide circle of onlookers. Not revealing any nervousness, more curiosity at the condemned, he smiled to his father.

Shahin held an ornate sword, a wide-curved antique called a scimitar. Then, because Khalaf probably believed Shahin did not want to become 'messy', he handed the sword over to his trusted bodyguard, a snarling Yemeni called Maj, who, with pleasure, aimed and swung the sword. The executioner's grunting effort sliced the man's head clean; it made a thudding sound, and pumping arteries spewed the victim's blood, spurting first a small hose-like stream, then easing as the pressure of life ebbed and like a dripping faucet, dark scarlet drops absorbed into the darkening sand.

Shahin took back the sword, wiped it against the man's clothes, and then strode over to Khalaf, who gave an impassive stare, showing no emotion, especially not the disgust he harbored.

"You see what we do with spies, Khalaf? The man was caught with a pickup full of ammunition boxes heading towards the capital."

"The evidence was overwhelming as to his guilt, I presume, even if you do not have a confession?"

"Yes, indeed, it was apparent."

"You realize the last words the man uttered were: 'I am innocent, as Allah knows'? Plus, he spoke a few words from the Koran."

"And the language he spoke, you recognized it? No doubt some form of Yemen dialect. We could not afford him to join the government against our revolutionary brothers."

Khalaf shook his head at the haughty ignorance. "Brother Shahin, he prayed in a dialect of Sudanese, from a small tribe in southern Sudan that is totally cut off from the rest of the world. Not only does that tribe ascribe to the holy words of Islam, but it is said the prophet Mohammed himself went to that region to bring the sword and to convert the people to Allah. I read about them when I attended Cairo University and listened to their recorded lyrical prayers.

"That man probably is, or rather *was*, purer in the original Faith than you or I. He was probably traveling to join his fellow Followers of the Faith, not the government. But you would not have known that, having graduated from the University of Virginia."

"Still, he was not one of us." Shahin shrugged indifference. Hatred among Moslems existed as old as the Koran, tribal schisms out of the blood of Mohammad, split apart by whose interpretation of the Koran was the True Word. Al-Qaeda sprung from Sunni doctrine, and all other sects, whether Shia or Sufis, were heretics, *takfir* (unbelievers), subject to destruction.

Brute slaughter did not impress Khalaf. He turned and walked towards the building where the al-Qaeda leaders were waiting. Behind him, Shahin reminded his followers of the justice done and warned them of what befalls those who do not follow the True Path. He handed the sword to his son to admire, fresh blood droplets still on the blade. Again and again, they all shouted, "Allah's will" and "Allah's is Great."

Scene 5: A Desert Committee Meeting
Setting: Late March, Yemen, at a village north of the city of Sayyan

"Thanks to our benevolent leader and his supporters worldwide," said Naser Abdel Karim al-Wahishi, "especially those who are technologically equal to our Western enemies. We have approximately three hours before satellites focus on this sector of the desert, and we must all go our separate ways."

He spoke from experience. Only last December, two American missiles had been fired on a militant camp at the Ghulam Khan sub-district of North Waziristan in Pakistan, wounding al-Wahishi in the arm. Two years before, there had been a similar meeting in Yemen, which al-Awlaki attended, and hours after its ending, government jets directed by a U.S.

communication plane circling overhead, pounded the buildings, killing innocents who had unknowingly reoccupied the space.

Here, today, the most imposing target of all was the greatest brain trust strength of the al-Qaeda movement in the Arab world, excepting the absence of bin Laden and al-Zawahiri.

Fifteen men sat in this room sipping coffee or ginger tea, several munching on *bint as-sahn*, the honey-covered puff pastry. Greetings of " مكيع مالسلا Aslamualikom" and " مكلاح فيك kayf halukom" coursed around the room. Khalaf was formally recognized by al-Wahishi, and a cooler nod of the head from the American, Anwar al Awlaki.

Fahd Mohammed Ahmed al-Quso, one of the collaborators on the *USS Cole* bombing, motioned Khalaf to take a cushion near him. Khalaf recognized Ibrahim Hassan Al Asiri, the Yemen Bomber, sitting in a corner, eating flatbread and fried eggplant as if he had not had a good meal in some time. Asiri, angrier and more blindly fanatical than anyone else in attendance, had tried to destroy cargo planes using PETN bombs disguised as copier machine parts. Similar bomb ingredients of his were used by the Underwear Bomber when he tried to blow up an America-bound commercial airliner.

Asiri had agreed to supply the destructive equipment for the *Crimson Scimitar* operation. Shahin would oversee its delivery into America and join up with a man known only as *The Professor*. Khalaf knew this much from the verbal messages he delivered between bin Laden and leaders of the Supreme Council. Of the operation's specifics, he knew little. The name, *The Scientist*, he had heard only once, and only in a whisper, not meant for him.

Discussions began, and it was like a corporate board meeting, with each attendee offering his report on various ongoing operations; after all, al-Qaeda boasted followers, commanders, and cells in more than 25 countries.

Ali al-Shihri, deputy commander of al-Qaeda in Yemen and former Guantánamo detainee, gave an overview of the build-up of armed al-Qaeda soldiers and other affiliated militants and their plan to make incursions against the Yemen southern coastal city of Zinjibar, seeking a softness in the underbelly of the government's defense forces.

Next, they heard from a courier who came from Northern Pakistan as a representative of Ilyas Kashmiri, the regional operations chief for al-Qaeda and its forays into Afghanistan. When not crossing the border, his soldiers and martyr bombers mounted attacks in Pakistan against Pakistanis; the goal was to undermine the American-stooge government. His report was positive, and all nodded assent at work well done. The American military had been publicly announcing drawdowns of troops in Afghanistan, with a total evacuation by 2012 or 2013 at the latest. Kashmiri, under bin Laden's direction, worked in the midst of formulating plans to coordinate with the Taliban to help capture regional towns in districts where the central government did not maintain effective control. The Supreme Council members gave their blessing, which reaffirmed bin Laden's titular power to give operational plan direction to all beneath him — at least to the few forces he could verbally issue orders to with a fair chance of compliance.

When the time arrived to present bin Laden's messages, Khalaf spoke sparingly and concisely, giving all the news that bin Laden wanted to be imparted, especially the ramping up of the *Crimson Scimitar* operation. He stressed that his master wanted the final say in making the launch decision and wanted full progress reports relayed to him for his opinions as the field operators initiated the attacks.

"We have heard your report, brother Khalaf," said al-Wahishi, "and we are pleased that *Crimson Scimitar* is going forward. We will do our part. With the anniversary of our holy brothers' martyrdom in America [9/11], we will launch our own regional attacks in remembrance of this new holy date."

Al-Awlaki spoke. "I feel our individual efforts, what we call the Lone Wolves, will bother the West more than your attempt at a master stroke."

Opinions of strategies differed within the ranks. The al-Awlaki contingent, which was younger and more technologically savvy, did not like the 9/11 attacks. A sleeping giant, the United States and its Western allies had awakened and thrown their military power to suppress the earlier gains, such as the Taliban's expulsion from power.

Before the websites of al-Awlaki were dismantled by Western authorities, they had more than 200,000 hits. His most famous utterance was, "If one killing upsets them so much, then we should have 700 followers killing 700 Americans." As recently as November 2010, he had posted a video calling for Muslims around the world to kill Americans "without hesitation."

His loyalty to the cause unassailable, Anwar al-Awlaki's teachings and personal encouragement caused the actions of the Fort Hood shooter, and he was the personal recruiter and handler of Umar Farouk Abdulmutallab, the attempted Northwest Airlines Flight bomber who tried to set off explosives in his underwear on Christmas Day 2009. Al-Awlaki, an American of Yemen ancestry, believed individual attacks — Lone Wolves — would be the most effective at undermining the security of Western countries. He agreed with bin Laden that America was the priority target — "The party of devils." But he wanted to do it his way, employing the famous line of a thousand paper cuts.

Osama bin Laden believed 9/11 to have been a success and had told Khalaf that another attack, greater than the Twin Towers, would be required to move the United States out of the Middle East and force them to abandon Israel. Hence, *Crimson Scimitar*. It was interesting that though al-Awlaki and bin Laden had never met, the Emir, in playing his politics, would give over the running of this operation to the young Iman, al-Awlaki, and his trusted deputy field commander, Shahin. That did bother Khalaf.

As young as al-Awlaki was, Khalaf believed in what the Iman espoused, for he thought of himself as an avowed fundamentalist, but he was also utterly loyal to bin Laden, and that was where his future of advancement lay. He did not have to like al-Awlaki nor Shahin, his protégé, yet Khalaf well understood his position and his ranking in this august meeting, a mere courier, one of three to his superior. Cautious, after everyone had given their opinions, he answered, "All attacks should be welcomed to keep our enemies in confusion."

"Yes," agreed al-Wahishi. "We support our leader in his goals to sow the greatest damage by his brilliant planning."

Khalaf felt this might be his opportunity.

"Whether it is your Lone Wolf attacks or *Crimson Scimitar*, it is my hope to go to America and be a foot soldier jihadist in one of the attacks."

"But it is not the wishes of your leader?"

"He need only listen to your agreement, and I will join with the others."

"It is well and good," said al-Awlaki, speaking in English, the common language of all who sat on the floor in the meeting, representing several nationalities. To Khalaf, it seemed unclean that al-Awlaki's casual speech used American idioms and analogies to basketball and rock and roll stars.

"Such loyalty is appreciated," continued al-Awlaki, "but this is an operation in the United States, and our most exalted leader has decided that what will bring success is our strategy of attacking our enemies using home-grown martyrs. We have a couple of agents in place that have passed as Americans for over a decade. To make changes will lead to mistakes."

The courier knew what was coming. It would be the orchestration of re-affirming the on-the-scene operational leader of *Crimson Scimitar*, this news for Khalaf to report back to bin Laden. And there at the door was Shahin, who spoke.

"I am ready to serve and will depart when the word is given."

Khalaf expected this choice. Not only was Shahin educated in America, but he was also a prized student from the Virginia mosque that al-Awlaki once led as Iman. Ten years ago, the acolyte Shahin had provided several stolen credit cards to be used by the martyrs of 9/11. And as the ultimate irony, Shahin had even accompanied the religious leader al-Awlaki when he was invited to the White House immediately after 9/11 to offer bereavement prayers for Muslim government employees.

"I will carry the word," said Khalaf, masking his disappointment, "plus the list of Lone Wolf attacks you have planned. Allah be praised for your efforts." In this, he was sincere, and he listened to the news from all who spoke, cataloging with a sharp memory what he must take back to Pakistan and to his future Emir of the coming First al-Qaeda Caliphate.

Plans were coming together. The current destabilization in the region would help their cause in rebuilding new regimes under al-Qaeda rule. The world would accept them as the formidable lion, there to receive the people's fealty, but only if America were to be humbled.

Crimson Scimitar would be the knife stroke to the neck against the weak and defenseless, just as Shahin had so adeptly demonstrated. So be it, accepted Khalaf.

It was Shahin's smugness of speech that Khalaf could not bear listening to. The operational commander gave only minimal details of *Crimson Scimitar*, speaking as though it were his own invention and not bin Laden's decade-old Master Plan of Attack, unknowing that by Khalaf's own suggestions, certain aspects of the operational plan had been modified. He might not know plan specifics, but the greater scheme bore Khalaf's imprint, and this rose above being a mere courier.

What happened after the meeting was the ultimate slap in Khalaf's face.

"A donkey?" He stared at the scraggly, emaciated beast of burden.

"Only a few miles to the pick-up point," grinned Shahin. "We must convey to the sky watchers that nothing of significance took place. Some of the Council will move to a school, among the children, and others will depart by fast jeep."

As Khalaf swayed and bounced over rocky terrain, a guide in the lead, he swore that his embarrassment would be avenged. He saw Shahin as the culprit — not a hawk, but a crow.

Scene 6: The Florida Cell of Misfits
Setting: Late March 2011, Miami, Florida

They were ten years in the making, and the Professor was somewhat proud of his three attack cells. Two of them, unfortunately, were criminal in composition, requiring money to be exchanged to gain uncertain loyalty, while the third cell gave blind faith, being made up of disillusioned, idealistic former students culled over the years and nurtured into his personal sphere of dissatisfaction mixed with fanatical fatalism.

The criminal cells had no idea they were being used nor that their final tasks would be nothing like what they had been told were their philosophical objectives. *The Professor* believed that al-Qaeda leadership — the Emir, bin Laden, himself — had imparted the ultimate 9/11 outcome information only to Commander Atta and the other chosen pilots. The rest of the attack cells that day thought they were going to hijack the planes, not crash them into buildings. It did not matter if a few of the foot soldiers were misinformed. If it assures success, ignorance for sacrifice is always a worthy axiom.

It was his Florida cell, if you could call it that, which gave him the most trouble. Its members acted more like 'weekend warriors.' They came in contact with the authorities in random circumstances and risked falling apart by arrest or internal disloyalty.

Hiding behind the excuse of another university conference on foreign policy, he found himself in an industrial section of Miami, seeking out the motorcycle repair shop. He had dressed down, slovenly, in dirty jeans and a plain t-shirt without logos. He parked his rental car several blocks away, and his walk in the humid air added a layer of sweat to his grimy appearance.

The repair shop, with only one BMW motorcycle up on a bay rack, looked more like a parts warehouse — probably because it was an illegal chop shop for stolen motorcycles hefted from other areas in Florida and nearby states.

The Professor's contact, Mike 'Gator' Donaldson, was the shop owner and primary mechanic. He was a stocky man with bad teeth and sharp incisors that gave him his nickname, while his physique portrayed him as a walking advertisement for a tattoo parlor, his tats having been poorly crafted in prison. His alma mater was the correctional institution called Glades.

Gator knew nothing about what was happening in the Middle East, but after an abusive upbringing and other sociological baggage, he hated all races and all religions. Outside of the occasional stereotyped racist epithet, he did not give politics much thought. More than anything else, he hated the Federal government. Pick some initials, and he hated them. DEA for his drug busts, IRS for his surprise audits, and FBI for stings he got caught up in. Local cops for expired license tags. He had no greater passion, outside of straight tequila shots and big-breasted biker chicks, than wanting to stick it big time to the government. This intensity provided the blind rage that drove him into the conspiracy, where the Professor gave him a specific destructive scheme to vent and destroy.

"Are the other clubs still in on this?" asked Gator.

"Just three of them, and again I can't name names. They hate the Feds as much as you do." The Professor passed himself off as a Cuban biker with an ax to grind, the ringleader from an outlaw club based out of Tallahassee.

"The more there are to help us, the bigger the body count," grinned Gator, displaying his tobacco-stained teeth.

"The other clubs will join you with their targets. Kill some, great. But we will achieve just as much by showing them as screw-up assholes when they can't catch us," the Professor assured him.

Walking from the garage into a fenced storage yard, Gator opened the door to a large aluminum shed, flipped a light switch, and pulled up a trapdoor hidden beneath an oil-soaked tarp. Inside, the Professor saw four wooden shipping crates piled atop each other.

Crimson Scimitar

"This came in last week as bike parts. Wherever you got this firepower, it's enough to blow up the entire Federal Judicial Center." Gator gave a gargled, congestive laugh. "Up until now, we've been practicing, playing around with dynamite that went missing from a construction company four years ago. You know, like blowing up stumps and fish in the swamp. But your stuff's gonna work like hot shit."

"In a couple of months, I'll get you word on the target."

The Professor saw Gator grimace.

"What's the problem?"

"It's Kettering. Busted on a meth charge. He's up for trial in a month. I'm afraid he might cut a deal — you know, and talk about our little blow-up escapades. Like me, he doesn't know what government building we're hitting. He might crap us out for holding unlicensed federal explosives. So far, he hasn't said nothing, but I know they're gonna put the heat on. He might be a good guy, you know, loyal, and a friend, but he's in a three-strikes situation when he goes before a judge."

Complications as they approached the *Crimson Scimitar* launch were unacceptable.

"Not good. We don't need a screw-up this late. We need at least three of you on this job.

And I'll be sending you one of my Cubans with explosive knowledge, but you guys are the soldiers, and you do want to send a message to the Feds, don't you?"

"Yeah, I know. So, I've been thinking. There's a buddy of mine, just out this week on Murder Two. Thinks it was a bum rap. Someone else pulled the trigger, but, you know, he was there when it went down, so they bundled them all up, and he got 15 years, but he was out in five because of a prison overcrowding release program. Still, he's more pissed than me. We're tight, and he'll keep his mouth shut. I can depend on him. Doesn't even have to know much."

"And your buddy Kettering?"

"I can move this junk to a storage unit I got. No one knows about it. Put it over there until your Cuban buddy shows up. I can start making the bomb packages to the specs you gave me. Kettering won't have anything to snitch about."

"I don't like loose ends. I know a guy...."

"Whatever." Gator glanced away in dismissal, his friendship with his buddy Kettering not so important as to derail blowing up the System.

"Yeah, whatever. You'll hear from me. The time is fast approaching."

"Can't wait to rock 'n roll," said Gator, locking away the explosives.

The Professor found the repair shop owner's statement ironic. Back in 2001, a 9/11 passenger, one of several that tried to save their aircraft from nose-diving into Washington, D.C., only to then crater in a Pennsylvania cornfield, said similar words. The Professor had come to learn post 9/11 that the cry, 'Let's Roll' is not merely a party but a call to action, and yet a rock in the highway, an impediment. A worn traveler, Professor Rogers looked for a gas station to change clothes, ready to rip off his t-shirt and use it to wipe off the day's sweltering mugginess.

Turning his car air conditioning on full blast, he placed a coded call, one he never thought he would have to make. He left a message for Mr. Fix-it, as he called him, the one-eared man whose name was Razzor Hassim. No rocky bumps for *Crimson Scimitar* And Kettering was one nasty impediment.

EPISODE SEVEN — Gang aft a-gley

Scene 1: Quid Pro Quo
Setting: March 2011, Washington, D.C.

Inside the hallowed marble halls of Congress, the closed session of the Appropriations Subcommittee for the U.S. Senate Select Committee on Intelligence had adjourned for the day.

Ronald Givens, Assistant Deputy Director of the Central Intelligence Agency, and several of his staffers were gathering up their presentation papers, having underwhelmed three of the five U. S. Senator committee members in attendance and sent them into nodding dozes with their data-soaked presentation: "Assessment of economic risk and estimated financial aid support required to countries impacted by the Arab Spring."

'Arab Spring' was the new speaking point nomenclature out of the White House and State Department, defined as recent events of populace agitation against single political party regimes. The word 'totalitarian' was thought unwise to impart in public speechmaking; it was better said that the U.S. sought, as an end result, a hybrid form of democracy. That, too, was unspoken, usually by lifers out of the State Department who saw more anarchy in the Mediterranean and Middle East news, with a tilt towards Islamic radicalism overpowering the democratic dissidents. After all, Lenin's communism consumed Imperial Russia, and they were but one of many minority parties vying for power. All history with qualified variations repeats itself, or so said the smartest analysts within the government, and then they would qualify 'repetitiveness.'

"Do you have a moment, Ron?"

Givens was closing his briefcase over the documents stamped 'Top Security, Do Not Distribute.' He looked up to see the fashionable and very powerful senior Senator from California smiling at him.

"Of course, Senator."

They found seats at the back of the empty meeting chamber. Ronald Givens was in his late forties and dressed 'pinstriped conservative' with the proper power tie and patriotic flag lapel pin. He felt at ease in his present rank within the Agency for the time being and was optimistic about his future. Expecting the President to win re-election next year, he envisioned that senior Administration officials would start resigning in the mid-term to accept high-paying private sector executive or consultant employment. A few valuable posts should become available, priming his ascendency; perhaps first to Deputy of the CIA, then with good fortune in a victorious second Administration, perhaps on a grander scale, why not a Cabinet post? Why not head of the CIA? A rare internal appointment. One part of his strategy of finesse and working the angles required paying careful attention to U.S. Senators.

"Senator Crandall, sorry for the dry numbers. At this time, we can only speculate. Any full-fledged revolution will require pointed infusion of aid for the new government. We just don't know at what point we can determine if they are our friends or not."

"No problem. I'm used to hocus-pocus and smoke and mirror budgets. After all, I am from California." U.S. Senator Lucy Crandall drew a deep breath, collecting her thoughts and weighing the political chits this conversation might cost her.

"Mr. Givens, I have an odd request, but one I think you and the Agency might be able to help with." She paused and then plunged forth. "I have one constituent, a young man who, through his charitable foundation, has been a major supporter to several of the environmental causes I publicly champion. Speaking candidly and confidentially, so far, he has not made any huge contributions to my re-election campaign. Nor, I should point out, to the President's re-election finance committee. However, I believe if I can halfway deliver on his interesting request, it might kick him loose, at least in a first step to be generous to our party's Political Action Committees."

And, through them, trickle down to her own future re-election coffers, thought Givens. He did not like playing the favors game unless it benefitted his career, but this was Washington, D.C., and his boss, the Agency Director, and above the Director, all those surrounding the President of the United States, were adept at it. They knew how best to disperse election promises, offering them first as tensile steel — which then, after post-vote counts, disappeared like confetti in a windstorm.

"Well, let's see what we can reasonably do, Senator." *Always equivocate*, he thought, mindful of the exit strategy. He heard her sigh.

"The young man I'm speaking of is Hugh Fox."

"Fox, of that Skilly video games empire? My two nephews are addicted, to the point they even have his games downloaded as these new phone apps."

"The same. Somehow, in his idealistic fervor, Mr. Fox wants to go hunting for real-life Islamic radical terrorists. His corporate lobbyist contacted me several days ago, starting a push to see if I can use my position to gain friends and allies in the intelligence community. They want expertise that might point them in the right direction."

"Mr. Fox must have let one of his games override his brain. If you're asking whether the Agency can open its files to some doobie-smoking geek, you know the answer would have to be a firm 'no.'

"I feel the same way, except for what I would call 'ramifications.' It seems Mr. Fox has hired or otherwise secured the services of Colonel Storm King."

"Colonel King, of that fugitive manhunt TV show?"

"Yes. And from my perspective, this means publicity, and maybe not the best for the Administration. The new super-duo's first target is none other than Osama bin Laden."

Ronald Givens showed surprise, which he quickly smothered.

"Crap, and pardon my French, Senator. That has to be headline hunting."

"No doubt, but you would agree that your agency hasn't caught the bastard. I don't want, and I'm sure your boss doesn't want, the perception of this inability to catch bin Laden paraded out in the media as a failure and maybe even comparing us to the last Administration's lack of success."

"I wouldn't say this in public, Senator, but bin Laden is a non-event. As you know, there are more lethal groups out there with fanatical hate-America agendas. Besides, we have dispersed or killed most of the higher-ups in al-Qaeda." He'd just told the Senator an outright fabrication and sensed she could see through his spy doublespeak.

"But the Supreme Council of al-Qaeda still functions, even if bin Laden is dead, or if he's alive and incapacitated in some way. As you can see, I *do* read the intelligence assessment reports you copy to the committee.

"What I am seeking, Mr. Givens, is a semblance of providing assistance without necessarily opening up any state secrets. This ambitious crusade, if one may call it that, will probably gain them a few pages of early publicity, but once their search goes nowhere, fans and the rest of us will get bored and change channels. Your department does not need to overtly assist, but you should be aware, and if the press asks, perhaps not come off with a negative response, but with guarded caution. Wish them well while saying one ought to leave the fight against terrorism to the professionals."

"I grant you, if handled wrong, it could become a dicey public relations issue. That wouldn't be welcomed. Our opponents, as you well know, seek any political issue to improve their polling numbers."

"Exactly my concern."

Givens saw himself being manipulated by a politician; damned if you do, damned if you don't.

"Senator, it's very kind of you to let me know what might be coming. I will have our staff formulate a response. As a token of our limited cooperation, very limited, you can hint to Mr. Fox and Colonel King, off channels, that we will see what we can do to aid these 'volunteers.' I might be able to find a few non-classified White Papers with general background on al-Qaeda to toss them as the proverbial bone."

"It's all I can ask. Thank you." The Senator rose and departed. The Assistant Deputy Director of the CIA pulled out his cell, punched in a highly restricted number, and made immediate contact with the Counter-Intelligence Division and, within that, the bin Laden Desk at Langley. In the public's eye, the search for bin Laden had waned since 9/11, and it had taken a back seat to major events, as today's report on Arab Spring demonstrated. Syria. Libya. Egypt. Even ultra-rich Bahrain. All were in play and at risk.

Governments in dangerous flux went to the top of the priority list, well in front of brainwashed vest bombers seeking virgins in heaven by vaporizing themselves into a bloody mist.

"Anything new on Geronimo?" It was the Agency's code name for bin Laden.

The man on the other end of the line responded, "Perhaps. As I told you and everyone in the Eyes Only clearance, including the President, we are tracking a courier who has a history of running errands for Geronimo. He's living in Pakistan, close to Islamabad, and still seems to be a message runner. We think he's staying at an al-Qaeda safe house. Even with no confirmation of Geronimo's presence, we have your Director's and the President's approval to prepare military contingency plans. That's all I have at the moment. In a nutshell, though we have a warm trail, we have no confirmation whether we've found a High Priority Target, al-Qaeda or Taliban."

Next, Givens called his boss, who also had been updated on this high-value lead.

"Yes, I agree it's worth a look-see," said the CIA Director, "but I told the Section Ops, 'Let's not let our allies in on the intelligence quite yet.'"

Givens concurred. After twenty years in the spook business, including seven years in backwater hellholes as a field agent, Givens did not trust any ally of America. They didn't bleed red, white and blue. He got to the point. "Nothing major, sir; just a nuisance glitch."

82   S.P. Grogan

He abbreviated his conversation with Senator Crandall. Hearing no immediate response to the Senator's request, he continued,

"I believe that, without fanfare, I can find a way to sidetrack them. We don't need gung-ho cameras filming a 'Great Chase' across the sands of Araby." Givens, in his mind, started formulating a response to the Senator's request. He would kill two birds; no, better yet, *stuff* two dead-on-arrival birds with one response.

He ended the call pleased with himself. He received no firm verbal authorization from his boss to proceed but rather a decentralized affirmation through silence. Givens took the conversation as good enough to take quick action. After all, this posse plan by a Gameboy brat and a drunk ex-soldier cowboy (he recalled hearing somewhere that King liked his whiskey) was a non-issue, anyway; they were petty players, a waste of his time.

There were more critical issues to confront in this unsafe world. The Japanese earthquake and resulting tsunami were examples of the critical need for contingency planning. Ronald Givens had been appointed to an intra-governmental task force to deal with potential future catastrophic nuclear power plant failures within U.S. borders, whether by natural or terrorist causes and to develop new protection safeguards to deal with damaged nuclear plants from atmospheric fuel leakage, cooling fuel rods and emergency radioactive storage disbursement. Representing the CIA on the task force, he believed, was a plum assignment. It was a privilege to be part of greater events in these nervous, historic times instead of consorting with reality TV trash.

Givens found himself once more contemplating the Senator's request and realized how to stifle the yo-yo stunt. Can't act too overt, can't even be seen to have a presence. It was better to toss cold water on it, artfully finessed, with sensitivity to the players. As a first step, he needed to find out what those jokers were up to, gathering intel on the ground and in California, of all places. Next, he needed to establish an anonymous agency presence; someone to 'look and report.'

Who could he choose for this babysitting operation? The name came to him quickly: Wendell Holmes. He knew Holmes was on his way out, about to be shoved through the door into early retirement with a Twenty-Five Year Service Badge. There were only a few months left before they turned him out to pasture — and in Given's mind, it was good riddance. It was a perfect ending to Wendell Holmes's spotty career, or so he told himself. Even he did not have access to Holmes's classified action files after he was posted as Senior Group Ops Leader and then assigned the CIA liaison to SAD (Special Activities Division) fifteen years back. Didn't matter. He had an unpleasant history with the man, and Givens felt his choice was a brainstorm, and technically by the org chart, Givens was indirectly one of his bosses.

His course of action selected, he phoned in his command call to Operations for an Assignment Order, wondering if Holmes would realize the reassignment came from his former field partner as a last 'gotcha.' He suddenly thought less of the Senator's situation, not caring if the solution — Wendell Holmes on the scene — solved anything. He considered himself now a player one step up. He had supplied an answer and assumed he had pocketed a political chit of future tangible value. Pleased with himself Givens straightened his tie, tugged his shirt cuffs out from his suit jacket to their proper length at the wrist, retrieved his briefcase, and headed back to his office, where there were genuine issues of world turmoil.

Scene 2: A Buzzed Rock Removed
Setting: Miami, March 2011

Kettering's head was rolling with a beer buzz, and he wanted to give his statement to the detectives and get it over with. With his testimony, he could avoid being found 'habitual' and possibly dodge doing thirty to life. He just needed to hand them someone other than himself, and his friend Gator seemed the perfect mark. Make the deal, his attorney pushed him, or you are in deep shit, and they slam the door behind you — that door with the bars and without a key. He had been in with Gator and Lewis, enjoying all their antics for at least five years. It was mostly small potato stuff, dealing drugs and motorcycle thefts. Cops had left them alone for the most part, seeing them as small fish, more like middlemen. Until he screwed up, that is.

He itched around his ankle where the monitor bracelet held snugly. Glancing out the window, he saw the patrol car at the curb and knew that on the hour, they would knock on his door to collect him. He had to make his story sound colorful. Not dynamiting in the swamps — building bombs sounded better, and that should get their attention. The Feds would go apeshit and make a big deal about the information. Maybe they'd stage a high visibility bust and call Gator and Lewis 'Aryan Nation skinheads' who were going to blow up banks because of the mortgage bust; whatever. Whatever got the evening news headlines. Whatever got him off the hook with a lesser plea.

Kettering threw his empty at the trash, missed, and grabbed another beer from the fridge. The television suddenly went to snow fuzz. Damn. He had been watching a rerun of *King's Retribution*. Not a bad show, he thought, and for a dishonest man like him, it provided insight regarding what to do if he ever went on the run. He enjoyed seeing how the bad guys got caught and the mistakes they made. He'd yell at the screen about how dumb some of the wealthiest white-collar crooks were.

His favorite TV show focused on strait-laced business jerk-offs who had their hand in the till and then went on the run. Television had its educational moments. He could learn to be

84 S.P. Grogan

smarter, know where to hide, and know how to avoid their stupid errors. It was the same with the other cop shows. You could learn a lot about how not to get caught by educating yourself at someone else's expense, by being a couch slug. Like this one show about how they investigate homicides. Maybe like today's interview. Kettering mulled over his possible 'tattle tale confession' and decided that if the cop in the interview room came up and put his hand on his, and said for him to look into his heart and find God to do the right thing, then that would mean they're trying to do that bonding thing and make him slip up. He'd have to be careful with them.

Focus on Gator and the dynamite. The D.A. would give him a break for that, his attorney said, and cut him slack on the other charge. He should have been smarter and not put his meth lab in his garage where it smelled up the place, as his sense of smell had been destroyed by meth chemicals. He should tell one of those television cop show producers that smells stinking up the neighborhood can trip you up. He heard tapping on glass. Someone was knocking at the back door. He stretched himself up, glanced into the kitchen, and saw some repair guy in uniform. Oh, yeah, the cable for the television. Must be down in the entire neighborhood.

Taking wobbly steps, he opened the door and said to the repair man, "Fucking thing won't work. Can't see my shows."

"Yeah. We know. It's an area-wide outage but should have been fixed. This won't take a minute. I'll check your connection at the set and then to the house. Sorry for the inconvenience." Kettering laughed, more about whom they were hiring these days. It was like those Ethiopian guys who drove the cabs and worked the corner convenience stores. It used to be

Cubans, then Chinks moved in, and now Sand Niggers. And this guy was strange; no doubt a foreigner. Even with his cable repair cap, anyone could see an odd thing about him: his ear was missing.

Wondering if they give you a handicapped parking pass for having no ear, Kettering turned to point the way to the living room and was too slow to react when the needle plunged into his neck. A bee sting, but no pain, merely a surprise. He found he could not speak at all as mobility drained from his limbs. The repairman eased him down on the floor, saying, "Scimitar will not fail.

"What's 'scimitar?' "What's a 'scimitar'?" Kettering had no idea. And why couldn't he move?

He did have his vision still. His eyeballs rolled, bug-eyed in their sockets, staring and then trying to blink as the repairman pulled an explosives package from his work bag, put it on the floor next to the motionless man, and set a timer.

"You might as well be useful as a distraction," said Razzor Hassim.

Kettering noticed, too late, that the man was wearing gloves. He should have been more suspicious. He had never seen that on television. He could not move to save himself and watched as color maps and photographs were scattered around the living room. And after the repairman exited the back door, shutting it quietly as if being careful not to wake anyone, a funny thing happened: the television rebooted and regained its clarity. *King's Retribution* flared back on with fast sequences of a chase scene. Kettering realized he had seen that episode before and wanted to laugh, but a bright light erased his confused thoughts and ended his wicked life.

Scene 3: The Reveal — Part One
Setting: Outside Colorado Springs, Colorado

"You want me to do what?!" Booker did not like ambushes, felt he had been sandbagged, and followed his first exclamation with: "You gotta be fuckin' kidding?!" Followed by his hands thrown up in the air, disbelieving exasperation added to his third exclamation: "No fuckin' way!" His first goal of having Booker buy into the project had succeeded. Phase Two, not so easy, now requiring tending to internal wounds caused by his having previously abused the facts. Hugh knew the sales job would be slightly difficult — and the reason why he had his private jet fly him and Booker Langston to Colorado from LAX, landing at the U.S. Air Force Academy. "We do some tech simulation stuff for some of their classified aeronautical projects," was Hugh's passing throw-off. The limousine SUV meeting them drove for thirty minutes from the mountain foothills to the prairie suburbs, south of Castle Rock, north of Colorado Springs, to the construction site.

The sign on the entryway, quite guarded, but humming with workers, stated without fanfare, 'Sand Creek Arapahoe Reservation — Future Home of the *Skilleo International Soccer Training Center.*' It was here he made his pitch while they were standing in the middle of the nearly completed stadium that would showcase world championships, itself surrounded by practice fields, training facilities, and player-coach-media housing. Langston did not have to be told to believe one of Hugh Fox's many projects was to have America soon dominate world soccer.

Without preamble, Fox had stated as if in a casual discussion of the weather, "This is a hypothesis. As I somewhat explained earlier, I, and a friend of mine, have acquired a television production company. The mock trial will be one of our new launches. They have another television show where we will use some of their personnel to search and capture bad people. Real bad people. But considering our lofty goals, chances are we will not be catching Public Enemy Number One and instead be dependent on using paid actors.

"Now, hold on for a second. As I said, we may or may not be successful. Either way, we are going to have a mock trial, televised to the public, and then regardless of the verdict, the script will show us turning the 'fake' culprit over to the proper authorities. So, what I want you to do is to step in as my Project Chief Operations Officer with specific duties: (1) oversee that this stadium is completed in record time (I will allow some overtime if necessary), (2) create the legal staffing of the mock trial, including reputable, I mean, the best defense and prosecution teams, and (3) as I said before, I want you to be the lead defense attorney."

Booker might be burned-out, bored with his daily circumstances, but he wasn't about to call Hugh 'crazy.' He knew that the young man was entirely serious and that usually what he started, and finished, made money and headlines, and in the end, with a product launch, the new technology or a cause funded all made sense and seemed to fit right into the kinetic frenzied tech world.

"So, I am *really* going to be a reality television star?"

"If circumstances say so."

"And am I likewise the detective who first captures these 'bad people?'"

Hugh gave a smirk, knowing he was drawing Langston in.

"No, I have lessened your load. As I said, I have hired a television show staff. You may have seen *King's Retribution* lead the chase and nab the accused. That's been their modus operandi in the past, but my idea is a take on *Law and Order*. *King's Retribution* catches them, and if they do or even do not, then we will create this 'mock trial.' And *King's Retribution*, or *KR* as I'm calling them, will bring the alleged malefactor to your...." Fox used his hands to express quotation marks, 'Department' to go to trial...publicly. I think this is a tremendous concept.

"This is short-term, a pilot only, one time, to pitch to the Sales Department to gain a network purchase of another season or two. You would be doing me a great favor. One of my ideas is being led by someone I trust, who is not prostituted to Hollywood."

"*King's Retribution*? But this *KR* are the TV fake bounty hunters?"

"Not fake; they are real bounty hunters, though a lot of their work is pre-planned, scripted like all reality television. Five Aces Studioz, which I now own half of, has their contracts. I've done my research. They are actually pretty good at investigations and capture. Far better than Interpol, if I may be so bold as to compare."

"Interpol? You are going after foreign criminals?"

"Just one."

"And may I ask?" The sun was in Booker's eyes, and he squinted as Hugh built the dramatics with pregnant seconds passing.

"Osama bin Laden."

Booker's exclamations now followed, with other various curses, almost to the point of calling Fox 'totally insane,' but hesitated, sputtering, left with only, "You gotta be shitting me!"

Hugh let his friend vent, knowing what he was hearing was from a man who thought he had abandoned his fiancée; a false assumption twisting in Booker's mind, tormented into believing that his inaction that day ten years ago this September indirectly killed her. That one name, bin Laden's, dredged up all that was evil in the world, all that took Booker's happiness from him, and had driven him, dare he say it, to admit his weakness, almost into alcoholic dementia.

Hugh Fox must now challenge a man's soul to be saved.

"Bookie, there is no guarantee that we will capture our friend, Sheik bin Laden, probably not, therefore after a reasonable time of searching, as we shall certainly build public interest, we will provide a copy of the alleged killer, a living mannequin of what people might expect, a paid actor and we then put on the mock trial, and…I want you to defend him, the doppelganger. I want Osama bin Laden to be your client. I want you to prove that Osama bin Laden, the most wanted man in the world, is not guilty of the crimes he will be accused of."

More incredulity led to an open mouth without words. The word Booker sought surpassed 'dumbfounded.'

Hugh appealed to the inner core of his friend's beliefs.

"Bookie, you were an outstanding defense attorney. You can see lost causes and bring them vindication because facts are most important to your creed. As a New York defense attorney winning nearly 85% of the cases you handled. I checked. Later, because of your personal anger, you reverted to a prosecutor, a rabid one if truth be told, believing you had to rid the world of evil, any evil, yet, again, the truth must spin the story. The guilty are guilty because you proved it so, again, with evidence.

"I believe you, attorney Booker Langston, are the one true person who wants justice, fairness."

Hugh rushed on, "Osama bin Laden on trial in America? Who will make that fair? It's a mob citizenry with a noose too small to avenge 3,000-plus victims. Probably100 million plus out there would be willing volunteer executioners."

Hugh had walked closer to Booker, who was in a half-trance, taking in the open skies of Colorado, of construction workers hustling, building new things. He put his hand on Booker's shoulder, hoping the black lawyer was absorbing his words, forming thoughts, processing in a linear construct.

S.P. Grogan

"Bookie, does Judy Yu and her memory need to continue to be smothered in hateful revenge, or does she deserve righteous justice from the man who can say to her: whatever happens, I gave a human being a fair and honest right to be proven innocent or guilty, based on truth?"

Booker had to laugh.

"That was a miserable pep talk and traveling salesman spiel. You are a clever asshole. But Osama is the biggest asshole threat in the world. If I took this supposed 'actor' bin Laden's case, whatever evidence was presented, I would lose in the most grandiose style."

"Before, during, and after the trial, you would be a household word. Women would...."

"Watch that." Booker still held memories close and sacred.

"Women would want you to handle their divorce cases. Start thinking lucrative private practice."

"Even if I backed a loser? Against public opinion, with a mountain of evidence, there is no hope for even a miracle defense."

"Want to know who the prosecutor will be?"

"Tell me."

"*King's Retribution* has had great success in their shows using the public servant, New York D.A. Cotton Matther the Fifth."

Again. "You're kidding. Matther, that son of a bitch. I always beat him when we went up against each other."

"Yes, I know. You even won with eyewitnesses saying your client stood over the bullet-riddled corpse holding a smoking gun. I think you are perfect for this project."

Booker was caving. "Yeah, my back story is the stuff for sob sisters. But you knew that. Of course, you did. And yeah, I guess DA Matther would jump at something like this. His middle name is 'grandstanding.' He is the most visible and ambitious bureaucrat who wants to be governor or President.

Hugh sensed conversion. He sought comparison. "Think instead of *Inherit the Wind*. Clarence Darrow against William Jennings Bryan. Spencer Tracy against Frederick March. A parable of the times, just like today. A true mock trial that has a message."

Two-second beat. "Yeah," sighed Booker Langston. "If Matther wins this so-called trial, he will have a national fan and registered voter base. The Golden Ticket. That man must be stopped. At least I would get to play a Sidney Poitier or Denzel Washington version of Spencer Tracy."

Hook, line, and sinker. Know your bait and the habits of your quarry.

"Did I just hear you say, 'if,' as in 'if he wins,' as in 'he might not.'" I guess I should tell you, though it probably does not matter to you public servants, but you and Matther will each be paid $1 million for the trial, another $1 million bonus to who convinces the jury, either direction, guilty for Matther or not guilty by your skill."

Booker saw it. "My God. This is not just one of your digitized 'shoot-'em up' games. No, you are crossing the line from fantasy to reality, going in the opposite direction of all of us who want to hide in a dreamland, escape our existence. You want to do a real-life game, take the worst of some reality TV show, prove that you could make tawdry fakery into award-winning entertainment, and at the same time gain millions of new fans. You are beyond diabolical." Booker paused, got serious, and took stock of what he might be stepping in. "But not me. I wouldn't do this for the money; it's a principle I would want to prove to myself. That the word 'justice' can find a place in this country and still have meaning for all."

Like himself, Hugh thought his friend was a little too jingoistic in trying to define this new cause, rationalizing why undertake a crusade of 'justice,' whatever that meant today. Hugh would go along as he could.

"Perhaps you have guessed my motives, deciphered my disjointed reasoning. Maybe not. But please take the money; my accountants don't have a line item that says, 'paid nothing for something.' Hugh saw Booker processing it all, thinking about his first steps.

"I can create my own defense team; you pay for expert witnesses, pay for quality research?"

"Both teams will have a fair budget for that. Enlisting the Queen of England as a character witness for our actor bin Laden may take some logistics and under-the-table shenanigans. But it might be managed. It's for a TV audience, after all."

"And where is this case going to be tried? A federal courthouse in Washington, D.C.?"

Hugh swirled his arms around in a grand motion, like directing the finale of Piotr Illich Tchaikovsky's *1812 Overture.*

"Here. You are standing in the middle of the largest courtroom in the world, 40,000 seats, never such a spectacle since the days of the Christians in the Roman Coliseum, or public executions more recently in the Middle East, during regime turn-over. The Sand Creek Arapaho, who own the underlying land, and I have made a special deal to host the event. We attract a crowd, whoever wins, I mean when you win, they win, I win — a neat package for all.

"I already have the Five Aces Studioz team setting up the camera angles, and the courtroom itself will be center stage, right where we stand, employing my final piece de resistance, which should impress you."

Booker realized he was now part of the show-to-be as Hugh Fox resumed the stepped-up tour of the soccer stadium under rushed construction, as he followed behind — the newly appointed Defense Attorney in the *Trial of Osama bin Laden vs. Everyone Else.*

The Trial of the Century.

"You know," shouted Langston, catching up. "You know this whole show won't come off unless you hire a realistic actor to play bin Laden."

Mentally, as he always did, entrepreneur billionaire and puppeteer Hugh Fox checked off another key item in his multi-tasking brain cabinet and opened another mental file.

"I am working on that. Count on it."

Scene 4: The Search Team Gathers
Setting: Santa Monica, California March 2011

Callie's first view of the War Room impressed her. Hugh Fox had leased half of the top floor office building at the corner of Third Street and Washington Avenue in Santa Monica.

Formerly offices for a stock brokerage firm, the layout held open workspace cubicles surrounded by VIP glassed-in offices. Moving quickly, a dozen or so youth-hip worker bees were plugged into computers, clicking away. Doing what? Callie could only guess they were siphoning off data on the 'enemy' and running the information through a filtering program created most certainly by some Skilleo Game engineering nerd. Three of them hunched over their keyboards, staring into the screens, and looked like 'exchange student' types. One woman worker wore a hijab head covering, and Callie assumed she could probably read Arabic script.

Callie observed this activity from the boardroom, where the principals had gathered for their first formal strategy meeting. J-Q acted as meeting secretary. As though it were a labor negotiation, Hugh and Samantha sat on one side of the table and Storm and Callie on the other. J-Q was at one end of the table, and *Retribution's* muscle, Clayton Briggs, was at the other. CAMERA ONE was there filming, supposedly unobtrusive. Abbas and Bennie found vacant seats.

King, who sat in the middle between the ends, believing that was the location of importance, started things off with a basic question:

"Okay, where do we begin?" His voice was dismissive, like he would go along with this joke, but just for a while.

Fox beamed, caught up in the project, and where the others sought common ground regarding what their purpose was, Fox exuded clarity.

"We start by excluding areas where bin Laden is not to be found. We are analyzing his most recent emails to give us direction. For example, heavy flooding occurred in Pakistan last summer. Bin Laden released a softer toned-down video calling for a new Muslim relief agency to assist flood victims. From that, can we infer that he is perhaps in or around Pakistan versus anywhere else?"

Samantha offered her endorsement of the possibility.

"It sounds like what you might hear from a neighbor to his friends," she said. "Trying to be the good ol' boy politician showing concern for his constituency."

"It's just as likely," offered King, "that he's shaved his beard and is working on a tan at the Royal Savoy at Sharm El Sheikh." That was an Egyptian beach resort in the Sinai Peninsula.

The night before, King had confided to Callie that if they were going to go on a wild goose chase, it should be to a five-star hideout.

Fox ignored the apparent lack of confidence in his cause. Even he might have agreed that the task before them seemed daunting. "I can assure you," he said, "that the people we have working on bin Laden's biography and personal habits." He motioned to the workstations beyond the conference room, "We are united in consensus that bin Laden will always be a fanatic, that he has an image to uphold to his base, his fans, and that this requires him to be near the action; not on a working vacation."

"It would help," said Clayton Briggs, slurping at a power drink, two empty cans on the table before him, "if the government would give us a hand. I mean, we all are on the same team. Let them send us a couple of James Bonds."

"Bond is English and fictional; nevertheless, it's a worthy observation," agreed Fox.

This meeting was called as an 'organizational gathering,' but Fox wanted just as much to delve more into the personalities he'd asked to assist. "In fact, I have made some overtures through my sources and have been assured that we can expect a 'volunteer' with expertise in the Middle East. But you cannot expect them to bless our project too openly."

"One would expect not," came King's dry comment, and everyone at the table understood who would take on the role of the project's skeptic.

Samantha spoke up. She disliked formal meetings without agendas and noted that Hugh's corporate style was a free-for-all bull session. She preferred chop-chop bullet point decisions. "I think we need to take the general topics of our research; each of us picks a specific subject, and then Hugh can assign a researcher to our ideas."

"Even 'bin Laden is dead' theories?" asked King.

"Even those."

Fox turned his eyes to the other television star.

"What guesswork do you think we should concentrate on, Miss Cardoza? You've been very quiet."

Callie saw all eyes in the room fall upon her and cast her gaze back to Hugh Fox.

The intensity in his face made him almost glow. For the first time, she saw beyond his aura of public success and saw instead a young man asking a serious question. He was not pandering to her fame and was treating her neither better nor less but on equal terms, in accordance with her own value. Samantha Carlisle was a lucky woman to have him.

"Okay," she said. "We should accept that the government is constantly monitoring all communications. They have billions of dollars and technological resources we do not have at their disposal. And that they are not going to share is a given. Still, they might be overwhelmed with too much information, and true clues may be missed. We, therefore, have as good a chance as anyone to find this murderer."

She brought them back to the truth — that this was not an adventurous lark but a quest — a mystery to find a boasting killer. As they pondered that sobering fact, she continued.

"I would like to work on tracking down the bin Laden family. As one man, he could hide in his cave and never be found. But he is a family man with multiple wives and many children. With such a large, extended family, one of them is bound to make a slip and, with good luck, may even lead us directly to him."

Silence followed.

"Yes, I like that," said Samantha. "We know the spook agencies are run by alpha males.

Probably none of them thought of looking at the women around bin Laden."

Fox nodded approval, his attention on Callie. "Your suggestion, your investigation. Go for it. After the meeting, I'll pull in some people to build your team. Now, let's parcel out the jobs, assign staff, and in a week, we'll see what proverbial sweet nuggets we shake loose from the date palms."

They talked for another half hour, taking on assignments. After the meeting broke up, Fox took them around to each of the cubicles and introduced the Hunt Team, as they called themselves, to all his employees, brought in from his own company, and calling themselves the Discovery Team. Callie marveled at the expensive computer equipment Fox had at his disposal. The government's equipment was from the lowest bidder, whereas Fox apparently owned the latest, all of it top-shelf. She began to look forward to seeing what systems and downloads he had amassed and to using her expertise in computer programming. It got her excited about starting her own research project: the bin Laden family tree. This could be fun escapism for a month or so, she considered. After all, she had nothing better to do and did not relish making the public relations swings to play politics with next season's future, especially following in King's shadow.

Crimson Scimitar

Scene 5: The CIA Sniffs a Crime Scene
Setting: March 2011, Miami

"You're from Homeland Security?"

They shook hands.

Wendell Holmes's cover story was only partly true. He handed his business card to the FBI agent, and at the same time, showed a photo ID badge, ridiculous since the laminated photo revealed a much younger self, taken many years ago.

"We are called in from time to time to determine if any incidents reach the threshold of concerns for greater response, you know, with international implications," he said. "I show up, look around and write a report."

He did not say that he was on loan to Homeland Security from the CIA nor that he thought that with this recent assignment, he had been relegated to the generic title of Field Inspector and banished to the hinterland.

"Well, the police called us in," said Harry Curtis, the young FBI agent. "For about the same purpose. You know, explosives, and wondering if there is some sort of national conspiracy. Better safe, with more eyes on the ground, than horribly sorry."

"I agree."

Both men were staring at what was once the home of the late meth dealer Kettering. After the walls blew out, the structure had caught fire, even though the police were sitting right outside the door. Their police car was heavily damaged, but they were still able to quickly direct the fire department to the scene, and most of the damage from the blaze had been contained.

"What is the police theory, and yours?" Holmes asked as he crossed the crime scene tape, making Curtis follow and wonder if his jurisdictional trespass was acceptable to the police and FBI forensic investigators.

"A homemade bomb gone wrong. Police are going to raid a motorcycle repair shop where they think the explosives are being stored. Today, in fact, if you want to tag along. So far, we have not officially been called in. Locals think it should stay local. Except for the materials found, we would have said yes."

Holmes stepped carefully through the blackened debris.

"And the kitchen here is blast center?"

"Not much left of Mr. Kettering."

"The police report said the bomb he was working on contained French-made plastique explosives."

"Yes, that's a little strange because Kettering told the locals that the explosives he had seen stored first-hand were boxes of dynamite."

"Think he was going more sophisticated?"

"Don't know. But you think a guy who could build a meth lab would be a little more careful when building an exotic bomb. They did find a few fragments of what we think is the timer mechanism. And oddly, pieces of pink paper, which, when pasted back together like a puzzle, formed scraggly black lines like thunderbolts, off-set by markings, what they say might be fleur-de-lis. Maybe French origins. We think it wrapped the explosives. We're checking with foreign manufacturers."

"On the timer, maybe he got a.m. mixed up with p.m." From the burned wood kitchen remnants, Holmes walked into a smoke- and water-soiled living room, taking quick looks into the bedrooms. Police were good at finding the big clues, like a burned, fragmented body in the aftermath of an explosion. Holmes had an excellent memory for cataloging what he saw, intuitive enough to absorb small details. Short of a photographic memory, he captured brief observational moments with his small Konica Minolta camera for later review. He had read somewhere that Nokia and Samsung were battling this year for maximum clarity; they called them 'megapixels,' to put a camera into a handheld phone. Not for him; he enjoyed his mastodon approach to field investigation.

And here, he didn't say it, but something seemed strange, off-kilter. He wasn't sure what it was. Couldn't quite define it.

"Yes, I would like to be in on the raid. And you said you had those materials found in the house?"

He let Agent Curtis drive while he reviewed the file.

The raid was a bust. No dynamite, no bomb-making materials on the premises. Holmes surmised that many of the motorcycle parts in the shop were stolen, but the warrant narrowed the search scope to defined particulars, and the U.S. Drug Enforcement Agency, with local Miami cops and their bomb squad and the SWAT unit on standby, called the shots as they rushed the building.

Holmes hung back from the proceedings, watching the shop owner and another employee glare at the invasive toss-apart, each biker throwing nasty thoughts with acid-laser stares, grumbling under their breath. They weren't reciting poetry. Holmes saw a mindset he knew well — hatred from a class of people who stayed alive by feeding on soul-eating maggot anger of everything they weren't. He hoped the local cops would keep these guys on their radar. This type seemed prone to graduate from petty theft to higher classes of violence and mayhem. He felt they were primed to toss a Molotov cocktail for mindless new thrills.

Excitement rose from the good guys when the bomb-sniffing dog hit on a storage trailer and tugged at his leash, and howled. Under a tarp on the floor, they found a trapdoor, and the DEA-Miami Police strike force thought they had scored. When it was opened, out came a small box of fireworks, pop bottle rockets, and sparkling cone fountains. Holmes saw a curled smile on the repair shop owner's face, a slight twinge of 'gotcha.' Us vs. the cops, and *us* won this round. The CIA agent, with his years observing human nature, saw the shop owner basically admit, without words, that there was more to what went on today. Holmes filed away everything he saw.

FBI Agent Curtis joined him, and they watched the DEA and the SWAT teams pack it in and leave.

"You have an opinion?" asked Curtis.

"More curiosity than theory."

"Think Kettering wanted to be another Timothy McVey?" McVey was the Oklahoma City bomber and mass murderer of hundreds of innocents, executed as an American-grown terrorist.

The file folder that Holmes reviewed on the drive over contained partially burned photographs of a Miami building and maps associated with its location.

The David W. Dyer Federal Building and U.S. Courthouse

"Possibly. Looks like he picked out a target."

"Local police say Kettering and this Gator and all his cronies are very anti-government. But search warrants on their homes turned up nothing. So far, the police see this as a one-man show, prematurely canceled."

"Keep digging if your office can. I have strange vibes about this one. Maybe it's too much incoming unfiltered data on this old brain of mine. Take the photos, for example. The ones you recovered. If this was to be a planned attack, planting a bomb, you think there would be more surveillance of the building. The shots in these photos are only of the front, basically taken, as it seems, by someone taking snapshots from his car while driving by, no side shots or rear views of the building."

"Maybe they burned up in the fire."

"Maybe. Another observation. Unless he had just developed the photos, there are no pin marks, no thumbtack holes on any of the corners. Again, if he was going to be a diligent planner, you'd think he would have put the photos on a wall, created a storyboard of his attack plans, and it wouldn't be in his kitchen. More likely a bedroom."

"There was nothing like that."

"Something else is odd. It was just the bomb? No other bomb-making materials?"

96   S.P. Grogan

"The police detectives told me that none were found here. You think it might have been made elsewhere and delivered to him to hide, but he started fiddling with it or shook it wrong, and ker-plooie!?"

"That's as good a scenario as any. But what started all this was his arrest for the meth lab in his garage, which the Miami police hauled off. You'd think they might have discovered any other unusual equipment, not for meth but bomb-making. And why build a bomb at all with the police sitting outside your house?"

"Maybe meth fried his brain. I'll check with the locals and their evidence lockers and see if bomb-making components were mixed in with the meth equipment."

"Please do. But what brought me here in the first place is the French origin of the explosives. The make-up is just too exotic for a meth-head." Holmes filed away all this information to be reconstituted later in his official summary report. He saw nothing for Homeland Security or CIA interest, no clue that a foreign power was now in league with biker gangs.

His cell phone played the James Bond theme.

"You gotta be kidding!" Curtis laughed.

"An early-retirement indulgence." He answered, listened, and then hung up.

"New assignment. California and right away, so I can't hang around and snoop. Please keep me in the loop on this. It just doesn't feel right."

On the ride back to pick up his rental, he mused about bringing up the subject of retirement to the Fibber. He was nearing the end of his career, and Holmes had no idea what he would do after he received his symbolic gold watch. He wasn't even that old; had his teeth, his hair and could get it up whenever candlelight and soft music set the mood, though he had for stimulus backup a prescription for blue 'energy' pills he got when they were released and marketed in 1998. As to the unknown tomorrows, he hadn't made plans or even contemplated any. Always on the go, even though his more recent assignments smelled more of paper-pushing bureaucracy than of hot gunpowder and saving wayward damsels. He had no vocations, and the only hobby, if you counted it, was an occasional short story he might write during field downtime, a release to let his mind wander into imaginary worlds. A large box in a closet at his apartment held his scribblings, gathering dust. He did not type his stories on a computer. His short stories, all handwritten, seemed to be a statement of personal connection. A lost art: idea from pen to paper, to be read, back to mind.

He had no idea what he would do when he was out on the street, and that scared him more than facing armed mobs. For the final countdown months until his retirement, they, the unknown powers above, let him work out of his one-bedroom condo in Alexandria, Virginia. The scuttlebutt was that they did not want him office-based at Langley. They gave him the title of Field Inspector and loaned him off to Homeland Security, where his assignment was to travel the U.S. and do follow-up reports on local law enforcement cases that might garner CIA interest. Very hush-hush. If a case was flagged as a 'threat potential,' then the investigation would be transferred to other agents, meaning the FBI, since, as CIA, he could do no snooping on U.S. citizens. Holmes accepted the direction, kept his face to the work ahead, fearful about his pending retirement, and diligently filed his reports. Not like the old days, just a few years ago, when he made a difference when in the field; governments might collapse because of his directed ops.

The report to Homeland on the self-bombing in Miami, copied to the CIA computers, would be classified as 'no further investigation warranted.' Let the locals do their job. Still, it was a curious death.

His mind shifted to tonight's expected phone briefing from Langley. He had no idea why they needed him in California. Another police investigation? Maybe, he pondered, they found a backwater assignment to park him in for a few months until they kicked him out.

Scene 6: Prep Work
Setting: Late March, Camp Pendleton, California

"Go! Go!" The shouted words blared into his headset, and he and the rest of his squad team repelled from both sides of the hovering helicopter into the darkness of the night. Rotor wash kicked up plumes of dust and dried out their mouths with the taste of dirt. The others carried light loads as the intervention attack force, but Pacheco and his partner bore the heavy weight of explosive charges. Pacheco's gloved hands heated up as he carried himself with a rush to the ground. After hitting with a bouncing thud, he was off and running toward the gates. They had been rebuilt since the last practice run.

Shawn Pacheco, lately of the war zone in Afghanistan, had been, he would later say, 'thrown' across the globe to unite with his new teammates of SEAL Team Six, located temporarily at Camp Pendleton, north of San Diego and west of Fallbrook in a giant training reserve used primarily for the Marines. His transfer paperwork said his placement fell under the Naval Special Warfare Development Group (NEVGRU) of the Joint Special Operations Command.

He had definitely felt the jet lag when he reached the base camp a week earlier. Since then, there had been two night operations of helicopters rushing over hills, barely scraping the coastal sage. His tasks were defined with precision. He and his partner, a SEAL operator named

Marco Vitali rushed the gate, set the charges, moved to cover, and detonated the satchel charge.

Vitali returned to the helicopter, taking up a security perimeter, while Pacheco sped around the walled building area, something the old men of multiple Iraq tours called a "middle-class *al-qasr* [castle]." His secondary job was to be prepared, if called upon, to throw another charge against the gate on the other side of the target al-qasr. And he was to keep his eyes open and prevent any escapes from the buildings.

Tonight, he had heard, this would be the last exercise at this location, with a planned deployment — again, a rumor — to Afghanistan. Pacheco had the smarts to realize the mission meant an extraction; attacking this building that was definitely highly fortified and extracting a person or persons. The SEALs had a history of this type of operation. The most recent and notable was in the Indian Ocean in 2009 when three SEAL snipers took out the three pirate kidnappers of hostage Captain Phillips, with simultaneous shots on the down roll of a ship, at a range of 75 yards.

Failed operations do not receive the same media notice but become teaching tools, as tragic as they might be — especially when errors are made by members of a SEAL Team.

In October 2010, SEAL Team Six made an early morning raid on a mountain Taliban hideout to rescue a Scottish aid worker held prisoner. During the raid, as kidnappers were being killed, a fragmentation grenade thrown by a SEAL mortally wounded the woman hostage. The exploding grenade had not been necessary, and, worse, the SEAL initially denied using it, the first report blaming a suicide vest. It was all caught on helmet cameras — the truth came out, and the sailor was disciplined, leaving the team's morale in a bad funk. Pacheco, accepting his outsider status, felt the underlying current when he was in casual B.S. chatter. He noticed a consensus that most of those he was now working with hoped that this new mission, whatever it was, would vindicate them for their mistaken killing of an innocent woman. Thinking about the death of Montoya, Shawn Pacheco agreed with that word: 'vindication.' It sounded nobler than 'retaliation,' but not by much.

To Pacheco, several factors gave weight to the importance of the upcoming operation.

The best clue: the civilians involved. Pacheco did not talk to any of them, but by their silent presence and low-voice discussions with the officers, these people definitely were not acting like they were under the direction of the military. On the contrary, the civilians were providing intelligence on whom and what was to be attacked. Shawn knew they were handlers from the Central Intelligence Agency.

The planned attack created its own curiosity. After the assaulting force neutralized the opposition, one team would be deployed to handle prisoners, suggesting that a significant number of people might be detained. A third SEAL group would consist of the CIA with its own 3-member team, those bearing only side arms — yet as he viewed them in these ops exercises, they came running in with empty duffel bags, even a box of heavy-duty garbage bags. So, he thought, it was to be a rescue and then picking up and bagging...what?

And not to forget the military dog trained not to bark in the middle of the night, even with the simulated weapon fire popping up to garner realism. A dog in its Kevlar to do what? For control, tracking? If a sniffer, nosing around to uncover...what? Digging a Taliban Saddam Hussein out of his hidey-hole? Shawn Pacheco reached his conclusion — something big was coming down.

A flare went off into the night sky, and at the same time, a voice came into his ear: "Stand down. Return to breaching point." He heard the reduction of the helicopter rotor noise. It was mission assessment time, and he hustled to join his comrades near the gate he and Vitali had surgically removed moments earlier.

In their post-op briefing, where they gave assessments of this commando course of action

(COA), the commander field judges said that everyone hit their tasked goals. Minor criticisms were heard, but there was no bawling out of any member like at boot camp. SEALS knew what to do. Mistakes, as he well knew, were deadly. Give me the job, and it will get done. The only thing of bother was timing, they said. We need to bring down the in-and-out to less than an hour, and we can't achieve this with a lean-to facsimile. You will soon be joining other members of this special force, and all of you will train on a realistic mock-up within the next few days. Be prepared to ship out tomorrow — regulated goodbyes only.

He knew what that meant. When he was in Afghanistan, the higher-ups monitored his email to Janet. *Being deployed on mission. Will be unable to communicate for some time. Will talk to you as soon as I can. Love, Shawn.* He wanted to say more, longed to see her, to hold her and seek her comfort. The emptiness from Montoya's death still hovered in his mind like a curse.

He hoped someday she would understand this turmoil and believe in him, as he was unable to do for himself.

EPISODE EIGHT — The Law and the Gossip

Scene 1: Lawyers with briefcases...
Setting: Los Angeles, late March

Harriet Eberhardt should have entered the Prosecutor's office with a little bit more finesse, but she had been caught on her only afternoon off, and the casual look had to suffice. To hell with them and their aloof stuffiness as being the only stars in the purported Crime Fighters League. But the call she had received, last minute, still intrigued enough to force her into hustle mode.

100 S.P. Grogan

Booker Langston, the hotshot 'Show No Mercy' prosecutor, had asked for her, called her personally on her cell phone, said something 'unrelated to work, a project for her to consider, could she meet him today, short notice, sorry.' She waited for him to finish his brief command, as if she would agree, before acting like she was considering it for only seconds, then said yes, she would re-arrange her schedule. Curiosity had gotten the best of her. No time to rush home and dress up. He could take it or leave it. Plus, she never ever had a sit down with the Prosecutor's office that wasn't adversarial. Was this to be a neutral visit, even social? She couldn't imagine that and spent her time puzzling over the six outstanding cases that would soon face trial. Which one had caught his eye? An offer to plead out? Only on her terms, she groused to herself. Strength of conviction combined with anxiety was the mixed message she showed to the reception when she presented herself. "I have an appointment with Booker Langston."

"Oh yes, Miss Eberhardt, counselor, let me see if he can see you now."

At this moment, Harriet noticed turmoil, a buzzing current in the office, interns and low-totem attorneys peeking up from cubicles, and the privileged ADA's from their cluttered offices. Retreating when they glanced her way, all seemed disappointed.

"Is something going on here today?"

"Oh, yes," replied the receptionist, "the office is expecting the arrival of New York District Attorney Cotton Matther. We're all excited to see a prosecutorial superstar up close."

"Yes, he is a poster child." Harriet left the rest unsaid, knowing someone in her workplace, the public defender's office, had a NY *Times* article and photo of Cotton Matther on their wall, with multiple dart holes sticking in the face. "I hear he has a strong conviction record," she found herself saying to pass the time.

"Oh, yes," the office receptionist, short of gushing, responded. "Yes, it is claimed so. But I think Booker, Mr. Langston, had more convictions last year than DA Matther." Harriet wouldn't be surprised to hear that there was an office pool running on who kept more conviction notches on their briefcases. But it was like prosecutors, LA vs. NY jurisdictional ego flexing, a turf battle over crime statistics, so not the best measurement tool. She just had to say something to make a point when she showed up in this office expecting to negotiate.

"You do realize I am with the Public Defender's Office?"

"Of course she does, Harriett," came the booming voice of Booker Langston. "Miss Halston here made money off you, betting you would win the Sievers case last year against me. Isn't that true, Miss Halston? She is quite your fan, at least when it comes to picking winners."

Miss Halston actually blushed and returned to her work.

"Harriet, let me show you the conference room we will be using."

When settled, with morning coffee poured and sipped, Booker came to the point:

"Hear me out. As you might not know, I have the highest respect for your legal mind and capabilities." She started to protest, if only slightly. "No, it is true. For that reason, I have asked the Public Defender's Office to lend you to me for a period of four months to help put on a mock public trial which will bring attention and hopefully a positive reputation to the work you highly espouse to."

"Saving the innocent from confined torture is a high calling indeed, and I don't see why I wasn't part of the discussion of where my time might be best spent."

"Well, that's why we are here, as friends, I hope. In this mock trial, I will be heading up the defense team as the lead attorney. I want you to sit second chair at my table.."

Now, that caught her off guard, but she recovered. But, to that statement, she could not resist. "Should it not be *I* as lead and you as my second since I am the one with the most recent experience in *defense* advocacy?"

"Good for you. I appreciate self-confidence in one's character. At any other time or court case, I might have deferred and bowed to your prowess, but don't take this the wrong way; this will be one of those 'Watch and learn' moments. Learning my trade secrets has value, I bet."

Before she unleashed a few choice words about his cockiness, there came a knock on the door, and as if a rush of bright lights and hurricane wind flowed into the room, one of the great legal megastars of the times, as prosecutors go, the Honorable Cotton Matther V, followed by a younger, business attired, either acolyte or the prosecutor's 'yes, sir' indentured servant. Harriet gave both men a curt smile. *What was Langston trying to drag her into?*

Harriet found herself rising as introductions were made; though it seemed like the good ol' boys club had just opened their session with a fake love fest, those little pointed barbs melted into the early pleasantries so well.

"Booker, you are looking fabulous. With all the smog, it can't be fresh air and California sun? Aren't you glad you made the move, not only to West Coast environs but over to the dark side of the law with the rest of us?"

"Cotton, let me introduce you to Miss Harriet Eberhardt, one of the stars in the galaxy of defense work within Southern California. We were just discussing our upcoming 'staged' trial. Miss Eberhardt is considering joining our Defense Team."

"Well, bully for you. This will be the feather in anyone's cap, as they say. Probably like me, after this, you will be in demand; definitely hire a face as pretty as yours as a Cable

102 S.P. Grogan

Television legal commentator. And Booker, here is my associate who will be my right-hand man. Sorry, Ms. Eberhardt, my right-hand 'person.' James Buchanan, who I believe is a Sixth to my Fifth famille scion. All the right law schools, but a tremendous lawyer almost as good as you *were*, Booker."

"As I understand, Mr. Buchanan, you were a former congressional aide to U.S. Senator Montgomery, and you made your legal bones out of the Department of Justice. Even two cases before the Supreme Court?"

"You have done your research, Mr. Langston. I can't wait to join the battle."

In these few moments, Harriet had 'read' both new arrivals and filed them away as oily and too gratuitous. At this point, Harriet was about ready to tell these prosecutor show-offs where they could put their kiss-ass exchanges and tell them she wanted no part of whatever scheme they were involved in, but then Cotton Matther put on his competitive war mask.

Quite serious, once the head prosecutor from the Southern District of New York, now New York City's visible prosecutorial litigator, he intoned, "Okay, fanfare over, let's get down to the Rules of Engagement." After that, the verbal exchanges were machine gun bullet points of agreement negotiation.

"You signed your contract with Fox?" asked Matther. Harriet knew only one Fox, outside the news and movie corporation, that might be involved contractually. A past coincidence came around: *Hugh Fox.*

"Yes, received 20% advance," responded Langston.

"Same here. He's good for the money," and Matther and Buchanan laughed to each other.

"Shall we run this like the Harvard Law School format for Mock Trials?"

"Yes, my preference also."

"Discovery exchange?"

"Yes, but assume, no surprises. All must be from the public record. No hidden secret transcripts from alphabet U.S. Govt. agencies." Langston shot a glance to Buchanan, who shrugged his muted acceptance.

"Have you heard who the judge might be?"

"Fox said he is looking at a few retired Federal judges. But if you have a candidate, go for it. I'm told we might draw names out of a hat, if that is acceptable?"

"Not that happy," replied Matther, giving a devilish smile to Harriet. "You know I was the best at judge-shopping a case."

Langston retorted, "That is why I suggested that blind draw method."

Matther was checking his calendar. "Are we still on schedule for a trial date? One month I heard for research and prep."

"Yeah, it'll be somewhat rushed, but I can live with that. It's reality television, after all. Nothing monumental to world security."

Buchanan interjected, "I heard that they are going to run some actors and television crew over to the Middle East to make a big show of searching, that sort of thing."

"Better for audience hype, the tease factor," grinned Matther.

Harriet just sat there listening, not knowing what was going on but realizing this 'invitation' to be involved was turning out to be something quite big, quite visible. Star-making qualities, even. And after all, in the courtroom, attorneys were entertainers, litigants in battle employing witty rapier finesse in cross-examination or brawling fists pounding out overwhelming evidence. The jurors or judge were the audience to be swayed.

After more details were bantered around, accepted, or postponed to, as attorney Buchanan quipped, a future 'script' meeting, the meeting broke up, neutral smiles of good-byes exchanged. And when the conference room door closed, Langston could only respond, "What a pompous butt-kisser, but a lethal cobra in the courtroom. I was in a criminal law firm back in New York, mostly white-collar stuff, a few celebrity arrests, high-profile shootings. Cotton always seemed to want to take on those cases I handled."

Harriet had to question, "You defended clients before, as he said, then joined the dark side of prosecution out here? And the reason was?" She saw him think of a response, so she added. "And in New York, did you fare okay? And against him, specifically?"

"We crossed swords in nearly twenty-five cases on the high-profile side. As a defense attorney, in a similar job to yours, I won all my cases, pled out two, and one was dismissed because of jury tampering. No one could ever prove who was trying to affect the outcome, but for my money, there was some concern about ethics in the District Attorney's office at that time. Don't let the good vibes distract you. He wants to see me grovel with my failure in this case, but we'll show them how wrong the outcome will be."

"Booker," that was the first time she ever used his first name but only to get his attention. "Mr. Langston, what makes you think I am going to drop all my present cases to go play at some televised courtroom drama for ratings and Prosecutor Matther's self-aggrandizement."

She actually saw a shy smile on his countenance. Was he begging her forgiveness for his oversight? Harriet now realized she never got a straight answer on why his career had shifted abruptly, why back then advocating for the innocent in New York, yet currently the aggressive attack wolf in L.A. courtrooms.

"Oh, I guess I'm sorry. I keep forgetting that you did not hear what I am offering. I struck a financial deal with Hugh Fox. I'm for the cause, not the dinero. We are going to split my initial payment. For me, it was going to be $1 million, but with you on board, you'll get half of that — $500,000 for three months or less work. And if we win, there I go again with that 'if' factor. Anyway, *when* we win, I will keep the proffered victory bonus of $1 million since I am in charge of production operations, like an Executive Producer."

"Me? $500,000 for one mock trial? That's ridiculous."

"Well, it's Hugh Fox's funny money, and he expects a true-life performance."

"Who are we defending?" They both heard that she used the word 'we.'

"Osama bin Laden."

"Oh, sure, I thought it was going to be hard." There was her natural wit that he had actually come to enjoy in the courtrooms where they had faced off, her sarcastic lashing out with verbal skill.

"They haven't settled on the main actor to play Osama, but I hear they are interviewing talent."

"And you say televised?"

"Worldwide."

"I don't think you can wave a magic wand and have my current caseload re-arranged."

"Being done as we speak." She accepted he could pull strings; he did have a rep.

"You think I will jump at this?"

"I know you like challenges, that your battles are against bullying foes, and that you, like all of us, are here to prove ourselves to ourselves, if not the whole world. We are very similar in nature, Miss Eberhardt."

As she considered his continuing speech of friendly cajoling to gain her consent while she countered his offer with how her own moral high ground could not be bought off for a measly $500,000. What a piss-poor counterargument. Such a sudden monetary windfall for any city public defender was manna from an unpredictable god, and such funds gained honestly. She thought of law school loans that would be retired.

Weakening, her final fallback questioning: why would she jump into an utterly whacko situation without consideration of her needs? She damned herself. Of course, the need satisfied was recognition gained by being in the same courtroom with two of the most recognized trial attorneys representing East and West coast criminal litigation clubs. An epic battle, the tribal competition fierce, and all televised. Within all these mental gymnastics, still having few details of what her responsibilities might be, she gave her acceptance half-reluctantly. Then, as they were shaking hands on the commitment, which she would quickly reduce to a legal document of services to be rendered, it suddenly came to her attention, the brain cell light bulb clicking on with illumination, for Booker Langston to have made this offer in the first place, he had been noticing her.

Scene 2: Loose Lips and Wagging Tongues
Setting: Santa Monica, California, Late March 2011

Perhaps overlooked in their first several meetings, the bin Laden 'Hunt Team' should have addressed one further issue — that of secrecy. King was a man who usually said yes to any headline, all publicity being somehow favorable, but he would not have wanted the world to hear of this crazy project prematurely before he could spin it to his benefit. So, he would keep his own counsel and say nothing overtly.

However, on this day, as meetings wound down, where research teams consisting of part-time employees began to shut down computers, someone at their workstation, diseased with that social addiction of one who must say anything rather than nothing, sent out an SMS, on a new short message service platform, called a 'tweet' to a friend:

@#sweetnewjob#CapturebinLadenhunt#Hunters-r-StormKing&HughFox#.

Within these modern times, there are two universal truths: That the world is connected and that there are no secrets in La La Land.

SnoopOnline, the media gossip consolidator for the tabloids, pried out more under the rocks and broke the story in the early morning hours, and it was immediately picked up by all the interbred tattler sheets. The news went viral before noon, with the bloggers disseminating their opinions. It received its final blessing of 'validity' from the television networks in the evening news hour slots.

In those brief, attention-grabbing television seconds, the public heard this:

TV Show to Hunt Bin Laden

The popular television reality show 'King's Retribution,' which tracks down and captures criminals, will next focus its attention on trying to discover the whereabouts of international terrorist Osama bin Laden and bringing him to justice.

Retribution's star, retired Army Colonel David 'Storm' King, said, "We have a successful track record focusing on criminals from the U.S. Who says we can't go after evil wherever it is to be found? As I see it, bin Laden is top of the list as the world's most diabolical murderer."

[Storm did not say anything of the kind, but at this point, the lede had life, facts and truth mattered little.]

A theorem about publicity says that any public notice designed to be positive will garner an untold number of dispelling negatives.

Reeling from media inquisition about the leaked information, Callie and Storm discovered that the publicity onslaught's downside was ridicule. Talk show comedians skewed the news with jokes about capturing bin Laden but having to do so between commercial breaks. They said that instead of torturing bin Laden by waterboarding, the same effect could be achieved by forcing him to watch American television reruns of *The Bachelor* or locking him in a cell where he had to listen to constant looping of *Achy Breaky Heart* and *The Macarena*.

News pundits criticized what they called the crassness of Tinsel Town making a game out of capturing a mass killer and said that the actual hunt should be left to government experts.

And this was the news tidbit that Khalaf, consolidating world news reports, felt relevant and had conveyed this to his boss at the Abbottabad, Pakistan residence. At the push of a button on a remote, the communicative world reaches all, beamed on waves of unseen currents.

Ensconced in cubicles, the Research Team, the fact-finders, found itself inundated with well-intentioned (or not) citizens calling to offer their insights as to under which piece of shit bin Laden had hidden his miserable self. Much of the information seemed miraculous in origin, whether by tarot cards, Ouija board, or dartboard guesses. Email at the *King's Retribution* fan site crashed, and an automated phone tip line put callers on perpetual hold.

Good news, though, was still good news, it seemed. That was the take from Hugh Fox, and in presiding over one of the group's 'sessions of progress,' handed a letter to King, who read it and announced, with a growing smile, "The network has renewed us for a third season, providing we launch the new season with our bin Laden hunt. Briggs, go and notify the rest of the crew. I'll work with the PR department later for a public news release."

Since they were between Season Two, which was complete, and taking time off before shooting and editing shows for Season Three, it was noted that new viewers were drawn to '*King's Retribution*' re-runs, and even Skilleo games had an uptick in sales; not necessarily fans, but the curious.

Storm King accepted that hunting the terrorist and the resulting television show — with or without a capture — would drive viewers to the season's premiere, and ratings should soar. And in the process, King believed he would become an even more recognized personage, a face for the magazine covers, the go-to military expert required for talk shows. He decided to text his agent about sniffing out possible movie roles, especially with Schwarzenegger on the outs as the action-hero standard.

King could see himself as a Harrison Ford or Sean Connery, though younger and on the cusp of being a strong, maturing character. To King's current way of thinking, capturing bin Laden was secondary to staging the process and managing the perception. If they came back empty-handed, as he expected, the show could be focused on al-Qaeda history as a back story and then a stock footage travelogue to the Middle East. Any search sequence could be televised with dramatic license — quick shots in and among empty buildings, dark alleys, maybe a cave or two.

The idea proposed by this small news story — that someone, government or a private resource like the *King's Retribution,* might capture Osama bin Laden and return him to the United States for trial — resonated throughout the country with mixed results.

The Northern California Attorneys' Association and the Law Club at the University of California at Berkeley questioned if a U.S. trial, which likely would be held to try Osama bin

Laden 'for crimes against humanity,' whether bin Laden could ever get a fair trial under American jurisprudence?

Elsewhere, and for their own purposes, were those who did not use the word 'alleged' and did not want to see the terrorist Osama bin Laden ever make it to trial.

Scene 3: The Wrath of the Anointed Righteous
Setting: Late March, Battleford, Georgia

Samuel Tate, pastor of the Church of True Believers, held his rural congregation of fifty parishioners in thrall. They saw their God as the only God and believed the Bible was the only word from God, not open to interpretation — except by Pastor Tate. When of recent the topic would arise, he preached against the presence of Anti-Christ bin Laden, and for such, to someday be a prisoner on American soil must be condemned as blasphemous. A government trial, he preached, would draw too much attention to the Devil and his accursed followers. Pastor Tate conveniently fainted, then revived with the revelation that he alone must bring the message to the masses: only those who joined the Church of True Believers would enter heaven; and there was no place in such celestial bliss for those who did not believe in God or the crucifixion and arising of Jesus Christ, as extolled through Pastor Tate's teachings. True, Muslims do not worship Jesus (Isa) but accept him, not divine or heavenly, but still as a messenger of God. Pastor Tate could not accept some latitude as to how others believed.

Jubilant with the Holy Spirit for giving him these thoughts, Pastor Tate asked his travel agent to book him a flight to Los Angeles so he could protest against apostate Muslims and this *King's Retribution* TV show, the Hollywood cesspool filled with radical anarchists. Then he called his publicist and told him to put out a press release saying that Pastor Samuel Tate would appear in front of whatever location he chose to announce before the cameras, and thus the world, that he would burn a Koran in protest.

When this press release hit the Arabic-language television news network known as *al Jazeera*, stating that an infidel would burn a Qur'an, the book holding the religious treatises of Islam, a mob rioted in Algeria, and three people were killed. At an ethnic newsstand in Chicago, upon reading about Pastor Tate's one-man book burning threat, Razzor Hassim told himself that somebody should stop anyone who might attempt to desecrate the holy words, words from God himself that were told to Muhammad through the archangel Gabriel.

Hassim had an appointment to meet the Professor in Los Angeles. It would be no inconvenience that he should take a detour to observe this sacrilege that sought, by its act, to curse his spiritual leader.

Hassim accepted the ridiculousness of this stunt, but it drew attention back to these 'bounty hunters' who, by their efforts, were defiling a 'Chosen One.' In his religious zeal, Hassim accepted in faith that no one would ever catch Osama bin Laden. The al-Qaeda Supreme Council and the Emir were inviolate. And by dedicated association, wrapped in the same cause of imparting political retaliation, Hassim considered himself equally invincible. And he would act as a tool of Allah's to smite evil as he saw its threat.

Scene 4: The President's Men Gather
Setting: The White House, end of March 2011

The President of the United States glanced through the updated memo entitled 'Anatomy of a Lead,' which had been prepared by the deputy chief of the Pakistan-Afghanistan Department of the CIA.

"Well, you have all read the report. Does anyone have any comments on taking action if the intel proves true?"

"I don't trust the intel," said the Vice President, thumbing through his copy. "Too risky without total confirmation."

The opinion was heard, smiled at, and dismissed. The President turned to his true off-shore intel source, the Director of the Central Intelligence Agency.

"Do you think bin Laden is at this house in Abbottabad? Says here it's a few hundred yards from Pakistan's West Point military academy. You got to be kidding! Hiding under their noses?"

"Perhaps it's a protective shield for whoever is at that location. As you have been briefed, much of their Intelligence Agency is compromised with fundamentalists," replied the CIA Director. "If bin Laden is there, it's certain he is under someone's protective umbrella. If we go forward, we can't let the Pakistani government get wind of any planned operation, or it will, for certain, filter down the chain of command. It's happened before. As to our 'Lead' report, it has been constantly upgraded with new data, and though on-the-ground surveillance has no confirmation of who's in that compound, as you might have read, it's my staff's firm opinion that it is an al-Qaeda sanctuary for some high-value target. Perhaps only an al-Qaeda field commander. Our preferred choices are bin Laden or al-Zawahiri. If either one, we must take action."

"If we have confirmation of the target, especially if it's 'Geronimo,' a drone missile would be the safest response," came the answer from the ribbon-medaled Chairman of the Joint Chiefs.

"We've been through this before," stated the CIA Director. "We have to capture the son-of-a-bitch. Bits and pieces of body parts won't satisfy the public or the press, I might add."

"Yes, I concur," said the President. "Where are we in initiating an operation?"

"Per your last instructions, our SEAL Team Six and my field personnel have been in training on the East and West coasts, and as we speak, they are being brought together and sent over to Bagram [Afghanistan airport] for final assault practice on a replica of the compound."

"Timing?"

"If nothing changes within the target location, our strike force will be ready by mid-May.

With the latest and final intelligence assessment, we can give you a window for a final decision."

"Okay. Apprise me of any new details. Trying to move troops out of Iraq and Afghanistan is a balancing act as it is. Ending up like Carter's failure at rescuing the Tehran embassy hostages is not an option."

"I agree, Mr. President. This operation is designed to be surgical, swift, clean. In-out."

"It had better be. And what's this I hear, and Michelle has to tell me, about some television cop show going after bin Laden?"

"Hot air, Mr. President. Headline seekers."

"We don't need any interference that could tip our hand about how close we might finally be."

"Yes, and in that vein, I have made sure that we have someone in the field who can keep a lid, if need be, on any vigilante antics."

"Good," said the President, and he opened another briefing folder to another world crisis needing to be dealt with.

If required, those *King's Retribution* yokels would be misdirected, the CIA Director said to himself as the meeting conversations buzzed around him. He understood the wall of plausible deniability he had to create for the President, not that this was at any level of national security.

He had agreed with Assistant Deputy Givens that putting soon-to-retire agent Wendell

Holmes out among the Hollywood nuts was a perfect 'kick-out-the-door' assignment. Holmes could be a thorn, so the farther away he was, the better. His mind drifted. The Director of the CIA could recall in his own experience that in 1998 after he had left the White House as Clinton's Chief of Staff but remained one of Clinton's private brain trust advisors, the name Wendell Holmes had surfaced in what became known as *Operation Infinite Reach*. It was a memory not pleasing to the Clinton White House, the Director distinctly remembered.

Scene 4: Flashback — Consequences of Questionable Action
Setting: Khartoum, North Sudan, August 20, 1998

As they approached the factory, the two men in flowing black robes hugged the buildings, obscured by the night's deepest shadows. With their white skin, both men would be out of place at any time of the day, so their faces were wrapped in cloth with only their eyes visible, peering from slits, each man burdened with a backpack.

At the warehouse door, one of them began jimmying an ancient lock. Within 15 seconds, it clicked, and the door opened with a creaking squeak. They froze. From an earlier reconnaissance, they knew a night watchman walked through the building at odd hours. The two men eased in, skirting piles of boxes marked in Arabic: 'Urgent: Medical Supplies.'

The name on the building said *Al-Shifa*, the Arabic word for 'healing.'

At the CIA, early data-gathering suggested this pharmaceutical plant might not be making medicine, but processing the deadly nerve agent VX, the ingredient that would, in later years, be known as a primary component for WMD, or weapons of mass destruction.

The two men went to their separate tasks. The younger agent crept over to what looked like waste disposal barrels and began scraping refuse into a test tube vial. Then he quickly scrambled to another part of the warehouse, near the rolling assembly line where products were boxed.

He crawled under the conveyor system and gathered caked samples of dried sludge.

Wendell Holmes, the older agent by seven years, had set himself the task of seeking out the small testing laboratory. He threw his robe over some cabinets, and under the cloth covering, he snapped flash photos of the bottles and labels with an old Pentax camera. He took a selective sampling of bottles from dispensary shelves and off the quality control tables, examined the Arabic-language labels, and placed bottles in his backpack, in specially segmented Styrofoam pockets to protect them from breaking.

When he rejoined his associate, he found him between boxes, running litmus test strips on his gathered vials. He was using an eye-dropper to add saline solution and then checking the chemically altered strips against a color chart.

"I found it," whispered the younger man excitedly. "EMPTA, for sure." It was the chemical base used in the VX nerve agent.

"Where did you find it? Maybe we can find some bottles to confirm."

Glancing at the vial in question, the young man shrugged.

"This came from the soil sample I pulled from outside."

"Outside?" Holmes's voice was hoarse with incredulity. "Not in the plant?"

"Near the street, but it must be connected to this building."

"You think so? In a busy industrial section of Khartoum? All I found were medicine bottles, all labeled properly, with shipping manifests going out to hospitals and clinics in this country. Nothing being shipped to Iraq."

"Well, I called it in when I had a positive sample." With a superior attitude, the younger agent pointed to his sat-phone.

"You did what?" Holmes bristled, and his voice rose above a whisper to exasperated shock.

"The strike. We have enough. That terrorist, what's his name, Osama whatever, we've been told he's the financial angel behind this factory."

Holmes knew that the Agency had made this a major push for clarification; they were seeking some 'retaliation' target for recent embassy bombings in Africa, those taking responsibility being a new Islamic terrorist group called al-Qaeda or al-Qaida. The Clinton Administration wanted to show the world that no one escaped this superpower's wrath; that they could retaliate with an 'infinite reach.'

But this clandestine incursion had been to gain evidence, nothing more, and had now been compromised and pointed toward a deadly conclusion. Holmes regretted being stuck with such a high-strung newbie.

"Ronnie, you idiot! Didn't you read the rough intel? The man's name is Osama bin Laden, and that was someone's guess. It's unverified! Shit! How much time do we have?"

"They acknowledged immediate launch. We should get going." The young man spoke nervously. Suddenly, playing Secret Agent had become a little tenuous because a cruise missile had been called in on his location, on his head — by him.

Despite his partner's stupidity, Holmes agreed it was time to hustle.

But then a flashlight shone in the young man's face, and they heard a startled Arabic voice. Holmes, off to the side, launched a fist and knocked the watchman to the ground senseless. Then, taking advantage of his partner's quick response, the younger man ran as fast as he could toward the door they had first entered. Holmes shook his head to realize that the boy's style of bravery meant 'save self first.' He bent down and slung the watchman over his shoulder, balancing the backpack on his other shoulder. Then he, too, moved as quickly as he could. *Move ass and avoid the incoming,* he thought.

Exiting onto the roadway, he crossed the street and lowered the factory worker to the ground. He could see his fellow agent leaning against a building a block away. Suddenly, the watchman jumped to his feet and tore back across the street, yelling as loud as he could, "Thieves!"

In Arabic, Holmes shouted a warning that made no sense: "Bombs are falling." The watchman did not understand or else did not hear. Familiar only with his job's routine, he ran back into the factory, seeking a phone to call the authorities.

Holmes walked down the street. In disgust, he watched his partner retch out his fear.

"You asshole! Did you really have to start an international incident based only on one glob of dirt?"

Agent Ronnie Givens gave no reply. Night turned to day and the Al-Shifa Pharmaceutical Plant and its dutiful watchman ceased to exist in an explosion of fire and rubble.

Scene 5: The Fall-out
Setting: Washington, D.C., 1998 to 1999

Holmes filed the internal CIA field report, and he minced no words. The destruction of the pharmaceutical plant and the killing of a factory employee had been initiated by a premature analysis of only one soil sample taken from outside the plant, not within the building, as requested.

Though Givens was named in the report, Holmes did not specifically draw attention to the ineptitude of the sampling conclusions. The implication of who was at fault was clear, leaving Holmes with an enemy for life.

At that time, and in announcing the single missile attack in Sudan, the Clinton government cited the following evidence as justifying its actions: (1) Contact between plant officials and Iraqi chemical weapons experts, who were thought to be using the EMPTA ingredient in their VX production. (2) Ties between the al-Shifa plant and the Islamist al-Qaeda group of Osama bin Laden, believed to be behind various bomb attacks on African embassies.

A report written in 1999 by the U.S. State Department Bureau of Intelligence and Research questioned the attack on the factory, suggesting the evidence offered was 'weak.' Bin Laden, who had been a resident in Khartoum in the 1980s, had left Sudan by 1996. Holmes had actually met bin Laden in the late 1980s in Pakistan and later Afghanistan, one of many idealistic foreign warriors, something not put into any report as being extraneous to this specific incident.

The connection with Iraq turned out to be a $199,000 order for veterinary medicines. One critic of the attack questioned: "What was the hurry to bomb? The factory could not be folded up like a tent and spirited away. The U.S. had diplomatic relations with Sudan.... Perhaps instead, someone [the inference meant Clinton] needed to look 'Presidential.'"

The Clinton Administration sought to distance itself from the intra-agency turmoil generated by Holmes's known 'report of doubt.' In 2000, Holmes found himself 'reassigned,' as they say, to the embassy staff in Outer Mongolia. Supporting Holmes and his report was an in-house CIA analyst who also voiced doubts and questioned the evidence requiring a bombing response even before the power to launch a strike had been given to Ronald Givens. In 2006, that analyst was fired based on her outspoken opinion. Not wishing to admit to faulty intelligence, or even more insidious, a Wag the Dog fabrication, the CIA Boy's Club closed ranks to silence and denial. And the benefactor? Ronald Givens was promoted, the first of many upward moves, not usually based on competence.

In 2001, the al-Shifa plant owner sued the United States for more than $50 million, saying he had detailed records of what the factory had actually produced and that it was medicine, not chemical weapons. He demanded a formal apology from the United States. The Sudanese government kept the factory 'as is' in its destroyed condition indefinitely, asking the U.S. to come in, investigate and prove its case. The U.S. government never responded.

As with many international incidents, the side stories were lost in the shuffle to what seemed more important on the world stage. One result had far-reaching consequences no one noted at the time. The medicines destroyed at the al-Shifa pharmaceutical plant never made it to the people in the Sudanese and Iraqi countryside, and after 1998, an increasing number of sick Middle East citizens died for want of treatment. Many of those people knew about the medicines lost and, seeking justice, turned to al-Qaeda, which was subsequently funded partly by wealthy Sudanese, some of al-Qaeda's monetary contributors that led to 9/11/2001. Holmes believed there was a correlation, a thin thread binding al-Shifa and the Twin Towers. He wondered whether Ronald Givens ever understood his small action of rushed inaccuracies was the catalyst, that he, Givens became the spark to the international powder keg, of why all things are still in such a rotten mess today.

Scene 6: Holmes is the Hunter
Setting: Santa Monica, California, First week of April 2011

In hindsight, Hugh Fox didn't exactly know why he decided to drop by the War Room around 11 p.m. instead of returning to his hotel suite. It was one of those fortuitous events that moved a person along a different current in the stream.

He had finished a late dinner at the French-American restaurant *Melisse* on Wilshire Boulevard, sitting at a private table with a small group of venture capitalists and film producers who were going home pretty well zonked on assorted Napa reds. Earlier in the evening, they had been at their best doing their "Luv ya, baby" pitch to him. What they sought were the film rights to one of his most successful video games in the Skilleo Games catalog, *Galaxy Slaughter*.

At this point in the industry, most comic superhero characters were already optioned out, with films in production or already released and seeking theatergoer buzz, and fingers were crossed for a surge of interest that would guarantee a sequel and a branding franchise of recurring royalties. The new idea pickings had been slim at Comic-Con the previous year, and the studio money seemed to be grasping at [idea] straws — one direction was moving back into video game themes. Even the toy company Hasbro was trying to resurrect old board games like 'Battleship' into a movie. "If they ever make a movie on 'Monopoly,' entertainment values and civilization as we know are doomed," said one of the inebriated execs, suddenly trying to take back his slurring gush of words, "No, no." Worried that he might have spat out a truth.

What impressed the moneymen and the mini moguls was that Skilleo didn't just create a game, but it also patented the 'art of gameplay,' developed around the patents' innovative methods to attract player interaction. Where Pixar had triumphed with digital clarity in the cartoon format, Skilleo held the edge in gamesmanship technology. 3-D, as an example, seemed to be reaching a peak in movie ticket sales; initial curiosity had leveled off since viewers had come to expect only jump-out-of-the-screen action. 3D advancement created a niche audience to be drawn into the experience. Skilleo had a large prototype IMAX-size movie screen in a theater where moviegoers could sit with high-intensity, spectral beam 'guns' and, at the appointed sequence cue, could join the hero and blast away at the flesh-eating, bloodsucking, inter-galactic androids with actual screen response from the shooter's weapon. Aim, fire, bad critter evaporated. It was incredible; another leap for the entertainment of mankind and also for Skilleo, from carnival sideshow shooting ranges and backyard cap pistols of cowboys and Indians to i-gaming commercialization. The checkbooks were open, and Fox was asked to fill in the amount. He left them soused, drooling and hanging out to dry without an immediate answer.

His restive spirit had brought him here to the War Room, his current hands-on project. In front of the building, he noted that a few lean-to's and sleeping bags bore testimony that 'protestors' had located the central locus of the 'Hunt Team' office. The Santa Monica night remained mellow with a few night owls holding soap box tepid arguments, muttering their opinions, mostly to themselves. A guard stood bored at the building's entrance. Tomorrow, Hugh would increase tighter security as he entered without challenge.

In the silent, dark War Room, Fox saw a single globe of light within one of the cubicles and walked over to find Callie Cardoza punching away at a computer keyboard. Her black hair pulled back into a casual bun; she was engrossed in the display screen and oblivious to his arrival.

"Late night?"

Whoa!" She jumped at his voice.

"Sorry. I wanted to see who was putting in overtime. Should have guessed it was one of the boss ladies and not any worker bee."

"Hardly a boss," said Callie, turning to watch him take a chair next to her. "And speaking of which, where is the boss lady, Ms. Carlisle?"

"She's in New York for some sort of Fashion Week. And your Colonel King?"

"He's certainly not 'mine.' We are, how would they say, 'close acquaintances.' Working at close quarters on a set can do that to you."

They looked at each other during an awkward silence, both perhaps realizing that, oddly, they had each qualified where their significant other was as a prelude to the conversation.

"And what are you working on?" Hugh asked. Her body seemed to emote the fervor of the hunt he had sought to impress on his staff and cohorts.

"Bin Laden's family tree." She turned her screen so he could see a diagram of multiple lines listing family relationships. She scrolled down several pages. "Over 600 *closely-related* family members."

"Amazing. I guess if he were Christian, the Christmas card mailing list would bankrupt him."

"Naw, he could afford it. His family's company, Saudi Bin Laden Group, is one of the largest construction firms in the Islamic world, with offices internationally. They gross about US $5 billion annually."

"The Saudi rich boy has time on his hands, so why not a little terrorism for fun?"

"Interesting, he's not a pure Saudi. His grandfather was a tribesman from Yemen, and his father was born in Yemen and then settled in Saudi Arabia before World War II. He started a small construction company that blossomed when he came to the notice of and fell under the benefice of the Saud family."

"As in King Saud of Saudi Arabia?"

"The same, but still confusing. To track the bin Laden progeny, I have had to break it into groupings based on the wives' nationalities: Saudi, Syrian, Lebanese, Egyptian. Osama is one of 25 children of his father, Muhammed bin Laden, by his tenth wife. So I categorized our buddy into the Syrian group."

"That's quite a lot of due diligence to go searching through every single name and background."

"Agreed. So we have to make some assumptions that a computer program filtering system might not have the capabilities to run."

"My engineers could certainly create anything you required."

"Sorry, but they could never duplicate the old stand-by 'women's intuition.'"

"Indeed, I hear it's a mystery of the centuries, if not eons." Their smiles met. "So, how do your female hunches beat out a Cray or an IBM supercomputer?"

"Think as a man might, then out-think him."

"Now I'm worried."

"Seriously, bin Laden has five wives and had about 22 known children, 18 of the children surviving. He looks to the children as his legacy, but when it comes to his personal needs — and certainly all men, including imams and priests, have some form of libido — I am going to make the nonscientific assumption that he wants warmth and comfort from his latest wives, from his wife Siham Sabar, and his last wife, Amal al-Sadah, a.k.a. Amal Ahmed Abdul Fatah."

"There seems to be sense to that reasoning. But I never could understand how a man could handle more than one woman, regardless of culture."

"You are a wise man."

"Though maintaining a short-term harem might have its merits."

"Ah, a typical male response, but a surprise from you. I thought for kinky needs, you would merely create digital avatar groupies and then program them to whisper sweet algorithms."

Fox accepted that this ex-cop had smarts, and he enjoyed her sharp-witted personality, but this banter had drifted toward flirty. It wasn't a bad feeling, but unsettling. He did have a girlfriend of sorts, or at least a bed partner.

"So how does Mr. bin Laden getting his rocks off with Wife #5 help us?"

Safely back on track.

"It is not so much bin Laden's proclivity as it is learning the character of his latest wife, Amal Ahmed Abdul Fatah. We know they married when she was 17 years old and that she came from Yemen as a gift from a powerful Yemeni family. What I read is that it was an arranged marriage to strengthen bin Laden's ties back to his ancestral home country. So, like a mail-order bride, she was taken out of her comfort zone, and her husband has her tucked away somewhere.

"Maybe with him, maybe alone. She and Osama have had children, all young still, so they most probably are with her. I'm betting she has pangs of homesickness, missing old friends and family. Actual members of his direct family, the older wives and children, know he's in hiding, and they know not to contact him, and he will contact them only in an emergency. Some of his wives are, I believe, stranded or political prisoners in Iran. But it's *her* family I want to concentrate on — to discover if they have made any unusual trips out of their homeland and where to. That may be the lead we need."

She held the best for last. "And there is one other element that might be the answer we are pushing for."

"And that is?"

"At 29, now she's still the youngest wife. There could be a jealousy factor among the older wives causing marriage dissension, or she could just be bored hiding out with him, thus cranky. Or if not, anxious to be with him, thus horny. I'm counting on one of these elements of disharmony to be the key to identifying his location."

She leaned back and sighed, looking to him for a confirmation of her train of thought. At this point, if she were in a discussion with Storm, he would have found something wrong with her concept. He was unable to offer any form of compliment.

But Hugh mulled over the machinations of her logic.

"It's a theorem to be proved, but strong on the equation. Yes, I like it, but how are you going to track her family?"

"Well, I've already been able to pull her tribal records, and I found passports issued to five family members: two uncles, an aunt, and two of her sisters."

"Passports? How?"

"There is the Europol database, which tags passports from countries that are defined as 'hotspots.' I'm sure the CIA and the U.S. State Department through Homeland Security have something similar."

He straightened up, alert.

"What? You hacked into the International Police database? Callie, that could have ramifications. That could backfire on us!"

She caught the fact he called her by her first name. It was a first, even if it was in agitation.

"No worries, I think."

"You think? Please don't stress me out."

"I went back into my old job's computer section at the San Diego Police Department. When the latest system upgrade happened, I was there and left a few back doors open, so any request to Europol would come from the Police Department email box and into a blind account I could access. And all I asked Europol to do was put us into an alert system on this group of family members and when they are on the move across international borders."

"Telling them what? A reality TV show wanted to be kept informed?"

"I built a story about several Arab family members being sought for forced female genital mutilation of a girl under 15 years of age. Given that most of Europol's computer data input clerks are probably women, I believe my request will gain some priority, perhaps some internal eyes on my targets."

"I am impressed." And he was, paying her a little more attention and wondering more about her.

"I am *also* impressed," came a gravel voice from the blackness. Hugh and Callie jumped, and she grabbed Hugh's hand.

A man came out of the darkness like a ghost forming in the dim light. He was an older man, maybe late forties, early fifties; what made him look old were touches of grey to his sideburns and leathered wrinkles on a craggy, outdoors face.

"I don't mean to interrupt, but the door downstairs was open, and the office door was unlocked."

"Unlocked? I don't think so." Hugh felt Callie release his hand and saw her hand inch towards the large purse at the side of her computer. It was a reactive response from an ex-cop but not a good ending for someone else, and Hugh found himself sandwiched between both.

"Unlocked," said the man, his statement firm and unyielding.

"And what can I do for you this late at night?" Fox sought to diffuse the situation, warily eyeing Callie as she pulled the purse to her side and snapped it open.

"Mr. Fox, I presume? My name is Wendell Holmes. I have been assigned to your group, team, or whatever you're calling your operation, as a 'Field Tour Guide.'"

"Assigned by whom?" Fox relaxed only slightly. He did not presume that this was a mugging, an irate fan, or anything more sinister because the man had come into the full light of the desk lamp with his hands at his sides, empty, his palms strangely turned outward. Hugh put his hand gently on top of Callie's as her fingers edged into the depths of her purse. Her eyes were focused on the man, gauging his distance, his bulk, and target points.

"If you recall, you had your public relations and your lobbyists seek experts who might be able to help if and when you left the U.S. on your search. I am the one selected to be your, as we are calling my position, field guide." The man called Holmes snickered with humor at his title.

"What makes you an expert to be guiding us?" Callie voiced direct suspicion. She was always cautious when she worked alone at night in an office complex. She knew both doors were locked, and there was no way Hugh Fox would have left them unlocked on his entry. B&E, breaking and entering, were not bona fide credentials they required as they pursued their bin

Laden caper.

Wendell Holmes gave them a disarming smile, knowing that less is more and too much, indeed, is distrust.

"Let's see. Tomorrow, you, we, the team were heading to Mr. Fox's office compound in Silicon Valley and then later meet with part of the show's planned legal team, a Mr. Booker Langston."

Fox saw the game. No resume would be offered. It was a test. A verbal duel, so to speak.

"That's common knowledge. There was a news story in today's *L.A. Times*. Suggesting I was up to something. Spending more time down here at this office."

"True, but are you aware that Colonel King is at the Zanzibar nightclub as we speak, fortifying himself with courage?"

"That's not that unusual," said Callie, irritated again at King. *Not that unusual for a vain man trying to drink himself young*, she thought.

"With this project, we shouldn't be talking about bar hopping," Fox said. "I expect this to be dangerous."

"Then you're holding hands with the right person." His words caught Callie and Hugh off guard. They looked at each other, glanced down, and then moved their hands from a warm touch both were unconsciously enjoying.

"Coming from a background of having been an office-based computer policewoman, one would be surprised to learn you are proficient in firearms, Ms. Cardoza, having actually shot someone," the mysterious man named Holmes said with a fatherly smile.

Hugh glanced at Callie. Before he went forward on this project, he had had his research staff run in-depth dossiers on the two stars of *King's Retribution*, but this was news to him.

Callie, surprised at hearing the ancient history, recovered and gave this Mr. Holmes a mean nod, acknowledging that the man had his sources. Point advantage to him.

More to Hugh, she said, "Many years back, a drunk boyfriend, 'ex' for sure, came at me with a knife. It was right when I graduated from the Police Academy. But the incident got expunged from my record as self-defense."

"'Expunged' is such a subjective word," responded Holmes. "Would it be more accurate to point out that the ex-boyfriend can never have children and that the police report was 'expunged' only after you were promoted to the computer section? A coincidence?"

"And while we're on the subject, I assume you gave up your regulation firearm upon leaving the San Diego Police Department. Their standard issue, I believe, is a Glock 22 .40 caliber. You have certainly downsized to something more feminine, yet still lethal, like a Beretta Tomcat. Yes, I could see you with that one. It's easy to hide in a purse."

This was too much, and her anger flared.

"How did you…?"

"Here are the bullets." Holmes dropped the live ammunition on a desk across from them.

Hugh and Callie were stunned at this trespasser.

"What the…? I went to the restroom over an hour ago, you son-of-a…."

"Another point in my favor?" Wendell Holmes, immensely enjoying this moment, turned his back and began disappearing into the shadows.

"Languages. I speak passable Arabic, plus a smidge of pidgin tourist Urdu and Farsi. If that's the part of the world we're headed to."

There was silence. Fox smiled and begrudgingly accepted the man as a player — but playing for whose team? And he had to ask, as if it were sealing the deal.

"You said three points of validation. And the other point?"

"I have met Osama bin Laden. Several times, in fact."

Somewhere in the War Room, they heard a door open and close, but they saw nothing.

REEL THREE

EPISODE NINE — The Players Gather

Scene 1: The London Cell Awakes
Setting: London, First week of April 2011

The apartment's panoramic view took in the Parliament building across the Thames. He could also see the revolving Ferris wheel known as the London Eye, with its 800 riders per revolution, all unaware that soon their world might change to more fear and uncertainty. They could only blame themselves, thought Khalaf. What could you expect when the Imperialist British trod across the Trans-Jordan and carved up the Ottoman Empire solely to suit the desires of allies that could be properly kept subservient to the Western need for oil to fuel their battleships? And added fuel to the fire by issuing the cursed Balfour Resolution creating the State of Israel, founded by terrorist Zionists.

"How long since you have been here?" asked the older man, sitting on the couch, enjoying his tea service. Khalaf likewise sipped. It was a silver tip Darjeeling tea, he had been told. He gave the man's question a few seconds of consideration. Had time moved that fast?

"About seven years. I did graduate-level Economics studies here in the city for two years, but I never finished the degree. The Brotherhood brought me back to Cairo to help form student protests against Mubarak."

"And, as you see, a seed planted becomes a flowering garden."

"Yes, Mubarak is gone. It's not so much flowers blooming these days as it is weeds springing forth, and some of them need to be ripped out by their roots."

"Will you ever go back to Egypt?"

Khalaf knew the answer, but pondering the question left an impression that such a door might be open. It wasn't. He had cast his fate with al-Qaeda, been recruited by Mullah Omar himself, and reported directly to bin Laden, which was a great honor.

"The Emir requires my presence."

"Future Emir. Bin Laden requires at least one country to affix his star and create his caliphate."

"That time is coming. *Crimson Scimitar* will define his greatness, his power, and we will either regain Afghanistan when the Americans leave, or Sudan or Yemen could come under our power."

"You mean 'his' power?"

"Of course, I am speaking collectively to our organization, with the Emir as supreme ruler." The older man smiled. He had been around many years and had seen so many youths spout rabid slogans, only to settle into the comfort of the system when age gave them the wisdom that the world could not be conquered; that one vest bomber sworn to Allah's cause would not alter governments.

"More tea?"

"Will your associate be arriving shortly?"

"Yes, any time."

"Then, yes please, two cups is my limit. It is very good."

The man, a banker by the name of Taher Abboud, poured for him, and both drank silently, each in contemplation.

Banker Abboud finally offered, "Your English is quite excellent," turning the conversation to trivial matters. "No trace of a Middle Eastern accent. Very Oxford in lilt. And your dress to visit me is certainly not that of a man of the desert, high mountain caves, or wherever our illustrious leader is now ensconced."

A test for him to slip and mention where bin Laden might be? Khalaf saw the sly humor in the smile of the financial man who was also a devout fundamentalist. The banker hid in the elegant dress code of suit and tie worn by those who do daily transactions with the Bank of England and its various correspondent banks. Khalaf dressed for this occasion in a late winter tweed sport coat and white turtleneck, trendier than what his staid conspirator chose as his business uniform.

"Yes, while attending school, I went out of my way to blend in. I thought it might be useful at some future date." Khalaf had trimmed his beard before flying to Great Britain by way of the Emirates and then allowed a barbershop on Mill Street in Mayfair to sculpt and shape it, close-cut, into fashion. People might see him as 'foreign,' but they would not be able to identify his nationality.

"I heard from another source, one of our brethren involved in *Crimson Scimitar*, that it was you who conceived this phase of the operation on your own. It is very brilliant, I might add."

Khalaf accepted the praise as his due and felt good that his talents were recognized. His recent trip to Yemen and his meeting with several members of the Supreme Council had not been as complimentary, nor as rewarding, as he had hoped.

"Let us just say that learning from our enemies led me to the concept. But indeed, I was blessed that the Emir approved and asked you to finish the structuring of the part of the component plan we call 'Pelham 123.' If it succeeds, it will be because we all saw the value."

"Yes, and 'value' is a keyword." The doorbell rang, and the banker, Abboud, rose to answer.

A young man entered, less Arabic in looks, more Persian, lighter-skinned, carrying two large suitcases, and they exchanged greetings. In the business world, he went by Zia Johnson, but his birth name was Ziad Mahoummed Barakat, and he worked as a stockbroker at one of the large brokerage firms in London located in the Canary Wharf financial district, with his firm's offices strategically located in New York and Chicago.

Khalaf listened in silence as Abboud outlined the role of Johnson/Barakat, the stockbroker. The young man gave a sheepish smile, realizing he was in the presence of a direct link to the head of al-Qaeda, which was an extreme privilege. Abboud finished by saying, "And he will leave for New York within a week before the launch of *Crimson Scimitar* so as to be in place on the attack date."

"Good. Thank you, Zia, for volunteering. Not all of us can serve as martyrs to our just cause, but believe me that I will pass word of your deeds, when accomplished, back to the Emir."

"I am most grateful," said the young stockbroker with an expression of joy. "I have longed to participate in the battle of the Faith."

Abboud walked him to the door, and Zia Johnson left, hesitant, clearly preferring to stay and know more about all that would come to pass.

The banker took the suitcases to the dining room table. Khalaf followed and saw they were filled with money: English pounds and other Euro currency.

"Taher, how much does this give us?"

"There are nearly two million Muslims in the United Kingdom, my friend. Our population grows at ten times the number of the Anglo-Saxon race. There are 1,500 mosques, and twenty percent of the Imams within those mosques are our supporters and say so indirectly whenever they can during Friday prayers. But as president of the Islamic Benevolent Foundation, I can tell you that almost all of them have contributed to us to assist the less fortunate. When I bank this delivery, our balance will be about $2 million in ready funds. And at the appointed time, I will make the transfer."

"And we can count on Barakat? Everything has to be timed so accurately."

"He is my wife's nephew. I saw his passion at an early age and directed it well. But realize he is more anti-Zionist than one of your al-Qaeda indoctrinates, those habitually unemployable and left only to cast hatred on others due to their own misfortune. Ziad is sharp. He's a good choice."

"You do not need to defend him. If he is your recommendation, I am satisfied and will report back as such."

"Thank you, Maulawi Jan." The man mentioned a name Khalaf had gone by several years earlier. It was a birth name, dropped for a one-word *nom de guerre* more in tune with a holy revolution.

Khalaf walked back to the window and the London skyline before him, wondering if any of the al-Qaeda-sponsored cells, the ones he knew nothing about, would be launching their own attacks on the anniversary of 9/11. The word had gone out for such attacks; he had delivered the message himself to various regional al-Qaeda commanders with supporters in Western countries.

Would the London Eye be such a target? It was so visible and offered so many possible deaths and injuries. Maybe attacks on the Summer Olympics in 2012? No, not his concern. He brought his mind back to his duties. The United States came first and would feel the might of *Crimson Scimitar*. If only bin Laden would give the word.

He said aloud, as more reinforcement to his commitment, "Abboud, we shall succeed. The infidel Americans saw 9/11 as one attack, yet there were several simultaneous operations consisting of four planes. *Crimson Scimitar* is an octopus with many tentacles. If by bad fortune, they cut one tentacle off, other arms will be out grabbing and strangling."

"Above all," he added, "the Emir, the head, is inviolate and will always be lord over us."

Scene: Magical Dream Tour
Setting: Silicon Valley, California, April 11, 2011

The caravan of limousines drifted south along Highway 280, away from the airport, veering off at Los Altos Hills and then winding its way west to the ten-acre Skilleo Game Technology campus, nestled against the Palo Alto Foothills Park.

Stretching her legs upon exiting the limo, Callie took in the environment. By now, the sunlight had burned away most of the coastal sea fog, yet there was still a smell of the cool, distant ocean carried by a feathery breeze to moderate the late spring weather. Before her, up a dozen steps on a slight rise, lay three buildings, each four stories tall and each curved in a wide arc; spaceships designed of brushed aluminum glinting with a chrome shine and accented with wide swaths of dark green glass.

Looking full circle, she saw hazy mountains in the distance, while to the south, on the grounds of Hugh Fox's corporate headquarters, there stood a phalanx of wind turbines of varying dimensions, and to the north, an array of solar panels. *California, 'politically correct,'* she mused.

King had been right to guess the place would be an enviro hangout, with 'greenies' trying to balance good deeds with acceptable levels of greed. What also caught Callie's attention was that the offices overlooked an immense landscaped garden, not of thorny roses or gentle petunias but boasting an elaborate maze of high hedges worthy of *The Shining*. Not menacing so much as a siren song to draw one in with curiosity. *For Hugh Fox, even nature must have its gameplay*, she mused.

The tour group consisted of Fox, Skilleo's majority [nearly sole] owner, leading the way and exchanging small laughs of conversation with Samantha Carlisle, who was at his side. Storm King took second position in stride, puffing out his chest, his face critical as if looking for a fault to point out. Callie could guess that King's attitude, previously braced by limo cocktails, held less awe at the man's success and more festering jealousy that youth was being so obscenely rewarded.

Perhaps King envied that the upbeat games inventor walked with a beautiful woman, one not as attractive as Callie thought herself as she dumbly tried to compare their attributes. Such insecurity put her in a funk mood, and she walked alone; or so she thought until she realized that the mysterious new addition to the team, this Wendell Holmes, if that was his name, opened the door for her. He wore a neutral smile and, throughout the tour, did not speak except once.

The visual videographers, CAM ONE and CAM TWO were ever present, cameras always on.

Something would be made from all the film they were amassing. A documentary, a reality show within a reality show; no one had told them what they were making or what to tape. Tasked without tasks, required to be their own creator, ONE and TWO said nothing and did their best to blend into the scenery to gain their best shots, still close enough that their directional microphones gained the best voice quality even during casual conversation. For those who enjoyed fame, these cameras and operators morphed into invisibility and were accepted.

Last to enter the building and receive the requisite Guest IDs was the bodyguard, Clayton Briggs, looking less 'muscle man' in a sport coat, and Bennie, the *King's Retribution* getaway driver. A small-framed man, balding and nervous, Bennie bore a weasel-narrow face with out-of-style tortoise glasses constantly being pushed back on his nose. He and Briggs took their status as the show's filler character actors and knew their best talent was shying away from others' limelight.

Handsome paychecks for their limited acting skills kept them thankful for jobs others could have easily filled. Abbas, of special effects skills, had studio work with the editing department and was absent this day, disappointed at missing the day trip.

The tour lasted two hours. Everyone participating retained a specific memory after seeing all the wondrous high-tech gadgets and the smiling 'hellos' from each employee they met in the labs or saw in the wide hallways, including those who skateboarded or roller-skated by.

Samantha Carlisle commented approvingly on Skilleo's daycare center for employees' children. She was amazed that the company operated a medical clinic offering preventative advice on carpal tunnel syndrome, exercise regimens for computer finger tendonitis, desk-side neck massages, and break areas with vibrating chairs near workstations.

The alpha males King, Briggs, and Bennie, had to be dragged away from the Testing Laboratory, a basketball court-sized, carpeted living room with TV screens mounted on the walls everywhere, and serious employee 'testers' sitting and playing games or standing in participatory action screen games of golf, baseball, or bowling. The three men each picked a game not yet released to the public and were excited that they could tell stories of what new Skilleo games the Christmas season would find under the tree (in departing, everyone received a gift bag of the latest games).

King played *Infamy 2*, portraying a superhero with the power to remove evil scum by striking them with bursts of electricity, ice, and other elemental ammo. The game was set in an imaginary city similar to a hurricane-ravaged New Orleans, where thugs and radiated swamp monsters needed to be obliterated. Bennie put on 3-D game goggles and played the baseball game *Triple Play* and kept exclaiming how realistic the hitting and pitching seemed as he swung wildly. Clayton's choice was *Vegas Noire*, a detective TV series-type game in which crimes are solved, and the player role-plays required guesses during gruesome CSI-type autopsies, where player hands can dissect anatomically accurate corpses.

Callie noted that Samantha deferred from choosing an action game and, in fact, looked away as if horror bred from such masculine excitement, whether it was sports or action gameplay brutality. Callie likewise begged off. Seeking to say something positive, Samantha commented to Hugh, "I have heard of your educational brands, that kids can learn cognitive skills by interplay."

Callie saw Hugh beam at the praise. She tried the same, pointing to a game that several second-grade testing subjects were animated about. "Is that one of your educational games? Those children are definitely enjoying it."

"A prototype game, *Angry Turtles*. The kids are using the computer mouse to skip upside-down turtles across a lake into the mouths of alligators to gain points. We will quiz players afterward and analyze their responses as to satisfaction levels." He gave thought as if processing the entire program the kids were yelling in glee over. "I am not that thrilled about the design violence."

Callie noted a genuine smile slip from his face as Samantha turned away and exited the room. Did he see the disappointment in her expression? That children were absorbed with cruelty as much as the gratuitous violence of an adult play game? Perhaps pre-game creation these days required psychological profiling regarding player response when the game was turned off. She could accept that logic.

Animation returned to Hugh's features, which Callie found herself enjoying, as Hugh Fox took over from the personable yet serious tour guide as they entered the Research Lab. He went through the game creation process, from idea germination to outsourced manufacturing in China. "The fertile mind of an individual dictates what the public eventually sees as their own tastes," he said, showing them a room — comfort again the priority — where in one corner, a group of people tossed out brainstorming concepts in friendly and rollicking banter; in another part of the room, researchers huddled over laptops. "We ask them to scroll to search the Internet universe and see what else is being communicated out there in the world. A disjointed fragment of an interesting idea might be given over to the brainstorming section of this department."

The bodyguard Clayton Briggs noticed a woman circling the floor in an enclosed booth, presumably soundproofed and with one-way glass. She seemed distracted, her arms waving, and muttering to herself. "What's she doing?" he asked.

"Oh, we take some of our smartest people as volunteers and have them enter what we call the Escape Room on a rotating basis. They speak about whatever comes to their mind, which we record and then sift for any germ of an idea."

Callie had seen this sort of behavior before. On the street.

"She's tripping." Callie frowned but relented at Hugh's direct smile.

"Only mild hallucinogenics, I assure you. Some of the world's greatest art, literature, and scientific ideas were created by people involved in chemically induced incidents that led to their creativity. Writer Aldous Huxley on LSD, the artist Van Gogh with absinthe addiction, and scientist Carl Sagan tripping out on pot. Baudelaire wrote in opium hazes, and Hemingway and F. Scott Fitzgerald had alcohol as their temptress muse…and demons."

Looking into another glass-partitioned room, Bennie asked, "And is this gentleman on druggie withdrawal?"

They all peered in to see a young man, the epitome of a surfer dude, lying on a tilted psychiatrist's couch, his head wired.

"That's our Dream Room," explained Fox casually. "We're trying to record a person's brain waves as he sleeps, trying to capture a dream sequence. And as he comes out of deep sleep, perhaps he'll start talking, and we can compare the sentence fragments, and perhaps someday be able to look into a real dream, and from there capture an essential, pure, virgin idea."

They all stared at him, not knowing if they were present among the most genius of geniuses or in Dr. Frankenstein's chop shop.

"You have to understand," Fox went on, seeing their reactions. "In order to compete in a crowded world of products, creation and delivery of any product must be totally unique for it to survive, though luck and timing are also important elements to a game release. It takes us three to four years to go from idea generation in this laboratory to the product being on a toy store shelf or sold online. In that time, public fickleness or new technology can make our product fail in the marketplace. We cannot waste resources by being wrong. Skilleo must always be ahead."

For the first time, Wendell Holmes spoke up.

"There seems to be a gentleman over in the corner talking only to himself. And he is finger-shooting. I presume he's playing a game, but he has no headgear on, and he seems to be talking to no one. I expect, as your rooms of Dreams and Escape exist, one would find the best subjects for ideas might be from the delusional, schizos, and psychotics." They all turned to the finger shooter and saw the man involved in a western shoot 'em up. Fast draw, dip and turn to shoot — it was like an old arcade game of hidden pop-up targets of villainous desperados. Callie accepted that to the Skilleo mindset, shooting red man savages was unacceptable.

Curious, they all gravitated in the player's direction as Fox explained.

"Another prototype in testing mode. It's two or three years from the market. As you all may be aware, the participant game player has moved from a joystick to a data-accepting handheld device, like a tennis racket. We're now to the point where the game computer can view the player's action and accordingly mimic the action. That's been the standard. Many are switching to VR [visual reality] gameplay. Here, we are merging systems with a modification. Moving from a contact lens microchip to the eventual implanted laser retina visuals with voice command."

"The man is generating computer play within himself?" questioned King, with a skeptical squint, "But I don't see it. Have you miniaturized it?"

"It's a Bluetooth capacity. The first major update since it became market acceptable in 2004. You can't see it because the visual is implanted in a contact lens in one eye, the motion receptor is embedded in his jaw, yawing the chin and tongue clicking creates a response." Fox saw disbelievers. "No, really. While iPhones are moving towards voice-activated responses to word association in order to discern a variety of questions, in the future, we might be able to dispense with the earplug or having to push a button to activate a device. For example, there are cars where you say, 'Car Turn On,' and the action will occur without a key. But since we are gameplay oriented, the central game box, again, in the near future, will be able to record your voice tangents and recognize you in the midst of group gameplay. Installation in the jaw might someday be a common outpatient procedure, not harmful and requires less effort than getting a tattoo, and with more application use. We are in early prototype with the contact lens camera slash jaw receiver transmitter."

Shaking their heads and accepting that they must be the ones who were Neanderthal Luddites in a Sci-Fi version of *The Twilight Zone*, they moved on. Some of them, amazed, brainstormed aloud about what uses such a jaw-implanted device might have. Callie saw that the last of them to exit the room was Holmes, who had walked up to the talking game player, and, after some deep eye contact, ran his hand along both sides of the man's jaw, seeking a bump or a blemish that showed where the device lay hidden under the skin.

He, too, was impressed. Callie thought the spook was absorbing perhaps one day to apply this new tech to battlefield or spy use.

Callie's stand-out memory of the day's tour was the walk-through of Hugh Fox's private office. Like a person's library or medicine cabinet, one's office revealed the subtleties of its occupant's mind and style; supplied clues that, in this case, laid open the personal myths of this supposed 'introvert genius.' She scanned the office in detective mode. To say the place bore a minimalist coldness, with its utilitarian furniture and lack of bric-a-brac, would be incorrect.

Even saying that 'functionalism' pervaded the style did not correctly convey the work environment.

Callie, who had been invited to many stars' abodes on the party circuit, did not see boasting, flaunted wealth, or executive arrogance. Fox's furniture, as a secretary explained, was of the German 'Bauhaus' movement design, with the consensus of the tour group being that office seating was designed for a visitor in sitting to speak one's mind quickly because easy comfort would be hard to settle into. Fox's smoked, cracked-glass conference table was oval, a sign of equality in ranking placement. She saw no wall of fame with photos that celebrated the boss standing with prominent politicians or sports figures. There were no family photos and, most notably, no desk photo of Samantha Carlisle. Callie found that telling, though she could not for the life of her decide what Carlisle's photogenic absence revealed.

The top of his desk lay vacant, clean of daily toil, if any such paper bureaucracy tedium ever did find its way to the steel and glass work area. Three wafer-thin computer screens were mounted on one side of his circular desk, with the novelty of an embedded touch-screen computer screen within the desktop glass. Rounding out the tech display was the large, mounted TV screen — more a movie screen — up one side of an office wall. A floor-to-ceiling glass wall behind his desk overlooked the garden maze. Callie wondered if Hugh ever looked in that direction; would he sit quietly, contemplating the puzzle garden, and could he trace a correct path from entrance to exit? Was he that kind of man?

Another long wall was bare except for three paintings — small, ink sketches in ornate gold frames. It took Callie a minute to recognize the significance of these three art pieces, styled by the same artist, being the only items in such a large, empty space. She knew her silent guess would be correct. *Leonardo da Vinci*. Originals, no doubt, and worth dollar signs of a million or two or more.

A hidden meaning? Perhaps it was acknowledgment or praise from one inventor to another; or, perhaps, daily inspiration.

Callie knew Storm King's thoughts were not on the host's fascinating character, which was intertwined in his personal presence, his office, his corporate style, of Skilleo Games and its amazing technology. Obvious glances at his watch made it clear that King was bored and wanted to head back to Los Angeles, back to the safety of his party world. As in times past, Storm

King's diligence required steady lubrication.

They waited for the limousines to appear for the ride to San Francisco's Stanford Court Hotel for a late lunch, then back to the airport, LAX before dinner, and more work in the War Room. Of the trip, King could only mutter, "The city," meaning San Francisco and its environs, "is a haven of yuppie commies," he had intoned in a bass voice as if his pronouncement blanketed all as unwashed.

Wendell Holmes stood next to Callie and gazed back up at the third-floor window of the executive office they had just left.

"Don't you find it interesting?" he asked.

"What's that?" She did not dislike him, but she didn't know him and felt it prudent to be cautious of whomever he might really be working for. A man with an agenda is always more dangerous because his interests are not for the good of the whole.

He continued. "That if you scan the pages of the game catalog of Skilleo Games

Technology, there are multiple choices for addictive game customers, but no war games. Yes, there are bloody, explosive battles with crooks and aliens, but not one of Marines or SEALS battling turbaned, dark-skinned terrorists. Seems almost un-American."

"And you are implying what? He's a liberal, sympathetic to Islamic interests?"

"No, not at all. Mr. Fox is a sincere young man in what he does well, which is to create satisfaction in entertainment. Like most, his core beliefs are sub-surface, not deep commitments. Future experience outside of his Skilleo bubble will bring him the knowledge that might shape him. Reality is a great wake-up lesson. Perhaps Mr. Fox is smart enough to realize he needs enlightenment, and that has piqued my curiosity."

"You're referring to this crazy hunt to find bin Laden? Are you saying it's a quest for Mr. Fox's personal, as you say, 'enlightenment?'"

"Can't say at this moment. Let me put it this way. It's curious that instead of having his game engineers draw up a storyboard of World War II battles, or fighting nasty North Koreans, or yes, corrupt Saddam Hussein and the Invasion of Iraq." He waved the catalog from the gift bag they were all given. "Perhaps Mr. Fox, once an inventor of originality, has become trapped as a corporate beast in his silicon castle. You might have entered into the creation of a new game, his idea of reality through rose-colored sunglasses, not from your perspective. And though flowing from his brilliant mind, per se, not one of his games has a basis in today's events, actual war, or insurgent experiences. Others similar to him at least make realism capture society's flaws, 'Grand Theft Auto' a prime example. In his world, he provides gratuitous Sci-Fi slash zombie violence within a Hollywood script; nothing, it seems, can be field tested by direct observations. You and I both know real life doesn't come with a hand-held portable console."

"I don't consider myself a pawn in anyone's headgame." Callie's eyes followed Wendell Holmes' stare to Fox's office, where they had left Hugh and Samantha in a tête-à-tête, and drew Callie's eyes upward. Were they up there for a quickie on that conference table? The woman's ass imprinted on the glass for the cleaning crew to wonder about? Callie shook the imagery. She did wonder about ulterior motives: *What were those rich folks up to? Putting her into a game? Risking her life?*

"No one is going to use me," she reiterated with a growl aimed more at herself than Holmes, and it was less about Fox's motives than in consideration of her current flagging relationship with Storm King.

132 S.P. Grogan

Scene 3: Choices Towards Violence
Setting: San Francisco Airport, First week in April 2011

Razzor Hassim knew that Fate had blessed him and shown him that he was to be an instrument of Allah's will. It could not be more obvious.

He had just arrived from Chicago on a flight delayed for forty-five minutes when the pilot refused to let two white-turbaned men remain on the flight. Their protestations of innocence, of their religious freedoms being violated, carried no weight with the pilot, Lord of the Commercial Skies. He was an extremely stupid man, thought Hassim, a poor excuse for a worldly, educated man if he did not even realize that these two men were not Muslims at all, nor Islamic clerics, but were of the Sikh religion from India. A pilot who can't tell religious Indians from Persians visibly demonstrated the shortcomings of their culture, where they praise what a wonderful place America is as the melting pot of the world. Hypocrites.

Hassim, wearing a Chicago Cubs baseball cap, sat in his window seat and continued to read a Western cowboy sheriff mystery by author Craig Johnson. No one bothered him. No one paid him attention except to ask what sort of beverage he would like to drink. "Diet Coke," he said, and "Thank you" when it was delivered.

As he walked the terminal, he looked at the overhead signage to find his way to Baggage Claim. As he proceeded, he saw two separate mobs of people coming his way.

The hungry media were pressing against Pastor Samuel Tate, and Hassim could hear the man ranting.

"I will be protesting outside the offices of *King's Retribution* TV show in Santa Monica. It is an abomination against the Lord Almighty even to give this ungodly evil called bin Laden any sort of guise of respectability or humanity. The man wants to kill us all and supplant our blessed Christ with the addled words of a mere camel trader, a desert brigand. It shall not happen! Tonight, after the gathering, I will burn this false book of theirs for all to see."

He raised his arms to the airport ceiling as he brought his voice to a higher octave.

"It is not for true believers, men or women, to make their choice in the affair if God and His apostle decree otherwise. He that disobeys God and His apostles stray far indeed."

A reporter took advantage of the pastor catching his breath and interjected: "And did you bring a Koran to burn? Can you show us what you intend to burn?"

Pastor Tate found himself coming down from his spiritual high to practicalities requiring some thought.

"I would not sully my luggage with such perdition. I will search out a bookstore and see if they have a copy. This town, based on sin and carnal pleasure with those of the same sex, certainly promotes such foul teachings." He paused. "And yes, I must buy a can of gasoline to anoint and sanctify this purging."

He took off down the corridor, his pulled suitcase inadvertently bumping into Hassim, an act the pastor ignored and did not look back. Several news reporters and their camera teams fell away, their story gathering complete, and confronted the second mob: an approaching gaggle of paparazzi falling in step with Colonel King of *King's Retribution*.

King stopped, allowing everyone to catch up with him and causing travelers to slow down to see who was attracting so much media attention and who the famous person was, who seemed to glow in the face of such recognition. Knowing his publicity people were coordinating his arrival, King had pressured Fox to offload his party at the main public ramps and concourse instead of at the more discreet corporate-based operations terminal.

Behind King, at a safe distance in order to stay out of the limelight, was Hugh Fox, likewise Samantha Carlisle, and Callie Cardoza, the latter feeling the moment required incognito dress in scarf and sunglasses. Minor players of the entourage followed, Clayton Briggs and J-Q. Behind them and off to the side was the interloper, Wendell Holmes, uninvited on the Skilleo corporate jet but not disinvited. They had all found him a man of few words, pleasant when responding but otherwise quiet. To Fox, the presence of Holmes offered the Hunt Team legitimacy. There was among them at least one person who seemed to be a professional, though he still had not provided written or confirmed credentials; his demeanor was his calling card. Fox appreciated the understated and the man's lack of boasting, which was refreshing in his world.

With the camera lights on and microphones thrust into his face, Colonel King pontificated for his fans.

"I'm pleased to represent *King's Retribution* and that we will be the ones to pursue Osama bin Laden and capture the ...." He left the last word to interpretation yet made certain his smile and features moved left to right to meet all the cameras recording.

"By our past actions, our past two-year winning series has demonstrated that evil cannot escape the best criminal fighters in the world. And to Mr. bin Laden, wherever you are, I will only say, 'You can hide, but not from *King's Retribution*. We are coming to get you.'"

With a regal air, he led the way, forcing the coterie of the press to catch up with him as he strutted and tossed out pithy platitudes and homilies of benign insignificance.

"Will you write a book of your experiences tracking down bin Laden?" asked a puffing, out-of-breath reporter.

"In *catching* bin Laden!" bellowed King, "I shall make history, not write it."

From a respectful, if not wished-for distance, Samantha turned to Hugh. "Our hero seems even larger than the celluloid time slot he inhabits."

Unable to keep up with the military fast-walk cadence, the reporters slowed and, looking around, finally understood that Storm King had formed a partnership with one of the richest 'couples' in the country. They descended upon Fox and Carlisle and the seductive Callie Cardoza, now recognized. King found himself alone, signing an autograph for a small child, who looked at him in worshipful awe.

Choices, choices. Hassim beamed at his good fortune. *They must be attacked, taught a lesson, and destroyed. But who first?*

His eyes fell on a man wearing sunglasses inside the terminal and standing off to the side, away from the press. He must have arrived with the retinue of the *King's Retribution* group, and he was standing with two or three others watching the interviews taking place, except —

Suddenly unnerved, Hassim realized the man was staring at him, and immediately, as he looked around, it became clear that people were passing him by, and only he stood in the middle of the terminal: set apart, conspicuous. Damn. He turned and hustled. What a foolish mistake.

And why had that man directed his attention at him? He was probably just a bodyguard to the stars, like the large man who stood near him. That was it. Just doing his job and identifying potential threats. Hassim looked over his shoulder, seeing no one suspicious following him, and he relaxed and slowed his pace.

Well, yes, he was a threat. The sooner, the better, since he had to meet The Professor in San Diego in two days. Again, he came back to the dilemma: *Choices. Who first?*

Scene 4: The Mission Moves Forward
Setting: California Desert, April 7, 2011

Pacheco lay on his belly, tasting the local dirt as small arms fire crackled all around him.

Mostly they were fake rounds, with a few coordinated bursts of live ammunition to signify urban battlefield conditions. Sweat grimed his hands. His fingers stretched and scraped two colored wires out of the dirt, and his upper body inch-crawled to the hidden IED. A wrong snip of the wire might set off a simulated explosion, or might not, or an 'insurgent' hiding on a floor above could use his cell phone to arc a signal to the explosive. Shit. Practice or not, he had the internal shakes, hoping his squad unit backed up behind him in the narrow street didn't notice his timing reflex lagging a few seconds.

From training at Camp Pendleton on the California coast, they had been ferried by a C-130 cargo jet over to the Twentynine Palms military base, located 175 miles northeast of San

Diego. This base was more than 900 square miles, but the two selected squads of SEAL Team Six were destined for its mini desert metropolis, unknown to the public, which was mocked up with 1,500 buildings and designed to resemble an Afghan city. Team Six was inserted within a training exercise involving Camp Pendleton's 2nd Battalion, 4th Marine Regiment, which was preparing for an August deployment to Afghanistan. Over three days, Marine trainers would run the SEAL Team members through an exhaustive alternative regimen to their planned objective, which was still to be revealed. It was basically an "If everything goes ape shit, what are the options?" backup scenario.

In the anticipated raid, assault, or whatever was planned for SEAL Team Six, imaginary helicopters were to have malfunctioned or been shot down after landing, and the SEAL Teams would need to extract themselves through highly-contested city blocks. That scenario gave Pacheco a hint about the job ahead: it was in a city, not the countryside. He could fight under any circumstances. His whole career had been shaped for him to react as a soldier facing a violent, merciless enemy, but he preferred to battle in hilly terrain, as opposed to inside a village where everyone hated you and they were possibly all armed to the teeth, including the women; the gooks just ready to take their potshots at you.

Pacheco snipped the wire without an explosion and yelled, "Clear." The squad rushed past him, leapfrogging down the street, rifles swinging side to side at unseen dangers.

"Brace! Controlled det!" shouted a "coyote," one of the marine trainers and exercise referees.

Suddenly, a rattling explosion shook the buildings, vibrating the ground. Even though it was mock practice, team personnel walked warily. Simulated war could be just as dangerous.

A fellow demolition squad member ran to Pacheco's side, out of breath, and looked at what Pacheco had faced when defusing the bomb. He gave an approving nod.

"If we get through these next few days," said the huffing SEAL, Pacheco's bomb tech partner, a grunt named Vitali, "I hear we're primed to launch out of here."

"Any word?"

"Naw, but I think they want us to go back and run sequences on that big white house at Pendleton. New intel, I think. Whatever it is, pretty sure we're going to be hitting it hard."

"About time," grumbled Pacheco, easing himself against the wall, wiping his face, and starting to follow the others down the street. In front, two SEAL members fired as an 'enemy combatant' appeared in an upstairs window. His right hand shook. That IED disconnect went too damn slow. *If this fakery had been live and hot*, he thought, *I could have been dead.* Not a good confidence builder, and when he caught a glance of a fellow SEAL across the street, for just a moment, he thought he saw Montoya's face and that dopey grin he gave just before he kicked the can, literally, and disappeared in that red mist.

136   S.P. Grogan

His reality was stilted, and he shook his head. Then, gathering up his skewed senses, he rejoined his fellow SEALS as they sought to escape the imaginary city.

Scene 5: Danger Downplayed, an Unsung Plot
Setting: Department of Energy, Washington, D.C., Afternoon, April 11

Ronald Givens didn't like being relegated to a lesser seat at the conference table; his presence required merely to be sure the CIA had been noticed and a representative requested. He already knew his pat answer to the invariable question.

"Our agency has no valid report of any foreign group, from any chatter we have so far analyzed, that would be a threat to your planned transportation operation."

Others had their own intelligence statement ready to put forth.

Around the table were representatives from the Department of Energy, U.S. Atomic Energy Commission, National Regulatory Agency, Homeland Security, Federal Bureau of Investigation and the CIA, with Assistant Deputy Director Givens attending.

The task force's point person, a take-no-prisoners woman scientist from the National Regulatory Agency passed around a photocopied clipping.

"As you can see, pursuant to the Department of Energy mandate and the approval of your agencies, we have started low-key practice runs. Our first hot run is scheduled for later in the year when all contingencies are in place."

Givens picked up the circulated paper and read a cut-and-copied Associated Press news article:

Las Vegas *Review-Journal*, February 2011

Low-level nuclear waste to be shipped through Nevada

San Clemente, Calif. — A 192-wheel trailer will make four trips hauling old generator parts considered to be low-level nuclear waste from California through Nevada and to Utah for disposal.

Officials from Southern California Edison's San Onofre Nuclear Generating Station said the levels of radiation from the old parts pose no risk to the public but that "they hope the public won't come out to see the lumbering trailer."

Its departure date was not released for security reasons.

The FBI committee representative piped up from the end of the table.

"Going from California to Utah by way of Nevada is not like going from the East Coast reactor to a Nevada depository site?"

"You have had a chance to look over the internal Environmental Assessment Report," said the scientist/chairperson, pointing to a large, stuffed, six-inch-thick binder. Each member had one before them, and each binder would be gathered up after the meeting as it was 'For your eyes only.' A glance, never expected to be read.

"The route is straight interstate, for the most part," she said, "until we cross into Nevada, then we can use less traveled highways. Each state's head of highway patrol will receive a four-hour advance notice of the trailer's passing over their state lines. Each governor has received a letter of notification, and there is so far no negative political response by any of them, though Nevada politicians, U.S. senator, governor, and Las Vegas's mayor are privately griping at the depository's location in their neighborhood."

"Of course, the manifest description, as I understand it," said Givens in his put-down voice, "still says low-level radiation canisters when in fact, the cargo might have to carry some high-level toxins."

Coming from the field of science, where fact is an indisputable truth and there is no equivocation, she never did like politicians, and this CIA administrator assigned to the working panel proved her case. She felt Givens added nothing to the discussion but instead just strutted his prominence. She was about to speak when the key technocrat from the Department of Energy, and her immediate boss, gave the final word.

"All this has been debated, Mr. Givens, and you and your agency voted for this direction. The time has come to test the operation. And you know, as well as I, that multiple redundant fail-safes have been built into this project. I assume that you have nothing new to report from your sources?"

Givens gave a clenched-teeth smile and responded with his pat answer — that from an international security survey, there were no concerns that put this truck carrier operation at risk.

The FBI rep gave his expected answer, that from their sources of information, there were no valid internal threats and that all existing home-grown terrorist groups had been identified and infiltrated. None had designs on a truck convoy supposedly bearing generator parts of low-level radiation.

The committee members had previously approved the operation, which came about after the tragic March 9th earthquake tsunami that wiped out Japan's Fukushima Daiichi nuclear plant and caused the world's worst nuclear accident since Chernobyl. In the U.S., there was political breast-pounding by alarmists in and out of Congress that forced federal agencies to revisit contingency plans for disaster scenarios, from earthquakes to terrorist breaches. It was a massive safety review since the U.S. had 104 nuclear power reactors in 31 states. Many plants were old systems, with the first built in 1960 and the last having opened in 1996. With rampant environmental and anti-nuclear opposition after Japan's disaster, the next plants would not come online until 2020, if ever.

The most pressing issue — less than an internal meltdown and equal to a natural disaster — was that of nuclear waste, the spent fuel rods, and other highly radioactive by-products that needed a resting place for permanent warehousing for a thousand years. In emergency conditions, when a major incident began, systems in nuclear plants would shut down automatically, and there were backup systems with manual turn-off buttons. However, nuclear waste protection was minimal at best, and no long-range, publicly approved, and vetted plans were in place. The rising public clamor for more stringent protection led the federal government to begin testing possibilities, and as it always has done in crisis mode, it turned within, conducting secretive discussions framed with tinges of paranoia.

This ex parte committee, formed for the betterment of everyone's security, had devised a test plan for a delivery system that would bring highly dangerous nuclear waste to a central depository in Nevada. The first action step before it went public was to announce a successful test run post-event.

"What's the timetable for the first shipment?" asked Givens, trying a conciliatory voice and not giving a damn about the importance of what was occurring, seeing merely another meeting to be checked off his busy schedule.

"September or October, maybe later," replied the Atomic Energy scientist, returning a weak smile.

"I suggest it not be on September 11th. Bad luck ramifications."

"We will take that under advisement, of course. A good thought." And the group turned to the mundane matters of implementation, with group concurrence that the first truckload would be generated from the New York nuclear power plant.

To reinforce that their committee selection had been correct, another news story was circulated at the table, this one dated three weeks earlier, on March 16.

What's the most at-risk U.S. nuclear power plant?

(*CBS News*)

The Nuclear Regulatory Commission recently provided MSNBC with an updated list of the American nuclear power plants at the highest risk of core damage (which can lead to meltdowns and radiation release) in the event of an earthquake. What parts of the country are most at risk?

You may be surprised.

Most might assume that California plants built around the turbulent San Andreas Fault line might be the most dangerous. However, the most at-risk plant isn't even on the West Coast — it's the Indian Point Energy Center on the Hudson River. With a 1 in 10,000 chance of a core breach, that's right on the edge of what the NRC calls 'immediate concern regarding adequate protection.'

The article continued, but, as reviewed, it drew a quick response from the FBI spokesperson, who was not a friend of the media.

"We don't need some investigative reporter starting to snoop around when we announce a 'low-level radiation shipment' to an undisclosed destination."

"No, we don't," said Homeland Security, "and I can assure you we are moving as quickly as possible to get this first run operation up and completed. We must be prepared to move more quickly if it is required sooner, yet we must not act precipitously and put the secrecy we have so far achieved at risk of media disclosure."

And they all agreed. Secrecy was essential.

They just didn't know that national security had already been breached.

Scene 6: The Scientist
Setting: New York State, April 11

As they had their Professor, they called this one the Scientist, and he did not like the moniker. After all, he was the Assistant Operations Manager of the Indian Points Energy Center, operated by a private corporation under National Regulatory supervision. And he thought it a joke that he must now report to an unknown person known as 'The Professor.' But the news was good for the cause. When he secured the date for the trucks leaving his facility, everything would be in place. He would know the date and have enough time to relay the information, which would set *Crimson Scimitar* on the road to its destiny.

The sub manager's name was Brahma Singh, and by a quirk in genetic features, he had passed as an Indian Sikh, though his ancestry came from the valley region of Kashmir. Before the 1948 U.N. boundary settlement in the First Indio-Pakistani War of 1947, the family name of his small shopkeeping family had been Khan. That was before his displaced family found itself trapped by the ceasefire in the town of Kotli.

New boundaries shifted their identifications and ability to survive the economics, and with the need to assimilate to the conquering culture as well, they didn't find it easy to suddenly be impoverished refugees back in Muslim Pakistan. Thus, he'd grown up giving lip service as a Sikh, yet a closet Islamic, and became politicized when attending graduate school in nuclear physics at the Indian Institute of Technology in Kanpur. A tourist trip to Pakistan when he was a youth further radicalized him under the mind control of the Lal Masjid mosque in Islamabad and its many calls of jihad against Westerners. His education and some good luck brought him into the nuclear energy industry, and he was determined to protect his hidden beliefs until he could find a way to strike out at India and its allies who supported military control of his parents' home of Pakistan — the underlying enemy, namely, the United States.

He hid well behind his public façade as a Sikh. He found it humorous how wearing the dastar (turban) confused Protestant and Catholic faiths. While the disguise left him faking another religion, he seemed to modify his own beliefs flawlessly to fit the circumstances at hand, that of being more the nationalistic spy and saboteur than the irrational religious extremist.

Brahma Singh knew that *Crimson Scimitar* was likely to succeed. And he relished the role he played, supplying, by happenstance, the main ingredient: high-yield radiation.

In 2011, Indian Point supplied nearly 30 percent of New York State's electricity, but Singh knew he could not sabotage it by himself. Since 9/11, all power plants have had safeguards aimed at preventing terrorism. When he heard about the transportation plan from the Atomic Energy Commission, he decided that his best opportunity would be to send a ticking time bomb somewhere else in order to maximize damage. With *Crimson Scimitar*, al-Qaeda could achieve more than a small nuclear plant 'accident' but, by its design, could wipe out a much larger swath of the American economy.

He was surprised when, in quiet suggestions through back channels, he offered the concept to a friend of an al-Qaeda friend in Pakistan. His idea was embraced, not for originality but for location opportunity, as it confirmed an idea, as he was told, that had been considered by bin Laden himself.

The main 'spreading epidemic' component of *Crimson Scimitar* would be poisonous nuclear waste. Indian Point stored its spent fuel rods submerged under 27 feet of water within 40-foot deep pools, each made of four- to six-foot wide concrete walls and with liners of half-inch thick stainless steel. The problem was that they had run out of pool storage for spent fuel rods. After five years in those pools, the spent rods should be moved to 'dry storage casks,' which again were supposed to be impervious to floods, tornadoes, and projectiles. A nonnuclear explosion in the main transformer on November 7, 2010, triggered the debate over moving the spent fuel rods to a safe sanctuary elsewhere. After the March 11, 2011, Tohoku earthquake, political fears hastened a quick decision to move them as soon as possible.

On the morning after the April 11 committee meeting in Washington, Singh's boss called him in and told him the spent fuel rods would move across the country in September or October.

Taking a long lunch break away from the plant, Singh went into the nearby Buchanan Public Library and joined an online discussion forum about his favorite team, the New York Jets.

"Can't wait to see the Jet Big Boys winning in September or October of the season," he typed.

"Yes," came a reply 15 minutes later. "Jet Big Boys victories sound good to me," typed the Professor from his home computer in Las Vegas, adding, "Any specific Jet Big Boys game and date you will be rooting on?"

"Let me think on that, will keep you informed about the Big Boys," typed Singh, who then went off for his own pleasure and started looking at game stats and fantasy match-ups. After all, the Jets were expected to have a pretty good fall season.

That evening, making a special trip to UNLV, the Professor accessed a computer in the faculty's Administration Office and joined a forum site about the Blackburn Rovers, an English professional football team in the Premier League. Transposing the Scientist's football vernacular into soccer speak, he posted: "Hope to get tickets to the Big Boy Rovers' games in September-October, but no specific date yet."

The cut-out at this point, the London banker Taher Abboud responded, "I will look to receive your specific game date and ask around about Big Boy Rover tickets. All is well here."

The next morning, April 14, messenger Ibrahim Ahmed sat at one of the old public computers in an Islamabad coffee shop and looked at the forum discussion in the Urdu language about the Pakistan national cricket team. One member asked if there would be a September-October charity test match, as he had heard. Ahmed printed out the communication.

As this trail of news circled the Earth, low-orbit satellite feeds streamed trillions of sentences written in that 24-hour period down to the multi-Cray computers owned and run by the CIA and housed in a concrete bunker under a Virginia hillside. Hundreds of program filters, designed to discover specific-sequence alarm words and instantaneously set these worrisome fragments aside in an alert folder of 'grey intelligence worthy of further review,' were unperturbed by multiple uses, in different languages, of the phrase 'Big Boy.' Had American alliteration and interpretive context scopes been in place — to define not what was there as is but what might be interpretive, such as aspects of coded black humor — filters might have noted that *Little Boy* was the first atomic bomb exploded over Hiroshima in August 1945. Its opposite, *Big Boy*, might suggest much worse. On his smoke-sputtering moped, messenger Ibrahim Ahmed chugged the latest report back to the whitewashed compound in Abbottabad.

The main recipient of the good news, Osama bin Laden, in turn, gave various command instructions to the returning Khalaf to share with the other attack team members regarding the approximate timetable of *Crimson Scimitar*. He was proud this was his plan, giving in his mind little credit to the part Khalaf had played in generating a source for 'attack' ideas. But when would this attack, these planned multiple attacks, be launched? Osama had a date in mind to correspond with the Big Boy travels, therefore in late September, perhaps early

October. An attack on the 9/11 anniversary meant nothing as a demarcation. The best strategic attack should be post-anniversary when security was again lax.

Unbeknown to all, as circumstances sometimes run a course of their own choosing, like a micro-burst rain cloud that produces a flash flood miles away through a dry stream bed and under sunny skies, Osama bin Laden would be facing an immediate choice of life or death, in just over two weeks. The flash flood was coming.

EPISODE TEN — The Hunt Quickens

Scene 1: Executive Prejudice
Setting: April 12-13, CIA Headquarters, Langley, Virginia

The night staffer at the al-Qaeda desk at Langley received the coded text message, recorded it, and placed it in the queue for morning review and action, if any. The one-paragraph substance, developed by members of the planning and legal oversight section of the military intelligence with CIA field input, those overseeing SEAL prep, had come to a joint conclusion regarding potential in-field operations.

By the next morning, April 12, the message had been sanitized with authorship removed. On April 13th, it reached the desk of Ronald Givens, who was preparing the day's briefing report for the Director of the CIA, who would be giving a worldview intelligence summary to the President at a mid-morning briefing.

The message read:

"It is our recommendation, upon recent analysis of legal circumstances within the U.S., that physical apprehension of Geronimo is not conducive to a favorable resolution for all concerned and that better circumstances would be the action taken of extreme prejudice."

Givens had no problem with that and wrote 'Concur' under the message and initialed the report. He had no reasoning in his sign-off but just felt it would do him no harm to support a finding for the termination of a terrorist.

With the critical information of the world reduced to bullet points for the Leader of the Free World, the Director of the CIA, reading from his notes, said simply, "Our legal and field analysts believe it best that, should any combat situation be initiated, Geronimo not survive."

The President of the United States had recently heard his own Attorney General state that he hoped the U.S. would capture and interrogate bin Laden, but that they also assumed, again for no known reason, to sustain the position. All collectively assumed the military strike force did not expect the al-Qaeda leader to be taken alive. Not knowing that a CIA analyst with a law degree had, in his analysis, used the term 'clusterfuck' to describe the legal situation if the U.S. government had a live and jailed bin Laden on their hands.

The President of the United States saw the world through politically tinted glasses (several days earlier, he had announced and launched his re-election campaign). To him, an end of a terrorist was a check-off on his to-do list, positive to his goals, not so damaging if nothing happened. This did not require a national debate on morality. With his silence, he accepted the advice of his top military leaders. And he was fine with that.

"Do we still believe we have him located?"

"Yes," came the reply from the head of the CIA. "Our assessment is that there is a 50 percent probability he is in that house. If he's not there, it's at least a command center and a target of the upper echelon."

The President turned to the three military men in the Oval Office.

"Are we ready to launch?" he asked.

"Training is being completed. Two more weeks at the most."

"Keep me informed at all times. When your people are in place, I will make a 'Go or not go' decision. We cannot make a mistake."

"Yes, Mr. President," said the military men.

The President turned again to the CIA Director.

"I am relying on your assessments being accurate."

"Yes, Mr. President."

Later, the Director of the CIA stopped at Givens' office.

"The Man accepted your position."

"I'll pass the word." Down the chain of command, this word circulated until the SEAL

Commander informed the selected Attack Squad leader: "If he's there, we've been ordered to kill the bastard."

Scene 2: The Eyes Have It
Setting: War Room, Santa Monica, April

From their day-long field trip to San Francisco and back, Hugh had scheduled another session immediately in the Santa Monica War Room to further complete the team building. However, on their arrival, those who greeted them were not on the agenda; a growing crowd, including a flash mob of media — with shouting from everyone. Placards of diverse opinions waving in the night, each protestor seeking to establish credentials to gain an interview. Media and agitators seeking their 15 seconds of forgettable sound bites.

The security team (only the best for stars and the mega-rich) formed the barriers to let the entourage dash into the building. No red carpet treatment tonight. Inside, the noise reduced to a muffle but not absent, followed them into their meeting.

As the group settled in for a wrap-up bull session of strategy and hypothesis in their search for an international outlaw, they suddenly realized that they were not alone. Sitting at the other end of the conference room table sat two people, unknown to them. Callie noted they were both in business formal; the African-American wore a coat and tie, distinguished. She guessed him to be in his mid-forties. Why deny it? She judged men, as an ex-cop might, seeing someone that one might stay cautious of, not threatening, just wary — serious facial expressions; full of brooding intent.

As Samantha saw the newcomers, to her, the woman next to Mr. Coat and Tie had taste. She wore not a drab business look but a sharp beige ensemble, a light long suit coat, matching blouse, skirt, and shoes, which seemed, to Samantha, to be from the Elie Saab Fall 2010 collection, all matching. Attractive in style, a subtle power statement made, more pleasing in countenance, as she gave a friendly light smile to all that looked her way. Callie and Samantha judged women as a woman might, from different perspectives. *Well-dressed, business-like beauty lightly diffused*, thought Samantha. Callie, the ex-cop, sensed a vibration between the two by body language, leaning in towards each other, something yet to define.

The answer to the group's silent queries was answered by Hugh's introduction:

"I would like to introduce you to an important part of *King's Retribution's* upcoming multi-part special; this, folks, is one half of the litigation team." He motioned at Booker Langston, who gave a head nod, and to Harriet Eberhardt. He scrolled through a quick bio of each and emphasized that they would be the Team in the planned trial of Osama bin Laden.

"That is if we catch the son of a bitch," offered Storm King with morose fatalism, maintaining his mantra on wild goose chasing, but not huffing as much about it these days, as his popularity just from the gossip rags had gained him new consideration by the public.

"As you all might keep your eye on the prize," replied Samantha, sitting next to Hugh, no one, it might be pointed out, sat at the head of the table. Not a round one, but an oval design had mysteriously replaced their previous formal rectangular conference table — no place to be the head of the table honcho. "*King's Retribution* is the collector of evil, and Mr. Langston and Ms. Eberhardt are part of the justice side. So, in your vernacular, Storm, you might say we are creating a new major launch to your show in a format that, for this Special Event, will be more '*Law and Order*' than merely chase and capture."

Samantha noticed slight indignation from Storm King, whose stature might face a backseat. However, she knew how to schmooze the insecure. "What comes from all this is that you are featured all the way through, as you will be not only the hero of the capture but certainly the prosecution's main witness, as a lead detective might be called upon. A very important role."

Fox rejoined, giving the background on the prosecutorial side, which impressed Callie as she knew Cotton Matther to be one of the famous, or at least a popular headline-hunting district attorney. Still, his major conviction rate of the high-profiled was worthy of significant national ink in the press and as an expert on the live cable trial circuit.

During this meeting, the background noise of the protestors could be heard, rising and falling with low roars or occasional muffled shouts.

In due time, Hugh turned over the floor, the meeting to give the outline, which no one of the King's Chase and Capture Team had seriously considered up to this moment. The preamble question: "Okay, the world's worst terrorist is caught; what comes next?"

Abbas of Special Effects had to interject, being the one in this group who knew reality from fakeness, "But what happens if we don't capture Mr. bin Laden, let alone find him? Don't we have production time constraints?"

Attorney Langston, Defense Team leader, rose and gave a baritone-rich overview of what they saw their roles to be and the structure of what a legal process might be. He held their attention, not realizing he was just practicing on them, salient points to convince their course would be proper, ethical, and legal, and the eyes of the world would be focused on their actions, with or without the real culprit in hand. During this interesting monologue, it became apparent that Ms. Eberhard visually gave subtle hints of admiration for her co-team player through her mannerisms.

"What is being produced, as I have been immersed into it, is drawing attention to the events of 9/11, the identification of the main perpetrator, your involvement in the location and capture, and then a world stage of, yes, as Mr. Fox envisions it, a show trial. Any inability to capture the fugitive, and we know you will do your best, will have little mass media impact, as the focus will quickly turn to the presumption he was caught and must now be viewed and tried in a televised trial. You all, I believe, call it a 'mockumentary' where fictional events are presented as a documentary. Here we have real events mixed with fiction." Langston could see they were seeking to digest what they were about to do, so he wisely put it into their multimedia lingo: "Mr. Fox's public relations people believe you may have one of the largest televised viewing audiences...ever."

Booker could see that all in the room started believing a 'hit' was pre-destined, and they would all be winners. Langston continued, "Mr. Fox and his Five Aces Studioz people have identified three possible actors to play bin Laden. I have seen the mug shots — oh, excuse me; the publicity department called them 'headshots.' I believe either one of the prospective candidates can act the role favorably. So you can have some satisfaction in the build-up for the

146   S.P. Grogan

hunt, that whatever the outcome will be followed by publicity that says *King's Retribution* made a valiant effort and a trial will be televised with the visage of bin Laden in the nefarious starring role."

"And if we are successful, what then?" Callie asked, somewhat defensive of their own goals.

Booker gave her a crooked smile, intent short of smoke puffing from the nostrils.

"Then Cotton Matther will use his enormous prestige to convict" — looking at Storm — the 'son of a bitch.'" Langston did not say the other alternative was the U.S. Government would come in with guns drawn and arrest everyone. And he would have to protect the man who hired him.

"But you're the Defense. You expect to prove he's not guilty?

Langston had them, like a great carnival barker might sell snake oil as a cure-all.

"Who knows what unfolds, what the final script says? That's why this is a premium television experience. You will have to buy the subscription or buy the ticket to be in the courtroom, and watch the fireworks, hopefully on the edge of your seat, even if the verdict is obvious."

On a question from the usually quiet Wendell Holmes about how such a jury might be impaneled, Booker turned to Harriet, who saw that as her cue. After all, Harriet saw herself as the worker bee in the prep work.

"As you might imagine, this is not an ordinary trial. The judge will be selected from a list of retired court judges. The jurors will be drawn from a pool, not just Americans but representatives of all countries impacted by their citizens' deaths on 9/11. But this is television and not the real world, and all will be compensated for their time.

"Our timing is related to your planned excursion to whatever location your team decides to pursue. As Booker said, 'success or failure' does not matter to us. We will have a stand-in ready to go two weeks after your return, and your publicity has built the anticipation."

Harriet paused. They did not need to know the details; the lengthy research. Her cadre of hired staff was knee-deep in researching all the past communication, speeches, and videos that Osama bin Laden had made since he first arrived on the world stage, if not his early youthful indiscretions. They, the Defense, were on the same page as the Prosecution, in building a picture of the character of the defendant they were to represent. Take the information and pass the highlights back to the Accused Team, who were also receiving information from Matther's Prosecution Team, so that the Accused (the actor) could get into character and best represent himself if called upon to mount the stand to give his side of the story (the Defense team opposed this consideration) to the fact it might be expected he'd give a carefully scripted 'I am innocent' interview prior to the commencement of the actual proceedings.

After Harriet sat down, she and Booker were peppered with questions, which they delicately side-stepped with, "We are in the process of working out the solutions but will be ready when the trial starts."

Two specific inquiries gained the most surprise. Again, the Discovery Team, sitting in their War Room, really had not gone beyond their charge of launching the search.

"Where is this trial going to take place?" From Bennie, who oversaw CAMERA ONE AND CAMERA TWO positioning,

Responded Hugh Fox matter-of-factly, "We are using an outside setting which will be configured to resemble an enlarged courtroom with special tech add-ons. All camera angles will provide overlap coverage, including the jurors. Think in terms of Super Bowl coverage."

"The words 'show trial' and 'large' have been bandied about. How big is your 'Skilleo courtroom?'" asked Storm King, with a half sneer, not kind in his phrasing.

"The Courtroom Stadium will hold 40,000. It is located in Colorado, and there will be ample parking, even outside facilities for overnight stays."

Whistles and surprised expressions floated around the room. No one caught the slight movement in Samantha Carlisle's face. It seemed impassive, but inside feelings masked her tinge of disappointment. The stadium-sized courtroom was news to her. Certainly, she took care of the responsibilities tasked to her and expected Hugh had his projects in development. But she thought he would have confided in her, be proud to tell her what was going on. Pillow talk meant openness. She did not know if she was saddened but definitely felt an uncertain unease, a surfacing doubt new to her with this physical and emotional relationship with Hugh.

Asked Callie, "How long do you think this trial will last?"

Hugh looked to Langston. Booker spoke from his seat.

"We are constrained by what the producers feel the audience's attention span will be. Current best estimation is a Monday-Friday event, First Day; with the jury we have agreed to, only two potential alternate jurors selected before cameras; Cotton and I will have done the pre- voir dire and made our selections beforehand. Second Day morning, Opening Statements, Prosecution begins. Cotton has a day and a half for his presentation. I and my co-counsel, Miss Eberhardt, get only a day based on the premise that there will be less new evidence to offer and fewer 'character' witnesses to come forth. On the Third day, concluding witnesses, and like a 'game show'" — Langston looked at Hugh — "each legal team will be giving the other side one surprise witness, with only 24 hours hours to learn their background, and each team to then present our own surprise witness, then cross-examine the others'. Don't like it, but it will wake up the audience and put our extemporaneous skills to the test. Fourth day, closing statements, and final day, juror verdict, and immediate judge sentencing."

148   S.P. Grogan

When any further questions were asked for, Callie kicked Storm in the leg under the table, knowing his paper cup sipping had not been coffee and any comment would be slurred and unwise. So, she led off:

"So, we are really going to do it. Locate the bastard and bring him back."

Hugh's smile, meant to be infectious, bore some hard love at the same time.

"This is not for a pilot show. I am quite serious about taking advantage of all your talent." He glanced at his partner-girlfriend-of-sorts. Samantha took her cue.

"Of course, as stated, there is the contingency that we do not find our target. As Attorney Langston has mentioned, we then film what you are all great at — a docu-drama, a reality television version with this substitute actor. Whatever the outcome, the public will know you gave it your best shot, and Mr. Langston and Miss Eberhardt will provide the courtroom ratings, which…" And she looked to the stars, "both Storm and Callie will participate in." King gave a lurching bow of recognition. Callie sat stoically, waiting for the curtain to collapse from some glitch.

Storm moved his legs away from Callie to avoid her reach, and because he could not stay silent, his ego demanded its own stage. "I mean, all of this is great. It's going to boost my show, but really, what's to defend? Just show film of the Towers collapsing?" Hugh could see Booker wince, as did Harriet. By now, she knew most of Booker's history, his fiancée's tragic death, his despondency-dependency once lost in the bottle, his keen senses now recovered. She did not want to see a morality play debated here, so Harriet spoke, soft, kindly, though everyone could sense there was ice in the underlying voice.

"I assume, Mr. King, you have nothing against America's values of honesty and fairness put on display?"

King took several seconds looking for a comeback, slunk back in his chair, and was just going to lash out with some jingoistic mantra when the crowd's noise pitched to a frenzied sound; shouts tore through the room. Hugh rushed to the window then hurried from the room, followed by Holmes. Clayton stayed protective of the remaining small crowd, including King, who never left his seat, in some kind of obliviousness to the commotion, not his cue to run towards the unruliness out on the street. He was only an actor, after all.

The rest went to the windows, staring down at the melee. Booker Langston now rushed out, his brief hesitancy at this roar of danger delayed by his fateful memory ten years previous where he was impotent to act.

At the steps of the building, Hugh saw a fight in the street, about five or six demonstrators brawling, throwing punches. Cameras were clicking, top-of-the-hour news media documenting an unruly crowd out of control. Fox's paid-by-the-hour security was at the front doors, of no real use, no desire to interfere, their responsibility only to protect the sanctity of the building's premises.

Fox, Langston, and Holmes were standing there, likewise smart enough not to jump in seeking peace, waiting for the approaching sirens to re-establish some semblance of order.

They then heard the curdled scream, high-pitched, one of anguished pain, flesh-tearing pain.

Glancing around, the three of them saw two figures on the sidewalk across the street.

Holmes understood the situation.

"It's a set-up, the fight a distraction." He took off running, ignoring the fight's violence, shoving his way unceremoniously, uncaring through the crowd, barreling over media vultures, noticing the 'staged' fight suddenly had mysteriously abated, with several men running off down the street. A staged convenience, agreed Fox, running up to the man on the ground, screaming, bloodied hands to his face.

Holmes ran past the victim, knowing others were following. He pursued a dark figure down an alleyway. He caught a glance, saw a fleeing face in a side-lighted window, a thought of recognition, but then smart-man-not-hero realization overcame his bravado — he was unarmed. His chase slowed to a halt. Besides, he was panting. Not 007 young anymore. He turned back to see if the targeted victim lived.

Fox was bending over the injured man.

"Good God, call an ambulance!" he said. "His eyes have been gouged out!"

"It's that church nut," said Holmes, returning, seeing strewn posters around them and regarding the bloodied, eyeless face. "The preacher at the airport. The one wanting to burn the Koran. Damn. Offend another man's scripture, and wrath will descend against the blasphemous."

Callie arrived, herself breathing hard, her pistol out of her evening purse, and started after the attacker when Hugh caught her arm.

"No. You have no backup, and there's a lunatic with a knife, maybe his own gun, out there in the dark. These are urban predators, much more dangerous."

She looked into his eyes, saw concern, and relented. They heard sirens drawing closer and saw a curious crowd surging toward them, the media of ambulance chasers leading. The Fifth Estate smelling blood, as the ground around Pastor Tate proved so. Fox's security guards finally did decide the guy writing the paychecks might be under threat. They threw up a quick cordon around their 'employers' dealing with the man moaning on the ground, blinded Pastor Samuel Tate, whose head was rolling side to side in excruciating agony, occasionally babbling weak entreaties for his god to perform a miracle for an enfeebled sinner.

150   S.P. Grogan

Holmes saw Samantha on her knees with blood soaking her dress, holding the man's grasping hands away from his face and the empty dark eye sockets.

"From what I can see," said Holmes, returning from his own survey of the attack ground and not realizing his poor choice of words, "there was no Koran burning tonight because some fiend objected to free speech, if not hate speech."

Booker had not been with them but now entered the scene. "No Koran, but I did find one of these…." He held up a bloody eyeball. "We need a cup of ice. I doubt it can be saved; maybe there's a prayer of a chance."

Scene 3: The Tunnel
Setting: South of San Diego, California April 15, 2011

Rows of concrete warehouses spread across the horizon, drab and dusty looking, like a maze of stubby monoliths where some god had press-punched out repetitive ugliness. Professor James Rogers turned off Highway 905 where it met Siempre Viva Road, and drove down a wide alleyway between a pod of buildings, reading signs until he found the D-2000 complex and the office/warehouse #2025, labeled 'Johnson Fresh Produce.' Informed by his cell that Hassim had just arrived at Lindbergh Field from San Francisco, he parked and awaited his 2 p.m. appointment.

He left the car running for its weak, blowing air though it offered little relief from the heat. Leaning his head back, he closed his eyes, his body heavy with exhaustion. He had arrived at this warehouse complex south of San Diego after a long, early morning drive from Las Vegas.

Five hours in travel, perhaps a one-hour meeting, and then five hours back with no one the wiser.

He even paid for his gas with cash.

He cleared his mind and willed himself to nod off for a few minutes. It surprised him that over the last month, he had become both eager and nervous in anticipation of *Crimson Scimitar*, a risk that, if successful, would mean satisfactory revenge. Thinking about this as he drifted into a semi-conscious slumber dredged up the history that had brought him to this day and its unfolding plot.

James Rodgers had not been born with that name. His mother was a Lebanese nurse, and his father a French Algerian doctor. His parents had a revolutionary fervor in common for aiding the underdog and, in time, found themselves working side by side at the Palestinian Ain al-Hilweh refugee camp in Lebanon. There they spent grueling hours tending to the undernourished and ill, performing operations with scant medical supplies. For the first nine years of his life, their son played with Palestinian children in the rubble of destroyed villages.

Crimson Scimitar

They were watched over by Yasser Arafat's Fatah militia, who patrolled the children's playgrounds and, after dark, drove their rocket pickup trucks toward the battle lines of the First

Lebanon War, often taking along 13- or 14-year-old boys who stood in the truck beds carrying the smaller rocket-propelled grenades. Their son watched the firework trails of the large rockets lifting off, red ribbons streaking skyward, in clapping glee. Sometimes he heard a distant boom and was told another kibbutz must have been destroyed. All his friends would cheer, but he did not understand. The drifting smell of gunpowder in the air intoxicated the impressionable youngster.

One day the rockets came back, deadly projectiles hurling in his direction, fired from contrail jets high above. And as he watched, the jeeps disintegrated, and the men and boys who had smiled at him vaporized before his eyes. As if it were comforting, he was later told that the attack was expected, a required response for some atrocity one side did to the other, the original offense long forgotten. In press releases, military strikes were always called 'precision,' except for this one time when an errant rocket fizzled in trajectory and found the refugee camp's hospital. By the time the boy arrived, the dead were being carried out, unrecognizable, his parents among them.

He was not an orphan for long. A representative of UNESCO who had known his parents in the camp rescued the shell-shocked boy found wandering aimlessly. The boy carried his Superman backpack filled with few clothes and a tattered copy of the Koran, the only surviving artifact of his mother's memory. The rescuing aid worker's name was Rogèt, with French pronunciation, and the boy was brought back into the UNESCO camp, where the common language among the humanitarian workers was English. He caught onto the language quickly.

A year later, an aid volunteer teacher from Alberta, Canada, decided a good deed for her own peace of mind was to rescue at least one refugee and that it should be the attractive little boy who spoke her language. He seemed bright, and they called him Jacques Rogèt, which she later Anglicized to 'James Rogers,' James being the first name of her deceased second husband.

James Rogers acclimated to his new mother figure, had a growth spurt, and accepted — as curious youth might do to repress violent nightmares — the good life of a suburb in Quebec,

Canada, where both his English and nearly forgotten French could be nurtured.

If he had not run into an Arabic-speaking boy at his private boarding school one day, he might have grown into someone staid and boring. He began to question his life, dragging from his repressed memories his early life circumstances, seeing before him the violence of his parents' death, and feeling he could smell the burned flesh that seared his nostrils. As he questioned his background, challenging his birthright and purpose, he picked up his dead mother's Koran and began to read with intensity. Eventually, he sought out a local mosque.

152 S.P. Grogan

Above all, in reliving his parents' death, he recalled who had flown the jets (the Israelis) and, more importantly to him, who had made the bombs and the jets — the American capitalists.

This knowledge did not take him down the road of understanding and forgiveness but instead down a darker route, where anger festered, became putrid, and turned into a hunger to seek revenge. To understand his enemy, he had to learn about them, and his schooling led him to political science courses and eventually, because the job market was stronger, found him settling in the United States.

Payback led to his nom de guerre, the Professor, and his dream of revenge had a nightmare aspect, that of waiting, never knowing when the call might come. In the many years which passed, he had enjoyed the comfortable suburban life and accepted it as a blessing in raising a family. His ancient nightmares became slowly replaced by fear of his own children as orphans, as he once was. James Rogers lived with inner conflict.

With a start, he awoke as knuckles tapped on the car window next to his head. The visage of Razzor Hassim stared down at him, causing him to shiver as if he saw Death, cold and unsympathetic to his own desires in life.

"Professor, follow me." Rogers did so, following Hassim into the Johnson Fresh Produce building. An older lady, looking like a withered piece of fruit, sat at the front desk reading a Mexican movie magazine. She clicked them in through a secured door. Near the loading dock, two workers loaded boxes of lettuce onto a flatbed truck. Hassim led him to the back of the warehouse, behind crates of food products and plastic sheets, into a cold room where fresh fruit was stacked on pallets. Hassim entered a small office and shut the door behind them. On a side wall, storage boxes were piled on a metal rack. He pulled the rack aside, revealing a closed, hidden door.

What time do you have?" asked Hassim, the Enforcer or Mr. FixIt, as Rogers called him, obviously only behind his back, replied,

"2:15."

"As do I." He pulled out a cell phone and placed a call. "Buenos Días, Manuel. Nostros estamos aqui."

For five minutes, they said nothing. Apparently, they were waiting.

The hidden door finally opened, and a young man peered out warily, his automatic pistol pointed at their chests.

"Señor Smith," the man said, lowering the pistol slightly.

"Luis, ¿Qué pasa?" the young man eyed the Professor, and the pistol eased up. "¿Quien es?"

Crimson Scimitar 153

"Mi amigo, Señor Jones. El pago port tu trabajo. *My friend. He paid for your work.*

He turned to the Professor. "And this is Luis Delgado, one of the best. A fierce man. Peligroso hombre, si? People down here fear his reputation."

The pistol went to the man's side, and he smiled. The door swung back open.

The Enforcer and the Professor descended a long ramp and found themselves in a tunnel.

Rogers viewed all, amazed. Electric light bulbs hung from the ceiling going down the corridor, a far distance. Dual rails lay flush with the floor, a mini-railroad track. The air felt sticky but tolerable, and Rogers felt a slight breeze and heard the hum of an electric motor signaling a cooling system in use.

They walked for five minutes, standing up; it was not a small tunnel. When they passed a red painted slash on the tunnel's ceiling, Hassim turned to him and said, "Mexico." They arrived at another ramp and went up. They were in a storage warehouse, mostly storage shelves piled in disarray with boxes of parts that seemed to be used appliances. The young Mexican brought them to an open area surrounded by crates, a meeting area with several chairs and a dilapidated couch with uneven cushions. A man, who Rogers guessed was in his late thirties, sat there, dressed in slacks and a floral shirt.

"Señor Smith, welcome," he said in rough English, and he bade them join him. The younger man went to a cooler and came back offering cans of Jarritos sodas, and Rogers felt he should not decline. Hassim, or 'Señor Smith,' made introductions. No hands were shaken, but there were nods of satisfaction. Rogers was introduced with his own alias, 'Jones,' and the man in charge had introduced himself as 'Alvarez.'

"Señor Jones, what do you think of what we built for you?"

"I am impressed, and thank you for your work." Hassim had prompted the Professor earlier that the less said, the better.

"Your payments to us have been timely and appreciated. As you know, crossing the border is extremely tough; it is well-guarded in this section. So, we built this like we would an American highway, but with our own builders who never knew where they were. Each night we picked them up and brought them here blindfolded. But my question is: When can we expect our last payment, and does your offer hold true as to our own use?"

"Soon, within three months or so," replied Rogers, "you can expect one major delivery to your warehouse, which is to be sent over to us. If our property arrives intact, with no problems, you will be paid. Then, wait for at least one month. Either we return and leave by this route forever, or we do not return, and then the tunnel, and any of our other shipments, will be turned over for your full use, and our obligations will end."

154 S.P. Grogan

Hassim spoke slowly, so his words and meaning would be understood. "Until that time, this tunnel will not be used at all."

"It is a valuable commodity," said Alvarez, "and should be used as soon as possible. Any time it could be discovered. Border Patrol uses ground penetrating equipment."

"Did you not show us your plans to string perpendicular piping near the surface to mislead their ground sensor sweepers?" Hassim gave him a serious stare-down.

"Sí," Alvarez shrugged. "I hope your shipment comes soon."

Hassim ignored him.

"And how are you doing on the people we asked for?"

"Sí, sí. Per your instructions, we have, how do you say it, 'subcontracted' out for five drug mules from the Sinaloa Cartel based in Tijuana. These are men without remorse, who like your money and will do as you say. We told them it will be some sort of attack on a DEA meeting in the U.S. They are eager to strike back for the losses they have been taking."

"And they will bring the firepower we asked for?"

"Yes. It's a strange request, but they would rather act tomorrow than months from now."

"Well, you have paid them well to be on standby. They will see action; that we can promise," Hassim assured him.

"I have decided to place Luis in charge of them. They will obey him, and he will obey me."

"And they will follow our direction and understand we are going to attack the Norte Americano Federales?"

"Your money has been good, and they can expect a large bonus when they are successful. Is that correct?"

"Our goal is success. They will be rich, and you will have your tunnel. And we will be gone, and you will never say we were here." Hassim's voice was clear and slow. His intent was clear.

Alvarez looked at both men and accepted that their agenda, these secret plans, would not be made known to him. He had accepted Hassim's earlier visits and funding for the tunnel, knowing the man was a foreigner. Just as they were when they were in the United States. Outsiders. And after several actions of vetting this strange man with one ear, Alvarez was confident, as well as he could be, that this was no gringo sting. What purpose would it serve?

No, he would not kill them and take their tunnel, though his men had pushed for such action.

There was money still to be made, and frankly, though he was a brave man, he feared the man who called himself the false name of Señor Jones. Alvarez feared that if something happened to Jones, others would follow to take revenge on him, his men, and even their families. He believed the others could be as ruthless and merciless as the cartels to which he acted as a middleman. And yes, if they were going to help kill DEA agents, that was not such a bad thing. And if it all failed, Alvarez knew he could recruit other soldiers for his personal needs, including a new lieutenant.

Like Luis Delgado, they were all expendable. There were more mercenaries out there, all greedy, all wishing to advance, with guns and blood, a proven résumé for the cartels.

The three of them inspected the delivered crate. Hassim exchanged a glance with Alvarez and checked to ensure the seals were in place. He left the box unopened as a test of Alvarez's curiosity. Hassim had his own exit plan, including mopping up, killing the tunnel builder, even the Professor, and all tracks of their visit would be erased, but he would have to wait until the dust settled on the fallout from the reaction of the *Crimson Scimitar* attacks. The tunnel was the planned retreat, and it must remain in his control until the end; then, he had these other plans that Alvarez would not like.

"Yes, this can be sent over to the other side and stored in the warehouse whenever you have the time. Expect a few more crates."

"Bueno. It will let us practice with the carrier system. A lot of merchandise can move quickly down this tunnel." Alvarez paused and smiled with an open-mouthed grin that revealed a grave robber's prayer: multiple gold teeth. "We will control a strategic money maker when we have control of the tunnel."

"In time. I will notify you when the major shipment will arrive," Hassim told him.

"Esta bien, nosotros estarenios preparados." *Good, we shall be ready.*

Professor James Rogers said nothing as they walked down the tunnel back to the U.S. side and saw that the lights in the underground corridor were switched off. Hassim secured the door and put the metal storage rack back in place.

At their respective cars, the Enforcer spoke.

"That tour was for your benefit. They needed confirmation from a higher authority. It gives them further comfort if they trust anyone initially. And if something were to happen to me, you must be here to carry out the first steps of *Crimson Scimitar*."

"I thought my goal was to provide the three cells, which I have done. Sadly, with this one, I have had to buy their services."

"If I am killed, because that is the only reason I would not make our timetable, you would have to be at this location to receive the 'shipments' across the border. Beyond that, all attacks will flow to their own simultaneous execution. Nevada determines the timing of both California and Florida."

156   S.P. Grogan

Hassim changed the subject, removing his ball cap and wiping his forehead.

"Have you heard from the Scientist?" Having a direct conversation between them was better than risking computer or phone communications.

"Yes, they have put their plans in motion for two months from now. The exact date is being held confidential until the truck convoy can be put in place. But we will know for certain since he is one of the project coordinators," replied James.

"Good. I am glad this attack is ready to be launched. It will be a spectacular success that every one of our followers can rejoice in."

"We can only hope so." Rogers hadn't meant to dampen his enthusiasm and knew the Enforcer would pick up on it.

"You have doubts?"

"Not really. There just seem to be more headlines drawing attention to, as they call them, 'terrorist sightings.' Did you notice a nut Christian religious leader tried to burn a Koran, and someone blinded him? And it was at some event where a television show was promoting itself to capture bin Laden. We do not need the public or the authorities to be on guard."

"Do you wish me to destroy those television stars?"

"No, of course not. I just wish we had the complacency that existed on 9/10/2001." It struck Rogers that Hassim had been traveling through Los Angeles, which would have put him near the location of the attack on Pastor Tate.

"You were just in L.A., weren't you?" Suddenly he felt he knew the truth, pissed he blurted out a veiled accusation. The phlegm of fear rose in Roger's throat, and he swallowed away sour bile.

"Not really. Flight stop-over to San Diego. But you are right that we must be vigilant. Hopefully, no more accidents like what happened to that unfortunate biker in Florida. Make sure your people are in line and faithful to our cause. Martyrs will be required for the glory of *Crimson Scimitar.*"

With that, Hassim departed for Allah knew where, leaving the Professor feeling uncomfortable. He realized that until this attack was successful, he would live on the edge, agitated. He had started a new habit of looking over his shoulder and expecting to see the killer with one ear.

Scene 4: Clues Point the Way
Setting: Santa Monica, California, April 16

Exuberance about the last month of investigating for real or imagined terrorists had waned, and the mood throughout the War Room, especially in the conference room, was a 'blah'

Crimson Scimitar

atmosphere. The attack on the pastor in front of their offices had left them all in a stupor. What had happened? What was their relationship to all this? They were certainly no longer on the periphery of national events; now, *King's Retribution* was an indirect component of the violence, with several critics calling them agitators and, worse, glory hounds.

The headlines, which mostly King noticed via his clipping service, portrayed the television show *King's Retribution* as stoking the fires of religious intolerance, and causing the fringe elements to ride along on the show's coattails for publicity's sake. Gone, misplaced from the public's clamoring view, was the honorable quest to capture an 'alleged' international mass murderer.

In the past several days, online and media pundits from both the left and right of the political spectrum decried their insensitivity. It didn't make them feel better to hear on the news that Pastor Samuel Tate was recovering, although blind in one eye. The found eye, contrary to Booker Langston's observation, had been 'miraculously' reattached thanks to the advancements of modern ocular surgery and a quick cup of ice in a customer's gin and tonic from the nearby Hillstone's restaurant. The alcohol was the preservative.

Fanning the flames of notoriety from his hospital bed, Pastor Tate, now believing himself a cyclops martyr, filled the airwaves with venom-laced press releases fomenting cries for a holy crusade against Islamic devils. No perpetrator had been arrested regarding the pastor's attack, and rumors abounded on what it all meant. The LA press soon moved the story to page three and, with no hard facts leading to the apprehension of the culprit(s) (and defining Pastor Tate as an out-of-town kook), downplayed the incident, and any follow-up was attributed to a 'violent mugging by persons unknown.' In this multicultural city, sustaining a narrative that might upset the Muslim community by pushing an Islamophobic conspiracy proved no benefit. Pastor Tate only grew more rabid when ignored.

From both sides of the eye-gouging perspective and the further fringes, a new flurry of hate mail dripped into the Five Aces Studioz offices, which set the tone when they all reassembled in Santa Monica War Room to make an effort to refocus on the task at hand.

The quiet team consisted of Hugh, Samantha, Storm, and *King's Retribution* staff members Clayton Briggs and Bennie. J-Q kept meeting notes. Callie Cardoza excused herself to answer an international telephone call.

CAM ONE and CAM TWO roamed unnoticed.

With Fox's concurrence, attorneys Booker Langston and Harriet Eberhardt were absent from today's session, flying out and moving their war room to Colorado Springs, near their future courtroom. DA Cotton Matther V, now on paid sabbatical, would join them later in the week to review a proposed 'script.'

In today's meeting, Wendell Holmes's position might have seemed subordinate, but his aloofness from the gathering gave off more mysterious vibes. No one dared to ask him: Who did he report to? What did he bring to the table as his expertise? Samantha Carlisle, who made it her career to study the human body, to see how to best dress a body's nuances to accent and draw out the best of its character, found herself at a loss as to how to define the man. Unlike Storm King and his flagging posture, Holmes looked rugged, giving off a more sublime countenance, less military aggression than King. She almost wanted to say it was a false beatitude, one that could easily mask sub-surface violence. Like a Zen cobra.

Yes, his smile reminded her of a coiling viper, a bush cobra, or maybe as a human, the manipulative corporate raider. She had met both, in different circumstances, one in the African bush, the other dating, and had dispatched such serpents in her own lethal fashion, one by machete, the other, the human, by verbal emasculation.

Holmes gave Samantha a nod, his mouth curling slightly upward. To others, the gesture might have been interpreted as a smile, perhaps meant to be disarming. Samantha, though, saw the man's enigma — alluring but not revealing. She shifted, uncomfortable, and turned her gaze back to the table, back to the security of Hugh Fox's defined personality of exuberance with occasional raw sex the dividend. Today, she needed to give him her support, and for that, she was content.

The Team waded through several staff presentations of gathered information and condensed world news reports by various anti-terrorist consultants. Analysts/employees came and left bearing investigative reports. By the end of the two-hour session, a large pile of folders lay in front of Fox.

"And the consensus of what we have uncovered so far?" Fox asked the conference gatherers.

"We don't know where bin Laden is any more than our own government does," King said, his voice gravely naysaying.

"I think we can be more specific on where we don't think he is," said Samantha, who had been paying attention and taking notes. "I would accept the premise, based on his past actions, that bin Laden is still directing from behind the scenes, not hiding, and more active than just giving out occasional sound bites to Al Jazeera television. So he needs his followers close at hand and an atmosphere where his followers can support or help hide him."

"Considering 22 percent of the world's population practices the Islamic faith, and they are on every continent, we might be able to reduce the search grid by 10 percent." King sipped from his constant friend, the plastic cup, and by now, everyone accepted that his drink of the day held spiked octane proof.

Trying to be helpful, the show's getaway driver, Bennie, said, "I say he's not in South America, Australia, or New Zealand."

Crimson Scimitar

"I don't think he's hiding in North America," said Clayton, who wanted to demonstrate that the lifetime use of bodybuilding steroids had not impacted his mind. "He has this persona to project. He's not going to shave his beard, dress outdoorsy and escape to Canada."

"Like you said, Ms. Carlisle, he's still the main honcho. He needs a stage to perform on."

King glanced up, bristling, believing one of his own had just put in a dig against him, but before he could snipe about it, the door opened, and they all turned and saw Callie.

"I may have something," she said.

"We only accept good news today," said Fox, trying to move the group's downcast attitude into a more positive temper. It was the way he led — moving beyond negatives.

"If you recall, I had some feelers out through the international police database about bin Laden's extended family."

"And?" cued King skeptically.

"Well," she said, and a smile spread across her face. She held it for a few seconds to draw them into the anticipation.

"A week ago, Ali Tameni Fatah, who is an uncle of bin Laden's last wife, Amal Ahmed Abdul Fatah, was granted a visa from Yemen to Egypt and then to Pakistan, returning by way of Saudi Arabia and Mecca. He could be on his haji, his pilgrimage to the holy city. But what is more interesting is that he is taking along a woman, not his wife. And more importantly, her age and the birthdate on her passport match the age range of this Amal Fatah's older sister."

"But she is not the sister of this bin Laden wife?" Samantha asked, seeking the significance.

"I'm guessing it's a fake name on the passport. Could be a mistress, yes, but my hunch it would be too flagrant for him to display a girlfriend that openly in their sort of Yemeni culture."

"So, if that's true, what do you think these bin Laden relatives are up to?" Samantha continued her questioning.

Callie responded, not gleefully but sure of her hunches. "Could be anything, but why is Pakistan on this itinerary? It does fit if he's making a swing of holy cities. Islamabad, the capital of Pakistan, is home to the Faisal Mosque, the largest mosque in South Asia and the sixth-largest mosque in the world. If he is flying under that cover story, maybe we can take the jump and say that bin Laden's fifth wife might be eagerly awaiting a visit from her Yemeni sister."

"Okay," said Fox, nodding and noting Callie's seriousness. He saw her building momentum toward a resurgence of interest in the hunt and the spark they had all been missing these last several days. "Okay, since we have no other lead on hard substance to date, let's say you're on the right track. If bin Laden's favorite wife of the moment is having family visitors, it should follow that bin Laden must be nearby."

160 S.P. Grogan

"Okay, they land in Pakistan, and then they all drive to a cave in Afghanistan for a family reunion?" King was not ready to be convinced.

Fox answered. "Possibly, but I can't see any bin Laden family member, especially the women, wanting to make a social visit in an active war zone. Nor do I see bin Laden cowering in a cave. We are not giving the man credit for the deviousness and survival skills that have gotten him this far."

"I've got more about where the uncle and his female companion are going." Callie wanted to be the center of the discussion; this was her scoop, something that put her above the fray. She wasn't seeking stardom but recognition of her worth. As she began to speak, it suddenly hit her: who was she trying to impress? Not King. That ship already sailed. He would never recognize her talent. Nor did she need to impress Samantha Carlisle; they were in totally different worlds of achievement. As she began to speak, she focused on Hugh Fox before moving her eyes around the table so as not to betray any listener preference.

"When I heard that this uncle might end up in Pakistan, I set up a team here to begin monitoring hotels where they might stay, both in Karachi and Islamabad. If they stayed with friends, then we would have no chance, but I was hoping that perhaps the uncle was not traveling on his own nickel but as a guest of the bin Laden family's generosity. If so, the uncle might want to travel in Arabic first class and enjoy a taste of the good life."

"And?" said King, a little more interested. His brain cells were grinding out the potential of a new script plot.

"An hour ago, we had a hit. That was the call I took. A reservation was booked under the uncle's name for two rooms in a small boutique hotel in a suburb just outside of Islamabad."

"I assume your source is accurate?" said the previously silent Wendell Holmes. They all looked at him. The Sphinx talked. "Just asking; we've been down a lot of false trails."

Callie exuded confidence, and her smile was just shy of a smirk. "My information is from international police computers and their filter programs. I flagged several family names in the system, which lists outstanding warrants for genitalia maiming of young girls. I assume my search matrix might be as solid as the ones you rely on." She raised her eyebrows. Holmes did not respond but waved his hand as if to say, 'Go on, it's your show.'

"Not in Islamabad, but outside?" asked Samantha.

"A small town called Abbottabad."

"I've heard of it," King said. "That's where they have their version of our West Point. No, I can't see it. A wanted fugitive hiding among the police?" He drained the last of his drink, tossing his cup at the wastebasket, a missed rim shot.

"Wait a second! Wait a second!" Fox jumped up, excited and tearing at the stack of folders before him. "I saw something here. Hold on." They all watched as the centibillionaire, in a half-crazed mode, tore through binders and piles of research, like a kid searching Christmas morning presents for his Daisy air rifle or, more likely, an iPad upgrade.

"Amazing! Here it is." He scanned it to make sure and then read aloud: "On January 25th (of this year), Pakistani intelligence, the ISI, raided a house in Abbottabad and captured the Indonesian and al-Qaeda-linked militant Umar Patek, on the run from a US $1 million bounty for allegedly helping mastermind the 2002 suicide bombings of nightclubs in Bali that killed 202 people."

"What's an Indonesian terrorist doing in Pakistan?" asked the bodyguard Clayton Briggs.

As if to finish the thought, Bennie said, "If not to confer on tactics with his boss."

"But here's where it gets better," Fox said, rifling through more papers. "The Associated Press says that earlier in January, two French al-Qaeda members, one of them of Pakistani origin, were caught in Lahore *after leaving* Abbottabad. It was suggested they were trying to reach Taliban leaders in North Waziristan. But then, on January 23rd, Pakistani ISI arrested their contact, a clerk in the local post office. Guess where? He worked in Abbottabad. Too many damn coincidences."

"From what I've read," said Callie, concluding, "the Taliban has been strong in the region just north of Abbottabad. The town of Buner, 30 miles from Abbottabad, fell to the Taliban in 2009, and they had an active training camp close to the town of Mansehra. That's only a few miles from Abbottabad."

"Why didn't we hear about this capture of the Indonesian terrorist before?" King asked, scolding no one in particular. "Or of these other captures? Certainly, that suggests a concentration of shit-heads that would be glad to hide bin Laden. Or to visit him and kiss his holy robes."

"Like relatives paying a social call," said Callie, emphasizing what had initially brought all current threads together, like a woven prayer rug.

"It is interesting to note," Fox replied, assuming the role of mood changer, studying the research notes in his hand, "that although Umar Patek was captured on January 25th, the news was not made public until this last March 30th, less than fifteen days ago. And only then, the columnist writes, as a slip to the Associated Press. And guess when the information about the capture of the two French nationals and the Pakistani postal clerk, Tahir Shehzad, was made public?"

"Surprise us," said Samantha, her voice adding humor to his upbeat charm.

"April 14th. Yesterday. What do you make of that?"

162   S.P. Grogan

Callie gave it her best shot. "The intelligence communities are keeping the public from knowing about these captures, and probably providing disinformation about the terrorist network, trying not to tip their hand. They must be closing in on the quarry."

"Osama 'The Skunk' bin Laden," said King. He swiveled in his chair to glare at Wendell Holmes, who sat passive, betraying no emotion. That seemed to grate on the ex-soldier turned cable star. He could show everyone a thing or two.

"Let's hightail it to Islamabad, and I mean pronto. We'll take a day trip to this Abbottabad and kick some raghead butt." King psyched himself up. This could be the real deal, and he wanted to be the point man before the cameras. Though they didn't match King's earthy response, the others found their collective spirits soar in agreement. All the facts seemed too coincidental, all closing in on that one town. Only J-Q, the boss's facilitator and go-to guy, had questions.

"How do you quickly fly to a terror-prone country and get past the airport and national security when they know your publicized job is to capture one of their folk heroes? And just where exactly is Osama bin Laden? I assume this town is not just a couple of desert tents but a city with many possible hiding places."

"We found the town," said King, rising and cinching up his belt as though to emphasize his readiness. "Locating the hideout is one of *King's Retribution's* specialties. That's why I'm here, and I am going. Are you all coming, or are you going to stay in Cali-fornication like a bunch of wusses?" With a dramatic flourish, he swept out of the room.

Callie groaned aloud about the display of King's massive ego. This might not be a cruise on 'The Love Boat,' but she had to agree, even if hesitantly, that doing something was better than sitting on their rear ends. And she did believe all the evidence pointed toward a specific geographic location.

What was the least that could happen? Bad intel and a bad choice of a vacation spot.

"I think I might have a way to get us all there under the radar," said Samantha Carlisle with an expression of smug conspiracy.

"The game's afoot," said Hugh Fox, laughing, and the rest joined in the infectious merriment. Except for Wendell Holmes.

Amateurs, he thought. *They're headed for trouble, and I'm the designated babysitter.*

Scene 5: Stop the Amateurs
Setting: The White House, Washington, D.C., April 19

The President of the United States cursed, snubbed out his cigarette, shaking his head in disbelief.

"They are going where?" He was in the Oval Office, which was filled to standing room only with all the key players: CIA, Homeland Security, Secretary of State, the Vice President, the Chairman of the Joint Chiefs of Staff, and core military commanders, who were keyed in on the upcoming raid preparations, including the Admiral in charge of the SEAL insertion. This was their fourth meeting of operational planning with all the power players present.

"They've decided Abbottabad is where bin Laden is hiding," said the CIA Director, realizing his boss was pissed. He felt the same way, and worse, he hated being the messenger.

"Do we have a leak? Is this operation compromised?"

"We think they figured it out on their own, with their own resources. We have an agent in the field. In fact, right in the middle of their camp. He is out of our agency's loop and has no idea what we are up to. He conveyed that information innocently in a daily report saying they were on their way to Pakistan via a few other countries."

"But this Abbottabad town...." The President ran a hand over his face, exasperated. "Can't we stop these Hollywood Rambos at the airport? Halt them at customs? The Pakistani government surely is not going to allow hotshot bounty hunters to go traipsing around their countryside."

"Zoos," said the Secretary of State.

"What?"

"Their travel request is for an official visit to Middle East zoos tied to the SammyC

Wildlife Foundation. The ploy, and a smart one, I might add, is to give each zoo they visit a grant to acquire modernized veterinarian equipment. Their press release went out already. If we find a way to cancel their trip, we will have a goodwill debacle with key allies. *Arab* allies."

"Good Lord."

"We can neutralize their trip," said the Navy admiral who oversaw SEAL team deployment. Everyone looked at him in shock, wondering how the military man defined the word 'neutralize.'

"We can launch Operation Neptune Spear earlier than expected. Our intelligence has not changed. The last report shows daily life as usual. What we do know is that someone big is living there."

"Bin Laden? Any confirmation?"

The CIA Director felt that the blunt truth was necessary. "I am now at about 65 percent 'yes' in our assessment."

"But that's not as comforting as a sure thing. Okay, around the room, what are your opinions? Let's have a frank talk; go or no go?"

164   S.P. Grogan

Most nodded assent in a wary fashion. The Vice President said, "I'm a more cautious man. I wouldn't launch until we were 100% certain bin Laden was the 'Tall Man' the observers have seen in the compound."

The President gave pause as he took in more one-word opinions, reviewing them all on his mental slate.

"Alright, caution is a wise practice, but I don't know if that's true in this terror war." He turned to the admiral. "How soon can we move up the operation's jump-off schedule?"

"Alternatives scenarios have been prepared, and instead of mid-May, I can have our people in place by month end. Interdiction and boots on the ground by April 30, or May 1, no later." The admiral sought to convey firm confidence. He knew firsthand that the SEAL teams had reached prime operational effectiveness a week before.

"Okay, give me a daily briefing as you get into place. I need 24 hours for a final review of all intelligence and our troop preparedness. And I will be the one making the final decision. Is that clear?"

Around the room came the affirmation of who was Commander-in-Chief.

"And you say we have a spy in their camp? I'm talking about the TV show people."

"Yes, he's accepted as an expert advisor. We were about ready to retire him and thought this was a quiet pasture to park him. But he will follow orders." Recalling who he had in this position, the CIA Director thought to himself, dismayed: *Holmes is a cowboy who follows orders as he interprets them, but sometimes you have to play the cards that are dealt.*

"Well," said the President of the United States, "see if your inside snoop can disrupt their schedule, and hear my words, nothing overt or harmful. Just slow them down. I am trying to exact justice for the American people for 9/11, and I won't find this government outmaneuvered for television ratings."

"Yes, Mr. President," they said in one fashion or another, leaving.

The Press Secretary to the President held back for a moment. "If we do hit him and succeed. You want full media availability?"

"Damn right," affirmed the President of the United States.

The CIA Director heading back to his office, wondered what sabotage directive the Agency should convey to Holmes. Whatever, he would direct Givens to convey it as point contact. The Director thought long and hard, concluding, *certainly this bunch of celluloid crook-catchers couldn't screw up an op sanctioned by the head of the Free World and undertaken by the might of the U.S. military. Or could they?*

Scene 6: I'm back
Setting: Bagram Air Base, Parwan Province, Afghanistan, April 22nd

The wheels of the Boeing C-17 Globemaster III military transport aircraft thudded heavily on the runway.

Here I am, back again, thought SEAL Six member Shawn Pacheco, watching moist condensation hiss from the overhead as the cabin's depressurized air absorbed itself into the desert's dry heat. And this was supposed to be springtime.

Whatever the assignment is this time, it'll be big. I don't dare speculate. The briefing will be soon enough. Tonight, maybe. My part is small. 1-2-3-4. Repel from the helicopter. Blow a hole in the house wall, help secure the perimeter, search for arms caches. Jump back on the helicopter. I can do the job in my sleep. What could go wrong?

EPISODE ELEVEN — Hot on the Trail

Scene 1: In-flight Entertainment
Setting: In transit, 35,000 feet over the South Atlantic

Hugh Fox prodded in a friendly manner. "Now that we have you trapped with only a parachute exit and a captured audience needing mid-flight diversion, let me ask. You mentioned meeting Osama bin Laden once?"

"Three times."

That perked everybody up as they sprawled in the leather seats of Fox's Embraer corporate jet as comfortably as they could. Samantha, Callie, and Storm made up the remainder of the passenger list. J-Q had remained behind as Hugh's corporate alter ego at Skilleo Games Technology headquarters.

A second executive jet, Samantha's, held Clayton, Bennie, Hiram Abbas, and CAM ONE and CAM TWO, various production equipment, and trailed a close 30 miles behind. The leadership had decided that a digital camera need not capture all moments and that privacy aboard Fox's jet would allow some candid conversation.

"We're waiting," said Samantha, putting down her *Women's Wear Daily* trade journal.

"I expect we'll get the sanitized Freedom of Information story?"

Holmes had not given much support to the fugitive hunt, and Callie was still suspicious of his agenda.

166   S.P. Grogan

"Yeah, tell us about the son-of-a-bitch," said King. A steward replaced King's empty Scotch glass with a refresher.

Holmes put down his audiobook reader and removed his earbuds. Later he would continue listening to 'The Life of Washington;' there were enough hours of historical biographical audio left to cover all anticipated and unforeseen travel spots in this entire *miss*-adventure.

Their first fuel stop had been Miami, and next, the Canaries. Then the first stop on their itinerary was Cairo and a visit to the zoo at Giza. Then they'd go on to their covert destination in Islamabad as the guests of the director of the Islamabad Zoo, located at the base of the Margalla Hills.

"The Osama bin Laden I first met in January of 1980 was friendly; shy even."

"Bullshit," said King, tepidly.

"No interruptions." Samantha scolded him lightly, and King gave off a low, feral growl.

"One has to keep in mind the historical context. In December 1979, the Soviets invaded Afghanistan. Bin Laden was only 22 then, and he showed up several weeks later, full of idealism. At that stage, he was not radicalized, and he was extremely loyal to the Saud family, from whence his family fortune had sprung. In fact, when I met him, he was known as a construction executive for the bin Laden family interests.

"We crossed paths when I was sent as a virgin neophyte under an exchange student cover to Pakistan to gather information on the tactical situation of who was in the fight, what tribes, and could we help, as we defined it: aiding the Afghan *Mujahedeen* in its resistance to the Soviet occupation of Afghanistan. This was still the Cold War, and Jimmy Carter was president."

"You said 'we,'" said Callie. Fox gave her a stare that said, "Do not dig too deep," and Holmes continued.

"I met Osama in Lahore. We were about the same age, he a few years older, and we were both determined to shape the world. We were loyal to our home countries, he to Saudi Arabia, and myself to Mom and apple pie. We were doing similar work when we crossed paths. He was collecting funds from Gulf Coast countries and funneling them to the Afghan fighters, and I was doing the same from another direction. Right after the Soviet invasion, President Carter started arming the mujahedeen with cast-off U.S. supplies. Several times, bin Laden and I had to coordinate logistics, making sure the right equipment flowed to the tribes who were going to be the best fighters. It was heavy political balancing for both him and me."

"I saw the movie *Charlie Wilson's War*," interrupted Fox, "with Tom Hanks and Julia Roberts. That was *you* somewhere in that story? Amazing!"

Crimson Scimitar

"Please. I was a young grunt in the trenches. More a supply clerk, whereas Osama bin Laden was already demonstrating leadership talent and he was a problem solver. And as he used funds to buy weapons, he also established hospitals for the guerrilla wounded, bombed villagers, and brought candy and treats to the widows and orphans. While we wanted to beat the Soviets through a proxy war and send them home with a bloody nose, bin Laden was building friendship networks."

"Is it true that we armed bin Laden and gave the Taliban an open door to take over Afghanistan after the Soviets left?" Samantha was trying to understand the mess called the Middle East.

"Not then, and not directly. What we left was a vacuum of leadership. The Soviets evacuated, and we left a leadership gap and created a civil war."

"So you two were friends?" King didn't like this story. "I thought bin Laden hated Westerners."

"Not in 1980. And yes, for a couple of years, we were coffee-sipping buds, respectful of our mutual goals. It wasn't until 1986, when he fell under the influence of the Islamic scholar Sheik Abdullah Azzam that his thoughts turned to the concept of world jihad.

"You might recall that in late 1979, radical Islamists captured the Grand Mosque in Mecca, espousing liturgical epitaphs that bin Laden would mimic years later. But at that time, he supported the ruling al Saud family to come in, under religious fatwas, to allow soldiers to recapture the mosque, using firepower in the sacred shrine and being supported by French military advisors."

They heard a change in the pitch of the plane's engines and could feel the beginning of a slow descent.

"It would have saved the world, and the U.S., a lot of grief," said King, "if the Commies had killed the bastard back in the 1980s." He drained his glass.

"That almost happened. In 1982, bin Laden was trapped with a small contingent of Arab guerrilla volunteers near Jaji, in Paktia Province. They were under bombardment by a Russian mechanized battalion, heavy field howitzers, aerial bombardment, and strafing by a MIG fighter."

On the intercom, the pilot gave landing instructions to his VIP passengers. Buckle up stuff.

Holmes picked up his audiobook.

"Well, what happened?" demanded Samantha Carlisle. She was intrigued, caught up in the telling.

168 S.P. Grogan

Holmes stuck in the earbuds. "I saved his life." He closed his eyes and tuned into the audio chapter about 22-year-old George Washington's fiasco as a military man in the surrender of Fort Necessity at the Great Meadows.

They all stared at this unassuming man.

Scene 2: The Long Watch Ending
Setting: Outside the Abbottabad Compound, April 28

"The old gardener has returned," said the observer, lowering his binoculars.

"How long has he been gone?" The other watcher turned to a notebook, written in coded notations, and thumbed back through the pages.

"About two weeks this time, unless we missed him coming in the evenings."

"No, that is not his routine. He comes when the weeds need whacking, stays a few days, and then he's gone."

"Where do you think he goes?"

"Probably has a poppy field to tend. He would make a lot more money cultivating opium than running a lawn care business."

Standing at the window, back in the shadows, the observer resurveyed the compound as best he could, with only a small visual angle of the grounds.

"Did you hear anything back from the vaccinations the doctor took at the residence?"

"They're not saying much, but it failed to get them to open up their doors for testing. Just concluded there are a lot of family members there, mostly women and children, mostly all related."

"It would've been a good trick, getting DNA encoded for future comparisons."

The other man began to write in his notebook.

"Okay, they want another count of the residents."

"The requests for information are picking up. Something's in the wind, I think."

"We are not paid to think but to watch, observe and report. I count no changes from last time except for the gardener's arrival. That makes five men in the compound, plus the Tall Man, who you only saw once. Plus, the women and children — there haven't been any changes. I don't know how we can make the 'status quo' sound exciting."

"Just write it up and report it. I wonder how long we're going to have to stay here?"

"Not long, I say. This all has to mean something."

Scene 3: Parting Words
Setting: Inside the Abbottabad Compound, April 28

"Are you rested?"

"Thank you for your concern, my Sheik."

"Is it true what I hear about our brother Umar Patek?"

"Yes, the government shot him when they raided one of our follower's homes. Patek was taken away injured, along with his wife."

"I am sorry that we did not have a chance to meet. What was your impression of him, Khalaf? You were my intermediary."

"Sadly, he seemed like a man on the run, too harried to be a sharp thinker. I think he wanted to see you in order to rebuild his confidence, to go back to Jakarta and plan more worthwhile attacks on the government."

"You do not think his capture will come back to haunt us here?"

"I am sure they will be tortured, but no. I was very cautious in my meeting with him. They did not know who I was, and I made a major effort to cover my trail. Besides, as you know, I traveled to see The Doctor."

"And how is our leader?"

Khalaf knew that bin Laden had the habit of minimizing his importance and portraying others in al-Qaeda as more worthy.

"He sends you his prayers for long life. Like all of us, he awaits your command to launch *Crimson Scimitar*."

"If I could, I would do it this minute. It is indeed frustrating that we must await the capitalistic system of the Americans to overproduce their nuclear waste products. The Scientist reports that they are preparing their shipment, but it is still several months off."

Khalaf said nothing. He felt a little jealous that he was not totally immersed in the planning of what would be al-Qaeda's greatest triumph and angered that his fellow jihadist, Shahin, was at that moment mobilizing in Yemen, poised to lead the main assault.

Bin Laden likewise held silent, as if pondering.

"I am disappointed that all other associations of our followers are not achieving great success; that those in Yemen and Somalia believe Lone Wolf attacks will lead to victory. And I am saddened we are losing so many good soldiers to the enemy. We must again regain the offensive." Bin Laden sipped at tea that had grown cold.

"I am considering," said the future Emir of the planned al-Qaeda caliphate, "that if we are successful with *Crimson Scimitar*, it may be time for us to approach the West and tell them I

170   S.P. Grogan

would be willing to put aside my 1996 declaration of war on the United States if they will accept two of my six Articles of Demands. And I may ask you to be a member of the delegation when al-Qaeda approaches their leaders."

Khalaf leaned back in shock, overwhelmed.

"What a great honor you bestow, my beloved Sheik. I know by heart your tenets. They have been my faith throughout the struggle. Which ones do you believe will be achievable?"

Osama bin Laden stroked his beard with a satisfying tug. Khalaf thought he looked worn and tired; under the assumption he rarely left his top-floor residence in the compound. Even he would be shocked to know about the escape tunnel and his leader's weekly midnight long walks.

"I think we have achieved one goal by the Americans making their misplaced demands against tyrannical Muslim governments, with their catchphrase of 'Arab Spring.' That is a joke and so typical of their need to reduce great philosophies into short slogans. Their demands for democracy underscore that we of profound faith will soon be in control of governments using elected Islamic majorities — Libya, Egypt, Yemen, and eventually Syria. When we gain such strength, then, like Iran's Ayatollahs, we shall ask for our own Pan-Muslim union, but it shall be the Caliphate."

"Yes, in my travels I have seen the disillusioned masses of the faith, ready to rise. I am sure they seek a single voice."

"*Crimson Scimitar* will reduce America economically, and for fear of another such attack, I shall demand, first, the removal of all Western military from the Prophet's homeland on the Arabian Peninsula."

"Your nemesis, the al Saud family, is being undermined by this *Arab Spring* movement. They will certainly fall if the U.S. Fleet is sent home."

"Exactly. You are, as I have always believed, an apt pupil and a future leader."

Khalaf bowed his head reverently and asked, "And what of your second demand regarding their retreat?"

"Yes. I want to control OPEC and raise oil prices for all the Western nations. I hear an economic recession is building across the world. Now is the time to agitate for increased energy prices. With the fall of the Sauds, we can pressure the Gulf States and our brothers in Iraq to raise their prices. If the American economy fails, then perhaps they will cut back their economic spending on foreign aid, especially to Israel. And that will be a holy quest for another attack, something the Iranians, who I deeply mistrust, still might be willing to initiate with a nuclear sword." He paused, rifling through several papers, one he held to the light.

"The attack plan on the oil tankers, if we can bring that about...." He let the thought hover unsaid.

Khalaf heard the renewed fervor in the Sheik's voice of his great plans. Over the last days before his presence in the compound, in his travels, he had begun to hear disgruntled voices, those who no longer would follow the Sheik's desires or even as supporters seeing inaction as a character flaw. Now how untrue; here was the active man of years past: the Caliphate again a true possibility.

"What do you ask of me? What can I do now to advance our cause?"

"I have sorely missed good conversation. The television reception is poor, and when I hear the news, it is not what it should be. There is much to plan in preparing to reach the Americans once *Crimson Scimitar* has succeeded. Let us talk and strategize, and then I will send you with messages to all our commanders for new battle plans, as well as to select a delegation to visit the United Nations. It will be time to bait the lion in his den."

"Who might join me on this mission?" Khalaf wished to purge one name from a planned delegation.

"Al-Rahman will decline, I am sure. In fact, I wish to see him become my true second-in-command."

To Khalaf, this suggested al-Zawahiri might serve in a lesser role; this was a surprise. The Sheik must be thinking in terms of a massive re-organization in the ranks. With the success of *Crimson Scimitar*, no one would question his leader's commands. Khalaf felt he must force the issue so as not to be undermined by the others appointed.

"And what about brother al-Awlaki? If I may be as bold, I met with him recently and did not see a man of great vision."

"His American upbringing does not sit well with me. If he were to take a sword and rush into battle, I would praise him and have no doubts. But I do have doubts; he may be too ambitious."

Khalaf had his answer and felt relieved.

"Again, I thank you for such an honor to be a delegate. Allah be praised and guide such our blade to be true and swift, crimson with the blood of the non-believers."

Sheik bin Laden gave a weary smile, pleased to hear a positive voice.

"Join me in prayer this evening. Today is the twenty-eighth, and I want you on the road no later than the third of May. By then, I shall have outlined the demands for the Americans to quit the Middle East altogether."

"I am humbled," whispered Khalaf, "and by your command, I shall serve you and our cause to my death." His head touched the floor, and tears welled in his eyes. His body surged

172   S.P. Grogan

with newfound energy. Finally, he had his calling. Soon he would be on the first step to becoming a leader, a statesman within al-Qaeda. His dream of power, of sitting next to the Caliphate throne, would become a great event. And all this new life would begin on May 3rd when he would carry his mantle of new duties and authority, blessed holy by Osama bin Laden, to all followers of al-Qaeda and then the world itself. Nothing could stop his ascendency; he would never again be known as Maulawi Abd al-Khaliq Jan. As bin Laden had proclaimed, he had the name of a "future leader:" *Khalaf.*

Nothing could stop him.

Scene 4: 'Go'
Setting: The White House, April 29th, 8:20 a.m.

The President of the United States moved quickly across the lawn to the waiting presidential transportation, call sign *Marine One*, a sleek VH-3D Sea King Marine helicopter.

One of the Marine military liaisons stood at attention at the foot of the steps, prepared to offer the customary salute to the office, the power, and the man who now held it just over two years into his Administration. Today much weighed on his mind. He was going to Andrews Air Force base to board Air Force One, flying to Alabama to tour storm-ravaged counties. Later, they will say, he looked serious but unperturbed, simply fulfilling those duties calling for a presidential presence to offer comfort to those now homeless. His cabinet and his security advisors knew otherwise.

There are many events that define one's legacy in this office, the highest in the land, political decisions that might backfire and lead to a humiliating downfall and ignominious resignation or stewardship where accomplished legislation defines the future of American character, like The New Deal or The Great Society. The President knew he was at that momentous decision with options weighed and a myriad of opinions sorted, where the percentage of confidence in a successful outcome still hovered around 60% odds; nevertheless, it came down to the simple two choices of being wrong with the aftermath of downplaying the error, a training exercise, as minor in the scheme of daily international events, or by luck making the right decision and becoming the Avenger, restoring pride by action to a neurotic and uncertain world power as was the United States this crisp April morning.

On the steps of the helicopter, he turned to make the obligatory wave to the few staff and press onlookers and the photo-clicking tourists beyond the fence. The time had arrived. He motioned over his chief National Security Advisor.

"Tell them it's a 'go.'"

The next night, the 30th, put him in one of those ironic moments of playing the consummate actor. At the White House Press Correspondent's Dinner, host comedian Seth

Meyers cracked the joke: "People think Bin Laden is hiding out in the Hindu Kush, but did you know that every day from 4-5, he hosts a show on CSPAN?" The President of the United States laughed along with the audience.

Scene 5: The Mighty Obelisk Comes
Setting: Evening in Giza, Egypt, April 30th

His arms eased around her, crossing, and his hands rubbed over her silk nightgown, grasping her firm breasts, aroused nipples, perfect handfuls. He buried his face in her freshly-washed hair with its scent of lemon and hint of lavender. She leaned into him with a pleased moan as her hands grasped the elastic in his boxers, pulled and slipped her fingers inside, rubbing and teasing him erect, hard and eager.

"A million dollars for your thoughts," Hugh whispered against Samantha's ear. He exhaled a warm breath and felt her excitement as her hands increased their play.

"I want you to buy me one of those," she said, her head nodding beyond the open balcony of the Presidential Suite, on top of the Mena House Oberoi in Giza. *The Churchill Suite.* The great man himself had stayed at this five-star hotel in 1914 but probably had not enjoyed the hands-on moment quite as the two entwined were.

Fox looked at the magnificent view of the massive Pyramid of Cheops, outlined by a blood-stained evening sky.

"One or all three? I might get a better rate on shipping if they come as a package deal."

"Do we have to go on?" queried Samantha, half serious. "Couldn't we stay in this idyllic setting for a week, ride camels across the desert, and have sweaty sex on a magic carpet? The one on the floor here, at least?"

Hugh responded with kind humor. "Perhaps go down to Tahrir Square on Friday nights and join the mob of 20,000 students and the Muslim Brotherhood demanding a new Islamic constitution based on Sharia law?"

"You certainly know how to take the romance out of a girl's wet dream of wanting to be deflowered by a Sheik of Araby."

He nibbled on the nape of her neck and continued the light banter.

"After today, I have the feeling you would rather be seduced next to a water hole with animals looking on, seeing if your screams can out-blast lions' roars and the yipping of hyenas."

"Wasn't that a fun zoo tour today? Seeing the North Sahara species of cheetahs and Dorcas gazelles?"

"The zoo officials were certainly appreciative of the grant you gave to initiate a state-of-the-art breeding facility."

174   S.P. Grogan

"Speaking of breeding...." She purred and turned into him, releasing one hand, but the other hand still stroking him. "I don't want to go, and I bet I can make you agree."

"The Islamabad Zoo is expecting us tomorrow afternoon. There's a long morning of flight ahead, but...." His kiss was intense. His tongue entered her mouth and flicked at hers.

When they came up for air, he gave his own rendition of a feral growl. "Let's see if we can cause an earthquake that will topple the pyramids with stronger tremors than destroyed the Lighthouse of Alexandria."

He eased her to the bed and raised her nightgown. He found her nerve endings easily, but she wanted the moments to last and rolled to his rocking motion. She kissed and tugged at his lower lip and felt the heat of her insides, where her muscles held him tight and brought the momentum of his power to her building climax of shudders and hoarse shouts. At the height of their released sensuality, she grabbed his hair in both hands and pulled back his face to stare into his eyes. She felt a warmth surge from him as he filled her. They were both satiated and breathing hard, their bodies glistening with salty moisture. He fell to her side, and she lay a leg across him with her head on his chest and felt her throbbing ebbing away with slight spasms.

She did not love him, and he knew it. His feelings were likewise at odds — the passion was eager, yet the tug of his heart was not so certain; uncommitted. They enjoyed each other's company and spoke the same intelligent language. It felt like they'd had to take their companionship to the ultimate conclusion, copulation, in order to satisfy their curiosity, explore, and revel in bringing each other pleasure. They were people of compassion and caring, yet they could not bring about those emotions between themselves and forge a bond of total loving, of opening themselves up and asking the other to absorb their essence, of making two into one.

They were having a good time during their adventure of trying to do the right thing, and sex was a beneficial byproduct. They seemed to have the perfect relationship for two Type A, bicoastal business tycoons. Passionate fusion when they met, business-like text and emails when apart.

Hugh spoke to this situation, but only in a roundabout way and analogous terms.

"If you lived 3,000 years ago, in the age of the pharaohs, you would be high priestess of the cult of Imhotep, who became known as the Healer." She responded in kind.

"You might not have been a pharaoh back then because you would not be able to stand the palace intrigue. I think I see you as the Architect, the one who builds the Great Pyramid."

"So I would have 30,000 workers at my command, and it would take 80 years to complete? That's a lot of 1099 forms to file, and I hope there is no OSHA."

"You'd find a way to build the greatest pyramid." She toyed with his chest hairs, playfully twisting. "But better, you'd find a way to build a replica all miniature, so all the citizens of Thebes and Luxor could afford their own backyard pyramid. And then you'd bring out Versions 2 and 3 and mint many Egyptian piastres." They both laughed and rolled among the satin sheets.

His hold on her was gentle and caressing. He mulled something over, and he was more serious when he spoke.

"The ancient Egyptians were actually correct in their religion in three instances. Far more realistic than what we have today. As befitting you, they believed that animals could be gods.

"Second, they once created a monotheistic religion based on the Sun as the only god — Aten; and they were correct, for, without that god, we are all nonexistent." Except for their matched breathing, silence drifted through the room, but street sounds came in from outside the window.

"So far, you are indeed astute. What is the third tenet of your new faith?"

He laughed.

"They had their worldly goods buried with them when they departed their mortal coil. They held to a religion that believed you could take it with you. Today that would solve a lot of material hassling among relatives and rid us of estate planners completely."

She gave him a supportive chuckle before she turned serious herself. Unexpectedly, she asked, "What do you think of Wendell Holmes? Is he for real? Did he know Osama bin Laden like he said, and even saved his life once?"

"I have no reason to doubt it. On tomorrow's flight junket, he will be forced to relay that tidbit. We are all too anxious. To think that by failing to let a basic stranger die, the future would have been altered, and 9/11 might never have occurred; the 'what ifs' are mind-blowing."

"I find him interesting," she said, and there was a momentary silence.

"'More than me,' asks the jealous lover?"

"Of course not, silly. It's just that he's a quantity yet undefined in this mission we're on."

"I would hate that the worldly older man is more of an attraction than youth and endurance."

Samantha leaned up on her arm and looked at the handsome, clean-lined face with wet, stringy hair across his forehead. Then she crawled up on him and moved over his hips. She rubbed against him, bringing a desire visibly back to life.

"A youthful cock prevails every time," she said, shifting to turn her back toward his prone position, anticipating, as she knelt across him.

176 S.P. Grogan

"I have found the tomb!" his mock cry of thrill. "And to its soft darkness, I bring the Mighty Obelisk!"

Scene 6: Priority Instructions
Setting: Early morning, Mena House Oberoi Hotel, Giza, April 30th

Holmes dropped off his single bag with the concierge. He would have breakfast on the terrace, he thought, while waiting for the others to arrive for the limousine ride back to the airport. He bought the latest faxed copy of the *New York Times* and the Egyptian-English written *Al-Ahram Weekly*. A quick scan bore nothing that would hinder their plans to arrive in Pakistan early in the afternoon. Local headlines screamed for prosecution and the death penalty for the deposed Egyptian president Mubarak. *Sic semper tyrannis*. Death to tyrants.

Though, he thought, Muhammad Hosni El Sayed Mubarak had been one of America's more supportive bureaucratic rulers with a 30-year run in power, toppled only two months ago.

What had been unleashed? How could the U.S. administration praise the rise of democracy in Egypt when the Middle East desk knew the strength building in the Muslim Brotherhood? They will take control, he surmised from his own experiences. Islamic law will stifle outside tourism, internecine anarchy will bleed out, and dictatorial theocracy will take over — slaying the innocent, like the Coptic Christians and then the moderates. It'll be Iran all over again. From his experience, he wondered if the Egyptian military would let their power be defused, place them under the thumbs of the Mullahs, and take away their perks.

Dominos tumbling and a more violent world at the precipice. Being shown the exit of his career, should he even care? He laughed to himself: *Do I have such an ego that I feel I really could do something about the world's turmoil?*

He returned his key to the front desk, knowing that his room had been covered by the Fox-Carlisle Traveling Circus, or however they were billing this farce. He had his instructions: tag along and take notes. And in terms of that request, he had performed admirably and had even a free around-the-world trip with barely any effort. He did not think they would succeed; the Pakistani countryside is too easy to hide in. Osama has many friends who would be willing to die to protect him.

A strange premonition crossed his mind. *Who best deserved to capture and deal with Osama bin Laden, a group of idealistic do-gooders? Or the U.S. Government?*

His brief reverie was broken when the clerk at the front desk took note of his key number and smiled.

"You have a message, Mr. Holmes," he said. He handed over a printed phone message.

He half expected a change in plans, a decision to abandon this wild goose chase, or maybe turn the jets towards South Africa. The attractive and personable Ms. Carlisle was definitely a 'Protect the Wildlife' enthusiast, and he admired that she put her resources behind her commitment. The Egyptian Zoo was definitely a zoo, with its unique 40 acres of lushness, but he viewed Samantha more in the big picture, where she could make a difference. Providing opportunities to send a new stock of animals into the wild to replenish wilderness habitats, maybe, or at least what was left out there. Still, he wondered about a ridiculous paradox: If fur stoles came back into fashion, would she rationalize that a mink farm was not the same as stocking the jungles with wild and snarling creatures? No, only for the short time he knew her; he believed she had a good heart. But like him, could she make such a difference, save the world, her world of wild animals, from man's slaughter?

He glanced at the note and then grimaced. *How in the hell?* How, with all their technology, did they send a phone message that could easily have missed him? And how did they expect him to accomplish what they asked? He wadded up the note, tossed it into the nearest trashcan, and then stalked off for a hearty, five-star breakfast. Maybe his last, he thought, before his meals became Pashtu cuisine.

Perspiring and with her t-shirt soaked, Callie Cardoza entered the hotel from her standard five-mile run. This one, though, was a little outlandish: she ran to the base of one of the pyramids, then around the Sphinx and back. This would be the closest she got to the attractions as a tourist since what was on the schedule now was a shower and packing for the airport. Next time, if there were a chance, she would return as a casual tourist. No, probably not.

From across the lobby, she watched as Wendell Holmes wadded up and threw some paper away. Her curiosity was piqued. There was no real reason for her interest except her wariness of Holmes altogether, including his most recent tale, which went towards proving her conviction that the man was puffery of the highly implausible. She pre-judged the man as a tag-along of no value to this project. Yet, though she was not a detective, she was a former cop, and her past experience in the computer field service required intelligence.

And most important of all, she was a woman, an ex-cop, where all curiosity needed a good sniff test.

After Holmes's departure, when she could not see him anymore, she went over and retrieved what turned out to be a phone message. It puzzled her, for all it said was:

Delay meeting until May 2. L.P. What was that about? She mused over the contents and turned the paper over in her hand. She didn't know of any meetings that were set up by either

Hugh or Samantha. Was it one Holmes was supposed to arrange? With all his fake buffoonery, was he finally going to be of use to them? And who, or what, was 'L.P.?'[*]

Whatever.

Callie Cardoza would not believe anything Wendell Holmes told them anyway.

Scene 7: Pre-Launch
Setting: Morning, Bagram Airbase, Afghanistan, April 30th

He was a sailor-soldier, part of a unit, part of a greater operation, but his training, his focus had been on one task. Other than a mission yet undefined, Pacheco knew little except rumor until the Commander stood before the assembled group of 70 assorted SEAL specialists and confirmed, "We think we found Osama bin Laden, and your job is to kill him." The serious-looking young men broke out into a cheer.

The curtain was pulled back from the wall displaying photos of what looked like a rural farm neighborhood, and a tarp was yanked off a table showing a scale mock-up of a house. *The House.* As Pacheco could see, as he stood off to the side in the crowded military-ready room, this was the house matching the life-size cut-out they had practiced on in the California desert, as other SEALS had trained on a similar façade building in Pakistan at a place called Camp Alpha.

It now became clear about the civilians who were now giving their report. CIA. He and his comrades would be storming this house based on CIA intelligence. Hope the damn place wasn't empty, Pacheco worried. The CIA men didn't identify themselves as spooks, merely 'intelligence collectors.' From them, he heard the operation called '*Operation Neptune Spear,*' something he knew, the trident being part of the Navy Special Warfare insignia. Yet, he had heard the name 'Geronimo' bantered about between two SEALS, not in his insertion squad but within his eavesdropping.

As he listened to the superior officer, they were given an overview of the operation, not just a segment, but now heard how it all would come together.

Tonight, the operation would begin, offering little moonlight. The 160th Special Operations Aviation Regiment (SOAR) would provide two modified Black Hawk helicopters.

Pacheco heard the word 'stealth' and thought it ridiculous that you could make a helicopter quiet.

Larger Chinook helicopters would be on the ground halfway between Jalalabad in Afghanistan and Abbottabad, sitting on a dry stream bed, poised with backup fuel or to be

---

[*] L.P. — *Leon Panetta, Director of the Central Intelligence Agency, February 2009 to June 2011.*

Crimson Scimitar

there if the operation went sour, to evacuate the survivors or to interdict with Pakistani forces those who did not use the word 'alleged,' if they were in league with bin Laden and tried to interfere. Another SEAL team would sit in a Chinook just inside Afghanistan, likewise ready to ride to the rescue.

Pacheco was to be in the first helicopter, Razor One, his sole job when they landed inside the compound was to run to the side of the house and detonate the wall for entry, even if the front door seemed to be unblocked. Once the demolition charge did the trick, then he was to do a quick check of the perimeter walls and look at the outbuildings for booby traps or hidden weapon caches. Report back to the helicopter to be on standby and ready for embarkation. Quick and easy.

Those in the assault force inside the compound were handed out plastic tie-on handcuffs.

Prisoners were expected: five to six men inside, the rest, about twenty or so, women and children. Check women for weapons, secure them all. Two SEALS identified themselves as the detainee section, and it was pointed out where all the captured non-combatants were to be held, so the interpreters could conduct on-the-spot interrogations.

Sitting on its haunches like a soldier at parade rest, Pacheco spotted 'Cairo,' the Belgian Malinois dog, trained to sniff out any hidey-holes for Sadaam Hussein-type characters or run down any escapees.

We are taking no chances, he considered, and whoever was in that building would be ours by morning. Pacheco grinned to a fellow SEAL and got a conspiratorial waving Hawaiian shaka, 'All's great, bro.'

"Okay," finished the Commander after the thirty-minute overview was laid out. "Break into your designated assault teams for your last verbal walk-through. Fall out formation tonight at 21:00. Lift off at 22:00. Religious services three buildings to the west available to all after you are dismissed."

Pacheco walked to the front of the room and viewed all the daytime photos posted on the wall. So, this is Abbottabad, Pakistan. Looks peaceful enough. Rural farm-like. How does that perspective help? It's going to be past midnight and no moon. Pitch dark, and probably gooks shooting back at us. Maybe they will be shooting off flares, and it will be sort of macabre daylight, and we will be sitting ducks. Oh, well, considered Pacheco, 'ours is to do or die,' and he started listening to the assignment tasking of Razor One for the umpteenth time, still wondering, *Will bin Laden have the light on and the welcome mat out? Fuck him if he opens the door.*

Two hours later, the report came down; cloudy weather obscured the strike zone. The bubble of anticipation burst among the SEALS casting a somber pall, not bitter, just disappointment. Neptune Spear postponed and rescheduled for tomorrow night, the 1st of

180   S.P. Grogan

May. Just great, was Pacheco's assessment: Murphy's Law at work in the guise of Mother
Nature.

EPISODE TWELVE — Opposites Attack

Scene 1: Wendell Holmes tells a story
Setting: Early afternoon approaching Pakistani airspace, April 30th

*We have demonized the man, and on the world stage, certainly for good reason. But back in
the1980's, the young man, as I met and knew him, was the construction executive under a
dominating family, trying to set himself apart from multiple brothers and sisters to find himself both
for his vocation and his beliefs. This made him vulnerable to many outside influences; the most
telling were the Islamic radicals who shaped their religion to fit the political goals to gain power.*

*So it was in the winter of 1983, after the Soviet invasion, when bin Laden decided he wanted
to be an Arab mujahideen, tired of being a Crescent relief worker and supplier of funds to the
Afghans battling the atheist Red Menace. As in our history, we had 'volunteer' brigades, like
Chennault's Air Force against the Japanese or the Abraham Lincoln Brigade, to fight against Fascist
Franco. Bin Laden saw romance believing he could form an Arab Brigade to become Afghan
Freedom fighters.*

*He soon had a cadre of a dozen enthusiasts from Yemen, Egypt, and Saudi Arabia that wished
to follow him as he went into Afghanistan to set up a guerrilla base camp. I think at this date, he
was a little naïve and premature, but then so were the Soviets in the war they fought. Bin Laden
rushed out to become a guerilla leader without a logistics supply line, just as the Soviets were
saturating the countryside with bulky mechanized military equipment. Two wrongs came to blows
in the wrong valley.*

*I was going in-country with a donkey supply team consisting of two proto-type Stinger shoulder
launch SAMs, the FIM-92B, new and approved over the 'B' model. Also, we carried a couple of
heavy machine guns and related ammunition and repair equipment. Tools were as valuable as
bullets. Sand and dust could jam any of this equipment, and a good supply of machine oil and even
battery hand-held vacuums were worth their weight in gold while out in the field.*

*Bin Laden was leading his Dirty Dozen to reconnoiter a base of operation outside Jaji in
Afghanistan, and we all happened, as coincidences go, to meet on the same smuggler's trail, and felt
our numbers more secure in joining forces. My mujahedeen contact would meet me in two days,
and the rendezvous point would be three clicks from where bin Laden had his objective.*

*The first night in bivouac, as was his nature, he tried to convince my pack carriers to abandon
doing the Western Imperialist lackey's job and join his cause of righteousness, with, of course, all my*

military stores. It was not so much Islamic slogans he espoused as a battle of good versus evil. The blessings of his cause by Mohammad would come in 1986.

That night we had a friendly argument; I warning him off to leave my job and my people alone. In the end, we reached a mutual truce, drank bitter cold coffee, nibbled on stale wheat bread, and slept without tents. The next morning the Soviet observers found us crossing a ridge line, and all hell broke loose. In the Soviet invasion, we tend to forget that the Russians actually did create a viable Afghan military force. Within those people were local citizens that kept their eyes out for invaders, us, coming in from Pakistani borders. Once the forward observers saw our line of march, they radioed in for air support and a military unit with mounted howitzer cannons one valley over.

One minute the crisp morning air is silent, except for a bird screech echoing down below on the valley floor, and next, the ridge above us explodes, a sun bursting with fireball and concussion. Military measurement by the forward observers, capable but not brilliant with mental math, made an error when they computed their trajectory fire, putting our coordinates where we had just been and not where we had just hiked to. That mistake saved our lives.

The phrase 'sitting ducks' comes to mind as the world around you goes to shit. And although there was no specific trail leading off the ridge line, we started scrambling down, and the next wave of fire again hit right where we had been — rocks and shards flying everywhere.

Bin Laden lost one man with a granite chunk of shrapnel to the head.

The exploding shells became a fiery orange beacon to the overhead MiG 21 Fishbed jet zeroing in on its bombing run. Had the Soviets flown down on us with a slower prop plane with their napalm or with a Hind Mi 24 helicopter gunship, we would have been Swiss cheese on toast since the pilot would actually have seen our rattled teeth. As it was, the jet's first run dropped his ordinance on the lip of where the cannon fire on the hill still was smoking, and with luck, the napalm ran to the other side, but not before vaporizing two of bin Laden's soldiers, too late off the top path, into crispy critters.

I knew a second strike both of howitzer fire — and these were most probably the Soviets D-130s throwing 122m shells, and another MiG bombing run was in the cards, and here is when I made the command decision, the gut call, the famous 'under-fire-in-the-trench cures all forms of atheism.' I told everyone to run back up to the path and go up. We did this running, trying to hold on to skittish braying donkeys. I had recalled that further up the trail, I had seen some sort of cut in the rock, like a wild goat trail, leading down, not the valley we wanted since this new direction was toward the Soviet mechanized artillery, but it would have to do since we still had targets pinned on our backs. Stumbling down a cliff is as scary as seeing the jet over your shoulder make its arc turn for another run. We could only pray in several languages, and by the grace of luck, prayer, Jehovah, and Allah, the pilot assumed, like I hoped, that the spotters were again calling in on us being where

182   S.P. Grogan

we had just left. I can tell you napalm heat is BBQ-searing when that sort of lighter fuel spreads across the ground, even several hundred yards away from our position.

All of bin Laden's remaining cadre were shitting bricks, a couple of them shell-shocked. They were volunteers from universities, their textbook reading limited to ancient authors spouting political science theory, and only with the smoke, heat, and smell of death could they comprehend there is no glory when you see a buddy holding in his guts. I speak metaphorically for the moment. That happened about five seconds later to one of his folks when the howitzers decided to carpet shell the entire ridge line. We had run out of time and positioning, and in the open, we just had to hunker down as shells rained like a volcano eruption with exploding rocks and blossoming lava, but the view was from inside the volcano. I had thrown myself down and found indirectly had done so on top of his mightiness, Mr. Osama bin Laden; it seems we both were calling dibs on the same overhang of a small ledge. Two more of his men met Allah, and I lost one porter and a donkey bleeding out.

When there was a moment's respite as we knew they were reloading and the jet making another turn, I yelled, 'Screw this shit!' into bin Laden's ear. We had no choice, nowhere really to scramble without tumbling down, and they had our position. No more running left, right, up, or down. I ran to one of the donkeys and hauled the boxes to the ground, and with my trusty Buck Hunter knife opened the box and pulled out the prototype Stinger. I couldn't do anything about the howitzers, but the MiG 21 still was a flying thorn, probably on a strafing run with its twin-barrel 23 mm machine guns, hoping to skewer us into shish-kabobs.

I crawled over to bin Laden and said, though he was probably half deaf as I was, "Want a battlefield lesson on the benefits of the upgraded Stinger FIM-92B? I'll give you guys one if we survive! And then, loudly, I went through the memorized manual of use; it requires two to operate. I made him shoulder the launcher, but I leaned over him to do all the work. And in the nick of time, we fired at the screaming MiG.

WOOSH! It was a beautiful sight to see the white trail take off and waggle before acquiring the target. Back in 1983, the Soviets had not converted all their jets and helicopters to anti-ground missile electronics. The MiG pilot probably received the incoming signal, and I saw his evasion tactic. Too late. They never did learn anything by studying air tactics from the Vietnam War, mainly since the North Vietnam SAMs weren't aimed at their allies but at us. The Russkie almost made it, but he was in too close, and the Stinger, at its rated speed of Mach 2.2, hit the plane's tail. The explosion shook him for a few seconds, he tried to save his ship, but the plane's tail fell off. I guess he ejected. Never heard. But I think the crew on the Soviet howitzer tank artillery batteries had followed the rocket action because we gained a brief silence in the bombardment. Now, the cannon commanders in charge had to start thinking they might be facing more firepower than a throwback rifle squad of British Empire sharpshooters with old Enfield rifles.

Immediately, I had to find the next target, the spotter team, whether Soviet or Afghan and had to believe they were on the higher mountain top across the valley. I finally spotted them with field glasses in a rock embattlement, several soldiers looking right back at me. This time, I had to do all the work. I had to reconfigure the directional gizmos not to seek out a heat or airframe registry but to fire the Stinger like a big bazooka. I was never a great marksman, but the projectile hit right below them, giving them a piss-in-the-pants scare and sending them running to a safer spot. This blinded their artillery for targeting, and that was enough time for us to regroup with our survivors, two of them critically wounded, and make the trek back the way we had come, back across the Pakistan border, and for me to get drunk, soaking in a tepid bath.

Bin Laden gained a good dose of education on that adventure. It wasn't until late 1986 that he came back to establish a working camp on that same mountaintop where the spotters had been located and, this time, brought along hundreds of wannabe hero martyrs. From his later battle of Jaji in 1987 to the battle of Jalalabad in 1989, he kept learning from his mistakes to establish himself as a battlefield leader, which stoked his reputation among his growing followers. To second-guess him as a tactician would be a grave error. 9/11 sadly proved the error of our leaders, discounting his concept of a world jihad. It is a very real threat today, as it was ten years ago. End of story.

"Did you ever hook up with him again," asked Hugh Fox, looking out the window, seeing the land of Pakistan reach up to meet them as they approached the airport in Islamabad.

Holmes shrugged. "Once or twice more, strictly business negotiations. He couldn't handle a Western Imperialist saving him from becoming kosher fried bacon. Definitely put me out of his Rolodex. No, after that, we went our separate ways, though, in 1991, his fledgling al-Qaeda tried to blow me up and the U.S Military Attaché in Karachi with a truck bomb. Tit for tat, in 2000, my friends sent Afghan tribal guerrillas to assassinate him, but that came to naught. But those are stories for another time, if they can be told at all." Wendell Holmes gave himself a satisfied nod in dredging up those memories, bittersweet, fading. He caught himself and glanced around at them all. Samantha wondered about the mystery of the man, while Callie did not believe his story's veracity except as a tall tale. Storm King had passed out an hour earlier and only woke up when the plane bounced and jerked unceremoniously down the runway in Islamabad.

Exiting through customs, a guide approached holding a sign 'U.N. Wildlife Federation,' their cover story, and followed him with all porter-carried luggage out to their assigned Range Rovers, *gangsta ghetto* power vehicles with darkened windows, each with an armed driver and a front seat bodyguard from an international private security company. One of the drivers asked for Samantha and handed her a note.

Her face showed disappointment.

184   S.P. Grogan

"What?" Asked Hugh, concerned.

"From the zoo director. Asked that our tour be postponed until tomorrow. 'Unavoidable conflict,' he says." Listening in, Callie gave Wendell Holmes a surreptitious glance for reaction. A sphinx.

"Tomorrow, it is. Not the end of the world. I'm sure most of us are travel weary." Hugh's cheery smile, his arm around Samantha's shoulder, edged her back to accept the delay. Her anticipation returned. She hated when someone else's schedule did not follow hers. She returned a halfway nod, yes, tomorrow would be fine, and all those around her gave reassuring smiles, except the one from Holmes. The twist of his lip bore the satisfaction that his call from Cairo, before their flight departed, to his agency station contact in Islamabad, another career man named Henry Kane, had achieved the required result. Holmes would have to think what would give him two more days of stalling before *King's Retribution* would take the drive to Abbottabad and find nothing.

Tomorrow was the 1st ... He was struck with a sudden idea as his glance fell on Colonel King (Retired), and retiring, wobbling, to his designated vehicle for the trip to their hotel. Not a bad idea, thought Holmes, easy to implement with no one the wiser.

Scene 2: Hotel mini-plots
Setting: Serena Hotel, Islamabad, May 1st, 9 a.m.

The two of them walked the stone pathway within the Jasmine Gardens of the Serena Hotel.

King's Retribution, aka the U.N. Wildlife Federation, had taken over the hotel's top floor. When Holmes had walked the corridor on his way to his meeting, he had passed the open room where Callie Cardoza, Clayton Briggs, and Bennie were unpacking their travel boxes of computer and surveillance equipment. CAM ONE was positioned in the corner, covering the scene and panning to Hiram Abbas, their special effects and disguise makeup artist, who had gone native and was parading around, modeling his mufti outfit, more Arabian desert than street Pakistani. The man would be laughed at unless the locals assumed he was an Arab foreigner. It might work. The hotel's location was in the Embassy district.

As they strolled the grounds, the CIA's station chief, Henry Kane, queried, "What's the word as you've heard it?" He was a man of middle age appearance, early fifties, prematurely graying hair, wearing black-rimmed glasses with thick bottle lenses. He was dressed in local business casual in a white short-sleeve cotton shirt with a thin black tie and carried a morning newspaper in his hand, downplaying his role as a mid-level office worker or an English-speaking manager of a telephone service center.

"I was going to ask you the same thing," responded Holmes. People walking in the garden were few, admiring the flowers, sniffing the floral aromas, or pacing quickly with the

Crimson Scimitar 185

determination to be somewhere; all looked like they belonged. To Holmes's wandering glances, nothing suspicious, though he expected a select few of the hotel staff were in the government's pay as informants.

"Something is going down," said Kane in a whisper, "the Ambassador has been notified to be on call this evening." Kane worked at the American Embassy as a passport official, his public cover. "And all essential personnel were asked to be in their offices by 7 a.m. tomorrow. Want to take a stab? You were usually pretty good at deductive assessment."

Holmes mulled over the information he had. Bits and pieces, nothing concrete.

"From what you tell me, it might be a regional operation that could have blowback. Add in that I have been brought on board to babysit some loose television stars who want to go parading around the countryside in the context of 'Ugly Americans.' Maybe these people I'm with are about to embarrass our government and destroy Arab relations. Then, maybe not." Holmes, inquisitive, pumping for information, dribbled out fake nonchalance and asked, "I assume the chatter between our field ops in country and Langley has picked up in recent weeks?"

"Well, yes, much of the incoming from along the border."

"What specific city?"

Kane showed reluctance.

"We are out of the loop for most of the satellite encrypted communication, but we get our fair share of ubiquitous questions, weather, known troop redeployments, that sort of thing. Must mean something to someone."

"What city seems to be the focus, Hank?" It was a mistake for anyone to think that all within the CIA family knew what the other office across the hall was doing. Kane had been stationed in Islamabad not because his talent was exceptional; he was a desk jockey on rotation, capable but limited, a passing agent of dispatches. Keep eyes and ears open. Holmes, the traveling nursemaid, nothing more, wanted to make his assumptions correct, to validate himself for just himself. He had this sneaky suspicion, so any info sifted might yield nuggets.

"Bilal Town, a suburb. A lot of retired military officers live in the area. We've had a surveillance team up there for the last three months. Farmed the job out to local talent, I heard."

Not what Holmes was thinking, but wait....

"Suburb? Of Islamabad?"

"No, of Abbottabad."

Bingo. Kane did not need to join a spy pact, and Holmes would keep what he knew to himself. It made him give Callie Cardoza her due on investigative results. To himself, he

186 S.P. Grogan

concluded this could be the Big Catch: the bin Laden desk had tracked down the world's number one terrorist. And here he was on the outside looking in, a mothballed dinosaur. Kane brought him back from his reverie.

"How are the stars of *King's Retribution* doing? I know they're keeping a low profile. Are they here doing some background research, a documentary? Something on the Taliban? Assume they're going over to Kandahar?" Kane did his own prying, more gushing than sleuthing.

"That's the plan, but the schedule remains to be seen. It's part junket for the troops, no big story. You know, USO-sanctioned. The main people, the trip's sponsors, are into 'save the world's wildlife' and presently are on a morning tour at your local zoo. The rest are hanging around the hotel. But perhaps," and Holmes gave his voice a serious bass tone, "maybe you can help me on two small items, no big deal."

"If it deals with *King's Retribution,* I'd be glad to help. I have Season One on CD. Would enjoy meeting Colonel King, if that can be arranged? I'm a big fan."

"Don't see why not." *How easy was this going to be*, Holmes mused. He still had the touch; he could do his spook boogie act with a clandestine zing.

They continued their walk in the garden while Holmes told the embassy staffer that he wanted to send a coded diplomatic message to Ronald Givens in Washington, a.s.a.p.

From a top-floor window of the hotel, Callie looked down on the two men. That government jockey, their official escort, Wendell Holmes, was up to no good. She just knew it.

Scene 3: Personal Issues and Betrayal
Setting: Serena Hotel, Islamabad, May 1st, 5 p.m.

Holmes savored his light early dinner, a local dish, Lahori Beef Karahi, with freshly-made wheat bread, tandoori naan. The day had brought about earned hunger as he saw his objective fall into place, awkwardly at best, nevertheless successful.

Callie, after breakfast, had been pushing everyone for an afternoon sortie to Abbottabad, about 30 kilometers distant, and with her computer equipment set up, wirelessly activated, and her data programs humming, she wanted a strategy session right after lunch before launching everyone on her Range Rover expeditionary force. Reconnoitering the terrain, she described the road trip.

Just before lunch, the first setback to her plan flew down the hotel hallway in gushing tears. Samantha Carlisle, fresh back from the trip to the Islamabad Zoo, wailed and stormed into her room, leaving Hugh in anguished pursuit. Before he rushed in to give her further comfort, and through heaving breaths, he spat out Samantha's tale of distress to the task force, who had hurried to discover the source of woeful crying.

"They had to put down a baby rhinoceros," explained Fox, "some sort of throat blockage. Sam was yelling that she had seen the same illness in a larger rhino on the Serengeti. And if they poured a soupy liquid broth down the throat, it would relax the interior muscles, and the baby would stop hyperventilating and catch a normal breath. The vet on the scene just didn't have a clue, he said it was a restricting inflammatory cancer, the rhino was in distress, and death was the easiest solution. She yelled at the doctor, 'You barbarian witch doctor!' but it did no good. After the rhino died, one of the vet assistants reached into the back of the baby's throat and pulled out a piece of plastic with a nail stuck in it. We all thought it might have come off a feed pallet. Both the vet and Sam were wrong in their diagnosis, but it was apparent the baby might have been saved with more testing. Samantha was just short of hysterical and kept yelling that she could have saved the animal. And, I think with the grant she was bringing them, they might have purchased an updated X-ray machine for larger animals and might have indeed discovered the obstruction. But it was too late."

Fox turned to Callie.

"I've got to go to her. Sorry, but we might have to postpone our logistics meeting until tomorrow morning, the trip to the town also." Fox tried to give Callie some positive words, a further excuse seeking her understanding, but at a loss, he went back into Samantha's room. They all heard her sobs before he shut them out.

"That's a bummer all around, but tomorrow's tomorrow," intoned Clayton, walking back down to their newly-established hotel conference War Room.

"At least we have more time to develop some lead concepts, maybe track down the relatives to a closer proximity," from Bennie, likewise trying to make Callie accept the change in plans. She just stood there, looking like she was running on empty fumes. She and Holmes exchanged a stare, and he walked away without seeking to make her feel better. What could he really offer?

No, he had nothing to do with the death of a baby rhinoceros, but later in the day, just for the sake of icing on the cake, Holmes accompanied Henry Kane and friends up the elevator to knock on the suite door that Storm King shortly opened.

"Some admirers of yours, Colonel," said Holmes and immediately brought the group into the television star's room.

"Indeed, a pleasure," offered Kane. When they were all inside and Holmes shut the door, the American Embassy covert agent made the introductions; of himself as just an embassy staff officer, but the other two men were media, a pool reporter from the *Associated Press* and a staff reporter for the *London Times*. And with the shaking of hands, King recognized these men as

188   S.P. Grogan

important conduits to the public who, with the right finesse, could ensure his further rise in international stardom.

To salute like-minded worldly men of action, to establish a sense of instant camaraderie, Holmes pulled two bottles of Scotch from a large grocery sack he had brought along, knowing the label was King's preferred peated cask sipping choice. No minibar to slake one's thirst; a flow of the good stuff would do the trick.

"Are you here because of your announcement to capture bin Laden?" questioned the *AP* reporter, pencil ready in hand, a man quick to the point, his trademark.

"When you capture bin Laden, will you take him to the World Court in The Hague?" inquired the *Times* man, more in tune with international protocol.

"How in *Episode 6* did you know the drug dealer was hiding with his sister-in-law?" asked Hank Kane, a stalwart fan. And King puffed up his chest, forgetting he had been warned to talk about zoo tours and not to draw attention to their real reason for being in Pakistan, and began to respond to each question.

After a while, Wendell Holmes, without being noticed, exited the hotel room. King, by tomorrow morning, would be in no shape to bounce along Pakistani roadways in search of his elusive prey that could bring him unimagined glory. Holmes now felt confident that the trip, when it occurred, would be on May 3rd, or even the 4th, just as he had been ordered. Mission accomplished.

As he sought the dining room for his victory dinner, he again glanced at the response from Ronald Givens that Kane had handed to him before they exited the elevator to King's suite.

Holmes's morning message had been brief: "K and friends desire going to A this afternoon."

Given's matching response, an implication of curtness, but unsaid: "No. Cancel trip to A. Imperative. — R. G."

Smokescreen semantics in sending his message to the Agency, just to tweak the snooty nose of Ronald Givens, give him a moment of jangled nerves, petty yes, but now more than ever, suspicions confirmed. *Abbottabad. Osama Bin Laden was there. And the American government knew it. Good for them. Even if sitting on the sidelines of probably the biggest show of the year.*

To himself, he affirmed *Wendell Holmes was still a team player.* Then, a slight wavering to his core. *Or was he? As was expected, he had betrayed trust to accomplish what he was told to do. But his employer wanted him gone. Was there any residual loyalty? And what about the attack on bin Laden?* Wendell knew the outcome. *This was not a capture, the search for public justice. Nope, this was a kill order, pure revenge for political purposes. Like what they did to Che Guevara, captured, assassinated. Perhaps King's Retribution might have a more honorable motive, but too late.*

Wendell Holmes mulled over this mental conflict during a very sumptuous dinner. After all, this was probably his last field mission; he had done his duty.

His last thought of this internal debate: *Damn, I really would like to see the show when the cavalry arrives. Maybe I could be of help on the ground if needed.* Wendell Holmes wanted to be of use, have value.

His dinner dishes cleared by the waiter, Holmes decided a celebratory tea was called for and placed his order for a Kashmiri chai, a pink, milky tea with pistachios and cardamom. As he was enjoying the relaxation a warm drink, even non-alcoholic, brought to a man's disjointed thoughts, he gazed into the hotel lobby and across to a small alcove where there was a type of Persian garden with ferns and miniature palms festooned with several ornate hanging cages of various colorful parrot species, who gave a squawk now and then. Samantha Carlisle stood alone, talking to the birds.

He did not mean to intrude into her quiet, reflective mood. Something drew him.

Inquisitive, most certainly, wondering how you talked to a classy multi-millionaire, where class might be an impediment. More to the truth, he had a heart and understood another's pain and the need for comfort.

"How are you feeling?" As lame as one could offer. He felt stupid.

She looked at him. Her eyes were still moist, sad eyes. She gave a light smile as she bravely stroked a parrot with its bobbing, darting head.

"Much better, thank you. I tend to wear my heart on my sleeve. Too sensitive when I know nature is straightforward with its random consequences." A momentary silence between them.

In a low-life Mafia voice, he said, "I can make the zoo veterinarian disappear if you wants?"

She gave him a quick stare of shock and then a releasing light laugh.

"That was a major effort on your part, thank you. You're always so serious."

"As are you underneath. You are a woman driven, as exampled by your success." He had rushed out his words and again felt foolish for it.

Samantha turned to him, regarding Wendell Holmes, finding something about him, curious since the first time he had walked into the conference room in Santa Monica. She almost wanted to say that word again, 'alluring.'

"You seem to have drawn a personal conclusion about me without much research."

"Dossiers. Psychological profiles on all of you before I stepped in. One must know the habitat before traipsing around with the wild creatures, correct?"

"You had us investigated?"

"As, I suppose, you had your people check out *King's Retribution*, and dare I even conclude, you did a background on Hugh Fox."

She did not get mad at such accusations, even the intrusion into her private world. Famous people are under the microscope, and she thought he was right, though slightly rude in his candor. Before any investment, for business or emotional commitment, nowadays, good research avoids wasting time.

"And what did your 'profile' conclude about me?"

"I'm sorry if I misled you. Others did the gathering; my specialty, I guess, is to interpret the acquired information. Make field decisions for an appropriate response."

"And?"

"And outside my traveling with you these last several days, my current visible analysis remains: you are a most attractive and intelligent woman, your dining habits are refined, you hold your fork in the proper manner, grip your wine glass by the stem, and you are outwardly, physically in good health."

She did not think with her hard exterior shell, her business brusqueness that she could color in the face, but she did, to a mild blush that she found somewhat unnerving.

"You said, and whoever you work for did psychological observations of us: what was your personal interpretation when you read my file? Am I too prone to emotional outbursts, as you saw this noon? Brittle inside?"

He found they were exchanging intent stares, her question sincere, not a sarcastic threat.

"You mean that one might interpret your human emotions of caring as a weakness? No, I do not see that. Trying to achieve in a man's world and yet still being a woman has always been the conundrum, the testing of the inner self. As I see it, a strong woman to the world is not necessarily your flaw but your challenge. Still, you do have one or two issues you wrestle with."

"Ah, now we get to it," she teased. "And I thought I was perfect."

He could only be serious and truthful, two of his own flaws. He could lie as a spy but not when sincerity was the best medicine.

"Your push for success is a good driving force, but now, this crusade to the far corners of the world to mete out what, the thrill of the chase, drama of a possible confrontation, and is the end, 'justice'? I am guessing this whole production is less for you than it is for Hugh Fox's needs.

"Like your African animal hospital, trying to save the world's defenseless animals from extinction by the ravages of mankind. I sense that your basic desire for caring, a good trait, has become an ideal that might've pushed you to the extreme of your actions. You want to be the doctor, nurse, a savior to all you focus on, man or beast. Hugh Fox or baby rhinos."

Her body stiffened, arms crossed, stern, back to the stone face. Not contempt but anger at someone probing where they should not be.

"Very perceptive, Mr. Holmes. You are suggesting I want to be 'God'? An absurdity in your conclusions. You should watch carefully where you tread."

He did feel he had stepped into sensitive quicksand and was going to apologize, then reconsidered; he had nothing to lose. He did not report to her. She was tough enough to take any crap someone could throw at her. Maybe that was it; he held this inward respect for her.

"Tell me this," he said gently against her sternness. "What one emotion, going back to your earliest youth; what one loss in your life was the most traumatic, that you did not necessarily cry out, and say I want to be 'God,' but you did want life restored, or you wanted your special happiness back like it was."

She had been edging away from him, ready to turn her back on him. She paused at his words and gave them thought. Damn, he was good.

A bittersweet expression from her.

"My first pet, a baby kitten; Snackers, I called her. One day she was in my lap; she coughed several times and died. I didn't understand death; too young. I cried for days wanting breath to come back to Snackers." He saw in her eyes the reliving of the tragedy. His heart went out to her, to retain such an impression all these years, to have it significantly mold your life force. He could understand where that part of being a 'rescuer' evolved from. She could also bear the weight; he viewed the re-transformation, saw her restore the mantle of her inner power, and watched her shoulders arch back and upright.

"It took my shrinks five years to get that out of me, Mr. Holmes, and you read a report, talked to me, and it's out in less than five minutes. I am impressed."

"As a wise old man, I have seen and lived all aspects of human nature and have a good idea of what makes some people tick."

Her look was wry, again appraising. She, too, could analyze, take a statement, and suggest other interpretations.

"You are not *that* old, Mr. Holmes." And she turned and walked away.

As Samantha Carlisle turned a corner, heading to the elevator, she literally ran into Callie. It was then she realized Callie had been watching them.

"A police spy amongst us?" she asked. "He's up to no good," Callie muttered.

192   S.P. Grogan

"Holmes?" asked Samantha.

"The same. In Cairo, he was handed a message saying, 'Delay them to May 2nd.' Then, I caught him with this embassy staffer, probably the same agency Holmes is part of, and he gave Holmes a message. I followed our 'friend' to the concierge, and he ordered a rent-a-van for later tonight. And on top of that, in checking in on Storm, I find he's already two sheets to the wind telling Hollywood lies to his Pakistani fan club. Our primary star bounty hunter will be in no shape to make any trip to Abbottabad tomorrow."

"Boy, Callie, you are good. What's up, do you think?"

"Not sure, but someone, probably Holmes's boss, whoever that is, doesn't want us out of this hotel tonight and tomorrow."

Both women smiled at a conspiracy joined.

"We follow Holmes tonight," said Samantha fiercely. Holmes had almost seemed caring, all misdirection, the bastard.

They went to find Hugh.

Scene 4: Final Confirmation
Setting: Washington D.C, May 1st, 1:22 p.m.

The Director of the CIA put the final call to the admiral, who from the very beginning was in charge and the primary creator of *Operation Neptune Spear*.

"No last-minute change on this end. You may proceed, by the President's order."

"Yes, Mr. Director. They'll be in the air in ten minutes."

"Good luck."

"Yes, sir."

Crossing the Afghan-Pakistan Border, May 1st, 11:25 pm

From the outside during the boarding process, he did think these new design helicopters, with their fancy hood wrap cowling, did sound less *pocketa pocketa* noisy, but inside, with all of them scrunched together, Pacheco felt the noise pounding down on them instead of outward, or maybe it was his nerves. His body was jostled by the constant reverberation.

The two helicopters whirled and shot through the night sky. Not up in the sky, thought Pacheco, but barely off the ground, darting down through canyons, over hillsides, scarcely a hundred feet above rocks and oblivion. He hoped the pilot's night vision systems were sharp. It was all coming together. His mind burned with intensity — what he was trained to do, what he existed for. The military in him started the mantra in his mind of each step of his sole mission, not his participation in some great historical tapestry that would be recalled in books and film — real life, a time to fight and survive.

Next to him, a fellow SEAL pissed in his pants, not from fear; Pacheco accepted that probably forgetfulness in the rush to combat prep his equipment, bodily functions were the last thing a SEAL prioritized on his check-off list; working equipment came first. The urine smell merged with the odor of grease on the oiled gun slides and black face makeup on silent and poised zombies.

An hour later, "Weapons check," came the shouted command, also blaring over the com headsets. "Hooyah!" a charged-up reply from all. Target sited. Next, in a minute, Pacheco would hear "Lock and Load" — the call back: "Hooyah!" He would sense more than feel the helicopter reducing speed; then the swoop pointed down, the gut drop to a slammed hovering.

"Hooyah!" Ready to deploy.

His helicopter crashed.

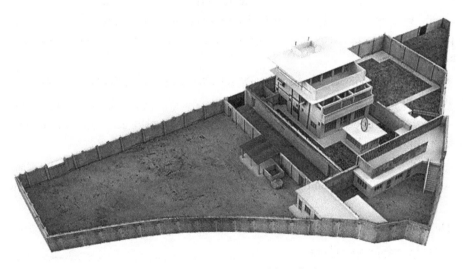

The Compound at Abbottabad

REEL FOUR — Attack and Capture

EPISODE THIRTEEN — The Attack at Abbottabad

Scene 1: A General Visit
Setting: Earlier, Serena Hotel, Islamabad, 7:30 p.m.

The knock on his door.

Before heading out on his unsanctioned scouting mission, Holmes was just finishing up checking his emails, all junk mail, nothing personal for him. A caller this late at night? Hotel staff? One of King's group? In the old days, his familiar Glock 17 would be at his side, his back to the wall as he would ask, 'Who's there?' expecting the door to be shredded with automatic weapons fire. Yes, it had happened once before, many years back, in a far and distant empire, long since vaporized by political machinations from lowly citizens wanting their voices to be heard.

He opened the door face-to-face with a Pakistani in a dark English Burberry weather coat. A military cap under his arm.

"Hello, Wendell, dear chap, it's been a long time." The voice accented pure British, a product of England's Royal Military Academy at Sandhurst.

"Brigadier Jamshed Khan. An unexpected pleasure. No, I apologize, *General* Khan. Congratulations on your appointment; what was it, two years ago, someone told me? Do come in."

He walked over to the dresser, where a bottle of Scotch sat unopened.

"May I pour you a small one?"

"No, you are most kind, dear fellow. But my driver is waiting around the block, and I can only stay a few minutes."

Holmes went back to his bottled water and sat on the edge of his bed, motioning the general to the only chair in the room, his accommodations not as opulent as the rich and famous down the hall.

"How may I be of service, as I may presume, to the future head of the Directorate of

Military Intelligence?" The cordiality was not so much an acknowledgment of a friendship of the past but that, at one time, Holmes was Khan's handler. Though he was no longer on active field service in this area of the world, he expected that Khan's current intel overseer, Hank Kane, would have maintained the special relationship that Holmes had first developed.

"Well, I must say, it is a surprise to find you back in the field. I thought they'd retired you to greener pastures. Or do they shoot old war horses?"

"It's coming, I am assured. But I am not on any covert job. Believe it or not, the State Department made the request, and I have been assigned to act as field liaison for a traveling group of television stars."

"Ah, yes, one of Mr. Kane's favorite heroes. I once watched one show of this *King's Retribution*. Found it, what would you call it, 'pre-staged artificial tripe'? So, you are not sneaking around my country, up to no good?"

"General, I am escorting wealthy people on a tour of zoos in the Middle East, with the television stars tagging along."

"Yes, I have heard that. But I just don't believe that this would be the Wendell Holmes I remember. What did the Syrians call you, "The Magic Assassin"? A man who could, by stealth, never be seen, his skill to cajole or induce others to remove thorny opposition or terrorists they might harbor. Never pulled the trigger himself. It is sad to see those days are over for someone so talented."

"I have no idea what you are talking about."

The general enjoyed the banter of old times and said so.

"Kane is not you, Wendell. Wherever the term 'foggy bottom' came from, he personifies it. This last week he has been highly agitated, totally unprofessional for the trade he represents, and those at MI seriously believe you chaps are up to something."

"Can't help you there, just a tourist." Holmes saw forehead furrows in Khan's expression.

"But assume I could help you? Like the old days?" Vagueness a part of the protocol.

The general liked to be a thief, not a beggar. This was hard for him.

"As you may recall, I have expensive tastes."

"You mean your friend Achmed?"

The general shifted uncomfortably.

"Wendell, you are so out of touch. At least Kane doesn't know, or he would have spilled the beans to you, probably make it all seem dirty. Well, as you foresaw back then, Achmed instigated a little blackmail. Sad to say, that relationship ended a year ago with an unfortunate accident. Poor Achmed. Drive-by terrorist shooting, you know. No suspects. Today, my time is quite pleasantly spent — Brian at the British Embassy, height of discretion, and the young man is quite besotted over me."

"Seeing you happy was always my selfless objective."

"Don't patronize me, Holmes. Through me, your people learned how we think and how to push the right buttons. Like, allow your drone flights over our sovereign airspace not become political flashpoints for the leftists or the imams."

Holmes put his contrite face on.

"You are quite right. You are still very important, even if others don't appreciate you. What is the issue, straight and simple?"

"Brian wants a sports car. I want to buy it for him but don't want to dip into my 'escape' fund, you know, the one you convinced me to set up, in case a change of government kicked me out, or worse, my situation became known."

"Which I have always protected."

"Yes, you have. I am still here, and God willing, still with a career future. And though it is an invisible sword you hang over my head, and the ghost of your connivance keeps me supplying tidbits to the unappreciative people like Kane and like that asshole who came through here muddling up the whole Taliban cesspool. You recall the man?"

"Indeed. Ronald Givens. Power on the brain, more ambitious than you, General. If I recall, as station chief here, he boasted at an embassy function about who the U.S. was banking on to run Afghanistan once the Taliban were defeated. His loose mouth precipitated, as you will remember, the assassination of anti-Taliban leader Ahmad Shah Massoud."

Khan joined in the reminiscence. "I believe it was September 9, 2001. Was it a coincidence it was two days before 9/11? Did he know something? An old score? Who knows? Sadly, a footnote, forgotten. And the talkative bureaucrat never punished.

Holmes had to concur. Even intelligence competitors could have mutual dislikes. "To me, Givens is the poster boy of how to stumble into war. Next to 9/11, he's the second reason we had to come to the 'rescue' of Afghanistan and commit 'surge' troops to this ten-year battle to seek 'peace in our time' stability."

"A peace you will never find. Vietnam once more, just with a new generation of armchair generals without a clue how to fight religious fanatics who fund their war with opium sales. And Afghanistan is made up of tribes with no desire to form a central government. Leave them alone. Besides, we need a neighbor where we can send all our own extremists to kill themselves."

"Thank your lucky stars; your other secret is safe with me. And only me."

Khan look perturbed at Holmes's need to bring up the unsaid.

"Why don't I just have our people remove your head?"

"Not so much, but I do keep recorded transcripts of my past fieldwork. But, for old times' sake, perhaps I can be of use to you. How much are sports cars going for these days? Any around you have your eye on?"

"We are not a backwater third-world country; we are very international. And we talk in American dollars. $25,000 will make him a slave to my desires."

"Don't your current stipends from us help?"

"A pittance these days. You've got an economic meltdown back home, so your budgets are cut. And you've so many operatives running around here, most we know about, wasteful spending; it is as if I am considered unimportant."

"Never to me, General. I will honestly see what I can do, but it may not be much."

"And perhaps I someday can do you a favor."

"In this part of the world, my power is waning. My political enemies list runs for several pages, and there are those who don't want to see me retired but rather pushed over a cliff."

At the door, they shook hands, not close friends, not adversaries, but respectful of each other's professionalism. Then, as he pulled up the collar on his coat to ensure the medals and insignia on his uniform were well concealed, the general had one final question, "You are sure you aren't up to something? Just before you got here, your Embassy started acting like a closet full of howler monkeys, and when I heard you were around, I said to myself, 'Holmes is back, and there will be a bloody mess, something the Directorate will have to clean up."

"I am up to nothing," affirmed Holmes, the truth within a lie. Some things never would change. When the general had departed, Holmes did his usual maudlin reminiscences, recalling the value that then-Colonel Jamshed Khan had brought into the Agency, a protected source.

Holmes was the only contact and protector of the soldier's secrets. Holmes would take those to his grave, shocking truths that gave him sway over Khan, leverage, to be a productive snitch. In a Muslim country and a high-ranking military man to boot, prison would be unhealthy for the general if anyone discovered his proclivities toward beautiful young men. Worse, it would be summary execution on the spot, on any public street in broad daylight, if anyone found out that General Jamshed Khan of Pakistan's Army Military Intelligence was secretly a devout member of the Church of England.

Holmes prepared for his night foray. Going to his closet, he grabbed his heavy parka against a chilly night. His suitcase lay on his bed, and he did his clandestine trickery, removing the suitcase's insides and packing a few 'toys' into his backpack after emptying it of his hardback and audiobooks, his old fashion writing material, his scribblings.

198   S.P. Grogan

Prepared, he went in search of his rent-a-van. At this moment, Holmes had concluded that something was happening in Abbottabad; he was sure of it, tonight, perhaps. And he wanted to be there, tired of being the traveling nanny for the rich and famous, feeling an inside ache to be back in the middle...of anything.

In retrospect, it would come as no surprise to hear from General Khan again, with the military man yelling at him through the telephone receiver when Holmes answered from his hotel room at 5:15 a.m. in the ugly morning hours of Monday, May 2nd, 2011. Holmes, not necessarily regretting it, found himself up to his neck in self-inflicted shit.

Scene 2: The Last Day
Setting: Abbottabad, May 2nd, 12:55 a.m.

After a day filled with positive snippets of activities, visiting with nearly everyone important in the compound, though not the women and children, of course, Khalaf settled on his mattress to read the English novel he had brought back from his last courier run. British-Irish author John le Carré's most recent thriller, *The Constant Gardener*.

Earlier in the morning, he had surprised bin Laden's son, Khalid, with an illustrated travel guide on France, three years out of date, but accepted with excitement by the young man, who immediately went off into a corner and started flipping through the colorful pages. "This year," said Khalid, "with approval from my father, I will accompany you on a mission, and when successful, we shall visit Paris as one of our return stops." Khalaf agreed and said he would look forward to also seeing Paris, although he found the city pretentious and over-priced and too 'Cathedral Catholic' for his tastes.

Khalaf spent the afternoon exchanging gossip with the brothers, Ibrahim and Abrar. The two men were not in the inner circle, as was Khalaf, knowing only the general concept of *Crimson Scimitar*, so the time was spent in animated discussion, perusing headlines in the Pakistani newspapers and wondering if certain suicide bomb attacks reported were the work of an al-Qaeda cell or merely Islamic sects with their own agendas against the central government.

On the other main subject, all three men felt the Afghanistan war proceeded favorably as a religious war should, with perseverance and patience. The Americans would leave soon. "They tire too easily of long wars when faced with enemies they cannot see," said Ibrahim, "besides, the Zionists control the government and want the American's foreign aid spent on them against our Hamas comrades."

The conversation ended with each discussing their next trip out of the compound. Khalaf knew that the brothers would be going in separate directions to deliver bin Laden's latest long-paged missives, one to al-Rahman; another would be the important directive announcing the creation of the 'peace' delegation to the United States upon the success of *Crimson Scimitar.*

Abrar would go out the day after tomorrow, his assignment, as usual, to visit the internet coffee shop and receive the incoming news via email.

The sanctioned al-Qaeda website alone received nearly 10,000 hits per day, seeking the latest spiritual tomes from their leaders, the Sheik, bin Laden, and the Doctor, al Zawahiri. The brother, Ibrahim, had a more dangerous trek, going into the disputed tribal lands of North Waziristan to seek out Atiyah Abd al Rahman, also known as Atiyah Allah, the al-Qaeda regional commander in that district and, as Khalaf knew, a long-time favorite of bin Laden's. Atiyah, by this new decree still in draft form, was to send his delegate representative Khalaf to America, as was another planned appointee from Yemen by the Supreme Council of al-Qaeda, expected to be the choice of Anwar al-Awlaki. Khalaf did not like the idea that the American al-Awlaki would impose his will into the negotiations with the U.S. He hoped, by planting seeds with bin Laden, the delegate selected would not be Shahin once he returned from his victory in the U.S. If and when that occurred, Khalaf would be overshadowed. He could not openly complain to bin Laden, as his position was tenuous until he demonstrated his implacable leadership in assisting in bartering peace terms against the Great Satan.

His day ended upbeat and blessed as he was asked to have a meal with bin Laden, served by his leader's wife, Amal. She beamed and made shy eyes at Khalaf. He knew the reason. A week before, she had been allowed to leave the compound with another woman, Abrar's wife, Bushra, to travel and visit Amal's sister, who had arrived from Yemen. After several airport delays and bus breakdowns, the women met finally at one of the town's more well-kept hotels, a luxury for Amal to enjoy before returning to the strict conditions of the compound. Khalaf had heard the reunion had been joyous and tearful, and when bin Laden mentioned it, Khalaf could see Amal's happiness. If only the world allowed Sunni family unity to rule, not governments, there would certainly be peace.

"I will finish the documents tomorrow," said bin Laden as the evening's last pot of tea emptied, signaling the close of the meal and the conversations. "That will create for you the position of one of our 'Delegates-at-Large,' perhaps the Secretary of the Proceedings. You will show those documents to whomever to establish your presence, and all will be required to give you immediate support to contact the Americans, but again only when *Crimson Scimitar* has been executed. Abrar brought news from the Scientist. Because of the meltdown at the nuclear reactors in Japan last month, the Americans are moving up their timetable. We shall act when they do and do so decisively but only by my command. Understood?"

"Yes, Caliph."

"I am putting the final brushstrokes on canvas for our masterpiece. *Crimson Scimitar* will set the name of the caliphate in history, so when they think of jihad, *Crimson Scimitar* will be the name that comes to mind, and our followers will shout it strong as they rush into battle. Khalaf knew bin Laden had been working late hours recently with his daughter Sumayya, who acted as proofreader to his messy script, and she, though young, was educated and had found a talent in organizing and editing many of the rambling revolutionary prose.

"It is late. Go and rest, my son. Tomorrow, we will go over the paperwork for your mission. Besides…" but he did not finish the sentence as he looked at Amal, his fifth wife, putting away linens on the other side of the room, and he gave a rare, mischievous smile.

Khalaf accepted this as a silent dismissal and, reverently bowing several times, backed his way from the room. Even great men must have a release from the pressures of leadership.

As he departed, bin Laden's and third wife Siham's daughter, eighteen-year-old Sumayya, entered carrying a sheaf of papers with penciled notations. Another internet speech finalized for posting? Perhaps announcing his delegate credentials?

On retiring for the night, Khalaf's bedroom was not a bedroom but a hidden closet on the second floor, which the occupants used mostly for media production. His cubbyhole was in a wall cut-out behind a desk, which he had to crawl under to access. A thin mattress jammed the limited floor space, and a bookshelf ran up one wall, filled with books and magazines. Not a library for all others in the compound to use, but his own restricted research materials for al-Qaeda business. This fake closet, when shut, disappeared into the wall as a hidden access, one of two in the compound. The other hiding spot, identical but on the first floor, held the weapons and ammunition. And then, unknown to almost all in the compound, including Khalaf, there was the false door near the rear of the house that seemed to lead nowhere but held the entrance to the small cellar, which went twenty feet under the back wall to an outside trapdoor exit beyond the compound wall in what looked like an assorted trash pile.

Within his own cramped space and from all his reading off the shelves, his ideas, when conveyed to bin Laden over the period of a year and a half, had been used in the most surprising fashion. And it was this help to bin Laden which brought the Courier Khalaf to the attention of the al-Qaeda leader, seeing in the young Egyptian a noble future within the organization.

Such heady thoughts kept Khalaf awake well past midnight, his breathing the only noise he could hear, for all residents of the compound were at rest. Lying on his mattress under a dangling light bulb on a wire cord, throwing off a dull glow, his English book lay on his chest unread for the last half hour, his mind racing to all the benefits and glory which soon will fall to him.

He must rest, and be prepared, so he put the book aside, reached up, and clicked off the illumination into engulfing darkness. He even slid the closet door somewhat closed for better privacy.

Silence.

No, a noise. Humming on the wind. Closer, louder.

He sat up and listened hard. Louder, a whizzing-ratcheting buzz.

Helicopters! Now approaching; here, now!

12:58 AM Nearby, in the early morning hours, S — A — , an IT employee working from his Abbottabad home, tweeted:

Helicopter hovering above Abbottabad at 1 AM (is rare event)

1:05 AM Tweet S — A —

Go away helicopter — before I take out my giant swatter :-/

1:09 AM Tweet S — A —

A huge window shaking bang here in Abbottabad. I hope it's not the start of something nasty: — S

Scene 3: Hunting the Hunter, homing in on Holmes
Setting: Abbottabad, a half-hour earlier

"What's he doing?" Callie asked Samantha, as the driver, stared into the darkness, the SUV pacing Hugh Fox ahead in an identical rental Range Rover.

"Hugh is still on his trail," said Samatha, looking ahead at the vehicle in front of them that carried Fox, Clayton, and CAM ONE. The ladies had Abbas in the back seat of their vehicle, who had been gabbing away with inane trivia of his life. It had been a two-hour drive, almost 139 kilometers from their hotel to the outskirts of Abbottabad.

"Holmes seems to be just driving around," Callie expressed growing disappointment. "He doesn't have a fixed destination. Maybe a bad source? This might be just a shitbag of nothing."

Samantha shrugged, understanding. "I might have pegged him wrong. He might just be doing recon for our trip up here in the next day or so."

"Not at 1 am. Just doesn't feel right about this guy." Callie's opinion.

They continued driving. Callie had to believe Wendell Holmes, being a spook, active or semi-retired, but on assignment, had to know by now he was being followed and wondering what not-so-smart people were doing playing at amateur shadowing.

202   S.P. Grogan

Suddenly, two black objects shot perpendicular across their vision, no more than 150 feet above their vehicles.

"Shit!" yelled Samantha, and probably meant it.

Seeing Fox's SUV accelerating and suddenly lurching to the right meant that Holmes, in the lead, had arrived at a conclusion about their destination and charged off in that direction, bouncing down a rutted farm road.

"What's going on?" shrilled Abbas, trying to hold on as the vehicle bumped and swerved.

Callie was speeding to keep up. "Holmes and his damn stories. I bet we just fell into one of them."

For a moment, they were hounds in the fox chase, then Callie shouted, "Roll down your window!" as she did hers. Three windows lowered, accepting dust from the vehicles ahead.

"Hear that?"

"What?" The vehicles slowed. Everyone in all three cars listening.

"Helicopters. I can barely hear them, but I hear them."

Both their rental SUVs edged forward more cautiously. Hugh, up ahead, turned off his headlights, they did the same, and then he stopped. Crazy as they were to begin with, everyone got out and looked into the darkness at a three-story house, seemingly white stucco in the night and encased by a surrounding wall, the whitewash hazed with a swirling cloud of dust.

They could see two helicopters had landed, blades whirling, the rotary dust obscuring, both aircraft positioned on two sides of the compound, the farthest one from them tilted at a strange angle.

Clayton and CAM ONE joined Callie, Samatha, and Abbas.

Where's Hugh?" Samantha worried.

"He went forward to confront, curse something at Holmes," said Clayton. When Samantha moved in that direction, he grabbed her arm none too gently.

"Mr. Fox made it plain I would be terminated on the spot and left here tonight if you go anywhere in that direction."

Samantha began her own curse but accepted whatever was going on up ahead was not just risky but probably deadly. She folded her arms in a huff. They all congregated without words, an audience, witnesses to events they could not witness.

Scene 4: Something's wrong!
Setting: The Compound, city of Abbottabad, 12:57 a.m.

Pacheco feels the helicopter start to oscillate, shaking them with a whipsaw effect, throwing a few of the SEALS into each other. Only a few of the rappelling ropes for descent have been thrown out when Pacheco hears the grinding noise crunch — he hears the helicopter tail shear off as it hits the concrete wall within the compound.

The pilot must have executed a hard landing because that's what comes next — a jaw-slamming hit. There is no time to wonder what happened. The lead elements are already out as the helicopter leans at an odd angle.

The firing begins — chatter from Heckler & Koch 416 carbines with attached suppressors.

Pacheco's line of sight, surreal green with the night vision goggles, catches a glimpse of the other helicopter hovering above, sniper SEALS covering the compound floor area. He does not need to blow the main gate; they're already within the house grounds. He scampers behind two running SEALS, heading towards the house wall, his secondary objective. Headset talk snipes with action commands. "Hostile Target." Another voice: "Acquired." From a small house, a man appears with an automatic rifle but is blown backward, his dying trigger finger arching up a stream of bullets into the dark sky. "Hostile Down." A flashbang goes off in the small hovel. No time.

Pacheco and the two SEALS pass through a gate and another gate. They are in front of the building at the base of the triangular compound. Three other SEALS are rushing behind them. He knows who they are: the Kill Team, find and eliminate. A man and woman appear at the building's front entrance. "Target." Both civilians are armed, one with an AK-47 machine gun, so they are the enemy. Pacheco, with the explosive satchel, has moved to the left to reach the side of the building. He barely hears the *phiffi-phiffi-phiffi* of automatic rifle fire. The man at the door fires back, narrowly missing Pacheco before he is hit. The woman standing behind him screams, and she, too, falls, her chest stitched and splotching with a dark mass against a white night garment.

He's at the wall. The plastic explosive charge placed. The three of them move quickly away, flush against the building near the back wall. "Whoosh!" The loud detonation shakes the ground, and before the dust clears, the Kill Team enters from the front; Pacheco's two SEALS enter through the blown hole. Pacheco scurries to the other wall and through the gate into what seems to be the garden area, nearly running into a cow as scared as he is, the animal desperately trying to pull its stake rope from the ground.

Pacheco runs along the wall, against the building, covering as instructed, only carrying a sidearm, his pack of remaining explosives still heavy on his back, and he moves out of sight of the downed helicopter. He can hear but can't see the covering helicopter and does not know where it landed. They must have given up on rappelling onto the roof and set down outside the compound. He quickly looks to the garden gate and sees no SEALS entering. Everyone must be on the west side of the compound. Has their covering sniper gained position? Gunfire reverberates coming from the building, which draws his attention, and as he is turning towards the sound, prepared, about ready to say in his comset, 'East side Secure' he senses something in his peripheral vision and glances up. He is hit full in the chest.

Scene 5: Chaos
Setting: The Compound

Helicopters! Above the building!

Khalaf jumps to his feet and, by instinct, closes his closet door behind him. He is naked except for black boxer shorts. He starts for the stairs, anxious to get to the weapons downstairs. Khalid is running up the stairs. He holds two Russian PP2000 submachine guns, one he hands to Khalaf. "It's an assault. I must protect Father!" He rushes up to the third floor before Khalaf can ask the all-important question: from which Army? It cannot be Pakistani; they have an understanding, an accommodation with certain military officers to keep them informed of such a raid as this. Americans! SEALS! Army Rangers!

Khalaf hears gunfire, from the sky, from the compound grounds, and starts toward the stairs, raising the machine gun into firing position. What of his future? Of his glory? To end like this, dead, ignominious, in his underwear.

Bin Laden's son rushes back down the stairs. His father close behind him, a pistol in hand, deep seriousness etched on his face, saying nothing, no battle cry. At the bottom of the stairs, they quickly separate, with Khalid returning to the uncertain courier.

"My father says he will hide in a special place. He has an escape route! He says you must escape over the wall. Launch *Crimson Scimitar*! This is his command. Here are the orders." Two USB thumb drive sticks for computers are thrust into Khalaf's hands. "Go now. I will guard the stairs and the compound for both of you!" He runs down the stairs out into the night, into battle. Brave young soldier.

Turning to make his escape, he has limited options. Why did bin Laden not ask him to follow? Should he follow his leader anyway? He is confused for a moment. No, in their practice, he had never been chosen to go with the Caliph. Ibrahim and Abrar would protect him. An explosion brightens the night. The noise of muffled gunfire comes to his ears. The courtyard is breached! For a moment, he freezes.

Suddenly unseen bullets ricochet into the stairwell. He makes up his mind. To go downstairs is now death.

The window is his only exit from this floor, too small, like a large mailbox opening but his only chance. He pushes it open, wriggling, scraping his chest as he edges out. He puts the two data sticks into each side of his mouth but can't pull the PP2000 with him and get out the window simultaneously. He throws it to the grounds outside, but it hits the wall and bounces back inside the compound. A glorious death behind him, no, a lost opportunity? He is willing to fight his way out, killing these infidel soldiers as he flees. Not now. Survival dominates his fear.

Barely clothed, cold, and now unarmed. If he jumps even the one story down, he is certain he will break or sprain a leg and be killed or captured, but there is a small ledge around the building, some architectural detail he is standing on. He glances back in the window just as he sees Khalid running back up the stairs, to see bullets tear through Khalid like a rag doll. Two helmeted-type spacemen, brown-black camouflage, alien in night goggles, all carrying automatic rifles, advance upward, stepping over the dying Khalid. Two seconds of thought, *the boy will never see Paris.*

Khalaf, on the narrow outside ledge, eases the window back into place, hoping they do not look in this direction. Above him, a large helicopter, all black, no insignia, descends into the field on the far side, away from him. They are being overrun. He looks to his left and right and sees that one helicopter has crash-landed into the main yard, and is leaning against the wall, while another helicopter sits, blades still rotating, outside the compound. He glances at the troops inside and outside the wall, all moving in quick coordination; several are pushing the women and children into the yard, all of them with their hands tied. He hears the curses and screams of the women, the children wailing. Barbarians, damn them!

Khalaf, crouching low, moves in the opposite direction, edging himself around the wall, an aerial artist on a thin strip of concrete ledge no more than a foot wide. He is now out of sight of all the soldiers as he turns the corner on the building's ledge. No choice, and he must take the chance. Jump from the building's side to the lower wall, quickly jump into the garden, and flee. He inhales a breath of courage.

Taking the first leap, his feet land on the top of the wall, awkwardly balancing and feeling a sharp pain. He feels a cut on his foot. He can't reset, can't regain his balance. *I'm falling.* His forward momentum flings him out, his arms flailing, and he lands with a thud on something that breaks his fall. He has landed on top of a soldier who will now kill him.

SEAL Shawn Pacheco gasps for the wind that was knocked out of him. Dazed, his pistol is knocked from his hand, but he senses a man rolling off him. Trained reaction causes him to roll back on the man and go for his knife. The man, he sees is without clothes. The half-naked man grabs at his knife arm as the blade clears the scabbard. Pacheco yanks his hand back to

206 S.P. Grogan

stab/slice, but the terrorist head-butts him, making him see stars, and he feels a bite to his arm, causing him to jerk, and the knife changes hands. The man stabs it into Pacheco's chest — and Pacheco knows he is seconds from death.

Khalaf stabs again, but his face registers shock that the knife bounces off for a second time. *What?* Of course, a Kevlar vest. Then, he is kicked in the groin with such force that he falls back as a deep pain racks him.

"Cairo! Cairo!" The soldier shouts. Khalaf is surprised. *Why is he yelling my country's city? Cairo?* It is code, calling for more soldiers. He cannot forget bin Laden's command: escape. *Launch Crimson Scimitar.* He hovers over the soldier for a second, spits the UBS sticks into his hands, and yells back at the prone man, "Khalaf! Remember my name, infidel. Khalaf!"

The knife will not help him now; he flings it aside and runs to the gate. He does not open it, fearing an ambush. *They will be waiting outside to shoot me.* He scrambles onto a barrel and hoists himself up to the tin roof of the stable in the corner, glances over, no one there, darkness before him, and back at the soldier who's rising to his feet. Khalaf rolls himself over the wall, landing on all fours on the ground outside the compound, away from the carnage and the death left behind. The Americans have probably massacred all the women and children — no witnesses to their barbarism. Khalaf hopes bin Laden has made his way to his hiding space. It is the first he's heard about this; why was he never told? He glances in that direction, where he guesses some hidden route might lead to the outside, but all he sees are forms in the darkness; he can't see who. More soldiers? They will find his leader. *Let us pray if they have taken bin Laden prisoner al-Qaeda can launch attacks to capture hostages as bargaining chips in a ransom.* Khalaf is thinking such distressing thoughts as he runs low, hobbling in his stride, his left foot painful with the deep cut. He runs through the open fields, escaping, praying he will not be seen.

What? Tourists are here? Gawkers. They are not Arabs. Two women, Western women. He runs past two vehicles. And hears an English voice shout in surprise. "What the hell?!"

He runs into the blackness. He prays for life, for his destiny.

His prayers would be answered. He could not know that the men in the nearby house, the observers, the Watchers, who knew him as the Gardener over many months, had vacated for good their premises only an hour earlier. And he did not know the 'tourists' he ran past would not even report their presence, let alone a fleeing unrecognizable specter.

No one shot at him. He ran past other curious who stood in their doorways or stared from behind windows. No one opened their doors to him; no one gave him shelter.

Pacheco scrambled to his knees and stared at the empty part of the compound. He had looked into the terrorist's face with his night vision view, and then when the goggle mask was pulled from his face in the tussling struggle — he smelled bad garlic breath. He would never forget the terrorist's face, as streaks of lights from the helicopters, from flash bangs illuminated the night in spurts of brilliance. The man had turned and ran as Pacheco went looking for his lost pistol, angry at himself, growling that he had been disarmed in a fluke attack, had been stabbed with his own knife, and the perpetrator escaping over the wall before he could respond. With his headset back on, the com's chatter returned, and he was surprised; the static talk was in the mode of operational clean-up. Two SEALS came running into the garden area and signaled to him.

"Anything of value?" Meaning intelligence, weapons.

"No." He hesitated, started to tell them what happened, but then saw how they would view his story, so he blurted out, "I thought I saw someone go over the wall, in the corner."

They looked and saw nothing, and one of the SEALS grinned.

"Shit."

"Yeah."

"No, I mean shit, you smell like cow shit."

You gotta be kidding, Pacheco inhaled. It was all over his knees. He stank.

Over the com came his name, "Pacheco, back to Razor One."

He headed back the way he came, the two soldiers doing a scan of the garden, seeing nothing, followed behind.

Back in the main compound, ordered chaos reigned. Pacheco saw the main gate open for the first time and another helicopter squatting near the stealth Black Hawk. An Army Ranger stood in the open copter door, manning a heavy machine gun as the SEALS took orders from two 'intelligence gatherers' and loaded the larger helicopter with black garbage bags of 'stuff,' computers, an armload of weapons. Over in one corner, a SEAL leaned over one of the dead terrorists, inking his hand for fingerprints, while another snapped photographs of the face, then turned and shot stills of the compound. About twenty children and four women huddled in a corner, guarded by the two SEAL designated guards; an interpreter trying to communicate with the women, but the children screamed, and a feisty woman shouted at them all in a language he did not understand, the tone definitely curses he would guess. He hustled by the dog and handler, both on alert, and griped aloud at the dog, "Cairo, where were you when I needed you?"

Brief direction from his Team Leader, "We have to blow the chopper. You set it, use additional ordinance from Razor Two."

Running over to the downed copter, he found the pilot bagging up documents from the cabin while the co-pilot pounded on the instrument panel with a tool wrench.

"Don't worry," yelled Pacheco, "I'll make a hot fire." And he started to unpack his C-4.

The pilot kept excusing the crash. "It was a vortex ring, stopped my rotor wash from diffusing, not a malfunction. Couldn't know, couldn't be helped."

Pacheco ignored him and focused on his job, and when he finished the last of the explosives, having to string contact attach wire to more explosives on the outside of the helicopter, he looked around to find himself nearly alone, and for the moment, thought he had been abandoned, left for his failure to fight an enemy and prevail. He shook the fear as he saw two SEALS herding the prisoners towards the building, away from the coming explosion.

Those two ran back to gather him up, and the three of them sprinted to the lone helicopter, overloaded with SEALS from both helicopters. The black ops helicopter had disappeared. Shawn had never heard it take off yet knew that the chopper would be far noisier than the stealth copter he was about to blow. Spooks are spooky.

He stood on the ground, turned, and, with the electronic detonator, set off the charge, and watched the night sky become a fiery day of flame. Well, thank God, he did something right. He did not realize he was the last American to exit the battle scene. He flung himself into the open door of the Black Hawk. The helicopter fled balls out towards Afghan air space.

Pacheco heard the Team Leader shout into a radio: "Geronimo not here. I repeat, Geronimo escaped. Shall we stay and pursue?"

Team Leader cursed the far distant angry response and shouted his last operational command order of the night:

"Let's get the fuck out of here!"

1:44 AM Tweet S — A —

All silent after the blast, but a friend heard it 6 km away too…the helicopter is gone too…seems like my giant swatter worked!

Of *Operation Neptune Spear*, in action on the ground, no more than 45 minutes between touchdown to liftoff.

But from that night into morning, May 2nd, 2011, what Pacheco found burned into his soul: an Arab man's angry face lit by night explosions, the man shouting at him a threat, a challenge: 'Calif or Caliph.' Something strange like that. And worse, as a SEAL, he had not effectively responded, and coupled with his recall of Montoya's not-meant-to-be death, from that time on, a disease of self-doubt about his adequacy began eating away inside him.

Scene 6: Protocol
Setting: Washington, D.C., May 2nd, 6 p.m. Pakistan, 3 a.m.

The Chairman of the Joint Chiefs of Staff put a call in to Pakistan's army chief.

"Sir, I am sorry to disturb you, but I must inform you that the President of the United States asked me to contact you. At this moment, the President has also placed a call to President Zardari to inform him of recent events. I am to report to you that the United States conducted tonight a military operation against terrorists around the city of Abbottabad."

The phone line held silent for a few seconds before the Pakistani military man commented.

"I was earlier awakened and informed. We scrambled jets to intercept your incursion."

Another silence. "But our aircraft arrived late to the scene. I am getting conflicting stories of a firefight and a drone plane shot down. I assume it was Taliban terrorists you targeted and not Pakistan nationals?"

"They were not Pakistan nationals," said the American four-star Admiral.

"And did your operation succeed?"

Lengthy silence from the Situation Room in the White House as a throat cleared.

"Strategically and tactically, the results could have been better. It is my personal opinion that both our countries may receive blowback, criticism, and protest." No need to say more.

The Chairman could hear voices on the other line, in the background, all talking at once, several phones ringing and being answered. "Admiral, I appreciate your formal courtesy, and I shall relay such communication to our people. You certainly are aware that we will object strenuously to your violation of our country's sovereign borders."

"I will be happy to let the State Department discuss the proper responses our governments might craft to maintain our need for mutual alliances. Good night, General."

The Commander-in-Chief of Pakistan's army looked to the distraught room full of high-ranking officers summoned from their slumbers or late-night clubs. Ramifications, that's all he could think of.

However we might spin the story, the Pakistani general considered, *the fact remains that the world's number one terrorist hid near a military town under our noses. It was a slap in the face to the government, to the military, to our intelligence network, who either knew or was totally and negligently ignorant. And if they knew, they should have hustled that man out of our country.*

One of his subordinates, among those in the room, asked the question they all harbored.

"Did they capture or kill bin Laden?"

The head Pakistani general mulled that for a moment.

210   S.P. Grogan

"My American counterpart strangely did not seem gleeful. Nor did he crow of their ridding the world of their Number One target." The general grimaced, knowing that al-Qaeda killed more Moslems than Christians. Personally, he would be glad if bin Laden met his doom. A political thorn of agitation removed.

The Army general turned to the country's acting head of military intelligence and vented the frustration of having no answers and, yelling at everyone in earshot, demanding a full investigation of this early morning 'attack' or heads would roll if he did not have the right answers.

The Pakistani intelligence officer, a general himself, though lower ranking within the Service, agreed aloud to a country-wide mobilization of all their controlled apparatus to gain answers and clarification immediately. This meant harsh responses to gain uncertain information.

He agreed with his Army superior about the absence of facts, saying, "Indeed, there is an air of bafflement." General Khan said the last in a stilted English brogue. He would soon pick up the telephone to call the one man he could, in turn, shout at and feel a whole lot better. And put to Wendell Holmes the troubling questions:

Where was Osama bin Laden? Captured or Dead?"

Scene 7: Unexpected Gift
Setting: Abbottabad, outside the Compound, earlier, 1:45 am

Just as the last helicopter lifted, visible momentarily in the glow from the burning sister ship below, then fading into the dark, Hugh Fox caught up to Wendell Holmes, who had walked from his van to be closer to the compound, but not too close. Showing no surprise, Holmes glanced at Fox's approach but reacted by turning his view back to the house and the pyre of military equipment.

The neighborhood, now awake, ventured outside their homes in various moods: wonderment, nervousness, upset, fearful, but all realized something momentous had occurred.

"Is this what I think happened?" Fox did not yell at Holmes for sneaking off, and Holmes did not complain about King's Retribution following him, unimportant to bigger issues.

"The U.S. military attacked this place and probably got Osama bin Laden," Holmes said almost wistfully.

"Got? As in captured?"

"EKIA. Enemy Killed In Action. This was never a capture mission. Unlike your high ideals of rightful justice, the U.S. government cannot handle 'messy political high drama,' scrutiny from the media, and especially the possibility of years wading through the American judicial system. Neat and tidy was accomplished tonight. I hope we had no causalities unlike *Operation Eagle Claw* [the attempted rescue of U.S. embassy captives in 1980]."

Feigning nonchalance, they acted like two Americans standing in a field, conversing as friends, successful in their own vocations, bearing skills where a crisis was assessed and dealt with as if they were watching the sun set or the end of a fireworks display. Ignoring for the moment that they were in a dangerous foreign country in the process of exploding.

Fox did not like setbacks. "With our primary actor off the world stage, I guess we will have to re-assess this whole trip. Our ol' boy Stormy [meaning King] won't like a hit to his reputation when I cancel this bounty hunter grab. I will have to reconsider this whole trial setup. My 'Trial of the Century' won't hold the same pizzazz. Let's see what Plan B looks like, audition the actors, hold a few rehearsals. See if I can salvage maybe a two-hour special of a mock trial."

"Sorry, but true. I assume a cold corpse does not bring ad revenues to the bottom line?"

"I guess I should go commiserate with our Team," said Fox, turning. "Wait, what's that?"

Both men looked to the house, against the outside back wall, to a pile of brush and trash moving, up and down, as if there was a wind. There wasn't. A pile of debris pushed aside.

Looking around, seeing no one in close proximity, Wendell walked carefully towards the movement, seeing some sort of door pushed up and to the side. A figure climbed up and out, cautious.

"Hello, Osama."

The escapee from the night's turmoil turned suddenly, and the CIA agent popped him, a hard fist to the chin.

Fox ran up to see Holmes standing over an unconscious man, face down, obscured.

Wendell, rubbing his knuckles, said, "Mr. Fox, one international fugitive delivered to *King's Retribution*, as you planned."

Fox stared for a long moment, abruptly shaken awake within a Homeric epic, a quandary before his eyes, that he, as Odysseus, will return to Ithaca, not beggar, not hero, but again a lost soul seeking purpose. Somewhat like actor Robert Redford's Bill McKay, victorious at the movie end in *The Candidate*. Blank-faced, Hugh turned to the action man who threw the punch.

"What do we do now?"

212   S.P. Grogan

EPISODE FOURTEEN — The Prisoner

Scene 1: What do we do now?
Setting: The Compound, 2 a.m.

My God, he thought, we've captured Osama bin Laden!

The smile from Holmes somehow brightened the Pakistani darkness. He shook his head in wonderment at the young man who had, until one minute ago, been playing cops-and-robbers, or more so Captain Avenger versus the Terrorist Head Honcho. Smart, yes, but not astute enough to yet learn that 'unexpected actions might have provoked at-risk consequences.'

"Hugh, could you grab my backpack from the van?"

Fox, out of his daze, dealing with what had just occurred and to whom, regained his wits and reacted not as the wealthy executive used to being the boss but ran, excited, like a pupil running an errand to please a professor. Holmes meanwhile put the escape trapdoor back in place and threw brush, and assorted trash, back over it. As he worked, Wendell said, "It will be our secret, Osama," to himself and to the quiet form on the ground.

Who knows if it might come in handy again?

The following circumstances were somewhat strange yet acceptable. Holmes's van made a U-turn and came up to the small waiting crowd of onlookers.

Fox spoke from the van, throwing keys to their security man.

"Clayton, you take our SUV and follow us. Samantha, Callie, follow him, and let's head back to the hotel. Show's over for tonight, and we don't want to be here when the police, military, and the world appear."

Samantha was worried. Instead of asking what had just happened, instead, she showed concern.

"Are you two okay?" Her look went to both Hugh and, then, included a glance at Holmes, who nodded to her but said nothing.

From the van window, Hugh gave her a smile more on the wry side, still trying to be comforting, but his expression came off as fidgety and stressed, something Samantha had rarely, no, never had seen before in his demeanor. The van moved off, seeking the highway and back to Islamabad and the sanctuary of the hotel.

They all departed, their vehicles not speeding, spread out to avoid looking like a suspicious convoy. Questions remained unspoken among the occupants: mainly, what had the U.S. military achieved with their attack on this unassuming house?

From the two in the first van, the contents of Holmes's backpack had done the trick. Plastic ties for hands and feet, a sedative shot, a porous black bag for the head, and a thin black plastic type of drop cloth as a covering in case they hit a roadblock checkpoint. Hugh Fox did not want to imagine what else a plastic tarp might be used for or to dispose of what.

At this point in time, early morning, May 2nd, the world remained ignorant. Only the CEO and President of Skilleo Games Technology, way out of his depth, and a CIA agent that no one in his shop wanted around, only they knew.

Collectively, the *King's Retribution* television show had captured the most wanted man on the face of the earth. Indeed, what came next? Calling a script conference seemed ridiculous in light of the magnitude of the event.

Scene 2: General Upset
Setting: Serena Hotel, Islamabad, 5:30 a.m.

"You bastard!"

"General Khan, good morning to you." After a long night and two hours of sleep, Holmes awoke to the shrill ring of the phone and shook his head of cobwebs. Not good news, he presumed, and he was right.

"Where is he? Did those elite killers cart his body off?"

"Who?"

"Don't play the Big Game with me. You are here; you must be involved."

"Wait. Slow down. Who, what are you talking about?"

"Osama Bin Laden. He's captured, dead, or fled and is in hiding. Some clown rodeo by your commandos landing on his roof. Killed all the grown men in the compound. One woman too. I have seen the bodies. And you knew this, Holmes."

"Jan, that's untrue. I knew nothing. Know nothing."

"I don't believe that, and it's General Khan. I have already dispatched a group of my men to keep you and your so-called 'zoo travelers' in your hotel until I decide what to do with you 'spies.'

"But you say they killed bin Laden?"

"If they caught him, he's dead. Even I know, through my sources, that any attack would be a 'kill-on-sight' order."

That bit of news of what bin Laden faced by a SEAL capture confirmed his previous similar statement to Fox, who had gone to bed, mumbling uncertainty about future choices. Holmes eased upright on the edge of his bed, fully cognizant of what was going to come down on his

214   S.P. Grogan

people, those under his protection. A crisis was at hand. He could easily see organized mobs sacking the hotel and the American Embassy, killing them all. *Think straight, man.*

"Okay, General, here is what my assignment was, God's and Allah's only truth. I was instructed by my government to keep the *King's Retribution* cavalry from going in-country until the 3rd of May. And now I can see why the delaying tactics. But General, I had no operational details. Do you think this new Administration is going to let me, an old-schooler, into the full plan? Please consider."

He could almost hear the brain wheel grinding gears through the phone. When the voice came back, the old calmness of the man he knew had returned. The rashness was gone from his voice, replaced with exhaustion.

"What you said is just so preposterous I actually can see the truth. It would be like your government to do something right for a change and yet farm out one of its best assets to latrine detail. You were being punished, laughed at behind your back, by your own people."

Holmes did not like that assessment of his assignment but could agree the general hit the mark.

"And we will not be arrested?"

"That remains to be seen…maybe…No, no, but you are all to remain in the hotel for your own protection. The office of our president has informed me your government will be issuing a public statement to the world in an hour or so. Bragging rights, but I can tell you, Holmes, the natives here will be quite restless. And our government is definitely upset."

"You think the hammer will come down on you?" Holmes understood where Khan's priorities lay — to his own personal needs and safety.

"The entire Military Intelligence apparatus will be under scrutiny from the world for letting bin Laden hide in our country, incensed at the U.S. actions whatever they did, with the radicals believing at this moment your military is torturing a beloved revolutionary. For the next month or so, this office will not be pleasant to work in. On edge, wondering if any of us might be arrested by our own ISI and disappear."

"General, you need to do something glorious for the cause to take advantage of the situation."

"You think like I do, Holmes. Adversity is opportunity. I have suggested suspending NATO supply shipments into Afghanistan, but that will take time to wind its way through the bureaucracy."

Holmes had no urge to argue in favor of America's continued need of Pakistan roads to fight the Taliban. He needed the good graces of the general, specifically to get his tour group safely out of the country with their 'package.'

Crimson Scimitar

"If I can think of anything for your benefit, can I get back to you?"

General Khan was not mollified yet understood the need to keep doors open. "Use our old code; come to me as Canadian press. Ask for an interview which I will reject, but will return the call."

"Sounds good."

"Holmes, bin Laden missing and presumed assassinated is not an advantage for me...yet. Think of something. At this moment, you do need my protection. Your life, in fact, might depend on it." And he disconnected, leaving the threat, serious and sarcastic, hanging in the air.

Holmes rose, went to use the bathroom, checking on the drugged 'prisoner' in the bathtub. He did not need the splashed cold water on his face to realize the danger he and everyone he was shepherding around faced. Any spur-of-the-moment reaction could be undone with an unannounced room-to-room search. He glanced out the window. A military truck was stationed outside the hotel, the troops not alert, merely loitering, the news on bin Laden not yet public, but General Khan's action made Holmes accept that the world today had turned very dangerous. And Holmes had to use his smarts to act quickly.

He heard moaning coming from the bathtub. He could only do one thing. He ordered room service. *Did Osama have any dietary needs, food allergies? Hadn't he heard bin Laden might have kidney stones?*

Scene 3: Negotiating an Exit
Setting: Serena Hotel, Islamabad, May 2nd, 6:30 a.m.

"Hank Kane." Over the phone, the CIA's embassy rep's voice brittle, out-of-sorts.

"And you were going to tell me when?" Holmes decided his own hurt façade would work well; act needy.

"Holmes, I knew little. Some agency people showed up last night, and we were closeted with the ambassador the whole night. I don't know the whole story, bits and pieces. We are out of the loop. Plausible deniability, I guess."

"Hank, I need to call in favors, old times' sake or whatever. You kept Colonel King from driving up to Abbottabad yesterday, considering what came down. They will probably give you an inner-agency medal if I spin it right in my report. But right now, I got to get these folks out of Dodge City before the crazies take to the street."

"You think it's going to be that bad?"

216   S.P. Grogan

"I expect some Washington announcement, beginning this morning, our time. What will be said, I haven't a clue. The aftermath will be ramped-up *Yankee-Go-Home* propaganda by the locals."

Kane responded, guarding his own position. "I don't know what I can do to help; the ambassador has us all getting ready to tell U.S. citizens to stay inside, something I think you should have your group act upon."

"Hank, I need exit visas immediately. All the paperwork approved, the airport called to clear our two aircraft, all the right palms greased. I don't need an Islamic baggage inspector going through all the camera equipment, believing they were part of the operation. What did they call it anyway?"

"*Operation Neptune Spear*. Dammit, Holmes, I wasn't supposed to blurt that out."

"Sorry, an old habit. But do tell me, was this *Neptune Spear* as successful as General Khan said?"

"Khan! Are you talking to that asshole?"

"Who do you think is threatening me with a dingy dungeon?"

"Just like him. Probably asked for a 'fee' to let you out of the country? That man would sell his grandmother for a bag of silver."

"Or a sports car."

"What?"

"Never mind; did the operation achieve its goals?"

"From the scuttlebutt circulating in the air, almost total success. I don't know what that means, but I hear the agency on the scene scooped up a trove of documents, videos, some of his speeches yet to be broadcasted. A year of analysis, and I bet, with this intel, we bag a few more al-Qaeda high-up muckety-mucks before the year is up."

"You said almost successful? What went wrong? Any of our boys killed?"

"No, they all got home safely.

"Great. So they got their guy."

"You know, I don't know, actually. Right hand dumb to left hand gibberish. This morning staff here seems to be working on getting access to bin Laden's residence. Seems there was some helicopter malfunction. It is a new model, some secret design that keeps noise down. The U.S. military is already screaming at us to make overtures to Zardari's government to get all the non-destroyed parts back. I heard the silent technology was up in the blades, and that survived. Our ambassador said he would make the call but in a few days. Pakistanis probably don't know what they got."

I wouldn't count on that, thought Holmes. The Pakistan military will be all over the attack site, collecting evidence, processing the area like a crime scene, preparing themselves to arrest someone, even the innocent. Holmes had to play the obsessed fan card.

"Hank, I bet if you were to expedite King getting out of the country, I bet he could reciprocate, maybe even find a bit part for you in one of the shows."

"You're kidding?"

"Hey, we've gotten close. I know he was impressed by meeting a real in-the-field agent. Get him to the airport and out of here, and he will owe you."

"Okay, but we got to wait out today; too much crap hitting the fan. Day after tomorrow is the best I can promise."

"That will have to do. Stay safe, Hank."

"You too, Wendell."

Scene 4: Tribal Jogging
Setting: Streets of Islamabad, May 2nd, 6:00 a.m.

As if there could be warning undercurrents in the air, Callie felt them blow across her face and picked up her jogging pace. She would not make the usual five miles today and turned herself around back towards the hotel. She could see the changing atmosphere for each block she covered — military trucks bearing armed soldiers as they raced down streets and started taking up positions at major intersections.

Callie had started her run 30 minutes early, hoping to take side streets and avoid the morning traffic. To be seen as demure or less Western in dress, she wore a makeshift variation of a shalwar kameez, a traditional dress for both men and women, basically a pantsuit, wide at the top, narrow at the ankle, and then over that, a long shirt or tunic. Instead of the tunic, she felt she could get by with an extra-large USC sweatshirt, her alma mater. Most logo shirts she had seen in the Arab world bore colorful branding and trademarks, from Gucci to Batman to The Terminator. To round off her ensemble, she hid her hair under a ball cap and thought herself totally devoid of femininity, though she did pick up several catcalls as she passed groups of men opening their shops and putting out merchandise. She sought to avoid this attention, but if the Islamic Fashionista Police tried to accost her, speed would leave them in the dust.

This increase in military presence gave her wonder. A coup in the making? Was this something that *King's Retribution* should be filming as background? She saw heightened tension in the faces of the citizens as she ran past them. Something's up, but last night's attack, if that's what it was, no, there couldn't be a reaction this quickly. Or could there? With that thought, she came around to thinking about Storm King with mixed feelings. She expressed relief he had not been along for the 'adventure.' He would have botched it up for sure. It was in this frame of mind she accepted that their relationship was at an end. She had no regrets, in fact, and she took it as her fault. Terminating her dependency on him should have occurred months ago.

She knew he knew. He had made no move on her since the trip began, and they exchanged coolness, not hatred, merely non-interest. All that had been the passion of the bed seemed an empty voyage, now being replaced with a caution about the man. Storm leaned more for the attention of the bottle. He seemed enamored with his own star-quality charms. In Cairo, she witnessed him in the hotel bar slobbering over two lady flight attendants who first found the star intriguing, accepted his mild pawing as part of the conversation, but later eased away from him as he began to slur his words. The disintegration leading to this break-up made no impact on his increased drinking. No, that was a constant. She guessed, and it was a good guess, that he found himself unable to match the hero status his television persona had to radiate weekly. Storm King perhaps was hitting the wall of his artistic limitations. Unfortunately, instead of overcoming such deficiencies and rising above, back to the star pedestal and fans he had grown accustomed to, he found solace in the liquor glass, which seemed to be leading him spiraling down a road where no heroes should travel. Callie was worried that an intervention might be required to carry the show through a new season.

Callie saw the hotel up ahead. Suddenly, from a side street, three young men started chasing after her, forcing her to sprint toward safety. Quickly, she outran two of what she assumed were attackers, only to glance over her shoulder to find the third boy gaining on her.

Who was this kid, Pakistani Olympic track and field? Ahead she saw the hotel entrance and saw the troops in front. What goes on? Could she get in? Would they stop her, roughly frisk her?

A tomato sailed past her. The guy was a lousy shot. Abruptly, she stopped. Bring it on, punk; if tomatoes were all he had as a weapon, she'd bust him bad.

The kid was laughing, pointing at her, then to his own shirt, and then ran off, back the way he had come.

His logoed red shirt: *Stanford*. And she was *USC*. Tribal rivals were a universal fabric of humanity.

After that, she thought everything else of the morning would be anticlimactic, and with her head held high, she walked past the ogling soldiers into the hotel lobby.

A message at the front desk. "Executive Meeting. Holmes Room 9 am sharp."

Scene 4: The Announcement
Setting: Serena Hotel, Islamabad, May 2nd, 8:25 a.m.

Callie hurried along the hotel corridor on the way to a quick shower to make this pop-up meeting and was surprised to find the entire contingent in the suite they had designated as their central headquarters and caught off guard to see a pleasing welcome smile from Hugh Fox, even a smile from Wendell Holmes, who busied himself fiddling with the room's television, changing channels.

"What are you all doing here? And does anyone know what's going on outside?" CAM ONE was at the window, camera pointing down on more troop trucks moving along the roadways. Two jets flashed at the horizon, their rumbled shrieks trailing seconds behind, there and gone.

"Here, quiet everyone. I think I got it," said Holmes, turning the sound up and stepping to the side.

On the screen appeared not the President of the United States but his Secretary of Defense, braced on one side by the Head of Homeland Security, and to the other side, the Chairman of the Joint Chiefs of Staff.

The Defense Secretary read a prepared statement:

Pakistan, 8:30 am May 2nd
Washington, D.C., 11:30 pm May 1st

"Good evening. Tonight, I can report that the United States has conducted an operation against the leadership of al-Qaeda, the terrorist group that's responsible for the murder of thousands of innocent men, women, and children.

"The raid which took place within Pakistan, and having the full cooperation of the Pakistani Government [not true] was coordinated and conducted by several branches of our military and achieved certain priorities including a substantial seizure of key documents and computers which will assist in our continued efforts to defeat this evil foe. I can also report that we believe that the terrorist, Osama bin Laden, had until recently been living at the residence where the raid was targeted. Intelligence suggests he had left the building shortly before our strike team's arrival and remains at large. He can continue to run, but he is not safe. The reward for his capture of US$25 million is still active."

The Head of Homeland Security stepped to the podium.

"I would like to read a statement from the President of the United States:

220   S.P. Grogan

'It was nearly ten years ago that a bright September day was darkened by the worst attack on the American people in our history. The images of Nine-Eleven are seared into our national memory — hijacked planes cutting through a cloudless September sky; the Twin Towers collapsing to the ground; black smoke billowing up from the Pentagon; the wreckage of Flight 93 in Shanksville, Pennsylvania, where the actions of heroic citizens saved even more heartbreak and destruction.

"And yet we know that the worst images are those that were unseen to the world — the empty seat at the dinner table; children who were forced to grow up without their mother or their father; parents who would never know the feeling of their child's embrace. Nearly 3,000 citizens were taken from us, leaving a gaping hole in our hearts. There's no doubt that al Qaeda will continue to pursue attacks against us. We must, and we will remain vigilant at home and abroad. And we shall not rest until all perpetrators of this tragedy are brought to justice and face the American people in our fair and transparent court system." The Secretary stepped aside to make way for the military's voice, the four-star admiral representing the Chairman of the Joint Chiefs of Staff:

"I can report to you that all soldiers and sailors involved in this action returned unharmed. Tomorrow, at the Defense Department, we will hold a further briefing on this successful mission. Tonight, since it is late, we will not be taking questions but will make ourselves available, as I said, tomorrow morning. Thank you, and God bless our brave military, and God bless America."

The television volume turned down before the talking head pundits began random guessing.

"Shit," said Storm King, dropping himself on a couch. "I gave an interview to the Associated Press saying how I was here to bring in bin Laden."

"You did what?" Callie had heard Hugh and Samantha's admonition that they must maintain the secrecy of their presence, or Samantha might lose creditability to her zoo visits, and what if they did not find anything worth televising? Her eyes cut into King.

"Hey, he got away; we still have a chance. Just have to dig up new clues." King realized what a pathetic excuse he had just offered.

Callie turned to Bennie.

"Check the computer for any online stories on our 'star.'" The last word said in derision.

Clayton Briggs shrugged his shoulders. "Does this screw up what we are doing here in the first place?"

"Probably," agreed Abbas, pulling off the jacket to his colorful outfit. "I guess we have no new information on finding bin Laden. And everyone," his look to King was not kind, "will

Crimson Scimitar 221

believe we were part of the military showing up. The local populace will think we were a diversion, culpable. We need to scram and fast."

Fox absorbed the news, compartmentalized the issues, and arrived at the main priority.

"I agree our first step is to get us all home safely."

"I put an earlier call into the American Embassy," said Holmes. "To start the paperwork."

Callie turned on him. "You knew what our reaction had to be before this press briefing?"

"Yes." Nothing more.

"And how did you know? And did you actually know several days ago? It works out swell for whoever you represent that we didn't get to Abbottabad any earlier. We just might have succeeded. Was this planned so we didn't get in the way of our U.S. military swooping in?"

He deflected. "How would you see the public reacting this morning to this U.S. incursion, invading their homeland? I am pretty sure the Pakistan government was not informed."

"I don't see how you can accuse Mr. Holmes of interference," Fox came to the rescue as if the secretive man needed rescuing. "I see nothing he did to slow down our progress. We are victims of fate, pure and simple. We did get up there, and CAM ONE got some great night videos, probably an exclusive."

Callie blustered, pointing to Holmes. "He's…he's devious."

They all heard the sound, indescribable, like an approaching flood, a noise building from a background to a rush of jumbled human voices, shouts, chants.

There was a rush to the suite's windows.

Marching down the street below them, sidewalk to sidewalk, were thousands of angry Pakistanis; the flow of the human tide passed the hotel and continued down the street. Not large numbers but enough to constitute a mob.

"They're probably marching on the U.S. Embassy," said Samantha, guessing their destination, likewise deflated, confused at what had happened to their crusade. What was going to become of their project?

"No stories out this morning on *King's Retribution*," said Bennie, looking up from the computer. "But al Qaeda on Al Jazeera just released a statement saying that" — and he read off the screen — "American troops invaded Pakistan and have kidnapped Osama bin Laden."

"Shit!" came a few voices in the room.

Bennie now chimed in, totally depressed.

"You realize this makes *King's Retribution* total fools. We will be the laughingstock of the industry. We will be pilloried for being outsmarted by our own government."

Clayton, downcast, joined in, "On the way back, I'm going to be working on my resume."

Fox, as Samantha noted, bore a grin, some trait of lopsided childish optimism. "Cheer up, everyone. Let me think our way back to being the Number One show on all entertainment platforms."

Callie, at the window, watched the angry crowds of clinched fists, yelling slogans, disappearing out of her sight. "These protestors already have well-printed signs denouncing the U.S."

"There will be a run on American flags at the stores for burning," said Clayton. King gave him a dirty grumble.

"The government, I am guessing," offered Holmes. "They must have had a few hours' notice to call out their hired mobs. Control the mob, and you avoid anarchy. I will be more worried when the fundamentalists who support the Taliban and al Qaeda take to the streets. I suggest that today everyone stay inside and just watch TV or video movies. I'll work on the visas."

"Call the American Embassy, and say there are hysterical American women having breakdowns who must flee back to their therapists." This from Samantha gained a pursed smile from Holmes.

Holmes used her weak over-dramatization as an excuse to exit.

"Let me call them again and take their temperature on what we can and can't do."

Hugh went over to Callie and whispered that the 9 am meeting was still on and on a 'need-to-know' basis. She then saw him with an aside, probably conveying the same message to Samantha. Interestingly, he said nothing to the show's star, Storm King.

Scene 6: Getting the Boot
Setting: Moments later, the hotel

From his room, it took Holmes five minutes and several re-dials before Henry Kane answered his cell phone. In the background, Holmes could hear glass break and the loud buzz of swarming wasps — human wasps.

"Opening champagne in celebration?" teased Holmes with his question, knowing the mobs had arrived at Kane's place of work.

"We're being bombarded with rocks." Kane was definitely worried. This was not in his job description. "The staff marines are on the roof, and the place is locked down."

"I know you're busy, but just to let you know, my tour group *does* want to leave. Today, if any way possible, tomorrow is a must. So, if you can prioritize, I would appreciate it."

"Paperwork is somewhere on my desk. If they don't set the place on fire, I'll get it going.

Crimson Scimitar

"By the way, another wire came for you."

"Oh, really? Can you fax it over to the hotel? Don't think you or I taking a stroll will be healthy."

"It's an "Eyes Only" transmission."

"Go get it and read it to me."

Silence from Kane.

"Don't think that's a good idea."

"Means you read it. No secrets between us, Kane. It's probably sitting right in front of you."

Silence.

"Well, yes. Okay, Wendell, here it is, and I am sorry, truly sorry."

'Attention: W. Holmes services no longer required. Retirement contract clause invoked. Report to Home Office Personnel for standard employment separation procedures.'

Brutal but not unexpected to Holmes; just a lousy bedside manner of notification.

"Bet it is signed or confirmed by the initials. R.G."

"Again, sorry, Wendell. He really wanted you to know how the pecking order was; he signed it: *R. Givens.*"

"Hank, what's my real status? The termination paperwork for this forced retirement can't move that quickly. He's mean with a long memory, but this can't be pure vendetta. I did my little dirty job to their satisfaction; they're pushing me out because I'm a bureaucratic afterthought in this *Operation Neptune Spear.* Dare I call it a fiasco?"

Kane spoke, reading: "'*Immediate Termination. Revoke Pakistan visa. 24 hours to leave country. Oversee personally. R.G.*' That was my message."

"And you are doing *what?*"

"You get what you want. Like a good employee, I will do my job and kick you out. But right now, I'm watching thugs climb our fences and be beaten back by the Pakistani police. I think R.G. and the Personnel Department at Langley can cut me some slack."

"Thanks, Hank. I will leave peacefully, but I need all my people to exit safely with me."

"All I can do. But tomorrow, if I'm still here." Another sound of breaking glass. The call ended.

Wendell Holmes knew fervently he had served his country well. For the good ol' U.S. of A., his body had taken a few bullets (literally, one still in there), he'd been beaten up several times, even thrown into the sea a long way from shore, a lot of good stories to look back on. Yes, it was time to leave. The writing was on the wall or, rather, messaged to him. But not like this. Not with a bang but a whimper. And this was not forced retirement; this was being cashiered out like he had committed some grave offense, had been a traitor to the cause, all because of one man's desire for petty retribution that could be hidden within bureaucratic channels.

He handled the closed bottle of Scotch. Looked at it, avoided opening the cap to inhale the enticing bad memory-laced fumes. After a long minute of temptation, he put the bottle down and found ginger ale in the minibar. Cold bubbles on his throat. One good point to all this; he had prepared for such an eventuality. He did not leave the Agency tied to a pension as his only income source to pay the basic utilities. In truth, Wendell Holmes was well off, no, be factual, not in the Fox and Carlisle category to achieve the *Forbes* list but enough to buy, if he so chose, a good-sized fishing boat and sail the world; a ski chalet perhaps; or even purchase a business to keep his mind sharp. You don't work for twenty-five plus years in the hot spots of the world, seeing political fortunes change hands, laundered money moving quickly from unnamed source to unnamed source; even money haphazardly discarded when palaces were overrun. His hidden and padded bank accounts gave him such a comfort level.

His real issue, as it had been months ago, was, what does a retired government intelligence officer, a field operative, do to keep the adrenalin flowing? He had no idea. No absorbing hobbies except for occasional stress-relief creative writing, with many discarded short stories to show for it. No love life except brief relationships with women passing through his assignments. One-nighters had lost their appeal. And sitting on the dock of the bay and fishing wasn't him.

The street surges would be growing with those violently aggrieved, who saw a 'kidnapped' Islamic warrior as a hero, shouts of volunteers willing to die, strap on bomb vests. Instead of his uneasy inner turmoil, Wendell Holmes shifted into General Khan's way of seeing such events: Adversity creates opportunity.

First things first, Holmes went to the bathroom for a talk.

Scene 7: Bathroom Surprise
Setting: The Serena Hotel, Islamabad

The knock on his door was at precisely 9 am, and he opened it to let in the newly designated 'Executive Committee' of Hugh Fox, Samantha Carlisle, and Callie Cardoza.

"How do we get out of this country fucking alive?" Callie's opinion.

"Did you have any luck with the American Embassy?" Samantha focused on what was possible. She smiled at someone who knew how to get results, so she hoped.

"Under siege, but they're working on it."

Fox asked carefully, "And what about that other 'thing?' Isn't it about time we dealt with the 800 lb guerrilla in the room?"

Callie sniped bad humor, 'Talk about me, and I'll kick you so hard you'll sing soprano."

That broke the tension. Samantha sat on the bed. Callie took a chair.

"What's up, gentlemen?" Since last night, early this morning, when Hugh had dropped exhausted into bed without so much as a good night kiss, Samantha reasoned that any rebuff of her negligee's charm and his sudden hanging with Holmes meant this new bonding had raised her bullshit meter. Holmes openly admired her for her astuteness.

"As I see it, regardless of what you might think of me," he glanced to Callie and then Samantha, "I believe we are the core group to making a winner out of this entire enterprise of Hugh's and Samantha's undertaking, the investment in Five Aces Studioz, support of *King's Retribution*, and this recent globe-trotting quest. Egos, not put aside, but tucked in a safe place, the four of us, are the most brilliant and deductive reasoning traveling think tank, which together could think us out of any dilemma.

"And, let me add, you might not yet trust me, but recent events have terminated my past loyalties. Take it as you might, but I am, what one might call, a 'free agent,' my future is my own choice, and I am presently willing to join your cause. And, whereas in the past, I may have been a skeptic, I do now see a future for *King's Retribution*. With humility, I am a convert to the unimaginable and unexpected."

"Quite a speech, especially your sudden conversion, and any help at this moment is appreciated," smiled Samantha. Callie added, "Get us out of here, and I'll forget all the nasty things I've said."

Fox was eager to face a strange reality. "That brings us back to the 800 lb. guerrilla and our combined four brains, correct?"

"Correct. Ladies, let me show you something." Holmes walked over to his bathroom door and opened it.

Osama bin Laden sat on the toilet seat, chained to the sink, a tray in front of him, calmly eating toast and, as Samantha Carlisle noted, calmly, with a free hand spreading strawberry preserves from a small bottle of Wilkin & Sons. He looked up at the open-mouthed faces from the doorway and ignored Callie's 'Holy Fuck! Mother of Christ,' spoken in Spanish. The Caliph of the future al Qaeda Empire gave them a curt nod and resumed eating and reading on his lap what seemed to Hugh Fox was the local morning Urdu newspaper, folded at the crease.

Holmes said to his restrained 'guest,' "Excuse us." And moved them back into the hotel room and shut the bathroom door.

Samantha began hitting at Hugh, more slaps than fist damage, then, for good measure, hit Wendell on the shoulder several times.

"Why didn't you tell me, tell Callie and me, last night? You…you both are…."

Fox held up his hands, begging for forgiveness. "For your own good. Protecting you both. And all of them down the hall."

Wendell came to the rescue, trying to placate them.

"He sort of sprung out of the ground into my van last night. Until he was ensconced here without trouble, who knew what might have happened, who might have caused disruption? The less you knew, the better chance a ruthless torturer would accept your story version of innocence," a pause, "or then he might not care."

That sobering explanation brought the room to silence.

"What Wendell, what we, the four of us, should be discussing and putting into perspective is, what is the next step for *King's Retribution*." Fox looked to Callie. "We caught the bad guy. What do you want to do? Somehow turn him over to the U.S. authorities? Maybe the military attaché at the Embassy?"

There was a long pause. The two women of the Executive Committee realized that they had never given a thought about what to do if they were successful. Finally, Callie put it succinctly.

"You're kidding," she snapped, amazed that such an action was even contemplated. "As Senor Holmes said, I am sure the SEAL strategy last night meant dispatching our 'prisoner' here with 'extreme prejudice.' I could kill in the line of duty, but I'm not a stone-cold killing executioner. And I have no idea, but *Dios mio,* he has to answer for what he did." She firmed her shoulders and crossed her arms defiantly as if to say that was that.

"She's right," agreed Samantha, returning to sit on the bed, letting the rush ebb back to decision-making. "Even if we made a public display of turning him over to the authorities on the steps of the U.S. Capitol or wherever for the cameras, you know the government's track record. They would drop him in the black hole of Guantanamo, and any 'fair trial' would be ten years out, if at all."

Fox made a decision. "We can't turn him over to the government, at least not here in Pakistan. It would be suicide for us, and, yes, I agree, if the U.S. Government gets its hands on him, bin Laden will probably be 'disappeared forever.' First things first. We get him out of the country, back to the U.S. Then, second, let me hear all your thoughts in the next few days, but I will take care of it and keep the risk minimal for you all. I will activate my personal resources."

Crimson Scimitar

"Why, just you, in charge?" Samantha's question a private feeling that a portion of their 'we' relationship was being modified.

Hugh, with a smile of understanding. "If we get our 'prisoner' out of here, I agree, he belongs to *King's Retribution*, and we follow through with creating some sort of judicial action. Like a trial. But the handling of all of it, and I mean the coordination, I believe, should rest on my shoulders, and I'll pick up the cost. *King's Retribution* will get full credit. This was my original idea, and I want to move the risk and any negative blowback from you all."

Samantha studied her lover. Though always the consummate gentleman when it came to their relationship, she noted a slight shifting, a separation, 'my risk' vs. 'our risk.' On the surface, it seemed he was only thinking of their safety, but was that all? Not now, but she would give this a heart-felt analysis to a deeper meaning here, but later, when they were back home.

Callie had doubts about Hugh's suggestion. "The minute we land on American soil, if we don't hand him over to the Feds, we will be in some deep legal shit."

"Whatever I do, I promise there will be in the mix a solid written agreement with the government to provide all of us a safe exit, a 'stay out of jail card' from any liability and gain blanket immunity."

Fox sought to seal the decision. "I have the financial resources and gobs of legal eagles to fight the system. It's for the best, Sam, Callie." Silence, for now was not the time to express opinions. Departure was the utmost requirement. Hugh looked to Wendell. "And what has our 'state prisoner' have to say? Does he know what's going on?"

Wendell had been silent within himself, laughing at three VIPs playing high-stakes poker, not knowing the rules. He replied to Mr. Fox, his new boss/client, he presumed.

"Per your direction, I told him he would face American justice. I got one of his two laughs this morning. He says we will never get him out of Islamabad. His supporters will be searching for him everywhere. Turn him loose; he'll forgive and forget."

"You said," asked Samantha, her mood recovering, seeing a challenge, several challenges to overcome, "You said he laughed twice in your talk. What was the 'other' that seemed so funny to him?"

"That it was *King's Retribution* who caught him."

They all smiled at each other, almost embarrassed as they were drawn, by this event, becoming suddenly closer, at least more dependent on each other.

"I hate to interrupt such a moment of a short-term victory," added Holmes. "But he did say something that gave me concern."

"And it is?" Callie prompted him, but more good-naturedly.

228 S.P. Grogan

"He said it might be too late for him, that his life is now set for martyrdom, but the United States will have to face the '*Crimson Scimitar*.'"

"He speaks English?" Fox had not thought of how they might communicate with bin Laden.

"Yeah, but he hides it for the global façade of being all Arab. From my knowing him and my dossier reading, he speaks fluent Arabic, his native tongue, then Pashto from his time in Afghanistan, Urdu from his stays in Pakistan, and some Persian because it's similar to both Urdu and Arabic. His English comes from his training as a civil engineer, and I heard he once took an immersion class in England. Been there twice, in fact." They looked at him. "Hey, I once read his intra-agency dossier." Samantha knew he would have and accepted the man knew things.

"But what is this '*Crimson Scimitar*'? You think it is something serious?"

"Who knows? The lion, cornered and caged, might spit out falsehoods to worry and misdirect us. Or there might be an operational plan moving from his drawing board to launch. I mean, since 2001, there really has not been an attack that has been equal in creativity and magnitude to 9/ll."

Samantha understood their prisoner had changed everything.

"This '*Crimson Scimitar*' would be a new dimension. Scary."

Wendell had been mulling possibilities. "I have to agree. At the right time, I will have to notify U.S. intelligence, my past bosses."

Samantha, "Whatever they did to you, will they have confidence in what you tell them?"

"Probably not, but I will work on a way so they will listen." Surprised by what she heard, Samantha also believed his remark, suddenly realizing she believed in him.

Holmes was not finished. "I must emphasize that I think I will have to be the person who goes and finds such information, if such a *Crimson Scimitar* plot exists. I need some evidence that they will have to listen to. The only place where there might be possible scraps of information is lying around back in Abbottabad. Tonight, I will have to find a way to search bin Laden's house."

The three Executive members of the Team of the High Council said, in one fashion or another.

"Not without us." Callie pointed her finger at him.

"It's too risky, said Holmes, careful not to say it was because they were women. He was old school, but he knew better.

Crimson Scimitar   229

"You have become part of *King's Retribution*. All for one and all that crap." Callie, in a forgiving mood, smiled at Hugh, Samantha smiled at Wendell, then Callie and Samantha gave their mantra, 'If a plot exists, it is still part of the *King's Retribution* story to deliver.'"

Asked Samantha, "But how do we pull it off? The country is a lit fuse on a powder keg."

"Okay, okay, if you want to do stupid things. You're not 'secret agents,' but I have an idea to keep all you bumblers safe. I have to make a telephone call. You three think of ways to get our 'guest' out of the country. And why don't you three peek in on our fellow traveler and give him some comfort level that we're not part of a Hollywood hit squad sent by Oprah Winfrey?"

Holmes left. As the remaining three began strategizing, Samantha just had to peek into the bathroom and reaffirm her eyes to believe. Osama bin Laden was still there, still sitting on the toilet, yet now using the facilities. Samantha accepted the fact that their prisoner was human after all. Past actions definitely questionable, but by the smell, a very human being sat on a porcelain throne.

EPISODE FIFTEEN — Tragic Adventures and Escapes

Scene 1: Bargain with the Devil
Setting: The Serena Hotel, Islamabad, Pakistan

Holmes made the call from the lobby.

He had been surprised at how it had all come together, almost like planning a road trip to a vacation spot back home. His first call that morning had been to General Khan, dialing in as a Canadian newspaper accredited newsman seeking an interview on the bin Laden raid. Sorry, but no interviews, said the military clerk. Minutes later, the return call.

Seeking to defuse any latent anger, Holmes moved quickly to set the tone.

"Sports car still that expensive? I might have a willing buyer?" Vagueness in case telephone calls were being monitored, believing a full-blown finger-pointing investigation was or would soon be underway.

The general took the hint and likewise expected prying ears.

"Yes. Now, it should be more costly, just because of circumstances. But the sticker price remains the same. What are the specifications?"

"I have a group of friends who would like to see the garage where you were this morning. Spanish and French journalists and other car enthusiasts."

230   S.P. Grogan

Khan balked, and for good reason.

"No, that would be impossible. I am in charge and do have access, but...."

"I might be able to help you out as we earlier talked, make you the hero beyond my buyer paying for the car."

"I am listening."

"I hear you have an old wreck up there, some vehicle that went flying into a wall. Can we have that?"

"Certainly not, and that comes from even higher sources."

"That's okay, I understand. What if I bring you another buyer, only to look at the condition, take a few photos, and get back to their bosses, who might up the purchase price with your bosses?"

"Mr. Holmes, you do sound like a Canadian used car salesman, not a journalist. And what are you asking, to have these other friends of yours, just look and see? Are they from your same news organization?"

"No, my ties with that news service have been cut as of today. These buyers are from the Beijing newspaper syndicate. Very motivated buyers."

"Oh, I see. That is intriguing."

"I see two prices here to quote; the first is a look-see, and I equate that to half the price you and I are settling on for the sports car purchase, and on the second value, you hook their bosses up with your bosses, and you take the glory for any sale. Your bosses can play one buyer against the other. New foreign subsidies, like that."

Silence, and then General Khan responded.

"Yes, I think the car could be acquired for that pricing. But a first look only." And, sounding even more obtuse, like two mobsters knowing the FBI was bugging the phones, worked out the details of the trip to Abbottabad.

"I will be there tonight, as I believe you Canadian car people say, 'watch that you kick the tires properly.' And Wendell, I am sorry to hear you are going to be unemployed. I am sure you would be welcome to stay and enjoy our hospitality."

Holmes begged off the invitation, not taking the schmoozing as sincere.

Next, he sought out Hugh Fox and, pulling him aside, pleasantly asked.

"I require U.S. $60,000 cash as soon as possible."

"Geez, is it going to cost us that much to bribe our way out of the country?"

"A little sprinkled everywhere. When I have the funds and work out the details, you will be the first to know, and it will be you only who will have to decide if my plan has merit. And this is between you and me, not your other fellow travelers. Yet, I think you will approve."

Hugh Fox had earlier taken the measurement of this on-loan government representative. Thinking 'intelligence agent' or 'spy' might be correct, but Fox saw more, viewed the character to the standards he sought himself. Holmes spoke only when he had something to say, and when he did, the comment was well thought out and succinct. When silent, the man must always be thinking, analyzing all scenarios, a puzzle worker like Hugh himself, and in that, he found genuine admiration.

"Okay," said Fox with an accepting shrug, the way people of confidence have in making a decision and having faith in the person, who, in turn, must have strong self-assuredness in the outcome.

Scene 2: A Fateful Decision
Setting: The Serena Hotel, Islamabad, 3 p.m.

The local news outlets throughout the morning reported, with their updates, that 'reliable sources' verified that the U.S. military had spirited Osma bin Laden out of the country to an unnamed location. One Pakistani talking head said he presumed it would be Germany where the CIA had black operations, specializing in non-Hague Court interrogation techniques. One guest spokesperson, the Taliban representative in Islamabad, stated, after a few minutes of impassioned ranting, that his organization was prepared to join with their al Qaeda and Pakistani brothers to launch attacks to save Osama bin Laden and gain his release. Such continuing news, in one hyperbole or another, *ad nauseum*, reached out to an enraged audience. It was apparent that whether bin Laden was dead or in captivity did not matter; it was the message of revenge, no real concern for the man's health that was being exploited to the masses. Basically, a recruiting pitch, and apparently, there were those in certain recesses of power who preferred a dead martyr, not a breathing imprisoned hero who might become talkative.

When all the *King's Retribution* Team had re-assembled in the late afternoon, Hugh Fox, with a lot on his mind and pre-schooled to the agenda, sought to lead the meeting.

"We are all painfully aware that our own country has usurped our original task of locating and capturing Osama bin Laden," explained Fox. "I assume for television production values, this looks negative."

"Assume?" King spoke, a familiar glass in hand. "It's a fuckin' disaster." Not his first drink of the day.

"Please, let me finish. Perhaps I have good news. We've been offered a second bite of the apple, but we should discuss the ramifications and risks. So how do I say this: we have been offered a chance to get inside bin Laden's house for a private tour; who's up for that?"

He held their undivided attention. Everyone stared at him; then their eyes shifted over to Wendell Holmes, the man seeming oblivious, reading a local English printed newspaper, and the realization swept over them that they might have underestimated this man and never gave him the value he deserved. The two most particularly re-appraising Holmes were the women, Samantha and Callie.

"I don't know if I am ready to jump at this," continued Fox, "but we should consider it a *King's Retribution* decision, and I will abide by the majority. But it seems for you all in the business, inside filming of the bin Laden house post-shootout should gain the high viewer numbers you are looking for to open Season Three of *our* show. Considering the mood of the crowds outside and what we might expect up in Abbottabad, this will be quite dangerous. There are some logistic problems. Only a few can go. We can take only one camera person, but it should be a lighter hand-held camera. All participants will have camera hats." Fox paused, collecting his strength for the next statement.

"Storm, if we do this, it's best that you do not go."

"What the hell?" King struggled to his feet.

"You are a known quantity. Your face would be recognized."

King seethed with anger.

"You need me. I am the only military man here who has fought and bled for his country!" Several glanced at Wendell but could not guess if he had ever bled out any patriotic fluids.

Fox responded, "And being an American soldier, even retired, is a negative, especially on this day, when nearly every Pakistani has a low and violent opinion of America's 'invasion' of their country by the military. And you, Storm are the embodiment of all the mob detests. Don't you see that?"

King didn't see it like that and huffed around the room; here was a new opportunity for glory, and he was no coward.

Callie, still reeling at the offer, the possibilities of such a visit, and her participation, yet seeing Fox about ready to enter a violent argument interspersed with spiced curses, felt she needed to offer a solution. Turning to their driver and field sound man, she asked, "Bennie, on any night footage that we shoot, can't we use Storm's voice-over, do some later close-ups of him in similar light settings, and no one the wiser that he wasn't there?"

Bennie ran with the suggestion, understanding the players and their need for stroking.

"Sure we can. Did it before; if you recall, our show going after the bank robber hiding in the Louisiana bayous? Studio Insurance wouldn't take the chance of Storm being eaten by critters. It was all second-unit shooting. Probably just like this. Of course, a few hundred more guns pointed our way."

King thought about the business he was in, an actor, a star, no longer a foot soldier, and the bottom line came into focus. Slowly mollified, he acquiesced but, in doing so, shifted to military leader mode, General Eisenhower before D-Day.

"Okay, maybe that's smart, but before we decide if this is worth the risk to anyone, how do we get there? Do we have a cover story?" Callie gave him credit; Storm could be good at changing from strategic retreat to tactical command.

Fox looked to Holmes, following a pre-established script, and continued, "A military truck will pick up those going at 10 pm. When we get there, we go in with CAM ONE, if CAM ONE wants to tag along (the videographer nodded a vigorous 'yes'); according to what's been approved, we run around for about one hour under close, watchful eyes and be rushed out. Three hours max, including up there and back."

"But do we have a cover?" asked Clayton, assuming the bodyguard always went where the stars went. Flexible, he also, when called upon, interchanged boom mike duties with Abbas or Bennie, though this night shoot would be with only a few shoulder directional microphones.

Holmes folded his newspaper. While Storm King knew military strategies for massive ground force deployment and Fox might know how to energize creative people sitting in work cubicles, the now *ex*-C.I.A field agent understood sleight of hand.

He spoke evenly with a crisp check-off as if the plan came from some game playbook he had personally authored.

"Foreign journalists. Miss Cardoza will go as Spanish press for *El Pais* daily newspaper, Miss Carlisle as French correspondent for *Le Figaro*. Laminated documentation forthcoming from a one-hour print shop."

"French, how do you know I speak…?" Samantha caught herself, knowing the man's penchant for reading secret dossiers.

He continued, "Hugh will come loaded with still cameras as a press photog. As previously stated, CAM ONE will be there, with that camera constantly running for immediate real-time spontaneity, and you all can edit to your heart's delight. Clayton and I will look conspicuous as personal guards to the women to keep the macho military men at arms' length so that no questioning can take place."

Holmes keyed on the politics in the room. For the sake of harmony, no one should feel slighted.

"And Colonel King will run the whole show from here, with CAM TWO. Bennie will be on the computer, and perhaps Abbas can work the streets for information, even scout the safest back way to the airport tomorrow."

From his backpack, he pulled out four small boxes.

"These are the iPhone 4S I picked up today. They have been pre-set for the country and checked. They will be best used only for intra-communication, like a walkie-talkie between us, not for long distances.

Abbas scoffed. "Hey, I have a 3G; there's no 4 out yet!"

Holmes deadpanned. "That is, the American released version will not hit the market until this October. Black market phones are on the street now, even here."

They all just stared at him, a few heads shaking, not in disbelief but in understanding, '*Of course, why not? We got the fuckin' spooks on our side.*'

Fox jumped back in.

"Now, we need to take a vote. I don't want this forced down anyone's throat. I don't know anything about the military truck that's picking us up, don't know what we will find when we arrive. When I say risks, I mean it seriously; I won't put anyone in harm's way just to gain a headline or win an Emmy."

"That's sweet of you, Hugh," said Samantha, patting his shoulder. "But our original trip was going to be, and you would agree, a naïve run-up into hostile country, all of us with no idea what we were really doing or what danger we would stumble into. At this point, I have a little more faith that a well-drawn-out roadmap is before us. Definitely an exciting one, so who, ladies and gentlemen, could say 'no'?" She looked to Holmes. Fox looked to Callie. All eyes searched the room for a sign of re-consideration.

"It's a plan I can live with," said King, speaking for *King's Retribution* and all. Of course, he could, thought Callie; his butt isn't being hung out there to be shot off.

Scene 3: New Mission Prep
Setting: The Serena Hotel, Islamabad

Holmes spent the rest of the afternoon and early evening in prep work for the night's foray. Samantha found him in the hallway outside his hotel room, overseeing a workman replace the door lock mechanism. She watched him for a few moments, studying the intensity on his face, even for such a small and mysterious task. The worker finished and departed. She approached. He noticed her, and they exchanged smiles, conspiratorial ones.

"Changed out the locks so only I can open the door. Have secured our friend better but gave him a longer chain so he can walk about 6 feet. Turned off and jimmied the water to the bathroom, so he can't start a flood. Best of all, I scrounged up a VCR machine, and he has five hours of one-year-old Disney films, his favorite. He has food and water. Even a prayer rug. He will behave. I left in his mind the threat of immediate execution by the several guards outside his room, which is untrue. But I will have Abbas, not knowing what's in my room, walk the corridor every thirty minutes as a precaution."

"When will we tell everyone about who we are entertaining?"

"I left that to Hugh. He is the new producer of this second phase of an extravaganza. It's his opinion, and I agree; we remain at risk until we have my buddy Osama on dry land in America. You know, 'loose lips, sinks ships' mantra."

She knew what he meant. "You mean letting Storm be aware of what's really happening?" Holmes nodded.

She continued, "Just to let you know, I have been thinking about the problem of shipping our luggage, *all* our luggage home, short of stuffing him in a FedEx duffel bag."

"I'd be interested in hearing your ideas. I've not had much time to join you all in a bull session."

"I'll let you know tomorrow morning when we are back safe."

She put her hand on his arm, if just briefly.

"I know tonight you will watch over us. But who's going to give you protection? Please, take care."

She turned and left. A wondering smile grew on his face. That was the first time in a very long time that someone had worried about him.

As darkness fell, with meals completed, the nervous wait for the truck rendezvous in front of the hotel began. Holmes made a last preparatory stop.

Callie opened the door to her hotel room, mildly surprised. Holmes handed her a wooden box, which she opened as she walked over to the desk in her room. A beat-up Smith & Wesson 642, a snub nose revolver, with two small boxes of .38 caliber ammunition.

"Oh, you shouldn't have," Callie said in a flat voice, almost snide.

"Sorry, couldn't get your favorite piece. My street vendor contact had a limited selection but said this was 'airweight' and perfect for purse concealment."

"Looks like it's gone through several wars and revolutions." She inspected it closely and saw that the revolver was clean inside and loaded. "Everyone get a popgun?"

"Only you and I. Range qualified over hobbyists."

"And are we going into trouble? Something you haven't told the group?"

"As far as I know, we are paying for an open house tour, nothing more."

"So, if someone knocks on the door with guacamole and chips and an AK-47, I have your permission to blast away?"

"My sort of girl."

"No, I'm not." They exchanged judgmental looks.

"Yes, in that you are correct." And he left, wondering what was in store for them all.

After he had paid the 'fee' over to General Khan, would he gain access to the compound house, take the photographic quickie tour, and head to the airport in the morning? That simple?

No, he sensed that would not be the case. He made a mental note to bring along extra ammo.

Scene 4: Khalaf Shaken
Setting: Abbottabad, May 2nd, 5 p.m.

Khalaf's nightmare revealed futility, a vision of tracer bullets flying past his head as he ran across an open field in broad daylight. He felt panicked. In turning, Khalaf saw the face of an American soldier firing at him, snarling, laughing, yelling at him above the rattle of gunfire. "Cairo! Cairo!" A round hit him solidly in the back, flipping him up in the air, landing hard, his face in the sand, his eyes open, searing pain that burned into numbness. And he could see the soldier walking toward him, reloading, and laughing. And, in a descending darkness that bore death....

His eyes burst open, startled, wondering why death left him with senses. Regaining his surroundings, he discovered his face and clothes drenched with nightmare sweat. He found himself sprawled across a small frame bed, noticing on the wall musical posters of the singing star Atif Aslam, another of the band, Roxen, and pinned to the wall near a small desk, a yellowing newspaper clipping of a photograph of bin Laden and the Doctor, al Zawahiri, at a Taliban press conference. He remembered the time and place. He had been there.

Khalaf was in the student's house on Iqbal Road, the student who attended Pine Hills College, a loyal follower, though the boy's parents were apolitical and not enthused with their son's rabid outspoken beliefs.

Khalaf lay back on the mattress and let the waterfall of emotions return and pour down.

His Sheik was either captured by the Americans or dead. It was late afternoon on the day of that raid, but he had been awake at the other house, his first out-of-breath stop, watching the television as the results of the raid were made known to the world. His tears were all gone, but they had been profuse, distraught at not being with his leader in the last moments, guilt-ridden yet expressed relief that he had made his escape.

The man who had first harbored him, who heard and saw a barely-clothed man pounding on his door at 2 am, could not at first contain his annoyance, even though his house had been designated as a hiding place for any al-Qaeda member on the run, those fleeing local police roadblocks or army raids. Later, after he heard the terrible news, the man's opinion changed, overwhelmed as Khalaf had been with their spiritual leader, their Caliph, but now awed that in the same room with him was the last person to see Sheik bin Laden, kidnapped or murdered.

Celebrity status was not something Khalaf was ready to accept because it was awkward: to him, fame had no satisfaction if gained by actions of no redeemable worth.

At this new safe house, before he had dropped off into an exhausted sleep mid-morning, he had sent the student out to find certain cell leaders of the local al-Qaeda militia. Even now, fully awake, Khalaf lay in the student's bed and sought to overcome his distress by concentrating on revenge and retaliation, and what came to mind was a poem by his mentor, bin Laden, a poem of the U.S.S. Cole bombing.

A destroyer: even the brave fear its might.
It inspires horror in the harbor and in the open sea.
She goes into the waves flanked by arrogance, haughtiness and fake might.
To her doom she progresses slowly, clothed in a huge illusion.

This is America personified. More than ever, *Crimson Scimitar* must succeed. He reached under his pillow to clasp the security of the two data port sticks bin Laden's son had thrust upon him before rushing unknowingly into the slaughter. Khalid would never see Paris. May Allah bless them all for such sacrifice.

The data and information Khalaf had been entrusted with were invaluable, yet what *wasn't* there was deeply disappointing, more than Khalaf dared to admit to himself. He had inserted the computer sticks into the student's laptop on his arrival. He knew the password by heart. Folders appeared with all the operational information on *Crimson Scimitar*, where, for protection, each element of the campaign was imparted in bits and pieces to those who would undertake the attack in the U.S.,

Khalaf could read each participant's role on the computer and, more importantly, how to contact them. The other computer stick provided more details on *Crimson Scimitar*, but this one was specific to the financial side and its importance, defining the roles of London banker Taher Abboud and stockbroker Zia Johnson, the latter who would be making a trip to the

U.S., as his part of *Crimson Scimitar*. Both of these men Khalaf had met on two previous courier trips.

Within his hands, he had all information on *Crimson Scimitar*, and its breadth and audacity gave him a sharp pain of sadness about the military genius of Osama bin Laden as a brilliant general, now gone. As a mentor and friend, his opinion of bin Laden became tinged with disappointment. Certainly, in the midst of an attack by the Americans, everything was rushed, hectic, and bin Laden, waking from a deep sleep, did not have time to prioritize the most important commands, not knowing they might be his last. What Khalaf did not see from bin Laden's computer folders was his own elevation in the al-Qaeda command hierarchy, his blessed new rank as an al-Qaeda delegate-at-large. And not having that written promotion that bin Laden must have completed, perhaps even signed, drove Khalaf to agitation and his first decision of leadership in a war lacking a supreme leader.

By 4 pm, three of the local al-Qaeda city militia leaders finally showed up for an impromptu meeting, all in grief, yet regarding the haggard young man as a living martyr.

They were a chorus of questions: Is he alive; who would now lead? What must we do next?

Those were meaningless to Khalaf, who said with deadly seriousness, "We must go back to the house and secure our secrets, recover whatever the Americans might not have taken. We must gather up our papers to protect the cause." Khalaf's thoughts were not only on the papers that might still be around in bin Laden's bedroom, as in his promotion document, or what might lie discarded elsewhere in the compound, but he was concerned about his own hidey-hole closet room. There were definitely secrets there, perhaps not overt, but collectively they should not be gathered up by the enemy.

"The Army has control over the building," said one of the al-Qaeda soldiers, "It is hard to get even close before you are ordered away."

"Let us use our contacts and soldier brotherhood. I must get back in. Isn't there someone in the Army that can gain us admittance?"

Said another, "Yes, we have built relationships. I have heard that one of our cells has developed a contact with several mid-level military officers that they have approached in the past for accommodation. But truly, it will cost us."

"I have the money but can't get to it until tomorrow." Khalaf was thinking that one folder on the database held information on several regional bank accounts to be used for al-Qaeda activities and coded so that they could be used by anyone with these passwords, now at his fingertips: open *sisma*, open sesame, the bank vault. Khalaf controlled over about 40 million Pakistani rupees, which he ought to convert to US$200,000 for contingency emergency use but understood little to his obligation of what he had been entrusted with, and especially if he had the right to use those funds as he saw best. But this was war and circumstances had changed.

His mind burned for retaliation and the power to accomplish such.

"Go, and establish our Army contacts, make the deal, do not pay too much to gain entrance, but above all, I must get back into the compound tonight."

He felt better; he would take action. Action could allay grief, and in a positive mood, a belief in himself that he could approach the al-Qaeda leadership and let them know what the Sheik had promised him, he would gain his place in the sun. And he recalled a line from another of bin Laden's jihadist poems.

A youth who plunges into the smoke of war,

Smiling,

Stains the blades of lances red.

Scene 5: CSI — King's Retribution style
Setting: Abbottabad, May 2nd, 11 p.m.

The military personnel carrier, carrying the 'journalists' and their bodyguards, bumped and swerved over the rutted highway, gears grinding between fits of slow and fast, traffic still busy this late. They entered Abbottabad and headed toward Bilal Town, the location of bin Laden's compound. The human cargo hid from the public's curious eyes, all sitting on bolted wooden benches in the bed of the truck, gaining pounded, bruised butts, and all nervous as hell as to what lay ahead. The convoy consisted of a Jeep in front, with an air of official importance, while the trailing Jeep bore four heavily-armed assault Pakistani Rangers, suggesting a do-not-mess-with-with-us attitude.

The first mystery to this entire trip was what in the hell were two Chinese men doing sitting with them, saying nothing, occasional smiles responding to the stares? Around their necks dangled press credentials, quite similar to those that Callie, Samantha, and Hugh Fox wore. They wanted to ask the obvious question of what was going on to Wendell Holmes, but they knew they would get some sort of run-around. Holmes would have told them if it had any bearing on their own job. And that's what Holmes focused on. He passed out a grainy Google satellite image of the compound and explained the layout, detailing where they should first go and what to do. CAM ONE toyed with camera preparation. Clayton Briggs would follow, carrying the camera bag of backup spare parts. Nothing better fail.

"We will start from the top floor down. Hustle to that location first; that is where Osama lived, and his wife was wounded. Take wide shots, then close-ups, and then further close-ups. Do so in a mental grid of the room. Everyone stay behind CAM ONE, and then Hugh, you follow with your camera, snapping away. If you can do it with low light resolution, do so, but if you use lights or flashes, do it with the camera pointed away from the windows, if that will matter much. Samantha and Callie have perhaps the hardest jobs. Memorize details. I would like you to visualize it all and recall each part of a room. I will ask you to write separate accounts of what you see, and we will compare.

"Insignificant items will have importance by someone else's interpretation."

"Seems you have done this before. Ever been a film producer?" asked Fox, seeking levity to all their worries.

"Crime scene investigation. Machete massacre of civilians in Uganda; they were just leaving church." So much for a light-hearted frame of mind as they entered the backyard of known Islamic terrorists. Holmes went back to the operation.

"Clayton, you follow last; always guard our backs. Stand at the door, smile, be nice, but keep out any military chaperones. There are three floors and two to three locations of ground-floor living quarters. Second and third floors are first priority."

"And where will you be?" Callie seemed intent on pinning him down.

"I'm the floater. I'll be around."

The brakes screeched, and the truck lurched to a ragged stop. The tarpaulin cover was thrown back, and they stared into the faces of intent soldiers, not police, all brandishing weapons. Beyond them, a green gate, guarded but opened, and the compound home of Osama bin Laden.

In a hustle fast-walk, they were escorted inside, two soldiers leading the way as they crossed the compound, quickly taking into focus a large canvas cover against the wall, with bright halogen lights shining, lighting up the interior, also under guard. They passed through two gates to the main building, and without waiting for directions CAM ONE with Fox did a rapid ascent, rushing past the soldiers who seemed unsure what their orders entailed.

As Samantha passed by her soldier escorts, she gave a lovely smile and said, "Merci beaucoup."

With notepad and pencil out, Callie, hugging onto her shoulder bag, followed the group, passing more stiff-faced action-ready soldiers with a "Gracias, señors."

Two steps at a time, they arrived at the third floor.

Holmes hung back from the group as General Khan walked out of the shadows.

"And these are your Chinese correspondents?" He gave a chuckle, eyeing the two Asian 'journalists' with suspicion as they gave short bows back at him.

"Their embassy would like them returned in excellent health."

"And you have something for me?"

Holmes pulled a folded envelope from his overcoat, the evening chilly.

"I hope Brian appreciates not only his new sports car but your generosity."

The general tucked the envelope into the inside pocket of his military jacket.

"And the Chinese contribution also included?"

"As we agreed. If they are satisfied, these men will notify their superiors, who will, in turn, contact you and let you initiate the high-level discussion between governments. And what you have is a NBP [National Bank of Pakistan] cashier's check for both amounts, $45,000 US total. $100 bills in a paper bag is so passé these days."

"I would agree. Very unrefined. I am still somewhat surprised, Wendell, that being dumped by one intelligence agency, you would adeptly go shopping to another without missing a step."

"Let's say I am now open for business as an independent contractor. But enough said, would you be so kind as direct your guests to the ill-fated secret stealth helicopter, or what's left of it?"

"Yes, indeed." Patting his breast pocket where the envelope was snug and secure, the general smiled, motioning as would a congenial host to the two Chinese 'journalists,' ushering them into the compound. "I can't wait to see Brian's face when I show him the car keys and ask if he wants to take a slow spin."

CAM ONE had to put the camera light on; there would be no sneakiness. The lights in the building had been shut off, or probably the attacking Americans had cut all wires leading in. After passing dark stains on the stairway, they found the third floor and began as Holmes, finally catching up to the group, directed the cataloging of the interior.

Samantha could not help but notice the dark stains on the bed sheets and floor, blackened pools, coagulating, not totally dried. She wanted to gag and fought the urge.

In this home, three men and one woman had died violently. She was used to the accepted deaths found in the natural order of jungles and zoos; even the bedside passing of an elderly aunt gave her an understanding that all life eventually shall cease. But the harsh death of bullets shredding apart a body and tearing asunder vital organs, the heart silenced. The image required a rationale that what occurred had merit, but she was not firmly convinced. Her jumbled thoughts were broken by Callie's observation.

"Take note. This place is not only trashed, it has been stripped."

Samantha could see that no papers seemed to be where a desk was, nor a television or computer. Holmes had said to observe and not pick up or take anything, as there was a good

242   S.P. Grogan

chance they would be searched on departure. She began to do what was asked of her, detailing, taking mental notes of the usual and unusual.

Fox snapped away with his camera, the flashes adding to a surreal strobe effect. Callie wandered to the room's edges, peering down at the minutiae of discarded trash. Clayton hung at the doorway, blocking, his back to the room, talking idiotically about football nonsense to the two soldiers who tried glancing around him to see what the others were doing inside.

The signal that the bedroom had been intensely photographed was when CAM ONE clicked off, plunging the room back into darkness, except for the flashlight shone by Callie and a random camera flash by Fox, likewise doing last-minute angles from the doorway. The group moved to the next floor down, passing the soldiers, more confused than ever and the process repeated.

The discovery, like uncovering the first step that led to King Tut's tomb, happened when in the second-floor 'media room,' a desk had been moved, causing Clayton, in the semi-darkness, to inadvertently nudge into Callie. As she stumbled, her hand went up against the wall to catch her balance. The wall bowed inward.

Fox came to her side as she studied the indentation.

"This is not solid," he said then to Clayton, "pleasantly shuffle our watchdogs downstairs." Seconds later, he began inspecting the find, borrowing the flashlight to check each corner. There, at the corner of the wooden molding, running up the wall. Using two hands, he pushed the 'wall' back and found it telescoping inward. Callie instinctively found her hand going to her purse, clicking it open, her hand sliding inside, feeling for security, prepared for a split-second response.

"A closet," commented Hugh.

"A hiding place," half-warned Callie peering into the darkness. The flashlight revealed a small library of books piled everywhere, a mattress on the floor.

"A major find. SEALs, if that's who they were, missed this altogether."

"Congratulations." The voice of Wendell Holmes, over their shoulders, coming out of the stairwell darkness. "Photograph it in detail, but take nothing. Have CAM ONE get it all."

Holmes pulled out his iPhone and took his own quick shots. He moved on to the other rooms.

Samantha saw Holmes pass by and wondered if he had taken his macabre private tour of bin Laden's home to later rub the sordid details in their prisoner's face. Did the man get his jollies off reliving the shoot-out?

Fox photographed a series of close-ups of the graffiti wall above the mattress and the bookcase, stood back when he finished, and made an interesting observation.

Crimson Scimitar 243

"All those book titles, many of them are in English. Some are even American authors. I recognize them as best sellers."

When the second floor had been documented, they came down to the ground level, but not before, at Holmes' insistence, the hidden closet be restored exactly as it was, hidden. "Let's see if Pakistani Intelligence is really intelligent." And although they were told strictly not to take souvenirs or remove any article from the compound, one of the *King's Retribution* team, when not being observed, slid a small wrapped package with pink striping into his camera case.

After twenty minutes of a quick documentary coverage of the ground level, basically in a fast pace swing, they were collectively at the front entrance gate, only to make a startling realization.

"Oh shit," said Clayton, looking up and down the roadway.

Their military ride home had disappeared. So had the Chinese.

"A long walk home," Callie gave Holmes her evil eye. "What did you pay for? A one-way ride?"

"Think whatever, but we should move on," Holmes thought General Khan's little joke not particularly funny. "The word will probably be out that more foreigners, meaning we, are in the neighborhood."

Fox saw every calamity from rose-colored glasses. "Let's start the hike to the nearest bus station or find a late-night taxi." He started the trek, and with no other recourse, they trudged behind, looking from side to side at darkened homes and alleys, knowing that dire consequences might befall them at any moment.

Scene 6: CSI — al Qaeda style
Setting: The Compound, Abbottabad, 11:50 p.m.

Khalaf, with his volunteer jihadist militia, were in two cars. They approached the compound from the opposite direction, missing the Americans by only fifteen minutes, arriving to the schedule set by the military officer who, through a series of communications, had granted them chaperoned access, no one knowing, except his people, that a high-ranking (Khalaf's implied position) al-Qaeda would be among the visitors coming to pay his respects to the future shrine.

This was not a tour of the curious. One carload of the militia stayed outside, warily watching the guards, one soldier, definitely sympathetic, striking up a conversation. Khalaf and three others entered the compound to be confronted by a military colonel. One of the

244 S.P. Grogan

militia members stepped forward with a paper bag marked with the printed name of *Euro Mart*, a local store.

"I hope this is what was requested?"

"Yes, but at such late notice, your payment for entrance came from one of our mosques, their donation fund for the poor. Small bills, almost all US $10 and $20 bills. I hope your recipient appreciates the sacrifice of our people for his greed."

"Please be quick. You are the last to visit tonight."

"Oh, and what, you have had other souvenir seekers?" The militia member, as well as Khalaf, was incensed at the desecration.

"Watch your tongue. Important foreign journalists came tonight who will tell the true story of the murders." And the military man turned away, the paper bag secured under his arm. He had the important job of delivering it to General Khan first thing in the morning, less his own cash fee for handling.

"Let's go," Khalaf's quick command, marching off.

They made two quick stops. The third floor confirmed what Khalaf feared, all of bin Laden's correspondence: videos, computers, all stolen. Damn Americans! His own promotion was now in the hands of the enemy, with no chance of return. What was worse, Khalaf realized if bin Laden had indeed put his name down for this recognition, for him to be noticed as an al-Qaeda sub-lieutenant, a proposed diplomat, that the CIA would add his name as marked for assassination.

On the second floor, with the proper push on the wall, his sleeping work area was revealed. Nothing, it seemed, had been disturbed. That, in itself, was a blessing. The American troopers had no idea what they might have learned if they had seized his library. He breathed a sigh of relief.

Crimson Scimitar remained undiscovered, which he was assured of by his quick inspection.

He turned to the men around him, who were in awe, dazed at the whole scene of seeing what a war zone within a residence looked like, and wondered why the only al-Qaeda survivor looked upon these strange books as if they were a treasure of gold.

"The soldiers won't let us remove anything, I am sure of that. Let me show you something that we must do." He took two of his most important books and walked back to the window, to the one he had crawled through. When was that? Almost 24 hours ago. He edged up the window and flung the book across the wall into the field beyond.

"I want you to gather all books up and do what I just did. When we leave, we will go around and pick them all up and take them with us."

Giving his orders, he supervised, and as he did so, a shock hit him. Someone, most certainly, had been there, for he saw something missing. But why just take that? Why leave everything else? Why make it look like nothing had been disturbed? The uncertainty of not knowing raged within.

Soldiers watched the al-Qaeda depart, not paying much attention as they drove around the side of the compound and began quickly loading up the thrown books into the car trunks. Men in the other car were excitedly talking, and one finally came up to Khalaf.

"One of the soldiers is one of us and said that there were foreigners touring the compound earlier taking lots of photographs."

"They were journalists, I was told."

"The soldiers heard they were that, yes, but our brother soldier overheard them talking when they left. They were talking in English, but not British English; they were talking like Americans."

"Strange, they were here. But considering we gained entrance, I would not be surprised the corrupt government let the CIA and their trash back in to gloat, to post more pictures of this tragedy across the internet."

"That's what we think."

"Too bad they're gone. I would order that they all be executed."

The militia member became ecstatic.

"Yes. Yes. They did not drive away. They walked. What it means, I don't know. But we may be able to catch them!" The other men crowded around, all talking enthusiastically about their chance at gaining revenge for their fallen brethren and their supreme leader. 'Blood for our leader, for the faith!' they began shouting, and Khalaf had to yell at them to be quiet. And believing that Khalaf endorsed their enthusiasm to exact punishment on the infidels, the first car rushed away, and Khalaf, throwing the last of his books in the back seat, had barely jumped in when the driver of his car sped off.

It was not what he wanted. His life should not be caught up in a misadventure, of running around the city chasing the invisible group of spies and killers. His main goal was to reach the southern tribal regions and make contact with al-Zawahiri, both to pay homage to whom he expected would be the next leader of al-Qaeda, but more importantly, to continue launching *Crimson Scimitar*, and bringing to al-Zawahiri's attention what bin Laden's last desire had been, Khalaf's ascendency. The first militia car raced far ahead, eager young warriors with no sense. "Catch up to them," he said, really wanting to say, 'Enough!' This would be a ridiculous waste of time, but he would feed their ardor. A good leader sometimes must be led by the rush of events.

246   S.P. Grogan

Scene 7: Firefight — Death of the puppy dog
Setting: Streets of Abbottabad, May 3rd, 1 a.m.

From the raid, now the night after, the government must have clamped on a curfew as they found, as they walked, tired and cold, few cars on the streets, especially no public conveyances. Up ahead, they could see more concentrated lights of a downtown market area of scattered shops and closed produce stalls, and their hopes grew that this adventure might soon be ending.

Not so. The old model Suzuki sedan flew past on the street, then began a long screeching brake stop, turning sideways. Armed men jumped from the car and began randomly firing in their direction.

"Run!" yelled Holmes, pulling his market stall-acquired Glock pistol from concealment under his jacket. Everyone took off down an alleyway full of refuse, knocking over boxes, scurrying toward another darkened street. He could only guess how they were discovered. General Khan certainly seeking more fees would not have given them away; Khan liked Holmes as a deal maker who brought cash. Most likely, a soldier at the compound ratted them out, and identified who to look for. "Keep low and to the sides!"

They had sought to blend in, the women in long Pakistani dresses and head scarves and the men with ball caps. You could not hide the bulk of Clayton Briggs, too giant-like for a late-night saunter, too much like an American jock, with swagger.

Gunfire rippled down the alleyway above their heads from the most dangerous type, amateurs. 'Crack!' The shot had come in front of him! Callie crouched behind piled crates, her revolver extended in a two-handed stance. The gunfire chasing them suddenly stopped.

"Didn't hit anyone, but they damn well know now we can fight back."

"How many?" Samantha came to Holmes's side. In her hand, she held a small cigarette-size derringer.

"What the hell is that? A Cracker Jack prize?"

"A .22 tickler for muggers."

"I count four of them," said Callie from across the alley, seeking a target. "One with an automatic short machine pistol, two with hunting-type rifles, old military, one unarmed, I think."

From where the attackers were concealed, another car drove up, distant yelling was heard, and the car sped away.

"Damn, more to join the party," said Holmes. "They're going to start flanking us; come around the block. We need to keep running to the next block, try to lose them. Callie, you take point; I will bring up the rear."

Rapid fire resumed, laying down a stitching carpet of thuds and ricochets, but the quarry was already in motion sprinting across the street into the next alley, just as the second car turned the corner and rushed towards them. It would be a long alley with very little cover.

"Get behind those boxes." Were they trapped? There were houses on both sides of the alley. Holmes turned and prepared for new attackers from the second car to enter the fight.

This driver must have had experience in military tactics or in gangsta drive-bys. He pulled up to the alley, looking down to see if they had found their targets.

Callie's shot hit the driver's side window, and the car edged slowly forward without control, a foot removed forever from the brake, as three car doors flew open, and men fell to the ground, scrambling away. A momentary lull.

"Let's go!" Holmes called out to all of them, and again at various sprinting speeds, they chased after Callie. At one point, Fox yelled in a loud whisper, "How about here?" Whispering did no good. Neighborhood dogs were yipping, a few home lights going on, but no one at the windows. Fox pointed to a garden area behind a house, and he opened the gate and rushed in. His thought was to get out of the direction of a future round of flying bullets. His posse followed. Hugh went to the back door and began a steady pounding.

"No, I don't think so." Clayton's foot slammed in the door, his drug-bust version of the Welcome Wagon. All went rushing in, Callie doing her room clearing swing with her gun, but kept them all moving, past screaming children, people rising from floor mats, out the front door into a wider street. Their position was not an improvement. They were parallel to the attackers, and Car One could send their people easily to the next street, as could Car Two going to the end of the alley, and they could be boxed in between two fields of fire.

"Another house," said Holmes, and they crossed, and he made a choice, finding another home with a garden on the side, this time rushing through dead plants and pulled-up vegetables. A chained dog at the back of the property started howling, lunging in their direction. Clayton hit it solidly in the nose, sending the dog flying, dazed and whining.

"Well, if they don't like Americans now…" observed Samantha running past, not ready to debate animal injuries over saving one's life from human beasts.

They were onto the next street, relatively quiet of night noises but void of gunfire. Two blocks away was the market center, more lights, and scattered nightlife they could hide within.

They took off running, Callie in the lead, then Fox, Samantha, and Clayton loping along next to out-of-breath CAM ONE. Damn, realized Holmes, the videographer has been

248 S.P. Grogan

recording it all. Don't they know this is real reality and real death? Commercial breaks don't fit into gunbattles.

In a millisecond, the window shattered, then brain gore and blood from the driver's head splattered over Khalaf, speckling his face. Most merciful Allah, am I hit? He fell out of the car onto the pavement, shaking, looking at his body, feeling his face — not his blood. Mercifully.

He had no gun; why should he? And the others with him held twenty-year-old Russian rifles pulled from the trunk.

"Pull him out," Khalaf instructed one of the men, "You drive." The other began firing aimlessly down the alleyway. When Khalaf hesitantly put his head around the corner to look, he saw nothing. "Stop."

At that moment, the first men in the chase raced from the alley, their car slowly trailing behind. They did not continue to pursue, no one fired. Instead, they all walked over and looked at their dead comrade. These were militia volunteers from the universities and the cities' slums; their mindset embraced broadly smeared idealism offering religious fraternal brotherhood, which bound them more than a promise of wealth or a heavenly condo of virgins. In shock that their cavalier attitude of chasing down infidels had resulted in the death of one of their own, they sought anger in their shame and loss of not being instant victors.

"They are no longer down there!" shouted Khalif, seeking to gain control. "They must have gone to another street. Back in the cars. You all go that direction, and we'll go this way. Honk constantly when the Western terrorists are located. Do not fire unless you have a positive target. We cannot have al-Qaeda condemned for killing any residents. Death to Americans! Death to non-believers!" Affirmed shouts, new pledges of faith to enact punishment: to disembowel, castrate, behead their enemies.

It was Khalaf who, surprising himself, brought about the revenge.

He directed the driver, oblivious to the blood-soaked seat he sat in, no time to clean it. He scanned the side streets intently as they slowly drove, looking one way then the other. The other two men each held a cumbersome rifle at odd angles, poking from the open windows.

They would have to stop to sight a target and squeeze the trigger.

Frustration built as they searched. They had lost them, except Khalaf felt he knew their direction. The central market square. Late-night produce deliveries were being made, and a few private coffee clubs were still open. Perhaps they had an arrangement, and the CIA army would be there to save them. Perhaps this was a trap? Again, Khalaf had to remind himself that this was not his true mission; it would be an unholy ghastly error if he were killed. The right decision came to him; he must find an honorable way to break off the engagement.

Then he saw the group of spies emerge from an alleyway, walking down the street, beginning to cross the wide street towards the maze of market stalls. Headlights off, he yelled at the driver to accelerate the car. Why stop? His men with rifles would not know how to shoot the running men and women. But a car was a weapon, backed by a plethora of deadly statistics. The hurtling metal projectile aimed at the middle of the group. They could not miss.

"Watch out!" Their hearing had been impaired by the night sounds of the market workers unloading produce for the morning sales, the motor noises of delivery trucks backing up, and backfire sounds like gunfire. The car was upon the Americans in a rush.

Samantha looked up to see the faces of two demented men, the driver's of glee and evil satisfaction, and seconds before the car's bumper plowed into her, she felt a rough shove and went up in the air, off her feet, landing with pain as she felt her ankle twist in the slam to the roadway.

Callie and Fox turned just as Clayton Briggs went up onto the car hood, slammed against the window, smashing it, and rolled up and off to the side, where he hit the road with a hard smack. He lay silent, no movement.

Callie reacted instinctively and fired at the rear window of the hit-and-run fleeing auto.

The first shot shattered the glass, but the car careened at that moment into a bicycle rack, humping over several bikes, popping the trunk open, scattering contents, and deflecting her next two shots. Around a corner, the car peeled out of sight, and Callie's footrace to catch it quickly ended, and she turned to find those of *King's Retribution* standing over Clayton Briggs, her bodyguard.

"I'm sorry, Callie, he's dead." Hugh Fox opened his arms to her, but she walked past and looked down at the inert body, blood seeping from Clayton's ear, his mouth. Inside, bones surely crushed.

What had she done? Callie wondered, an agony of grief. Why, by her actions, had she brought them here? To all die? For what purpose? For a damn television show? To make her a star?

She kneeled and held Clayton's hand, desperately trying to recall all her memories of the living man, so many times taken for granted as just being there on the set as supporting background.

Clayton, I am so sorry.

"Let us go back and kill them all," yelled the jihadist from the back seat.

"You fool. Did you not see the ISI police running out to them? They are reinforced. We would be the ones greeting Allah tonight, not those Americans going to hell."

250   S.P. Grogan

"No, I did not see that. I am sorry, my leader."

Khalaf let the lie do its work. He needed no more of such risk. At his direction, the car pulled over to the side of the road, and he inspected the damage — front window damaged, back and driver's side windows demolished. He glanced in the car trunk filled with the thrown-in books from the compound, picking up one volume, one of his graphic novels, *Cairo*, noting a bullet had pierced the cover, going all the way through to exit. Allah's miracle, if not simple fate, even with tonight's fiasco of inept men playing gunmen, he began to believe he might indeed be omnipotent, and these books continue to serve their holy purpose.

Slamming the car's trunk tight, they drove off. After a few moments of silence, his commanding presence reestablished itself against the earlier trepidation of a bullet ending his life.

Not tonight.

"Call your brothers. They can continue to search, and may Allah be with them. You are now tasked, as my bodyguards, under edict from The Sheik's last will and testament. We need another car. You must drive me to the border. I must make contact with Doctor al-Zawahiri."

The two men, in renewed awe, looked at Khalaf's hardened visage as he drove on towards the darkened horizon. How honored were they to be giving homage and duty to such a man. May Allah protect him. *Yes*, Khalaf thought, *yes, they must be thinking that.*

Scene 8: A Sad but Hasty Farewell
Setting: Serena Hotel, Islamabad/Airport, May 3rd, 7 a.m.

Callie lay in her bed, the sedative numbness wearing off. Last night, she thought her cop training would let her rise above the personal tragedy, bring out the coldness required to act swiftly in a crisis. Instead, the death of a friend took Callie to a far place of her inadequacies, and she let the born leaders take charge, and she became a mere robot following instructions.

She could recall all the events, even if in a haze of short jerky scenes.

Damn that Holmes! He got us all into this! No, her ambition did; she accepted that guilt, but still, Wendell Holmes played his part, and we were led to bin Laden's compound for some additional mysterious purpose that Holmes deemed important for himself.

But damn Holmes, he did have quick reflexes to the attack.

She remembered him going over to a fruit truck, a dilapidated pick-up. He did not commandeer it at the point of a gun as much as he haggled, like buying a trinket in the market.

Dickering with shouts in street buyer-seller haggling, he struck a quick deal, and a weathered man, the truck owner who had no political views, could care less of world views, but who understood money and contract handshakes, dumped the remainder of his boxes into a pile at the market.

Callie did not help to lift Clayton's body; she still held his hand. Fox and Holmes accomplished this sad task, easing Clayton's body gently into the truck bed, covering him with a tarp, not a worthy shroud, she knew, for such a good person. Fox and Callie crawled into the back of the truck and hunched down.

Quick snapshots of odd moments came to her mind. She remembered turning to CAM ONE and saying plaintively, 'Please turn off the camera.' But Fox said gently, 'we must remember all, if anything, now for Clayton. But, I promise, it will be ours and not be seen on any television screen." She nodded, not really there, and she saw him take the gun from her that she had been holding while at the same time she held Clayton's hands, both cold, both of death.

What had Holmes said to Samantha, she had not heard. But she had seen Samantha take Holmes's Glock and approach the growing crowd of curious, shouting at them. Callie caught the drift, if not the waving gun attention grabber, something like: "Stay away! We are I.S.I.! Security Police! Chasing and killing bandits!" Holmes must have conveyed a similar warning in Pashtun and everyone drifted away, back to their illegal clubs and marketplace jobs, not that eager to find out what really was going on, at least knowing a man, the big man who had died, had very white skin.

Callie heard a siren in the distance. She found herself pushed up next to Hugh Fox in the back of the pickup, across from CAM ONE, a covered body in the middle. Samantha sat in the truck cab next to Holmes. The fruit delivery man, a somber scowl on his face, scrunched down in the passenger side at the window, worried protector of his livelihood, once in a while telling Holmes with hand motions to slow down. Prudent advice.

The fruit truck started off, but after only going half a block, it stopped, and Holmes jumped out and picked up something off the street. He threw it in the back of the truck, next to Callie.

"Take care of this," he said to no one in particular. Callie glanced down, hardly seeing the title in the darkness, the pages flipping back and forth in a rising breeze, but finally, under highway lights, as they entered Islamabad, she could read: *Dead or Alive* by Tom Clancy.

An American novel discarded on a Pakistani suburban street.

What was that all about? As the truck sped closer to their hotel sanctuary against the biting wind, she found herself leaning into Hugh Fox, less snuggling, more a burrowing desire to escape this miserable world.

252   S.P. Grogan

Scene 9: Departure Drama
Setting: Islamabad Airport

The details of their exit from Pakistan will perhaps come from someone else's forthcoming memoirs.

What was seen by the public that day was a somber exhibition, with no acting. The dark-tinted windowed SUVs brought the *King's Retribution* group to the private tarmac where their two jets had been fueled and prepped for departure. Led by Storm King, for once sober and serious, the team boarded, this time in a different grouping. King, Bennie, Abbas, CAM ONE, and CAM TWO all boarded Samantha's executive jet, and with the cabin door barely secured, the plane began taxiing for takeoff as if it was racing to clear Pakistan airspace.

A few minutes later, a beat-up 1950's hearse entered the airfield and made its way to the rear lowered ramp of what might be perceived as a US military C-130 cargo plane. The attention that this might be U.S. military with some nefarious intentions brought out a squad of Pakistan's elite military commandos with several officers that certainly had to be attached to ISIS, their military intelligence. General Khan exited a military car, be-medaled in his glory, even slapping a riding crop against his knee-high black spit-polished boots.

Behind the hearse came the SUV bearing the mourners, Hugh Fox, Wendell Holmes, Samantha Carlisle, and Callie Cardoza. And behind the SUV came a large cargo truck covered with a tarp.

General Khan paid his respects.

"It is unfortunate that I heard one of your film crew passed." He looked to the group, which he had to admit did look bereaved. No one acknowledged him with a 'thank you.' Callie, in her mind, apportioned some of the blame for Clayton's death to those who had deprived them of their returning vehicle at the Compound. She was in a foul mood, grief and anger, a bad mixture.

From Holmes, "An accident. Slip in the tub. We will be returning him to his family as soon as possible."

"And the need for a military cargo plane? U.S. Air Force?"

Fox handled this part.

"No, not at all. This is privately owned. I rented it…to carry cargo and Clayton's casket. And it is a smaller version of what the military has. This is a Lockheed C-130J sold for commercial aviation." The funeral staff was unloading a large coffin, putting it on a sturdy gurney — the coffin covered and secured with a black blanket. A draped American flag was inappropriate, considering the present political atmosphere.

General Khan eyed them all, unsatisfied, with several 'officer agents' behind him also suspicious and determined soldiers behind them awaiting orders.

"And this cargo? Do you mind if I take a look?" And without receiving a response, he strolled over to the large crate being unloaded by forklift. He motioned to his retinue, who motioned in turn; several soldiers yanked back the tarp, and several brave men jumped back with shouted screams.

They had screamed as two ferocious hissing, snarling large cats bared their teeth, just a foot away, safe, thank the Prophet, that heavy plexiglass with air holes protected all who crowded closer to view.

"As you might know," explained Samantha, approaching the general, raising her voice as the Rolls Royce engines on the cargo plane started their propellers rotating, "they are native to arid parts of Pakistan. These are wild caracal cats. Your zoo was generous to loan them to me as one is female and the other male, and they are for breeding. There is a zoo in Spain with an infertile pair, and we want to see if we can create some romance. I am very grateful to your government for this kind gesture of goodwill for the zoological world."

General Khan had to recapture his bearings and compose his thoughts.

"Why are they in such a large container?"

Samantha pointed. "See the hole in the slanted part of the box? That leads down to their artificial burrow? Caracal cats are nocturnal. I hope that on this journey, they will stay out of sight and sleep. You don't want to get near them. They can do serious damage if they feel threatened."

General Khan motioned for the tarp to be replaced and the rope secured, and turned his attention elsewhere. He saw the coffin on its bier approaching the ramp.

"I must pay my respects." He turned and made his way quickly towards the funeral team and their silent duty.

At the coffin, Callie said, serious and defiant, knowing what the general wanted.

"Is this necessary?"

"I insist." He again motioned to the men, who removed the black draping. To the horror of the funeral director, the soldiers started fiddling with the side latches until Callie nodded, and the funeral employees moved in front of the soldiers and carefully undid the secured bindings and then the side clasps. The lid raised. A body lay in repose, flowers on his chest. Clayton Briggs.

Callie turned her head away. She had already kissed her friend's forehead with a sobbing goodbye.

General Khan remarked to nobody. "He is a big man. I am sad for such a young man to meet an untimely end." He looked more closely at the body. "It is interesting that my office was made aware of a firefight last night back in Abbottabad. The details are sketchy, but I heard there was a lot of shooting, deadly ordinance flying."

Fox choked lightly. "Damn bathtub. And he was an excellent athlete."

Callie, bereaved hardness. "He was a sweet puppy dog to us all."

Without asking permission, Fox pointed, and the funeral staff closed the casket and moved it up to the base of the ramp, trying, with difficulty, to get it over the ramp's lip. General Khan, frustrated and exasperated, motioned, and several soldiers went forward to help with the pushing. Then, as they all stood in silence, unsure of what came next, the forklift brought the container of wild beasts behind and also ascended the ramp.

"General, here are my stamped papers of exit for our entire party, even copies of my lease of the airplane." The general did not take them but had a subordinate glance at them. He returned them without comment.

Samantha and Callie turned and walked towards the nearby Skilleo private jet owned by Fox. They did not say goodbye. Wendell and Hugh started towards the C-130J ramp to depart.

General Khan was suddenly bewildered about what was going on and what command decision he should make. Detain them? For what?

Hugh turned back after several feet and walked towards the general, who made strides to meet him halfway.

Beyond any listeners, deaf from all four propellers pushing noise and blasted air at them, the general could only sneer his fatalism in shouts,

"Am I going to regret letting you go?"

Instead of answering, Hugh waved towards the apron of the airport, to the fence where people stood watching planes arrive and depart. He waved as if saying goodbye to an acquaintance. A young man sitting on the back of his red sports car convertible waved back, a face full of happiness, jumped down behind the steering wheel, waiting. Wendell turned and followed Hugh Fox onto his rental air ride. The ramp closed, and the cumbersome bellied cargo plane taxied. All three aircraft were seeking the sky heading home.

Watching the takeoffs, at this moment, General Jamshed Khan knew he had been duped, but just not how or what had happened — he was at a loss. His distracting conclusion: this sports car better produce excellent dividends.

Crimson Scimitar

Scene 10: Tasks of Subterfuge, Tasks of the Future
Setting: In transit

At 28,000 feet, they went about a sad task. The C-130J gained its altitude, and with a hum of the propellers, the flight settled into a more tolerable level of comfort, allowing Hugh and Wendell to go about their work.

First, to the large wooden crate cage that held the caracal cats, they inserted a slat that blocked off the entrance to the 'burrow.' Then, removing the large latches that looked like permanent fasteners on the side of the plexiglass, they positioned large round poles on either side of the enclosure, and like carrying a paladin and with extreme effort, almost to Hugh's level of strength, they lifted the cat cage as a separate unit and placed it on another pallet brought on board the plane earlier. There they fastened the rigid plastic box to the wood base. The cats hissed and growled and paced nervously but would soon calm down as the tarp was thrown over to provide the darkness they so often craved to find rest. Indeed, they would disembark in Spain for relocation to the Madrid Zoo founded in 1770 by King Charles III, and hopefully, scents and urges would create a family for the preservation of this endangered species. Samantha Carlisle, at her best doing good works, motivated by a memory of a kitten named 'Snackers.'

Next to their task, they finished off the leftover base of the cat box into a new crate configuration, with new sides hammered, leaving one side yet to be put in place. Into the interior, they placed a battery-operated lamp, an easy chair they could bolt to the floor, left multiple Arabic books of fiction and history, and a three-day food supply. Two empty gallon plastic jugs for a portable urinal, a covered pail for body waste disposal, and toilet paper. The final touch was chain manacles for the wrists and ankles, but enough give that there was some room for movement. Fox hoped they had provided minimum 'jail' accommodations, acting on such short notice.

As the before mentioned 'sad task,' they opened the coffin and, gripping the underlying burial shroud, lifted the body of Clayton Briggs, again a heavy lifting effort, in silence. Beneath, where the body had lain in the coffin, under a hard molded plastic cover, lay the inert Osama bin Laden, unconscious, an oxygen mask to his face, a small bottle at his side.

Quickly, bin Laden was placed into the leather chair, and tilted back into a semi-inclined position, shackled, the light turned on. His vitals were checked and deemed acceptable. A letter was put into his hand informing him on awakening that he was in a crate, he had a two-day trip ahead of him, what supplies he could draw on, and materials to read. A fax printout, hastily supplied, was several pages long on how a trial in the United States was usually conducted and told him of the rights he had as a defendant. In the fax was an abbreviation of the charges he would face. The main indictment was first-degree murder as the planning

256   S.P. Grogan

mastermind, and conspiracy leader, in the deaths of approximately 3,000 innocents on September 11, 2001. As such, said the printed paper, in any U.S. jurisdiction court, it would be expected that bail would be denied. However, he would have counsel of defense and would meet them within a week.

Clayton was reverently placed back in his casket and sealed. This time an American flag was brought out and draped over the coffin. Any of the curious on their arrival would view and probably accept that a departed soldier, having made the ultimate sacrifice, had returned home from one of America's many far-flung battlefields.

Holmes and Fox sealed up bin Laden's crate, and various official stamps and papers were affixed stating that the machinery inside was destined for a location outside of Colorado Springs.

The two men, now physically spent from their labors, found upfront seating in the crew's quarters. They ate boxed lunches and took short naps. A long, loud, bumpy flight to endure. Wendell spent his awake time writing in his pocket notebook, outlining personal thoughts, structuring random ideas, scratching, editing, and rewriting. Hugh Fox had his own writing stylus — a laptop. At the height of his talent, Hugh busied himself with planning out the next steps to what would become *"The Trial of the Century"* television programming. Different writing formats from each man, and though diverse thoughts, both efforts would congeal as One Monumental Climax, as to say, an ending which might start the beginning; where some media critics would expound about and ridicule "The Greatest Show on Earth" (implied a 'circus' — albeit, usually sold-out entertainment), where others more erudite sensing the impact on history would see a coming Divine Transformation. Yet, not yet. So much still to live through before any audience forms their conclusion about the conclusion.

INTERMISSION

REEL FIVE — Jugglers in Rehearsal

EPISODE SIXTEEN — Intermission's Over

As this *intermission ends*, it would be well to note that if a future historian or the History Channel were recounting the upcoming disparate events as a whole, one would see a book or televised program in lengthy chapters or on streaming television as a weekly series sprinkled with dissimilar characters involved in seemingly unrelated plots, all resolved by the book's end, the play's final act, or shooting in the film can. All are woven by these individual scenes into a strengthened literary rope of *epic* consequences. The word 'epic' is entirely appropriate, with the definition succinct as the narration of deeds and adventures of legendary figures of the nation's history, or in this story-telling, of the world.

Under these circumstances, the Islamic radical revolutionary group known as al-Qaeda and the U.S. television show *King's Retribution*, the former seen today in occasional resurgence still vying for that comeback legitimacy, and the latter these days, as in all reality entertainment, their past frozen in time by recurring syndication deals. However, it is important to recall that in the summer of 2011, al-Qaeda and *King's Retribution* were destined to meet again in spectacular fashion.

May 4th *Associated Press* News Release (Editorial Sidebar story)

As the world learns more about the attempt to capture terrorist leader Osma bin Laden, it might be ironic to note on that same day, May 2nd, when SEALS were attacking the hideout in Abbottabad that an American television crew and its reality TV stars of King's Retribution were secretly in Islamabad, only 80 miles away, on their own hunt to capture bin Laden, and do so on camera.

According to sources, they missed their quarry, as did the SEALS, but the U.S Government retrieved valuable intelligence into the world's most nimble escape artist.

Not so, King's Retribution, who returned empty-handed today to Hollywood without the fame and fortune they sought. If they had stayed around, perhaps the Taliban or al-Qaeda would have furnished more potential primetime moments.

258   S.P. Grogan

TMZ Television

Host Commentator: Guess the vacation King's Retribution cast and crew took to Pakistan didn't pan out. They wanted to surprise us by bringing bin Laden back wrapped in one of their spiffy TV specials, but the American cavalry had the jump on them. Next, we hear Storm King is going after Hitler's ghost.

Commentator #2: Their best seasons are behind them. With that egg-on-their-face farce, they will be lucky that the network will let them apprehend overdue parking violators.

Variety Newspaper Headlines

[May 6] *Retribution Flops in Packy, SEALS are Hit*

[May 8] *Obits: Retrib Star Clayton Briggs — Car Accident in San Fran, Private Services Set for May 11th*

[May 24] *Bigelow-Boal 'Hurt Locker' Team to do Bin Laden Op/Sony Signs Up*

[June 12] *Relative Media buys in-can real SEALS Flick for $13 million*

Scene 1: The middle finger salute
Setting: Central Intelligence Agency, Langley, Virginia, Friday, May 6th, 11 a.m.

The CIA head of the U.S. Foreign Intelligence Analysis Section, Matthew Brady, found what he held in his hand awkward and explosive, and worse yet, the materials were addressed to the man whose office he entered after a slow knock: Ronald Givens, Assistant Deputy Director of the Central Intelligence Agency. Brady considered Givens a limited man, consisting only of being an asshole and butt kisser, but with ranked privilege and himself desiring a long career, Brady knew the system enough to put on his mask of being a lowly executive worker bee in the spy hive.

"Yes, what is it? Did you have an appointment, Brady?"

"This came into our Section this morning with a request to review and verify, which we just completed, but what was unusual was it was addressed to your attention for an immediate delivery once we confirmed background."

"Well, let's see it." Givens held his hand out, demanding, not requesting. Brady complied.

Givens gave off a superior attitude 'huff' at being interrupted, ripping opening the large folder marked: 'Confidential.' A large photograph, black and white, grainy with night features, fell into his hand, and he glanced at it with a quick dismissive study. He froze, suddenly sat upright, startled and upset.

"What the fuck?!"

"Yes, sir." Seeing his superior's discomfort, Brady realized he could have fun with this.

With masked innocence, he replied, "We were quite surprised when I showed this to *everyone* in our section for their input."

Givens snapped, flustered.

"You showed this to others and did not bring it to me directly?"

"Protocol required our vetting. You can see it shows two Chinese men, both holding cameras, who we suspect must be intelligence agents from the Chinese embassy, standing in front of our stealth prototype Black Hawk, the one that crashed during the *Neptune Spear* Operation. Notice the distinctive hub look around the blades."

"Yes, I see that."

"And do you recognize the man standing off to the side? He's smiling, as you can see."

Givens knew on the first look. Hesitantly he glanced again and then threw down the photo.

Goddamn it, Givens thought to himself, almost apoplectic.

Brady maintained his faked benign detachment. "I believe that is Agent Wendell Holmes, isn't it? But I heard he was discharged?"

Givens could not admit to what he saw.

"When did this hit our Middle East desk?"

"Oh, it didn't, sir. As you can see by the envelope, this is an Inter-Departmental circular. It was put into the Langley mail system early this morning, around 0830."

"Holmes is here? Get Security to find the bastard; he'll be on his knees before me within minutes."

Brady fought back the buried guffaw seeking release.

"I am sorry, sir. I did think the method of delivery was somewhat odd; you would expect it to come through our bin Laden desk, but it came to my section, so I made inquiries. Seems like he was here to sign all required paperwork for his retirement release, then left our facility, but not before dropping off several of these memo mailing packets."

"There are more? Damn it, find out who got them, go around and collect them all. This is highly-sensitive material, not meant for others."

"Oh, you mean the Director should not receive this photo?"

"The Director received this photo?" Givens stumbled, then caught himself. "Well, I guess that is okay."

As if on cue, the phone rang, Givens answered, and his voice immediately shifted to humble subservience. "Yes, sir, I did receive a copy. No, only a few moments ago. Yes, I will be right over." He hung up, and Brady thought he could see a tinge of perspiration on the man's forehead. After all, inner-office scuttlebutt knew Givens, even if, as punishment, had

260   S.P. Grogan

assigned Holmes to a dirtbag job, who suddenly surprised all by surfacing in Pakistan in the midst of a top-secret operation. Was there a leak, or was Holmes that wired-in good?

"That will be all, Mister Brady."

"Oh, one other thing, I don't know if you saw the small detail surrounding Agent Holmes."

"He is no longer an agent of this agency."

Brady handed over a magnifying glass, and Givens squinted at the photo.

"Damn. Damn him to hell."

Ex-CIA agent Wendell Holmes stood to the side of the rotor component of the downed helicopter, away from the Chinese 'agents,' his arms folded. Only on close magnified inspection could it be seen both of Holmes's hands were 'flipping off' the camera and the world beyond.

Scene 2: Triaging Political Damage
Setting: Washington D.C. and Pakistan, May 9th-16th

Three days later, on May 9th, U.S. Senator John Kerry, Chairman of the U.S. Senate Committee on Foreign Relations, announced he would lead a delegation to meet with Pakistan's Prime Minister Yousuf Raza Gilani and President Asif Ali Zardari.

Asked if, on his visit, he would push the Pakistani leaders on whether they knew that bin Laden was in hiding for years next to their military academy, Senator Kerry replied, "We have a huge agenda, we have huge interests that are very important to try to keep on track, and there's a lot to discuss."

The next day, on May 10th, *ABC News* reported that an unnamed Pakistani official, thought to be a military general, said that the Chinese were 'very interested' in having a 'formal second look' at the helicopter wreckage at bin Laden's compound. That same day in a Senate hearing, Senator Kerry was quoted as saying that the continued search and capture of bin Laden was "a potentially game-changing opportunity to build momentum for a political solution in Afghanistan that could bring greater stability to the region and bring our troops home."

On May 16th, after his initial meeting with the Pakistani leaders, Kerry spoke to reporters: "My goal in coming here was not to apologize for what I consider to be a triumph against terrorism of an unprecedented consequence. My goal was to talk with the leaders here about how to manage this critical relationship more effectively."

A Pakistani reporter pressed: "Al-Qaeda said they do not know where Sheik bin Laden is, and your White House says neither they nor the military has him in custody. Who is correct?"

Senator Kerry did not respond, but an aide made a later 'background' side comment, "The White House has already issued a denial that we [the U.S.] did not capture bin Laden on the Abbottabad raid, and active operations are still ongoing to determine his whereabouts."

Later in the day, a smiling Senator Kerry informed the press "that Pakistan will return the pieces of a U.S. helicopter that went down during the Abbottabad operation."

A U.S. delegation official said at the time that he would be 'shocked' if the Chinese hadn't already been given access to the damaged aircraft.

Scene 3: I'm Not Worthy
Setting: Ft. Campbell, Kentucky, Friday, May 6th

Pacheco sat in the bare room with its metal desk and chairs. A quasi-conference room turned interrogation center, at least, that was his view.

He was into his third debriefing. The first one had been, like everyone else's, a quick interview analysis on their return from the mission, one-on-one at Bagram Air Base. There, he spoke the qualified truth, which was causing so much trouble up the ranks. His verbal and taped report followed his actions upon his rushed exit from the crashing helicopter until embarkation and liftoff. What stood out were two salient points: one of assumed truth and the other a question to which he had no specific answer.

Recorded Testimony:

"I am pretty certain that I saw an undressed individual, wearing shorts, and underwear, run across the garden, scale the lean-to stable roof, and jump over the wall." No further elaboration.

He did not mention the struggle, of his nearly being killed, of his failure to kill his enemy. That lie of omission to him was a dogging canker sore.

He was asked: "If this person, in fact, existed, and you did, as you say, see him, was that person Osama bin Laden?"

Recorded Response to Question: "No, it was not him, but a much younger individual, but I saw this person only briefly, and it was dark."

Another Question:

"And why did you not put a satchel charge around what we have called the 'hubcap tail rotor'?"

Caught off guard, when this came out of nowhere in the second interview, he had moved from an 'I don't know' to an answer with a little more thought, but it still sounded like an excuse for his failure.

"The crashed helicopter was at an angle up against the wall, and to reach the tail rotor section would have required a ladder. I assumed the charges I had set and the resulting fire would have been hot enough to melt all vital components. Perhaps a thrown charge might have done more damage, but there was no certainty it would catch and hold on, and it might have prematurely exploded, setting off the remaining set charges [killing me, he did not say]. Plus, the 'withdraw' command was given as I was putting the charges within the helicopter."

A weak excuse. For him, there was no acceptable explanation. He had failed twice.

Three times if you count Montoya's death.

A man and woman entered the room. By their business attire, coat and tie for him, dark skirt and jacket for the woman, he sensed his previous debriefings were unsatisfactory. The first had been his own unit's officers, basically to analyze the operation, compile for the history books, and then seek further eyes-on-the-ground intelligence. From his comment about the compound escapee, if that really happened (skeptical looks at him), this led to the second interview, with what he guessed were the regional spooks and their suggestive accusation that he could have done more to destroy the helicopter.

Today, more prying; maybe the lady taking notes was a psychological profiler. He could use one. He did feel he was going nuts, no, more that he had lost his SEAL fighting edge, and internal doubt was fatal on a battlefield.

They began the routine, the repetitive questions, and he thought they were trying to trip him up by asking in different sequences. What? Gain a confession? Okay, yeah, he screwed up, big time, as he saw it. But it was not coming from his lips. This was something he knew he had to find answers to.

Outside, he could hear the military bands booming over the crowd noise. The President of the United States had entered the base. He was going to give a speech of 'job well done' and then, as Pacheco had been told, all those who had participated in *Neptune Spear* — from the Rangers of the 101st Airborne to the 160th Special Operations Aviation Regiment, the Night Stalkers helicopter strike force to the Fifth Special Forces Group that housed SEAL Team Six — all were going to a private handshake moment with the President. Pacheco already had decided if this investigatory tribunal of giving him the fifth degree dragged on, so much the better. He had no desire to receive a pat on the back from the Commander-in-Chief. He didn't deserve it.

The session was an hour long, some questions asked several times, and when he finally felt they were at an end point, another man entered the room and handed over a file folder. The man and woman both reviewed the contents.

The man stared at Shawn, seeking by his serious, narrow-eyed expression that he could extract the truth by mind games.

"Do you have any Chinese friends?" *What was this,* wondered Pacheco; *where in left field did that come from?*

"No." Both of them stared at him as if he had just lied.

The man in the black suit took what seemed to be a paper photo, like a faxed photo, folded it in half, and pushed it across the table to him.

"Do you know this man? Ever meet him?"

Night shadows encased a vague man standing in front of what Pacheco could see was the rotor section from the helicopter he had failed to destroy. He stared long and hard, committing the man's features, stance, and actions into his memory.

"No. I don't know who that is." And the interview ended.

Pacheco struggled through the crowd, hardly blending in since he was in his field dress uniform, his only clean one left. The people pushed to the hangar where the throngs were breaking up yet hanging around, waiting. He had missed the President's rah-rah speech. It would not have made him feel any better. He sought out the mess hall room where he, along with the rest of his SEAL Team, had been told to report this morning. He had probably missed the President doing a personal High Five to his buddies.

An MP stopped him.

"And where are you going?"

"SEAL Team Six. I'm supposed to be in there."

"Yeah, go ahead and try, but they got it locked up tight. The Commander-in-Chief is visiting with you boys. By the way, great job."

Pacheco nodded and made it a few more yards to the hall door, where there were two men in black, very similar to the 'suits' he had just left, but these were Secret Service, with their earbuds and lapel pins.

"Sorry, no admittance."

"I'm in SEAL Team Six."

"Yeah, that's what everyone's coming up to us is saying. You should have been cleared a couple of hours ago. Just wait. He might be passing by."

"It's not a big deal." Pacheco deadpanned and realized the president's bodyguard was giving him the once-over inspection of a potential threat.

Applause. Multiple shouting of "Hooyahs." And the door opened, and out walked the President of the United States, beaming, leaving the men who had just accomplished the impossible, at least, that's the way a supporting media was portraying a half-successful raid, with the main target unaccounted for. Still, everyone came home safe, physically, that is.

Like a good stump vote-getting politician, he began working the crowd of soldiers, surrounded, in these close quarters, by more Secret Service agents. Pacheco could see television cameras jockeying for position. The crowd pressed him against a rope barrier, and in an instant of handshaking, the President of the United States held his hand out to SEAL Shawn Pacheco.

Both men looked at each other. Pacheco did not extend his hand. And the political President took momentary regard, then flawlessly, not skipping a beat, moved to the other soldiers, handshaking, standing buddy-buddy for digital photos. The Secret Service agent who had stopped him at the door, and was in the passing procession, gave a quick stare.

"What's your name, sailor?"

"It doesn't matter. I'm not important." And he let the jostling crowd swallow him up as the President of the United States moved on, very pleased with the day, forgetting the refused empty hand. It didn't matter. It wasn't important. Cameras fawning and crowds cheering always mattered.

Others did not think so.

Pool television coverage caught the brief moment. To some, the one second of awkwardness between a soldier and his commander became interpreted as a refusal to respect the office. To others, the dissing of the man of the office, perhaps dislike of the President's politics, even to some as implicit racism; it was Kentucky, the South, after all.

As a small item in news coverage where balanced news was the required formula, the refused handshake act of the unknown soldier made national news snippets and universally became an example, an act of disrespect to the country during this glorious celebration of a positive spin on a distant battlefield action against those that meant harm to U.S. citizens. To his comrades, once they saw the clip, but not knowing the mental reasons for his rebuff, as even Pacheco would agree he did not understand why he had reacted as he had, Pacheco once again became an outcast to his military family.

To retired Army Captain Russell Mosswood, watching television at his home in Cleveland, Ohio, with his daughter Janet, he said in disgust, "I don't know what you see in that man!"

Janet had to admit that her fiancé, Shawn, did not seem himself on the video phone calls over the last several months but was very distant and morose. She loved the man she had last held and kissed goodbye before he left on his travel orders, but with the disapproval of her father and seeing her betrothed's metamorphosis, including what she had seen on television with the President of the United States of America, this was not the man she knew. She was confused in her emotions, and these were only further strained by her ignorance of the situation. Because of strict military orders of secrecy, the Mosswood Family continued to believe Janet's fiancé, Shawn Pacheco, still served in the SEAL Team Four unit and did not participate in the bin Laden operation. Captain Mosswood, a Bronze Star veteran from Viet Nam, expected any man worthy of her daughter, and a soldier at that, to have a character of higher standards, insert himself into the action, not just sit on the sidelines of the battle. Captain Mosswood began his campaign to separate his daughter from this ungrateful loser.

Scene 4: A Farewell and Reset
Setting: Forest Lawn Memorial Park, Hollywood Hills, May 11th

Remembering the good in a good man should have been the overriding sentiment that brought them to the grassy hillside dotted with gravestones. Sadly, in various degrees, *collective guilt* bound them briefly together as they watched the coffin lowered into the ground, and listened to a solemn minister speak, who had never met this Teddy Bear personality, once alive as Clayton Briggs. Those who knew the real story, that Clayton sacrificed his life to save a life, could not tell the world, not yet, perhaps never.

The only outflow of visible grief, hiccupping sobs, came from Clayton's secret male lover. He was being consoled by his sister, who was at a loss to understand the depth of her brother's bereavement, accepting that a strong friendship between them both had existed and nothing more.

Everyone from the *Pakistan Folly*, as the recent overseas trip was called by many friends and enemies, and dutifully headlined by the media, had earlier expended their sorrow, accepted their share of guilt, and parceled out blame, right or wrong, as they felt it justly deserved.

At the funeral, Hugh Fox felt sick to his stomach. He lived in an artistic non-real world of vampires and space monsters where you could kill thousands and become a winner on a high point system, or if bored with repetitive violence, just turn off the machine. Being shot at, which he had never experienced, and seeing men die violently should not be dismissed as a novelty. He had been standing right behind Callie as she fired and saw the terrorist driver's head explode. For her to rise, turn, and walk past him as if killing another human being did not faze her at all, left him inexplicably empty in his comprehension.

At the side of the grave, Samantha Carlisle held a red rose, soon to be tossed into the dirt on the coffin. Death, she reflected, has such lack of imagination, much formaldehyde, and make-up color; such drab rotting in a dark box. She paid for all the funeral expenses, hoping that this could be some sort of penance, knowing it would be very little. Clayton had exchanged his life for hers. He had known Callie better than her, and Callie would be a person he could relate to, knowing she was worth saving. Samantha had barely spoken to Clayton, mere smiles when he opened a door for her or helped with her luggage. And he saved her life by his sacrifice. His job perhaps, but so much more. Samantha had succeeded at all business endeavors she had undertaken, made millions, multi-millions, but this bodyguard to the television show she had administrative power over, he never knew her personally, she never knew him. A stranger saving a stranger, without debate, an instantaneous decision made on the value of life. And her guilt? Could she have made the same choice? Could she have sacrificed herself for another? She did not know the answer, and that bothered her conscious.

From the night of Brigg's death and the days that followed, Callie Cardoza floated, acting as if she was dealing with it all, but not really. She dealt as best she could with the loss of a very close friend. She was hurt; yes, that was part of her malware psyche. More so, hurt fed into anger, and she, of them all, stayed silent, using her mind to pass out blame. Could she have made a quick shot and killed the driver who ran down Briggs? Why did Holmes take us back to Abbottabad? A much bigger can of snakes had been opened; she was now a co-conspirator in an illegal abduction.

And then there was Storm King. Fox wisely had put him in the jet, where she was not, and let Bennie, Abbas, and CAM ONE babysit him. King's guilt in all this was in *faking* guilt — that Clayton's death would not have happened if he had been leading the troops.

And later, just as they landed at their final destination in Los Angeles, he had seen the *Associated Press* news story, revealing and ridiculing their presence. None of that would have happened, he lectured, if they had all stayed home. He felt he was in error for not being strong enough to make them do so. Callie saw him standing there at the gravesite, slightly swaying. She wanted to be far away from this drunk.

Callie's worst guilt was a silent wish, a very wrong one indeed, that the car should have hit Samantha Carlisle instead of Clayton. That would have solved several problems, and she cursed herself for being so low to think like that. And only when she looked across the grave and saw Wendell Holmes, his head bowed in some form of silent prayer, did she dismiss that sacrilege and let another evil arise in her soul: she wanted to kill someone, and she knew who that was. The service ended, dust-to-dust in the form of dirt sprinkled in the grave by some, roses dropped by others.

What happened next was remarkable, but maybe not so unexpected, considering who they were.

Hugh Fox went around and thanked all the employees of *King's Retribution* team, even the part-time office research staff, and softly told them they would meet again in Los Angeles at the Santa Monica War Room office. One Month. No later than June 13th. Everyone still paid. There were mixed feelings; some felt Fox's callousness of the timing, and others were quietly relieved they still had a job. Most suddenly grasping that the television show so recently belittled and savaged would fight back and produce 'something.' Uninformed employees were fearful that *King's Retribution* would make a new plan to go back into the field looking again for bin Laden.

But they, the key executive committee survivors of Abbottabad and bin Laden's compound, knew a 'Big Something' event would occur to make a new season launch, so all went their separate ways and would not meet again until summoned. But when they finally gathered, all hell would break loose — the foundation of America would hang precariously in the balance, and *King's Retribution* would have a featured role in the outcome.

Scene 5: Road Trip Arrival
Setting: Tribal Lands, Southern Pakistan, May 9th

Five days of everything going wrong with his transportation choices, Khalaf reached Lahan, a small village a few miles from the Tribal Agency town of Wana in Southern

Waziristan. While back in Abbottabad, he enlisted, if not drafted, two youthful zealots, those car passengers with him in the firefight against the American spies. He gained their blind allegiance by intoning bin Laden's final command for him to go and meet with al Zawahiri. He did not tell them that to reach the Doctor, he had to go through Ahmed Abdul Rahman, son of the 'Blind Sheik,' the father imprisoned in the U.S. for the first attack on the World Trade Center in 1993. Rahman, the son, a senior al-Qaeda operative, acted as a layered in-between, a gatekeeper to the securely hidden al Zawahiri. With bin Laden's supposed kidnapping and presumed eventual execution, Khalaf had to reach them quickly, primarily to gain his new delegate appointment, and secondly, to see who he eventually would report to, for someone had to assume the mantle of al-Qaeda leader. Khalaf feared the passion for establishing the caliphate would dissolve into infighting and regional guerrilla war, with random acts against NATO forces, no mighty strike at the heart of the beast. *Crimson Scimitar* was at risk.

His two disciples had gone forward to make travel arrangements, but still, nothing went right.

For safety reasons, he could not go directly west into the northern federally administered areas and then go south. It was a pure war zone, almost all travel by night, and the higher smuggler routes would require donkey travel, and from his Yemen trip, he despised riding on the back of any four-legged animal that smelled and had a mind of its own. Instead, he would take the train south to Pezu and then west to Kazur. The trains broke down twice, requiring an overnight stay, and the final leg of his rail trip reminded him of cheap commuter travel in India, crammed and overflowing with human cargo, smells of sweat, greasy foods, and excrement. Things looked up when his two men greeted him at the railway station with three dinged-up BMW motorcycles, not in great shape, but road-hog durable. This he could enjoy, the coolness of the air streaming past his face, his eyes soaking up the landscape, apple orchards and goat pastures shaded by Neem trees, wide-leafed, their bark suffused with medicinal powers. Once when they had stopped along the road for mid-afternoon prayers, a small animal called a pangolin, like a miniature scaled armadillo, scurried past them, a good omen — and good eating if you captured an adult.

Before they began their ascent into the mountainous area of South Waziristan, where they might meet bandits or rival tribes who, by blood feuds, had no love for al-Qaeda factions, the three travelers stopped in Manzai. Here, a local shopkeeper received a hefty payment from Khalaf, and they purchased automatic pistols, stuffing them into their side saddlebags.

From this point on, they were in the midst of an area of Pakistan that the central government admitted they had no control over, a land of lawlessness and extremist religious fatwas, many placed against another's neighbor. In this part of their trip, they would cycle through two Pashtoon tribal lands, the first, Mashsud, and the second, Ahmadzai Wazir, to reach the town of Wana. All this territory fell under the control of the warlord, Mullah Nazeer Ahmed, who hated the U.S.A. and could not tolerate the Pakistan government and had a spotty history with any loyalty to the Taliban, but on this day, this month, he served as a member of the Central Council of the allied Taliban groups in Pakistan.

Khalaf and his men sought to ride only when darkness descended, the best protection against the high-flying Predator drones. He had never heard of an air strike against fast-moving motorcycles, and the decision to travel in this mode brought them up to the roadblocks. The first, controlled by a ragged group of Burkis, an ethnic group assimilated into the Pashtoons, were equally armed as Khalaf and his men, and when he saw that they wanted only a 'road passage fee,' he understood they only sought enough money to buy themselves their next meal. The descending face of rural poverty had been evident the last twenty miles. To save face, they dickered and haggled, and he finally paid them a few rupees, whining, as they expected he would complain as a formality, decrying that they had stripped him of all his money, which they had not. As they drove on, his men rode up to him to extol his skill, the art of a chameleon, 'You are such an actor!' they yelled at him and said he was as good as the famous film star of the '60s, Waheed Murad.

Pakistani soldiers manned the second roadblock, more a slowing down than a stopped inspection, soldiers eyeing them carefully as they passed. It dawned on Khalaf that perhaps the word had gone out that he was expected. His own worth rose in his mind. Yes, that is why we weren't hassled.

Scene 6: Disappointment in Lahan
Setting: Village of Lahan, May 10th

Evening dipped over the ridge lines as they drove down onto the Wana plain, circled through the military district town, and a few miles later came to the village of Lahan. Most of the locals seemed to keep to their small homes, made out of Pucca bricks slathered with mud. The village had no electricity, and concerned eyes peered at them. But, curious to identify the strangers, Muslim hospitality soon overcame fear, and the weary travelers were nibbling on maize bread, followed by small bowls of rice and mutton, all soon devoured.

While Khalaf pondered the next step on his journey and how to make contact, he was surprised to face menacing armed men as he and his group entered the small house they had been led to as guests. He had not expected to see Ilyas Kashmiri, a handsome bearded Pakistani, wearing shaded eyeglasses though darkness deepened outside. Around him stood a cadre of fierce al-Qaeda fighters, ready to growl and lash out as if they had just come in from a vicious battle with the enemy, but against which opposition they fought was not apparent.

Kashmiri addressed him loudly in recognition.

"Maulawi Abd al-Khaliq Jan." Khalaf felt uncomfortable being addressed by his formal name, which only a few within the al-Qaeda organization knew. For the last year, he had been encouraging all to call him 'Khalaf,' which meant 'Successor.' Recently, he had begun to wonder if his battle name held more true meaning these days and whether he could use it to his advantage.

"You are alive, and the Emir is gone to Allah, or so we have been told. Do you not think that unfair?" Khalaf, who had met Kashmiri once before on a courier run, decided on the spot he did not like the man, but this leader of many attacks was his tactical superior, the best strategist, and the best chief military commander of al-Qaeda. Khalaf had his response prepared, for he expected this question to come often: why did he not die gloriously alongside bin Laden?

"It is Allah's Way, and I would have died to save him if it was not for his command to come to see my brothers and bring my Sheik's last command."

Kashmiri stared for a moment and then nodded at the words, accepting the answer.

"*Crimson Scimitar*. I have heard only a few details, an overview. Yes, it will be our revenge for the Sheik's martyrdom. Yes, perhaps there will be a journey to heaven for all of us, taking as many Americans with us as possible."

"It is my wish to speak to the Doctor." Khalaf would not mince words and must make it sound important.

270 S.P. Grogan

"Rahman shall speak for him. There will be a meeting in one week with regional commanders to discuss the ramifications of this tragedy, kidnapping, and murder and seek Allah's inspired guidance.

"And you must, of course, be present to tell us the tale of the Emir's last hours. And the Doctor says we all must exercise caution, especially after what has happened, not only in Abbottabad but also in Karachi yesterday."

"What? We have been on the road, racing to reach you all with my report."

"Yaqub was taken."

"Killed?" Abu Sohaib Al Makki was the fourth courier that bin Laden used between himself and others, most notably up along the Pakistan-Afghanistan borders and interchangeably with Khalaf's assignments.

"No, arrested by the I.S.I. in Karachi on May 4th. There is no doubt by all the public relations they put out that the Pakistanis wanted to show their masters, the Americans, that they, too, are still fighting us and not hiding us in Abbottabad."

"What was Yaqub doing in Karachi? I last heard he was up here meeting with our brother Rahman."

"He was awaiting a ship from Yemen, the arrival of one of his fellow countrymen, Shahin, and his attack force."

"Shahin?"

"Shahin was not captured and should be here within a few days."

Khalaf felt the opposite would be better for the man, yes, if Shahin had been killed honorably in a shoot-out, but he swallowed his prejudices. *Crimson Scimitar* came before all other pettiness, and Khalaf must accept that Shahin would most likely become the international hero of the jihad when the attack succeeded.

"Praise to Allah for such deliverance," said Khalaf, seeking to sound sincere.

"Well, it leaves you with a great honor?"

"I am sorry I do not follow, honorable commander?"

"You are now the last of Sheik bin Laden's personal couriers, and the Supreme Council, after they select a new leader, must decide what to do with you."

And with that, Illyas Kashmiri turned and left with his bodyguard. Khalaf did not know what to think. He had to recapture the high ground and tell this shura when it met of bin Laden's last command to him, his new position of 'delegate representative'. Beyond that, he sensed this gathering of al-Qaeda leaders would have those present who did not support him. He must be wise and shrewd. As he prepared to sleep that night, exhausted, his body still vibrating from the day's bumpy ride across pocked roadways, one thought came to him, and he could not fathom if it were a positive revelation. He knew al Zawahiri, ever wary, would be close by, but would not make an appearance, instead using Ahmed Rahman, a fellow Egyptian as he, as the Doctor's spokesperson. Rahman derived his power from being both an al-Qaeda commander and a facilitator between the warlord Haqqani family network of the area who aided and abetted the al-Qaeda with the tacit support of the Pakistan security agency, I.S.I., on a secret agreement that they must stay near the Afghanistan border.

And then, from tonight, on the scene was Kashmiri, the most violent of them all, founder of the feared 313 Brigade and the brains behind the Mumbai, India attack in 2008 and effective suicide attacks on many Pakistani government institutions, boasting many civilian casualties with the plan to destabilize central power and in the anarchy to follow bring about the rise of the caliphate. Zahwari, Kashmiri, and Rahman each wore a US$5 million price on their heads for capture, dead or alive. At least Khalaf was in good company with men judged by their enemies to have great worth. His goal was to stand among them as equal, but that would require great deeds.

EPISODE SEVENTEEN — Wandering in Place

Scene 1: Samantha and Hugh
Setting: United States, May 12th-June 13th

The month respite gave all a chance to forget and retrench. Re-energize the batteries. Only three of them, Holmes, Cardoza, and Carlisle, knew of the prisoner secluded at an unknown site under the supervision of Hugh Fox, himself incommunicado to the team. They had let him run with it, or rather he took off on 'his project,' and they knew next to nothing, except something, as they say in Callie's business, was in the 'development stage.'

Samantha Carlisle, as a titular 'showpiece' head for marketing purposes, attended the opening of two SammyC boutiques, one in New York and the other in West Palm Beach. She skipped over a slew of charity fundraisers at the height of the beginning Summer Season. Without fanfare or want of publicity, her foundation had shipped, to the surprise of the Islamabad Zoo director, who received the shipment without prior notice, a portable X-ray machine, one able to check the stomach contents of elephants or the throat obstructions in rhinos. In a second shipment, the Pakistani zoo received from the SammyC Wildlife Preserve two pigmy hippos saved from illegal trappers bent on capturing exotic species for unlicensed wildlife parks. She did not acknowledge their profuse 'thank you.'

Her relationship with Hugh Fox cooled as sometimes happens with long-distance affairs, where mutual interests had parted. To Samantha, the chase and capture of a 'wanted terrorist' satisfied her, so she would let Hugh handle the next steps, take the praise, and manage the fallout. She did not ask but accepted he would make some colorful splash of turning over bin Laden to the Federal authorities, perhaps on the steps of the U.S. Capitol. It did not matter. Her foray into adventure had reached a plateau, and she was ready to move on; again, she would accept fashion designer chores and save animals as a charitable hobby. Less excitement would be fine with her, and she created a shell of that belief to crawl into. Yes, she would go back to L.A. just to see what the Team might have uncovered and, expecting little, and would close that brief, exciting 'fling' chapter of her life. Her decision processes seemed firm; she would return to her glam monotony, a star in a narrow couture field of high-priced fashion.

Sam and Hugh cordially exchanged the obligatory emails on a weekly basis; more or less, what are you up to; how are you doing type of missives. She missed the steamy exchange of bodily fluids, one of his finer points, so to speak, but she could, and did, focus her mind on ongoing projects. There was one day on a Manhattan street, as she exited her limousine, she witnessed a purse snatcher make his grab, yank personal property from an unsuspecting woman and take off amidst shouts of 'stop,' with other pedestrians shoved out of the way in the culprit's getaway.

Instinctively, she reached for the small derringer in her purse but stopped. What could she do, run down the perpetrator in high heels, kneecap him? For a moment, she wondered and knew that Wendell Holmes would have stopped the thief; somehow, he would. How, she did not know, but she knew he would have. And it surprised her to think of him in that odd way.

Across the country, Hugh Fox fell back into running his Skilleo Empire with ferocity.

He held good memories of Samantha and, in his mind, likewise wished her well, and being not an ordinary man, he wondered if he should have done more in the relationship, but if it were to be, it would have happened, she would have been the one to give him a signal, but she did not, and he moved on…back into game play.

Upon his return, Fox found his glass-top desk piled high with unresolved decisions. That the ever-efficient J-Q could organize was apparent, but crossing the line to sink millions of dollars into funding prototype games that might be obsolete by the time Research moved them to manufacturing was too great a burden. J-Q was quite happy to make the shop hum with directional memos, and he bubbled with relief on his boss's return from what the administrative assistant considered a lark, or worrying that this was the boss's first mid-life crisis which must happen when youthful tech entrepreneurs hit their late twenties. This must be so, as J-Q saw some subtle changes in the returning Hugh Fox.

One of the directives he got from On High was to set up a target practice range in one of the outer buildings and establish after-work, free, and optional martial arts training for anyone who would sign up, with the suggestion, which usually meant compliance, that all female employees take a basic course in self-protection, which rapidly and enthusiastically gained full classes for the weeks the program was offered. 'Scream' and 'Kick the guy in the nuts' seemed to be the mantra the instructors taught. J-Q found it somewhat disquieting that Fox had reduced his company gym regimen and offer training classes in martial arts. Those signing up would recognize the teachings of famous movie examples employing Shaolin Kung Fu and Taekwondo. Those seeking hard core status, going beyond colored belts, learned hard core, the Brazilian *Vale Tudo* ('Everything Goes'), and the Israeli Army's *Krav Maga*, a lethal skill of eliminating an armed attacker close-up.

Another aspect of the 'enhanced' Hugh Fox was more daily trips to the Research and Game Development Departments, checking on what progress had been accomplished, encouraging more innovation, and thinking outside the box. J-Q overhead Fox once ask his Head of Research a nonchalant question, though J-Q felt otherwise. "Does this concept," inquired Fox, "have any military applications in the real world?" J-Q did not register what the answer had been. In another uncharacteristic act of market share positioning, a team was created to study and generate ideas on what worked in the war gameplay market, a highly profitable arena to enter but one that Skilleo had previously considered irreverent as pro-military and had not offered any games series with battlefield themes.

These moves might seem strange, but they raised no suspicions to the company employees or the world outside, and the machine of success which was Skilleo Games, continued to manufacture and release fascinating products of role-playing delight, which the game box and I-gaming world hungered to devour.

The one mysterious aspect of Fox's return, as J-Q saw it, was that The Man closeted himself with a new team, totally off-grid. Ten people met for one hour daily in closed sessions, with no paperwork, only verbal instructions. J-Q recognized one participant who made stealth visits as the President of Cre8ive Networks, a top producer of major televised live events.

Hush-hush projects were often the norm at Skilleo, but J-Q was not asked to participate this time. There were mysterious private jet plane trips, or scheduling itineraries made off-calendar; again, no J-Q requested. Vexed and a little miffed at not being asked to be part of this inner sanctum, J-Q had to accept that whatever this mystery was, 'it was going to be colossal big.'

Scene 2: Cardoza and King
Setting: Los Angeles, May 14th

Back in L.A., like nothing had happened, they hid their feelings as best they could. Callie and the rest of *King's Retribution* went back to work on scripts left hanging out in pre-production.

Clayton was no longer there though the coming season would be dedicated to him in the show credits. Bennie, the chase driver, added to his duties the role of supporting muscle, although that wasn't his strength, literally. Well, he rationalized, he could when confronted Taser with the best of them. Abbas filled in the gaps beyond his special effects role. All looked like it would go back to the normalcy of search out the crook and capture him, except for those underlying issues surrounding the two main stars.

In filming the capture of a serial child molester, hiding out from federal warrants, and discovered leading an unassuming life as a small-town postal delivery man (the more opportunity to scope out young children at home), the *King's Retribution* team let the 'snatch and grab' get away from them. King showed up at the shoot, tipsy, and when making the demand for the pedophile to come along peacefully, the mailman took off in his truck, and a high-speed chase ensued, more comical if risking other motorists and pedestrian lives on the street could be seen as such. But it was a small electric mail delivery truck and its getaway most of the time was curb jumping, weaving through flowerbed yards and picket fences.

When finally, the vehicle hit a tree, Callie, in the lead chase car, jumped out and, instead of handcuffing the jerk, ended up beating him senseless, requiring his hospitalization. An ambulance-chasing attorney of the lowest dregs was talking about a multi-million lawsuit against the network, the television show, and casting Callie as the real criminal. And even though the tabloid newspapers and television media like *Entertainment Tonight* — the scandal sheet type of television show — crucified the guy with Xed-out photos of all his under-age victims, the word coming down was that the show's insurance company might have to settle on a small sum to make the story go away, which infuriated Callie even more. One of the aspects of the settlement was that she would have to go through an anger management course.

What came out of this additional attention and notoriety surrounding *King's Retribution* was that the media had to subtext the story by recalling to its viewers-readers the recent 'scandal' of trying to capture bin Laden. Now, two weeks later, the story slant suggested that American taxpayer dollars might have been wasted getting *King's Retribution* safely out of Pakistan before angry mobs tore them apart. This incensed Colonel King, and with his reputation being challenged, a major component of his ego, he could not let a false story go unchallenged, plus he could garner free ink with his name attached.

On May 13th, from CAM ONE, he demanded that all the footage of the trip to Abbottabad, specifically the film segment from the tour of the bin Laden compound, be sent to Production. He had studio editing grab snippets of the inside of the Compound with grainy night shots of bloody floors, and King did a voice-over, with the finished product sent to their Public Relations Department for release. Hugh Fox heard of the usurpation of control. He could have deep-sixed the flagrant boasting, yet he thought about it and instead offered a subtle touch, a minor edit, so as not to offend a primary star.

King's blind focus was that this visual teaser would tout his continuing stardom and guarantee the precarious future of the Season Three launch. Who would object? As he saw it, *King's Retribution* might not have captured bin Laden, so he thought, but they were in the 9/11 mastermind's home the day after the attack, and that ought to have some heavy Nielsen rating weight from viewer interest for a kick-off show for the Fall season.

When King went to Production to record his voice-over for the 20-second video release, a new script was slipped into the reading, which he did not notice, and read what was before him. [low voice whisper] "This is Storm King of *King's Retribution*. I am standing in the bedroom where Osama bin Laden lived. It is the night after bin Laden escaped. The SEALS have departed, and you can see the destruction they caused. We showed up and took action. What else did we find that no one else, including the CIA missed and is not talking about? Tune into *King's Retribution* press conference on Monday, June 6th." After two takes, King turned to the production director, "Wasn't I supposed to say something about tuning into our new Fall season premiere show? Hell, I guess this will do. I'll put something together for the end of the month."

[May 15th] Los Angeles Times, Weekend Section: Surprise to us, but King's Retribution may have indeed pulled off a coup that even our best foreign journalists could not have accomplished — a private tour inside bin Laden's home the day after the SEAL attack. We all will have to wait for this so-called press conference, and no doubt Colonel Storm King will keep reminding us to watch their new Fall season. I, for one, will be interested in what they did find.

The good news: King had regained mixed favor with the fickle public. The curious masses would probably tune into the new season opener. The network realized they had been boxed in, understood they could build a fair amount of hype around the original search for bin Laden and the tease King had left hanging out there about this press conference, and again reconfirmed they would renew for another season. The bad news: King had no idea what to do next. All the raw footage, all that he had, lay around on digital copies in a studio editing bay. The production crew did not know what to do about putting together the 'bin Laden

276   S.P. Grogan

tour' footage, especially if there was a June 6th press conference. And no one knew anything about that.

Hugh Fox did.

Scene 3: Stroking/stoking the lawyers
Setting: Conference call

On Hugh's arrival back in the United States on 6 May, he had contacted attorneys Booker Langston and Cotton Matthew in a conference call. With Booker on speaker phone, Harriet Eberhardt listened with cautious trepidation, seeking what was going to be required of her and where she fit into this Alpha fest.

Matther began immediately with his bombast.

"I expect, Mr. Fox, that we are together to discuss disbanding our television judicial grandstanding. The press has not said kind words about your cohort of TV stars."

"No, counselor, we will be proceeding as previously stipulated. I assume, counselor, that you have not been lax in preparation."

Matther humphed with slight discomfort. "Certainly not. You paid the upfront, and I work."

"And we are being paid well, aren't we, Cotton?" interjected Langston, enjoying making a slight dig.

Matther recovered. "Indeed so, paid full weight regardless of the outcome. I look forward to duking it out in the courtroom before the cameras. Considering we are using actors, including the terrorist role, I assume the show will be rehearsed, edited, and taped."

Hugh heard, not saw, a lawyer waffling. "Per your contract, it's a live audience, live television. Maybe a 15-second delay for bad language and temper tantrums."

The prosecutor, used to publicity and showmanship, accepted such conditions, confident he would prevail. His scathing reply set the tone.

"It will be my satisfaction to take this mock trial and shove it up Booker's legal briefs."

"Ah. The flow of competitive juices. I like it," said Fox in a very congenial mood. "So, the reason I called you both, and you, Miss Eberhart, is that a schedule has been set for this 'mock' trial commencement on Monday, July 25th. Will you all be prepared for voir dire to select four jurors prior to the opening, say on the 21st, then again on the 25th for a public battle over choosing two alternates who will join the six jurors already selected, then Monday afternoon, give your opening statements?"

"Yes," both men responded. They had in their hands a 'rough script' of the time allotted to present, prosecute and defend their case.

Cotton sought confirmation. "So, we will have an impaneled jury Monday, the 25th?"

"I would hope you realize selecting a jury might have taken weeks, and we would have lost audience share, so having a quiet selection process overseen by the judges was the smart way to go. Just remember, when the gavel bangs and the trial opens, everything is fluid, and you are all on your own. No re-do's, no edits; this is live. Play your parts well. Our primary 'presentation' is you all in legalistic jousting to save or condemn the defendant."

Harriet asked, "The actor playing bin Laden, is he prepared?"

Over the phone, they could not see Fox's surprised countenance and then flawless recovery of his 'lie,' which could have been a dead giveaway. He gave them an update. "Our bin Laden will be ready, as required."

As required, the appropriate words, since Hugh, on his return to the U.S., with his prize secreted away, had his people put the actor who would play bin Laden into a paid holding pattern, telling him to learn a few parts he might utter in the public limelight, watch film to catch bin Laden's nuances in speech, how he carried himself. Fox called the actor my 'back-up quarterback.'

Harriet continued, "I do have to say I was impressed with your Colorado Springs 'courtroom' set-up. Aren't you running a risk everyone will feel this is some type of 'sweeps week' scam, and no one will watch? The critics could be merciless."

"As I said, you people will provide the sizzle of drama, and I expect a turnout based on your performances."

"Thanks a lot," joked Langston. "After this, I may not be taken seriously ever again."

"Oh, I doubt that. On another matter, I appreciated both the defense and prosecution submitting a list of judges I could select by pulling names out of a hat. As you noted in my email, we will have three judges sitting; one head presiding judge to manage the courtroom and two additional judges as experts in the law to help carry the load. In this selection, I have gone ahead and relied on well-respected legal experts [he had not], and the judges they selected are:

Judge V. Behan; he graduated from Colorado College, gained his Legum Doctorate at Harvard Law; then there is Judge Georgia 'Skye' Raven, JD graduate of Oklahoma University, and practiced on the bench for over 20 years."

"I haven't heard their names," asked Matther, perplexed, since he kept tabs on the most prominent legal bench warmers. "What court or district are they practicing in?"

278 S.P. Grogan

"Interesting enough, their jurisdiction is where the trial will be held, northeast of Colorado Springs. They are tribal judges for the Sand Creek Reservation. They are Arapahoe and Shoshone Native Americans by ancestry."

Before an opinion, comment, or complaint could be raised, Hugh offered his final reveal.

"And for Head Justice of the Tribunal, if we can call it that, I have persuasively asked, and she has accepted, retired Supreme Court Associate Justice Scottie Sanford. All three are being prepped, and, as I am told by the triumvirate of these judges, the gavel will pound down promptly on July 25th, barring the unforeseen."

To both sides of the coming legalistic throwdown, the appointment of former Associate Justice Sanford caught the legal trio by surprise. She was a race mixture of Korean-African American, her father a Korean War veteran, returning with a war bride. She voted on the high court to the liberal side, but as Booker Langston recalled, she was the go-to resource when it came to criminal cases before the jurists, and in that, she had been seen as a moderate, believing in the Constitution yet feeling instead of strict interpretation felt it was a 'living document' that could be re-imagined for modern times. Justice Sanford, now retired, had fooled court watchers several times when she ruled the opposite and strictly interpreted past laws, mainly on military rights issues. In their minds, both defense team Langston-Eberhardt versus Cotton Matther were impressed at CEO Hugh Fox's deep reach into the inner circles of power. Themselves proficient court watchers, they could not anticipate the prejudices three trial judges acting in modified concert might bring to the bench.

"I expect to see you all at your new courtroom near Colorado Springs no later than July 19th to become familiar with your environment. Best of luck to all three of you." The call ended.

Scene 4: Booker and Harry
Setting: Los Angeles, Langston's law office

After the conference call, when Booker and 'Harry' were walking through her research on bin Laden and al-Qaeda political messaging, their mood was buoyant, excited about the challenge. Booker could appreciate his co-counsel even more for the ability to lay out a possible defense, as impossible as the quest might be. Early on, Attorney Eberhardt had dismissed mental issues and incompetence as plausible arguments, instead she said their battle strategy should be focused on three themes: (a) Osama bin Laden by lack of evidence, or hearsay, did not create or otherwise order the 9/11 attack and (b) any statements he made or wrote to the contrary were done so in an atmosphere of political expediency as a leader, and politicians are known to boast and lie; and (c) try to humanize the man versus the myth. The theorem she felt they should argue: if a politician pontificates, then query: what is true and what is the lie? The answer is obfuscation which must imply evidence of innocence. A fine point of a string like tightrope to walk. Having put that concept forth, she had to admit, "Running with this plan is still an uphill fight to convince any jury of innocence who have had daily doses that Osama bin Laden is the personification of evil."

Booker Langston's take on a strategy meant a contrarian theory of who is really guilty. "From my perspective, I believe if we can show, though jurors may not want to hear it, that the United States in their foreign policy has been as reckless in its applications whereas a foreign political party has been likewise abusive to their actions, even violent, then how can two wrongful entities make one more guilty than the other."

"It will be hard for anyone not to think of 9/11 as the lesser of two evils."

"True, one must be subtle in the application. I'm just supposing. Keep in mind; we only need one juror to have doubt for our side."

"Yes, if the defense is to prevail. But we are back to that argument: does an attorney have the moral right to defend a known guilty party?"

"Ah," smiled Booker. "Though your right to question principal is admirable, our system was created to mandate truth, then facts must define justice, and justice is paramount in our national beliefs. It was that which defined us as Americans above all else. And yes, historically, we have had a bad sense of justice, like the 'Dredd Scott' case or sending Japanese-Americans to detention camps, but society nevertheless prevailed, and in time justice was rectified. Our primary, laser-focused goal is to convince the jurors and America that there may be a lingering doubt. And we must face a vigilante mob to do so."

"Is that the beginning of your closing argument?" Both laughed.

"Thanks, Harry, for bringing me back to the tasks at hand." They had grown close in the last month of prepping, he being 'Bookie' and she 'Harry.' Harriet realized something between them was growing, but at the same time knew if she wanted to pursue a relationship and gain intimacy, she had to expunge a ghost — that every telephone call would relive that day of his doomed lover's screaming terror. How could a new relationship replace the deep hurt she could sense still created a somber personality? Even with this focus on trying to save a look-alike bin Laden actor, she could see that his obsessive determination brought back memories of ten years ago. Having an emotional addiction to heartbreak depression was hard to kick, and she did not see an upside to being the one to cure his doldrums.

Out of the blue, Langston said, "I want you to make the opening statement. You deserve it, understand the material, and can create the right vision we want to try to convince jurors with."

She was taken aback. A plum assignment indeed, to be the center of attention and on television right at the start. In her world, she would jump to the head of the line, whatever verdict came down. She leaned over with a quick kiss on the cheek, no prelude to anything more, a friendly peck of a friend thanking another for a favor. While they were united as co-workers and equals, she sensed an ebony blush on the black man's face.

Scene 5: Guest Relations
Setting: Sand Creek Arapahoe Reservation, near Colorado Springs, Colorado

In preparation for all that was coming, Hugh Fox had hired a corporate security service to interview, vet, and then hire a protective detail of twenty professionals, men and women, all highly capable and trained. One particular condition of their employment — they had to be citizens of Hungary or Bulgaria. None of those two countries had victims who died on 9/11 by any attack, and the supposition was that these country-specific employees had no ax to grind. He wanted to wean out the unhinged who might seek revenge or otherwise interfere in what he was 'producing.' Approximately 400 people from 101 countries besides the United States had died on 9/11. It might not matter where they came from, but he could take no chances that something unforeseen could set off a member of a victim's family. What he was doing was protecting his own self-confidence. To this end, two assigned bodyguards would always be in close proximity to each of the stars of *King's Retribution* and to Samantha and himself. Fox laughed to himself at this decision. But no one for Wendell; Holmes could take care of himself.

While traveling, as today, two bodyguards accompanied Hugh Fox, then stationed themselves at either side of the door, as they knew this routine from the last two weeks of such clandestine visits while Fox entered a room they could not see into — the 'prison cell' of Osama bin Laden.

Perhaps a little bit understated, the several rooms were future offices under the Skilleo Sports Stadium on the Colorado Native American reservation, which had been temporarily converted into a very comfortable double suite by a Marriott Hotel décor designer.

"How are you doing? Need anything from us?"

Bin Laden lounged on a sofa. The television was on, showing the 2004 Pixar-Disney *The Incredibles* movie, a computer-animated superhero film. Unbeknownst to the viewer, Fox's company made a brand deal and had come out with a kid-aged video game of *The Incredibles* fighting robotic monsters that still sold well around the holidays.

Bin Laden responded in slow, accented, yet credible English. "My mind is active, my body getting in better shape with the treadmill." He pointed to the machine over in a corner. "I guess we are just waiting to see what the U.S. Government is going to do with me. As I see it, my life as a revolutionary is over. My supporters believe I am dead and a martyr to them, and if my face is ever seen in public again, many will think I have been turned, brainwashed. Don't ask me to make a statement. Whatever I say will do no good for me. I know your government; they won't swap me for a busload of kidnapped Israeli tourists if that were to occur. I am just here, enjoying as I can, my impending doom."

Hugh walked over, checked the refrigerator to ensure it had been stocked daily. No stove, all hot food microwaved. He left meal planning to bin Laden's own reasonable requests. Osama reacted, settled in, no rant ideologue to the walls; why initiate a hunger strike against the conditions of his incarceration? No one in the outside world would know. Such were the Americans. So, he acquiesced and ate very well. Hugh looked around the room, saw everything was in order, and sat in a chair near the couch.

"I am here to tell you that your trial will begin at the end of July. It will be a public event. If you want a comparison of fairness, put it in the context of maybe the Adolph Eichmann trial in 1961 by the District Court of Jerusalem."

Bin Laden did not like the comparison. "I will not accept any court in this land to have the right to try me. I am a political prisoner who still has rights as an international citizen."

Hugh smiled. "I see you have been reading all the legal paperwork we gave you. Good for you; I want an educated defendant. No, Mr. bin Laden, this is what you feared it might be; this is a show trial, tightly choreographed. I can give you slight comfort and point out that there is little chance of you being exonerated. However, you have to trust your two defense attorneys. They are highly skilled and dedicated by honor to giving you the best representation.

"But if you are found guilty, then there will be a debate on the consequences of punishment you might face. That will be out of my hands. A jury will have decided and given you an honest verdict, as their prejudices might allow. Frankly, if you are found guilty, the death penalty is too clean and final a punishment for all the pain and suffering you put 300 million of my countrymen through. If asked, my idea is that you are placed in the middle, say, on Interstate 70, in the middle of Kansas, dressed as a white-robed cleric, and let's see how the average motorist might react.

"Yet, as I say, you and I have put the conclusion in motion, and I have no desire to stack the deck against you or pre-empt justice, and that's what this country will decide: how shall a society act against the horrendous? Please talk in all seriousness about your defense with your lawyers."

"Mr. Fox," said the non-state prisoner, "I am ready for anything your damn failed society forces upon me."

Hugh ignored the declaration. "Mr., or Sheik bin Laden, I have come to tell you the agenda as I know it. You will have one meeting with your defense attorneys one week before the trial, then daily afterward if you wish. Before the trial, wardrobe and make-up will put you into a pristine condition the world can admire, if some wish to do so.

282   S.P. Grogan

"And I'm honest. At the end of the trial, I don't know what comes next. So, treat every day as precious. Write your manifestos, write poetry. Just don't be harsh on we of *King's Retribution*. Remember, if you were caught by the SEALS, you would have most certainly been killed. If we had turned you over to the government, even last week, you would have been assassinated on the way to their maximum security. Or, otherwise, dropped into a deep black hole. Here, under my direction, the court will allow you to give any statement you wish, at a time of your choosing, preferably part of a closing argument, or upon the verdict, whichever way it goes."

That caught bin Laden short.

"I can say what I wish?"

"Yes, no muzzling, but it has to be done on my cue, and to your advantage. It will gain you the largest televised audience ever assembled."

The prisoner thought for a moment and smiled. "I may talk of the glorious coming of '*Crimson Scimitar.*'"

"Ah, yes, you mentioned that several times before, but without explanation. We found you, and sooner rather than later, we will discover your other secrets."

"I doubt that. It is in motion. I cannot even stop it. An unsheathed sword swinging in many directions draws blood at every slash." On that note of bravado, Hugh got up to leave. From his sport jacket pocket, he pulled a sheaf of papers and put them down on a table.

"Something for you to look at and consider. No pressure."

"I won't sign any confession or any document to be manipulated against me or al-Qaeda."

"Nothing of the sort. This is a brand licensing agreement from my company, Skilleo Games Technology. It gives my company total rights to use your image, a lot of gobbledygook language, but the gist is: I can put your face into any of my games. Done tactfully, of course."

"You think I would do anything of the sort? Be a target to be shot by the children of America. You are only a self-serving evil capitalist."

"Read the document, is all I ask of you. It is in English and Arabic. Of the revenue proceeds, 5% goes to you, and if you are convicted, or speaking honestly, become deceased, the 5% revenues revert to your large family. I have heard that you personally may not be as wealthy as they say, that most of your funds have gone to bolster your organization's causes. Osama, that might mean millions of US dollars to provide for your wives and children. Not from the bin Laden family of your parents, but a gift from you."

"Get out of here."

"Someone else will do this, without your permission, create you as a Devil Ogre, steal royalties meant for you. I am afraid the whole world has become crass; there are those who will seek clickbait to attract advertisers, trading on fame and controversy. Today, you have that currency. Do not lose sight of what you might do with the bin Laden brand. Consider us as 'partners' in that I will defend your name, not turn you into a cartoon, even if I gain by it."

Hugh had just opened the door to leave.

"You are the lowest of lows, lower than the piss of a scorpion!" shouted the prisoner at his jailer.

Hugh Fox pled to his guilt as he departed. "Yes, I am an entrepreneur, unfettered."

Scene 6: Wannabe Swashbuckler
Setting: off Catalina Island, California, May 19th

"You look like death."

"I think my insides are coming out."

"I don't think buying this boat would be your best decision."

"Do you think?" said Holmes with stomach-in-his-throat pained sarcasm.

He had once run the Marine obstacle course at Paris Island. Nor would he forget freefalling into Venezuela to meet with opposition leaders, pulling the parachute cord at 1,500 feet. On this day, the gusting winds and the high wave swells mixed his breakfast like a blender, shortly to be his undoing. This had been the second of his 'trial' New Life experiences. Golf ended at Pebble Beach when he found the ocean or the bunkers more than the fairway. What did they say of the sport, 'an endless series of tragedies obscured by the occasional miracle.' Buying a 2011 26-footer Skip Jack sports fishing boat for a hundred grand was going to be his Hemmingway moment — catch (and release) blue marlins, sail off to an island, drink mojitos, dance with the native girls. Now, he might never make landfall alive.

He leaned over the railing. God, there went breakfast!

"I think we ought to put into Avalon, let you get your land legs back." The boat charter captain, and sales agent, knew after the first mile out of Long Beach that this landlubber would not be buying the boat and changing his lifestyle to a Captain Ron. It took Holmes, as the prospective buyer, past the point of no return to realize the weather conditions were not even severe, modest at most, and this was not the best idea in contemplating a change in his priorities.

"Yes, I agree. I will sleep in a hotel tonight, and if you don't mind, I will take the ferry back tomorrow." As a larger ship with a deep draft to cut the waves, the daily ferry had more life jackets to grab for.

And here he was, mid-afternoon, overlooking the small harbor, sitting outside at a seafood restaurant, enjoying a club soda, still calming his gurgling stomach. It was time, he thought,

284   S.P. Grogan

to take stock of himself. He was not *that* old, mere rocking chair retirement on the porch did not suit him, and as he was finding, idle time did not keep his mind functioning as he wished.

Hugh Fox had asked him to help out, temporarily, come back in around the end of June. Probably needed help gift-wrapping bin Laden to his former employers. Though that might be short-term satisfaction as he did not feel he was part of *King's Retribution*. His whole life had made him an outsider. Thus, he had started the trek to discover a new life. It wasn't going well.

Before him was yesterday's copy, May 17th, of the *L.A. Times*, and one article stood out, just two small paragraphs, under the fold, at the bottom of the International Section, but the headline said it all "*CIA To Search Bin Laden Compound.*" He chuckled, wondering if King's puff piece several days earlier of 'revealing' what he had seen that night in bin Laden's home had set the Agency into reviewing their operation; did they, in fact, leave anything behind? It would be just like the government to rush back and see what they might have overlooked, forcing them to defend their efficiency. Holmes had seen the CIA publicity gristmill, sympathetic journalists, milking their intelligence coup to the max of positive goodwill in the public's eyes. The headlines and planted stories this the last week spoke volumes.

— *bin Laden tape on new uprisings*

— *39 Terror Plots Foiled Since 9/11*

— *al-Qaeda minus bin Laden still deadly*

— *bin Laden knew of European plots*

Didn't the public understand that the intelligence community engaged in subtle propaganda to accept that spies are needed more now than ever? And oh, by the way, tell your congressman to maintain our appropriations, if not grant us more funding.

Holmes wondered, with good reason, if Givens was behind this screen of currying more favors with Congress, a skill that Holmes conceded his ex-field partner excelled in, banal schmoozing.

As he watched the tourists cavort around shopping for Chinese-made souvenir trinkets that Wal-Mart back on the mainland was selling for less and taking photos of the idyllic harbor with its water parking for day tripper sailboats, none of them realizing that the water slapping the expensive hulls was rated yearly as one of the most polluted harbors in the nation. What looks photogenic on the surface can be deceiving.

Clicking cameras brought his mind to tumble back through the night of May 2nd into the 3rd, still upset that his last operation went so terribly wrong. Poor Clayton Briggs, to be another unheralded statistic in the War on Terror. He hoped that Briggs would be avenged along with all others of 9/11. Holmes wondered if he would help if called upon, but he did not see himself as a focal participant. What worth did he have left to contribute?

Holmes did admit to himself a lasting loyalty to the Agency, even if he considered a few in the upper leadership were pricks, understood the intelligence gathered in the bin Laden raid would lead to more operations, definitely an increase in targeted missile launches from the drones. He felt a little envious to be missing out. But did they have all the information? He picked up his cell phone, called the central switchboard, and gave his old code check-in.

"Sorry, sir, but that number is not active."

"Oh, yeah, it was a good try, though. Could you do me a favor and leave a message for the bin Laden desk?"

"I'm sorry, sir, we do not have anything like that. If you would like to send us a letter, perhaps it might be directed to the right party." Gee, obfuscation continues to reign.

"Okay, let's try this. "My message is this: 'the Chinese ask — do you have any more Black Hawks to photograph?' Here is my name and number. Have someone on the bin Laden desk call me back." He hung up. He knew all incoming calls were taped, and his message could only be interpreted as suspicious; he definitely would get a quick assessment analysis.

Five minutes later, as he expected, the call came in.

"Wendell, is that you trying to get the Espionage Act thrown at you? Want to see Guantanamo this time of year?"

"And this is?"

"Matthew Brady."

"Oh, Matthew, right, I heard you are a new Section Head? Terrorist Analysis? Mid-East Desk. Thought I would get some tech grunt dealing with me, read me the riot act, and shuffle me out the door."

"I caught this as it was going across my desk. You realize, you are persona non grata."

"Still taping all interesting conversations?"

"Of course."

"Well, I will guard my vapid tongue against cursing certain employees using their family's anatomy as a reference point."

"Most helpful."

"My greater fear is that I hear Director P. is being tapped for Defense. I would hope the President looks to a successor from beyond the Agency instead of promoting bad apples from within."

286   S.P. Grogan

Brady skipped the social visit knowing the unstated animosity between Holmes and Givens. "And your call pertains to what?"

"Just like you boys, sift the general bull for the hard crap. And how is the bin Laden desk going these days?"

"You know very well there is no bin Laden desk. If so, it is a minor desk in a storage closet."

"Oh, please, let's not have Wild Bill Donovan roll over in his grave. So, now it's renamed the al-Qaeda Desk. Am I close? But here's my reason for calling. I note you boys are going to take the same tour I and a few of my *closest* television star friends took a few weeks back. The Agency P.R. planted it in yesterday's *L.A. Times*. So, when you folks climb to the second floor, there is a hidden closet in the hallway. Push on the side wall molding, and it will open. What I want to know, only in a general sense, is what you guys find in there. I am waking with these nightmares that I saw something in the dark but just can't get my brain to click the light bulb on."

Silence. "If you can hold, let me get back to you in a few minutes."

"Okay." Seals frolicking in the harbor kept him amused until the connection came back.

"Tell me what you saw." A new light bulb from a part of his brain he had planned on unplugging beamed to brilliance.

"Matthew, I am impressed, so you guys already went in there. When? Probably on

Kerry's visit on the 16th. Am I correct? The press release was just safety wallpaper to deflect any possible leakage. Keeps with your improved good-guy image."

"Holmes, what did you see?" Brady knew his side of the answer, and in this regard, Holmes accepted, for the moment, they were on the same team.

"Books. A kind of bookcase, three shelves, and they were filled with books and magazines. Also, some graffiti on the wall, not much, no 'Kilroy was here,' more doodling, reminder 'to-do' notes, Arabic political slogans, maybe other muddling."

Silence.

"Give it up, Brady. Quid Pro Quo, and all that."

"Door was open. No books. Graffiti still there. Looks like the Pakistani army came back in and did a clean-up or a cover-up."

"Maybe, maybe not."

"Holmes, you know something?"

"No. And I am retired, remember? Thrown under the bus. No one to bounce my ideas off." And that was the truth. What could he really deduce from that empty closet? But he could not lose this door opener.

Crimson Scimitar

"If I do come up with something, is there a faster way to make it through to the proper decision makers? I wouldn't want to be shuffled around on a merry-go-round; after all, the Agency is a part of the Washington, D.C. mindset. That's why I always tried to stay in the field."

"You were a good agent, Holmes. That's the word from some of the other old mastodons around here. Anything you got; someone will listen. Let me give you some numbers. By the way, your hands in Abbottabad were quite photogenic." The flipping-off photo.

"Your people did finally realize those were local Chinese shopkeepers. Nothing nefarious."

"Yeah, a good gotcha gag. Took a week before facial recognition came up with zilch. Even though we were played, a few of the team were definitely spouting fire. Lucky for you, there was nothing in the Regs that would have cooked your goose, literally." Holmes chortled aloud that someone appreciated the inside joke, Brady, being recorded, could not laugh.

Holmes jotted down the numbers, and the call ended. At least all bridges weren't burned.

Books in a secret closet, and two weeks later, they're gone. Why?

He leaned down and pulled *the* novel from his overnight bag. The one picked up off the street in Pakistan. At least I brought something to read on the trip home tomorrow, thumbing the pages, noting several words written into the margins *in Arabic*. But maybe I should wait, I'll probably get seasick reading, and besides, I'm out of work, plenty of time on my hands. Maybe in a few days I'll start it. Maybe download it as an e-book. No, I like the feel of this one, hefty, good paper, hard cover. Tangible worth. It's seen a lot, and I need it to talk to me. He dropped the book back into his bag, unread.

EPISODE EIGHTEEN — The Plan and The Hunt Team

Scene 1: The Scientist's Good Fortune
Setting: New York State, June 1st, 2011

"They have set the date for the shipment, September 30th."

"Plenty of time for us," answered Brahma Singh.

Plenty of time to get the Crimson Scimitar team in place, thought the Scientist.

"Yes, but I want to have secondary plans ready to leave earlier, if need be, just in case. After talking today with the staff working with the Nuclear Waste Alternative Task Force, I get a sense they are a little freaked out and running in place without a roadmap."

Singh, the Scientist, as al-Qaeda hierarchy gave him this cover name, was responding to his immediate superior, the Operations Manager at the Indian Points Nuclear Plant.

"What makes you think that?"

"Have you read the series *The New York Times* has been running on our industry?" The manager did not wait for a response but pulled from a file folder and handed over a faxed copy of an article, the headline read, [June 1st] *Changing Nuclear Picture After the Tsunami*

Singh assumed this article arose from the decision last week by German Chancellor Angela Merkel to end the country's nuclear program, making Germany the biggest economy to abandon nuclear power.

"Well, I don't expect a tsunami in inland New York State."

"Don't count out Mother Nature," corrected the Ops Manager. "Just recall that the 5th largest grossing film two years ago was *2012*, filled with earthquakes, volcanoes, tectonic plate shifts, and the climax with the largest continent-destroying tsunami in the universe."

Singh was constantly reminded by his boss that the man was a movie trivia freak, less the scientist, more the generalist data-absorbing bureaucrat who could, as Singh knew, list all movies that teamed Veronica Lake with Alan Ladd and still have the time to operate a nuclear facility on the side.

"Grant you that. But I would guess the first *Times* article was really what set off the Task Force."

"Indeed." And on cue, he pulled out the article.

[May 11th] *A Dangerous Fusion: A Crack in the Safety of Nuclear Reactors*

Singh refreshed his memory by scanning the article, shaking his head at the fear-mongering teaser sentence, '*Since the Three Mile Island accident, at least 38 nuclear power reactors have been forced to shut down for a year or more because of safety problems.*'

He handed the article back.

"At least this time, we were not mentioned by name." He donned his 'them against us' editorial positioning. "Why don't they write something positive about what we are doing, like supplying all the electricity the public demands?"

The Operations Manager nodded in agreement.

"Well, with this shipment, we are being proactive and disposing of nuclear waste into a program that might just be the answer to our overflowing stockpile problem."

"Yeah, but the government doesn't want to let everyone know we *do* have an answer."

"Unfortunately, the State we are sending the waste shipment to doesn't want it, even after $1.5 billion was spent there to build the repository. U.S. Senator Harry Reid is Majority

Leader and has clout with the President, who's facing his second term election next year, so the Task Force has deemed this a 'National Emergency Priority' and 'Top Secret.' Everything is being couched as an 'incomplete transit shipment. The public manifest will state it's just being stored temporarily until it moves on to the final waste destruction facility."

"Which plant the government hasn't built yet. So, the shipment may sit for years waiting for its final destination."

"When we succeed with this test shipment and let everyone know after the election what we've accomplished, I think we'll have the votes in Congress to reopen the repository. I hear a bill will be introduced tomorrow just for that purpose, but it will take a year or so to be veto-proof, at least until after the election."

But you won't succeed, thought the Scientist, *we will*. That evening, at an office store with computer rentals, he emailed out an invite-gram, 'Aunt's Birthday, September 30th. Please arrive a month early to visit old friends and family.' He knew the Professor would receive this message, but on the other end, he wondered, who in the al-Qaeda network would step in to run *Crimson Scimitar*?

The same day, a coded email from the NRC came across the computer screen of Assistant Deputy Director Givens at Langley, and he read, "September 30th Shipment Date set, any changes in conditions?"

"No." Givens typed in the simple email response sending it back to the Task Force Chairperson without even glancing at the Daily Briefing Reports from other security agencies, but knowing the CIA had no high interest in international traffic chatter about possible domestic strikes within U.S. borders.

Scene 2: Skilleo Geek Squad
Setting: Los Angeles, June 1st

Holmes had decided to take a break from his self-journey of discovery and drop out of sight. The timing was right; he was not a public figure, always behind the scenes. And the glory, if not the infamous, was about to occur, so it would be wise to make oneself scarce.

Once again, he was at a loss about his future. Holmes had spent a week of his mandated California vacation experimenting with New Life Experience #3, traveling up into the Los Olivos — Solvang wine country behind Santa Barbara, touring vineyards, and staying in a trendy B&B. In Los Angeles, he became the tourist, visiting the La Brea tar pits, sympathizing with prehistoric animals sucked to their deaths in asphalt, and later following a ribbon of modern asphalt, he drove the I-405 up above the smog to visit priceless works of art at the Getty Museum. Spending all his free time exploring did not resonate well with him; a lack of exhilaration from not directly participating, he found himself unsatisfied even in the midst of fascinating educational sojourns.

At the airport, prepared to return to his unused condo in Virginia, he discovered his plane on a five-hour delay, something about a cockpit light not functioning and maintenance without the correct fuse replacement, the cost being a mere $25, as he overheard. He did not consider inconvenience could be a prelude to fate. Holmes accepted this unscheduled blip stoically, placing the blame squarely on his shoulders, for without his government credit card to expense such business-class flights, he had sought the most economical fare, bringing him to a cut-rate airline, which, to make ticket costs so low must have scrimped on all parts, without a back-up inventory of spares, including this $25 fuse. The ticket counter clerk gave him a limp apologetic smile, but all service people did that when your world had just been made miserable, but theirs had not.

He wandered the airport, avoiding the bookstores that blared out in print all forms of gossip, lies, false reports, and pundit essays for and against. Even the airport's public television feed blabbed the same mishmash. Holmes could laugh that soon *King's Retribution* and Storm King would gain the notoriety so long sought to make next season a must-watch smash. He laughed; he would not be a part of Fox's grandiose schemes. Fox had only asked one thing of him. Since he knew their guest and had a history with the squirreled-away prisoner, he would be tasked to babysit, a bodyguard of sorts when called up in a couple of weeks, so he had been told. That was fine with him — a firm job assignment at last.

With time to kill waiting on the plane repair, which made him nervous, and lunchtime coming up, Wendell decided to grab a cab ride over to Santa Monica and have lunch on the 3rd Street Promenade. Coincidentally, as he well knew, this was only a few blocks from where Hugh Fox and his Skilleo team had opened up the War Room for the bin Laden search and escapade. Was it only two months ago? Was it still operating?

Poking around the old stomping grounds, he found guards in place and was definitely surprised to find the door to the War Room's office unlocked, and more so, that there were people inside. Four of them, to be exact, each to their cubicles, and they seemed to be busy at work, no slacking off, even if though selected staff of *King's Retribution* was to regroup in the Colorado Springs area no later than the 20th of July.

He looked into the nearest office work space at a young man with purple-slashed dreadlocks, large earlobe plugs, and wearing a band shirt; some group called Maroon something.

Feeling good to get back into role play, he introduced himself as a friend of Hugh Fox and that he had accompanied him to Pakistan, downplaying that he had only gone as a favor, nothing more.

"What are you all doing?" he asked. "I thought Hugh would have boarded this place up and taken the key with him."

All youth is innocent or expects the world to be the same, so why hide anything?

"We all thought that too, and as you can see, he did downsize to the max. But, no worries, everyone else went back to the campus HQ, no one lost their job."

Good ol' Hugh, thought Wendell. *The boy genius can do no wrong; no one hates the guy.*

They exchanged name introductions and firm handshakes. The geek kid's name was Gizmo, saying with pride, "Everybody calls me that."

"Yes, you are, I'm sure, but what specifically are you doing? Still working on discovering bin Laden's new lair?" Wendell had to keep the Big Secret until Hugh made the Big Reveal.

"Definitely a bummer, man, for *King's Retribution*, but as Mr. Fox said to us four, 'the war ain't over until Armageddon, or Bruce Willis says it's over.'"

Gizmo waved around the room. "All four of us do different tasks. Bridget over there, the blonde, she just enters all the news, worldwide, everything about terrorists, wars, all this Arab Spring shit, who's who, who's killing who. Mark, next to her, takes the news and runs scenario programs, all those simulations of potential outcomes, using variables. You know, like war games, assassination probabilities, you know?"

Holmes did not know but found it fascinating that Fox, even with You Know Who under wraps, was not letting go of his 'catch more bad guys' obsession.

"And what do you do, and I assume your partner there?" In the cubicle across the way, another young man sat hunched over his computer keyboard, rapid-fire typing. A part of his costume of rebellious independence was that he wore a braided ponytail and a multi-colored tattoo down the length of his arm, which Holmes might take a wild guess at what was a lavish display of comic book heroes. He could spot Wolverine gracing the young man's shoulder.

"Lars and I are programmers. We've been asked to design a 'kill the terrorists' urban combat game." Holmes had been correct in the earlier assumption about Fox being anti-war, anti-military. A real war zone is a great eye-opener to a preconceived West Coast Richie Rich group mentality. Holmes guessed that Fox's recent in-the-field close proximity to murder made a convert out of him, redefining his interpretation between good and evil, no longer that evil was just misunderstood or that America was the real bully in the War on Terror. But to reconstruct his beliefs into a video/mobile game, what does that say?

"Fox told me that there was strong competition out there already?"

"Yeah, don't know why Skilleo didn't jump into the field earlier, but hey, we'll catch up. Games with SEALS or Delta Force shooting up the landscape, wiping out terrorists, blowing up this bin Laden dude and his gang of cutthroats, those may be the next generation of fad. We just need to be ready with this if it's the next hot ticket item."

The geeky programmer was a fount of info, definitely seeing an adult human in near proximity the button to launch his tongue to chatter. That brought up a new line of inquiry that had resonated with Holmes since the tour of Skilleo's Research Labs.

"And I assume this new game will have all the high-tech whiz-bang stuff, and pardon the joke, but all 'the Gizmo high tech,' like Wii Game meets *Futurama*."

Gizmo was honored to be identified with a TV show like *Futurama* and that this man even knew about it. Holmes didn't know, never watched consumer TV, and had just thrown out associated wordplay off the top of his head.

"Yeah, like, from the mall or from across the country, I could say a code and my computer thousands of miles away, could log me in, and start a game mode, and I could play it in my head, or with remote sensor glasses. Real futuristic stuff, man."

"You're talking about the jaw implant?"

The kid was impressed; to have that inside scoop, Mr. Holmes must be a really close friend of the super boss.

Holmes gave a quick glance at the kid's workstation.

"What's that?" Holmes thought he knew; in fact, he *did* know.

"That's a bad night shot inside bin Laden's compound. We've been asked to pixel-enhance it and make the shot look like it was a daylight photograph. More resolution for a sharper image."

"Looks like you're getting there. That's quite remarkable, night into day." He pulled his cell phone out of his pocket. Went to the 'Camera' app and scrolled back past Renaissance paintings, reconstructed saber tooth tigers, and up-close snapshots of wine labels. He offered his camera phone to the programmer.

"Do you think you could do the same with these? I think there are five shots."

"Wow, man, you were there?"

"Just a tourist, tagging along with buddy Hugh."

"Well, sure, won't be a problem."

"Can you download these and email me the do-overs?" There came a look, the one separating youth from age, where without saying anything, this zit-faced IQ dudester had thought, '*What planet were you born on, old fossil? That's kindergarten play for me.*'

Holmes let the expression slide and thanked him, paying kudos to such brainy abilities, and then, almost as an afterthought, said, "Could you include in what you send me, what you did for Hugh, so I can compare, and can you send him a copy of mine and his together? I think he would appreciate your special talent; give him a great souvenir to review. Oh, and while you are knocking out copies, there were a couple of other people on that trip. I'm sure Fox's office has their contact information. Send a copy to Samantha Carlisle and Callie Cardoza."

"Yeah, sure, don't think that would be a problem. After all, that's a pretty historic souvenir for them to have."

LAX to Washington Dulles. When later that day, with Wendell Holmes seeking comfort, crowded into his economy class seat, the great coastal basin metropolis of Los Angeles shrinking in size and then slipping behind him over the western horizon, he pulled out the book. Finally, he decided he would give a proper amount of 'trapped' time to reading; best-selling author Tom Clancy's 2010 published *Dead or Alive*, his latest techno-thriller. Maybe, this will be my Life Experience #4, an author's research expert on espionage, or better yet, a book critic.

Scene 3: Games for Small Thrones
Setting: Village of Lahan, outside the town of Wana,
South Waziristan, Pakistan, June 4th, 2011

Khalaf hated rudimentary democracy. For several weeks, he had been trapped in the village, listening to various sides put forth their tiring arguments, and stump for preferred candidates to take over al-Qaeda to fill the vacancy left by bin Laden's disappearance, his presumed 'murder by the Great Satan.'

It was apparent that two camps were forming, those of the old guard, a conservative wing that favored al-Zawahiri as being the logical heir. After all, did not bin Laden defer to the Doctor's direction and input on the 9/11 planning? On the other side, a Young Turk revolt seemed to be building strength, with the candidate being Kashmiri, with planks in his platform for more aggressive war taken to the enemy within Pakistan. More quick surgical thrusts into the belly of the Pakistani government carried out by greater numbers of suicide bombers. Destabilize and conquer, and to Khalaf's horror, Kashmiri began shifting away from total enthusiasm for *Crimson Scimitar*, not openly negative, just more circumspect. The plan ought to go forward, his supporters said he said, if only to keep America paranoid and let them know al-Qaeda still could deliver a far-reaching blow. But whether such a grandiose plan had any chance of success (a backward slap at bin Laden's strategy), the war had to be first won on the local ground where we live; this was said by many al-Qaeda within the village, and Khalaf noticed that those starting to show up for the *loya jirga*, the political gathering of great importance, were coalescing in this opinion.

The jirga was set for the 7th of June, and at that time, it was expected that a new al-Qaeda leader would be chosen. By then, Shahin would be on the scene for his final briefing on the *Crimson Scimitar* attack, gain everyone's blessing, and begin the process of putting the wheels in motion; the first priority was to have the attack team make a safe and unchallenged entry into the U.S. Khalaf had heard this might be difficult, as the southern border, their planned entry point, was quite guarded.

The grand council meeting would be interesting. Khalaf believed Shahin would again fire up the naysayers to support bin Laden's final plan of attack. Would Kashmiri oppose Shahin's role and go into an open play to take over al-Qaeda?

Towards this important meeting, al-Rahman appeared yesterday on the scene and, like Kashmiri, brought with him an escort of scraggly yet lethal bodyguards and, more important, news directly from al-Zawahiri.

To those gathered, he said, "After our beloved leader's martyrdom (he had no evidence of such an occurrence), the decision was made that if the CIA found anything compromising upon his body or in his home, the Doctor ought to seek another location, and taking no chances, that is what he did. While he is incognito, I have been delegated to speak for him."

At the appropriate time, when they could be in private conference, Khalaf gave his report in more detail than he had been outlining to Kashmiri and his followers, including the command from bin Laden that Khalaf be appointed as one of the al-Qaeda delegates to the United States to participate in the negotiations after *Crimson Scimitar*'s success. Rahman had no love for the United States. His father, the blind cleric, would spend the rest of his life in a U.S. prison for coordinating, if not blessing, the first attack on the World Trade Center. When Khalaf finished with his report, Rahman spit out,

"They should all perish."

"There should be a few left to surrender. Remember, bin Laden's plan is a good one; to have America withdraw is a great defeat in itself and allows us to rise to power."

"Yes, you are right; the Sheik could see the greater vision while we only could see the haze of the battlefield a few steps before us."

In a gesture to mark his obedience to al-Zawahiri as the leader he would now wish to follow (instead of Kashmiri), Khalaf made a great ceremony of handing over the computer thumb drive, consisting of all the plans, contacts, participants, and codes to *Crimson Scimitar*.

"You have done our cause a great service to rescue this information," said Rahman, holding tight the gift received. "*Crimson Scimitar* has many disjunctive parts kept separate to protect everyone, and here is the key. It would have failed had you not brought this out safely. I will convey to the Doctor all that you have said. I do not know if those in our meeting will wish to give you so much power as an envoy, and it is unfortunate from your perspective that the Sheik did not set such a high commission into writing, but I will be your advocate and make a case for you when I next talk to our future leader."

There it was, a little camel trading. Rahman gained Khalaf's support for the Doctor to be the anointed successor to bin Laden, and Rahman would present Khalaf's petition. If Khalaf were going to move up the ladder within al-Qaeda, he accepted he would make choices, and doing so meant taking sides, which translated into fresh enemies. He had now done so.

Khalaf did not tell his fellow al-Qaeda compatriot, or anyone for that matter, that he had made copies of the information on both thumb drives; that Rahman and the Doctor would only see one, that of *Crimson Scimitar*, and Khalaf, protecting himself, would keep the other data stick to himself, the original on him, another copy hidden back in Abbottabad. This data stick contained the banking information for certain secured al-Qaeda accounts, those accounts once under bin Laden's control, now no more. The amount in question being $US 200,000, and in terms of Pakistani worth, Khalaf could believe himself a wealthy man, but he saw the money not as his to covet but as his to apply towards his goals. For all he had recently been through, he sincerely believed what he wanted was best for the jihad, and he took the position that he was a trustee of these funds, to use as he saw fit, and such personal confidence begat by ready cash continued his forward momentum.

But these final days before the *loya jirga* scheduled for June 7th, the grand council meeting made him impatient, restless. He could not stand the petty politics of impoverished zealots brandishing guns while arguing before and after prayers, even during the meal hours. Nor was he appeased with the entertainment from the gathered men who extolled their war stories or sang ballads of close calls and sacrifice in battle.

Scene 4: Emerald Eyes
Setting: Outside the Village of Lahan

While waiting, Khalaf had begun to take long walks from the village, limited in exploration, clearing his mind to again study from memory the computer files bearing all nuances of *Crimson Scimitar*. He felt this attack, even if completed by others, there must be some way he could attach his star... but only if he could convince the Supreme Council that he should be a spokesperson for al-Qaeda when they sat down to negotiate with the Americans.

There they were again, the four girls, barely women. Days earlier, he had seen them on a trail leading out of the village but attached no importance to them. He took other trails, including once the roadway into Wana to buy coffee from a vendor, sit under a shade tree, and listen to old men talk about the weather and how poor the harvest that fall might be, as he surmised, old men had done so for several millennia.

In his third sighting of the young women, he noticed a pattern. Two women would walk out of the village from one direction and run into the other two women, all four in a single file procession. One woman carried on her head a large clay jar with a wide mouth; another woman balanced a small crate with some sort of cloth-wrapped package. The next time, they carried the same, yet he sensed they switched who was carrying what. That seemed odd. In their manner of dress, all four wore the niqab wardrobe, with their faces completely covered, all in black, except one of the women, the tallest of the group, who wore deep blue. He approximated only by height, stature, and their walk that three of the women must be 13 to 14 in age, while the one in blue could be slightly older, maybe close to16, maybe 17; he knew little, had no experience of how to guess what lay behind a veil.

But their masked outings intrigued him. An imbalance to a set order — and with nothing better to do, Khalaf followed them out of curiosity, hopeful, for variety, they might know another route he had not traversed before.

After about a half mile of walking through rocky terrain, the path barely visible, where he thought they might be doing a circuitous route into Wana, they branched off in another direction.

Soon, he could see they were approaching what looked like a large ruin, what he deduced was some sort of British Raj-era military outpost, most of the place reduced to rubble with several remaining walls standing in various forms of weathered erosion.

He hung back so as not to be seen, and when he moved forward again, he caught a glimpse of the last woman treading over a crumbled wall, going down inside, out of sight. Ready to turn around, his eye spotted a rusted sign, and he went forward to read the wording, both in Pashtu and English: *Warning! Mine Field!*

Instinctively, he quick-stepped backward, fearful of where he stood. Before the outpost, he surveyed a large open area, and as he saw, most of it was strung with barbwire, aged and broken in many places. Indeed, a minefield must have existed, either emptied of explosive ordinance, or there was a good chance a few unstable devices had been forgotten, ready to take a leg or a life. Yet, here, surely the women had crossed unhurt, but no man, like himself, would take such a risk just to be curious about what lay beyond the wall. In this dilemma, he spotted a few black threads caught on a metal barb. Here is where they entered, and bending as a tracker after mountain sheep, he studied the ground seeking the mark of a footprint on rock. No tracks. But what's this? A colored pebble, hand-colored, not natural rock, he could spot them every few feet, the short gait that might be the length of a woman's step. To step to the side, right or left, or step on the stone, was a life-or-death decision, and with trepidation, he chose the latter, the first step with a catching breath.

Nothing happened — next small step, and another after that.

Near the wall, he heard a rare sound: laughter.

Securing a hiding place, he moved over the fallen wall stones, accepting he had passed through the abandoned minefield, agreeing it was a good ruse to keep people away.

Carefully, he peered over.

Football. Soccer, it was called elsewhere.

The four women were having fun, laughing, not loudly but enthusiastically kicking an old soccer ball around on the dirt of a small enclosure. Khalaf soon enough figured out their deception. The large jar had carried the ball; the small balanced crate hid tennis shoes which they now wore, their sandals off to the side. Stimulating something deep inside him, a perverse reaction, he saw they had hiked up their skirts, wearing white pants underneath, loose-fitting pants, and had removed their face veils, still covered but more modestly by hijab scarfs. His eyes quickly were drawn to the blue full robe outfit. And as she turned in a parrying, rapid kick demonstrating she was the most talented of the other three, in fact, probably a teacher-coach, Khalaf saw her face and found it beautiful. He watched transfixed, the motion, the gracefulness in making her ball strikes artistic, like it might be set to music as a frenzied quick-step folk dance — and dance throughout time conveyed sexual innuendos, invitation.

One of the untutored kicks of another girl bounced the ball into the rocks, and the young woman in blue, shouting out a laughing scold, walked over to retrieve it, and when she did so and glanced up, her eyes locked into Khalaf's gaze from his hiding place, her entrancement overwhelmed him. Both reacted by not reacting: what should he do? He recalled his Qur'an:

O Prophet! Tell your wives and your daughters and the women of the believers to draw their (jalabib) veils all over their bodies that is most convenient that they should be known (as such) and not molested: and Allah is Oft-Forgiving Most Merciful.

First stern at their discovery, she froze and waited, but he did not jump up and shout Qur'an scripture or try to stone them as violating heretics or curse them as licentious. Suddenly, he wondered, feared she might think him a *munharif* (pervert or deviant). The thought mortified him. She said nothing, saw not his anger but a face full of his embarrassment. Finally placing a smile of mutual conspiracy between them, he hoped, she returned to their game. Though at this time, she raised her veil to cover her face, beneath it, she started to sing loudly a song, not a chant of scripture, but something else; he recognized it, a new popular tune, *Afghan Pesarak* by singer Aryana Sayeed. Modern music, certainly forbidden in this village. If not among all conservative Islamic tribesmen.

You are so tall, Tajik girl

You are beautiful and you have drunk (weedy) eyes

Seriously, I would die for you and your ancestors

You are the legacy of your father and your ancestors

You are so tall, Tajik girl

Khalaf, only weeks ago believing he had the courage of a lion, been in a running street battle that killed an infidel with a car, fled in utter cowardice from four women playing sports, mostly shamed that his spying had been discovered.

What he had seen must have broken some sharia law, which one he did not know, but women in competition, in athletics, must be a taboo since he had not known of any other such examples in Afghanistan or Pakistan. Yes, Muslim women he knew in Egypt were more progressive in mimicking Western women's dress and saying they were equal to men. As he was taught and must agree, he still accepted, by Mohammed's writings, that men's actions only sought to protect a woman's virtue. He had heard rumors that some Saudi women wanted to participate in the Olympic Games. Knowledge of perceived sin, such as playing soccer, had at this moment no influence on his morality, for Khalaf's mind focused only on the uncovered beauty in the face of the Woman in Deep Sea Blue bearing bright green emerald eyes. He must learn more about her.

By his later discovery, reality is seldom a friend of happiness.

Scene 5: The Mystery of the Strange Request
Setting: War Room, Santa Monica, June 3rd

Two suited men and a nattily attired young woman, all three with briefcases, arrived at 10 am, standing at the office entrance, looking around, gaining a perspective of who was working within. The *King's Retribution* people were back on their production lot doing catch-up, leaving mostly the four IT geek people and a receptionist answering the phones, doing odd job clean-up from the Pakistan trip, or otherwise cataloging some of the Hunt Team research work for the archives.

From one of the stranger's briefcases was produced and handed over to the five employees copies of an official-looking Memo from Hugh Fox of Five Aces Studioz. The young woman read aloud what turned out to be a directive: All data on all machines to be copied and handed over to the strangers. Bridget whispered these were definitely 'corporate suit' types from Skilleo; attorneys was Gizmo's opinion, and, being a wise mouth anti-authoritarian-at heart, demanded a call to his boss's office to confirm the memo was indeed from the mind and hand of Mr. Fox. Finally, bowing to the boss's unusual request, after several hours of this scramble, disks and thumb drives were collected and placed into one of the briefcases of the attorneys, who had merely sat around chatting among themselves while looking rigidly officious.

Then, the moving men showed up. Having been annoyed by all the data retrieval and copy requests, the Skilleo IT people became incensed when all their pet computers were unceremoniously carted off. And while they were yelling 'theft' and proletariat slogans damning the elites against the masses, a second wave of movers, more Best Buy-looking fellow geeks, arrived with dollies pushing boxes of the latest computer ware, followed in turn by several IT friends from the Skilleo home office who assisted in a massive set up.

The lady attorney told all the grunt workers present:

"For the next thirty days, your sole work will be to discover, improve, and enjoy what you find in the installed programs." The curious began their exploration, resentment turning quickly into glee.

The computers were loaded with historic video games. And then, surprise of surprises, Skilleo games, several of them prototypes at that, virgin coding yet to market.

The foursome geeks, and even the receptionist, caught the gaming fever, and challenging banter brightened the large room as games were played, critiqued, and coded to improve.

Heaven shined this day as game and player voices reverberated their credos:

"It's time to kick ass and chew bubblegum…and I'm all outta gum." — Duke Nukem

"If history only remembers one in a thousand of us, then the future will be filled with stories of who we were and what we did." — Battlefield 1

"Nothing is true; everything is permitted." — Ezio Auditore, Assassin's Creed

From a Skilleo licensed game, 'Wizard's First Rule' — *If anything goes wrong, you die first.*

And other games of warning. *"It's dangerous to go alone! Take this."* — Old Man, The Legend of Zelda

By this time, two of the attorneys had left, but the woman remained, commandeering an empty cubicle. She did not play kid stuff or try to forget that she once enjoyed My Little Pony. Instead, she pulled her own assignment from a Barnes and Noble shopping bag: three best-selling thrillers with terrorist plots. The young attorney, with the barrister-proper name of Lisa Goss-Scott, who had caught Gizmo's attention, but ignored by her, thumbed the pages of her assigned office work. *The Judas Gate* by Jack Higgins, UK edition, September, 2010; *The Lion's Game* by Nelson DeMille, published in 2000; and a very battered, well-read copy of *Mao II* by one Don DeLillo. In the margin of one page, she found the initials W.H. with the margin note: "In a repressive society, a writer can be deeply influential, but in a society that's

300 S.P. Grogan

filled with glut and repetition and endless consumption, the act of terror may be the only meaningful act."

Not enthused by a glance at a book cover of multiple Warhol Mao images, she decided, 'Of all three books that should keep me occupied for a month, I'll read this last.' She never did. Within seven days, as Hugh Fox anticipated, the U.S. Government struck, in unusual speed for the wheels of Washington, barging in, macho bluster and guns waving. And what had initiated such law enforcement fanfare was a short film.

Scene 6: An Earthquake Like No Other
Setting: Mann's Chinese Theatre, Hollywood Boulevard, Hollywood, California,
Monday, June 6th

The press conference was not a crowded affair; in fact, it looked pitifully small when housed in the large seating area of the Chinese Theatre, a venue that opened in 1927 with Cecile B. DeMille's *King of Kings* and, in 1973, saw the launch of *Star Wars*. Today, there was to be an announcement about a television show, presumably about their Fall season, maybe allowing the reporter-types to ask mocking questions about their failed Pakistan terrorist hunt.

Interestingly, the public relations push came from the Five Aces Studioz, not the juggernaut of what could have been the combined strength of Skilleo Games and SammyC Fashions, which seemed to have gone off the radar these last 30 days. Instead, the focus was to be on *King's Retribution*, their reputation alone, which still seemed tenuous among the showbiz crowd.

To the expectancy of anticipated re-hashed news, the Hollywood and national press corps responded in kind and sent their second-stringers and intern reporters. The AP provided a news person, a woman reporter who usually handled celebrity obituaries. The *L.A. Times* had present their Life Style Editor who had a short time gap in her daily schedule. Local television Fox News had a camera crew in training show up as a teaching lesson. No entertainment section representation from East Coast Media, including the *NY Times* or *Washington Post*. Why would they?

All were served coffee. A two-minute warning. At the appointed time, a young smiling PR woman came to the podium and announced:

"Thank you for coming today for this important announcement. You will be receiving a complete digitized copy of today's press announcement. Any questions after seeing our film can be submitted to the offices of Five Aces Studioz." The lights of the theatre dimmed, and the curtain parted. The audience began tittering in disbelief that they would be watching a film. A few thought the gimmick beneath them and began to leave slowly, still watching the massive IMAX screen as the program began.

Storm King's voice-over. "King's Retribution in Abbottabad the nights of May 1st and May 2nd." The darkness was punctuated with flashing lights and the sound of gunfire (the couriers within the compound fighting to a quick death) — camera shots, jerky, of fast walking through a house, the torn-apart rooms. Cut back to the explosion of a helicopter being blown up, lighting the sky. The next shot, the downed helicopter. Cut back to helicopters lifting off into the night. Splice to the chase in the streets of Abbottabad, the fast snaps of gunfire in a street chase, people racing through houses, the town market with cars racing, more shots fired, being in the back of a truck racing into the night, fade-out.

A close-up shot of Callie in front of a green screen shot of the bin Laden home hideout.

"I'm Callie Cardoza of *King's Retribution*. We have a history of tracking down those alleged individuals culpable in crimes against the innocent. [pause] On May 2nd⋅ we captured Osama bin Laden. [pause] He will be facing justice in a trial to be held on July 25th. This will be a public proceeding, televised, and tickets available for those who wish to attend in person."

The press audience is reacting in shock, no more so than from the next scene:

Osama bin Laden sits in a chair facing the camera. He looks serious. In his hand, he holds a newspaper. Close-up. The newspaper is the United Kingdom's *Daily Mail*, dated May 20th. [misdirection, designed confusion]. The camera pans back to bin Laden who seems to be in good health but speaks to the camera, definitely unrehearsed, in Arabic [subtitled in English]: "I am innocent of these preposterous charges. I reject any U.S. court. I speak only for the truth as the spirit of al-Qaeda. I ask my supporters to not yet seek revenge but await *Crimson Scimitar*, the day to come when all of the Faithful will arise to establish the Caliphate."

Cut to the legal counsel, looking uncomfortable, not pre-prepared; a statement made earlier not knowing that the *real* bin Laden would be the defendant.

"I am attorney Booker Langston, and my co-counsel, Harriet Eberhardt. We have been selected to act as the public defense counsel for our client, Osama bin Laden. It is our sincere goal to provide Sheik bin Laden with an aggressive defense."

Next cut: "My name is Cotton Matther; I am a lifetime prosecutor. I have been asked and have accepted the solemn task of prosecuting the world's greatest terrorist, who participated in the planning and direction of a crime against humanity on September 11, 2001."

Cut to: A long aerial shot, then moving in closer to the stadium near Colorado Springs, the camera moves into the stadium, showing the seating for 40,000 — then the surprise. At one end of the stadium, out on the field, is a large plastic-type bubble, maybe 100 feet in circumference, a large dome, and within is what is perceived as a typical type U.S. courtroom, á la Perry Mason, similar to numerous television courtroom dramas. People can be seen in the stadium doing those tasks in preparation for an upcoming event.

Young woman's voice-over: "Tickets for the 'Trial of the Century' to be held on Monday, 25th of July will go on sale tomorrow, June 7th, at all major ticket outlets. The event will be televised live. Please visit our website shown below for more details [the unique website address, perhaps a homage to the defendant's boast — www.CrimsonScimitar.com viewed on screen center as final notification].

The video film is over. The lights come up. Press reactions are mostly shock as mobile phones reach out to the world with a true 'scoop.' Others run to grab a DVD of the video film just seen. A few cheers, but a rushing crowd to exit. The lowly interns and cub reporters will yell back at their offices that this is *their* 'story' and they must be chosen to be *The Face,* report the momentous, and yell the cliché, 'stop-the-presses.' They are ignored.

And so it starts. Such news travels fast but comes slowly to other parts of the world.

EPISODE NINETEEN — Fate Intervenes

Scene 1: Khalaf Besmirched
Setting: Village of Lahan, June 5th

To Khalaf, Shahin's entry into the village seemed like a Roman conqueror returning to receive laurels of victory. Rewards not yet earned.

The attack leader for *Crimson Scimitar* arrived with his squad, and most noticeable, all the men were clean-shaven (except one), beginning to shift into their role of appearing unassuming, as they were expected to look as they entered America, coming in from of Mexico, according to Khalaf's reading of bin Laden's plan.

They arrived with a great deal of uplifting buoyancy for all, as al-Qaeda in Yemen had scored a major victory and had captured Zinjibar, a regional town of great import. The war there was going their way, and Shahin made sure that all of the Supreme Council members on the Arabian Peninsula — including al-Wahishi, Saif al-Adel, and even al-Awlaki received Shahin's praise of great leadership. So apparent was his boasting it became evident that another slate of candidates was now in the running, but which of those might be offered up as bin Laden's replacement? Not al-Awlaki, prayed Khalaf, not the American.

Both Shahin and Khalaf exchanged mutual greetings in cool courtesy. Maybe he was just an ethereal reminder of the ghost of bin Laden that Khalaf found himself, which he deemed nevertheless as his rightful due, to sit in private council when Shahin updated Kashmiri and Rahman on the outline of his planned travels, kept general to avoid the ears of spies.

"I received word today that August will be the beginning of our travels, followed by the anticipated date-to be determined by circumstances in the field — of our major attack."

"And what do you need from us," asked Rahman, in sincere differential respect to someone who might not be returning.

"With our Sheik gone, I made this trip for a final ratification from the rest of the Supreme Council based here. Yemen still remains in support of the operation. And while I am here, you have a certain landmark that would assist us in our final training exercise."

"And you feel, even with our Sheik in heaven, this *Crimson Scimitar* will succeed?" This from Kashmiri, unafraid to show his skepticism, certainly positioning himself if failure were to come.

"More than ever, dear brother. We have no word that they suspect us. All others in our plan are preparing. My men and I are ready."

"As we will confirm at our meeting on the 4th," stated Rahman giving off every confidence that this would be the supportive decision.

"Yes, we shall see, when everyone gathers." Not a rebuke from Kashmiri, but putting such matters in the proper perspective of the larger assemblage having the last word.

"Our late and beloved leader wished that Khalaf, here, be elevated from his important position of Council courier and act as one of the representatives to our delegation when we treat with the Americans…after our brother Shahin's great triumph."

Khalaf was stupefied. He assumed that Rahman would speak to al-Zawahiri, and behind the scene lobbying would gain his post. This was too open; he was too defenseless from scourging attack — which began.

"Khalaf is one of the best of our couriers, and to lose him would not be best for all our interests." The backhanded compliment from Kashmiri was too transparent, and from this quarter, there would be no support for his advancement.

"Khalaf does not even like Americans; he has said so," said Shahin, sensing from Kashmiri which way the winds would blow for the young Egyptian. "To negotiate with an enemy by first grabbing at their throat is not my idea of tact." Shahin laughed at his joke.

"I have seen Khalaf in many disguises," Rahman came to his defense weakly, "and he has the skill to mask his face from the emotions he really holds inside, as he does now."

"The Jirga on the 7th will certainly offer many choices and consequences," said Kashmiri, and they said nothing more, drank tea and ate wheat cakes, and let Shahin tell glorious stories of al-Qaeda's battles in Yemen.

Quite later, when Khalaf and Rahman walked alone, with only two bodyguards trailing at a discreet distance, he had to ask, "Why did you mention our Sheik's wishes for me? Was the time appropriate?"

"Khalaf, if you are to become a vital political representative at some point in time it is important to know that as you guard your front, you must keep eyes in the back of your head to watch out for your supposed friends. And please, Khalaf, if I can be frank, by putting you into play as a pawn, you can be offered for sacrifice, not literally, of course, but the only move at this time is to have the king crowned. When the king is enthroned on the chess board, we will all be glorious under his banner."

Khalaf felt the analogy poorly constructed and wanted to say the Queen was the strongest of all chess pieces, but he nodded his acquiescence, and thinking of a female chess piece brought him to a far more serious question, one to be asked with the delicacy of a future politician. He looked at his surroundings.

"I have noticed all the new people who have been arriving over the last weeks and seek to put names to faces, but I have seen a woman walking through the village, taller than most, and her dress does not seem to be of this territory. In fact, made of finer cloth. Is she here to join a future martyr brigade?"

"Ah yes, I know exactly of whom you speak. *Sabz*. The green-eyed woman-child. No, she will not be strapping on any bombs and flinging herself at government leaders." Rahman thought and laughed at his private joke coming. "Yet, she will be strapped on and explode with babies. Her uncle brought her here and acts as her guardian. Her father was brother to the Emir Tahir Yuldashev of the IMU (Islamic Movement of Uzbekistan), who was killed in 2009 in this very region by a missile strike. His deputy, Abu Usman, has taken control of IMU. Usman and al-Zawahiri decided one positive way to rebuild the strength of IMU and give a closer relationship to the al-Qaeda of Pakistan is through a blood marriage."

Khalaf did not like the way this conversation was going. Rahman, a consummate storyteller, continued, oblivious to his listener's mood change.

"She is married, then?"

"No, not yet; they are still haggling over the dowry. The ceremony will be a rushed one, wartime conditions as you can expect. The engagement is scheduled to be several days after the jirga. She is to marry Gupta."

"Gupta? He may be Pakistani, but does he not live at the border near Punjab (India)? And he is a lieutenant to Kashmiri. The marriage will give Kashmiri…extensive connections, a stronger power base."

"I do not disagree, but the Doctor feels he can control all the tentacles that we have out there, again, if he is chosen to lead." Rahman thinking Khalaf's mind was worried about the outcome of these strange internal politics, put his hand on Khalaf's shoulder.

"Do not fret, my young brother, such a marriage, if it does happen, will be miserable for both. And if a failure, there will be shame on both families, and no power will be consecrated. This Sabz will be a hellcat. I heard among the women that she had voiced her opposition to her father's wishes, though he himself did not have much say in the decision. A forced marriage sinks to its own doom. One of her uncles attends her, more a guard to keep her from running away or killing herself. What's worse, she is educated, was sent away to a university in Kyrgyzstan. Would you believe before these wedding plans, she was halfway to a degree in mathematics and only in her 17th year, and she knows several languages, including English and Russian? I ask you: what's all that have to do with birthing tomorrow's heroes?"

Trying a tactful way to move away from his dismay, Khalaf offered a supportive answer, "Yes, a smart woman for an uneducated soldier will bring ill luck. May Allah protect our brother Gupta."

Rahman had an idea, seeing the conversation offered another perspective and an opportunity.

"Perhaps you may be of service sooner than later. Tomorrow night, Kashmir and Sabz's uncle and the prospective groom will be meeting to discuss the dowry, hopefully, a small celebration to follow, perhaps a few crude Sitthniyan songs. If you were to show up, perhaps offer to be a witness and offer congratulations that might disarm any antagonism because you are an outsider, or better yet, those who harbor suspicion on why you did not perish with our martyred Sheik." He gave Khalaf a serious look. "As we who believe in you know you saved yourself to help further our cause."

To protect his own story, Khalaf tried to recall, what was that saying? That bridge, once crossed, where there is no turning back, what is it called? The Rubicon, that's it. He had crossed his own Rubicon. He had become someone else's pawn.

"If you feel it helpful, I will attend."

Scene 2: Heaven Asunder
Setting: Village of Lahan, June 7th, evening

He made it through the day, concentrating on all the bustling activities around him as if this meeting of al-Qaeda leaders would be some sort of colorful festival.

After lunch, Shahin took his six men, with a curious fan base of another ten men, to travel twenty miles to a highway bridge flung over a mountain gorge, where they would do mock

306   S.P. Grogan

attacks all day long, coming back well after dark. Shahin, in mock grandiosity, invited Khalaf along, both knowing his proper refusal would be interpreted as weakness on his part. He bore the low-voiced derision behind his back as Shahin and his men departed. Khalaf felt belittled that his task in this war was to attend a party.

Preparing for tomorrow's critical meeting and with the inflow of attendees and visitors, a goat was on a spit roasting in a communal fashion, and those hungry were allowed to cut slices from the cooked flesh — and tasty it was. He heard a voice near his head, *English*, and his whole countenance froze.

"Thank you." He heard the words repeated, English with a Russian accent; he was sure of it. And from a side glance, he looked into two deep emerald pools.

"Thank you for not betraying us. It was only a simple game for our health." And she was gone, carrying a large plate of meat and vegetables to a group of men sitting a ways off, lounging on the ground, one of them Kashmiri's man, Gupta, the future husband of this girl named Sabz.

Her voice childlike but strong in such brashness to talk to a non-mahram man (not of her family/tribe). Her uncle could beat her for such a breach of etiquette. Khalaf placed that voice, replayed her words, to a face he had briefly seen happily kicking a football. How did she say it? 'For our health.' A woman who thought for herself, about her needs; remarkable, and such a waste to have her legs opened to such a lout as Gupta. Yet, it was Gupta, in his anticipation at marital and conjugal bliss, who had later walked over to him and made the invitation to Khalaf directly, perhaps a seed planted by Rahman, a need for many dowry witnesses, or that the foreigner might want to enjoy the local customs of the neighborhood, or a sly hint of making the foreigner, the Egyptian, jealous of Gupta's good fortune. The latter was much closer to the truth, Khalaf reasoned, and properly accepted the smiling offer to join the men later in the garden behind Kashmiri's house.

An hour later, Khalaf made his toilet preparation. He accepted his own body smells as part of the heritage of field service where no baths were easily accessible. For the approaching gathering, he cleaned his upper body with a wet rag and put on his best, his only floral silk coat. He felt relaxed. As the customs dictated, he knew he would not see her there, so he would not have to avoid looking at her.

Shouts were heard outside. He wondered what had occurred, by the yelling; something important must have occurred. Another jihadist victory?

He walked to the steps of his small house and inhaled the night air, not for freshness, as the smoke of banked cooking hearths still rose with seasoned aromas. No, the air intake was to push his chest up, his back straightened, and hearing men's voices screaming, more tumult coming from behind Kashmiri's house as he walked to his duty. A mujahideen he did not know ran by in tears, shouting, "Our beloved leader lives! Bin Laden lives. The Americans have him!" Voices were heard, 'Death to America' and 'Jihad to free him!' A few scattered gunshots, celebratory *feu de joie*. Khalaf was overwhelmed, confused. What does this mean? *'My Leader alive? Has Allah shown his mercy? If true, all will be made right!'*

Khalaf's sudden and growing elation was interrupted — his world, his small universe, made unright. There was the brilliance of a thousand stars exploding, bringing a frozen time laced with sharp pain; he was floating through fiery clouds into a dark world he had never seen before.

Scene 3: Warrant of Power
Setting: Washington D.C., Afternoon, June 6th

The Head of Homeland Security took it upon himself to make an independent decision, rare and dangerous. He put a call into the FBI Director with his command. The Attorney General likewise concurred. Field forces were mobilized. A legal document for the seizure of one fugitive and any related papers concerning him or his whereabouts to be confiscated was signed off by the FBI's go-to amenable judge. The writ of seizure was broad-based, with only one address listed in the rush to readdress a wrong the SEALs and U.S. military had failed to first accomplish.

Scene 4: The Rushed Raid
Setting: Santa Monica, The War Room, June 7th

At 9 a.m., in a flurry of over-exuberance, if not ex-parte overreach, twenty-five or so members of a quickly assembled task force, a representative mixture of FBI, U.S. Marshalls, Justice Department officials, DEA agent, and even an IRS representative, stormed in with guns drawn to brace the occupants.

The routine intimidation was yelled: "FBI. Everyone freeze!" The next directive, a question: "Where is he?" The armed personnel began to spread out, severe in intent.

Attorney Lisa Goss-Scott put down her absorbing book. At first flustered, she had been told what might happen, thus putting grit into her spine.

Her voice raised. "Hold it right there. I am the legal representative of the tenant of these premises; who are you, and what is your purpose in trespassing?" She considered this a good comeback. She held her nervousness in check.

"We have an open arrest order for the fugitive Osama bin Laden. Please show us where you have him detained."

"And you have documentation to back up your request?"

308 S.P. Grogan

That caught the speaker off guard, and for a moment, he stumbled, muttered angrily, and turned to a fellow official officer, who reached into his jacket, produced a sheaf of papers, and thrust them into Attorney Goss-Scott's hands. She took a long moment to read.

"First of all, as I have been informed, Osama bin Laden has been arrested. A citizen's arrest. A judicial hearing might say otherwise, but not you people. Second, the arrested person of your interest is not here. Third, your warrant language to seize papers and communications relating to Mr. bin Laden is broad-based and requires more specificity. And finally, this is a working office of Skilleo Games Technology, having nothing to do with this Mr. bin Laden, and any disruption and seizure of work papers of the company, many of which are proprietary, will be deemed unlawfully seized and a disruption of the company's ability to conduct proper business."

The head honcho of the FBI, et al. task force had raided California drug dens and porn factories; he had heard such hired legal babble before and had gained a hard shell not to let anyone else's message legal jargon interfere with what he and his team were going to do, regardless.

"And turn off the camera," he yelled at meek CAMERA THREE. Two FBI agents went over to verify the camera was not recording. They failed to note a bank of unobtrusive mini-cams hidden throughout the office. A *King's Retribution* hallmark — record everything.

Attorney Lisa Goss-Scott bristled.

"You may have a right to search, but as long as we do not interfere, we have a right to view and record your actions…for future evidence. Again, I am warning you not to interfere illegally with the normal course of business. And we have the right to record your illegal trashing and seizure."

As if to support her, and Gizmo was smitten with her barring the lions at the gates, all the tech nerds pulled out their phones and began making Tweet snippets of a trashing search and building frustration when no criminal from the Mid-East made an appearance to surrender.

"Get those people out of here," was a frustrated order, "She can stay."

He turned to the Skilleo attorney. "I also want to speak to the owner of Skilleo, Mr. Hugh Fox." He glanced at a list and read off Samantha Carlisle's name and that of Colonel Storm King and one Carlita Cardoza.

Lisa shrugged. "I have no idea where they are. You have an arrest warrant out for them?" She did wonder.

"No, but we would like them to show up voluntarily at our offices for an interview."

"I will pass the word." No more was said between them.

As the furor ensued with searching units returning empty-handed and computer equipment detached and carried out, Attorney Goss-Scott, having fulfilled her task, replaced her book into her shopping bag, gathered up her briefcase (establishing her personal property as client work material) she stood at the office door, watching the proceedings as she made a cell phone call with the simple message. "They are here now, doing exactly as you thought, sir." One spoke respectfully to the paying client.

Later that day, legal documents were served by process servers at the headquarters of the Department of Justice, the FBI, and Homeland Security, then to the U.S. Attorney General as the legal officer for the President of the United States. The U.S. Government was being sued for a minimum of $100 million in damages; the main claim of the suit, property theft and tort disruption in the release of the Fall catalog and related sales of new Skilleo Games. A press release soon followed. This made national news, with many comments unfavorable to the U.S. Government and their bullying, dare one say 'fascist' tactics.

That same afternoon, a personal letter was hand-delivered to the Assistant to the President by Skilleo's main Washington lobbyist. The letter was addressed to the President of the United States.

Scene 5: Repercussions and Untenable Options
Setting: Oval Office, White House, Washington D.C., June 8th

In attendance: President of the United States, Head of the FBI, The Head of Homeland Security, outgoing Director of the CIA, recently appointed Deputy Director of CIA (Ronald Givens), the National Intelligence Director, Assistant to the President, Secretary of Defense, Chairman of the Joint Chiefs (note: the Vice President, not present, in China with family on an official visit.)

The President of the United States was not a happy camper.

"I just don't know where to start. First, we are informed — publicly, as is everyone else — that supposedly the terrorist Osama bin Laden is not in Pakistan as our intelligence community swore he was and may have been, but is somewhere in residence in our own United States.

"Second, without *my* knowledge (he looked to the Head of Homeland Security), we raided the headquarters of this Five Aces production company who supposedly 'kidnapped' a foreign national to bring him to the United States for a supposed illegal trial for his crimes and to be televised, internationally, I might add. But in conducting this 'knee jerk' raid, and that's my phrasing (and he looked to the FBI Director), we later discover this morning that there is no Five Aces leasing the office in question, but instead, we, the government, according to the

310   S.P. Grogan

morning newspapers, have allegedly stolen all the equipment of this kid gaming company, Skilleo Games Technology, which will prevent them from selling their games this Christmas. Katherine [the President's personal secretary] says our switchboard is swamped, for the first time in history, by children and parents upset they may not be able to have the latest released hot video games for the holidays.

"And finally, I receive a hand-delivered letter which wins the prize of prizes, but we'll get to that later."

The President, if recalled, had been a lawyer and worked to find solutions by managing the evidentiary points of a case.

"I don't want to hear excuses or lengthy explanations but give me concise answers:

1. How did this happen? Why did the SEALS fail?

2. Are we assured that the person in the video is, in fact, Osama bin Laden? And not a stunt?

3. It seems our first response to this raid in California backfired. Do we have other options?

4. And this snafu about video games not on the holiday store shelves; just remember, ladies and gentlemen: disappointed children have voting parents."

He stared around the room. "Okay, first: how did this happen?" His gaze landed on the CIA, then his top military officer.

"To #2 quickly," said the Director of the CIA, "Our facial recognition people confirm this *is* bin Laden. He seems well and fit." Not waiting for discussion, he rushed on. "As to how our intelligence and SEALS missed him in Abbottabad, we have only conjecture. Most obvious, he was not there when the SEALS showed up. It is surmised he arrived later to survey the damage and got swept up — pure luck — by these dimwit TV bit players."

"Dimwits who did capture the most elusive terrorist in the world, the one our government was seeking for over ten years," from the CIA Director.

The frozen smile on his President's face was not a kind one. "These so-called 'dimwits' of the *King's Retribution* television show have bin Laden in their fake 'custody,' and they have gained all this free publicity of wanting to put him on some kind of mock public trial, with a quick summary judgment. Do we think when they find him guilty, as they definitely will, will they execute him in front of a televised world audience? I don't see it. Everyone hates bin Laden, but the public might turn on any brutal no-fair trial murder. But who knows? That concerns me. But we'll get back to that shortly." His fingers touched a letter lying on his desk.

National Intelligence responded, "I concur, Mr. President. Our analysis says that is not the purpose of this reality television show — A. This television program has never shown a propensity for violence — B. We have discovered that the producer of the show, Five Aces

Studioz, by the way, Studioz with a 'z' instead of 's' (the president's stern visage said he could care less), is owned by billionaire Hugh Fox and multimillionaire Samantha Carlisle. It would damage their brand value if they were to go off the rails. And C. is the letter you received, sir, which you will be addressing momentarily."

The Attorney General provided his input. "By our review, and what we have learned, this is going to be a hybrid sort of trial, not a true U.S. judicial proceeding; it may be illegal, a trumped-up kangaroo court."

"You say a 'may be illegal.' Why isn't it totally illegal, and we go in with court orders and Federal Marshals?"

"Well, Mr. President, I don't want to say this, but our people got a little over-eager, hero-seekers, but I have since put out a notice that no actions are to be taken until we, you, reach a decision on how to proceed. One of our own people in Colorado jumped the gun, also yesterday, and did so without notifying his superiors."

"Jeez." The President of the United States, in times like these, lit a cigarette.

The Head of Homeland Security sought to make sure he would not be the only one in the dog house.

"One of the Assistant U.S. Attorneys in Denver, hearing that the trial was going to be held in Colorado Springs, rushed out and gained a judicial order from the Tenth District Circuit seeking seizure of a detained suspect, being held without his permission, suggesting a kidnapped situation. On his own volition, he showed up at the construction gate near Colorado Springs, presented the papers, backed by two U.S Marshalls."

"And what happened?" The President hoped taking a slow drag would bring control.

"Turned away by armed tribal police officers of the Sand Creek Arapahoe Reservation. Turned over to a tribal judge. Said we had no jurisdiction, that the upcoming trial on July 25 was under the auspices of the Tribal Court, and that the reservation is sovereign territory, and our papers were unenforceable. It did not help that we were being filmed by a dozen national news media outlets who had arrived to film this 'stadium being built' and questioned our people about their strong-arm 'Gestapo' intimidation. I was waiting to talk to you, like today, about the next steps."

"Great. Just great, an *expanding* fuck-up," said the President, letting a slow breath of smoke curl around his head. He had to ask again about options.

"So a military incursion is out of the question?"

"To attack where?" commented the Admiral, the U.S. Chief of Staff. "We don't even know where bin Laden is being held. We have placed a no-fly zone around the reservation to keep out any helicopter or small plane bringing him in. And again, sir, using SEALS or the Army

312   S.P. Grogan

Rangers for a tactical 'rescue' to gain hold of bin Laden probably would not be looked on favorably by the public. They want this TV spectacle. My current opinion is 'wait and see' for an opportunity to strike."

"But don't I recall we had one of our CIA agents on the ground when bin Laden was seized?" To that question, no one noticed CIA resource expert Givens shift on his feet and push himself against the back wall, seeking obscurity.

"Just a rumor," said the CIA Director, "We had embedded an asset early on with those TV people to help protect our own strategic plans in Pakistan from discovery. But he had no effect and is now retired and out of the picture."

"Which brings us to this letter I received and which has been checked out as to its originality and veracity." The President picked it up and read:

Mr. President,

We of Five Aces Studioz need to inform you officially that we have acquired and detained the wanted fugitive, Osama bin Laden, now an Indicted Defendant. It is our intention to have a responsible court of jurisdiction hold a trial before independently selected jurors to gain a fair and balanced verdict seen before the world. We hope you applaud our good intentions and that all your representatives will act peacefully and transparently to allow us to continue and complete our search for truth.

On the completion of our trial, set for July 25th, estimated duration to be five days, whichever verdict is rendered, we will provide the defendant from the jurisdiction in which we currently operate, to the boundary of that jurisdiction, to be turned over to United States authorities as they deem appropriate, at which time said representative(s) of the United States government will sign a release of liability and indemnity of Five Aces Studioz, its employees, hired expert consultants, and shareholders, from all actions we have taken, within or without U.S. borders and that we have indeed provided said Defendant alive and in healthy condition into your custody.

Prior to our release of said Defendant into the control of U.S. authorities, a deposit shall be made into an account of our choosing in the amount of US$25 million, the announced reward for the capture of said Defendant.

"Do they believe Osama's life might be forfeit if they turn him over to us?" Inappropriate question. A quick survey of the room, and the fixed faces, reminded the President that *was* the prime directive on the Abbottabad raid. No prisoners taken. So, the President quickly said, "And what about this lawsuit I hear about against the U.S. government, from this Skilleo company, about their lost toy income for Christmas?" (He looked to the Attorney General). "Do we ignore this as a definite frivolous lawsuit and a shakedown?"

"I would suggest, sir," said the AG, "if we were to take this letter you just read seriously, perhaps the lawsuit might go away. My recommendation is we don't go through a very nasty and public civil lawsuit where children might even testify before the cameras, and we don't go for a military option in any form, and after five days of fame for their TV show, damn them, we get this despicable person who, as you said, has slipped through our hands for over ten years." The military chief could not relinquish his responsibilities: "It is imperative that we at least have several contingency plans with military intervention strategies. If feasible and needed, Mr. President."

The President stubbed out his cigarette and again picked the letter off his desk, "Or do we, as was suggested, after this July 25th publicity trial, pick up bin Laden, no fuss, no muss, and I emphasize, no casualties? But I add, during this month or so of waiting for this trial to be exploited and concluded for ratings, we are all to be on alert, on deck, and we try to avoid political flaming arrows and sharp knives thrown at us by the neo-con war bloc who want us to go in, guns blazing."

Looking for ideas, someone said, "What happens if we do not pay them the reward? There must be some mitigating circumstances where we can walk from paying out that much?'

The CIA Director was wary. "However we might disparage them, these are the guys who snuck a terrorist out from underneath the nose of Pakistan's I.S.I. and now surprised everyone with an elaborate televised mega-show, so you must believe they will make a big deal if we try to shortchange them. There is a posted reward of $25 million. How would this Administration look if this Fox and his cronies televised to the world *King's Retribution* giving bin Laden to another country, say England or Saudi Arabia, or redeem him to the Taliban or al-Qaeda, who would gladly scrape up $25 mil from their oil-rich supporters? Do you want to chance that?"

"I hate anything or anyone going by the name of Fox," said the President's presidential aide, seeking to lessen the room's temperature.

The FBI Director griped, "Why not just sweep everyone up once this trial is over? Throw them in a deep hole?"

The President's aide chimed in, more to the truth. "To gain bin Laden safely into our hands, we will have signed a liability release to these people. If we renege on the reward or a liability release, I am sure the media and Mr. Fox's millions could make our life miserable, especially since the President is facing a second-term election."

The aide continued, "As to this lawsuit, I see where your thinking might be, Mr. President. You know, as we all do, that harassment legal action could take years to resolve, but with this presumed delay in delivering games timely to kids, that could give us a political black eye,

314 S.P. Grogan

something we don't need now. And as I read the lawsuit, they may have some merits, but I'm more inclined to believe it was done to give us a stern warning that this Hugh Fox can match wits with us and do so effectively (he also looked at the Head of Homeland Security) but I truly believe it may be no more than a bargaining chip, something to negotiate into this letter as a settlement resolving all issues. Sir, keep in mind, our goal should focus on getting bin Laden as you said, 'no muss, no fuss.'"

"Alright, enough," concluded the President, "Those who have reasonable suggestions get me a memo in 24 hours. I will review. We may need another meeting if there is a brainstorm out there."

As the meeting broke up, the Secretary of Defense asked, having not seen the demand letter.

"Who signed that letter?" He assumed it would be Skilleo's CEO, Hugh Fox.

"Let me see; I didn't pay it much attention. Some scribbled signature." The President read, "Someone named 'Wendell Holmes, Esq., owner of one share of Five Aces Studioz'."

Hearing an unpleasant gagging noise, they turned to see the previously silent Acting Deputy Director of the Central Intelligence Agency, Ronald Givens, throwing up on the President's Oval Office rug.

Scene 6: Taking Care of Business
Setting: Skilleo Games Headquarters, near San Jose, California, June 10th

The next day, Hugh was humming *Take it Easy* by the Eagles when he received a computer disk from the Santa Monica office with the note: "Mr. Holmes said you would like this as a souvenir." Being in multi-tasking mode, he did not readily pull up the contents on his computer. In fact, he could guess what the disk might hold, Wendell Holmes's photographs from Pakistan. He went over to a cabinet, punched in a code, and a file drawer opened. He looked inside at the souvenir he should not have brought back from his trip but was at a loss what to do. The sudden reappearance of Holmes, his name, brought back all the guilt of Clayton's death and stealing, if that's what you called it, the small package in the pink wrapper. Wendell Holmes would be the perfect person to deal with this matter, but every once in a while, when procrastination can do no harm, postponement is inevitable. Hugh Fox shut the cabinet and secured the combination. Some other time, he considered, and filed that thought away.

He went back to his computer and cluttered desk. It was wonderful to see media relations overwhelmed with thousands of demands for interviews with bin Laden himself and private offers of bribes to gain access. All ignored. As of today, he was in the midst of event management, decision-making, and project juggling, as usual. The courtroom stadium was nearly sold out. His attorneys were sending out threatening letters to shoot down attempts of scalping tickets. The price set at $35 would not be altered; equality to all, and all gained a view, of sorts (limit of four tickets). Housing was an issue. Denver and Colorado Springs hotels all being occupied with price gouging on rooms in play. His temporary mobile village for campers, busses situated a half mile from the stadium offered on a 5-day short-term residence — $25 cost per parking spot per night. On the positive side, every tribal member who wanted a job at high pay was employed.

Hugh Fox spent the day dealing with these executive decisions on an average of one every minute, it seemed. His games world took a back seat as the primary objective was the upcoming *Trial of the Century*; everyone said it was so. This was IT. Everything else could be managed by his other efficient team members, including the management of his investment portfolio, one of them, Five Aces Studioz.

In that frame of mind, he sang aloud to no one but himself, '*Don't let the sound of your own wheels drive you crazy....*'

Scene 7: Callie Clean-up
Setting: Los Angeles, June 11th

Everyone tried to let go, to put Clayton's death behind them, unwind until the trial, but they couldn't, and in some twists and turns, all the key players were drawn back in.

For Callie, the moment was a call from the Editing Department.

"What are we going to do with all this footage from your trip to Pakistan? The way Storm built it up to the public we gotta start work on it soon, to make any sense of it all."

No one in production was really talking to King; he just wasn't fun to be around if and when he showed up at the *King's Retribution* offices.

Callie empathized with their dilemma.

"Get CAM ONE and CAM TWO in with you, and cut out all the superfluous garbage. They have a feeling for the good stuff. Next week, I will come over and start working on a storyboard and make sure they send me over a scriptwriter, preferably Halsey; she knows Storm's turn of phrase and pacing, since this, I am guessing, will be his voice-over in the show." She gave a momentary thought, inhaling, as all the memories of that trip ripped through her emotions. Damn it all.

"How much of the bin Laden compound night shooting do we have?"

"Not a lot, maybe 30 minutes, really — like you guys were running through the place."

"Well, we were. And, let me make this perfectly clear, when I show up, I don't want to see any footage of what happened after we left the compound. Understood?"

316   S.P. Grogan

"We don't have anything like that."

"What?"

"CAM ONE told us that Mr. Fox, who was paying for the trip, took all the footage of that camera work once you guys left the compound; there's nothing on the return to the airport or covering the flight home or arrival. He has it all."

That was interesting. Hugh was keeping the public, keeping *her*, from ever having to relive Clayton being killed, murdered in front of her. There could be no other reason, and she could only feel, and did feel, a sense of wanting to thank him, somehow. But she had not seen him since their return, at the funeral. Only yesterday, a disk with photos of bin Laden's compound came over by regular mail, no note attached. Probably an afterthought coordinated by his Admin Assistant, his ever-present J-Q. She accepted that *King's Retribution*, in Fox's thinking, was now only an investment for the Skilleo accountants to fuss over. As B.B. King's song went, '*the thrill is gone.*'

A sliver of an idea came to her, probably would lead nowhere, but the only gesture she could offer, letting him know she was out there....

"Ms. Cardoza." Reminding her she was still on the phone with Editing.

"You do have CAM ONE's footage of the compound tour?"

"Yes, rough as it is."

"Clean it up the best you can. Make a copy, two copies, no four copies, yes, four copies, and send them to me posthaste. Got that?"

"Your wish is our command. Good to get something going."

"Don't hold your breath. We've time to create the season opener. I'll take a look at everything else in a couple of weeks. Bye." The call ended. Four copies. She knew the list: one for herself, one sent to SammyC Fashions only as the proper courtesy; hell, none for Storm King, let him get his own. Another copy for Wendell Holmes, but she didn't know how to reach him and expected him to be off on some exotic adventure.

The fourth copy she would express deliver over to Hugh Fox, no personal gift note, simply — *Thought you might like this* — *Callie*. He would get it; he would remember she existed. That was the real message.

Scene 8: A Favor Requested
Setting: SammieC Fashion Flagship Store, New York City, June 15th,

"Any other man would consider this a bribe."

"Moi? Bribe the New York City Police Commissioner? Don't be absurd."

Crimson Scimitar

317

"There's something you are after, Ms. Carlisle?"

"See, that's why you are the policeman and I, the simple dressmaker."

"Hardly." And they both laughed.

"When I sold my company, one of the small contractual stipulations to my benefit was that I got a monthly dress allowance, befitting my rank and the need to personify my own label when I went out in public. It is not my fault I am thrifty in choices and not a clothes whore, so I have this huge surplus of clothes credit and no caveat that prevents me from bestowing some of my good fortune on my friends."

"As I was saying, what are you after?"

"I bet you always got a confession out of your suspects?"

"A good rubber hose without witnesses helps, but in your case, I am sure you would never confess to your ulterior motives, correct?"

"I am more transparent than most believe. A month ago, I ran across a gentleman who worked, I believe, for the federal government, in law enforcement. I was impressed with both his attitude and the job I saw him perform for a friend of mine. He's left government service, seems to be out of touch, his office unwilling to give out his home address or phone number, let alone acknowledge his existence. My people have already tried going through the normal channels of inquiry. I have something that recently came into my possession that urgently I would like to discuss with him, of a personal nature."

"If it is blackmail with compromising photos, extortion, or your company has clothing design espionage, that would be a police matter."

"*If* only compromising photos; that would add spark to my dreary existence. No, nothing like that."

"If your job is non-official investigative work, I know of several ex-detectives now in private consulting."

"That is most kind, but this is more of an international nature. I just need to track him down, so we can have a sociable meeting, lunch at Le Cirque perhaps. There, would that request be so hard?"

"I do have contacts in Washington, up in the Justice Department. I could...."

They were distracted. A woman entered from behind a curtain, not a model nor a matron, but dressed in exquisite taste and her smile well suited to her fashion, a teased hint of naughtiness which had the Police Commissioner ogling the woman with blatant lust.

"I will find your man. You can count on me," said the Police Commissioner, his eyes fixed on the woman coming toward him.

318   S.P. Grogan

"Your wife looks spectacular, doesn't she?" cooed Samantha Carlisle, accepting she had not lost her touch — with men or the fashions she had created.

Scene 9: Bittersweet words, ill-timed
Setting: Suburban Cleveland, Ohio, June 16th

It was awkward. She was waiting for him to drive up in the rental car. When he arrived, she hurried down the steps and gave him a deep hug, but not with a passionate, longing kiss; no kiss at all.

Shawn felt cool civility in Jane's touch, the fondness but at the same time a holding back.

"I think it best you not come inside."

Shawn looked up at her house, and there was her father, the captain, glaring from the window; ready to do what?

Shawn started, "I want to try and explain myself after all these months. It is difficult. And much I want to say; I can't."

"Were you on a mission, were you hurt?" The concern was still there, and that made him feel better.

"See what I mean? Strict silence by orders. I thought you knew that when I went off and couldn't call you." It came out sounding like he was putting her down, but if she were to be his wife, there were certain limitations she would have to come to accept.

"You seemed to have changed." There, she said it. Shawn even knew that would be the observation at some point.

"Yes, I think I have. I don't know if it is bad or not, and I am working on it."

"Over the phone, there was a distance, like some wall between us. And in the Skype calls, your eyes were wandering, like you didn't want me to see you."

"This last deployment has been very hard."

"Were you upset that you couldn't go on the bin Laden mission?"

There it was, the crux of it all, that she even believed he was a no-show at the greatest publicized *failed* raid in SEALS history. He almost exploded at her and wanted to say, 'I was there; I almost caught a terrorist all by myself.' But his silence let her draw her own unfavorable conclusion, leading to the next condemnation.

"My father says you disrespected the President."

Of course, he would; anyone would say that who saw the multi-replayed television cut.

"What do you think? Do you feel I'm that sort of man?"

She paused. "I don't know…No, I don't think so. But all my friends…."

"Jane, it's not what your father or your friends think. It's what you believe inside, what you believe of me. I still love you, but…."

"But…what are you saying, Shawn?"

"I'm on medical leave."

"You were wounded!"

"Yes, and no. I have to go to San Diego and see some Navy shrinks. My problem is me, not us. I want to come back to you; I want to marry you."

"What are you saying?"

"What I think you wanted to say, is the pressure your father lays on you. Perhaps we both need a break, just some time off."

Tears welled in her eyes.

"I don't want that, but…."

"Yeah, those 'buts' are relationship killers. I think we both need to get our priorities straight. I need to bring back the old Shawn; he's there somewhere. And you need to separate yourself from your father's control. I never really understood it. When I see you and him together, it's a bond I can't compete with, nor do I want to live up to his *Go Army* standards."

"And our engagement, the wedding?"

"Ah, Jane, you are the realist, the best part of you." He raised her head with his fingers to look into her eyes. "This will be the hard part. I will try to stay in contact with you as much as they will let me. You will have to have strength for both of us. Anytime you can't wait, I will try to understand. Probably devastated, but you will know what's best for your happiness. That is important for me to accept. My goal is to come back to you. Will you try for me, to wait?"

She was crying now. The front door opened, and her father stood there, ready to intervene, to throw a punch, to prove something.

Shawn hugged her, kissed the top of her head, and drove off without looking back. Only when he turned the corner did he pound at the steering wheel and let his tears escape. He did not want to lose her, would not, but he had to find himself first. He was lost in spirit and inner confidence, but the good news was, he knew it.

REEL SIX — New Horizons in Play

EPISODE TWENTY — Arise, arise, and do great deeds

Scene 1: Back from the dead
Setting: Jihadist field hospital, Wana, Pakistan, June 20th

"So, what are you waiting for? Save yourselves and your children because the opportunity is here."

The voice; he knew who that was; it was his beloved Sheik speaking to him. He must open his eyes. But wait, bin Laden is alive, or is he dead? Are we talking in heaven?

"Let the truth ring out. Remember those that go out with a sword are true believers, those that go fight with their tongues are true believers, and those that fight in their hearts are true believers."

Dry lips mouthed his mute cry, 'Yes, yes, my Sheik. I am your devout follower." His eyes fluttered open, and he saw the world around him was that of the living. He lay in a small room, bare of everything, a small table with nothing on it. The smell was strong, of disinfectant, of medicine. He sniffed, the smell came from him, and he realized that a swath of bandages covered his chest, a bandage covering one side of his head. He now felt the pain, constant throbbing. Fearfully and slowly, in ordered concern, he moved a hand to feel if he had been deprived of his manhood and, thankful, went on to wiggle his toes.

"Back from your conversation with the Prophet?" An elderly woman with a red crescent insignia on her dress moved to his bedside and offered him a glass of warm water, the glass dirty.

"I heard my Sheik's voice," his voice raspy. "He was in this room."

"The radio. I turned it off. The Americans are boasting that they are putting our beloved leader on trial and on television. What shame. But they can't fool us; he is still strong until they kill him and then a battle cry for us."

He whispered, "He is alive?"

"Yes, but hidden somewhere. The CIA released tapes of where bin Laden lived, where he worked. We saw a quick glimpse of you in one of those videos. We are honored to have you here and have you back from the dead."

"Where am I?"

Crimson Scimitar

"A small medical clinic inside Wana. We are funded to take care of our injured fighters. This is as far as she decided to have you moved."

"She?"

"Your wife. She has been at your bedside daily. A truly remarkable young woman. You are quite lucky."

"My wife?"

"Yes, rest some more. I must inform the leadership you are recovering. They said they must visit when you awoke. Those who survived, that is. What sadness. The Americans drop death from the sky. Killed almost everyone."

My wife? He did not understand but closed his eyes and remembered his Sheik's words, asking all his followers to act immediately, from one of his old speeches. Yes, that was it. *"A delay may cause the opportunity to be lost, and carrying it out before the right time will increase the number of casualties."*

Crimson Scimitar. For that, he must recover his strength, but what happened? How did I get here? His eyes closed, only to open and see angry eyes staring at him.

Abu Hafs al-Shari, divisional commander of al-Qaeda, operational coordinator between al-Qaeda volunteers and the Taliban in Afghanistan, another man with a U.S. million dollar plus award on his head, stared intently at him before speaking.

"This has been ill fortune for all. But, once more, you are the only survivor. First at the Sheik's house in Abbottabad and now the missile on Kashmiri; I wonder if you are a bad omen sent by the Devil to test our resolve."

"Kashmiri?" But what was al-Shari doing here? He's based in Afghanistan. Oh, yes, a memory flooded back, the Jirga. Was it held today?

"Everyone dead at the man's house when the infidels struck, stinking body parts still being found, after nearly two weeks."

"Two weeks! I've been here that long?"

"Concussion. Shrapnel in your chest. When the doctor said you would survive, it was decided you must get back on your feet. Al-Zawahiri wishes to command you personally. He must hold great stock in you." The last was said with mild disdain. "You must be prepared to leave for London by July."

"London?"

"The CIA. They are making use of all the intelligence they took from Abbottabad. I assume you and our Sheik were taken by surprise." He squinted at Khalaf, "because you all left around a lot of computer information and files." And books and movies, Khalaf did not speak up to mention, but at least he had retrieved and destroyed his own materials.

322   S.P. Grogan

Al-Shari continued, "Seems like there were several plans for future attack operations in Europe, and they have been warned. But in England, they arrested a young man al-Zawahiri informed me through Rahman that you had recently seen. You are to go there and re-establish contacts to follow through on this part of our Sheik's plan, what Rahman called *'Crimson Scimitar.'*

Good, the containment of the plan is still safe, if an operational commander like al-Shari has little knowledge.

"Rahman, he is safe?"

"Yes, he said, "he was fortunate that he felt only you should attend those festivities, and he was spared, thank Allah, as well as that fellow called Shahin. He and his people came back to the village, searched the rubble for any other survivors, and sent all our key people away for better safety. I was coming to the Jirga, only a day away…if I had come a day sooner, so I too am fortunate. The meeting was canceled, but a proxy vote taken by those fast departing. With Kashmiri killed, and bin Laden facing a show trial on television, no one was in opposition to al-Zawahiri. The Doctor is now the acting head of al-Qaeda. I assume that will please you since you are both Egyptians?"

"Praise Allah for some good news. I am pleased, Commander al-Shari, because our plans go forward, and America will suffer. Can we free my Sheik?"

"Forget that for now. I hear Shahin is creating a new second squad to infiltrate as close as they can to this trial to see if anything can be done to free your Master.

"It is important to continue a battle, even if generals are lost. Fazul Abdullah Mohammed was also killed this week in Somalia in a roadblock gun battle. Dedicated soldiers win most battles, but we are taking losses of gifted fighters."

Khalaf knew of Fazul, a reward of $US 5 million to capture or kill him, a man with over 18 identities to escape, but it seemed all such measures failed him. With a quick thought, he wondered if the soldiers who killed him would share in the reward. Do Americans split up such millions of U.S. dollars when they kill us with their missile attacks? By now, if that were true, there would be many millionaires among the American soldiers who oversee the drone and ship-launched missile programs.

Al-Shari took notice of the wounded man's glazed look and waited a moment until he again had his attention.

"For myself, I have been tasked with taking over Kashmiri's goals to strike back at the heart of the Pakistan government. But first, there is one plan in Kabul I was working on. We, the Taliban and those of al-Qaeda are going to go after NATO tourists and their press lackeys, catch them where they sleep, so to speak." He said no more, protective of his own secrets, perhaps distrustful of the injured man in the bed.

"Power to your success, my brother," Khalaf commented as sincerely as he could.

"And to you, heal. I will send your wife to you." He left the room, and Khalaf felt he had been tired by the exchange, bluster, and suspicion aimed at him. And he would sleep again, except a strange anticipation kept his mind seeking his wife's appearance.

Covered in blue cloth, only those hypnotizing eyes were visible. *Sabz.*

"You."

"Yes, my husband." He started to speak, but she put a finger to his lips. "Nurse, will you give us time alone?"

"Yes. Yes. A good wife's care is better than antibiotics."

When they were alone, she sat beside him and said,

"Let me tell you my story, and you tell me if I did correctly."

Scene 2: Sabz's story
Setting: Town of Wana

"I blame my curse for all that happened. I did not like this arranged marriage. My father is a weak man and sold me for his honor. This Gupta was a mountain pig. I would have had to keep my eyes closed if he had put his body on mine. And my body is precious to me. It is a gift from Allah and should not be wasted. So, I cursed Gupta and prayed that some divine act of Allah would save me, and Allah sent the Americans and their bomb. But you want to know why you are here?

"I was across the village, waiting to be summoned. Once the dowry was set, I would be paraded in front of everyone as a great catch for Gupta, but then I heard the explosion. All the women ran out of the village, but I knew what had happened: the death from the skies. I had been in the same circumstances when the missile killed my other uncle, Yuldashev, leader of IMU. One missile, never more than one, that is all they need. They seem to know on whose head their missile must fall.

"There was great death when I arrived. And not very pretty. It was too bad, Allah's will, that one of the young girls to assist with my wedding was serving them food and chai. She died.

They all died swiftly, and there were few whole bodies to be recovered. Gupta's head was found on a roof. Kashmiri, they identified by a ring on a separated hand in the wreckage. My uncle, my 'protective escort,' perished. Too much fire to identify all of the bodies.

"I was the one who found you a short distance from the destruction, covered in blood and metal pieces, shrapnel, they call it. You were alive, and I recognized you. Yes, I admit, I had seen you around the village. I remember that you did not betray us for playing our game. You were the important man, the one who escaped the Americans when Sheik bin Laden, we hear now, was captured. It must have been a feat of great daring, you must tell me sometime. I must admit I did not run to your side and begin to take care of your wounds. I thought only of myself and such an opportunity. I found one of my friends, one of the girls I was teaching football to, and I asked her to get you immediate medical assistance. 'One of our heroes still lives!' I shouted. With her help, I fled to the old fort and, for two days, I hid among the ruins.

"It was craziness in the village, no one knowing who had been killed; all your brothers fleeing for safety. They thought I was dead in the blast because of all the women's body parts they found. After three nights, my friend and I got some villagers to take you to this fighter's hospital here in Wana. That is when I made my next major decision, a smart one, I think. I told them I was your wife. Who was there to say otherwise? So I hid, right there at your bedside. I have no wish to go home and be sold off again, and for what? That my children might someday die in these mountains? I am not a peasant woman, Sheik Khalaf. I would make you a very good wife.

"And it is even better that we travel to London. I can speak fair English, much in a Euro-Russian accent, not Arabic sounding. You need me. It will look less suspicious if you travel with a woman, young that I may seem to them, who is taking care of her invalid husband."

Those green eyes, the deep of the spring grasses, held him. He was overwhelmed with his pain, the tiredness of his body, the news of all that had happened, and now this, a woman imposed into his bachelor life, where his dedication had been for only one to share — himself.

"How old are you, Sabz?" More a loud whisper than a healthy voice.

"Seventeen. But I have one year of the university, and I would like to complete my degree in mathematics. And I am still a virgin, though if you know such life, you would not expect me to be ignorant of flirting, which should not shame me."

"As much as I would like, Sabz, I can't take you with me. It is dangerous where I go. Those Predator drones may find me someday."

"Not in London."

"But the police or the CIA might kill me."

"Then, you would have a widow who would cry and shred her garments every day in your memory."

"I live and travel as a pauper to go unrecognized."

"In London, you must look successful. In the West, one gains respect through money. And that you have, my Sheik."

"What?" He groped for his clothing, realizing he was wearing only a dirty hospital smock, his clothing certainly destroyed, rent from his body by the explosion. "Where, Where — "

"You mean this?" She held up the computer thumb drive. "They gave me your clothing here in the hospital. And I remembered how the American news reports boasted that they knew that your leader, bin Laden would sew money and information into his clothing for a future escape. And I looked through your nasty, torn clothes, as would any concerned wife, and I found this. I was hoping, I must admit, that if you had died, there might be money sewn in your clothes so that I might go somewhere, far away from here, maybe Karachi or Mumbai. But this told me that you are a wise man to have somehow made this much money in the fight against your enemies."

"You opened these files?" He was mad or thought he should be, but something in his mind began to work, a plan, that as she spoke, he realized they were talking and thinking along the same lines. And after all, she was beautiful and offering herself, in her way, to him. What sane man would forsake a golden apple?

She sought to close the deal.

"You have money, you are to go to London, and it will be difficult for you to move around unassisted for several weeks. You need to concentrate on all your secrecy, which I could care less about, but I know duty, and I am smart. In a few days, a good car, a large auto they call an SUV, will come to take us to wherever you wish to go. And it will have a strong bodyguard to protect us, worthy of the Sheik who fought at Abbottabad to save bin Laden and was ordered by bin Laden to carry the truth to all the rest of your jihadist army. I don't know if that is the truth, but the men I hired were very eager to serve Sheik bin Laden's wishes, and thus you."

"You paid them?"

"Of course not. As I told them, you will pay them only when we arrive safely at the nearest safe airport. Then, when we are in London, you can plot and scheme and seek revenge against the Americans. I only want a better life of my own choosing." She paused for effect, put her hand on his arm, and gave him a coquettish smile. "My beloved husband."

Scene 3: Mission Accomplished Revisited
Setting: Washington, D.C., June 22nd

Today, the President of the United States gave a major policy address. The primary emphasis was to live up to his political campaign pledge of withdrawing all U.S. troops from Iraq and begin in 2011 the slow disengagement of U.S. presence in Afghanistan. In his delivered remarks, he said, "We have broken the Taliban's momentum and trained over 100,000 Afghan National Security Forces. As a result, the U.S. will withdraw 10,000 U.S. troops from Afghanistan by the end of 2011, and the 33,000 'surge' troops approved in December 2009 will leave Afghanistan by the end of summer 2012."

326   S.P. Grogan

The President was in a favorable position as his poll numbers indicated that he could make this policy decision citing supportive evidence which he put forth in his speech:

"We are starting this drawdown from a position of strength. Al Qaeda is under more pressure than at any time since 9/11. Together with the Pakistanis, we have taken out more than half of al Qaeda's leadership. Although I am not pleased with the circumstances, we are currently in negotiations with a private third party to hand over bin Laden to the U.S. Government and to resolve all issues in favor of our citizens. One of our soldiers summed it up well. 'The message,' he said, 'is we don't forget. You will be held accountable.'

"The information we recovered from bin Laden's compound shows al Qaeda under enormous strain. Bin Laden expressed concern that al Qaeda has been unable to effectively replace senior terrorists that have been killed and that al Qaeda has failed to portray America as a nation at war with Islam — thereby draining more widespread support. Still, al Qaeda remains dangerous, and we must be vigilant against attacks. But we have put al Qaeda on a path to defeat, and we will not relent until the job is done."

"Well, that about sums it up," said an elated Roger Givens listening to the speech played over the C.I.A's internal video feed, "we got them running with their tails between their legs." He said this to no one in particular in the small social after-work gathering, a subdued celebration, except for Givens, who basked in conceit with his new-found promotion.

The word had come down that the President was moving the CIA Director over to serve as Secretary of Defense, effective July 1st, and everyone in the upper echelon shifted temporarily. Givens found himself waiting for the Congressional confirmation that his position as Deputy Director of the CIA would be changed in several months from Acting Deputy Director; the best position to run the show to those politicians who come and go in the CIA-appointed leadership. He was not after the top job of CIA Director, which had too much public visibility. His power would come when he was confirmed in the near future as Deputy Director, his political aspirations finally achieved.

In that position, he was informed, he would be rewarded with oversight of all intelligence dealing with potential terrorist threats and, as such, would serve as the Agency's primary contact to the head of Homeland Security, a prestigious platform by which he could establish public esteem as he testified before Congressional committees, and become a quoted go-to 'unnamed source' to certain friendly media contacts. If further upward advancement was not his next goal, political largesse and financial interconnectivity with donors were at his fingertips — the thought of which made him ebullient.

The only thing that could go wrong was another 9/11 on his watch. With bin Laden out of the picture, in custody, and the world touted to watch spectacle television, this promoted

Trial of the Century, ninety percent of viewers no doubt seeking victim revenge, while a disgruntled ten percent had started screaming epithets about an assumed tortured political prisoner. However, Givens cared little for populace fanfare, looking instead inward at navigating the minefields of the Agency, Congress, and this Administration, not outward where real danger might lie concealed.

Scene 4: Expressive Thoughts
Setting: New York City, June 12th

"I once asked a young man, 'should not *creativity* be used for a higher moral purpose?' and it got us into a mess of trouble, and I now question that premise, but with you, I think I should rephrase, 'Should *experience* be wasted when it could correct great wrongs?"

"And, Ms. Carlisle, to whom should I infer that question is addressed?

"Mr. Holmes, I have discovered, as best I can, that you are a skilled professional in what should we call 'interpretative analysis of facts' and one who then takes the appropriate action. Would that be an acceptable generalization? And yet, when I track you down, I find you skydiving over the Virginia countryside, at what I understand is your new hobby."

"Not a hobby. Call it a Life Experience investigation. I was seeing if a person could get seasick at 5,000 feet."

"I don't understand."

"Private joke. But definitely, a parachute tonight would be in order if required. In receiving your strong, very firm invitation, I did not expect to be standing on the top of a New York City skyscraper at the end of Manhattan, looking down on the Hudson River, with our Lady of Liberty brightly shining. So, why do I get the feeling that I am going to get more than I bargained for?"

"Patriotism, nothing more, Mr. Holmes. I thought this vista would remind you of what your past government service has brought to your fellow citizens, I being one of them."

"And that is?"

"A sense of security taken for granted and that you are unheralded for accomplishments I could dare not guess at. So, I am here tonight, setting the stage, to let you know you are indeed appreciated." She gave him a look, smiled, and then handed him a bottle of champagne, the custom of opening still relegated to the man. "And why don't we skip certain formalities? Please call me Samantha, if I can call you Wendell?"

The champagne cork popped, not a single drop bubbled forth in waste. He filled her glass, and both leaned back on very expensive lawn furniture.

This was not her apartment balcony. This night atmosphere came from a friend of Samantha's who owned a major stock brokerage and investment banking firm, the offices situated under the rooftop terrace where they now lounged.

"Let me ask you a question, based on your years of being 'out there,' seeing the darker side of human nature," she remarked.

He sipped politely; when she was not looking, he would find a way to dispose of the flute's contents. He had not had a strong drink of alcohol in ten years. Every so often, he would test himself with an open bottle in front of him; his internal battle, maintaining willpower, had to be closely regulated to keep his edge. Two months ago, witnessing Storm King in the process of liquid disintegration had reminded himself of how close he had once come to such depths.

"Ask away…Samantha."

"How are we, political governments, we the people, how are we actually going to settle our differences and find a general peace without wars or these terror attacks, the killing? I mean, yesterday, in Kabul, terrorists attacked a hotel, the same hotel chain we had stayed at in Islamabad. Twenty killed. Wendell, don't give me canned platitudes or spouted jingoism. Somehow, from you, I think I might discover a basis to believe in."

They exchanged glances. Since the first time they met, there existed in him a subtle charisma of understatement she still sought to define. From Wendell's view of her character, he had come to be impressed by the serious-thinking woman beneath the sophisticated beauty. Like the bin Laden search and capture, she really did want a solution that had viability, a real possibility of true implementation. She sought to be a savior, whether of kittens, animals, or, as he had seen recently seen demonstrated, of young men seeking goal satisfaction.

He did not take another sip, instead thought for several seconds and drew in his breath.

"We shall always have wars because we are tribal. Though we are a human species of the mammal genus and blessed with a thinking mind, we have filled our brains with the need to form associations in which we can seek supremacy over others. Over eons, two fundamental conditions have contributed to our failure to cohabit with our neighbors peacefully."

"Two? I would expect many issues of faults within us."

"Two at their extremes are overriding. The first is to seek the best advantage and comfort for ourselves, translated in the extreme that is the search for economic wealth. The discovery of the New World was in search of China's gold. Planting crops seeking the lowest level of expenditure to increase a better return on the harvest led to the business of providing slaves to tend the fields. The collective tribal stress of seeking and obtaining wealth leads to coveting the resources of your weakest neighbor. This will not end, and you and I can do nothing to prevent the rise and fall of world economies."

"I'd better ask about your second extreme. I need hope that there is hope. It bothers me that I can do so little."

"Saving wildlife from poachers is a very honorable quest, and I admire you for that. Sincerely."

"Why, thank you, Wendell. I do think you mean that."

He felt suddenly uncomfortable, cleared his throat, and launched into the hardest of all discussions, the threat of religion.

"Again, as the thinking animal and more so with the truth of science available to our understanding, we should have achieved a sense of peaceful enlightenment. Unfortunately, we are limited with a very prehistoric trait we have been unable to purge, and that is 'superstition.'

"In the basic sense, it is a false belief that there is more magic in the unknown, and if we can't understand it, then through superstition, what we can't understand must be more omnipotent than we mere mortals — either to accept the existence of a 'Creator' figure or rationalize why bad events happen the blame must arise from an evil spirit, so to speak, a 'Devil' incarnate.

"I don't know your religion," said 'Wendell.' Everyone called him 'Holmes,' but for her... He caught himself wondering. He continued his thought. "Nor am I here to argue how we create religions, but I would say religions are sustained by an unknown no one can repudiate, and that is faith. If you have faith, all things imaginary exist, all questions have answers, and when all else fails, the unknown Creator understands what we don't and can forgive us for human errors, including genocide. But let me get back on track, and apply it to a real situation as I see it.

"Islam and Christianity have always been at war against each other. It is one big tribal slugfest feud. Who cast the first stone is irrelevant, as is the second person who had to retaliate with equal violent force. Each side of these faiths believes the other is the infidel, destined for a brimstone lava abyss called Hell. Still taking sides, the Believers say at the End of Days, when the Creator ends all, and the good people embrace Heaven, and all the non-repented non-believers on both sides and everywhere else, however remote and not part of these present contests, will likewise be consigned to the fiery pit. Most not knowing there was a judgment aspect to their uncomplicated lives."

"So, you are saying, even though most religions preach goodwill, there can be temporary peace, but not lasting? Then, we are doomed to wars without end. How depressing."

"Not necessarily. I think if someone could bring new change to one side or the other of the embattled faiths, present an altered perception in their beliefs, there may be a chance, slim but possible."

330   S.P. Grogan

Samantha leaned over and let Wendell fill her glass. "Indeed?"

"You know you have stumbled onto a track of thought I have been trying to construct — part of my recent retirement hiatus. Recently, before I left my old job," they both smiled, knowing which place of employment that was, "I obtained a draft of a White Paper entitled, 'Countering Violent Extremism, Scientific Methods and Struggles.' It will be released this September, an ironic date, I suppose. In the reading, I was able to see the scientific relationship of terrorism as it impacts local civil wars.

"But generally, let's look at the currently most violent; the Islamic fundamentalist with a gun. The moderate Muslim can see a cooperative position with Christians of 'each to their own,' but the jihadists cannot, and we kill them as they try to kill us. But, just hypothesizing, what if they were to gain a new interpretation of their religion? Stay with me on this for a second.

"What if we found a new all-knowing Prophet? Jesus came out of the Jews, Martin Luther, a Catholic, changed the fundamental dogma of the papal church. Even in the last two hundred years, John Smith and his Mormonism rose to suggest a better life for 19th-century Protestantism.

"But do we want to take orders from a ruling Scientology mage or find holy direction by forced mass weddings under Reverend Moon veneration? I don't see those fringes bringing world peace," he told her.

She laughed lightly, remarkably impressed with the depth coming from the man she knew was a former spy. Of all the surprises.

He could not stop himself and tamp his enthusiasm. "This is a modern world where movies create believable zombies and lovers of vampires thrive. Based on superstition and imagination, one could even call such entertainment 'cult' religions, and like a religion, the consumer masses gobble up the unknown mythology as true belief, as a Comic Convention readily proves each year.

"So it goes. Advertising preaches and convinces us that whatever we buy is something we need desperately. It would not be, I believe, so hard to define a Newer New Testament or a 'heavenly revelation' of a Revised Qu'ran, perhaps the same lesson but repackaged, something like, 'rise above tribal thinking and love thy brother and sister and put down your assault weapons.' Simplistic credos might be the easiest answers to package up."

"You want a new religion for Islam?" Samantha asked.

"No, never disrespect the good influence of some of Mohammad's teachings, those which can still be applied to today's civilization. But could we not have another perspective vision from a New Prophet? Or even a new burning bush vision that updates Christianity. Hey, even Hinduism or Buddhism could stand a 21st-century make-over."

"And you want to be the leader of this, as you call it, what, a 'spiritual make-over?'"

Holmes, ready to tilt at windmills, got off his eager high horse. He sighed and relaxed back into his chair.

"No, that is the problem. I am a speck of sand on the beach, quite unnoticed. Society will not let an ex-government worker become a visionary. Great ideas must find viable platforms from which to launch."

Samantha jumped in.

"But when this new manifesto comes about, can I have a hand in it, rid the world of male chauvinism, give women the right to make their own decisions? Wear a veil or not, have babies or not, but their choice, yet still support the sanctity of life. Not interpretive words written by a male monk or imam from three thousand years ago."

He had met his match. "It shall be called the Book of Samantha." They exchanged glances. Sometimes serious diatribe must simmer behind innocent jest.

"Before we go writing a new Bible, you mentioned the jihadists a minute earlier. That brings me back to a real reason for this invitation."

"I did wonder why I had been brought back from my wanderings." He had been really, really wondering where her summons might lead. She continued. "I received in the mail two separate correspondences, one from you, a disk of the photos of the inside of bin Laden's compound, and perhaps coincidentally a day later, a copy of the video shot by CAM ONE under Callie's signature."

"Intriguing."

Samantha seemed slightly sad.

"Callie did say she had a copy for you but did not know how to reach you, meaning you had not been in further contact with *King's Retribution*, and I felt I had better resources to locate the mysterious Holmes."

"I am not a mystery, merely a closed book."

"Perhaps, not closed, but one not read properly."

Holmes again shifted his body uncomfortably. He parried.

"Speaking of books, I read an interesting one recently; it dealt with Islamic jihadists and an attempt to detonate nuclear weapons. And one feature of it that perked my curiosity."

"And that was what?" She felt at ease in his presence. No airs, no pretense. Not a manufactured man of society, no snob playing mind games; he was not even trying to come on to her, and that absent expectation seemed to her a letdown.

"I found this book on a street in Abbottabad and believe it came from bin Laden's house."

"Yes, I recall. Now you have my rapt attention."

"Maybe not tonight. I would appreciate just sitting here, with you, enjoying the urban skyline you and I are trying to save." She could accept the need for him to seek more quieting atmospheres.

She agreed. "Let's do lunch tomorrow. I will show you mine if you thrill me with yours." The innuendo in her tease was left hanging.

They enjoyed each other's company, talking about the small things they might have in common; she sensitive to his life of classified secrets, and he asking why fashion designer Alexander McQueen who had just died, was more popular in death. It would have been the perfect night for a couple to sit close and hold hands. Unsaid, they both thought that but did not do so.

Scene 5: Coming to America…
Setting: Claridge's Hotel, London, July 2nd

"But I do not like America."

"You must go," said banker Taher Abboud, sweating, wiping his forehead. "I know I will come under the scrutiny of MI 6. It is only a matter of time, and with their persuasive measures, that Ziad will give me up. Probably, there is already a hold on my passport." He pushed back the copied disk of *Crimson Scimitar*, the financial aspect of the attack. "Our Sheik, may Allah hold him close, entrusted the entire operation's secrets to your safekeeping. That suggests to me that you were to become an integral part of *Crimson Scimitar*. As I see it, you are now the facilitator of this operation, not some guerrilla fighter in the Solomon Mountains. And what you told me does demonstrate leadership.

"To protect us from Ziad's confession, I have changed account names, not to my name as you asked but to your passport cover, and moved out the last funds we deposited from the Islamic charities, ran them through the Cayman bank and back as new investment accounts at several brokerage houses as planned. Ziad's role has always been limited, courier and collector. I was to go with him for the paperwork on the final trades. You now must do that."

Abboud's appeal went directly to Khalaf's base desires. After all, the germinal idea for this part of *Crimson Scimitar* had come from his late-night reading and movies he watched at the Compound. Sheik bin Laden must have thought highly of him to include his 'plot' ideas in the operation, which spoke of great trust. Besides, above all others, he not only knew the intimate details of the plans, but he could be on the scene to carry them off, even travel to America, and that held added importance. What took him over the edge, perhaps the opportunity would present itself that he could find a way to see, even approach his leader, as bin Laden went on trial. Yes, he would travel to the belly of the beast, seeking its vulnerable heart.

This task, if he undertook it, would be as important as Shahin's attack, though he still himself hungered for military action. At least he would be in North America when Shahin carried out the violent part of *Crimson Scimitar*, and if his team achieved victory and crowned themselves with laurel garlands of victory to wave to the world, they must say he was there and give him his share in the glory. And if Shahin failed and Khalaf succeeded in his part of the attack, he would now take over. Certainly, his membership, up from courier onto the Supreme Council, was could be obtainable.

"Yes, I will go, for the sake of the mission and retaliation for the kidnapping of Sheik bin Laden." *Yes, that had a nice nationalistic ring to it*, thought Khalaf.

"Then, this is yours." The banker deposited the suitcase next to Khalaf. "This is the last of the monies we have collected from the charities. The monies are secreted behind tear-away leather."

"And again, I am to do what?"

"Here is the address of our Islamic Benevolent Foundation contact in the Bronx. His name is Nidal. He knows very little and is looking only for a payment, no questions asked. He will convert the cash into cashier's checks for deposit to the bank and brokerage accounts, the lists in your hand. He will assist you with the planned investment strategy. Using our secure email address, you will be coordinating with the *Crimson Scimitar* leader in the U.S., the Professor, who will text a 12-hour notice before the first attack, which will be your signal to start your operation. As I have been told only a minimum of facts, these actions by you are the reaction to the first 'attack' but a distraction for the secondary and main attack."

"And I must say, I do like this new cover, the businessman, traveling with his wife. Very smart of you, Maulawi Jan."

"No, I am now Sheik Khalaf bin Zayed, oil trade negotiator from the United Arab Emirates, advisor to the President of UAE. Wherever I must travel, and if I am going to the U.S., my cover would be this: I have been chosen to meet with American commodities trading firms. And yes, traveling with his bride."

Not yet, but very soon, she said so.

"And she is here? I would like to meet her."

"Oh, I am sorry; I believe she is napping. But on our return, there will be a dinner for all of us to toast our success."

"A pity, I may not be there to enjoy such fruits of victory."

"Oh?"

"If the police come knocking at my door, for the success of *Crimson Scimitar* and to protect its secrets, I must take my life." He stared at Khalaf. "I assume you have taken such an oath?"

Another test of loyalty? Khalaf would not fall for such games. No one seemed to think he was capable of such great accomplishments.

"As once a courier to the Emir bin Laden I took a blood oath to die to protect al-Qaeda."

"Even a man with a new bride can have second thoughts about sacrificing all?"

No delay in his response. "She will accompany me to heaven."

Taher smiled his admiration. "A dedicated man as you is to be shown great respect."

"My allegiance is to the memory of my Sheik and prayers to see him released to see his plan secure a victory, and if they kill him, prayers for his immortality."

"Then, indeed, Allah willing, perhaps we shall celebrate again soon. May He go with you."

"And He with you, Taher Abboud." The banker bowed slightly and made his exit.

Khalaf, traveling under the passport of Khalaf bin Zayed of the UAE, put the suitcase from the banker on the desk near the window. He and Sabz were ensconced in the Victorian-decorated Davies suite at Claridge's Hotel, one of the finest in all of London. Sabz's idea; she had Googled the top-ranked accommodations and chose this one befitting a UAE emissary.

Actually, the whole itinerary planning had fallen to her as Khalaf nursed his wounds and caught up on world news as they traveled. Not that he minded her travel maintenance or her hovering to see his bandages properly changed. Dutiful.

At their stop in Islamabad, he found himself being measured by a tailor brought to his hotel room to provide several expensive Kandura white robes, and, before flying out, destination the U.K., he had undergone a transformation into the perfect Emirati businessman, clean-shaven face, left with a proper mustache, acceptable to Western customs. Arriving in London, he added a Saville Row pin-stripe suit to better blend in. Surprised and quietly pleased, for casual times, Sabz bought him a pair of jeans, not looking like brand new, but more a distressed raw 'vandalized ripped' denim jeans, the latest rage at €500. Weeks earlier he thought he saw the same look on a beggar in Kabul, but Sabz's eagerness to dress him over-rode any desire to his opposition.

He was not ignorant of others' customs. He had traveled widely in Europe in his college days, even a stop in the United Kingdom, but found himself, as he watched Sabz, likewise devouring their surroundings, inhaling all that was different. Where in these past times, he merely had tried to get between here and there, negotiate airports and local languages, ever wary of secret police who might pounce on a young Islamic revolutionary. In this travel, he saw the enthusiasm of a young girl transfixed by all that was new, giddy with a world outside the poverty of Central Asia. Whether it was good or not, he noticed her influence providing a lightness in his heart. Behind him came her voice and not a *soft* voice.

"So, if you fail, you are going to kill me; for what, your mistakes?"

She had been listening from her bedroom. He turned and found her standing, irate, hands on hips, and absolutely divine, beautiful even in scorn.

"What are you wearing? It is sacrilege."

"What, that I am not covered head to toe, hidden where you cannot see my expressions, judge my temperament, either to bask in my glow of your wisdom or notice my evil eye and to protect yourself from my wrath. And this fashion, you see, is completely demure, maintains proper shyness, and at the same time is what any Muslim woman who is married to a husband of rank should be seen in public wearing, to show through these styles" — and she twirled showing off her outfit — "the value the husband places on his married property."

"But the colors? They're so...."

"Vibrant? Yes, do you want your 'bride' to be wrapped in a black funeral shroud? Do you like it? The head scarf is Hermes. The coat design, if you have not realized, is from the latest Egyptian fashion magazine, though the pants I bought here locally, from a boutique shop called SammyC Fashions, very, what do they say, 'hip couture,' the latest. But looking the best for my husband means nothing if he is going to kill me in New York?"

"What? You are not going to New York! This is the beginning and...."

"And I know it will be 'dangerous.' But what will you do with me? I know your mind. Give me a few Euros, stick me in a lesser hotel room than this penthouse — and you like my choice here, I know that — and then expect me to fend for myself, in a lesser style, having to use my womanhood to survive, just like back in Uzbekistan and Pakistan. No, thank you, I would rather follow you and your stupid project."

He was on her in a second; his hands grabbed her arms and shook her violently.

"What I am doing is not 'stupid'!"

She looked him hard in the eyes, fierce.

"Isn't your option that if all fails, then death is the appropriate measure? The Japanese, when fighting the Americans, killed themselves after every small failure, but they could have been a lot more victorious if they had stayed alive to win future battles.

"And what of your al-Qaeda?

"Every day in the newspapers and television, I see where they are killing your leaders. You just have to wait your turn; you will be the last one, eventually their leader, and then they will kill you." She did not laugh at him, her lips pursed. "I do not want that, your death. And I do not want to die."

336   S.P. Grogan

He let go of her arms, frustrated, tired at her back-country logic.

"I will not fail. And I…what I said about you was for an old fanatic's ears; I did not mean it."

She smoothed the fabric of her outfit, shook off her anger, and reposed her smile.

"I hope you do not fail." She went over to a coffee table and picked up a guest guide.

"You control the bank accounts. And I would like to shop in New York."

"New York is out of the question. I may go out beyond there." A plan had been formulating in the back of his mind, percolating since learning of this trip. He would try to join Shahin in the attack in Nevada. He believed that with the timing coordinated, he could accomplish his part in New York and then go to the battleground. He wanted to fight, to be a warrior hero, to prove his merits to himself, to al-Qaeda, to bin Laden, and yes, to Sabz. She would want him if he were a true hero of the cause.

She looked up from the magazine, noticing his attempt at sternness, believing she understood what drove his needs.

"I will give myself to you." Casually, said as if a comment on the weather.

"What?"

"You were planning on taking my virginity at some time. You are healed well enough to perform the sex act. In some ways, you have been the proper gentlemen, expecting at your call my eager willingness. I would rather give my purity to you than have you become mean-spirited or drunk and, like a ruffian, rape me and believe I would like such beastly brutality. I have seen women who have been raped by soldiers from both sides, soldiers who believe they are the righteous army; these women's souls are damaged, their spirit for life extinguished. So I have decided you may have my body… but in New York, in a nice hotel, a king-size bed like we have here… and not in our separate bedrooms." She gave him that child-like come-hither glance, her eyes to the floor, the female tigress offering submission to the docile male, but not so fast — "and we will have the night you so well deserve — after you return from whatever success you seek. But to have me, you must come back alive."

He did want her. During their few nights in close proximity, he had thought about kicking in the door to her bedroom and found himself hard and excited with dreams of ravishing her, and here it was, handed to him, she to be in his bed… her rules but his dream fulfilled. He could live with that. After all, the ending to *Crimson Scimitar* was in sight. His belief in its ultimate outcome had not wavered. Victors do not sacrifice themselves.

"New York," he stated in a firm voice as if he were the one in control. "We will leave in a week."

"And I shall have an allowance there." Not a question.

"Reasonable, yes, but no foolishness."

The notion struck him, odd and unnerving, that he had made no plans beyond *Crimson Scimitar*. What of Sabz and himself? What fate would follow? What did Allah have in store for him, and worse, he wondered if even Allah knew what was coming.

"Let's go out for dinner," she bubbled. "The guide says 'Amaya Restaurant' has top-star Indian food. And Khalaf, my dear husband, do you think we could go to a football game this weekend? Act like normal people, cheer for a team?"

Could he deny her anything? And in her innocence, which he knew was a lot more calculating than her purring sounds, this young thing had great insight; she offered an alternate choice in perspective to his narrow mindset and what cause of Islam was to tell him that he must suffer and be stoic and not enjoy life to its fullness before the epic battle began? So, why not with a beautiful woman to show off, to show to all that he was a man of impeccable taste? Taste he would soon savor.

"Yes, we could do that."

There was a yip of joy, and she ran to him, hugging, kissing his cheek, and skipped away to the window, looking at the wide world beyond the suite's glass and balcony.

"Oh, one other small thing, my dearest Khalaf," she paused for his attention, then patting the suitcase on the desk, she gave him that devilish smile, and in a whispered kitten voice, "Do you have to give up all that money for this Red Sword project of yours? Don't you think it is wise to put some aside for the next battle?"

EPISODE TWENTY-ONE — Storm Clouds Gather

Scene 1: Introducing the Unknown Threat
Setting: Santa Monica, California, July 5th

"Our work may not be finished."

They were all reunited in a War Room devoid of most of its equipment, a linoleum bare coldness. With their 'Hunt' target captured, sitting it out in some hidden cell, under their, well, Hugh Fox's control, the atmosphere wavered between letdown and animosity. Hugh Fox was absent from this gathering. That said a lot. There were those there who assumed the original mission was over.

"And by this mini-reunion, you are referring to all of us?" Storm King sneered at Wendell Holmes, not happy about joining the alumni group of terrorist hunters in the desolate War Room and knowing he would be more pissed off to be left out.

"What Wendell is asking for is a little of your time," piped up Samantha. "We have had a chance to review all the materials, the photos and video of the bin Laden compound sent to us, and interesting questions arise that we want to present to you, gain your input, and decide if there are next steps to be taken by *King's Retribution*, or just send our findings to the Federal authorities."

Callie found it interesting that Samantha said 'Wendell' instead of 'Holmes' and 'we,' not 'Hugh and I.' You would think she would have gone to Hugh. What was going on?

"I have no problem," agreed Callie. "We still have to make a show come together since the public is now demanding one. And I have no idea what this 'trial' is really about and if we have any role to play. So I have the time and the curiosity. After all, by achieving a *King's Retribution* success by capturing our quarry, we are on the minds of a greater television audience." She glanced to the end of the table where the morose King sat in a grumpy mood.

"Something new as a lead into the storyline would be helpful."

Everyone around the table, one way or the other, gave approval. They could dampen down their disappointment knowing the always enthusiastic Hugh Fox was absent working on what they now all considered 'his project.' So be it.

The conference room was filled. Besides those who went to Pakistan like Bennie and Abbas, J-Q was there representing Fox and the four Skilleo workers who were actively cleaning up the trash carnage in the War Room left by the Government raiders, re-establishing systems to the outside world with new equipment, again bare bones, replacement terminals but only for them. The War Room had been downsized, as close to 'mothballing' as one operation could get.

A new face had been added since bin Laden's capture, the quiet yet attractive young lady, the attorney Lisa Goss-Scott. Fox had decided all new *King's Retribution* actions would have to be through the lens of possible legal ramifications. Samantha accepted that Hugh wanted a layer of scrutiny and a closer eye kept on one of the stars by the name of King. Before the attorney sat three books, not law books, but novels, as the participants noticed.

And last but not least, seen but unseen, CAM ONE and CAM TWO were back at their jobs, recording all that was said for posterity and future show footage. CAM THREE, they heard, had come from production obscurity to be packed off to Colorado Springs to set up the 'inside-personalized' camera work to be layered and integrated within the national trial coverage. CAM ONE and CAM TWO, it was acknowledged, would soon follow.

Wendell turned off the conference room lights and started the PowerPoint slide show against a large screen in the War Room.

"I have taken out the *King's Retribution* entry to the country and our safe, speedy departure. Nothing stands out, in my opinion.

"Most of what you will see are the brief shots from the videos and then still photos from our individual camera phones. First, bin Laden's bedroom. Unless you all can see something Samantha and I missed, and please make the assumption we overlooked a valuable piece of evidence (and we will supply you with 8x10 blowups for your later study), then the conclusion we can make is that this was thoroughly ransacked by the SEALS and anything of probative value long removed."

"Except missing is the bastard's bloody head," a turgid comment from King, ignored by Holmes.

"Going down one flight, the second floor, which will hold our interest, is the discovery in one of what they call their three media rooms, next to the balcony, of the false wall and hidden closet library slash mattress bed. Since we all found this unusual and a true discovery by *King's Retribution*, overlooked by the SEALs, we took many photos and have many different angles. Later, we were told that this closet was stripped and left bare, either by the Pakistani military or al-Qaeda, or both.

"Let's do a role-playing game, a little Sherlock, a little Columbo. You all have paper and pencil in front of you; as I go through the next ten views, write down what you think you see. The last two shots are close-ups, thanks to our friends here at Skilleo."

"This is stupid," said King, ignoring him and not picking up the pencil.

During the five-minute drill, staring and scribbling went forward enthusiastically.

Like a quiz master, and on the last view, Holmes told them, 'time's up; please put your pencils down.' Then, he started around the room, ladies first, with Bridget, one of the geeks, honored to be part of the illustrious group.

"Graffiti on the wall, Arabic, which I don't understand. A couple of art drawings, red ink maybe, but it's too dark to tell, of looks like a sword, curved. Three shelves of books, several titles in Arabic, but, and this is crazy; the rest are all English or American books."

Said Holmes, "We will have the Arabic translated. The few I could read were al-Qaeda slogans seen on posters at rallies."

From Callie, "I can recognize the names of some major best-sellers." She read off a couple of names: "Tom Clancy, Clive Cussler, someone called David Baldacci, another is Robert K. Tanenbaum. A few more. Like Brad Thor."

Samantha passed out sheets of paper to everyone.

"Here is the list of author names we could read on the spines. Some we can't make out."

"Maybe our main laboratory could try further digitizing," said Bennie.

Gizmo, the geek programmer that Holmes first had met, looked affronted — *of course, they could* — but he said nothing.

340   S.P. Grogan

"Anything else?"

"Well, if you consider the mattress and look at the photos," said J-Q, "then what I see is someone staying there but not living there. I don't see extra clothes hanging up. One toothbrush in a glass, nothing else medicinal, no shaving cream, probably wears a beard."

"We can assume he is a man," snorted Callie. "No woman would live in such conditions unless she was a sex slave in bondage."

A few of the men raised their eyebrows. But Wendell recalled that as a cop, she may have seen something as terrible.

"Could you get any close-ups of the magazines, know what they were?" The question from Bennie, replaced from security, once Clayton's position. With Hugh's concern for everyone's safety, there were eight bodyguards floating the perimeter outside the conference room. Bennie enjoyed the relief of being the show's getaway driver again.

"A couple are folded, as you see, and we believe they are jihadist tracts; another, judging by the writing, and the head of a blonde female, probably could be Dutch porn."

"Our mystery man is lonely," suggested Samantha.

"A man into self-love is never lonely," intoned King, then caught himself and quickly added, "That's what I've found in inspecting barracks."

Abbas of Special Effects held up and pointed to his sheet of paper. "There is another pile of something over in the corner, holding up some books on the shelves. Smaller books?"

"I think they are old VHS tapes," explained Holmes, pointing. "Only two or three names on the ends. One I could figure out: 'Villain.' An old British gangster film back in the 1970s. Starred Richard Burton."

"Why, a movie video over 40 years old?" asked J-Q, wanting to feel included. "A favorite?"

Holmes shrugged, not knowing. "More digitizing and close-ups are required to see what's on these shelves. I am sure Gizmo here can handle it." The tech kid smiled back at his new-found friend.

"Okay," Holmes getting people back on track. "Ready for the first analysis?"

"Here comes the Sherlock part of the Holmes," Samantha lightened up, knowing where their joint postulations might be going. Wendell gave his overview:

"1. Our closet guest, let's call him 'Ali Baba,' knows how to read English and thus should be able to speak it.

"2. If he can read novels with American or British slang, chances are he had a college education. From the newspaper reports — and yes, I don't have access to private channels anymore — none of the 'known' couriers or bin Laden's son had that sort of study of Western pop culture; in fact, Pakistan universities certainly do not teach the lifestyle of American writers.

"Someone wants to take a stab at the first deduction of facts?"

From nowhere, Gizmo's game partner, Lars, dutifully raised his hand, seeking permission to speak. This would be the first time anyone had heard the Silent One respond.

"Ali Baba was a traveler, a visitor, passing through, and since it seems he read a lot and had a mattress, he came there a lot, but he was a rank higher than the rest, staying on the second floor, closer to El Supremo."

"Very good; a star for that man. Ali Baba might have been the third or fourth courier bin Laden used, or maybe more so, he might have been a sub-military commander, a strategist for al-Qaeda, who had come to consult with his leader and take back their battle plans to the field commanders to implement. And now, the Slumdog Millionaire question: do we know what plan or plans bin Laden handed to Ali Baba to give out to the field army?"

Negative shakes of the head.

"I think," Holmes began, then looking at Samantha, corrected, "*We* think the answers were in these books. Sadly, many titles we can't discern."

He pointed to the last PowerPoint image of the book shelves up close. Callie could see Samantha positively beam as he continued. "Think on this hypothesis which came to me as a revelation recently obtained when observing the oneness and harmony with a sky full of stars."

Callie saw Samantha give a silent laugh under her breath. Something was going on between them, and Callie wondered: Gads, Holmes probably didn't even realize he was being stalked. Samantha Carlisle, Callie concluded, having previously had years to develop her skills into being a woman detective, concluded that the fashion design lady wanted both men. Hugh and Wendell. No way, way. Ménage á trois or at least the fashion designer as the femme fatale ménaging un and deux at her leisure. She turned back to Holmes's lecture.

"…after 9/11, al-Qaeda certainly can't go to America and start planning the next attack. No, they have to wait until our guard is down again, let years go by, and maybe believe the best attack date would be the 10th Anniversary of 9/11…wouldn't that tell the world that al-Qaeda had not been weakened and could attack at their pleasure? And maybe this attack will be a doozy, more than airplanes crashing into buildings."

Even Storm King was listening. He understood long-term military strategies. The North Vietnamese suffered through twenty years of guerrilla war, proxy through sacrificing the Viet Cong, and aerial bombardments to prevail against the South Vietnamese and the Americans, the latter worn down, as King would always remember, by anti-war pinkos.

342 S.P. Grogan

Holmes continued the analysis, "Where would al-Qaeda go to gain research and intel to develop the most thought-out audacious attack plan to be launched in the United States since 9/11?"

Pregnant pause for the dramatic effect; he was enjoying having an audience who thought his experience still had value, and to Samantha, he was grateful for this second chance, to be assured he was correct, and damned if he was incorrect.

"Drum roll," said Gizmo.

The answer. "Why, from the best-selling authors of terrorist thrillers."

"Oh, come off it." King thought the man must be the silent kind of megalomaniac when they first met, now to grasp out so foolishly.

"Again, here me out. Ali Baba starts reading these British and American potboilers where they usually kill the foreign, typically radical fundamentalists, or shoot-outs against a crazed army seeking world domination, but for our strategist, they do more: they conceive plans where one of them might actually have a chance of succeeding. Bestselling authors these days have their own investigative teams who research all the minutiae detail to make the plot realistic. In some ways, the British or American author has done all the leg work for al-Qaeda without one of the real bad guys having to step into the country.

"Samantha, if you please."

She stood and advanced the PowerPoint to the cover of the novel, *Escape* by Robert K. Tanenbaum. She explains what they see. "Published 2009, where a terrorist character called *The Sheik* is introduced and ends up in the subsequent plots of two separate novels. I read this on the flight here. Strong plot, but a lot of carryover characters from books going back to 1993." She shows another slide. "Like in 2005, in Tanenbaum's thriller, *Fury*. [An orange-black cover featuring the Brooklyn Bridge was viewed]. Here, a terrorist cell is trying to set off a bomb on New Year's Eve in New York City's Times Square."

She moved the PowerPoint forward. Tag teaming, Holmes stepped in, taking his cue to add, "New book. *Dead or Alive* by Tom Clancy. 2010 in which the CIA and Jack Ryan, Jr., our protagonist, are trying to capture the terrorist called *the Emir*.

"The plot is fascinating," he explained. "The terrorists go to Nevada and shoot their way into the nuclear repository at Yucca Mountain, with the intent to explode a bomb, cause an earthquake, and let the nuclear waste seep into the groundwater. That plot is flawed since there is nothing at Yucca Mountain yet. But we have to ask ourselves, what if Ali Baba read a book and took it with him to do more intense research or hand it off to a conspirator to double-check the plot's accuracy? What worries me more is that Clancy's 1991 techno-thriller, *Sum of All Fears,* has Arab terrorists finding a nuclear bomb lost by the Israelis, and they detonate it in America, using non-Arabs."

"Yeah, man," said Gizmo, "Ben Affleck starred as Jack Ryan, and it was a scary scene, the bomb blowing up in Denver and almost starting a war between us and the Russians."

"Therein lies our problem, folks." Holmes had to bring the whole presentation back into a reasonable focus wrapped into a challenge.

"I think al-Qaeda is planning another strike against the United States, aimed at the 9/11 anniversary or around that date. The answer is in these books, maybe in a VHS movie Ali Baba and bin Laden watched together — from public media photos, the TV seized upstairs in the compound had a VHS system built-in or was attached. And as you can see from the list in front of you, there are twenty American and British authors, and I am guessing each one has some sort of terrorist plot. Many of these authors, like Flynn, Thor, and Le Carré, have multiple books dealing with some sort of bad guys planning an unholy act of terror. And one of those plots has been thought out so well by the author's research team that in actuality, it can be duplicated and with minimum effort."

"If you can see your way clear to this point and are starting to believe as we do," Samantha gave off a light plea, "We need you to read all the books you think you can devour. And no Cliff Notes summary write-ups, a paragraph unread might be just as critical. We would meet back in...hate to say this, but it's a short fuse, I would say one week, back here. After that, the next time we can meet and have Hugh present is at his 'project' near Colorado Springs."

"We should contact the Government, give them a warning." said the fourth geek guy, Mark, the one partnering with Bridget It was a throw-away question since this computer nerd was anti any government.

"And what would we say?" said King, still a non-believer. "Hey, we have a list of fiction plots that will lead you to save America from Islamic bookworms?"

"For once," said Bennie, "the Colonel is right. We are lacking hard evidence." King scowled at this lesser actor employee.

"Read the books," said Samantha. "We will have a staffer secure all the ones on the list and the ones for the titles we can decipher. Then, we will divvy them up."

"Okay, if we do stumble into something tangible and must continue, it means meeting at the Stadium," interjected Callie; her mind had been on different tangents. "Just in the time for this trial. I'll call Hugh and see if we can set up a temporary satellite War Room."

"Good idea," Samantha's reply was all business-like; conversing with Hugh at this time for her was an uneasy idea. Yet, she noted, Callie had begun using 'Hugh' more and more versus her usual 'Fox' or 'Mr. Fox'. Samantha gave this personalized shift no more attention.

"I'll watch the movies that were on that list," said King, setting the tone and standard for non-expectations that this literary exercise would lead to any great discoveries of immediate

344   S.P. Grogan

threats. They all knew someone else would have to surreptitiously re-watch any movie King took as his assignment.

Scene 2: Another Package to Deliver
Setting Fort Calhoun Nuclear Plant, Nebraska, June 27th

Jumping back to the end of last month, one such threat had already occurred and was to impact all that followed.

Flooding from the Missouri River surrounded the nuclear plant with two feet of water, six feet more, and the potential of contamination might occur. The good news was that the plant had shut down, in accordance with safety plans, anticipating the flooding. Yet it was the fear of a major accident, as demonstrated by Japan's tsunami destruction in March this year, that sent a tremor throughout the nuclear industry, pressured by anti-nuclear energy activists raising horrible specters of what climate disasters like tornadoes, earthquakes, and floods might do to nuclear energy plants, to cause unimaginable human tragedies, leaving the surrounding countryside an abandoned radioactive wasteland.

To this headline, fueled by increasing paranoia, the manager of the Fort Calhoun plant contacted the manager of the Indian Point plant, where the Scientist worked, and requested to join their planned convoy of spent fuel rods as their storage facility would be threatened throughout the long summer. The decision would be coming down in early July, actually, the 10th of July, approved by the Nuclear Waste Storage Taskforce Committee, of which Roger Givens was a member. They agreed to allow one trailer designed for radioactive transport to meet and accompany the Indian Point vehicles in Denver before proceeding south to Albuquerque, New Mexico, and west through Arizona, into Nevada. Thus the caravan convoy was expanded by the additional trailer truckload, and the trip pushed up to mid-September.

Again, the elevated CIA Deputy Director Givens scratched his initials to an inner-governmental memo once more, stating that his Agency *had no evidence of international threats that would substantiate a reason for the caravan not proceeding.* The same day the FBI taskforce representative also concurred by signing off: *No discernible known risk from any internal national chatter.*

In the bureaucratic details of configuring the radioactive waste shipments, the Scientist suggested at one sub-committee meeting, matter-of-factly, that each tractor-trailer in the patchwork fleet should be identified as part of the convoy with similar markings. After the usual committee debate, it was agreed that a large descriptive American eagle, screaming, diving, talons bared, should be predominantly displayed on each truck's side panels and rear door. The meeting's memo suggested this design should be for all future shipments of nuclear waste, affirming the look and giving off a patriotic sense of guarded security. The Scientist merely saw his approved suggestion as the I.D. for attackers to distinguish their targets.

Scene 3: Tele-Looping the Loop
Setting: Santa Monica

As the Santa Monica War Room group went separate ways, three lines of communication went out, none telling the other about their actions, each involving Hugh Fox.

And Hugh Fox, as much as he was multi-tasking with a magical flair like the Sorcerer from Disney's *Fantasia*, trying to undo apprentice Mickey's unruly magic brooms, he still had time for his friends, still cared, even when not there.

Samantha reached him first. As she expected, an awkward time.

"I am sorry I have not talked to you in a while. However, I feel what we are now doing is as important as your trial prep, which I know is important to you, so I hope we can continue to be professionals and business partners."

His response was an attempt at magnanimous self-blame. "Regrettable but understandable. This was a no-fault relationship. Last week I checked my schedule and was surprised that not one minute could have been carved out for personal time."

"A true commitment would have found the time." Malice not intended, she quickly added, "The same sort of restraints prevented my communicating more often." She really wanted to say, why did you freeze me out of working with you, side by side, on *The Trial of the Century*? All too late in expressing what would have seemed at present a nasty jibe, and that wasn't her.

He gave his own lame excuse. "Maybe I'm just worried about what a commitment means." What he meant to say was, 'If I gave this deeper thought, I'd realize I blew it.'

"I can understand. My issue is still not knowing what I really want." What she meant to say was, 'You would be a great as an occasional one-night stand, but I am still unfulfilled.'

He chided her, which she accepted. "You have the good-bad habit of wanting to save everything, from animals to rain forests to people. I think I was more of a project for you, but at least it was full service." Holmes already had made the same analysis.

They both laughed. Samantha moved back to safer ground.

"I know you're busy, but I would ask you to glance at Tom Clancy's books; he is very techno, very detailed writer, something you would appreciate."

"I will do so. And I plan to see you all at this next meeting J-Q has planned unless a late-night romp is in the cards?"

346

S.P. Grogan

"Sorry, no deal. I'm becoming a nun again, and this new project is my catechism. But the invitation recalls great memories, ones I will sincerely treasure and recall on cold, lonely nights."

"For myself as well." He sought his own form of neutrality. "From what you are telling me there is now the consensus that al Qaeda is planning another attack? I tend to accept the possibility. Our friend 'OBL' has repeatedly mentioned '*Crimson Scimitar*' as a warning, suggesting that '*Crimson Scimitar* is coming.'"

"In what we are calling Ali Baba's cave, there are several wall doodles in red ink, which could be viewed as a 'red sword,' and red meaning blood."

"You guys follow up on your hypothesis. I will support it since OBL seems confident that a supposed plan in the works by his side might just succeed against us."

Their call ended politely. Professionals could do that. Fox told his secretary to track down all Tom Clancy's books and then instruct one of his researchers to read them and give him two-page summaries. Then, any one of them which might seem more interesting, he would read it himself late at night, if he had time.

A few minutes later, Callie's call. To her, his voice came across as pleasant, as if the world outside his door, trying to beat it down, did not bother him.

What Samantha had not done, Callie gave him the gist of the War Room meeting and asked if he could assign someone ("I know you are busy with a good cause") to set up a quasi-War Room in Colorado Springs at the Skilleo Stadium. She quickly read off those who had been present and, for confidentiality, wanted them included in the 'new team.'

She mentioned they were going to hold their last Santa Monica War Room meeting in a week; if he could break away, his presence would be supportive, and said, "And *we* (meaning her) would enjoy seeing your happy and inquisitive face, leading us down the correct path."

She added quickly to lessen her hidden message, "As much as you are concentrating on the trial, *King's Retribution* needs to follow up on leads, and if this pans out, there may be another big show down the road. After your own television spectacular, *King's Retribution* may need some follow-up show concepts. So let us do the footwork for now. Maybe see us in four days, or if you can't, join us down at your trial." She again restated. "I know you're in your creative mode, but if you can make time for us, everyone would appreciate it." Again, she meant, wishing to say, 'me.' She had no real agenda, except she had to come to enjoy his upbeat moods when he was around. A little safe flirtation maybe.

"I will send you my notes by fax. You will be getting a FedEx copy of the PowerPoint we saw today. Take a quick minute to review. I do have ulterior motives."

"And, should I guess what? Or let my imagination wander?"

"If only."

She smiled, a smile with a lot of interpretive nuances attached, but he could not see her expression. "No, for your staff's viewing are the last two seasons of *King's Retribution* shows, including outtakes. I heard from one of the crazies here, Gizmo, I think, that you are mocking up some Warcraft-type games, and I felt you might just consider a 'shoot-'em up' bounty hunter game, and if you are interested, I am sure the Five Aces Studioz attorneys could work out the licensing."

"Ah, that's right, I am part owner of Five Aces Studioz, so I have to out-negotiate myself. A definite challenge. Does Storm support this direction?" he asked.

"I don't talk to Storm very much unless it's scripting dialogue on set."

"Cooling down between co-stars? Should I fear for my investment?"

"I can tolerate it, and Storm is the main star, as he keeps telling us. So, the show will go on."

A few seconds on his end, digesting ramifications, considering the unsaid.

"Good to know. What about all this book stuff? You think there's merit here?"

"As much as I have never trusted Wendell Holmes for his loyalties, I can't hide the fact the man is one of the best I have seen as a 'field operative.' He could cover my back anytime. Don't tell him that. What he is starting to suspect is a good path to follow. Gives us some fresh energy."

"And, as you said, good for *Retribution's* third season?"

"Can't be ignored, but there is something more sinister that rises above, at least puts my own vanity in check. I mean, what would you think if you ran across an al-Qaeda strategist who only read best sellers with terrorist plots? So, yes, something is there. And I've got this concern that we need to hustle."

"Why's that?" she asked.

"If I were planning a super-major attack, and as Holmes suggests, the best publicity angle would be on or around the anniversary of 9/11, I would have all my people in position well ahead, so nothing would go wrong, and that's a super worry."

"Meaning?"

"They're already here." That comment had them silent for a moment, the seriousness of her statement pervasive, but something more existed, and Fox turned his view back to the computer screen, where Clancy's *Sum of all Fears* plotted the explosion of a nuclear bomb in Denver.

Unknown to all, Fox was working from his new office at the Stadium near Colorado Springs. A real worry *here*? With this distraction, Callie Cardoza said goodbye and disconnected. Some signal vibrated in his mind, undefined, back to the present time. He, of all people, mastered such a high I-Q; it was a rarity when came moments of ill-timed brain farts where fundamental human nature eluded his thought processes.

What did he know? Fox recalled Callie's relayed worry of an attack plot perhaps already in motion. He had gotten to know her personality and her bona fide acting talents. If she was concerned, that had merit. Who could they warn? Key and reliable information was desperately needed, and Fox knew he had one piece of the puzzle.

This secret had been nagging at him since Pakistan, and believing on rare occasions that baring his soul to correct a mistake would give him feel-good redemption or some bullshit like that, he went searching for Wendell Holmes, who probably was still on premise in Santa Monica. His office tracked the man down, and Fox said immediately, "I have a confession to make."

Holmes put Fox on speaker phone. He continued culling through a stack of Vince Flynn novels. He told Fox of his homework. Fox had indeed read a few of them. Mitch Rapp, Flynn's main hero, is an unsanctioned assassin of terrorists, usually of Middle Eastern ethnicity, having nothing nice to say about the perversion of Qu'ran teachings to fit fundamentalist dogma. Fox considered that Holmes indeed had several of Rapp's characteristics, one being an immovable credo: good is good, and there are no grey areas when it comes to bad.

"I have a confession to make," Fox repeated.

"The confessional stands open," said Holmes, giving his attention to the games inventor.

"You said not to take anything when we were in the compound in Abbottabad. I sinned. I saw something that could be used against innocent people in the future and did not want to leave it just lying around."

"Sin to prevent sin; this is why mankind created rationalization. And what is your sin, my son?" giving the phone receiver a mock beatifying gesture and then folding his hands into a temple.

"I have sent you an email with a photo attached." Holmes opened his computer and searched.

The silence made Fox ask, "Did you get my attachment."

"A mighty sin, indeed. You know what this is?"

"Plastique explosives. C-4. French origin by the writing. I just couldn't let it sit there and be used later as a roadside bomb or something."

"Be careful and do not touch. It's still fragile, even without a detonator. I will have someone pick it up carefully and remove said sin. Where did you find this in the compound?"

"At the foot of the mattress, under a bed cover, where, what are you calling him, your Ali Baba read and slept."

"Your sin is forgiven. You have been wise, and we've been fortuitous. I have seen this similar brand before...and recently."

"Where, Pakistan?"

"No, here...in the U.S., in Florida...in a bombing."

Scene 4: Arrivals of No Good
Setting: San Diego, California, July 20th

The door creaked, opening with caution. In his hand, the gun felt comfortable as it readied itself, poised and aimed. On the other side of the door, several guns pointed at his chest.

"Buenos Dias, Luis," cordiality from Razzor Hassim, always a faked emotion from the Enforcer. "Did you bring me some important gifts?"

"Si." Luis Delgado stood aside as twelve men climbed the stairs from the tunnel, all unsure of their surroundings, wary, prepared for a trap set by undercover agents, but no shouts to surrender greeted them.

Razzor said, "Welcome to the United States of Infidels. May your stay here be fruitful."

The leader did not smile but looked at the olive-skinned man, noticing one of his ears was missing. He had no time for cordiality.

"On the day of victory, no one is tired."

"Ah, yes, quite correct." And Razzor replied in Arabic, "Days will show what we were ignorant of, and news will come that you have not sent. In the name of Allah, the Benevolent, the Merciful."

Only with the final words of code did Shahin lower his weapon; a set frown remained on his face.

Razzor did a quick head count of the newly arrived. Ten of them, eleven counting their leader, dressed in American-style slovenliness.

"I thought the team was six?"

"Change of plans," said Shahin, inspecting the duffel bag he had carried through the tunnel. "I will visit with you later, but as you know the country, you will lead this new team. Three of them for you, our most faithful, ready to die for al Qaeda glory. They have an

350   S.P. Grogan

important task. If completed, those who remain will rendezvous at the Bridge on the target date."

Razzor Hassim did not ask who the new people were or what was the additional task but had an idea. The news still saturated everywhere, the approaching tribunal. Where his sole focus had been on *Crimson Scimitar*, he had no choice but to follow the orders of this 'field commander' sent directly from the Council. *Crimson Scimitar* plans had now expanded. And if his guess was correct, this new team had been sent on a suicide mission. Razzor Hassim, on the other hand, had no wish to become a martyr anytime soon. He was a terrorist who enjoyed a paycheck.

He let his apprehension be muted and only responded, "Then let us begin a glorious journey," and led Shahin and his team, these underground tourists to America, out into the sunlight.

Scene 5: Feeling Better
Setting: Same day, San Diego Harbor

Keeping fit to offset the proscribed daily psychological talk session, Shawn Pacheco jogged the sidewalk leading from the Marine military base where he was housed to make a hard-impact run alongside San Diego Bay near Lindbergh Field. In the distance, he could see the aircraft carrier, *U.S.S. Carl Vincent* anchored; an ironic circumstance to Shawn, as he knew this naval vessel was on station in the Arabian Sea as part of the attack effort. He had heard, mostly gossip, that if bin Laden had been killed in the raid, the body would have been laid quickly to rest off the carrier into the dark watery depths, a murky grave no followers could pilgrimage to as some Mecca-type mausoleum.

Sometimes coincidence, however fated, bypasses the onlooker. As Shawn gazed at the beauty of the bay and the sailboats on tacking courses against a mild breeze, he looked away from the street where taxis and cars hustled to and fro at the airport terminal. Just then, leaving a truck-car rental agency, two vans with tinted windows passed by him, men staring out the windows like first-time tourists, as they were. Their destinations had been first to drop off two of their comrades who had a flight to catch to Florida; the others in the vans, carrying student visas, on a long haul to Colorado, to different locations, and with different objectives. *Crimson Scimitar* was slowly being tugged from its scabbard, to be bloodied by its sharpness.

Scene 6: Follow-up Concern
Setting: FBI Field Office, Miami, Florida, July 15th

"And to what do we owe the pleasure?" asked FBI Agent Harry Curtis, his hand extended business-like to welcome a fellow of the law enforcement fraternity.

"Let's say I'm on a whirlwind tour, going through my recent cases."

"I heard you were no longer with the Agency. A pity."

"Greener pastures, they're telling me. Cleaning out the desk, so to speak. My real reason for showing up is somewhat serious in nature. Where do you stand on that biker's weapons cache bust?"

"Which we never did put together, with our intended witness vaporized. Everything quiet, just a repair shop with bike repairs. Two weeks ago we pulled surveillance."

"I don't know if that was a good idea." Holmes gave the lawman his hard, no-nonsense stare.

Even for a Fibber on the front end of his career, Agent Curtis locked eyes with his own tough-guy stance.

"You and your former employer know something we don't?"

"Not the Agency, just a hunch on my part. Do you have the files? I want to look at the bomb scene photos again, and then will be happy to share."

The two men flipped through the photos from the case file: Coroner's Inquest verdict: 'death by misadventure.'

"Here, see, this coloring, very faint, mostly scorched."

"Yeah, we determined that was part of the covering for the explosive charge."

"Take a look at this." From his pocket, he pulled out a photo, folded in half.

The F BI. agent compared the two photographs.

"Yeah, similarities, pinkish lines. I could make the stretch and say it was the same type.

"What? Same manufacturer?"

"C-4 plastique explosive made exclusively by a French company, mostly used under special contract by French Special Forces. Some, however, must have slipped through the cracks and gone missing."

"Where did you get this?" asked Curtis.

"This small brick of C4 was discovered two months ago in a known terrorist hide-out in Pakistan, an al-Qaeda base."

"Jeez. What are you saying, Holmes? That these Waco-whacked bikers are in league with foreign terrorists?"

"Hey, I wish I had more, but this link being so recent gives me pause. But I might suggest your office needs to ramp it up again. At least through the 9/11 anniversary, if you get my drift?"

352 S.P. Grogan

Curtis felt himself unsettled. No threat, as crazy as it might sound, was that crazy.

"You really think something might be coming down?"

"I have some other intangible evidence that I am trying to verify." He could not very well say: 'we're reading books.'"

"Well, I know your background; you still have the rep you left office with. What do you think we should do about it?"

"Surveillance, wiretaps, if you can get them. And keep me informed. And, believe it, you guys will be the first on my speed dial for any smidge of a hot wind I hear about blowing in from the Arabian Desert," Holmes assured him.

"We can handle the home-grown guys. Usually, they trip up with a snitch, or we get them with a sting, but if there are fanatical nuts out there, they're going to be hard to identify, especially if they don't wander far from their cell group."

"If the agencies around here are on alert, we might gain an edge on whatever might be out there. Again, it might not be anything."

"It would be nice if you could put your own Agency into the local mix here; every bit will help," suggested Curtis.

Holmes shrugged. "That might be hard for me, again having lost my Double Zero rating and license to kill. But consider this; if you hear from Washington, can you voice my concerns as yours? Don't drop my name. Sometimes, the second opinion becomes the substantiation."

"If you stand by your 'guesses,' yeah, they certainly would be a valid concern to us."

"Final question, and don't go ballistic on me and think I'm the kook. I'm just fishing here, but do you have anything nuclear around here?"

"My God, you think that might be the target?"

"Never said that, part of the general background investigation."

"This will kick up my peptic ulcer. Well, there is the Turkey Point Generating Station here in Dade County. Out of four electric generators, I think two of them are small nuclear reactor units."

"You might find a way to let them know your concern, at least through 9/11."

"Wouldn't hurt, I suppose."

They talked socially for the next thirty minutes — interesting cases, budget cuts, family life at the Curtis household. Holmes said little of himself; what was there to offer? He was a mere unemployed nomad on a questionable quest for answers. When the agent offered him a ride to the airport, he declined. It would be the wrong signal to be driven to the private aviation terminal to board Samantha's jet, on loan for the project's quickie tour de force. Next stop, change of clothes from his Great Falls condo in Virginia, plus by hitchhiking on her jet, he could return to California with greater firepower from his private arsenal. Just in case. And on his arrival in the Washington, D.C. area, he needed to make a new acquaintance, work on building new friendships.

Scene 7: Car Talk and More
Setting: Alexandria, Virginia, near Washington, D.C., July 20th

"Studebaker?"

Matthew Brady of the CIA, on one of his seldom days off, looked away from washing his antique car in front of his Georgian-style home, situated in a quiet neighborhood of Alexandria, Virginia, and turned the hose nozzle off.

"Studebaker 1941 Commander and President."

"Classic for the war years."

"And what brings Mr. Wendell Holmes to my house on a beautiful Tuesday?"

"Office calls are monitored, and I'm off the clock. Hell, I'm out of work, unemployed."

"Thought maybe those TV stars might want you around, you know, consultant pay? Especially since they did capture the world's number one bad guy. It's strange your name wasn't in the paper as one of the bounty hunters. Say, that could be a great new career for you."

"Hollywood and reality television are not my cup of Scotch, but no, I will always be a background sort of guy, just like now, trying to make sense of what I saw in bin Laden's hideout that you guys missed." He had shown up to be friendly, but thinking of his forced exit from his job, his only career work, his voice was tinged with seeping bitterness.

Brady ignored the tone, accepting the ex-agent had not received the best treatment.

"And what do you, and I know you were a good agent, deduce by what we did not find, specifically in that closet that you said was full, and we found, on our return, completely empty?"

Holmes did not like the statement with an emphasis on the words '*were* a good agent.'

Does ending the term of employment end the skill? He did not think so and had an urge to prove his worth. Like a good poker player, he ran a bluff.

"Tell me about the guy who got away?"

Brady reacted with surprise.

"How did you know about that?" Holmes hadn't, but by deduction of who had been identified as residents of the compound, who survived and who did not, there was one unaccounted sleeping space. Who then used that closet for sleeping accommodation? And now Holmes confirmed his suspicion of the unknown guest, and that individual might have been present the night they grabbed bin Laden. Bennie and Abbas both swore some near-naked man ran past them. *Interesting.* So, Holmes gave up some free analysis.

"I think the guy came back to retrieve his belongings because they would have led us — I mean you and the Agency — to the real bombshell success of that raid."

"And that is what? Though we missed bin Laden, wasn't *King's Retribution's* success the high-water mark of the op? Regardless of who gets the credit?" Brady, like all Agency insiders, was still miffed at the embarrassment they'd had to endure from this 'op' gone sideways. He turned back to his chore; he could not let soapy water spots form on his classic car, and once more began rinsing it off.

"I think a major attack on the United States is about to be launched by al-Qaeda."

Again, the hose turned off.

"I don't know where you are going with this, Holmes, but be careful. Scaremongering can be a federal offense; the boy who cried wolf, and all that."

"What if I am right? And if I am not right, tell me so now, and I will happily shut my trap and not call the *New York Times.*"

Brady had also seen *Three Days of the Condor*, a spook movie, and chuckled at the weak effort in a threat from an ex-government man who certainly must have always despised a media that had a rep for slamming all U.S. clandestine operations.

"Okay, you are still family, if now alumni. All I can say is that we have no intelligence about any immediate threat within the United States. So the FBI informs us."

"What if I could tantalize you? What if you could take it up the ladder and look like a hero? Maybe not uncover any bad guys, but better safe than sorry."

"I'm listening, but don't expect much from me."

By Brady downplaying his management role in intel-gathering, Holmes knew he had found his 'inside' contact.

"One: explosives found in bin Laden's compound by Storm King and his posse were similar in make to those used in a bomb killing in Florida. Two: your mystery man who escaped the compound was studying terror attack strategies against the U.S., within the U.S."

"How do you have those facts? Where's your evidence?"

"Contact the Florida FBI on the bombing. Did someone escape from the bin Laden compound that night? Answer that, and I can give you more."

Brady did not like playing these games; he was one of the CIA analysts on foreign terrorism, had just been promoted, recently added to the Bin Laden Desk, now the Mideast Anti-Terrorism Desk, but he was starting to realize that Wendell Holmes must have been regarded as more than a simple field agent.

"A SEAL said he saw a man escape over the wall," Brady admitted. "At the time, the claim was discounted. The SEAL had been diagnosed with battle fatigue, a variation on PTSD, and after the attack, those symptoms seemed to have heightened. It seems they dismissed it as delusional to what he might have actually seen."

"From my side, I am still looking at the evidence. But what was in that closet, which was later stripped clean, seems to suggest to me some sort of attack involving a nuclear plot."

"Nuclear?"

"Maybe."

"*Maybe* led to WMD, which led to the invasion of Iraq and no WMD. *Maybe* doesn't cut it these days."

"Better than raising a banner on the bin Laden raid, 'Mission Completed.' I am working with what I have, but I do urge preventative caution. You have the 9/11 ten-year anniversary coming up. I'm sure the terror alert will be heightened, but you just might start the paperwork for more field agents now."

Brady likewise decided he had a source, and in the intel business, that was your gravy train.

"What can we do for you?"

"Nothing yet, but someday when I am surrounded, I may call in the cavalry to the rescue, and I don't want to have to fill out request forms in triplicate."

"Agreed." He gave a second of thought. "Use the code words 'Retirement Benefits' to reach me."

"Appropriate. By the way, if I recall, the Studebaker Corporation failed because of poor management decisions. Let's hope no one up the ladder at your 'corporation' is dense to the risks we still face against our security."

As they partied cordially, and Brady turned his hose back on, he had to ask, "Are you going to this big shindig, this *Trial of the Century?*"

Holmes turned as he was leaving and replied, "I'm the one who gets to pull the switch on the electric chair they're building on stage." He left.

The hose went off again.

"Shit." Matthew Brady knew he would have to ask for any flyover altitude photos of Skilleo Stadium. Just in case. Damn Holmes; that was probably a bad joke. Wasn't it?

Scene 8: CYA Posturing
Setting: Washington, D.C., July 21st

Density, as in 'head in the sand,' existed in one bureaucrat's office.

"I'm not going to recommend raising the terror alert just because of unverified evidence."

For ten minutes, Brady had sought to make his case based on his recent call to Florida and his conversation with FBI Agent Curtis, but Deputy Director Givens would have none of it. His casual defense: 'since there is no incontrovertible proof of a threat, then no need for undue alarm.'

"But the FBI Miami office seems to think there is a valid threat worth further checking, and the need for us to maybe put out a Pink Sheet Notice of Concern."

"The relevant phrase is 'seems to.' No, let them keep their concerns local. If I can't see it, and remember, Brady, I have had field experience. We don't need to be spooked at any little twig snapping in a gigantic forest. Remember, prior to Pearl Harbor, there were so many false signals that no one believed the actual warning signs."

"Pearl Harbor still happened."

"Be that it as it may, I don't want to see us go off stampeding. I will grant you this, around the 1st of September, in precaution to 9/11, then and only then we ought to remind people to be watchful; it will go well with any presidential comments on the anniversary. Yes, that sounds right. In fact, I will write the text myself, a press release announcement to raise the terror alert in anticipation of the 9/11 anniversary."

When Matthew Brady returned to his office, like the dutiful yet wise bureaucrat he was, he drafted a recollection of the just-held meeting with Deputy Director Givens, a 'cover-your-ass' memo. From his perspective, he now believed that Wendell Holmes, whatever his sources, had better analytical insight than Givens, but Brady prayed that Holmes was wrong in his worries.

Brady placed a long-distance call on a roundabout strategy and left a phone message.

"Agent Curtis, I would like to recommend you call Homeland Security's headquarters directly. Here is the phone number that takes you to the top. Please convey your concerns as we discussed. Thank you." He made a notation to have this call highlighted in the telephone logs, self-preservation habits essential in the shark-infested back halls of government.

EPISODE TWENTY-TWO — Mounting Clues

Scene 1: Movie Night at Sam's penthouse
Setting: New York City, July 20th

Samantha's genuine and fresh smile greeted Holmes, the returning traveler, the guest bearing gifts, when the door opened at her penthouse condo. "I wondered when you might appear." She walked back inside, and he followed. She did not try to figure out how the concierge doorman failed to call her on Holmes' arrival in the lobby; she assumed Holmes had the character flaw of skirting even limited authority.

He saw that she dressed comfortably in slacks and wearing a hip-length dragon-design silk shirt, which to Holmes looked like a man's pajama top, though he quickly decided it must be some hip couture mini kimono. Then, as was his inbred training, he gave a quick, all-encompassing scan of her residence, finding a well-furnished condominium overlooking Central Park, where outside the floor-to-ceiling windows, the day's brightness faded over a skyscraper horizon. As to furniture styling and art on the walls, he saw she lived to higher tastes but not flaunting the ostentatious.

Samantha's expression asked for an answer to the large shopping bag he was carrying.

"Homework and dinner," he replied. "I had to run down some of the books and movies on our Ali Baba list. In two more days, our team meeting resumes, then we are both off to Skilleo Stadium and the "Extravaganza of the Century." You are attending? Of course, you are. You have not abandoned your friends for a fashion show?"

"Of course, I will be there. Both places." That came off snippy, and she recovered somewhat. "I did think I would hear from you when you returned from Washington." She did not want to sound peevish; she was glad to see him.

"You are correct in chastisement if that's your direction. A man borrows a woman's executive jet, and when he returns it, he should express his gratitude immediately." He held out the shopping bag he had been carrying.

"And so?" she wondered aloud.

"Movies and popcorn, to be interspersed with Italian salmon pasta salad and a bottle of mid-priced Pinot Grigio. I was hoping your evening might be free."

"You presumed my calendar would be open just for you?" Her reaction was more startled at his brazenness. She did not know if she liked this take-charge sort of approach from this mysterious Spy Man. She had always been the one in control.

"I sleuthed. A couple of discreet calls using bare-faced lies, and you will be surprised how quickly information can be gleaned. Last night you were busy, tonight open, tomorrow night some charity kowtow, and the next night we are off to Colorado, if I can bum a ride."

She smiled, took the bag from him, and walked to the open kitchen.

"What's this?" After she had removed a jar of popcorn, the food and the wine, she found a gift-wrapped box at the bottom.

"A gift; for the woman who has everything."

He enjoyed seeing her rip off the paper in delightful glee, absorbed in the anticipation.

"Wendell, you shouldn't have." In the beryl wood box nestled a small handgun.

"It's a Ruger LCP, which stands for 'Lightweight Compact Pistol.' 9.4 ounces unloaded, but a lethal punch to put a bad guy down. Far more practical than your dainty derringer popgun."

"I hear you provide these little gifts to all those who might face danger. Callie told me about hers. Worried about me now? I love it. You are so thoughtful." She looked at him, almost in a new light of appreciation, seeing a sensitivity, male though he was. She grew more serious.

"Do you think there is a chance, all that we are looking at, the possibilities you are alluding to, all that could put us in danger? That I might really use your gift?"

"'Preparedness only' should be the motto. Chances of finding us surrounded and fighting a pitched gun battle with hostiles is remote. However, you do live in New York, and you do travel to strange destinations like the wilds of Africa. I hear Hugh Fox has installed a target range at his Skilleo complex. I am sure he will welcome practicing firearms with you."

An invisible wall of unsaid complications descended, tempering the congenial atmosphere. She could not tell if he referred to Fox to quell the possible urges beyond tonight's business 'date' of investigating movie plots. And she was unsure what she wanted from him; was it to maintain the arm's length acquaintanceship or something more? Certainly, she assented to herself; her seductive powers would manipulate down any defenses. They had never failed her before. Samantha accepted she found Holmes desirable; he looked in top physical shape, and was he not a man of the world, traveling among the exotic locales where women made love through teased, rutting rituals of animal dominance or subservient bondage? She began to create her own eroticism of what he might be like undressed, hard before her, ready with friction to stroke, to thrust inside.

"Samantha, want me to open the wine or heat oil for the popcorn?"

Pop...corn.

With an almost disappointed sigh, she said, "You, the wine, I feel like boiling scalding oil."

When later seated before her wall-sized TV screen, she inquired. "Why do I get an undercurrent that with all this fanfare, you don't seem to be in the mood for a movie? Even with my fabulous company?"

"I apologize." But he was in a mood. "And it certainly should not cast aspersions at the wonderful hostess, and yet...."

"What's wrong, Wendell?"

"For the first time, maybe I am realizing the scope of this project. Perhaps I have been too cavalier. Maybe *King's Retribution* thinking has rubbed off on me, that this is some new great adventure for me. Instead, the magnitude is sinking in. As you know, as a businesswoman, with any well-thought-out project, you have to begin with research. What I have found brings up the word 'impossibilities.' What I recently uncovered in my research was an abstract written in a publication, *Perspectives on Terrorism*. He pulled from his pocket a crumpled paper where it seemed he had scratched out some notes. "It's entitled: *Through the Lenses of Hollywood: Depictions of Terrorism in America*. It's by Thomas Riegler, a journalist from Vienna."

"That title sounds ominous to our direction."

"Even more so, this article was published less than two months ago. It depresses me as it goes through the history of how many movies with terrorist plots were produced and reached a worldwide audience. In fact, too many for our little group to go through under any sort of deadline. And what's horrifying, the author can point to examples of where terrorists may have gained inspiration from watching these films. So yes, it does sound like a familiar theme we are pursuing."

Samantha was sitting up, visualizing their vague guesses at a threat that might have real validity.

"Let me give an example, and the movie I want to get my hands on is the 1965 *The Battle of Algiers*, a dramatization of the real-life conflict between Algerian FLN rebels and the French army. It may not fit with a scenario set for today, but it illustrates a movie's power to hypnotize and motivate radicals. Supposedly, it inspired terrorists like the IRA and the Tamil Tigers." Holmes referred to his notes, "even 'the Black Panthers screened it to their members for training purposes...as to the effectiveness of urban terrorism.'"

He began pacing.

"I am feeling overwhelmed, even powerless to quickly solve this puzzle of Ali Baba; there is too much data to sift through." Back to his notes. "Did you know in 2006, and that's only five years ago, in a British trial of an al Qaeda sympathizer, they played a video he owned — *Die Hard with a Vengeance* — and sixty minutes into the film, it 'abruptly ends and instead begins to show views of New York landmarks, while a voice in the background imitated sounds of explosions.'"

She saw his dejection. She realized that his hitting a brick wall of not knowing might be unacceptable in his character make-up. She assumed his job description was to solve mysteries, find answers and provide solutions.

"You, *we* have to try. Wendell, you have just proven our concerns are justified. This search must go on. Please, see how important you being a leader now is vital to us all, to maybe many innocents. Please, relax. Let's watch a movie. Save the world, again."

"What's our headline feature for the evening?"

Holmes inwardly regained his balance, now concerned he may have upset his, did he dare say it, 'date?'

"Tonight, for your watching pleasure, we have a double feature, but we can fast forward past any lame back story." He laid out several blown-up photos. "Here and here are the titles we are going to view." The close-ups were of the interior of Ali Baba's hide-out, and visible and circled on the shelves were two names on what must have been VHS tapes.

So, they munched on fresh popcorn; she drank wine, he a Diet Coke, and watched *The Taking of Pelham One Two Three,* filmed and released in 1974, starring actors Walter Matthau and Robert Shaw. The plot unfolded to where four armed men hijacked a New York City subway and demanded one million dollars, which had to be delivered in one hour, or passengers would start to be executed.

One hundred minutes running time later, both Samantha and Holmes dissected the plot.

"Good thriller for the times."

"You still don't seem that enthusiastic," she remarked. When the film started, he had sat on the couch, and she on an adjacent deep chair, quite proper. When she returned with a refilled glass of wine for herself, ice water this time for Holmes, she moved over to the couch and sat near him; her feet tucked up underneath her.

"It's not that. I'm focused. I am trying to put Ali Baba's mind into adapting this script into a terrorist scenario, and it doesn't seem to fit with the al-Qaida template."

"How so?"

"Al-Qaida would not take prisoners and bargain, especially for ransom. They'd kill outright for the publicity value."

"Hijacking a subway car, even if to blow all the passengers up, seems like something they might do."

"Yes, I grant you that. And it is New York City, home of 9/11, the poster child of all terrorist wannabe targets. But, if we are to presume al-Qaida wants to make a statement even more diabolical than 9/11, just bombing a subway doesn't work. They did that in London, backpack bombs in the tubes and buses. Lots of fear and confusion but negligible disruption of the transportation system."

"Shall we go to the next movie and see if the puzzle is solved?"

"Let's; if this is not boring to your highbrow idea of cultural stimulation?"

"To me, boring is only found among people who talk about themselves."

During the next movie, the body language on the couch sought ease, and midway, Samantha was leaning on his shoulder, and without import, he put his arm around her, and she snuggled. Both, though, were odd in their respective thoughts.

Samantha felt encased in a mantle of warm protection and said to herself, 'So this is what stay-at-home comfort is all about.'

Wendell Holmes could only keep his eyes glued to the screen and wonder on the nearby warmth, 'What the hell is going on?'

The next showing, *"Rollercoaster"* (1977), tells the story of a young terrorist (an American psycho) who is blackmailing companies by placing homemade radio-controlled bombs at amusement parks, specifically on the main attraction, roller coasters. George Segal, Richard Widmark, Henry Fonda, and Timothy Bottoms were the stars, and Samantha pointed out actress Helen Hunt in one of her earlier roles.

With the movie ended, Samantha put in her critique.

"Fair. Stop the bad guy before he kills more people, race against time sort of thing. But you are right; if al-Qaida were plotting, they would hardly just blow up a roller coaster for attention."

"Perhaps I am reading too much into these movies; maybe Ali Baba only wanted to be entertained on cold Pakistani nights?"

"You don't believe that? After your research talk, I certainly don't." Holmes had taken the movie's end as an excuse to rise and again walk the living room, thinking, unsaid but obvious, to move away from her luring-alluring charms...which he enjoyed.

"VHS movies from the local al-Qaida Blockbuster are the old ones like that Richard Burton *Villain,"* 1971. I can't find a copy of that without making an Amazon purchase. I don't know how to do that; I don't have an account.

"Maybe all these books and movies do offer ideas; maybe they were ideas rejected. Or, on the other hand, ideas to be sent out to the training camps for the Lone Wolf infiltrators who indeed could take a bomb to the soft underbelly of America, an everyday tourist location, or a school just to undermine America's confidence of security."

"Where do we go from here?"

"For me, for the evening, it is time to go. My hotel room next, then a hitchhike ride to Santa Monica to learn what your stalwart *King's Retribution* task force uncovered, and then, to Mr. Fox's beckoned call, on to Colorado by the 23rd or 24th. Maybe all heads are better than one."

She took the plunge; why not? The evening had been pleasing.

"You could spend the night here." A lot was said in the statement, and his glance at her let her feel that she had torn something inside him, a wavering of his confidence.

"Samantha, you are in a relationship."

"And, I said earlier, it had ended, the issues being distance and commitment. I am not looking to start anything long-term. If you can accept bluntness, I need companionship, for tonight...only."

His eyes eased over her. "A beguiling invitation. And tomorrow, the one-night stand is over, no regrets, and everyone moves on? Tempting. More than you know. But Samantha, not for me. I am not around for the bounce-back from a broken relationship or just pure sport fucking with someone I admire. Perhaps someday, when you can see yourself clear from the thrills of short-term gratification, your perspective might be enlightened. And while I go home and take the proverbial cold shower, we have to refocus on our little quest. Something is going on bigger than we can imagine. I am going to spend my hours reading through the footnotes of the journalist Reiger's article. I thought these movies might have a 'nuclear threat' subtext, but they don't. One of my hypotheses fell to the wayside tonight. Truly, I thought al-Qaida had graduated to a nuclear plot; I was sure of it. But I'm not sure anymore, and to me, that's unsettling.

"It *was* a wonderful evening." He tried to show a facial expression of sincerity beyond his usual inscrutable mask.

"Yes, it was." She had nothing to be ashamed of, she asked for something, and it was refused. He did not make her feel small; no man could do that. He had just stated his position. She could accept that and think in terms of 'other fish in the sea' sort of thing. Why then did she have this emptiness in her body, somewhere above her stomach? The upset gurgle must be a repugnant fear that the man might have accepted her offer if 'monogamy' or 'domesticity' was the endgame and to her current lifestyle, settling down invoked horrid, unspeakable thoughts like losing her independent nature, like sharing emotions, like losing her heart.

Resuming her composure, she sought to make the parting neutral, all business-like.

"Oh, there is one thing I thought of."

He turned to her with the door opened.

"*The Taking of Pelham One Two Three.*"

Crimson Scimitar

"Yes?"

"There was a remake. I don't know when, a couple of years ago. Starring, I believe, John Travolta and Denzel Washington."

"I didn't know that. Probably I was out in the field, below the radar, somewhere in the bush. I'll track it down and see if there are any variations."

"Our friend Ali Baba could have picked up the new version of *Pelham* when he was on the road; what if he saw it on a hotel movie channel? There could be other movies or books out there he picked up and discarded. Ones we didn't find in his room. And what about those on the shelves we couldn't read? Maybe they had the nuclear bomb plots."

They were back to even keel, discussion among associates, or so they thought.

Wendell Holmes gave a slight head nod of profound sadness.

"Yes, that's what I am afraid of, that we have no clue on what's coming down." And he was gone.

Samantha Carlisle, in the silence of her home, before her the lights of a city where eight million people were settling down for the night, as she would do so, alone, she could only think, 'I would like to have slept with him, if only to know him better.'

Wendell Holmes, flagging down a taxi to take him back to his hotel, kept muttering to himself, 'What did I just do? What did I let slip out of my grasp? My scruples can't be that noble.' He began to imagine yoga positions that might allow him to kick himself.

Scene 2: Dangerous Gossip
Setting: Santa Monica, July 18th

With the 'Osama Show' about to go live, yet without sufficient hard evidence from the intelligence community, Homeland Security, even after talking with a local office of the FBI in Miami, Florida, did not see the necessity of putting out any press release of possible internal attacks within the United States. One loudmouth changed these dynamics.

The old World War slogan: *Loose Lips Sinks Ships* more accurately in today's climate of buzz-saw media frenzy would be so apparent when Colonel Storm King, showing off his new public 'date,' took to the red carpet at a movie premiere featuring a romantic comedy.

Storm had moved on from his tempestuous relationship with co-star Callie Cardoza without missing a beat, as there were so many young things in Tinsel Town that would give their virginity, if any true purity still existed, to be seen in the limelight, even with a reality show TV star, with mixed credentials of moral fiber and lucidity. Storm beamed as the cameras and reporters interviewed strolling stars, while utmost in his mind with its alcoholic buzz of the night, is that he would get laid.

364   S.P. Grogan

In the Q & A, while passing among the reporters, one well-known gossip interviewer, after complimenting his date on her revealing breast extrusion and hip-cut dress, turned and pushed the microphone into King's face with a throw-away question, expecting the customary, 'No comment.'

"Do you know where bin Laden is?"

King never liked the reporter, never liked any of them, but also accepted everyone here on tonight's red carpet had to make kissy-kiss face. King knew he had to give more of the tease to attract viewers, and the microphone was the tool, too addictive to ignore.

"Yes, I do. And he's close by [a lie]. And I can tell you there was more to our Pakistani trip than people are aware of. From our on-site investigation, we intend to reveal what the items discovered in bin Laden's compound told us."

The reporter, following the glam trail of this premiere, had the smarts to recall that no one had mentioned *King's Retribution* had found anything. Quickly, the question was asked:

"What items did you find? We thought the SEALS removed all the secret stuff?"

King basked in the glory of having the upper hand.

"Our team believes bin Laden is planning a new attack on the United States and…." His buxom, ditzy date paying no attention to the interview dragged him away to gain camera time with a fashionista mother and daughter tag team who gushed over his date's choice of a minimal see-most sequined wardrobe. When paparazzi photographs were scrutinized later, they showed Storm's date wearing no underwear, which required the tabloids to airbrush back in the propriety they so detested.

King felt he had done no harm, satisfied he had planted another show teaser for the eager public. He gave it only a passing thought to have the production crew splice together 'what if' video vignettes of terrorist hypothetical plots and intersperse them in the Pakistani footage. With his date, he entered the theater and snored through the last half of the film.

The fallout from King's casual comment had greater repercussions than the television star could foresee, from the top to the bottom.

Scene 3: Don't Piss Them Off
Setting: Washington, D.C., July 20th

The President of the United States, when informed, fumed and cursed aloud.

"What do they know that I don't?"

"We have no intel to suggest any attack within our borders," said the new CIA Director, having already yelled at subordinates down the ladder, including newly-minted Deputy

Director Givens, demanding assuredness from his staff. He wanted their assurance of no foreign plots before he met with the Commander-in-Chief.

"This King is a drunkard, and his TV show is tanking [not anywhere the truth]," assured the reluctantly forgiven head of Homeland Security. "It's all last-ditch showmanship. My people have no evidence to collaborate his off-the-cuff remark."

The President spoke to the top officials in the Oval Office.

"We don't need to have our citizens living in a constant state of fear. Let's nip this in the bud." He turned to his Press Secretary.

"Don't turn this from rumor into panic. After all, we have about ten days of low-key before, if our negotiations hold true, they turn over bin Laden. Downplay and laugh at it in the Press Room; suggest what was just said here, that though all government security agencies are vigilant, there is no fact to this comedian's wild guesswork. Laugh King back into the hole he came out of."

"We *are* planning on a 'cautionary' warning for the 9/11 anniversary," affirmed Homeland Security, gaining likewise a 'yes' from the CIA Director.

"Good, but issue it now. That we are on the ball. And make sure these two, the TV star's mouthings and any anniversary statements, are held completely separate. Sometimes, and I am halfway kidding, for national security and the peace of mind of our citizens, I wonder if the FCC couldn't find a rule to shut down fearmongers. And for the sake of all our intelligence, unplug reality television."

On July 23rd, 2011, the U.S. State Department issued an update to its Worldwide Caution Report of places where Americans should and should not travel. The warning amendment stated in part, "There is an enhanced potential for anti-American violence given the upcoming trial of the terrorist known as Osama bin Laden. Current information suggests that al-Qaida and affiliated organizations continue to plan terrorist attacks against U.S. interests in multiple regions, including Europe, Asia, Africa, and the Middle East. These attacks may employ a wide variety of tactics including suicide operations, assassinations, kidnappings, hijackings, and bombings."

No warning alert was issued for Americans living or traveling within the borders of the United States. Most Americans, by polling numbers, believed that with bin Laden in custody, anyone's custody, the threat of another 9/11-type attack within the United States was less than a 15% probability. A comfort zone they could live with and go about their daily lives unruffled.

Scene 4: To Take No Chances
Setting: Los Angeles, July 19th

Before they had all gone their separate ways, to the airport, out onto the highway, the Attack Leadership had assembled in a small temporary warehouse in the industrial side of East Los Angeles. Shahin, Razzor, and now attending, the Professor. The morning newspapers were being passed around.

"What do we do about this?" The question from the Professor, who found himself nervous and intimidated by the power of the other two men who had stone-cold eyes, and frozen hatred on their faces.

The *L.A. Times* newspaper headline, from the National Section, read: '*TV Star Says bin Laden's troops Seek Revenge*' followed by a short story speaking of unknown evidence found in bin Laden's compound that the TV show would reveal with the season opener. The final sentence in the article from an unnamed government source belittled the source, a television star, and assured the public that all the proper people had the situation of guarding the nation's security under control.

Another news story, more in the gossip, said that the star, King, had alcoholic abuse issues and cited several unnamed sources about on-the-sets incidents.

"It's that damn Khalaf's fault," grumbled Shahin. "If he were here, I would execute him on the spot." They were all talking in English, a part of the overall disguise of being perceived as shopkeeper Americans. "Our beloved Emir conceived *Crimson Scimitar*, but it was Khalaf who abandoned bin Laden during the attack, and he, not the Emir, must have left incriminating evidence behind."

"Will it affect our attacks?" The Professor was the outsider looking into the plans of the operational leaders. He had played his part in creating the sleeper cells, accepting he had to pay off the Mexicans to gain that cell's loyalty, but he now wished to step back and let the attack team accomplish their goals.

"As I see it and have since understood," Razzor Hassim spoke calmly, sounding more sinister with his slow, deliberative voice. "This television show, *King's Retribution*, does not air again until October. And I don't see how they could have uncovered all our plans. We have broken each segment into smaller attacks. I think we should be cautious, but there should be no stopping. We have come too far."

Shahin did not like loose ends that might threaten his attack.

"It would be better to blow them all up before they stick their nose further under the tent."

"Such could be accomplished. Certainly, their main star is the news source," said Razzor, with an air of confidence, thinking back to a situation in Florida he had cleanly taken care of.

"No," piped up the Professor. "*Crimson Scimitar,* focus on that. After that, you can blow up whomever you like."

Both men smiled back at the Professor. They both knew something he did not.

Conveyed separately, directly from bin Laden, even side-stepping Khalaf's input, if any, was the last order for the operation. There would be no survivors of the attack teams except Razzor and Shahin. No one would take the glory but al-Qaida's top leadership; no one would be captured who could compromise the organization's future abilities.

Razzor's smile was the most insincere, for he had been chosen to eliminate the Professor, whom he thought was weak, too Americanized.

Shahin had come with four rabid 'volunteers,' ready for the total sacrifice to achieve all conditions of the *Crimson Scimitar* plan. Shahin's point man and one volunteer for the East coast operational plan had since landed in Miami to be attached to the Florida cell, and he would coordinate the removal of any surviving bikers after their task had been accomplished. The man assigned extolled himself as a rabid Islamist who once had volunteered as a suicide bomber, now blindly dedicated to renewing that vow for al-Qaida's glory, but only after their target was destroyed. Another three 'sacrificial volunteers' would be spun off from the main attack team to accompany Razzor to Colorado. The third volunteer would go with Luis Delgado and his LA planned attack.

No loose ends.

Razzor would leave with the newly formed third team tomorrow for Colorado. The problem they faced: they had no idea what they might do to free their leader.

The Professor performed his last duty, so he hoped. Handing the envelope over to Shahin, "As requested, for you. These were hard to get, nearly impossible, but I was informed early enough and had the time to stay on 'call holding' at the ticket center for over an hour."

Shahin looked inside the envelope. Two tickets for *The Trial of the Century.* He handed them over to Razzor. "My man Maj will accompany you. He is quite useful."

"And by your direction, I got closest to this 'bubble,' sitting midway up, behind the jury box, facing the defendant's special holding area." The Professor knew he had talked too much, rambling from nervousness.

From Shahin to the Professor. "You have done well, but since we have added a new dimension to our plans, you must be prepared to join us at a moment's notice as the changing situations dictate. We still do not have a firm date when the trucks will start their cross-country trip?"

The Professor swallowed hard. He just wanted to be home with Marcie and his children. At least he must prepare for any inevitability and send his wife and kids to stay with his parents.

When asked, Shahin replied. "No, no word yet from the Scientist. I expect a departure date and transit map in the next 30 days."

Nodding as if all previous discussions were settled, all three men rose and went to a low table covered with cloth.

"Good, invite in our fellow brothers." Shahin opened the door and, with jovial comradeship, invited six members of the first attack team, the Main Team, who had been assembled in Yemen. The room soared with an air of anticipation; all training and planning had come down to this. The cloth was pulled back to reveal a topographical model of their objective. *The Bridge.*

Scene 5: Recovering Idleness
Setting: San Diego County, July 19th

Not the dream vacation he had hoped for. The doctors had given Shawn a provisional clean bill of health, meaning *clean,* barring surprise relapses. If even he believed they had muted his anxieties, feeding him a mantra that he had conquered his demons. He halfway accepted all this, gratified for their paperwork discharge, more accepting the necessity of proving his worth to someone, a call to duty to remove his previous lack of confidence once and for all.

They told him he would report back to his unit, and being medical people, they were proud of their treatments, omnipotent after allegedly curing a patient, and believed he deserved an R&R reward of thirty days furlough to visit friends and family. Part of the healing therapy, they told him.

His call to Janet, brief without satisfaction as she told him the time was not right for him to visit. He accused her of being a daddy's girl without a mind of her own. She hung up on him.

That did not go well.

So, for thirty days, what to do? Daily he kept in physical shape, more gratification to his career specialty than a sport. Still, he did deserve to do something decadent for himself.

Unfortunately, he mused, a chocolate overdose did not seem appropriate for the SEAL elite.

Shawn Pacheco, in the end, decided what the heck; he would visit every amusement park in Southern California; none of these parks had this Ohio native ever visited. Discover the kid within. Sea World first, Legoland, San Diego Zoo, and by the fourth day, he was at the Safari Park, with roaming and grazing animals, from giraffes to gazelles in a large park-like setting, and in his travels jostling the too many park visitors enjoying the near end of summertime. Like the wild beasts, people abounded, defined best as a mass of families. Being alone yet amidst carefree children made him miss Janet, visualizing all that might be, like having children with her, settling down. With her, he could find happiness. He was not going to lose a good thing.

With African-type heat swirling up the temperature, he was sitting on a shady bench near the gorilla enclosure, enjoying a rare treat of cotton candy, watching an ape female suckling her baby, feeling vexed he could not even escape images of family life even when staring at the wildlife.

Pulled from a trash container, he scanned headlines in the San Diego *Union* newspaper, seeking news on the Afghan war, wondering where his next deployment might take him when the article on King's gabby riposte from the movie premiere caught his attention.

My God, he read, *they are right*. He vividly recalled the night in the compound, everything that went wrong, his allowing one of bin Laden's inner circle to escape. He knew the fugitive existed even if the military did not believe his story. He knew what the terrorist looked like.

Someone should be told. Of course, there would be revenge against Americans for Osama bin Laden's capture and the man who escaped, that is the man who is going to attack America.

While reading the newspaper, Pacheco had skimmed over a capsulated small news article, obscured in the back pages that seemed unimportant as it might affect his life and choices, like most all Americans that day. A warning only to be recognized in hindsight, yet, beneath the surface, infecting a nervousness within the nuclear energy industry to rush along its plans for nuclear waste disposal.

Workers find ultra-high radiation levels at Fukushima Daiichi plant

Tokyo (CNN)

The operator of Japan's crippled Fukushima Daiichi nuclear plant has detected the highest radiation levels at the facility since the initial earthquake and tsunami five months ago, a company spokesman said.

The radiation levels — 10,000 millisieverts per hour — are high enough that a single 60-minute dose would be fatal to humans within weeks....

What Navy SEAL Shawn Pacheco read instead that caught his interest: *King's Retribution* leaving L.A. this week and will be on-site before bin Laden trial begins. King may testify.

He finally understood that there was a direction to follow. If his own commanders, the U.S. Military, or the government he swore an oath to, would not follow up on his nightmares, then he would go to the people who might just listen, help him, prove him right, bring him solace or redemption. Or bring him....

S.P. Grogan

Scene 6: New York State of Mind
Setting: New York City, July 20th

Khalaf sipped at the hot chai noomi basra tea (dried lime) just offered him on a silver platter by room service, a perky young woman. Her manners, he found after she departed, were not subservient obedience but an attitude of trying to do her job well. So refreshing to feel unpretentious service just for himself, not by stern command of indifferent obedience. He had given her a generous tip.

Nevertheless, his training translated this brief interaction as his mental acceptance of decadent America, and he thought smugly of their bold, provocative population of very attractive females. From his London stay, he had become acclimated to the sight of women traipsing the streets unprotected from public stares; even his own eyes constantly strayed, much to the humor of Sabz, who often, when accompanying him on his outings, teased him about his double standard. But, thanks to his prodding, she looked the proper Arab woman, though of modern times, dressed colorfully, her head wrapped, face uncovered, striking in its clear-lined smoothness. Khalaf did not understand why he felt upset when other men cast their eyes on her, probably urging their beastly imaginations to guess what lay beneath her garments.

And here they were in New York, at the final stage, to create history. He was unprepared for the menagerie of people, multiple races, and the cursed Jews, in constant motion, seeming to rush as if they had no time, yelling, not speaking, as if no one could hear them. Hell must look like this, he believed, and he felt satisfaction that 9/11 had come to this city of the damned.

In the uncertainty of his new role, from courier to key player, he went on his assignments by taxi, where he could sit in relative peace, and at all other times secured himself in the suite at the Waldorf, two bedrooms as they had agreed, for the time being, as she suggested, until the mission was successfully completed, as he now prayed, not for the Islamic cause but for very selfish reasons of fulfilling personal gratification.

Sabz did not know of the mission in New York nor of his plan that he was going to expand upon his responsibility and go beyond, traveling West into America's heartland to add his support to Shahin's brigade. Sabz, in ignorance, held the role of the wondering child, taking in all around her as a festive dream of happiness. When confined to the suite, she could be satisfied with fashion magazines and speechless at the voyeurism antics of reality celebrity television.

She did not accompany him on this day's appointment. With him, in the next chair in the richly decorated office of the head of the stock brokerage office, sat his new contact, Lawrence Nidal, a greedy little man, more interested in the commissions he would generate from Khalaf's transactions. He was sympathetic to Arab causes in general but was unaware of

Crimson Scimitar and believed he was a mere middleman, doing currency exchanges and securities trading for the several benevolent charities which Banker Abboud had set up to promote refugee assistance. He knew there was a plan but not of *the* plan. Dreams of great wealth from his guiding advice held the man's silence.

"Your account is completely in order and activated, Mr. Rasil," said the designated stockbroker to both men. The paperwork and new account information were slid across the desk to Khalaf, a.k.a., *Rasil,* one of three false identities that he would use to establish accounts at other stock brokerage accounts in the city's financial district. All business mail addresses went to the same post office box, and any trading funds could be wired to the same bank account, his account back in London, which then had instructions to make simultaneous transfers to very secretive off-shore banking locations, once more under Khalaf's direct control with a specific access code. Until the Supreme Council requested, all funds would be under his control for the foreseeable future. That was heady enough to cause him to closely inspect all documents pertaining to funds and fund transfers.

"Thank you," came Khalaf's response, seeking to heighten his normal English-Egyptian tone with a more Edwardian lilt, speaking in an upper-class accent, suggesting an Oxford education and, more important to this meeting, the voice of wealth.

Nidal pushed a paper across the desk to the stockbroker. "Here is the list of stocks Mr. Rasil would like to invest in with the funds he has deposited but at a future date, perhaps in a week or more."

Mr. Nidal, a stockbroker in his own right, acted as the facilitator of all the paperwork and nuances of the stock exchange's inner workings. "Mr. Rasil or I, under Mr. Rasil's power of attorney, will be calling you in the near future to make several initial trades, buys, sales, maybe even some short sales, dependent on market fluctuations. Is that acceptable?"

The head of the stock brokerage firm, who dealt with millions of dollars in trades, still knew when to give deference to any new client who opened a personal account with a $1 million cashier's check, verified and deposited.

"Of course, at your or Mr. Rasil's pleasure. You mentioned this account might be making short sales. You are aware of the new SEC rules on short sales?"

"Yes, of course," affirmed Mr. Nidal with confidence, knowing that the trading mechanism was the featured part of the strategy that 'Rasil' wished to do. Quite risky, but it mattered little to Nidal, who would garner a fee whether buying or selling, and if even all funds were lost in trading.

To satisfy the head of the stock trading firm that his client was fully apprised and the firm would take no responsibilities at a loss, Nidal explained, "Short selling involves the selling of a security that an investor does not own or has borrowed against. When shorting a stock, the investor expects they can buy back the stock at a later date for a lower price than it was sold for and cover, making a profit on the spread. The Securities and Exchange Commission, the SEC, to avoid driving down market prices on bad news, created an 'alternative uptick rule,' where covering on short sales might be frozen if a stock, in a short period of trading, dropped more than 10%."

The stock brokerage president reviewed the list of the planned first purchases on behalf of his client and gave a wry acknowledgment of the hefty commissions they would generate for the firm when the 'short orders' were placed.

"I see you will be a player in the entertainment industry, but expecting a drop in pricing in those markets. However, I must warn you; stock analysts believe this summer will be very strong for entertainment stocks, especially the Florida amusement park industry."

"Yes," said the fake Mr. Rasil. "My children like taking the carnival rides. But my strategy is to map weather patterns and see where storms might impact outside operations."

The stock brokerage president smiled a smile of silent ridicule but said nothing except, "An interesting strategy." In truth, he had seen crazier theories in betting on market fluctuations.

Outside the brokerage house, Mr. Nidal beamed.

"That went extremely well. Two more such meetings today, each with $1 million in new accounts and everything will be in place. When will you place your short sale order?" Meaning that on the information the stockbroker Nidal did not have access to, though he felt by past experience that an insider trading scheme was in play, the fee earner would only offer advice on trades, not pry further. Ignorance could be a legal defense.

"Soon", replied Khalaf. His actions, separate from Shahin's attack on the bridge, were to be coordinated to occur a few days earlier, the date tentative to early September, perhaps late August. Khalaf decided, though not astute in this capitalistic system, he might have a little fun playing with the stock market, buying and selling, just dabbling, only enough to show account activity and whet the appetite of the greedy capitalist stockbrokers who would later jump to his command when the actual play began. After all, he was playing with other people's money.

"I am sure you will do quite well," Nidal's comment of too eager hope.

They sought out a taxicab for their next appointment, something he dreaded. He could not stand this man he must work with. Khalaf's primary dislike was Nidal's aftershave, too fruity to inhale within close quarters. He would be pleased when this operation was completed, and whether successful or not, and it had better be a success, Nidal would receive his payment and be gone. From reading through bin Laden's battle plan against Wall Street, and his discussions with banker Abboud, Mr. Nidal would be compensated in a separate transaction that Khalaf would have no part in. A courier with Mr. Nidal's commission would be sent to make the final payoff. Khalaf seemed to recall the courier's name, Hassim something.

Scene 7: The War Room — Last Time?
Setting: Santa Monica, California, July 20th

Once again, the place was jammed with what could be called the revised 'New Hunt and Discovery Team.' Instead of joviality and singleness of purpose, the meeting began acrimoniously, with Callie Cardoza snapping at Storm King.

"Can't you just keep your mouth closed when you get out in public?"

"It's not like I said anything profound," King bit back. "There's nothing here. You are all playing a game where there is no game."

"One way or the other, you aren't helping. If there is no terrorist attack planned, then you are making us look like a laughing stock; and if one occurs, and you've told us to dismiss the possibility of an attack, we will be labeled non-caring fools and klutzes. Just let everyone here try their best, so we can go home satisfied we gave it our best shot."

Lawyer Goss-Scott, who said very little in the last meeting, merely commented, "There is a clause in all Five Aces Studioz contracts that stipulates," she seemed to quote from memory, "An actor may be terminated for cause if their actions are deemed a detriment to the harmony of the company's productive work."

King opened his mouth to curse and rant, but today he was more alert (sober) than usual and understood that in the reality television business, perpetuity of star power was fragile, indeed flexible to the need of a reality plot to change on a moment's notice to better improve plot line or ratings. He glowered as usual but stifled the outburst lodged in his throat.

With the uncomfortable silence in the room, Hugh Fox sought control. But Hugh Fox was not there, physically, that is. CAM TWO was pointing a camera at everyone, which then sent the feed to Fox in Colorado Springs to appear on his computer screen. Everyone could see Fox sitting at his desk in his new Stadium office, and he appeared on everyone's War Room computer screens. Real-time.

"What's this?" Storm jumped, looking around the room for 'his boss' whom he detested, finally to settle on Fox staring back at him from the facing computer.

Gizmo beamed at everyone. "This is our first commercial video conference platform from Blue Jeans Network. Someday, we will all talk to each over our computers, send little video vignettes to our friends."

King dismissed and ignored the laser speed of changing technology, though it engulfed him every day. "Too Star Trekian. Tick tock tick tock. Time wasted. It'll take decades to amount to anything. Next, we will have Dick Tracey wrist computers. Tick tock. Not in my lifetime!" Such declarations often become self-fulfilling curses, usually to the recipient's surprise.

Gizmo dismissed this poser Luddite, but he liked the man's phrase, *tick tock*, and scribbled it down, misspelling it. Domain internet naming these days was still a valuable commodity play, and if not taken, he could register it for about $12 and sell it later. Technology in any form had opportunistic value.

"Okay, can we re-focus," said Samantha, now the mediator, "we have two days before we have to head to Colorado Springs. From what everyone has submitted, here is a matrix of all the plots and subplots."

She motioned to Gizmo, who pulled a curtain back from a wall to reveal a large graph layout of author and movie names, central plot feature, primary target, and action taken to thwart the bad guys.

"As I was saying. The chart is very impressive," said the very small Hugh Fox, admiring the work that had gone into the informational analysis.

"Yes," agreed Samantha, "A great deal of thought went into this." She smiled, then so as not to suggest Holmes was her focus, gave Gizmo, the computer nerd, a friendly acknowledgment when she added, "Is there some sort of consensus of where we think this Ali Baba might have been concentrating on his ideas for a good attack concept."

Holmes stood and went to the wall chart.

"Let us agree on a few 'non-starters.' Ali Baba will not discover any religious icon or extraterrestrials that could destroy this country. Agreed?"

Several voices in the audience nodded, a few saying 'Agreed.' Hughes wiped two movies off the chart, *Raiders of the Lost Ark* and *Independence Day*.

"And I previewed and dismissed," offered the special effects coordinator Abbas, "that the Bollywood film where a master thief and his gang sing and dance while robbing a train of museum treasure. That certainly would not, as Mr. Holmes has pointed out, create a maximum 9/11 effect."

Holmes erased the Bollywood film and train robbery as idea generators, while Abbas added, "Dancing routines weren't half bad, and I liked the costumes," a statement which brought out laughter and moved the Team back into a more pleasant affectation.

"I think we all see what the preponderance of the evidence is pointing to," said Holmes, making sure they all felt what seeing the truth meant.

"Something nuclear," spoke up Fox's assistant, J-Q. Silence again, at the ramifications of what this might mean, if true.

"There are, however," said Samantha, pointing at the matrix graph, "some of these that are either too far-fetched for what our reality is, or if they are conceivable, beyond our reach and out of our pay grade. For example, *The Hunt for Red October* is definitely nuclear, but I don't think Islamic terrorists would be able to hijack a nuclear submarine and explode the missiles.'

"A good point," said Holmes. "There is so much redundancy built into arming a missile it would be near impossible. Even sabotage might cause an explosion, perhaps like the *U.S.S. Cole*; they might try to sink a sub, but radiation, if any, would be contained and thus not catastrophic."

The eraser removed *Hunt for Red October*.

"From looking at the photograph blown-up," said Gizmo, pointing in the photos to several books on their side. "There is a pile of magazines and at least four books we can't identify.

There is one book on its side, the spine perhaps sun faded, where all we got out of the title and author was a partial, *Spring* and *Hawk*. I am still trying a computer search algorithm for matching possible word combinations. Nothing yet to report."

"Hawk, with an 'e' on the end of it, might be 'Alex Hawke,' the main hero in the Ted Bell spy adventures." Everyone, in surprise, turned to look at King at the end of the table. He merely shrugged but continued, 'Bell has, I think, written seven Alex Hawke thrillers. In T*sar*, a killer known as Happy the Baker wipes out an entire Midwestern town with sabotaged computers. A little far-fetched, but, hey, you guys are flailing away. There's my two cents."

"Not bad, Colonel," and Fox from the computer. Holmes added the author's name 'Bell' and the hero 'Hawke' to a new line in the matrix and instructed J-Q to find all the appropriate novels, and they would be parceled out to the Team members for quick reads and summations, stressing to his listeners, to seek out what looked possible with a nuclear plotline.

"And now," said Fox, "Let's have a report from what everyone read or watched and ask the question: what is reasonable to be turned into a real attack? And yes, we don't know if the bad guys have stolen a nuclear bomb, which seems to be a central thread in several of these works, like George Clooney in *The Peacemaker*, but it may have occurred, and we might not even know it. That's when we have to call the government if we remotely think we have hard evidence."

For the next hour, they went back and forth, listening to storylines, discussing if such fiction could be turned into a real-life threat. At one point, Callie leaned into Samantha and whispered, "Wendell Holmes comes off like Brad Thor's hero, Scot Harvath, ex-SEAL, ex-Secret Service, just more mature, hopefully, less lethal." Samantha did not know how to take Callie's comment, deciding it was a good-spirited observation. Extremely curious, she would have to borrow a Brad Thor thriller and compare this Scot whomever against Wendell.

376 S.P. Grogan

At the end of the session, they were all brain-drained. Several more books and a movie had been crossed off the chart, but too many remained, meaning indeed such possibilities with dire consequences seemed patently feasible.

Fox finally, from afar, threw up his hands, feeling the dejection among the Team members, and asked, "Okay, which plot do you think it is?"

A new voice.

"It could be one strategy, but more than one plot." They all looked to the door and the young man who stood there, sheepish and awkward. He again made his point.

"9/11 was not one event, but four separate attacks carried out."

Sailor-Soldier SEAL Shawn Pacheco had joined the conversation.

Scene 8: Storming Doubts Explode
Setting: Santa Monica, July 20th

Pacheco had first tried Five Aces Studioz, the production office, seeking to locate the central star, Colonel Storm King. He was told at the receptionist's desk that the stars might be up in Silicon Valley, outside San Francisco, at the headquarters of Skilleo Games Technology, where they might be working on production scripting for the next season. An aside from one secretary to another at Five Aces led Shawn to overhear that co-star Callie Cardoza was the better of the two, and Storm King never showed up before noon because of his 'snootfuls.' Shawn Pacheco had heard of *King's Retribution* but had never watched a show, agreeing with his fellow troopers that the show never could measure up to SEAL combat qualities of stealth and technical prowess, so why waste the time?

He telephoned the Skilleo offices and learned of Hugh Fox (he knew of him and even played his space killer games for eye-hand coordination) and that Fox was the owner of Five Aces and indirectly the main man over the television show. That Mr. Fox was too busy to interrupt, that he was leaving town later in the afternoon, destination unknown (they knew he was already in Colorado Springs). Anyway, they said, the *King's Retribution* cast and a Ms. Samantha Carlisle, his business partner, were still in Santa Monica. That location was close enough, so he drove in that direction from San Diego.

A SEAL is not just a mere mastiff brute with a capacity for tolerating intense pain or dispensing it. Self-survival training also honed a SEAL's intelligence, and upon his arrival at the War Room, Pacheco, as any good recon soldier might, gained a lay of the terrain, noting a meeting in progress with a large following of spectators in animated dialogue, and felt it the prudent strategy to ease quietly within earshot and to develop an understanding of what was going on, an adaptation of the tenet, *know thy enemy*. At one point, he had heard enough; they were friendlies, except maybe one.

"And who are you?" King's voice was commanding and arrogant. He thought a reporter had discovered their lair, and Callie would be right; he would be portrayed as a buffoon.

"Shawn Pacheco. And I was there." He played his trump card up front; he needed them.

"Where?" King voiced confusion.

"Abbottabad."

King assumed the worst: a reporter.

"Yeah, you and the whole world have been there." He laughed in put-down disbelief.

"Yes, but the night before you all went there." He did not know they had been there, too, that same night.

Everyone seemed confused until what was said soaked in, and Samantha put it into perspective, the ah-ha moment.

"The night of the raid on bin Laden's compound?"

"Yes, ma'am."

"Yeah, right," scoffed King, knowing his first assumption must be the right one.

"And you are…? " Fox from the computer, which freaked Pacheco, put forth the question, dangling, letting the answer fill itself in.

"Specialist E4 Shawn Pacheco of SEAL Team Six. And you are correct; I mean that gentleman over there (nodding towards Holmes). I believe there is going to be an attack on us. I saw the gook, the one you are calling Ali Baba, escape. I was there."

Conversation erupted around the room. Discrediting doubt from King to palatable fear from the younger people who now realized this role-playing of a presumed mock *what-if* game was no longer imaginary; real terrorists were fomenting an actual plot somewhere in their own backyard.

"Main Executive's Meeting," intoned Fox with stern command in his voice, even if from a computer screen. "Right now." Pointing to their 'guest,' Fox emphasized, "You, stay."

With the fast exit of the uninvited, Pacheco understood the hierarchy of who was who as the room emptied, and introductions were made by those remaining. He was surprised that King did not stay, not because he wasn't invited, but that he mumbled that they were all being 'hoodwinked' and 'off on a wild goose chase' — again — although his 'again' had led to the capture of the bad guy. As Samantha offered a seat to him, Pacheco, looking at a computer screen, saw Hugh Fox scribble a note, passing it to someone off-screen. Wise move; they were going to check him out.

They all looked at Pacheco and he at them, no one knowing where to start until Holmes initiated the inquisition with a wide grin. During the grilling by the man, Pacheco had a hallelujah realization of who was talking to him — the man in the photo, the one standing beside his own downed helicopter, the man his government seemed...*in fear of.*

"Can't tell us too much about what happened, can you?"

"No, sir."

"Under orders of complete secrecy?"

"Yes, sir."

"But you told us that you did see someone leave the compound, one of bin Laden's comrades? But that would be against the edict you were given, correct? So, why did you tell us?"

Pacheco did not know anything about Holmes and his background but accepted that if he made Pacheco's military inquisitors concerned, he was, therefore, a very smart yet dangerous man who had perhaps practiced field interrogation — ex-military? The SEAL thought back to a course he had once gone through, where he had to react as the captured prisoner in front of shouting tormentors. Today, the truth would release a great burden from him, not all of the story, for he would never mention he was the dunce that allowed this 'Ali Baba' to escape his grasp.

"No one believed me when I told them."

Holmes remembered back to his conversation with Matthew Brady of the CIA. Well, surprise of surprises.

"And this would be because of what...your mental condition?"

Pacheco's jaw dropped open. Who was this guy? He saw various forms of awe among those around the table, especially the fashion lady, Samantha Carlisle, who exhibited a devilish look of idol worship in her expression. Not at him, but at this Mr. Holmes.

His words came out slower, now cautious.

"Yes, sir. The doctors called it battlefield stress. PTSD. It still surfaces sometimes. I have just been released with a clean bill of health. I think. For the time being."

"What caused the stress, Specialist Pacheco?" asked Holmes, no sympathy to his voice.

"Having traded places with a buddy and seeing him blown up instead of me." There, he had said it to strangers, and he could say it, and no depression welled over him. Was he really cured?

"Yes. The conundrum of all fighting service men and women: why did I survive and others, my friends, die? No one here will condemn you for having a human heart. But, why, indeed, are you here?"

"I have medical leave until September 15th, when I have to report for assignment. I believe I had some information to impart to someone, and I was right; you all are on to something, and I want to help in any way I can." Then, Pacheco did the one thing he felt would put him on equal standing: he folded his arms across his chest, imitating Holmes in the photo, hoping no one caught him and would take offense.

Pacheco himself was waiting for the Google search to reveal that he wasn't a fraud, but would they....

"He passes muster with me," said Holmes, chuckling at the inside joke between them that he had similarly deciphered. He could guess how the kid might have been shown that photo during his debriefing of him standing there with the two Chinese agents. Fed gooks just can't take gotcha.

"That's good enough for me," said Samantha.

"We could use an upgrade in military intelligence," this from the Spanish-looking lady, Cardoza, her name, that Pacheco felt had something of a military bearing about her, and then realizing her comment might have been aimed at Colonel Storm King. What was he getting into?

"Welcome, Specialist Pacheco," said Hugh Fox over the computer. Holmes offered his hand in a firm shake to the young military man, "Welcome to the *King's Retribution* Team, or what I now believe is the 'Stop bin Laden's Revenge' or what he calls *Crimson Scimitar*. And that was pointed out from the compound photos; there are a couple of red graffiti swords on the walls of Ali Baba's postage stamp-sized room. Definitely a planning and strategy cubbyhole."

Holmes agreed. "And Specialist Pacheco might just have stumbled on what we have missed, dimensional considerations. Of course, one strategy, multiple plots. That's what 9/11 was, wasn't it?

King had reentered the room and listened to everyone else's acceptance of the young military man and could not let all the high IQs in the room dismiss the obvious lack of verifiable intelligence.

"I'm still not buying this guy or buying any of this 'follow the books crap.' I don't see a plot here — only guesswork. You still don't have a solid lead nor a hint of time and place. That I said before and hasn't changed." Fox would have none of the negatives. He now put explicit trust into Holmes's inner gut.

"Let's take a break." He spoke to Pacheco. "You're a military man. We'll bring you up to date. Why not give us an opinion if our ideas are sound?"

Being usurped by a kid, an implication he was not *the* military man, finally broke Storm King, and he blew up.

"Hey, wait a minute," King visibly sat straight in his chair. "You don't expect a private to run a battle simulation. I have the experience, and it is my team, my people. If anyone heads this up, it's going to be me." His face turned towards the ever-present CAM ONE, jutting out his chin, knowing that conflict drew more viewers.

"The problem is," said Fox, having had enough, his voice carrying the sting of rebuke, "Is that Colonel, from the very start, you have not believed in the possibility of another terrorist attack in the United States, and the evidence has been mounting towards this conclusion."

"You just don't believe or can't see what's coming down," said Callie, trying to be tactful but not so artful.

King bristled. "You are now going to put your faith in a mentally compromised soldier. And you all think Mr. Holmes here is the Almighty General in Chief. My god, that man has been canned, not retired, by our government. They must know more than we do about him. And what do we know?" King, agitated, was standing. "That he can get our people killed."

"That's unfair," said Samantha.

"And what of you both, the new owners of Five Studioz? This has just been a lark for you bored people. We had a good television show going before we started running around following your scripts. And what are we now, the butt of all late-night comedians. Well, count me out. I don't believe any of this. We are wasting time and will now be wasting government resources, our tax dollars down the drain. And for what, chasing this imaginary Ali Baba?" and looking directly at the SEAL, "all based on the fact of being seen by someone who's probably going to get a medical discharge from the service."

With that, King, true to his name and nature, stormed out. Those in the conference room said nothing for a full minute.

"Let's take that break," said Fox and disconnected the screen to black.

With nothing better to do for the moment and like the walking dead, they all adjourned in silence, taking the stairs to the streets of Santa Monica. Callie had led the small group's exit, debating whether she wanted to chase after and confront her co-star and beg him to return, tell him he's an integral part, stroke the bruised ego.

Ahead of them on the street stalked the angry star of *King's Retribution* heading towards his muscled and tricked-out SUV, with a parking ticket shoved under the windshield wiper, which only infuriated him more. They watched him turn on them with dagger eyes, tear up the ticket, toss it to the ground, grind it into the road, and throw himself behind the wheel. They all realized it was an omen, seeing a former military officer disregarding and abusing civilian authority; even with the small act of civil disobedience against a municipal parking infraction, they all knew *King's Retribution* had an uncertain future.

Just great, thought Callie, as she surrendered to the greater cause of soothing his ego. Shrugging her shoulders to those around her, a nod to them, yes, she knew she had to be the one to re-establish group harmony. She started to walk towards him, a task she did not relish.

Storm King's vehicle exploded.

Scene 9: Grieving the Living
Setting: UCLA Medical Center, Santa Monica, July 21st

Like the television drama set in a hospital emergency room and played out with an ensemble cast, vignette scenes heightened the tension. In the hallway, two bodyguards, diligent and menacing, guarded the inter sanctum to protect the privileged, to inform the ER staff about who was who and what duties brought them here, and most specifically, to roughly handle any sneaky journalist rag sniffing for the million dollar photo shot — the more gruesome, the better.

Oblivious to the turmoil, Hugh Fox, after an emergency flight back, looked through the glass at Storm King, swathed in bandages and hooked up to myriad machines which could monitor his weak pulse and other vitals. Yesterday into this morning, the doctors had a touch and go time of it, but the prognosis after a lengthy repair on the operating table was at best 'critical but guarded'.

Fox's gaze fell more intently on trying to decipher the meanings in Callie's tear-streaked face. He had thought the relationship between the co-stars had ended but with the bomb's explosion and Callie's distraught reaction, he felt that between Callie and Storm, a fractured bond had been re-forged.

Not that it mattered to him, he thought, or tried to believe so. In the last several weeks, when he was with Callie, the times were enjoyable, with the ease of their being able to talk and, yes, laugh. That's what Hugh thought was unique; he had not really laughed much in his lifetime outside of the pleasure he derived from his satisfaction in hard-working creativity evolving into the tangible.

Laughter with Callie, he found, gave him a new dimension of appreciation of the world around him; his universe he found was larger than a laboratory, more colorful and animated than a mere computer screen. Callie, with her own struggle from the barrios, and yes, including this band of funk warriors called the *King's Retribution* Team, had made his recent journey seem worthwhile, but now it was at an end.

Callie looked up and saw him, offering a weak smile, but Fox, not noticing, had turned away. He was confused and depressed. He now believed he was getting everyone killed or at least placing them in danger. Storm King had been right, after all; this terrorist hunt game was self-indulgent, letting Fox play cops-and-robbers for real out of the comfort zone of his game world while using his own money; the risk element was with other people's lives. It was time to call it quits before anyone else got hurt. Well, not quite.

No, the trial was the most important. Its outcome would validate all that they had sought and, yes, accomplished. His mind was set. He would return today to Colorado. The show must go on.

Finally, in the late evening hours, Storm King stirred and opened one eye. He was pretty well drugged up and enjoying the numbness, though he could feel someone squeezing his hand hard. Callie, still in the room, next to his bed, looked into his face, hoping he recognized her. He whispered, 'Okay, bad guys do exist.' And then added, 'Some water, please.' Callie fed him some ice chips, praying he was back from the brink, and she began chattering aloud.

"Storm, you did it, you big lug. All the press in the world is out on the hospital grounds tracking every single doctor's report they issue. How's that? The rumors are that you were targeted because of what the fall show premiere might be about — secrets from the bin Laden caper. Can you believe that? It will probably be the most watched season opener. And don't worry; you are going to pull through. You better.

"We are partners; you are King of *King's Retribution*. Those big bad terrorists forgot that the bomb they stuck under your car would not disintegrate you into nothingness. Didn't they understand that a *King's Retribution* vehicle is a military-grade Hummer, just like what they drive around in war zones? With your stupid bravado and being a star with your background, you had the damn thing jazzed up with all the gadgets, including armor-plating everywhere, especially under the body frame!"

King, sleeping again, was no longer hearing Callie's rambling.

"And Holmes says the terrorists think you are the body and the rest of us are just the supporting legs, meaning you are the center of our Team, and we need you; I need you back. Please."

She had lost Clayton Briggs, now a close call for King. Her disdain for him lapsed into concern for a person who had been so close so recently in her life. The tough shell she had always wrapped herself in felt brittle. Within her was a need, a desire for immediate revenge, a great need for someone to hold her. She looked up, but no one was around to love or to kill. And she needed to satisfy both emotions.

REEL SEVEN — The Trial

New York Times — Bin Laden Trial Today, Historic Event 'Sold-Out.' Record Television Viewers Expected

Colorado Springs Gazette — Traffic Gridlock on I-25 New OBL City. Tribal Leaders Hire More Security

Daily Mail (UK) — Al Qaeda Leader's Trial Will Not Stand; Followers Demand Release or Else

Variety (Hollywood) — Five Aces Talk TWC Movie Deal, Parks/Rec Pratt To Play Storm?

Publishers Weekly — Qmyst Author Tapped to pen bin Laden Capture — Trial Book, Random House high 6-figure contract

EPISODE TWENTY-THREE — THE ATMOSPHERE

Scene 1: The Stadium
Setting: Near Colorado Springs, July 22nd

For those who attend world soccer matches, NFL championship and baseball World Series games, and *another* Rolling Stone concert, the event announced to run July 25th to July 30th, 2011, would, in comparison, rank up there in attendance, cumulative 210,000 attendees over five days through the turnstiles, and the estimated live television coverage audience, world-wide, expected to break all records, even surpassing the 1.1 billion people who watched the Sydney, Australia New Year's Eve coverage, just this past 2010-2011.

Physical attendance was limited by stadium size. Online ticket sales only, no-resale scalped tickets in front of the stadium. At two entry checkpoints into the Reservation, the road arrival, and the parking entries, there were redundant scans of IDs against the ticket registered purchaser database, with all attendee names registered and limited access. Actual tickets (no bar code or paper downloads) were scanned for an embedded strip; 825 counterfeited tickets were seized, and the holders turned away after facial photos were taken. All ticket holders were logged into an online data collection site for future retrieval for yet-to-be-decided marketing strategies — to similar 'entertainment' events? Who knew?

The Skilleo Games Events Stadium, touted as the most modern world center for soccer training and world-class competition, just (barely) completed was the envy of all with its techno bells and whistles. Seating was 42,000 person capacity compared, for example, to the People's Football Stadium in Karachi, Pakistan, home to the national football team, or the home of the Chicago White Sox baseball team. The Stadium was configured with forty VIP boxes situated twenty on each side. The three press boxes seemed like luxury suites to the media, who overwhelmingly demanded access. However, entry to one of the press boxes would be limited and hand-selected (by Hugh Fox) from international journalists who had been pre-qualified to elucidate the positive 'hero' status of *King's Retribution*, with delayed shout-outs post-trial of Skilleo Games and SammyC Fashions to their respective industry base. All other badged Official Press Corps were housed in their new headquarters, with large television screens, computers, and direct outside phone lines (no charge) for future world matches. They were only a few steps from an outside walk-up balcony where they could overlook the bubble dome of 'the courtroom' for photo shots. Any inconvenience was mollified by the press rooms having a complimentary buffet and fully stocked bar (at lunch only).

Housing was perhaps the only lack. Soccer team on-site housing sat like steel skeletons unfinished on one side of the stadium. On the other side were massive modular convention buildings compartmentalized for individual mattress cot-type sleeping, curtain privacy screen niches for the press. Another modular held 'chaperoned' mini-rooms for the hired stadium staff. One journalist, seeing the accommodations, remarked, "No house mother will dampen rampant libido-fueled juices from colliding." For the five days of The Trial and the five days of post- clean-up and shut down, Stadium employees, having their own modular hostel, would have evening access to outside movie screen first-run features, nightly live entertainment of local bands, and of course, a Skilleo Games Center, offering both classic arcade amusement as well as the latest in Skilleo interactive products.

Even to be featured was a debut of Skilleo games embedded in the new-to-market virtual reality (VR) Oculus Rift headset (three years later, Fox turned down Facebook by declining a $3.5 billion buyout of all of Skilleo's high cash flow operations including patents. Rebuffed but eager to at least enter the VR market and gain a tactical advantage, Facebook turned around and acquired Oculus for $2 billion).

Brilliant as he was, Hugh Fox could not stage manage everything with perfection. The incoming flood of traffic snail-crawled, providing close-in parking for travelers who would leave each night and then return the next day or sold-out remote parking for the campers, RVs, and SUVs with sleeping bags, making it one of the world's largest tailgate parties. Electric shuttles hummed everywhere. For off-site housing/hotels, bus transportation ran into Colorado Springs every night after the court's daily recess, even driving up from Canyon City and down from Metro Denver. Popup B&Bs were making a fortune.

The local paper wrote that the 'Been Lāden' Colorado city (a bin Laden play on words) had sprung into existence. The mega uber-stars received little favorable treatment. With the Feds banning airspace near the Stadium, the elites could not helicopter in but rather join the common folk on the highways, though stretch-limousines added a surreal touch when sandwiched between compact cars and pick-up trucks. When the attendees finally approached the stadium gates, staff helpers pointed them in the right direction and handed them a 'souvenir' program with details, for example, a vignette write-up of the players involved, like Attorney Booker Langston, and all the main participating characters. There was background on the formation of al-Qaeda, which was the primary interest today, and to balance that information, a two-page color spread of the events of 9/11. And composite bio sketches of the stars of *King's Retribution*, with gossipy snippets, a little public relations 'truth' of the behind-the-set filming of their television series. Storm King's bio featured an update that he was recovering well and might make a surprise appearance (he would not).

And outside the two main entrances, before entering the gates, stalls had been set aside to sell tourist trinkets. Products offered by the citizen hawkers included everything from the expected *'F-U Osama, even F-U this job'* coffee mugs to Twin Tower *'Never Forget'* t-shirts. Even for the event: 'Where U bin Laden?' and *'Skilleo Games Score'* bumper stickers. Exercising prudent sensibility in their product themes was expected, but there were a lot of loose, unenforced interpretations of what might offend prudes or 'piss off' words that might cause a scuffle. Monetized free speech reigned. Tribal security kept the peace as they could. Pure political protests were contained in their own soapbox preaching area, and what was allowed into the stadium was strictly screened, with body scanners and walk-through portable airport X-ray machines. This too, slowed down flows, as did the traffic, and a decision was made that the trial on Monday morning would be delayed until 1 pm. This news was conveyed over a designated low-frequency radio station set up for all seeking event information.

Scene 2: Pre-Trial
Setting: California and Colorado

American jurisprudence is a dysfunctional dystopia. One could easily postulate that for every action taken, a lawsuit is possible. Professor Paul H. Rubin wrote in November 2010, "The United States is already the most litigious society in the world. We spend about 2.2 percent of gross domestic product, roughly $310 billion a year, or about $1,000 for each person in the country on tort litigation, much higher than any other country." Nowhere did this manifest itself so apparent as during this period, before and after '*The Trial of the Century.*'

The process server, dumpy-looking and disheveled, one paycheck short of homeless (but a good disguise), showed up at the Santa Monica 'War Room' office and smiled innocently at the one building guard who was looking for evil miscreants but did not see one here. On entering, the process server began walking around, searching, before finding an unlocked door, which, when opened, showed clean desks and empty chairs — totally vacant premises.

The phone call to the law firm seeking service received valid questions: "No one's here; what do I do next? Where do I go?" There was no good answer.

The Five Aces Studioz was closed until next week after the trial. The Skilleo campus, still buzzing with worker bees, was impenetrable. No officer was present to officially take the legal documents, and if given to the wrong person, legal issues of proper service would be argued, causing delay after delay, and perhaps a counter lawsuit filed, open damages of harassment might be one thread of pursuit, wherein at least court costs might be affixed by a sympathetic judge, especially playing on Skilleo's home turf.

Any law firm, and there were many elites as well as ambulance chasers, pursuing target-focused litigation for clients bearing grudges or a mere feather of cause, were doing so for contingency fees, being cautious to minimize their expenses. It was a gamble; yes, rewards from judgments, like a high-profile payday, might be possible, but in their arrogance, believing they could find a statute to make their case, had not considered that lawyers on the other side were being paid substantial fees to minimize those who were trying to out-fox a Fox — preventive finesse, believing, as their client intoned, 'A good offense is the best defense." Who said that? George Washington in 1799: "Offensive operations, often times, is the surest, if not the only means of defense." Litigation is war, and Hugh Fox's 'offense' would have made Sun Tzu ('the Art of War', 5th century BC) pay bowed respect. Point in case:

Several signs were visible as the crowds began to converge on the Skilleo Stadium. Most directional, but a few, like ancient Burma Shave road advertising, were formal postings:

You are entering the sovereign jurisdiction of the Sand Creek Arapahoe Nation. All laws have been promulgated by the Sand Creek Arapahoe Constitution under the auspice of the Tribal Council and Tribal members.

Please have an enjoyable stay. Respect our laws and our culture. Hohóu[*]

---

[*] note: Hohóu — Thank you

A half mile down the road, now quite a crowded roadway, was another posting, recently created:

This event at the Skilleo World Soccer Stadium is operated under a treaty agreement between the Arapahoe Tribal Council and certain private parties. A copy of all event rules and regulations is available at the Tribal Information Booth, 2 miles on the right.

Another posting, within one mile of the information booth and related office:

Any legal documents dealing with this event must be filed at the satellite Tribal Office at the Tribal Information Booth, or they will not be considered by the Tribal Court.

It would be insightful to give an example of who first ran into these posted 'roadblocks.' Immediately after the public shock that bin Laden was alive, looking well, and would appear before some sort of hybrid court trial in Colorado, and before the 'hands off' memo quickly circulated from the Department of Justice in Washington, D.C., an ambitious Assistant U.S. Attorney scanned through his law books. He created a writ of habeas corpus (asserting that one Mr. bin Laden was being held against his will, therefore, this was not legal, and a judicial hearing must be held). He then scurried to a U.S. District Court (District of Colorado) magistrate judge, a squash playing friend of his, and gained a notice of hearing, date (immediate), plus an injunction tied to a writ of prohibition, forbidding the proceedings of *The Trial of the Century'* to go forward.

This headstrong, cocky Colorado District U.S. Assistant Attorney, dragging along two U.S. federal marshals, got as far as the first event gate (a vehicle checkpoint), asking to see their entry tickets which the three legal officers had not purchased. They believed their badge credentials and judge-blessed documents would open any door. It was not even a fair stand-off since the tribal gate bouncers were armed and looked menacing. By chance, several media cameras were rolling; even the prepared and the rarely roaming CAMERA THREE made a show of pushing her videocam into their faces. The attempt at legal ambush had failed. The confrontation was tense yet brief. The U.S. attorney now doubted his bullying tactics would be enough and, in fact, could be seen as 'politically improper,' especially against tribal employees. With pleasantries, the writ carriers were directed to turn around (difficult to accomplish) and travel back down the road to the Tribal Information Booth. A tribal judge was called to meet the 'government gentlemen.'

Perusing the documents handed over, Tribal Judge Georgette 'Skye' Raven gave her unofficial opinion.

388   S.P. Grogan

"I appreciate your diligence in trying to right a perceived wrong, but unfortunately, I will be ruling that these documents, the writs, and injunction are non-enforceable." The attorney sputtered, trying to argue, but was interrupted by a raised hand.

"You are probably unaware since you chose this direction that the U.S. District Court cannot interfere with a tribal court case, more so as we have defined this event by our recently signed treaty to be held under tribal law and jurisdiction. This new treaty recently filed as of record with the Bureau of Indian Affairs. Even with that document, our sovereignty pre-dates the U.S. Constitution, and our ability to handle our own affairs has been ratified several times by the U.S. Supreme Court."

"But…" the attorney, who could be very convincing, felt a sinking feeling.

"Please, since you represent the Federal government, I presume (giving a hard glance if such were true), let me hand you a copy of our latest treaty. We call it the: *Dancing Rabbit Treaty*. A court might interpret this as a 'contract,' but as you know, historically, we Hinono'eino sign all our agreements in good faith. And our word has always been our bond." No doubt the judge's eyes said many things. "But I would like to point out one clause in our treaty. Here:

'At the conclusion of this event of approximate five days duration, the defendant of this investigative trial, one Osama bin Laden, a foreigner of our land, shall be remitted to the jurisdiction of the United States for its own formal legal adjudication.'

"So, you see, your writs and posturing are premature to a conclusion that will support your position. Therefore, I will be issuing an opinion and dismissing these documents you propose to file with the tribal court, that is, if you are leaving them for us to rule on?"

The Assistant U.S. Attorney felt flustered, swallowing frustration. Filing his documents with this 'Indian' court might cause conflict with other governmental action he might not be aware of, a potential career-ending mistake if there were any missteps. He looked for solid ground, a safe withdrawal.

"No, we are not filing today. But you stated this event is an 'investigative trial,' what does that mean?"

"Good point, counselor. This event, this trial, is being held under what one might call an expedited process of law. It is being held in the semblance of a trial, with all rules of courtroom process being adhered to, but the court actions will be, if one might put it, abbreviated. All evidence entered shall be weighed as to its veracity, and selected citizenry as jurors will make a judgmental decision as to guilt or innocence, but in the end, the three-judge panel, of which I am one, will rule if all conditions were met in fairness to the accused, and to the legitimacy of the law being exercised under our tribal statues." A two-second pause in handing the attorney's documents back was dismissal.

"If that is all, I wish you all well in your return journey to Denver. Of course, you are welcome to buy tickets, if any are left, but I don't think so. And I might point out that your concern raised today has already been put forth and considered in Washington. Were you aware of that?"

"No, I wasn't aware. Which Federal agency is reviewing the legitimacy of this 'event'?" Today's defeat was heard in his tone.

The judge smiled as judges do sometimes, all-knowing.

"The Office of the President."

For a while, Judge Raven stayed around the Information Booth, watching event arrivals ask questions of confusion, gain directional answers, pick up the souvenir event program, even a brochure on tribal history and local tourism suggestions, and depart for the Stadium and outlying field parking. She chatted with the Tribal Clerk sitting at her make-shift table, and before leaving, the judge glanced at several lawsuits which had made their way into the tribe's possession as 'official filings' for the court's consideration. The Clerk, of her own volition, had read through the complaints, and knowing the law, she had officially stamped them as 'received and date of filing,' returning a second marked copy to be mailed back to the filing individual, representing the plaintiff against the defendant. Going to online law school in her spare time, the Clerk could spot how they should be categorized: (a) worthy of a serious response, or (b) frivolous, destined for quick dismissal.

During the next several days, lawsuits would be filed against Osama bin Laden for various complaints of damages on his assumed guilt for 9/11. One lawsuit processed against thirty different defendants (including corporate entities and executives: Five Aces, Skilleo, all the main cast members of King's Retribution, etc.); the shotgun approach of casting a wide net. Two lawsuits dropped off, claiming an unstated position in the still unresolved $25 million reward, seeking injunctive relief against any 'rash' decisions. By the end of the fifth day of the trial, over fifty lawsuits would be left with the Tribal Clerk. The majority of them were 9/11 survivors or relatives of victims, or victim's rights groups, represented by a slew of injury firm attorneys who had solicited clients with blank contingency fee forms — all demanding a financial piece of the *Trial of the Century,* contending a myriad of 'profiting from a crime,' seeking forfeiture and/or restitution. Several lawsuits were aimed at any legal claim that could be made on bin Laden's family construction conglomerate (a long shot). Already all legal parties of interest were conference calling, planning to hold a 'convention' of merging all their lawsuits into class-action status. The tribal court, in a short time, would give them all a quick wake-up call.

It was the U.S. Assistant Attorney who discovered the 'devil in the details' bombshell. On the drive back to Denver, in the governmental car's backseat, trying to cool down from his perceived humiliation, he was skimming through the 32-page *Dancing Rabbit* Treaty, seeking any little nugget which might create a brilliant opening to file a new case, to satisfy himself and to demonstrate to his bosses his true caring for this 'injustice now occurring.'

"Holy Shit," he said aloud, not really talking to the U.S. Marshals in the front seat, not caring if they understood the magnitude of this one small print paragraph. He summarized, in near shock:

"In addition to payments for the 99-year ground lease for the Stadium, a new entity, Skilleo Partners, for all rights to holding an event approximate July 20th thru August 5th (blah, blah more details on that, an addendum attached), Skilleo Partners shall advance $10 million to the Sand Creek Arapahoe Economic Development Corporation, to be applied for supporting and funding the necessary legal requirements and permits to gain a license for casino gaming, wherein, etc., etc. Skilleo Partners shall have a 25 percent gross profit ownership in the operation of said casino for a period of thirty years" — more boilerplate — "and provide and/or guarantee all funding for said construction of any casino/hotel resort." In addition, "Skilleo Games Technology, as a separate party, will have an exclusive license to use all tribal images and related tribal historical memorabilia, if approved by the Tribal Council, for use in various casino gaming machines and/or internet games. Again 'see related addendum.'"

"What's going on here?" He now began mulling ramifications over to himself. 'Is this a quid pro quo? A cash payment to hold this terrorist trial under the tribal courts, who will then protect their investment by keeping all the legal shit coming down placed under their control. Hell, I think we (career litigants and payday barristers) have all been royally snookered." The word 'snookered' was not used.

Scene 3: Arriving
Setting: Skilleo Stadium, Sand Creek Reservation, near Colorado Springs, July 20-24

The leading legal players of whatever this had become, a search for justice or televised farce, had arrived between July 19th and 21st. The corporate offices were unfinished except for Hugh's office, and the conference room had been converted into small bedrooms for *King's Retribution* and the two legal teams, advocates, and two of the three judges (another lived on the reservation). Jurors would be housed in a secure nearby location. Everyone within this broad executive umbrella was now under 24-hour security coverage by Fox's designated Security Force Alpha, backed up by roaming Tribal Police and police cadets.

Crimson Scimitar   391

For the key cast members, roommates were Abbas and Bennie, another room for CAM ONE and CAM TWO, though one was always in a freelance roaming mode covering the action but sticking close to the stars. This was their bread-and-butter gig.

Two mini-suites were set aside, reflecting the relationship between Samantha Carlisle and Hugh Fox, which had dissolved into a respectful friendship, business-like (still Five Aces Studioz partners) with lingering memories of the good times. Bicoastal did not work, especially in this frantic time when Hugh disappeared immediately after Clayton's funeral to take care of *The Trial of the Century* logistics, and Samantha discovered she was not an executive in this next phase of *King's Retribution*. Where *King's Retribution* had been a joint all-hands effort, buddy bonding, *The Trial*, the formal public nickname, had morphed into a Skilleo Games show with one production boss. Samantha accepted this with reluctant grace, learning personally how Hugh could become easily fixated and distant, not a lovie-feelie attribute. So, with new conspiracies of something out there called the '*Crimson Scimitar*' plot presently exciting the Search/Discovery Team of *King's Retribution,* she concentrated there and took stock of where her personal life might be leading.

With all the key team members re-assembled in a special VIP box, they ate, overlooking the playing field, in a bar garden-like setting, box lunches, simple and definitely healthy with organic overtones.

Most of their lunchtime chatter was not of the 'new evidence' in their conspiracy hunt but in outright wonder at the humongous bubble with a made-for-TV official-looking courtroom under glass, so to speak, or was it under Plexiglas? There was a debate on the composite.

Pacheco, as the newbie, found himself immediately awkward trying to fit into the group's social structure, observant in curiosity. They peppered him with questions that he could not answer, and several thought the secrecy shtick was ultra cool. Eventually, the younger set discovered that they all appreciated video games and found a common denominator for discussion. And just when Pacheco thought he might acclimatize into a fun crowd that could bolster his spirits with camaraderie, his cell phone rang. Hugh Fox wanted to visit with him.

Scene 4: First day
Setting: Skilleo Stadium, July 25th

First Observations: Callie and Samantha

The two of them sat in the primary seats in the VIP luxury box. Callie had noted the brass door marker: "Reserved," but not any ownership stated like *Skilleo*, or *Mr. Fox*, certainly not Five Aces Studioz. She had passed by another skybox door, identified as *Sand Creek Arapahoe*

EDC. She was unsure what 'EDC' meant, but she and everyone else were guests of the tribal leadership, the Stadium sitting on their land.

Callie heard cheering in the stadium, ticket-holders still arriving.

"Smile but don't grin, and look up slowly," said Samantha turning towards her, a demure, passive look on the fashion designer's face.

Callie raised her head to see her face on a giant Jumbotron* screen across and on top of the back rim of the stadium, and on another at the other end of the stadium, and then her 'mug' smiling back from multi smaller screens strategically placed so the crowd could see all, including unaware candid shots.

"What the...!" Her response was interrupted by a hand placed on hers.

"Careful. I am sure some of the talking head coverage might have hired lip readers to cover the trial testimony. Who knows?"

Callie could hear scattered cheering. That was for her. And it just wasn't one big live shot of an actress, but a split screen, her sitting in real-time, and then the other half of the screen a *King's Retribution* publicity still, of her looking tough as nails, running, firing a pistol. Damn, one of her 'Lady Rambo' looks she had asked Abbas in Special Effect to produce for her, hoping to make a point of being more than a pretty face with a breasty bod. Well, yes, the front of her blouse was missing a few buttons, but that 'badass look' was inappropriate here.

She noticed something else.

"Why aren't you in this photo op embarrassment?"

"Side deal with Hugh to nix the field producers to cover the two of us. You are the talent; I'm the money. Behind-the-scenes. You are center stage. They will probably mention my name, but marketing my persona should be laser beamed to the fashion industry. Couture will not be on the runway this afternoon."

From her bag, she pulled a fancy pair of expensive Swiss binoculars, and her gaze meandered around, looking at people and the signs they waved. Pretty blunt and nasty ones displayed, not one that said, 'Go, Osama!'

Callie accepted she was part of the show. She was an actress. Recognition for *King's Retribution*, with increased notoriety, the 'co-capture' of bin Laden, was a new claim to fame that she could deal with and feel good about. She noted the empty seats marked 'reserved' around her and Samantha.

---

* Jumbotron is now a generic word for HDTV-LED large sizing. The two Skilleo screens by Daktronic are 72 feet tall and 160 feet wide, 1920x 1080 resolution, 55 plus pixel clarity.

"Where are the boys?" An innocent question, no agenda, no drama. She knew where Storm was, recuperating, still in the hospital. Now, to be part of the television audience, watching, going cold turkey.

Samantha kept her eyes hidden behind the lenses, finding the stadium seats slowly filling as the traffic out on the highway and entrance road was being sorted out.

"I think Hugh is handling last-minute production value crises in his office in the bowels of this place. Wendell said he was tasked with a 'delivery system role,' whatever that means. They both should be wandering in."

Callie noted Bennie was munching away at the buffet table, as well as finger-feeding CAMERA TWO, who adroitly had the shoulder cam...focused on her. She gave a crazy, lopsided goofy look, then turned away. She missed Clayton; he made her smile for real. Okay, she was ready; now was the time.

"I read in the online *New York Post* that you and Hugh were no longer an item?" That was safe gossip.

Samantha watched vendors walking up and down stadium steps, selling water in paper cups and munchies. No plastic bottles to throw. She didn't miss a beat in her reply.

"*National Enquirer* said you and Storm are, how did they put it, 'Burned out, greener pastures or rehab. Guess which?' Today, they noted, you weren't at his bedside as a grieving...what? I read the headline. I didn't read the lies below that."

"Dating an office associate, or in my case, a co-star does not bode well for longevity. Besides, the days were coming where I might have shot him...in the foot." Callie cursed herself at the bad reference. Both of Storm's legs had been shattered in the bomb blast.

Samantha seemed sympathetic and offered, "I can relate. Relationships in the A-list category are fraught with career entanglements. Sad when a night at home means working with your lover and their PA (personal assistant) going over matching his and your calendars. But there were good moments I don't regret."

"Good for you. Sadly", said Callie, "I can't remember the tender times, merely a bed trampoline fucking haze. I'm screwed up. I thought I was going to live the fairy tale of a poor Mexican immigrant who succeeds first as an L.A. Uber driver, then becomes law enforcement with computer skills, and finally, with a break, smashes the glass ceiling for Latinos arriving in better television roles. Instead, I'm part of the bad side of the tattle sheets, less the role model for young girls and more the wet dream for adolescent boys who forgot about good manners, tenderness, and respect. They need to learn: amigos, it is important to first win someone's heart."

"Ah, I'm guessing you are now in a renewed search for romantic love?"

Callie scoffed. "Don't be messin' with me — a futile search. I want to believe in the ideal of wanting a good man to really care and show it. Unfortunately, true world situations are harder to discover."

Samantha lowered her binoculars and looked at Callie.

"Yes, that would be nice. In my world, I am now going through an inner debate on what I really want in the next relationship and if I really want the long term at all. It's difficult to change the philosophy of being the woman comfortable with her alone-ness."

"I understand such choices. Perhaps I need a surprise." She motioned, and Samantha handed her binoculars. Callie re-focused for clarity. "Maybe I can spy me a new target for *King's Retribution*."

They both laughed. Callie started her search among the restive crowd.

"Call me Sam," said Samantha. "My friends do."

"I'm still Callie, one friend to another." They had been through a lot.

"Hello, ladies." Hugh Fox joined them, not sitting next to Samantha or Callie but behind them. A Solomon's judgment, mused Samantha.

"Are you here for your opening credits?" asked Callie with a chuckle, still staring outward, not wanting to display too much in this close contact, to be too open.

"Yeah, first, I think I'll get a bite. Haven't had breakfast or lunch."

"They put out a good spread here."

Said their host: "I hear the chef for this box is from the Broadmoor Hotel. What do you recommend?"

"Shit!" yelled Callie.

Both Samantha and Hugh looked at her in disbelief.

"Look, look!" She lowered the binoculars and raised them again. "Look at middle row of seats just below, to the right of the Jumbotron across from us." She gave one last glance and handed them to Hugh, who focused and stared.

"Damn."

"And yes, what?" asked Samantha, holding her hand out for her property. She did the same, zeroing in where Callie had directed. Four men, dressed in variations of black, sat together, looking too serious, as if being present was disgusting with the boisterous crowd surrounding them. Then, it clicked, and she identified one of the four.

"Shit. Damn. That's one-eyed Pastor Tate. That's not a good sign."

"Excuse me, Sam, Callie. I'm going to check in with Security. We already have a Watch List of about twelve face recognitions, questionable as up-to-no-good suspects. I'll have the Eye-in-the-Sky give them priority." And he was gone.

"There," said Callie. "I didn't even spot it. And there's another."

Both women looked up and spotted two hovering objects barely visible against the bright sky.

"Camera drones," explained Samantha. "Hugh mentioned those in passing, but I forgot about them. I guess these are his prototypes, small, silent, but with a telescopic lens and television feed. Someday they might be everywhere."

Callie teased. "Please, please, can you get a couple of these from him? They would be perfect tech toys for *King's Retribution.*"

Sam gave back, "Why don't you ask him yourself? I think he likes you."

Callie's silence of processing became overshadowed by a stadium full of booing.

"What's the reason for that?' she asked.

"They are booing the so-called bad guys."

The show was starting, an invisible curtain rising.

The Defense Team entered the court.

Scene 5: The Defense — Booker Langston and Harriet Eberhart
Setting: Stadium Courtroom

"Don't let them get to you, Harry," said Booker as he followed her up the side steps through a secured lower-level door inside the clear plexiglass-type bubble to the courtroom floor.

Harriet tried not to look beyond the protective dome. That they needed protection *did* bother her. She had always felt safe in a courtroom, even if her low-life defendant client was charged with multiple murders. Here, not so much. She appreciated that 'Bookie' was thinking of her, hopefully with heroic concern, damsel distressed, not 'fatherly.'

"I'm fine. Just have to put myself in the zone."

They sat at their designated seats and opened their briefcases.

"I guess it is surreal in a fashion," Langston commented. "That we have 40,000 plus yelling their worst, and yet when we have our 'defendant' before us in two closed meetings, he says absolutely nothing. You'd think he could at least rant and rave about his being innocent or ramble out his mantras."

"Booker, the point is, he was listening. He did understand. I think you would have heard his wail if he thought we would just lie down and let Cotton stomp all over us. He might not have appreciated his circumstances, but any accused person wants to be placed in the best possible light. Instead, I saw manipulative coyness, more like the aggressor waiting to spring in a planned attack. That's been bin Laden's entire career modus operandi."

"Astute observation. Who knows, he may even help us keep him alive?"

The crowd switched from blood lust to cheers of support.

Prosecutor Cotton Matther V entered, reveling in perceived glory, unabashedly turning his body, circling to acknowledge his 'fans.' Waving to the stadium roars of an arriving Caesar. In his element. His associate, James Buchanan, took a seat. Two staff acolytes carried in the prosecutor's file cases of evidence presentations and began stacking his color-coded case papers. Cotton walked over to the Defense. Booker rose, but Harriet remained seated, looking over her paperwork. Nods were exchanged, no 'touch gloves and come out fighting,' but such sentiment lingered in the air.

"This will be fun," beamed Matther, still looking out, taking in the adulation of the Coliseum. "I would wish you good luck, but the bonus money for victory will be a great down payment for my future aspirations."

"Cotton, don't go measuring the drapes in the governor's mansion just quite yet." They exchanged serious pugilist stares. Booker sat; Cotton walked to his table and yelled at his minion staffers, who promptly departed. His second chair, Buchanan, said nothing, arranging papers for his boss.

The defense and prosecutor bent to prepare their paperwork, exchanging last-minute thoughts about documents and witnesses. Each team, if that's what they were, curious as to what the other side would spring as the 'one surprise witness' that would be allowed outside the approved witness list. Only 24 hours would be allowed to prepare for cross-examination. Sort of like speed dating, but speed witness, like a college speech meet where one draws a topic to launch extemporaneous support to a position. *All for the show* thought Harriet. Other watchers wondered about the same strangeness.

Scene 6: Girl Talk
Setting: Stadium VIP Box

Watching the preliminaries from above, Callie covertly tried to feel out possibilities.

"Why do you think Hugh took control of everything post-capture instead of turning bin Laden over to the Feds, FBI, or Justice? I argued for that, washing our hands of a massive migraine headache."

Samantha watched the attorneys confer between themselves, waiting as was everyone.

"I don't think I completely figured out what makes 'Game Boy' run." Meaning Hugh, the event's producer, her partner of Five Aces Studioz. "An observation or two. Hugh gets caught up in his creative world, single-minded focus, and perhaps life's perception merges with non-reality safe escapism. His form of a security blanket. Is that bad? Not necessarily."

"Ultra smart I'm sure has its own set of hang-ups."

"Somewhat true. To him, the chase and capture was a distraction from a hard corporate world of administrative detail and stress of profit achievement. But this," Samantha waved her hand around the stadium. "This might have begun as more escapism, omnipotence in control, but I believe this is no longer his version of fun. Clayton's hit-and-run murder was a wake-up, a call to Hugh's multi-universe of heroes but stark realism to us all. Even with the attack on Storm." She noted Callie's face tightened but continued. "So, Part 2, with the prize in hand, agreed, he gained short-term self-satisfaction, but then he learns that if the U.S. Government had captured bin Laden, it would mean terrorist toast. Outright summary execution. Even for bad dudes that doesn't compute with his world of tinkering: why did the bad guy commit the crime, what was the motivation, are there any extenuating circumstances that warrant a lenient re-do?

"Fry the motherfucker," Callie's opinion.

"What any pragmatist executioner would say."

"Hugh should think that way."

"Not if you are dealing with a noble person. Look around you. Again, this is not just a television show; an extravaganza boosted out to the entire world. This is Hugh's sense of pure justice, fairness, something that he, even I, feel has been misplaced in a cynical world of commercialism, bait-click platitudes, and empty-head ignorance. Is it just Hugh Fox against the U.S. Government and Hugh Fox against blind fanaticism? Yes, but likewise a Hugh Fox interpretation of what should be corrected, the polishing off our collective tarnished idealism. The question is, Callie, are you ready to ride the tornado, reap the whirlwind, join his version of 'noblesse oblige'? Or worse, be in love but be a second banana to his creations?"

Callie realized Samantha Carlisle had been there and seen all that within this man she was now slowly, somewhat methodically, being drawn to. With his wealth and good looks, upbeat personality, and his notice of her, did she have a need herself for a 'safety blanket'?

Callie Cardoza shook her head back into her own reality, her microscopic stage in the cosmos.

"I don't know what I want."

EPISODE TWENTY-FOUR — It Begins

Scene 1: Defendant in the box
Setting: First Day, Monday, 12:30 p.m.

The crowd on their feet, yet the noise slackening, returning to their seats; time to listen. The moment: three black-robed figures had entered the courtroom bubble. *The Trial of the Century* was underway.

The gavel sounded hard, a reverberating echo across the stadium's speaker system. Harriet unobtrusively checked her jewelry pin-styled lapel mike. Booker wore a microphone in a 'Blind Justice' lapel button. Cotton's was an American flag. Earlier sound checks days before gave her confidence; her voice, when called upon to speak, would reach beyond her nervousness.

The judges discussed small details among themselves and dealt with a few housekeeping items on the calendar for this day and tomorrow. Then, Judge Sanford, in sonorous tones, sang out. "Let the defendant be brought forth." To this anticipated put-on show, the stage-managed circus atmosphere, the drum-roll building to the crescendo of the Big Reveal, the main star of it all, the defendant, Osama bin Laden, could have cared less. Bin Laden had previously explained his 'predicament philosophy' to his jailer, Hugh Fox, when he told him that he considered his life and his career forfeit. He saw himself fated as a 'living martyr,' better off now as a symbol to continue the struggle than an old, forgotten prisoner. Freed, he would be suspected of having been 'turned' by his captivity, and no *Letters from the Birmingham Jail* [MLK] and no tome of *My Struggle* written in Landsberg Prison of his diatribe on prophetic plans of world conquest (Hitler-Mein Kampf) would repair his reputation to all the propaganda now demeaning him more so into the Devil Incarnate.

Having some access to outside newspapers and television, it had been confirmed to him by the 'free press' that in the failed attack on his home (which included the killing of one of his sons), his own murder had been sanctioned by the U.S. Government. And to all this, with all the current publicity of his capture and being detained, when Fox and his TV gang would turn him over to the U.S. Federal authorities, and he saw through the ruse of a 'fair trial,' bin Laden embraced his fatalism, resigned himself that whatever happened before a screaming stadium audience, whatever this kangaroo court passed as judgment on his head, bin Laden accepted he was a dead man walking.

"Are you ready?" came the familiar voice.

"Hello, Wendell," said bin Laden, rising from the couch, prepared. The defendant stood and smoothed out his garments, pleased that he could dress again immaculately in the descriptive role of an Islamic cleric. It was his original thought if he was going to be paraded around. His decision confirmed by a surprising source, his legal team, who had suggested in one of their brief sessions, that it was their strategy to plant reasonable doubt in increments, one such being a man facing religious persecution.

In his play role as 'Imam,' bin Laden knew his followers would envision the 'Emir,' the 'Caliphate' still possible. He walked with his escort Holmes through the tunnel under the stadium. He was pleased that his attorneys had walked him through *his* 'script,' all optional, they said, with only certain limited freedoms. One, being he would sit in the Box of the Indicted, without leg manacles and handcuffs. A victory of sorts, again managed by his attorneys, by this stern black man and the diminutive little woman lawyer with the sharp tongue, both desiring to educate him about their battle plans. And that's how he eventually came to accept that the Big Show was just another battlefield to wage his war of beliefs upon. He must bide his time and then act appropriately.

"Everything alright with you so far?" asked Wendell, who had not much to say, just doing his one assigned job.

"I have been in better circumstances, even in my Tora Bora office cave, but once I figured out how to use the remote and then learned how to record shows I wanted to watch," he paused, "then daily activities become more tolerable."

During this whole action against him from Abbottabad to this place and day, he, as prisoner and defendant, had only talked to two of his 'jailers,' Hugh Fox and Wendell Holmes. They were the masterminds of his incarceration, the true leaders, for the women he had read about, he believed they were subservient to these powerful men, the capitalist and the spy. Wendell he had known over the years, an indistinguishable personage, a rumored name, the "Silent Assassin," a CIA toady, nevertheless dangerous, who did not cause death but orchestrated the demise of his fellow patriots.

He tolerated them the same way he acknowledged without praise the two spokespeople of his legal rights (in America), he knew they had their agenda, and he had his, *Crimson Scimitar*, to be his legacy, pleased to himself that part of his agenda was in motion. And that his plan, yes, with Khalaf's first kernel thought of an idea, but his design, that these actions would soon be revealed as his public answer to this humiliation.

As he and Holmes approached the elevator (there were no guards accompanying them), he had to ask, trying to dampen his nervousness before it showed.

"Are you coming with me?"

"No, Osama, you know I am a man always behind the scenes." He did not try to give empathy or give the al Qaeda comfort except to say, "Consider this; you have the audience you always wanted."

The defendant entered a small elevator, not closed in but with glass sides. Wendell leaned in, pushed the G (Ground) button, and stepped back. No smiles between them. The door closed.

Scene 2: Grand Entrance
Setting: First Day, Afternoon Session

Some firebrand announcer had built anticipation. Forty-two thousand voices raised a cacophony of shouts, curses, boos, derisive cheering, each blasting lung trying to overwhelm the volume of all the others. There were also faces in the mass bearing silence. Disgusted? Awed? Supporters?

The see-through elevator rose to the courtroom floor, situated against the interior side of the dome. The defendant had been prepped. It was seen and reported that as he stepped out of the elevator, he straightened his back and stood taller to face the world, his judges. Osama bin Laden took a few steps forward into a plastic boxed booth; some might say, 'bubble within a bubble.' The elevator, as if on cue, went back into the floor, back down to B (Basement). Two guards now approached him. He saw they seemed to be of some nationality, an ethnic coloration to their round faces and black braided hair. They were all serious. They shut the door of the cubicle he entered and locked him in, standing to the back, silently on guard. Bin Laden then sat in a very comfortable chair and faced the small desk console before him, which held his microphone, and the head set for translation. Also provided were a small desk iPad in Arabic for reviewing evidence as presented and legal pads, pens with felt tips for any note-taking, but nothing sharp as a writing instrument.

Within the courtroom bubble, the stadium roar lessened to an acceptable modulating hum, like a nearby hive of agitated bees. More so in the defendant's plastic box, a clear 'cage,' added further soundproofing, so the angry mob without would have been agitated to realize their chants and screams to him were unintelligible, and, out there, he saw only small bodies gesticulating and open mouths making silent epitaphs.

He now took stock of his surroundings. All within the Dome were in their appointed places, as the earlier tutorial video he had been given had shown. The Defense table across from him, the high jurist bench with three judges seated, and facing them was a table where bin Laden assumed these were his Prosecutors, a silver grey-haired man, flanked by his associate 'flack,' the defendant decided. Across from him was an empty jury box, ready to receive the real judges of his fate.

He looked upwards. It was a beautiful sunny day, with a few clouds and no late afternoon showers, as he was told might happen this week. He could see mountains in the far distance. He wished he could have stood before such a crowd of his followers like this, but upon an elevated dais and sing lilting oratory that would move al Qaeda and then the Islamic world to let him lead them. A noise broke into his reverie — a gavel, pounding truth to the forefront.

Scene 3: Points of Law
Setting: Courtroom

The main charges of the Indictment were re-stated: *Conspiracy. Attacking Civilians. Murder in Violation of the Law of War. Hijacking an Aircraft. Terrorism.* If convicted of one, even two of the charges, the death penalty could be levied.

Judge Sanford: "How does the defendant plead?"

Harriet rose. "The defendant has informed us he does not accept the jurisdiction of this court, nor any court jurisdiction within the United States. He further believes he is a political prisoner brought here against his will. Although he will not participate actively in what he considers an illegal show trial, he has agreed to accept our advice, and on his behalf, may the record note, a plea of Not Guilty should be entered." Boos and derisive shouts across the stadium, all muted within the bubble.

Judge Sanford: "The court will enter a plea of 'Not Guilty' on behalf of the defendant. "Before we move forward, are there any other motions or comments to come before this court?"

"If it please the court," Langston rose to put forth for their side, an objection.

"The court has seen fit to accept from the prosecution a bill of indictment which has been entered for the record. However, we would like to dispute one of the particulars which we do not feel needs to be part of this trial."

With a nod from senior judge Sanford, Justice Behan, who would be the expert on both tribal law and Federal statutes in this trial, responded, "Mr. Langston, it is our understanding that you had an opportunity to review the indictment which would be the basis of this trial?"

"Your Honors, we accepted that the prosecution would throw the kitchen sink of charges against our client, for it is and will be our position to defend on the evidence that Sheik bin Laden did not plan nor approve the events of September 11, 2001. In fact, to this point, Sheik Osama bin Laden until this trial has never been indicted for the crimes of 9/11." Boos again from the audience, but again barely heard. The gavel sounded with little effect, more theatre to play to the world audience who heard stadium reaction as well as the court dialogues.

Booker proceeded; only the court need hear. "But Prosecutor Cotton most recently, within the last day, amended the indictment to throw in the U.S. Federal Court of Manhattan's 1998 indictment that charged our client for his role in attacking U.S. embassies in East Africa. This is found on page 31. This new charge is scatter-shooting in the least, creating guilt by

402 S.P. Grogan

association, which has nothing to do with the events of 9/11. Furthermore, if sometime in the future our client may be tried on those existing charges by the U.S. Government, he would be in a position of double jeopardy. Finally, the U.S. Government's 14-year-old indictment cannot be merged into what we face today, as the U.S. Government does not have jurisdiction with this court."

Justice Behan was reviewing the 25-page single space indictment against Osama bin Laden until his scan caught the paragraph of charges in question near the end of his perusal.

"Counselor Langston, I am well aware of the sovereignty of our nation and its rights. Yes, I do see the 1998 reference to an existing indictment in another jurisdiction. It seems to me that combining two cases into one was not the intention of this court and this trial. If my colleagues would agree, this portion of the Indictment, paragraph #83 on page 31 will be stripped from the indictment, and no reference to the events or related statements to the bombings of the United States embassies in Nairobi, Kenya, and Dar es Salaam, Tanzania, will be made during this trial or by the two counsels or defense outside this court as it pertains to this trial.

"Counselor Cotton, do you wish to make any contrary argument?"

Prosecutor Cotton rose to address the court.

"No, Your Honor, we believe all evidence of the character and past actions of the defendant deserves to be put before the jurors, but we will abide by your ruling. We believe we have enough evidence to gain a conviction."

Judge Sanford: "Are there any other matters either side wishes to address before the indictment is read, the jury called and impaneled, and opening statements?"

"Two minor matters. A small matter of court courtesy, Your Honors," offered Cotton. "My honorable colleagues for the defense keep referring to the defendant as "Sheik." We see here no honorific title to be applied. We believe he should be addressed as the 'Defendant' or 'Mr. bin Laden".

Judge Sanford: "Mr. Langston, your response?"

"Indeed, the court has the right to set court decorum and apply terminology as they see fit. 'Sheik' is a well-known cultural name and refers to a leader, particularly the chief or head of an Arab tribe, family, or village. *Sheik* is similar to *Mr.* or, as such here, a tribal chief. The prosecution will be trying to prove our client is a leader of a political entity, wherein we see him as head of an extended personal family unit. In their burden of proof, they must argue he is a father figure and leader of a political organization; therefore, the title could still be regarded as appropriate. I might point out another known appellation to an Arab male would be something like "Most Respected Osama bin Laden.""

"The word 'Sheik' in our opinion," Cotton shot back, "intones some mysticism, a romantic figure, and neither 'Sheik' nor 'Most Respected' would be proper here. 'Mr.' suffices."

"Enough," said Judge Sanford, "Court will accept the word 'Defendant,' the word "Mr." and the word 'Sheik' either/or if used correctly and not with derision. Either side may use those titles as they choose.

"You said you had another matter?"

Prosecutor Matther: "Your Honors, to prove our case, we will be entering into the record a great deal of communication and speeches of the Accused. If we read it into the record, one of our clerks or I will do so. I will even argue for the Defense in saying my reading of *Mister* bin Laden's words might be interpreted as prejudicial, depending upon my intonation. Therefore, I propose to use a neutral 'reader' if Mr. bin Laden does not wish to accommodate us and speak his own words."

"What are you proposing, Mr. Matther?"

The prosecutor pushed a button on the computer before him, and an image of a Muslim man appeared, with a beard, not looking like bin Laden, but business formal wearing a coat and tie.

"Professor Ibn al-Ahbar of Yale University is a qualified Islamic Scholar, and we would also have him as a witness to testify that the defendant's words are not the words of belief of a majority of those of the Muslim faith."

"Our first ambush," whispered Booker to Harry as he arose, "Objection, Your Honors, but I would like a moment to confer with my client."

That caught the court off guard. Booker did not want to see a verbal fistfight between sides but could use the moment to humanize bin Laden as a person fighting for his life, and his opinion mattered.

Langston strode quickly to the prisoner's box, plugged into earphones on his side of the glass, and pointed the same for bin Laden, who reluctantly responded. He could have just remained frozen, snubbing his defense team and the court, as this jurisdiction not deserving of his attention. Curiosity won over.

"Sheik, I am willing to fight the prosecutor's attempt to have someone read your words; I don't want them to convey any acting or nuances in speech, or intonation, that are not your own meaning. You must object. However, I think I can use this to our advantage if you would allow me. And at any time, remember you push that yellow button if you wish to talk to Miss Eberhardt or me. Meanwhile, if you have nothing to say, just nod your head, affirming that you understand. And we will see where we go. All right?"

404   S.P. Grogan

Bin Laden gave a decisive nod, and for the first time, Booker saw a small smile crease the Arab's face. *My damn client*, thought Booker as he returned to the defense table, *is actually enjoying it all.*

"Your Honors, my objection to Mr. Matther's proposal would have been on prejudicial grounds. However, we would like to put forth our own response." He turned to Harriet. "Defense Evidence video clip 220." The quick video of a man appeared on all screens, who actually looked like bin Laden, dressed as a cleric, and moved with several of the same mannerisms the world had seen in recent months from old film footage. It was Fox's bin Laden actor.

"For the defense presentation, we offer our own reader to better portray our client, and who will speak concisely and without drama."

All three judges looked at each other. Their microphones went silent as they conferred.

"If the defendant chooses not to testify and speak in his own words, we will accept that either side may use a reader of the defendant's words into the record. However, to avoid any 'live' misspoken presentation as we are dealing with Arabic language and translation interpretation, both defense and prosecution will submit said readings in pre-recorded versions for our and counsel's review before being introduced as evidence.

"Mr. Langston, will your reader also be an expert and testify?"

"He is an expert and will testify only if Mr. Matther's expert witness testifies."

Asked the judge to the prosecution, "Will your reader still testify to other evidence other than reading the defendant's past writings?"

Prosecutor Matther hesitated as he rose to answer. He turned to his so-called associate but did not seek a response. He would be the lead arbitrator, no one else.

"At this time, we would accept the court's ruling for the use of these 'readers' for the purpose of establishing a record. And, no, our witness is not prepared to testify to other matters."

Everyone resumed their seats. Harried leaned into Booker, "I think we stopped Cotton from grandstanding. But what expertise does our own 'witness' or 'reader' have to speak to?"

"Other that he is a great improvisational actor, an expert in characterization? No expertise beyond being a paid thespian."

Both looked up to see that tight smile and a hint of laughter on their client's face. The victory of the moment was that the accused, Osama bin Laden, might actually start participating in his own defense. But was his controlled mood of mirth laughing with them or at them with disdain?

"Now, if counsels have no further issues before us, will the bailiff please read the filed indictment into the court record?"

The reading of the Indictment took 20 minutes.

As the Indictment verbiage scrolled across the jumbo screens or was read by those in the audience who went to the designated court website to read for themselves, the reporter for the *LA Times* turned to the legal expert from *Court TV* and asked, "What was all the pre-word play about?"

"Adversarial jousting. The prosecutor knew trying to add additional charges would be challenged, but by doing so, he drew the world's attention that the U.S. government thought this 'Sheik' bin Laden was guilty of other crimes, multiple bombings no less. Cotton is after, if it is really required, winning the public opinion toward his position. One point in his favor. On the other hand, Langston raised an interesting defense strategy: up to this date, why hasn't bin Laden been charged with 9/11? Why wasn't it issued years ago an outstanding warrant based on a Grand Jury indictment? A guilty verdict requires a 'beyond a reasonable doubt' verdict. If the jury had been present, perhaps a lingering question might have been raised.

"As to trying to add color by bin Laden readers testifying, I think it was a draw. Again, Matther lunged; Langston parried. Personally, I don't see how either of those two characters on the screen could be used to speak like or imitate bin Laden. The image of him is set in our minds. Today, he looks like a diminutive old man in the defendant's box. No one could impersonate bin Laden and fool the public."

Scene 4: Jury Selection
Setting: The Courtroom

It came as a surprise to most that the number of jurors in this trial would be six instead of twelve, with two alternates. Six jurors was the national average in U.S. courtrooms. What was more so was the process of selection. In the two weeks prior to the trial, and without televised introspection, a process was put in place to select jurors from a wide pool consisting of citizens of neighboring El Paso, Pueblo, Elbert, and Douglas Counties. Selecting only Native American jurors from the Reservation would have been viewed as somehow discriminating and unfair.

Today's selection was for the two alternates. Potential Jurors #55, #83, #88, and #92 were seated in the jury box and were going through the voir dire process of questions by the attorneys.

Prosecutor Cotton led off with easy questions such as, what do you do for a living, asked about their children, if any, and asked them a loaded question, expecting an affirmative response from all four when he asked, usually an interrogatory asked by the judge: "Do you

406 S.P. Grogan

feel you can view the evidence, and the evidence only, and come to a just decision based solely on what is presented?" When they said 'yes,' he passed them over to the defense, and Harriet Eberhardt approached them with a smile.

Question #1: What is your opinion of the U.S. Government being involved militarily in the Middle East?"

Replied #55: "I don't really pay that much attention." That set up the others to answer carefully, such as, 'Only what I read in the newspaper' or "It is sad all the violence about religion against Christians." This latter from #88.

Question #2: "Do you know what happened on 9/11?" All answered yes; #83 was sad about all the first responders who died trying to save people and the brave fighters who took on the terrorists on Flight 93 above Pennsylvania."

Question #3: "Who do you think was behind 9/11?" Their answers varied. "Muslims." "Crazed Terrorists." #83 answered firmly, "I think this bin Laden had something to do with it." This answer would have been an almost automatic dismissal by the defense, but, in truth, whether they said it or not, all probably thought that.

These questions all had a purpose. In selecting other jurors, both counsels realized everyone knew of 9/11 and even held the opinion that Osama bin Laden was evil and, if a Muslim hates Christians, then by default, the United States of America. That's what Booker and Harriet had to deal with. And those prospective jurors in the previous voir dire who said they knew nothing of 9/11 and supposedly did not know who bin Laden was were challenged and dismissed by both sides as being outright liars with nefarious plans to sneak onto the sacred spots of the final jury.

Cotton Matther had the upper hand where all questioned assumed the accused guilty. Harriet had to find that needle in the haystack, not a pro-bin Laden possibility, they did not exist, but a person who's feelings were empathetic to a particular moral compass. Perhaps someone who would listen fairly to two sides of motivation.

Harriet was now focused. Question #4 to the prospective jurors: "Are you religious, do you attend church regularly, which faith?"

"Objection. Prejudicial."

Judge 'Skye' Raven had been overseeing jury selection, sub rosa to the court.

"I understand the religious overtones of this case, but to go beyond whether a person believes in Christ or Islam and dissect a specific tenet of those faiths does seem to go beyond the general scope. The objection is sustained but with a caveat. General questions on religious beliefs can be asked but not the specific name of a particular faith."

Harriet rephrased, "Do you believe in the religious precept where we must 'forgive those who trespass against us?' Most gave an affirmative answer. #88 answered smugly, "I'm really not that religious, but no atheist." #55 stated firmly, "That's in Matthew 6:12. We must try our best to forgive sinners."

Harriet's final questions were usually standard in defense practice: "Do any of your friends or family members have any association with law enforcement? And, if yes, were any hurt by a criminal element while on duty?"

Prospective juror #55 had a distant cousin who was a game warden in Wyoming. #83 had a brother who was a police officer in Littleton, Colorado and had been wounded when responding to a domestic dispute call. He survived, Harriet was so informed.

"Would any of you be able to reach a fair and honest decision towards acquittal if evidence was presented that the U.S. Government's foreign policy or agents of the U.S. Government directly, even indirectly injured people? And could you see a citizen have bad feelings, even by their religion, a desire for revenge, if their loved ones were hurt, even killed, by what is referred to as 'collateral damage?'

The four in the jury box had to think on that line of inquiry. When prodded, they responded by trying to state their views as well as they could.

#55 "Oh, I guess so. It depends on how strong I believe in the evidence."

#83 "I believe the U.S. Government would only do what they feel is right."

#88 "Yes, I could." ('Could what?' probed Harriet, "See where someone whose loved ones were hurt, directly or by mistake, by the U.S. Government. Could you understand their anger and desire for revenge?") Answer: "I could see where they might be really pissed off at America."

#92 "I know we make mistakes, but you have to believe in the U.S., right or wrong? I am sure I can sort through what is presented to us.?"

As Harriet returned to their table, Booker gave her a 'Well Done' smile. Several reporters perked up at her last questions. *Did the Defense actually have a defense?*

Within this patchwork format of jury selection, Judge 'Skye' Raven asked each side to concurrently write down their choice of selection, the first being the person most wanted, while the fourth was a challenge and to be dismissed. The judge tallied the selection against each, chose the two with the highest rankings, and dismissed the lower two. Harriet believed she won with #55 selected, and Cotton accepted any choice would be fine but smugly felt #92 would be open for conviction regardless of how good or bad his country had behaved on foreign soil.

408   S.P. Grogan

Papers shuffled, the courtroom waited for the entrance of the six selected jurors to take their seats, along with the added alternates.

Osama had seen a list and description from his lawyers of the six jurors chosen. From the six, with two alternates now seated, bin Laden saw he would face a United Nations mix of this hated nationalistic cauldron — most certainly, he guessed he would face a Jew somewhere within the grouping. What were their backgrounds? Inconsequential to him.

Judge Sanford then read to the jury a lengthy menu of instructions of conduct to be followed by them during this legal proceeding. The stenographer was present to record an Official Record. Relevant highlights were stressed by the judge as follows:

"Because of the short duration of the trial, all jurors will be sequestered for the duration. No outside communication. No reading or hearing of news. No discussion of the case between fellow jurors, except in final deliberation."

Jurors must base their findings only on the evidence presented; no previous assumptions must be used to reach a conclusion.

This is a capital case. In the event that the verdict is guilty, you will be asked to return to the jury room and decide on the severity of the punishment.

If you have any questions concerning your well-being during this period, please give a handwritten note to the bailiff."

After a litany of 'legalese' warnings, the jurors stood and were sworn to their oath:

"We, the jurors, do solemnly swear that we will well and truly try under the jurisdiction of this court to render a true verdict according to the evidence, so help us God."

Even juror #88, the agnostic, swore to a higher judge he did not believe in.

"Not happy with what we have to work with," whispered Harriet to Booker, "I think it's pushing a boulder uphill. I did not sense one friendly face in these accepted jurors."

"You did great," Booker patted her hand gently, then withdrew it, avoiding lingering and noticeable familiarity. The television audience did not need distractions, including allusions to romantic subplots. "What we must deal with is 'creating doubt,' and if not, then saving his life from a hanging mob."

"As to our opposition, what I am seeing, attorney James Buchanan the Fifth or Sixth, seems to be window dressing."

"Yes, Cotton will hog the glory, but I hear Buchanan is handling their own war room somewhere, overseeing the evidentiary order of presentation. Look to Cotton's right ear, the same with scion James Buchanan the Whatever Number, and you will see earbuds. They're both wired to the hidden staff to help choreograph his case. These are dangerous foes we face. Don't treat them lightly. Let's just focus on our brilliant team prep."

"You mean the team of you and me?" They smiled at each other, ready to do battle.

Scene 5: Press and Audience Observations
Setting: Stadium Media Center

The Court TV talking head back in the studio gave her opinion. "The prosecutor holds all the cards. No one will vote to release Osama bin Laden as an innocent. Not going to happen. That's why Cotton Matther could accept any warm body to serve. On the opposite side, the Langston-Eberhardt team has to be seeking someone on the jury whose belief is anti-death penalty. This is a capital case, after all. If convicted on all counts, the jury will resume deliberations between life without parole and the needle. Just one defection, and they must let bin Laden live, not a palatable decision to a majority of the country's polling views. The jury pool was pre-tainted towards conviction."

New York Times coverage, aloof and doubtful of all legitimacy, huffed out a tweet: "Native Americans won't allow a death penalty of someone they might even consider an oppressor against the U.S. Federal Government. 9/11 is not their battle." Of course, in a later front-to-back section column tracking the trial, in paragraph 20, they did point out that on 9/11American tribal leaders were in Washington, D.C. for a conference and that in the 1960s to 1970s, hundreds of Mohawk ironworkers were hugging the sky helping to construct the twin towers.

As sporting events might go, Razzor Hassim had a pretty good view of the Dome courtroom from their ticketed seats, especially a full view of his organization's leader. With him sat Shahin's right-hand killer, stern-faced Maj, who said little, and who Razzor accepted as being an 'enforcer' for the Council's attack team. Like himself.

Both men had left three of their companions discreetly hidden at a motel on the south side of Colorado Springs, away from public notice. It was the intention of Razzor and Maj as they entered the stadium and found their seats that as they watched the ongoing proceedings they were looking at methods on how one might stage a jailbreak.

At the moment, Razzor thought it was a hopeless impossibility. Osama bin Laden paid little attention to the audience before him, and eye contact could not be established to convey: 'We are here, and we will rescue you.' Razzor sought inspiration.

Although winning its time slots against its competitors, *Fox News Channel* still noticed its primetime shows were down in total viewers over the same time period of 2010. "Fox Report with Shepard Smith" and television commentator personalities like Glenn Beck, Bill O'Reilly, Greta Van Susteren, and Sean Hannity all were percentage points down. Fox News producers, therefore, decided to go all in on wall-to-wall coverage of *The Trial of the Century*. Headline

410 S.P. Grogan

stories like the landing of Space Shuttle Atlantis ending NASA's Space Shuttle program or a massacre at a youth camp in Norway all were pushed to the bottom of the screen in scrolling chryons.

As part of this coverage, a graph had been created for several program insertions followed by opinionated commentary

The bin Laden Jury

#5 Latino male, 52, truck driver, divorced, two children

#18 White male, 35, grocery store manager, married, three children

#22 Asian woman, 27, nurse, in a partner relationship

#34 Black woman, 45, banking executive, divorced, now married, one child

#37 White woman, 39, advertising executive, single

#50 Native American, 72, retired military, tribal board member, married, grandchildren

Alternates

#55 White woman, 62, home craft business; church volunteer, widowed, one child

#92 White male, 48, construction worker, veteran, divorced twice

Analysis by Fox Television guest speakers:

"Don't you see it? This is the makeup of the American spectrum, one beating heart forged by the diversity of ethnic origins."

"I don't see the Arab juror? But then they were ostracized and prejudiced against after 9/11, not part of our woven national fabric."

"I think Cotton Matther got what he wanted. A guilty victory pre-ordained and a ticket to the New York Governor's mansion or beyond."

"What does any outsider know what a sitting jury is thinking? "

Fox Host: "But we have our experts in the Stadium to give you impressions of their facial tics and body postures as they hear the evidence and what that might suggest towards a verdict."

THE SIDESHOW

At this point in the few minutes before the fireworks began within the courtroom, it might be important to note one behind-the-scene activity that received media play.

Beginning in 2004, with the rise of broadband internet access and the public entertainment use of portable digital audio playback devices, there rose in widespread usage something called 'audioblogs,' later to be known as 'podcasts.' From 2009 to the show trial in Colorado Springs, podcasting boomed and now was an integral part of entertainment and news dissemination.

In March 2011, the comedic *Ricky Gervais Show* in the United Kingdom had a record 300 million unique downloads. The *Benjamin Rush Podcast*, based somewhere in New Jersey, USA, had a strong following of 200 million downloads, mostly pitching oddity news stories off the wire services or buried in the web chatter. Benjamin Rush was attending the *Trial of the Century* as an accredited journalist, which was a stretch, but he was a big social media star among the legacy media pool.

Rush had recently started a podcast thread, asking listeners, "How Would You Defend Osama bin Laden?" The site traffic was overwhelming, and downloads soared; Hugh Fox heard about it and decided it was a good spin-off to monetize.

Fox bought the title query concept for Five Aces Studioz and any related marketing rights for an undisclosed amount and went beyond the podcast format into mass marketing beyond what was going to happen in the courtroom, and Five Aces created a "real-time contest."

"How would I defend Osama bin Laden?" A winner and runners-up would be chosen from all entries, and prizes awarded. The winner, beyond receiving a cash prize, would have his selected write-up printed as 'My Defense Strategy' as an appendix in the expected softbound publication of the tell-all book spin-off, working title, *"Official Proceedings of the Capture and Trial of Osama bin Laden,"* to be compiled and edited by the QMyst historian who would be publishing the official story, sanctioned by Five Aces Studioz.

EPISODE TWENTY-FIVE — First Salvo

Scene 1: Opening Remarks: The Prosecution
Setting: Stadium Courtroom

Judge Sanford: "We will hear now from the Prosecution."

The stadium quieted. Slowly standing, providing the dramatic flair of seeking out the courtroom, his eyes scanning in deep intent, prosecutor Cotton Matther embraced his milieu, the audience, the courtroom, even sensing where the television cameras were. His stare ended harshly on the defendant before turning to the jury and walking to them.

"Ladies and gentlemen of the jury, the morning of September 11th , 2001, across the eastern United States was bright, clear for the most part, the air fresh, an innocence of everyday living for millions of Americans who headed to work, to school, and boarded airplane flights to reach their destinations to meet loved ones. But it was not an ordinary day. Behind the commonplace, the act of day-to-day living, there was unfolding an insidious plot designed by evil men, carried out by fanatics with no moral base for human life.

"Ladies and gentlemen, on this day, September 11th , ten years ago this year, 2,978 men, women, and yes, children died at the hands of an organization called al-Qaeda. It was horrendous pre-meditation; the attackers who learned how to fly commercial jets turned them into weapons of mass destruction. And the mastermind of the diabolic mass murder sits before you today, the defendant, the leader of al-Qaeda, Usama, or Osama bin Laden.

"We also must point out that there are more uncounted victims whose voices need to be heard. All those First Responders who may have survived trying to save those who died, but who ten years later we are finding they are doomed by respiratory diseases from the chemicals and dust spread by the tower's collapse, and by site clean-up. A poison environment was another culprit brought upon by the attackers, and sanctioned by al-Qaeda, headed, here, by *Mister* bin Laden.

"Our goal is to provide you with the facts to prove his guilt. It is your responsibility to take these truths presented and by law find him guilty of all elements of the indictment presented, including the fact that the defendant boasted of his organization's, this terrorist group's involvement, under his direction."

Matther then began a slow recitation of the history of al-Qaeda ("the base") and how in 1988, bin Laden assumed the mantle of power to focus on symbolic acts of terrorism instead of military campaigns. He sought to show the differentiation between the religions of sermons and going to Sunday schools, learning dogma and good habits of good behavior to your fellow man, and that of extremist jargon, of what a 'fatwa' meant, and the core belief of Sunni jihadists.

"These are not men believing in good deeds, but people with hatred in their hearts, who take a religion, any religion, and poison by words and pervert the minds of its followers, to preach that killing your opponents is a blessing, fighting under false banners, the worst of their teachings: 'Death to all non-believers.'"

During this part of his presentation, and to prepare the jury for the ideological speeches, Matther introduced and explained the role of the 'reader,' allowing that the defense would likewise be using their own expert in capturing the intonation and spirit of bin Laden's words. The reader, the older Arab, more like a professor, appeared on the screen, speaking bin Laden's words. He did so first in the Pashtu language, then repeated in heavily accented English:

"It is no secret to you, my brothers, that the people of Islam have been afflicted with oppression, hostility, and injustice by the Judeo-Christian alliance and its supporters. This shows our enemies' belief that Muslims' blood is the cheapest and their property and wealth are merely loot.

"Men of the radiant future of our umma of Muhammed, raise the banner of jihad up high against the Judeo-American alliance that has occupied the holy places of Islam. God told his Prophet: 'He will not let the deeds of those who are killed for His cause come to nothing. He will guide them and put them in a good state; he will admit them in the Garden. He has already made known to them'…The best martyrs are those who stay in the battleline and do not turn their faces away until they are killed… The martyr has a guarantee from God: He forgives him at the first drop of his blood and shows him his seat in Heaven. He decorates him with the jewels of faith, protects him from the torment of the grave, keeps him safe on the day of judgment, places a crown of dignity on his head with the finest rubies in the world, marries him to seventy-two of the pure virgins of paradise and intercedes on behalf of seventy of his relatives…."

Matther clicked off the video.

"We will show more of bin Laden's spoken words or quotes from those authoritative sources who guided him. But in this instance, what is being stated by the defendant is the incitement to violence. Keep that in mind as you will hear more during our direct presentation, including in his own words, admitting to these crimes."

The prosecutor, then using *The 9/11 Commission Report: Final Report of the National Commission on Terrorist Attacks Upon the United States*, summarized that sad September day in bullet points and a poignant recital of each attack element.

Towards the end of his historic recalling of events, he spoke, "I can continue with historical details, but what best expresses the impact on our national psyche as we relive what our fellow citizens faced, how they survived and died on September 11th are best expressed in their own words." With that, he clicked on the screen so all could hear the audio of voices from that day, for the court, jurors, stadium, and television, to remind them of the scope of the horror.

Message September 11 at 8:59 am

"Hey, Beverly. This is Sean. In case you get this message. Uh, there's been an explosion in World Trade 1. Uh, it's the other building. It looks like a plane struck it…um, on fire at about the 90th floor. And it's, it's horrible.

This is Sean again. Um, looks like we'll be in this tower (Trade 2) for a while."

He did not survive.

414   S.P. Grogan

"It was pitch black. I went to get up but I was literally walking over bodies. So many people died, just died at that moment." She survived.

Witness: "And while I was walking down, they [firemen] they were going up to their death. And I was walking down to live."

Flight Attendant on Board Flight 11, "I don't know, I think we're getting hijacked. The cockpit is not answering their phone. And there's somebody stabbed in business class. Our number 1 has been stabbed…and our number 5 has been stabbed…."

Flight 11 hits.
Answering: "Betty, talk to me. Betty? Betty?"

"Jules, this is Brian. Listen, I'm on an airplane that's been hijacked. If things don't go well, and it's not looking good, I just want you to know I absolutely love you. And I'll see you when…" from NBC Nightly News Report

"I want you to do good. Go have good times. Uh, same to my parents and everybody. And I just totally love you. Bye babe. I hope I call you."

From Mohamed Atta- Leader of the Flight 11 hijackers:
Atta: "We have some planes. Just stay quiet and we'll be OK. We are returning to the airport."
Controller: "And, uh, who's trying to call me here? American 11, are you trying to call?" Atta (on inner-plane speaker): "Nobody move, everything will be okay. If you try to make any moves, you will injure yourself and the airplane. Just stay quiet."

9:02 am — Flight 175 — air traffic controllers
"Hey, can you look out your window right now?"
"Can you see a guy at about 4,000 feet, about five east of the airport right now,… looks like he's — "
"Yeah, I see him."
"Do you see a guy — is he descending into the building also?"

"He's descending really quick too, yeah."

"Forty-five hundred right now, he just dropped 800 feet in like, one sweep."

"What kind of airplane is that, can you guys tell?"

"Another one just hit the building."

"Wow. Another one just hit it hard. Another one just hit the World Trade."

"The whole building just came apart."

"The Pentagon just got hit."

Telephone call from Victim in Tower 1:

"We can't find an exit; there is smoke all on one side of the building. Someone said a plane hit the building — what am I going to do? I love you. Some of us will try all the stairs; the smoke is getting bad. I love you."

Harriet felt Booker suddenly tense next to her and start to jump up with a "What the...?" Then, not knowing, she grabbed his arm and, with an effort, pulled him down to his seat.

His loud whispered growl, "That's Judy's voice!" Harriet instantly knew. Her partner's fiancée, Judith Yu, was killed in the North Tower collapse.

She matched his whisper, with her own ferocity. "Booker, he's fucking with you. Rattling you. He thinks you are going to be giving our opening. I got this."

Booker slid back in his chair, seething, staring back at a newfound nemesis as Matther concluded, "Ladies and gentlemen of the Jury, it is time to bring justice back to those innocent lives lost on September 11th. Too long in coming. All they were seeking on that beautiful day was to enjoy the American Dream, without fear." Silent steps as he returned to his seat. Then, the stadium erupted in spontaneous applause. The judge could have begun gaveling for a return to decorum, but this was good television. The applause and cheers went on for several minutes, then died off.

A hard 'act' to follow.

Scene 2: The Defense Responds
Setting: Courtroom Stadium

"Does the defense wish to make opening remarks?" questioned Judge Sanford.

"Yes, Your Honor," replied Harriet, rising, one last hand to Booker's arm, giving reassurance.

Her demeanor was not as dark as Matther's; still, her approach had intent. She had to change opinions, not accept a blanket acquittal because the evidence favored her. It did not.

She launched:

"9/11 was everything our honorable colleague said it was. Nobody will deny that mass murder took place. But…not everything in the 'why's is simple, or answers we accept that are provided in one or two succinct sentences. The Mid-East is perhaps the best example of competing interests; what is one's perception is not another's, where people and governments forge alliances, then change sides and later switch again; where propaganda is truth, and lies might become history from only one narrator. What you, what all of us have received are 'impressions' of the person who is on trial.

"That is not enough, nor what is asked of you. You have sworn a duty to listen to the facts presented here, even to hear and listen to the facts from our position of believing in innocence. By your oath, the U.S. military or highly charged media headlines of ten years ago, even yesterday, bear little weight. Only the facts presented. It is our belief in the American judicial system that you will reach an honest verdict.

"Our case, as we will present it, is to form an understanding of a man with deep religious convictions who was betrayed by his own country, who sought meaning and found a cause rooted in his personal religion, and sought to throw off the yoke of a brutal foreign government, the USSR. When that empire was defeated in Afghanistan with the help of his humanitarian efforts, he could not rest because a coalition of countries decided to impose their economic interests on various regional countries he perceived as the downtrodden. This was what he believed. Fighting back, we tend to see the revolution or war from the 30,000-foot view and not perhaps wonder at the defining role of character — of family and home life. It will be his family of 22 children which clears our vision and allows us to show you the real Sheik Osama bin Laden. Not the man of headlines or propaganda, nor even that of his own press releases conceived to attract fans and followers. There is something more to the story, and we ask you to remain open-minded in your decision-making. We have faith, as you should, in how we seek out justice that has made this country's legal systems the best in the world. Thank you for your service."

Harriet returned to her seat. Booker gave her a positive congratulatory look, something the jury took in as they turned back to the judges.

Scene 3: Foundational Witnesses
Setting: Stadium Courtroom

"Is the prosecution ready to begin?"

"We are, Your Honor," said Cotton Matther. The first witness was called.

The prosecution's strategy was to build a foundation.

The initial witness was a survivor from the South Tower. Lucky for her, she was a paralegal on one of the lower floors. Still, her testimony was riveting, especially when many of her attorney supervisors had told her it would be best to stay at her desk and let the elevators and stairways be left open for the firefighters. She only fled with several female co-workers when one of the elevators was heard crashing through the shaft on a fatal plunge. She admitted to her fear and panic and became teary-eyed, asking for tissues as she concluded her story.

Testifying next was the retired Assistant Battalion Chief from New York City Fire Department Ladder Company 3, which took the heaviest casualties among all firefighters who died on September 11th. The firehouse, located on 108 E. 13th Street covering Manhattan's East Village, had two crews going into a shift rotation when the morning alarm call came in, so those who usually went home to families stayed and went to help at the Towers. The Chief, trying to be factual in his account, choked up, saying that the communications he had with those on the scene reported Captain Patrick Brown and his men had climbed to the 35th floor of the North Tower when it collapsed. Being one of the few survivors of a well-honed team leaves ashamed guilt, and remorse when thinking of fellow lost heroes.

Reporters listening gleaned two ironic comments. First, the Ladder 3 Company was founded on September 11th, 1865, and second, one of their surviving ladder trucks, stored for over ten years, was to be part of the exhibit in the new 9/11 Memorial and Museum, which would be dedicated this coming September 11, 2011.

The defense was cognizant that any intrusive cross-examination might lead the jury to see them as callous.

Attorney Langston put only brief questions to both witnesses.

"When September 11th occurred and for a week afterward, did you have the name of the individual who might have led or created the attacks at the World Trade Center?"

"No, I did not," said both in one fashion or the other, the former assistant fire chief only quickly added. "Not until later did we hear a name…but had no real official confirmation."

Prosecutor Matther saw no reason to ask follow-up questions to establish the purported name of the alleged ringleader. The jury knew the unnamed name.

418   S.P. Grogan

These two witnesses took the afternoon to its close of the first day. The judge suggested they adjourn for the day. Matther said that his witnesses would be ready for the morning. The defense had no issues, so the jury was excused with the mandatory warnings of not discussing matters of testimony, nor reading or speaking to any outside party, including family members, by phone, as they all would be sequestered at the stadium site and guarded. All rose, except bin Laden, as the jury and then the judges exited, and the defendant was led to his elevator and he descended from sight, listening again to muted 'boos' as he disappeared.

The courtroom was soon empty of the remaining participants. Stadium music played as the onlookers moved towards the exits to find restaurants or campsites and eventual sleep, as the next day had already been promoted as the prosecution's main case.

Scene 4: Quick Observations
Setting: Around the Stadium

Callie, from her seat watching the audience depart and having had two television seasons of her show behind her, part of her career, or as they say on her 'resume reels,' understood the pace of what she saw today and imparted that to Samantha.

"Damn, if they didn't program a minute to two-minute commercial breaks between lawyer opening remarks, judge's rulings, and witness testimony. Came across as seamless. Seems like Hugh is learning how to manage a Five Aces Studioz production. As long as he is not turning into President Snow of *Hunger Games*, a master manipulator of pre-planned action."

"What is '*Hunger Games?*" queried Samantha, fashion magazine consumer, not until now a reader of action novels.

"Best-selling book, movie coming out next year. Dystopian novel of an annual game of young people killing each other off to become a winner and gain food and fame, but in the end, no one mentally wins except our independent archer killer heroine, a teenager named Katniss who has two men competing for her, and could care less."

Like her already."

Razzor Hassim was walking to the shuttle that would take him and Maj to the outlying parking lots: "I have an idea. Let's see if we can pull it off and see where it leads."

"Is there anything else you need?" Wendell's question to Osama while bringing him to his 'hotel room' style prison cell suite for the evening.

"Can you find me a few Mr. Bean comedy shows? They're distracting."

"See what I can do. That's right; you do like VHS, and especially your action thrillers. Tom Clancy, Le Carri, Tanenbaum, a lot of best-selling terrorist plots to watch and read about." He saw a pause in bin Laden's step. "Oh, yes, we guessed they are *Crimson Scimitar* planning guides." Whether true or not, the premise was yet unproven, but why not indeed play a little psyche-ops on the guy; he was going nowhere. Interrogation-Lite.

No response from bin Laden as he retrieved a can of Saudi Arabian 'Mirinda Citrus' (Hamdiyat) drink from the refrigerator. Holmes would have only offered bottled water and dried naan bread, but Hugh Fox believed in quality accommodation and service for the 'condemned' or rather the 'defendant.'

"You CIA clowns think you're so smart," bin Laden reclined on the sofa, looking for his remote channel changer.

"Sorry, it's the *King's Retribution* team that's on to you. We'll figure out this next 'big show' plot in a few days. No worries, or I guess, you should be worried."

"Wendell, I don't know what you are talking about. All I can say is that Allah's will shall be revealed in a timely fashion for the world to see."

Holmes had pushed as far as he wanted and shifted subjects.

"I hope you feel your attorneys have Allah behind them. They're going to need Him."

"Actually, I thought I would be a character in some sort of al-Aragoz theater (puppetry), but they seem competent."

"Take it from me, and not something I want to admit, but Osama, they are going to do their damn best to represent you, but I don't believe finding you innocent is anywhere in Allah's bag of tricks."

"Don't forget Mr. Bean, any you can find?"

"We'll see. No promises. Good night." The door closed on the prisoner.

After the first moment of silence, he threw his empty soda can across the room and cursed Khalaf. *They know about the books and movies! How? Have you betrayed me?*

Early evening, the new Director of the CIA, the Head of Homeland Security, and the Head of the FBI held what could be a 'top secret' clandestine briefing with no transcription taken of the meeting. An aide showed recorded television highlights of the first day spliced together

From Homeland Security as their consensus summary: "Let's see if there is a quiet way to help the prosecutor lock in his verdict. Get this charade over with."

"The weather forecast says a chance of afternoon scattered rain showers tomorrow."

"God's will be done." intoned Pastor Tate, hobbling on his crutches towards his church's rented camper van and the barbecue grill smoking hot dogs and buffalo burgers for him and his three 'apostles'.

Scene 5: The Reading Club Meeting
Setting: Stadium basement

The attempt to gather together a 'reading club for new clues' by going over all the possible books found in Ali Baba's hidden room was not so much a fiasco as it was not prioritized to the other excitement of *The Trial of the Century* now in progress.

Disorganization proceeded.

The first thirty minutes consisted of a discussion of what happened on the first day, comments on the Stadium events, chatter stories of what they saw out among the crowd, and jokes about the slogan banners that were waved about — like an NFL playoff game displaying fan passions.

In an attempt to see who had read what, and their impressions, they found most had not completed their reading assignments. Again, too much other stuff happening. Admonishments were given to all to spend their nights reading the books taken from the raided compound in Pakistan.

Hugh Fox made a quick entry, asking how it was going, receiving glares from Callie and Samantha and a non-committal re-statement from Holmes, "Something is here; I know it. Even bin Laden this evening inferred as much." Fox soon departed after receiving several calls of perceived showmanship issues that threatened everything towards the next day of the trial's production values.

Someone asked where Pacheco was, and the gossip soon revealed that Fox, who had just left and probably knew the story, had asked Pacheco to miss everything in Colorado and be in California to work on a special *King's Retribution* project. Hush-hush.

'Bummer for him to miss all this,' someone's opinion.

In the end, they all promised to do better at looking at their reading lists. The Skilleo Team of Gizmo and other computer jocks were to use the days working on cataloging which book titles they might be able to enhance from the compound photos. The nights would find them in the Skilleo Game Centers at the Stadium, detached from reality, lost in their world of competitive gameplay.

The reading club adjourned. All were exhausted from the first day, and all would soon be in bed by themselves, which spoke much to the confusing times and stress they faced.

All they knew, as Holmes repeated, 'something was there, there.'

EPISODE TWENTY-SIX — The Second Day

Scene 1: The Sign
Setting: The Stadium Courtroom

Sheik bin Laden listened to the prosecution's first witness of the day drone on about the history of al Qaeda. Not interested in opinionated lies, he felt that he and the defense could agree on one truth: Cotton Matther was a pompous ass, a strutting peacock. He found himself doodling with the paper and marker, nothing critical that might be captured by the camera always focused on him.

Back in his 'cell,' he had begun preparing notes to pontificate a new manifesto if they were really going to give him an opportunity to state his views publicly, perhaps for the last time. He knew the U.S. government would not have let him reach the outside world, so for this freedom of speech, he was halfway grateful to this capitalist Hugh Fox, though no enemy would ever gain his full appreciation.

He let his eyes wander beyond the dome. Yesterday, he did not make eye contact with those in the mob seated around the stadium, not eager to set them off with their blood-lust shrills, pointing at him as a baited lion being teased behind zoo bars. He laughed to himself over the screamers at the far end of the stadium, those waving crude homemade posters and placards — he could not read any of them! The joke's on you!

Closer in, some signs said, as expected, that he deserved his fate to be meted out in horrible punishment. One sign said — bin Laden froze in recognition — one sign was in Arabic!

يوم النصر *On the day of victory*...his jihadist recognition code of ten years back! He stared, not believing, more confused, that those holding the small banner were...two small American kids with sports logo ball caps with embroidered initials *CR*. He then noted beneath the code words were, in English, *You Will Get Yours!* He got it — deflection of attention by disguise.

His people were here! To do what? Explode a bomb or attempt to free him? No, impossible. Even he knew the protection in the stadium, of him, the object of their 'show trial,' was severe. Such security against suicide bombers would force attacks on the outside of the stadium, away from the cameras, and not do enough damage to shock the American public, not like *Crimson Scimitar* will do. He took a deep breath and analyzed.

His people here were from the *Crimson Scimitar* team, and though their originally planned attack was their primary objective, trying to free him would be a slap in the face to his capturers, further proof that al-Qaeda had its grasping tentacles everywhere. Even if an attempt were made to free him, that attempt would focus the CIA and law enforcement back on the Colorado area and not at the Bridge. *You will get yours.*

422 S.P. Grogan

For the first time since his capture, he felt a return of self-confidence. He was their leader. Time to re-assert his power and control over the organization he led and would rebuild. Only he could be there when *Crimson Scimitar* succeeded. Only he could speak for al-Qaeda, the Arab World, and the new Emirate. All was possible.

He considered his dilemma and found he was not happy with his thinking, tinged with jealousy, for he had wondered: How would Khalaf use his special tools to create an extraordinary plan?

Osama bin Laden began writing on the paper in front of him.

Scene 2: Writing on the Wall
Setting: Stadium Courtroom

Harriet had been taking notes on the first two witnesses of the day, again mostly background, heading towards evidence presented against their client.

The retired military officer gave a political overview of the Middle East and the various political entities and revolutionary groups. His presentation was short, with more bullet points, and provided a few maps on the screen that were meant to give the jury a basic understanding of the countries and where many of the players came from.

Matther also used him as the expert on the attackers of 9/11. The officer noted that fifteen of the nineteen 9/11 attackers were from Saudi Arabia, two from UAE, one from Lebanon, and one from Egypt.

"And," asked Matther, "who were these perpetrators affiliated with?"

"The militant Islamist group al-Qaeda."

"And who was the leader of al-Qaeda at the time?"

"Osama bin Laden."

"Objection," defense attorney Langston did not even arise, "Foundation. We have yet to hear factual evidence of who was the leader at this time."

"Your Honors, we were proceeding in that direction," Matthers did not like his examination being interrupted when he was building to the crescendo. Booker had figured him out a long time ago, in a New York court many years back when they tangled. He could be rattled.

"Objection over-ruled. We will see if we are being led to the answer," ruled Judge Sanford.

Matther asked the question of the witness he should have perhaps led off with.

"Are you familiar with the *9/11 Commission's Final Report*? A copy I will now enter as our exhibit." With fanfare, an exhibit sticker was affixed to the hefty book by the court clerk.

"Have you read this book?"

"Many times, yes."

"Would it be correct that you actually helped to collate the evidence as part of the Commission's work in bringing it to publication?

"Did you also testify in part of the Commission's findings on some of the footnote preparations?"

"Yes to both."

"From your familiarity with this document, who does the Commission state was the head of al-Qaeda at the time of 9/11?"

"Osama bin Laden."

"No further questions." Matther gave a smug smile to Booker and passed the baton for cross-examination.

"Just one question." Booker rose and approached the witness.

"Isn't it true that the FBI and CIA, prior to the 9/11 attacks, had information that might have thwarted the hijackings?"

The witness digested the question, formulating his response.

"There were several incidences where information was misinterpreted or not exchanged between agencies. But whether having any pre-evidence would have led to a conclusion of pending attacks would be speculation on my part."

"By speculation, then, one might construe U.S. Federal Agencies were aware that an attack was going to occur and did nothing?"

"Objection!" Matther rose indignantly and was forced to use the word he didn't want to use. "Speculation. No evidence offered to suggest such an outlandish assertion."

Before the judge could knock him down, Booker gave a resigned nod and said, "I withdraw my last question, Your Honor." And returned to his seat, looking abashed but not rebuked.

"Doubt, create doubt," he whispered to Harriet.

The next witness was live up on the screen, not present in the courtroom. It was the Arab scholar who, as a translator even with coat and tie, had at least a beard, the only semblance to bin Laden and was supposed to speak in bin Laden's voice of past writings, tying him to the encouragement of terrorism. Instead, prosecutor Matther wove a different story, that the jury and audience would be listening to the writings of Abdullah Yusuf Azzam, a Palestinian theologian, the father of global jihad, and bin Laden's spiritual teacher.

424 S.P. Grogan

By questions made to the scholar, as foundational to his readings, the jury were informed that bin Laden had been a student at King Abdul Aziz University in Jeddah, Saudi Arabia, from 1976 to 1981 and would have listened to Azzam's lectures. It was Azzam who first preached for a pan-Islam trans-national movement, the future Caliphate, that bin Laden embraced so publicly. They were also unaware until this testimony that it was Azzam who encouraged bin Laden to help him support the Afghan mujahideen when the Soviet Union invaded Afghanistan in 1979 [see Holmes's Story]. Azzam, who had a Ph.D. in *Principles of Islamic Jurisprudence* (1973), began teaching in 1981 at the International Islamic University, Islamabad, Pakistan. Bin Laden, now a novice revolutionary, listened again to Azzam's lectures.

Even when Azzam went to the United States in the 1980s on a whirlwind fundraising tour and preached the value of jihad against the Soviet Union (America's perceived threat at the time) — and gained a sympathetic ear — it is evidenced that Osama bin Laden made his first trip to America to assist in Azzam's travels, and by this time was thoroughly indoctrinated as a jihadist.

The scholar read passages from several of Azzam's books (he wrote over 100 books and major treatises on the validity of global jihad).

Matther was showing bin Laden as an accomplice to violent philosophies. Know the mind, understand the actions.

Among the writings selected, the scholar quoted Azzam: *'Muslims do not have to stop an attack if women and children are present.'* And Azzam's slogan: *'Jihad and the rifle alone: no negotiations, no conferences, and no dialogues.'*

Harriet moved her view from the large courtroom screen and lyrical Arab words as the scholar read from Azzam's 1979 classic, *Defense of the Muslim Lands*. She saw bin Laden mouthing certain passages, memorized verbatim. She noted a sudden look on his face as if a magical idea had been imparted from the assassinated jihadist theorist. Bin Laden began to scribble, a rarity for him.

In 1989, as testimony was elicited, Azzam was killed in a careful and targeted roadside car bomb that killed him and his sons. The assassins were unknown and still unsolved to this day, but the suspect list was long, filled with Muslim political groups, if not the Israelis or the CIA. So, she mused, and guessed who benefited and became the anointed successor and leader of al Qaeda? Our client.

Matther was now going through a bibliography of Azzam's writings, putting them in sequence, then placing selected passages into evidence, with the prosecution's scholar reading them. The last readings were from Azzam's *The Signs of the Merciful in the Jihad in Afghan* (also stated in a later edited English version as *Ayat al-Rahman fee Jihad al-Afghan (God's Signs in the Afghan Jihad)* that wove his evangelistic support with a fundraising call to help against the Soviets. The idea sought to build the confidence of the Afghan mujahideen by portraying them as super-heroes, invincible against the enemy by the battlefield miracles he had heard, with witness testimony: scorpions that did not sting the Muslim fighters; corpses of martyrs that did not decay; fog that arrived to shield the Afghan and Arab fighters; enemy rounds that did not explode. Azzam writes: *"The liberation that placing your individual fate in God's hands that jihad provides liberating the believer from the shackles of material endeavors..."*

Harriet came alert. The scholar had stopped talking and looked to his side. Cotton Matther, questioning, followed his witness's gaze. Both men were looking at the defendant, then to the screen, and back again at the man in the glass box. The camera had shifted for a close-up.

Sheik Osama bin Laden held up two sheets of paper against the barrier, facing outward, so the courtroom, the world, and certain special people could see and read.

أنا لست متعب

II جراد البحر

يطلب

Scene 3: Is there a Translator in the Audience
Setting: Stadium VIP Box

"What the fuck?" Callie said to Samantha.

Hugh, sitting with them, started to reply, but his production phone rang.

"What do you want me to do?" wailed the floor producer, "Do you want me to cut the feed?"

Judge Sanford, perplexed but a judicial trooper, broke the silence in the courtroom and the mumbling in the stadium of the querulous: What was this?

"Since it is almost lunchtime, I think we will take a break. And while we are out, if the defense could instruct their client, if he wishes to communicate with you, that is what the yellow button in his cubicle is for, attracting your attention. Not paper notes. We don't need unwarranted interruptions. Court is in recess for one hour and a half."

"Break to commercial," instructed Fox. The jury and then the judges filed out, all looking back at the defendant and his small 'messages.' When bin Laden saw the stadium screens flash to a musical group singing and dancing, he put down the papers, and for once in a long while, he smiled with feeling. The prosecutor smiled his patented 'gotcha.' The defense team was

426   S.P. Grogan

floored, their expressions masked but certainly not seeing this as anything positive for their side.

For all, consternation, bafflement, and questions were the primary lunchtime topics. The trial, of course, had been seen as unique, having an actual court trial a watchable curiosity, but here was a surprise within a television show, and every era of viewers saw it differently. It was the reveal on *I've Got a Secret, Groucho's Secret Word;* and *Who Gets the Bachelor's rose.* Many who absorbed TV game shows like crack cocaine thought bin Laden was throwing out a Lifeline like in *Who Wants to Be a Millionaire?* But to whom? Two things the audience realized: bin Laden was coming awake and participating, and two, this *Trial of the Century* was unscripted unlike most reality television — thus, anything could happen.

Hugh Fox should have been elated, expecting viewership to soar when word spread of the — what? — the mystery message, a red herring? But he was flummoxed. He did feel he had coordinated basic scenes where actor movements were blocked out, following a rough script where ad lib and extemporaneous could occur with spontaneity, but not this, not events out of his control.

He finally regained composure and went to his phone. "Find our bin Laden look-alike."

Everyone in the VIP lounge sat, waited, and noshed at the luncheon buffet table.

Wendell Holmes returned from delivering his charge to his guarded quarters.

"Our guest is having lamb kabsa with garlic hummus dip for today's entrée."

"What's kabsa?" asked Bennie, munching cold shrimp from a large bowl.

"It's a national communal dish of Saudi Arabia. But, in this case, for him, without the 'communal.'

"Also, I heard from Booker that Judge Sanford expressed a firm warning to him, Booker, Harriet, and Matther, about trial disruption. She does not know, like us, what bin Laden was conveying, but said if it was an attempt to influence a jury, Osama could watch the proceedings from his plush hidey-hole for the rest of the trial. I know Osama likes the crowd he's attracting, probably even a new fan base when televised to the Middle East. Harriet told her client he was risking any public statement he would be allowed to read. For what it's worth, he gave his famous nod of understanding. So, what about what he wrote?"

As if on cue, the look-alike entered, shy if not nervous, at being before this prestigious crowd of TV stars and a wealthy games tech guru, one of his heroes.

Hugh Fox didn't mince words, no friendly intros. Instead, he clicked on the VIP box's television screens, and bin Laden's message popped up. He had been taping his own show independently from the audience stream.

"I don't know."

"What?!"

"Makes no sense," said the wannabe actor, now believing his acting career might be tanked.

Wendell intervened.

"Help us here. Three lines. First line says…?

"I am not tired."

A pause from the group. He, or bin Laden is 'not tired.' He understood.

"Bin Laden said, 'He is not tired.'

"And the second line, that reads…."

"Really weird…"

"Go on — ."

"Crayfish."

"*Crayfish* in Arabic?" Callie's questioned response.

"Crayfish like the little mini-lobster?" Abbas did not speak Arabic. He might look like someone from that part of the world, but he was Persian, brought to LA as a five-year-old when his family fled Iran with the Shah's fall and the Ayatollah's rise. He didn't need this job; his family was now wealthy in high-end coastal suburban real estate. His two brothers, both realtors, had their own *Flip This Million Dollar House* reality television show, selling home security services during commercials. But this was an action job, and his family was proud of him.

"You mean like one of these?" Bennie, from the buffet, held up a small crayfish used as a cold seafood platter garnishment.

"I guess," said the look-alike bin Laden.

"My grandparents called them 'crawdads,' said Wendell.

"Enough," said Hugh. "Are those letters or numbers next to the Arabic two I's or the number eleven?

"Or the Roman numeral '2'?" questioned Samantha, "And since we are crazed to know, line number three, I'm afraid to ask, what's that say?

It's the Arabic word for "ask.' Like 'ask me the question.'"

"Indubitably," said Samantha, motioning the catering staff to bring her a glass of white wine for her lunch.

Fox ruminated in exasperation, "Ask. Ask K. Who's K?"

428 S.P. Grogan

Scene 4: Call out for a Lifeline
Setting: The Waldorf Hotel, New York City

Razzor Hassim had heard of 'K,' of how he fit into the larger equation, mostly what Shahin had recently relayed to him, bringing him up-to-date on how the Nevada and New York components of *Crimson Scimitar* came to be. Razzor was not happy. He put in a call to Shahin's burner phone. Shahin was quite upset. Still, reaching out to K was essential, and the call would be made.

Khalaf, like the curious and television-sated world, had been glued to the TV, watching the *Trial of the Century*. Sabz, not that interested, had her head on his lap, reading the Fashion-Entertainment Section from the *New York Times* Sunday edition.

When they had arrived in New York, and after both slept in separate bedrooms the first night, she had realized that he might not come back from any trips taken away from the city on his secret project. She liked him. He had gotten her this far to a new life, away from danger. She could not hold her body hostage against his desires. Her debate within was of short duration. As Lord Byron once wrote: 'A little still she strove, and much repented — And whispering, 'I will ne'er consent' — consented."

Thus, she had not gotten around to all the glitzy fashion magazines for the last several days, having participated in marathon sex romps to please her husband's appetite. She was not unhappy, as she had read enough online and watched one restricted television channel to gain an idea how to achieve multiple orgasms and where he must specifically touch her, even chiding him, 'want me, think of my needs.'

Having 'consented' she was pleased with her New York stay; she could keep herself busy while her 'lover'(?), boyfriend (?), went to his business meetings or found a stock brokerage office to gain, as he said, 'knowledge on market plays.' He even bought several books on how to become wealthy playing the stock market. Even Sabz had been glancing inside the pages of graphs and charts. Numbers excited her like this new found sex and the multitude of clothes stores who treated her, with her own credit card, like a princess.

Whatever he was reading, or his television business news shows, or the rolling around, sweating, at least with her, his mood now satisfied, produced a pleased man and an upbeat verve, even charming, she thought, not so stern-faced. *This is the life,* Sabz thought, nestling against him, but a dark cloud hovered in the distance. She wanted to ignore the impending gloom. This leisure, a comfort of security, could go no further, it would not last, and she dared not ask to see the future. She must accept what is and enjoy each day at a time. Make the most. Pray to Allah.

She felt a sudden tensing of his body, rigid. He sat up; she pulled herself up next to him, worried. She glanced at the TV and saw the words on the screen.

"What's wrong, dear Khalaf? Have you seen an evil Jinn, a Ghul? And what is that on the television? It is Arabic. What does it mean?"

"It is a message. For me." He rose, nearly panicked. Back and forth, striding across the room. "What's it mean? Why me?"

She looked at him now with genuine fear. All that was safe might be at risk. And this fear, not so much for herself, but for the first time, she worried for him, not for her needs; yes, her needs perhaps, she wanted him, her affection had been growing over the weeks. Sincere desire. But what is this about? What message? From whom? A commercial came on.

The telephone rang. His cell phone in the suite's bedroom. His second phone, not his business phone, but a special phone given to him in London by the banker. For special use.

Khalaf hurried to retrieve it. Sabz's anxiety for them both; *it was a Ghul*, she knew.

Khalaf talked in Arabic with curt replies; all phone conversations still with obtuse paranoia.

"Yes. Yes, I saw. No idea. Yes, that line must be for me. I know; let me think. Can you call back in one hour?" He held the phone from his ear as a loud curse was heard. "One hour." The phone clicked dead.

"What is it, my darling?"

"The Caliph, my Sheik, in the midst of a trial where he will be condemned to death, has sent a message for me, but I don't know what he means. I must think. He went over and, pulling out hotel stationery, wrote in big letters:

II جراد البحر

Crayfish II

Beneath that, as thousands of puzzle solvers around the world were doing at about the same time, he wrote:

II 2 11 ii

After twenty minutes of staring, with Sabz sitting uncomfortably, turning pages but not reading, Khalaf said to her, "Look here, you went to the university. Do you see anything mathematical in the name, any letter configuration to a number that might be created? A code? A cipher?"

She had played with the small laptop he had bought her to play games on when he was not around. Instead, she had wandered as a child in the internet toy store, everywhere,

430   S.P. Grogan

learning, soaking in the lives of other cultures. Fashions, and yes, how to buy stocks. If he was interested, she ought to be a helpmate.

After ten minutes, "I came up with an anagram of crayfish — Sharif. You are Egyptian; wasn't there an actor like ...."

"Omar Sharif, yes."

"Oh, yes, Doctor Zhivago."

"And *Lawrence of Arabia*. But I never showed Calif bin Laden those movies."

"Movies? You watched movies with your hero, bin Laden? I am so envious. Let's go to a movie here or even a play? One of these Broadway musicals. I would much enjoy seeing *The Lion King*."

He had forgotten that he would say nothing to her of his 'library' and its contents, but it did not matter now, and his mind was elsewhere, running scenarios. It had to be something bin Laden had seen with or without him. With him, something new, one of Khalaf's selections. Without him, something his Sheik might have enjoyed earlier than my presence on the scene. Yes, perhaps while bin Laden was in the University, even earlier, when he was young. Impressionable times. What was in my closet library that I have not seen, but he might have, even in a movie theater as a teenager? And then later, he maybe picked up a copy as a favorite. I've watched them all, but this might not have been important to include in *Crimson Scimitar* plans. He grew frustrated. Was it instead a book?

Khalaf closed his eyes and started indexing in his mind, shelf by shelf, going through all the books and videos he had accumulated, what was acquired, some by bin Laden's direction, including the silly Mr. Bean shows the family liked to watch — he would let the children watch comedies, slapstick, and the adults watched action and war movies, but not anything truly gratuitously violent; those were rare — like....

Sabz walked over and picked up the Fashion-Entertainment sections she had been reading. She would show him the *Lion King* advertisement. When she returned, she looked down at the desk, back at the words on the paper.

"Have you tried 'separation'? She picked up the hotel logo pen and wrote Cray fish in Arabic, then English, and she separated the II to I I.

"Perhaps it is not a number or letters, but maybe it suggests two of the same thing. Two fish, or, and I don't know, two cray?"

Khalaf stared at the stationery and his writing, her writing, then stared at her. He was smart, but she was brain smart; where the math could work the abstract, it all clicked. Not what it meant, but where it directed him to consider. His mentor loved the misdirection of war. The answer had lain behind the word, not by meaning, but by inference that led to a story, that led to…. What could be done with what he now knew, he had no idea.

With a whoop of joy, يصرخ من شدة الفرح, he jumped up and twirled Sabz, her newspaper scattered to the floor. He hugged and then kissed her quickly, and then looking into those fathomless eyes, his mouth lingered on hers.

The phone rang. Time had raced only to a half hour gone. Anxious conspirators sought to move unspoken events along.

He answered. She saw his strength. She admired people who were strong in their own minds.

He could not contain himself. "Yes. Yes, I do know. But to let you know, when my task is completed here, I will be coming to help you all on your venture."

There was grumbling on the other end. "I insist," he said. Her lover was strong, bargaining from a position of strength. He knew the answer. There was grumbling in her heart; he was to leave her on his damn jihadist mission. If he died, where would she be?

"Thank you. May Allah bless our endeavors." Pause. "It's an old movie," Khalaf explained what he had found. Maybe this man, Razzor, who's been in America for more than a decade, hopefully, he or Shahin knew what to do with the information.

When he put the phone down, there was a smile of accomplishment. His glance at her spoke of resolve.

"*Lion King*," but bed first."

Sabz thought it a fair exchange.

Scene 5: From his own mouth, sort of
Setting: The Stadium

The afternoon session resumed. Bin Laden sat stoically on his best behavior. With little movement, his eyes wandered back to the small banner. The kids were still there, now bored from holding the sign. One of their parents waved it carelessly as part of the cheering and then put it down as she sipped some drink in a paper cup.

The opposing sides in place in the courtroom rose as protocol dictated as the judges and jury were seated. He paid close attention to that section of the stadium. He saw what he was looking for taped to a railing on an upper-level balcony, all in English. And he recognized the error, the message back to him.

We know and will remember 9/11/2011

432   S.P. Grogan

Not 2001, not looking back, but looking forward. By that message, his part of any upcoming plan was understood. He must be prepared, from any direction, at any time. They were going to do something to free him. May Allah give them courage.

Strange notions crossed his mind. *If their plan succeeds with my idea, then I will be able to personally lead Crimson Scimitar. If it were to be so, and yes, what a surprise for Wendell Holmes and all his blasphemous ilk.*

Sheik Osama bin Laden leaned back in his chair, listening to the continuing evidence presented. He looked to the sky and saw scattered dark clouds over the mountains. Was it going to rain today?

"It looks like the storm cells are moving directly west," commented one of Pastor Tate's followers. They gazed upward and agreed. Tate's three followers, his apostles or deacons, who had accompanied him, assisted him with his crutches to navigate the elevator to their high vantage point and helped him hop down the few steps and work his way into the middle seats of the row. All four of them could see the storm lodged on Pike's Peak, providing summer theatrics of lightning, but the other storm, a microburst, had moved between Colorado Springs and the Air Force Academy and was blowing out to the plains and dissipating, a welcome relief for the farmers and ranchers, their crops and the growing hay to be cut and baled for the cattle. Not so for Pastor Tate.

"I will pray tonight for Noah's deluge."

Judge Behan, one of the three judges on the trial bench, the one handling the flow of the trial and acceptance of the documents, and the scheduling of time allotted to keep with the conclusion on Friday, July 29th, added the next layer into *The Trial of the Century*.

"We expect, Counselor, that you will be finished with your primary case this afternoon?"

"Yes, that is our hope also, Your Honor."

"After the defense cross-examines, we will have allowed each side to present what one might call a 'Final Witness Presentation.'

Prosecutor Matther quickly reached the apex of his case, using the translator scholar to read into the record various speeches and writings where Osama bin Laden spoke of his violence of war, especially against Western targets.

The culmination of these was a video presentation by bin Laden.

"Ladies and gentlemen of the jury, I would like to draw your attention to a video provided to the Al Jazeera news channel on October 29th, 2004, in which the defendant addressed the people of the U.S." A photograph of bin Laden appeared on the screen. He was dressed in a tan and yellow robe against a brown, nondescript background. The screen split, and the face of the prosecution's scholar reappeared. He read the following:

"You, the American people. I talk to you today about the best way to avoid another catastrophe and about war, its reasons, and its consequences. Although we are ushering in the fourth year after 9/11, Bush is still exercising confusion and misleading you and not telling you the true reason. We never knew that the commander-in-chief of the American armed forces would leave 50,000 [bin Laden's error, 17,400 more accurate] of his people in the two towers to face those events by themselves when they were in the most urgent need of their leader. Your security is not in the hands of Kerry or Bush, or Al-Qaeda. Your security is in your own hands. Any nation that does not attack us will not be attacked."

When the reading finished, Booker noted that the scholar had obviously been told to elevate the emphasis of words to the shrill annunciation as an impassioned orator might foment a rabble.

Matther then asked his witness, "Professor, what you read, is that not a confession?"

"Objection," Harriet took the lead this time, "This calls for a conclusion when we previously had a ruling from you that the 'reader' would not be called to testify as an 'expert witness.'

Matther responded, "Your Honor, we are asking a witness to give an observation of opinion as to how the speech given by the defendant should be interpreted by any educated citizen who might hear it."

Judge Sanford gave thought.

"As long as it is a general observation and does not extend into trying to divine the meaning, the reading must speak for itself."

Matther took this as approval and restated his question.

"In reading this, what is your general observation on what the defendant said about the attack on the twin towers."

The professor, a paid consultant, knew what was expected of him.

"It seems to me that he is saying that al Qaeda attacked the buildings in New York City."

"Thank you. No more questions. The prosecution rests."

"Your Honor, we intend to cross-examine this witness under the same guidance you gave our colleague, that is, not seeking an expert opinion, but questions on the materials he read or did not read."

Matther hesitated, ready to reply, his face contorted. This was not in *his* game plan. He sat slowly.

Judge Sanford, "Keep it narrow, counselor."

"Yes, Your Honor."

434   S.P. Grogan

She stood in front of the defense desk and addressed the professor.

"Professor, let me play an excerpt from the speech that you recited." Immediately, on the split screen, the actual video with bin Laden appeared, and for the first time, the jurors and audience heard the defendant's voice in Arabic, only speaking for about 15 seconds.

"Is that indeed the voice of our client, Sheik bin Laden?" questioned Harriet.

"Yes, it is."

"But to me, it seems his intonation seems more calm than robust as you portrayed him?"

"I interpreted his words as I heard them." The professor sought a defensive role.

"And would you say you only read about three sentences of his speech? How long was his video speech?"

The professor paused, then admitted, "The speech was about 15 minutes."

And you read it all, and specific passages were selected versus other passages. Correct?"

"Yes. I was directed to do so." Harriet let that answer lie, to grow in the minds of the jury.

"And if we were to hear the entire speech, wasn't then the context, as you read it, actually a political speech made in October, designed to make an impact in the 2004 national election between President Bush and Senator Kerry?"

"He did refer to that election." The professor was now wary.

"Let's hear how Sheik bin Laden opened his speech in English." Immediately the screen split and the defense's look-alike appeared as a cleric, showing some mannerisms that might be construed as being tics of the defendant. Then, the actor began speaking, calmly in Arabic, then repeated in English.

"Praise be to Allah who created the creation for his worship and commanded them to be just and permitted the wronged one to retaliate against the oppressor in kind. To proceed: Peace be upon he who follows the guidance: People of America, this talk of mine is for you and concerns the ideal way to prevent another Manhattan and deals with the war and its causes and results. Before I begin, I say to you that security is an indispensable pillar of human life and that free men do not forfeit their security, contrary to Bush's claim that we hate freedom."

The look-alike bin Laden spoke in a quiet, slow cadence that seemed to match the video's bin Laden's demeanor versus the rushed, elevated professor's screed of moments earlier.

Harriet returned to the prosecution's professor.

"In the video you quoted from, and from the excerpt you just heard, bin Laden spoke of 'preventing another Manhattan.' Did you hear a confession in that statement? Could not another person interpret that as one political person speaking on how to avoid trouble versus someone issuing a threat? Could not several interpretations come from what was just heard by both of you?"

"I am not sure, perhaps."

"Thank you, no more questions of this witness."

"Mr. Matther, any rebuttal examination?"

The prosecutor wasn't sure if there was anything to gain, and his concern was that he would open up the professor to more challenges as a potential 'expert.'

"No, Your Honor, the prosecution still rests."

Judge Sanford turned to the defense.

"Will you be ready to open your case-in-chief tomorrow at 10 a.m.?

Harriet nodded; Booker said, "We will be ready."

Judge Sanford turned to her counterpart, Judge Georgia 'Skye' Raven, who looked to both defense and prosecution with a glance to the jury.

"By our schedule, tomorrow we will hear the defense make its presentations. On the following day, Day Four, both prosecution and defense will each have the chance to present your new and last witness, a 'surprise witness,' so to speak. Each of you will have the right to cross-examine the other's witness. Then, if there is time in the afternoon, we will hear closing arguments, and then jury instructions and the jury will retire to render their verdict." Judge Raven motioned to the court clerk, who produced two large envelopes, and delivered them to Prosecutor Matther and Defense Langston.

Pure television theatrics. Like the Oscar ceremony letter-opening for winners, the envelopes were opened with dramatic flair. Booker handed the envelope over to Harriet to do the honors. Though she sought to give an impassive look at the name within, the camera recorded instead a facial shock. She passed the surprise to Booker, who did better at covering his reaction to the 'prosecution's last witness.' And a surprise it was.

Matther took the name of the surprise witness of the defense with a smile of confidence that spoke volumes that he would handle this, like brushing off an annoying, pesky fly. He dropped the letter in front of his associate, James Buchanan, who would have the task, with a time limit of a day and a half of research, to supply strategic background materials to his boss, who would launch a presumably 'brilliant' cross-examination.

Court adjourned. As the jury and judges departed, Harriet turned to Booker and whispered her anxiety about this new crisis at the forefront.

"We need *King's Retribution* team on deck immediately."

EPISODE TWENTY-SEVEN — The Third Day

Scene 1: Defense Strategies
Setting: The Stadium

"Mr. bin Laden seems to have sucked on a lemon," Samantha Carlisle's appraisal of the lone man sitting in the defendant dock waiting for the day's proceedings to begin.

Sitting next to her, Callie agreed, adding her own input. "He does look like a grumpy old man. I have heard that Booker and Harriet were going to lay out their plans to defend him, not pulling punches and telling me he would not be happy. It seems like they succeeded in alienating their client, if even to save his life from a well-deserved firing squad."

"Any word from them or anyone on these 'Surprise Witnesses'?" Samantha asked.

"No, everyone's tight-lipped. But I heard the defense team asked Hugh for some researchers, and they all burned the midnight oil conducting their own investigation to prepare for their cross-examination."

Final words can have lasting impacts, and bin Laden received a double dose before his ascension into the courtroom bubble.

"Slow and serious," his defense attorney, Harriet Eberhardt, told him, "Doubt, doubt, we must provide the jury with doubt, even challenging what they might perceive as their deep-seated beliefs. And we will not be promoting your cause. Not making you a hero. And since you are not helping us, you must accept that our strategy is multiple scatter-shooting, throwing every alternative against the jury box, just to change one juror's mind." Their client clinched his face and said nothing.

Next came his slow walk with Wendell to the elevator.

"Your little demonstration of showing notes to the world, conveying coded instructions, that was a smart move," said Wendell. "I assume your cadre received the message. We know they are here. Our intelligence people are on to them (meaning *King's Retribution* not the Feds). Just like *King's Retribution* knows one of your people escaped from your house — and that we have most of his books from his special library. As we speak, we are deciphering your *Crimson Scimitar* plans. And within a few days, we will know what your 'Crayfish II' means."

"We will see, Wendell, we will see."

"Yes, but if we do succeed, your scimitar will be as potent as a butter knife."

Bin Laden again gave no response, but to himself, he again cursed Khalaf.

The defense called Professor Hiram Smith of Brigham Young University (BYU) in Provo, Utah. Harriet qualified the professor as an expert in world religions, and his testimony focused on the overview of the Islamic religion, portraying how close the similarities all faiths were.

"Is Islam a terrorist philosophy?"

"Of course not; that is ridiculous. That would be saying that 23% of the world's population who are Muslims, nearly 2 billion people, are terrorists. It shows the usual bias of ignorant Islamophobia."

He continued, "A fellow professor in religious studies, Kelly Pemberton at George Washington University, was quoted as saying, 'Islam is arguably the most misunderstood religion of the 21st Century.' The beliefs of Muslims closely track with those of Christianity: one God (Allah), angels exist, each with their Holy Book (The Holy Bible and the Qur'an), accepting prophecy from prophets (Jesus and Moses are prophets to Muslims).'"

Harriet: "Of these two major religions, Christianity and Islam, certainly there has been extremism to each, Professor; certainly there are fringes?" Her questioning had been light, attempting to make educating the jury like a friendly talk among friends.

"Yes, of course," Hiram replied, "Various cliques and movements have historically defined religious doctrines to specific goals as they interpret them differently from the majority. There are conservative and liberal interpretations. Muslims, since the death of Muhammad in 632, in a dispute over succession, created the Sunnis and Shias. Christianity saw the creation of Protestantism in difference to Catholicism."

"But by extremism, to get to the point, one side wants to kill the other side for their religious beliefs."

"Yes, of course, there are examples. Again, in both religions. In the overview, each religion believes the other faiths are going to hell, to purgatory. Tolerance of the faith is in the middle spectrum, a type of live-and-let-live. That God/Allah will reward me for my good deeds, but I will have to wait until after death to be told if I was right or wrong about which religion was the right one and if God/Allah exists. Or are they all right, as God/Allah might define true righteousness?"

"Are you saying, then, that extremism in religion which promotes violence against their adversaries, that those people are a very small minority?"

"Yes."

"For example, how many jihadists publicly espouse violence and within political organizations exist in numbers?"

"It is a hard number to quantify, dependent on so many variations of political philosophies in totally different countries and different cultures within those countries. Many who espouse

438   S.P. Grogan

religious hatred are actually probably anarchists, and if you dig deeper, their philosophies are more similar to cult atheism. But again, only a very small percentage gains the public forum by employing terrorist attacks. There are two recent surveys that go to my point that almost all of the Muslim world seeks peace through their religion. One survey showed a large separation from those in Muslim countries who wanted to impose the strict constructions view of the Quran by making Sharia law, the most conservative interpretation of Islam, the law of that country. In Afghanistan and Iraq, it is 90 percent in favor, but in Turkey, it is only 12%, and in Azerbaijan, 8%. There is no consensus to spread Sharia law to their countries or the rest of the world. More so, in another survey, the significant Muslim population had an unfavorable view of this most recent resurging ISIS political and terrorist group. 94% in both Lebanon and 94% in Jordan were opposed to this new form of an Islamic State."

"Thank you, Professor. No more questions."

Prosecutor Matther rose, more of an aside dismissal.

"Professor, in your view, would a political group that crashes planes into buildings and kills innocents, would that be your definition of a religious-based terrorist group?"

"Certain political organizations have combined political goals with religious fervor."

"And by that, you mean 'violent acts' to gain their goals?

"Yes."

Cotton Matther sat down, a silent excuse of dismissal, and the judge let the witness go.

Booker rose to call their next witness and another professor who had written a research book on the impact of television coverage on forming public opinion.

Defense: "After 9/11, did not the Bush Administration co-opt the national media to justify its eventual invasion of Iraq?"

Witness: "Yes, and they were quite effective, and the public perception, the polls, were convinced that by attacking Iraq, they were going to defeat those responsible for 9/11."

Defense: "But that was not correct at all?"

Witness: "No."

Defense: "And after 9/11, from the previous administration to the current one, has not the U.S. government supported the entertainment industry to produce a form of propaganda that made the Arab world the villain aggressor? Do you have such examples?"

Witness: "Those in various administrations and the military went out of their way to support Islam's phobic movies and television shows. As an example, as you asked, one month after 9/11 and the terrorist attacks, the FBI asked Hollywood producers and screenwriters to create various terrorist plot scenarios for intelligence training. The White House sent one of its top officials to meet with the leadership within the Motion Picture Association of America

(MPAA) to enlist their support to portray America's courage and patriotism against evil foes. Over the next decade, we have seen the rise of jingoistic patriotic plot sequences, America against foreign political extremism. One early film in this period, *DC 9/11: Time of Crisis*, overtly portrays President Bush as a man's man, snippets of the film showing him in masculine leadership poses, the man in charge to save the day. During this period of government-entertainment cooperation, a symbiosis best describes it, Hollywood moved from the 'war is bad' motif, graphically brutal, like *Saving Private Ryan* (1998) or *Thin Red Line* (1998), into more romanticized heroic war as in *Black Hawk Down* (2002), *Windtalkers* (2002), *Jarhead* (2004), *Gods and Generals* (2003), as well as, during this time, the creation of three pro-military history television channels. Also, you saw the rise of military killing-blaster video games. What the audience did not catch onto was an encouraged movement against the political context of gory wars towards more about themes of you and your buddy in righteous, good vs. evil, war situations."

Up in the media boxes, *The Denver Post* reporter asked the *Chicago Sun-Times* political columnist, "What is the defense trying to do here? You'd think they were attacking the media, as well as this show's producers, Skilleo Games, and *King's Retribution*."

The *Sun-Times* columnist replied, "Smokescreen legal gymnastics. They need other scapegoats. Though 9/11 occurred, their strategy is to suggest that we, the media, and the entertainment people perhaps had some measure of fault in the process that led to the attack, before and after. For us, it was due to our reporting in crises being un-sourced inaccuracies, written into frenzied headline speculations."

"Well, that didn't occur. Did it?"

The parade of witnesses continued when the defense called General (retired) Lionel Kincaid, an international political scientist and Patton Fellow, now teaching at West Point. This witness seemed a surprise to the reporting media, who saw the contrarian approach of bringing in a military person who might speak favorably to bin Laden's actions. They need not worry, but they wondered, many wondering as before, what was the defense doing?

Booker's first question set the tone:

"Would you consider Osama bin Laden an effective political and organizational leader?"

"No, I would not." Very crisp, soldier-like bearing.

"Please explain."

"Bin Laden was basically the titular head of al-Qaeda, which was more a mixture of rural tribal factions, and held together by the press and video propaganda releases. From what the U.S. government has uncovered, he may not have held oversight of the 9/11 planning, but that was left to others."

"You mean someone like Khalid Sheik Mohammed?

"Yes."

"Wasn't the original idea of 9/11 from Khalid Sheik Mohammed?"

"Yes. The 9/11 Commission Report details that he took part in his first planning of an airplane hijacking and destruction while in the Philippines in 1994. But the plot was uncovered in 1995."

"This was before Khalid Sheik Mohammed had any contact with the al-Qaeda organization?"

"Yes." During these questions, Cotton Matther was looking for the right point to object when Booker adeptly changed subjects.

"Let's talk about post-2001 and al-Qaeda and bin Laden. What is your opinion of bin Laden's leadership during, let's say, from 2002 to his capture several months back?"

"He was a failed leader. His organization was more talk than substance."

"Examples?"

"Well, the two-year absence from the world stage or encouraging his followers."

"His absence from the public until the 2004 al Jazeera video?"

"Correct."

"Any other examples?"

"Frankly, the decimation of al-Qaeda leadership between those times. When the U.S. Government went after al-Qaeda leaders, they targeted and killed at least 30 top hierarchy leaders. The central core of any organizational leadership has no longer existed since the beginning of this year. Any residual attacks are, if I might use the expression, unassociated franchise brands in other countries. They might make a terrorist attack for their own agendas, but al-Qaeda seeks or is given the credit to substantiate its legitimization."

Booker: "So, in your opinion, outside of sending out P.R. comments to supposed members, who are not card-carrying or dues-paying, but in fact are quite a distance from his actual sphere of influence, Osama bin Laden is a de-fanged has-been, not some diabolical plotter and threat to the world."

The general parsed his words carefully.

"Post 9/11 Osama bin Laden is not the great leader the world views him as."

"Thank you. Your witness."

A lightning strike was seen in the distance, where a dark storm cloud, part of a concentrated system, had formed quickly over the mountains and rushed towards the plains, billowing and roiling, growing in size — moving towards the Stadium.

Matther to the witness: "General, is it your opinion that Osama bin Laden was one of the two accepted leaders in the founding of al-Qaeda in 1988, the other being Abdullah Azzam?"

"Yes, his public pronouncements speak to that."

"And by the year 2001, he was the sole leader?"

"Yes, but he acts in concert with a Supreme Council, and there were several sub-leaders who led independent functions."

"You say 'sub-leaders,' like any organization, para-military types; so, there were departments like media and military operations?

"Yes, but in general organizational construction, again, many had their own leadership independence."

"Under the military committee or command structure, for example, there were sub-commanders for 'projects'?

"Yes."

"Mohamed Atta, the leader of the 9/11 strike team, wasn't he a military commander within the military command of al-Qaeda, under the leadership of Osama bin Laden?" Cotton Matther's arm swerved with a stabbing pointing finger at the defendant, who showed no response.

"It is my understanding, from the 9/11 Commission, that Ayman al-Zawahiri and Khalid Sheik Mohammed were part of the political and military planning committees."

"Along with Osama bin Laden?"

"Yes. He may have served ad-hoc, but yes, he was active in committee functions of his organization."

Cotton Matther could have ended there; his point made that bin Laden and al-Qaeda were one and the same, so his general questioning continued but with no major substance gained.

Scene 2: The Rain Attack
Setting: The Stadium

With the first raindrops, the Stadium crew put their inclement weather plan into motion. The Jumbotron screens announced:

In case of rain, weather garments will be provided, or please move under the nearest Stadium covering.

"What are they passing out," asked Bennie, munching on an early lunch while comfy in the storm-protected VIP suite.

442   S.P. Grogan

Samantha had an answer. "They are small plastic rain ponchos for those who want to enjoy the trial and the cloudburst at the same time. If there were a chance of lightning close by, then the trial would be postponed until the storm passed, but it would be wrong to send people out into the storm. Notice flagpoles around the stadium; Hugh told me they're state-of-the-art lightning rods."

"Our boy has thought of everything," came Abbas's comment, half-joking. "Say, those ponchos they're starting to wear, they even have a logo."

"Jeez," said Callie, "he monetized the ponchos with advertising." Instead of ridicule, she thought a moment and considered the 'he' she was discussing. "It's pretty brilliant, I guess. Self-paid for."

Samantha had to agree. "And it promotes the state's semi-pro soccer team, a future Stadium user."

The rain went from a drizzle in a moment to a downpour, sheets of water obscuring everything. Judge Sanford thought it could be the proper time for a short break and was starting to interrupt Matther's long-winded cross-examination of the general...when it happened.

Of those in the Stadium who saw, three of them understood and, in an instant, reacted.

A small spidering appeared on the courtroom bubble, like a crack in a car windshield from a rock, at an angle just above and behind the defendant. The crack became a small hole, then enlarged, and a second later, enlarged again, and mysteriously another spider crack appeared directly behind bin Laden seated in his plastic-type box.

Booker Langston had looked to the judge for his recess announcement and, by chance, had glanced at his client.

Samantha Carlisle, somewhat bored with Matther's monotone questions, was wondering if Wendell was watching the television somewhere, as he had not yet appeared in the VIP Suite. Her eyes were fixed on the bubble, watching the rain run down the sides when one raindrop began to grow and not move.

Callie, with Samantha's binoculars, was focused on bid Laden, seeking by laser focus to zap the s.o.b., when her ears picked up the faintest sound from the courtroom microphones, indiscernible, but a recognition lodged in her distant past.

Booker yelled, "Osama, look out. Duck!" Bin Laden glanced at him, confused. Langston jumped from the table, waving his arms for bin Laden to go down, down.

Callie registered when Langston reacted. "Gunfire!" That was it: a bullet striking a solid object. And she could do nothing. Her focus through the binoculars clarified what she saw;

one shot after the other in nearly the same spot, enlarging the strike, widening a hole, so the next bullet would not be stopped and would go on to the inner bubble.

Samantha hit her phone to the emergency code Wendell had programmed into it, gifted during the Abbottabad adventure. The emergency code beeped out to all that still had their phones, like an Amber Alert. "Wendell, Hugh, shots fired! We think at the bubble." She could do nothing.

To the surprise of the court, Booker ran past Cotton Matther, who was disgusted at the interruption. Finally, Booker reached the yellow communication button designed for client-attorney privileged talk. Bin Laden was smart enough to already have the headset on.

"Gunfire behind you. Get on the floor now!" Osama bin Laden ducked. A second later, a high-powered rifle fired, and the bullet, fired from far away within the Stadium, pierced the defendant's box through the previous centimeter-sized hole of the outer bubble shield and slammed into the opposite side of the box at the approximate height where Osama's head had been previously.

The bullet struck in relation to where Booker's chest was, but its speed and the wall of the cubicle acted as interference, and striking the glass-type wall, it spidered where it hit, and then dropped to the desk, as Booker looked down at the spent round before him, realizing it was at the position of his stomach, and had there been just a little more force, into his stomach.

Another factor that saved Booker from injury and bin Laden from being assassinated was that one of the guards behind bin Laden's enclosed seating arrangement had made a delayed move. To do what? Interfere with Booker's odd actions, or wonder why bin Laden was on the floor? As he reacted and reached for the door handle that housed and protected bin Laden the bullet pierced the fleshy part of his upper arm, a clear-through shot that added to the trajectory's slowing.

Hell did not break loose, but unrestrained chaos blundered in. The judges crouched behind their solid wood desks. The bailiff hustled out the recorder and yelled at the jurors to run to the exit stairs leading down and out to safety. Was there a full assault on them, many wondered in panic as they fled?

Booker turned to see three deer-in-the-headlights frozen caricatures: Harriet, Cotton, and his aide Buchanan. Harriet responded first and grabbed and pulled at Cotton Matther, who still did not understand the situation but complied as all three hid under the prosecutor's desk. Cotton looked out with a sense of fear tinged with spite — did he feel he should have been the center of attention from the attack? Was that what he really thought?

Seconds lingered with no more shots or noise of plastic cracking. Or, a new concern by some, fearing the whole bubble might collapse, pancake in...like...did they dare compare it to the Twin Towers?

Booker took charge. Silence within the court was the reprieve, his client hopefully safe. "Everyone out, now! Quickly!" And they complied, the attorneys, then the judges, less judicial now, and the injured guard with his partner supporting him. The guards had not been hired to remain and throw their bodies in front of a lethal threat.

Booker crouched, awaiting armed reinforcements. *Weird*, he thought, he still had on his headphones, and maybe did bin Laden?

"Osama." The first time he had used the man's first name. "Are you okay? Injured?"

A silent moment, then, "I am fine." Another moment, a chuckle, "These were amateurs, maybe smart ones, but I know if this had been Wendell, he would have found a way to make me dead. But he doesn't like martyrs." The most the defendant had ever said to his defense team.

Booker could only shake his head in disbelief at their situation. Prisoners together from the circumstances, surrounded by 40,000 wet people, but he did not hear, or looking out, see a mass panic to the exits, deaths, and injuries from trampling. Wasn't that what these terrorists wanted? The attention of the world stage watching.

Surprisingly, moments earlier in the control booth, the cue that a recess was certain to take a rain-delay, television cameras had cut away, and the stadium monitors went static, replaced with the announcement about rain protection as well as refreshments available, while pleasant music filled the air, beginning with B.J. Thomas singing *Raindrops Keep Fallin' on My Head**, and Booker heard a snatch of the catchy lyrics — "it won't be long till happiness steps up to greet me." He laughed.

While waiting, he asked bin Laden, "Wendell Holmes told a story that he once saved your life?"

"Did he now? He is the Silent One, you know. If he speaks, it must have been true. I guess that is two Americans I owe my life to. That is bad for my reputation."

Booker held back any mirthful response; he was not in a bonding, buddy-buddy mood.

"My fiancée Judy was murdered on 9/11 by your Mohammed Atta." Silence behind the narrow wall of protection, two men on the floor talking, one seeking an answer he had never gained closure on. Finally, to the silence, Booker responded coldly, "I am going to save your life a second time if I can. It is my duty in your representation."

They could hear the rain hitting the dome, heard distant thunder.

*The Burt Bacharach and Hal David song written for the 1969 film *Butch Cassidy and the Sundance Kid.*

Crimson Scimitar

"Duty," answered Osama bin Laden, "is doing right with no praise."

Right back at you. Booker remembered a quote from one of his favorite writers, Lois McMaster Bujold, that he used in many of his jury summations: "The dead cannot cry out for justice. It is a duty of the living to do so for them."

The tribal police rushed into the courtroom, guns drawn. Hugh Fox close behind.

Callie spotted the shooter before anyone else. Whether from her police training, *King's Retribution,* or watching actor Benedict Cumberbatch in deductive detecting as 'Sherlock Holmes,' her smarts kicked in, and she saw the angle of the shot which had to be made, created in her mind a trajectory and angle and in her vision moved the line of sight up into the stands, up and up. It seemed hopeless. Those in that area of the stands, as elsewhere, were hunkered down in their ponchos or as a makeshift tent under them, snuggling with a friend. They all looked the same.

Her binoculars went to the top of the stadium, the nosebleed seats, and started down, searching. Then, it struck her; she whirled around, looked at a particular spot across the Stadium, and stared up at the seats where she had viewed 'suspicious characters' several days ago. Those seats were empty.

Samantha was on speaker phone with Wendell.

Callie went back to her original guess. Close inspection. She began speaking to Samantha, who relayed Callie's thinking aloud.

"I am guessing they are up in Section II, probably in the first level. The top level is too distant; the shot would be a different angle."

"I'm on my way." Jumbled noise of Wendell running through crowds seeking shelter from the rain.

"Not alone, you aren't," snapped Samantha.

"Got two plainclothes with me."

Callie relayed to Samantha, "There may be four of them, not just one. And the shooter, I'm sure, has military sniper experience." She found herself saying loudly to Wendell, carrying his phone, "Be cautious."

"Yes, ma'am."

"Douche," she responded with a smirk to Samantha. Then she saw the tarp.

"Spotted them! Under a green-colored tarp. More than one. Wait, they are starting to move. Yep, guessed right. It's Pastor Tate and his posse. One of them just put down a long

446   S.P. Grogan

silver tube, guessing a rifle of sorts, on the seat under the tarp. They're leaving it there. Quietly exiting as if nothing happened, the bastards."

Pastor Tate swore an oath. Oscar thought he had hit bin Laden; the monster had fallen to the floor. But there was no blood splatter. Had Oscar missed? If they could, they would find another opportunity to finish the revenge meted out by the Lord's Hand.

"We are outta here," was one man's nervous response to the escape plan. As casual as they could be, excusing their way through the seated people hiding from the rain, the brief storm now passing, clear blue skies soon to arrive, warmth already in the air. Pastor Tate, miraculously cured of his limp, his crutches left behind, could walk just fine, hurrying.

At the top of the first level stadium stairs, the exit to their van, and escape, only fifty yards away, they met Wendell Holmes and company, three guns leveled at them.

"Bet I can blow a hole right through your other eye," said Wendell, seriously, meaning it. His finger was wet on the trigger. Slippery. He was out of breath from running around the Stadium interior, shoving aside those returning to their seats. Wendell was rusty at close-quarter kill shots, but yeah, he could do it.

Scene 3: The Group Therapy Relief Party
Setting: VIP Suite, the Stadium

The Charles Court Restaurant at The Broadmoor catered to the private VIP box a fine dining experience for the early evening buffet , but at this time, except for Bennie, Abbas, and CAMERA TWO, who snarfed at the rare roast beef sandwiches, most of the small crowd nibbled but tippled heavily. This was an 'unwind, unburden oneself, release the nerves' event.

When all had settled the small talk, Harriet Eberhardt led off with the anticipated main question: "How did they do it?"

Hugh looked to Wendell, but he shrugged off an expression: 'It's your production, mate.'

"First," began Hugh, "they bought eight tickets, four for one side, the other four their targeting point. They needed the rain storm to hide under cover, to mask the rifle length.

"The there were the crutches. Not just one set, but two sets, rifle parts hidden inside hollowed aluminum crutches, brought in with the bullets over two days, secreted near their seats. A sniper scope created from break-apart binoculars that could be re-attached to make a long telescope. It was a jerry-rigged rifle with small magazines of seven bullets each load; they were not automatic rapid fire but could make the shot every five seconds. The tribal police investigators even found a homemade sound suppressor, not a pure silencer, but enough to make it sound like a loud cough, which they say was muted by several of their fellow conspirators shouting during the firing.

"It might have worked," nodded Wendell, "a good plan. Their sniper boy was ex-US Marine trained, knew his stuff. A zealot of God and Pastor Tate's visions of hellfire."

"What really stopped those bullets?" a serious question from Booker. He and Harriet sat near each other. She had given him a hug, her expression one of relief when he emerged from the courtroom.

Booker's gaze went to the bubble courtroom below the VIP suite. It was not in darkness but bathed in floodlights as workmen repaired the holes in the bubble and the close call in bin Laden's enclosure.

"I think I might be able to answer that," Callie chimed in. "I talked to the investigators then made my own observation first hand. The shooter and Pastor Tate saw a plexiglass bubble and thought several shots would cause it to fall apart in sections, and they'd have a clearer shot, but if their first shot barely punctured the plastic material, several subsequent shots in the exact same place would provide a hole that an excellent marksman could make an entry shot again and again. Except," and she gave a sly inquisitive stare at Hugh, "that wasn't just ordinary plexiglass, was it?"

"No," Fox conceded, almost shyly, thought Samantha. Still the boy with his toys.

"It's two layers each, at 0.5 inch thick. One layer is polycarbonate, the center is polyurethane used to bond the inner and outer layer, and the outer layer is a 1.5 inch layer of acrylic."

"Of course it is," said Abbas. They all laughed in sighs and emotional release. They needed to recapture the upbeat.

"It's not so much a bubble," explained Fox, with a little more pride, "as being the world's largest jet fighter cockpit canopy. And, as you all should know, jet cockpits are durable but are not bulletproof; they're not impervious to flying projectiles."

"That's huge; where does something that big get made?" Bennie was now into the éclairs.

"Well, I can't say much. It is sectional and can be fused seamlessly. Skilleo has a relationship with the Air Force; training videos, gameplay, hand-eye coordination, and improving response times. You ever hear of something called Area 51."

"You're shitting me," marveled Abbas.

"Maybe, maybe not," deadpanned Hugh Fox.

"If it's a 'maybe,' a secret government agency hit squad might come after you," deadpanned Wendell.

And again, laughter, not as jovial, as some were not so certain what was true and what was not.

"Okay, what happens tomorrow?" Samantha, out of the loop, felt the loyal people here required straight answers. "Hugh"?

He nodded. "The bubble will look fine in the morning, not a scratch. But the world will know the scoop, and the world will be watching. Our press release and the one from the Tribal police will try to downplay it as just 'shots fired by a crazy person who was immediately detained and arrested.' Back to the trial, let everyone wonder. Pastor Tate and his gang are held incommunicado. None of the press has an inkling of who or what; that will drive them mad."

And more hype for your *Show of Shows*, thought Samantha, seeing for the first time Hugh's drive for project recognition bordered on obsessive-compulsive or mere self-gratifying ambition at its limits. She did not know if she liked that in him, if it was true.

"You might expect that piranha, Attorney Matther, to paint himself both as target and hero and embellish his actions," Harriet's viewpoint.

Booker added. "Cotton told me — and he *was* a little shaken — that he finished with our general expert. So we will go on to our 'surprise witness' and his cross-examination. Then Cotton will present his witness, and we will take our best shot. Then summation, late afternoon, is the plan. But you saw the plans today got pushed back."

"And you can't tell us who these witnesses will be?" From Callie, curious as a member of *KR* might be.

"Confidential agreements preclude, but there will be fireworks."

"Please, no more surprises," said Samantha.

Yes, no more surprises, they all agreed, and all felt better, as more light social camaraderie brought them closer together as a team. As finally, did the buffet table.

Scene 4: A Surprising Day
Setting: The Stadium

Razzor Hassim had to read in the morning paper that shots had been fired at the stadium and the perpetrator arrested. It was reported that Osama bin Laden was not harmed, and the trial would resume for the 4th day. No further elaboration. He cursed, believing the U.S. Government was trying to assassinate their leader. Action must be taken.

So, he would miss the morning courtroom session and have it on television in the background as he formulated a plan. He and his group of three 'attack' members knew any last-minute mission would be limited in scope. They all re-pledged their lives to al-Qaeda and would do anything to free their spiritual master, but this thrown-together team had very few directions to go. The attack yesterday, or whatever it was, would heighten stadium security with no chance of smuggling in weapons. Creating a mass terror attack by spraying a stadium with machine gun fire was not viable with the goal of freeing their leader, and too much publicity might indirectly put the *Crimson Scimitar* national plan in jeopardy. They agreed that when the trial was over, that would be their best option; yet, how would they know the method by which bin Laden would be removed from the stadium? Both he and Shahin's pit bull, Maj, would have to do surveillance, pick up random conversations, and gain gossip on how transferring the prisoner would be staged. To keep his people alert, they went over possible scenarios and how they would conceive a tactical ambush that had any chance of success.

The 'Crayfish' stratagem was discussed and prepared, if needed, and could be implemented in a moment's configuration, hopefully with the intended result.

As to weaponry resources, they were more than well-armed. From a tunnel between Mexico and the United States, this al-Qaeda squad had brought along enough firepower to overwhelm any opposition short of a military brigade. A drip, an ounce, of intelligence, was now the most valuable weaponry they lacked.

The Stadium crowd was festive and curious. Questions about the shooting brought watchful eyes, suspicious of anything looking threatening. They noted more guards were now at every stairway exit, more walking the perimeter of the playing field, which had been used in the past few days as a performing area to keep the crowd entertained during courtroom downtime. They had all experienced a heightened concern as all ticket goers were screened more carefully as they entered to find their seats.

For some, while awaiting the trial's opening gavel, they found distraction in watching the small drones hover and fly above the Stadium. This morning they drew the crowd's attention when two drones, flying in tandem, came flying high above, dipped down together, and in one fell swoop grabbed up another drone in a netting device attached behind the two radio-controlled flying machines, like a volleyball or tennis net scoop.

Hugh Fox sat in the VIP suite this day and informed his fellow associates, "I felt the government might decide to do their own monitoring, impose some intimidation. They can buy a ticket or watch television like everyone else." He said no more. Not arrogance, more an attitude of retaining operational event control. It would be interesting to note that it took the U.S. Government, through the FAA, another fifteen years before they promulgated regulations about drones flying without permission over private property.

The next surprise of the morning came from the judiciary, not from any witness.

450   S.P. Grogan

Judge Sanford addressed the court and the jury.

"Please note that we have dismissed a juror, and, per our rules, another juror was selected by a drawing to replace the juror." She turned to the jury.

"The Court must re-emphasize its past direction to you — that you are not to read or listen to any outside communication. Further, you should form no opinion except from the witness testimony during this trial. And you must not share any thought or opinion with another juror until you are sequestered in the jury room to render your verdict."

The housewife, #55, now sat as the replacement juror. The press took note Juror #18 was missing.

The judge turned to the defense. "Please call your first witness of the day."

Attorney Harriet Eberhardt rose.

"The defense calls Sumaiya bin Laden."

"Who did they call?" asked the reporter from the *LA Times*, the question directed to the CNN international reporter who was the go-to Mideast expert to all within hearing as they sat scribbling or emailing stories from one of the media suites overlooking the courtroom within the repaired bubble.

"Of bin Laden's 20-25 children, she is the daughter of Siham Sabar, born in, I believe, 1992.

"That means she's 19 years old," said the *Times* reporter, doing mental math. "But how does she help the defense?"

"I am guessing they are trying to humanize bin Laden as a family man. I don't see tugging at heartstrings will impact the jury. But who knows?"

Harriet moved to introduce Sumaiya, who was dressed not in black, nor in a face-covering burka, or even a head-covering hijab but a muted multi-color dupatta, which is a long scarf loosely draped across the head and shoulders. Perhaps a little more South Asia in cultural styling, but an acceptable clothing style. Sumaiya's face revealed a very young woman with dark eyebrows, no lipstick or facial powder, none needed, as her face was lovely and her skin smooth. She was not of the sun nor the desert, but an urban dweller, from somewhere, it was learned, living with her mother at another location in Pakistan, having been just released by the local police from supervision after the Raid, as Harriet elicited in the introduction.

The television screens produced captions, and an unseen woman spoke as a translator.

Further established was that she was born in Khartoum, Sudan. That she came willing, that she was not threatened or forced. Did she receive any compensation? Only the cost of travel and housing for herself and a close female relative.

"So, what you are saying is that you came to speak on behalf and for your father?

"Yes, he is innocent. He only thinks for the best of the Arab people."

"Were you with him during his stay in Abbottabad?

"Yes, along with my sister, Miriam, and my brother, Khalid."

"Your brother, Khalid, was killed in the attack at your family home?"

"Yes, he was unarmed and murdered by the U.S. Government."

The public and jury accepted she held extreme views that were not favorable to the military people they accepted as heroes.

Harriet shifted. "Tell us about your family life at the Abbottabad compound and times with your father.

Sumaiya began talking animatedly about pastoral living, the love of an extended family, and how bin Laden, the father, was kind to all his wives and children. How they took family bus trips, bin Laden in the car ahead, the rest in a bus following. That he sought to bring those family members held against their will in Iran to the compound, but this did not happen. Still, under the tapestry woven of bliss were short comments of the misery attached to following the warrior's path, fleeing countries ahead of the secret police, or hiding in remote locations, including barely tolerable caves for some. This led to Harriet's follow-up question.

"As was reported, did you lead the life of a pampered wealthy girl since your father was related to the wealthy bin Laden construction company family?"

"No, we suffered great privation. And moved several times, lived under bad conditions, and the mothers and children were threatened by airstrikes several times."

Harriet then went through several stories before coming back to bin Laden as a dutiful father taking care of multiple wives and separate family units.

Her final question, "Do you feel that your father was a cruel father, and do you see him as a murderer?"

"No, he was always a loving father to all his children. As to his politics, I am not that aware, but I can say he was a Soldier of Allah."

Booker took stock of bin Laden's demeanor. He knew he was agitated that his daughter would be dragged into this show trial but sensed there was a proud moment of his Sumaiya being so brave. The real test for the young woman would be the assault that was coming from the prosecutor, whose smile at sensing a target reached almost gleeful proportions.

Cotton Matther introduced several papers to the Court as evidence and a copy to the defense.

With fake paternalism, he asked the witness: "Did you ever have disagreements with your father? Most children do?"

452   S.P. Grogan

"Sometimes we had mild disagreements as most children who love their parents might."

"Could you read this passage that is underlined?" And he handed her a document which she studied, nodded to some understanding, and read:

"What are the negative and positive effects on the jihadist as a result of these revolutions? It is possible that some among the new generation will believe that political change could occur without jihad, that we must speak out in support of jihadists and against Western intervention as is now occurring in Libya?"

"You wrote this, did you not?" asked Cotton.

"Yes."

"What you seem to be saying — no, let me correct that. This is not some young girl telling her father that she wants a bicycle and he won't buy it. You are trying, by your letter to Daddy, to tell him that jihad must come to distant Arab countries, as you say, Libya, and not this so-called 'Arab Spring' which was supported by Western democracies like France and the United States."

She did not answer. He smiled.

"Let's go on; you have a sister, Miriam, I believe, two years older than you?"

"Yes."

"And you both, together, or separately, helped your father, and more specifically in the time you both were with him at your home in Abbottabad, say in the Spring, March-April, 2011?"

"We were both there. Since he did not have a staff for his papers, we helped to keep them in order."

"It was a little more than that, wasn't it, Miss bin Laden? Did not your father often turn to his daughters to generate ideas for his public statements?"

"I don't believe he said so as you suggest, but we would help him to formalize the papers he wrote."

"More than just secretaries shuffling and filing papers, or correcting misspelled words and syntax, weren't you and your sister Mariam actually his speech writers? You wrote out the jihadist philosophy of al-Qaeda, and your father cleaned up your words, not his."

"Objection," Booker stood. "He is leading the witness, if not providing his own conclusions."

"Sustained. Mr. Matther, more questions and less of your own statements."

"Yes, Your Honor." Cotton handed Sumaiya another document. "Is this one of your father's speeches that he recorded on video in March 2011?"

She read the photostat copy of the handwritten page.

"Yes."

"But isn't the handwriting of the speech, in your handwriting, not your father's, and he makes corrections, improves what you write, and will later deliver that wording in his speech to the public?"

Booker could see her thinking, seeking to anticipate the thrust of the prosecutor's question.

"He dictated, we transcribed. He made corrections. Mariam or I made editorial corrections of what you say are 'miss-spelled words.'"

"Is it not true that your sister once wrote a letter to Iran's Supreme Leader criticizing him for not letting go the prisoners he held in detention, the women and children of jihadists, so their husbands would be free to fight against the Western Imperialists?"

"We were concerned about family and friends held against their will under house arrest."

"And didn't Miriam guide your father on how to respond to this Arab Spring uprising? And did you not help write the communication that eventually went out as guidance to al-Qaeda branches throughout the Middle East?"

She perhaps rushed her answer. "Miriam and I have opinions that always are the positions of my father."

Matther knew he had her and drove home the impression he sought to make; one of 'you are damned' one way or the other.

"But Miss bin Laden, the truth is, is it not, that you and your sister, nineteen and twenty-one-year-old women living under Sharia law, actually steered the direction of al-Qaeda, it's public responses, from March 2010 to May 1st, 2011?"

"No, that is not true."

Above the give-and-take in the courtroom, Samantha had to ask as Hugh and Wendell joined her and Callie in watching the proceedings below.

"How did Booker and Harriet find bin Laden's daughter?"

Hugh answered, looking to his new-found male bro. "Wendell went back to his contact at the U.S. Embassy in Pakistan and was able to locate the survivors of the Abbottabad raid. There were several volunteers who were willing to testify to protect their father. I heard that of all interviewed, she was the most feisty and bright."

Callie asked, "Yes, I see that, but what is going on with Matther's attack?" Her question directed more to the ex-CIA agent who might know the subject matter that the prosecution was lobbing at the young girl, towards daughter Sumaiya who seemed unruffled, holding her own as best she could.

454 S.P. Grogan

"He is undermining bin Laden's leadership abilities but aiming more at the Arab world out there. Demean their hero. Women may have an equal say when the bedroom door is closed or in the sanctity of a private residence, but they are to be invisible in the male world of Islamic law. He's doing a pretty good job of it. Harriet showed a family side of bin Laden; whether that plays with the jury is hard to say, but Matther is scoring points, that daddy's little girl is a radical jihadist, cut from the same cloth. The real bombshell, folks — " and Wendell looked to the 'Executive Committee' — "are the documents the prosecution is providing for her to respond to."

"What about them?" from Callie, not seeing the bigger picture.

"He quoted the dates as being written in March 2011."

"Oh, I see," said Hugh. "The only way those papers could have been obtained...."

Samantha finished, "From the SEAL attack on Abbottabad on May 1st and 2nd."

All four now understood the big picture.

"This is not my production anymore," realized Hugh Fox.

"No," agreed Wendell Holmes, "This is Booker and Harriet against the power of the U.S. Government being brought to bear. I fear whomever the prosecution's surprise witness will be is being coordinated from the CIA."

"Or by the higher-ups," said Callie. *The Trial* had entered a new dimension.

Razzor Hassim cursed the television as the proceedings continued with Cotton Matther's questioning. Hassim and his plotters were going over satellite maps, most recent of the area surrounding the Stadium, and drawing on road maps of the Colorado Springs, Denver area. The Professor had been told that he might be needed to fly to Colorado on an hour's notice, depending on whether or not they could launch any sort of rescue.

Razzor looked to the television and spoke to the subordinate, the heavy lifter.

"Maj, that man deserves your sharp blade, disabusing our women like this."

Maj grunted agreement; his finger raked across his throat, demonstrating his proven art.

Cotton Matther felt he had to deal with Harriet's attempt to build a *kumbaya* family life, where a sign above the door might have said, 'Home Sweet Terrorist Home,' He enjoyed his humor.

"Miss bin Laden, let's talk about your extended family for a moment. On the day that your home was visited by the American military, there were eleven children and four women in the compound. Correct?"

"No, you can't count Miriam and me as children."

"Yes, a good point. Let's dwell on that fact."

Is it not true that your father's son married the daughter of," — he glanced at his notes — "Muhammed Atef, and another of your father's older children, Saad, married a friend's daughter in Sudan, and Hamza bin Laden married the daughter of Muhammad al-Zayat. Does that seem correct?" He rushed on, not waiting for her in acceptance of facts.

"But all those 'arranged' marriages, they were 'arranged' not for love between the partners, nor even personal family reasons but to tie al-Qaeda closer to Egyptian extremist jihadists?"

"Objection," said Booker.

"Rephrase, counselor. Certain words can be incendiary without foundational proof."

"Your Honor."

To the witness: "These marriages were alliances with political leaders who can help your father's organization. Is that not true?"

"Are not most American weddings blessed if marital alliances come with connections and wealth? Our cultures pride ourselves in gaining tribal alliances that help our overall security and comfort."

Not the answer he wanted, so a new tactic.

"About the marriages of your many step-sisters. Did Osama's daughter Fatima marry? Did Khadijia marry?"

"Yes."

"When they married, wasn't Fatima only 12 years old, and wasn't Khadija only 11 years old? Would you call a father who married off young children a responsible family man?"

He turned to the jury to let those facts sink in.

Sumaiya did not hesitate.

"It is part of our culture, to respect our religion, the wishes of our family."

Cotton Matther walked away as if finished, as he was, but he stepped over the line to make a personal jab, perhaps uncalled-for.

"But you are nineteen and not married? Does your political activism prevent you from finding the right husband?"

She answered in a voice dripping with ice. "My brother Khalid was to be married in 2009, but the U.S. government hunted my father, and Khalid was murdered and will now never marry. I await my father's blessing when he chooses for me the right man to strengthen our family."

456 S.P. Grogan

Matther could live with that answer; it supported his belief that he had uncovered a radical element brainwashed by bin Laden. The jury would see that, he believed.

Harriet felt there would be little value in trying to strengthen Sumaiya's testimony, and the judge dismissed her. For an instant, father and daughter exchanged eye contact, and silent messages exchanged. Hers of concern, his of pride in his daughter. He accepted she would be strong in a world where he might not soon be her continuing guide.

Scene 5: From a Dark Past
Setting: The Stadium

Spending his lunch hour, Razzor wandered under the concrete stands seeking access points. He was wearing a Denver Broncos ball cap and had a soft drink cup in hand. He had his story down pat as one of his stops took him to the cargo load ramps at the back of the stadium, where all concessions and heavy materials were transited in and off-loaded.

"Hey, who's in charge here?" he asked with swagger, trying to give off a heavy Chicago or East Coast accent.

"I'm a drayage supervisor." Said a burly man in work clothes, carrying a clipboard, directing some pallet shifting.

"I came earlier to scope out the system. Have interior finish paneling coming in on my truck, parked in the Springs, once this shit is all over with. How do I do it, and what day is best?"

"Well, it's up in the air, depending on when their trial is over. A day after the public leaves, the VIPs will come through here on their way out. So can't be then."

"Including the terrorist?"

"That's what I'm told; somebody from the government came by yesterday, just like you. Just checking out the logistics."

"Thanks. Good to know. Will wait a day or so and coordinate with you people when the construction crews come back in." He started to leave.

"Wait," said the supervisor. "Make sure you have an approved and signed bill of lading. They're still pretty security conscious; expect it to continue to keep away nosy tourists wanting to tour this historic site. Historic? It's all bullshit TV hype, that's all."

Razzor nodded to the supervisor in what was interpreted as agreement and walked away. He had one piece to his puzzle. Could they pull it off? Only if....

Afternoon. The Fourth Day

"The prosecution calls witness Khalid Sheik Mohammed."

Up in the stands, Hugh Fox looking down upon the scene, said, "Oh my god, what a coup: the smoking gun." Samantha sensed that in his new role as a television producer of one of the top three most watched live shows in television history, Hugh felt personally he had been outdone, blindsided, and though the following testimony would benefit his ratings, his ego must feel bruised that it was someone else's idea. Her ex-boyfriend's chutzpah is extraordinary, her not-so-kind opinion.

Appearing on the television screen, being viewed at home and the Stadium, appeared a thin and gaunt Khalid, his beard streaked grey, wearing a pumpkin-colored plain robe, while seated in front of a nondescript background to mask his location. Better known to the press and the government agencies as just 'KSM,' he looked far different from the standard full-faced bearded visage from an old passport or the stock photo of him captured in 2003, disheveled and not happy — his beard shaved to gain better facial recognition to verify the authorities had grabbed the right man.

Matther's Arabic professor appeared in the bottom right of the screen as translator. This would soon be dispensed with as unnecessary as Khalid was fluent in English.

Matther ran through a quick biographical sketch. 'You joined the Muslim Brotherhood when you were 16. You then enrolled at Chowan University in North Carolina and transferred to North Carolina Ag Tech State University, where you received a Bachelor of Science in mechanical engineering in 1986. In 1992 you received a master's degree in Islamic Culture and History from Punjab University."

A smart guy. He answered those questions in the affirmative.

Matther then pressed him on his radicalization.

"You found America as a student to be decadent?"

"Yes."

"That started your movement towards Islamic radicalism?"

"Not towards radicalism, but truisms towards more enlightenment."

"But it was when you went to Afghanistan in 1986 that you first met Osama bin Laden? But though invited, you did not join al-Qaeda at that time?"

"That is so."

Matther offered a pregnant pause and referred to his notes.

"I am going to ask you several basic 'yes and no' questions."

"Were you, at some point, a member of the organization known as al-Qaeda?"

458

"Yes."

"Was the accepted head of al-Qaeda during your time with them, Osama bin Laden?"

"Yes"

"Did you serve with him in some committee structure that was dedicated to military planning?"

"Yes"

"Were you present when the attack strategy that became 9/11 was conceived?

"Yes."

"Were you there when Osama bin Laden supported and approved the plans to attack the United States?"

"Yes."

"I have no further questions."

Cut and dried, right to the point. Was this the famous game, set, and match? Harriet wondered. Even in the media boxes, a quick consensus was the disappointment of not hearing a long, informative diatribe from the 'terrorist' but agreed he spoke to the facts that the prosecution wanted to convey to the jury.

Booker Langston, attorney for the defense, took his time in rising for his cross. He stared hard at the witness on the screen in front of him as if analyzing his inner soul, on how his actions deserved such recognition. He knew he was looking at an evil man.

"In 1994, you were in the Philippines, and while there, were you not one of several who devised something called 'Operation Bojink?' Is that correct?"

"Yes."

"And wasn't this 'Operation Bojink' a plan to hijack twelve commercial airliners flying in Southeast Asia, many going to the United States? And if the math serves me right, bombs were to be deposited on the airlines for a later explosion, and at least 2,000 deaths could have been caused. Wasn't this your plan?"

"It never happened."

"Yes, because after a test run with a bomb that killed a Japanese passenger on a flight in 1994, the plot was uncovered, and you were indicted on terrorism charges in New York Federal Court in January 1996. My question is: were you an indicted terrorist before you joined al-Qaeda?"

"My attorney has instructed me that I cannot discuss outstanding legal issues."

Langston accepted the parrying. That KSM had been coached was apparent.

"Let's then talk about another issue we should be informed of. You were apprehended in 2003. Is it not true that while in captivity, including the present time, the United States Government tortured you over one hundred times?"

Carefully considering the question, the witness worked out the proper response.

"I was not treated as a military prisoner under the Rules of the Geneva Convention."

"Isn't it true that because of this torture, you confessed to almost all crimes that your interrogators accused you of? Even some you were in no way responsible for? So, how can we believe what you previously testified to about our client as being the truth?"

"I have been asked to speak truthfully to this trial, and I have done so."

"You said you were 'asked to speak'? Have you been paid or received any special treatment that would allow us to doubt your testimony?"

"No."

"Are you certain?"

"Yes."

Booker made a sarcastic, disbelieving stare at KSM as he walked back to the defense table, picked up a paper, looked at it quickly, and turned to the witness.

"Khalid Sheik Mohammed, it seems to be the current belief among many in the world intelligence community you indeed were water boarded multiple times, perhaps a hundred times, and water boarding, for whatever reason, is horrible. Is it not being drowned and brought back from death?"

KSM did not respond. "However, beyond that past torture, aren't you currently being psychologically tortured that they, the U.S. Government, have threatened you; number one, threatening *not* to give you a public trial so that you might defend yourself, and number two, isn't it true that they have threatened to move you from your secure incarceration with fellow Islamic prisoners at Guantanamo Bay to the less secure, general American scum prison population you so despise at the Supermax prison here in Colorado, the place they call the Alcatraz of the Rockies? Isn't that the deal they offered you to speak against your former associate, Sheik bin Laden? And isn't it a fact that you are in that very prison, the one right down the highway from us, in an attempt to persuade you by threat as to your testimony?"

The witness paused and regained his voice. "I know nothing of any such arrangement."

Whether it was true or not, Booker had planted a cancerous seed of doubt that the jury must now realize that KSM could perjure himself, and for him, it did not matter; the only goal he desired most of all was to gain a modicum of comfort after all that he had been through in what was known as the CIA's black site *Extraordinary Rendition and Detention Program*.

"No further questions," intoned Langston.

460   S.P. Grogan

"Redirect, Your Honor." Prosecutor Matther to the witness: "Did you answer the truth to the questions I put to you?"

KSM recovered somewhat; his head began moving, side to side, as if trying to process, what? A past rehearsal, past memories, an uncertain future?

"Yes, the truth."

"And that was: Osama bin Laden, as head of al-Qaeda, authorized, approved, and participated in directing the 9/11 attacks on the United States and citizens of the world?

Wavering, but a 'yes.'

As Cotton sat down, satisfied, Booker launched himself to stand.

"One final question of the witness, Your Honor," and before the Judge could rule, Booker rapid fired, "Khalid Sheik Mohammed, as one human being to another, would you want Osama bin Laden to face the same torture by the U.S. Government that you went through?"

Cotton Matther began to protest, Judge Sanford pounded the gavel to interrupt the outburst, and KSM, visibly emotional, began to answer the question that Booker did not really expect an honest answer to. It did not matter; the screen and the face of Khalid Sheik Mohammed disappeared, as the screen had gone dark.

And that was that — the end of the evidentiary part of the *Trial of the Century*.

Scene 6: Wrapping Up
Setting: The Stadium Courtroom

After a luncheon break, the afternoon proceedings went to format. Closing speeches were given, too long to transcribe here, but repetitive of their opening remarks.

At the disadvantage of little refutable evidence, Booker spoke first and noted that all the facts were not yet available and made several claims of doubt, even suggesting that his client was in disagreement with his defense. 9/11 was a tragedy, but perhaps others were at fault; those who flew the planes had the greater guilt and were already punished, rightfully so. That bin Laden was not in control of al-Qaeda and a mere figurehead.

He knew their strategy of portraying bin Laden as the docile family man and loving father was weak but offered it up anyway. And when it came to politics, he said, one must consider the possibility that what we conceive as someone's adherence to an extreme position; in another country, that person might be called a 'freedom fighter.' And the evidence must be put in terms of geo-political understanding of the people of the Middle East and their beliefs. Thus, in his closing, he brought in the religions of Christianity and Islam, and that bin Laden had the right to believe in Allah, and all his writings merely expressed interpretation of the Qu'ran scriptures. Christianity, which preached forgiveness, could see that taking a life for a life was medieval and not part of the modern world. Punishment, yes, but the death penalty was barbaric. Booker's final jab sought to invoke the United States Government's position that the raid in Abbottabad meant that there would be no system of fairness using the American judicial system, and what had transpired over the last several days in this court was an attribute supporting the spirit of fair play. Booker's closing, more an appeal, bore a masterful touch, and everyone seemed impressed at his voice and tenor, his passion, but the consensus suggested it would fall on the deaf ears of the six crucial people who held bin Laden's fate in their hands.

In his turn at the pulpit of the court and the world audience beyond, Prosecutor Matther nearly belted out anguish as he focused on the individual tragedies of the victims, re-posited the highlights of his evidence, demanded justice and a verdict of guilty on all counts.

Judge Sanford read the jury instructions, which restated the articles of the indictment that they must view and render separate verdicts on the ten articles of the indictment, which would include, as a general recap: terrorism, hijacking aircraft, conspiracy, the genocide of Americans, hate crimes, mass murder in violation of the laws of war, attacking civilians, attacking civilian targets, intentionally causing serious bodily injury, and destruction of property in violation of the laws of war.

The jury was directed to the jury room to select a foreperson and ensure that all evidence and court exhibits had been provided. They were then expected to retire for the evening, with the subsequent full day to be one of baited anticipation outside of the jury room, and hard work, argument and debate within.

The King's Retribution/Skilleo people met to discuss what would come next, the verdict not primary in their plans as Wendell and Samantha presented their case of new action.

"*Crimson Scimitar* is real," said Samantha. "We don't know what bin Laden is telling us, but another attack plan is out there, and so far, the government is not taking your *King's Retribution's* previous success as good enough reasoning to raise the national alert. I am pissed that no one sees the danger."

Those in the suite listening to this pep talk were not so enthused. The week of trial had lost its uniqueness as the jury went into seclusion, a letdown of spirits, agreeing with both polls and television editorialists of the probable outcome. Booker and Harriet had done their best, but according to their contracts, their work was done. A verdict would be rendered. There would be no appeal process. The death penalty if given would stand in limbo as the U.S. Government would take possession of the accused. All would go home. The Stadium would be silent and empty before construction resumed toward its original usage of sports training and competition.

It was finally agreed that all would meet in a week at a newly-designated War Room to discuss whether, by reading books and watching movies, there was actual validity to a plot in motion by terrorists within the United States. Again, enthusiasm waned. *King's Retribution* had its third season locked in; they had strong opening shows of the bin Laden hunt, the Abbottabad attack, the capture, and then a few local domestic bounty hunting chases and captures. An Emmy-winning success odds-on-favorite, thus, going further in becoming an anti-terrorists think tank was not a plot line they felt would retain viewer interest in their standard reality show scripted format.

When they broke from their general meeting, the 'executive committee' of Hugh, Samantha, Callie, Wendell, and now Booker Langston and Harriet Eberhardt motored over to the Garden of the Gods Resort Club for dinner. It was a casual affair, with jovial and light bantering conversations, though it was apparent that in this social outing, there was an interaction of heads turned and smiles exchanged that suggested that the human species were cautiously pairing up.

To keep the dialogues upbeat, there was an obvious effort to avoid running on about any legal discussions or deep delving into trial issues or thoughts on how the jury might go — no one ever knew. Work and projects were taboo as the six of them visited with each other, and there were subtle personal questions about their private lives to understand the character of how a certain person 'ticked.'

Only once did they touch on *The Trial* when Callie had to ask Booker, "How did you know KSM was threatened with the loss of a comfy cell to be housed in a general population prison?"

There was a simple answer and no more to be said. "Mr. Holmes made a call," Samantha smiled, as did they all. They were Masters of their Limited World, accepting that each offered extreme talent to lost causes. Yet, later when the evening ended, a cool breeze on a Colorado night, where even a visible Milky Way shone bright and offered celestial majesty, suggestive of a thousand romantic allusions, each of these brilliant people returned to the Stadium, seeking their own beds, mellowing confused thoughts into fitful dreams. Unfortunately, smart people sometimes cannot reconcile the heart to action.

Scene 7: The Verdict
Setting: The Stadium

Now in the early afternoon on the fifth day of the *Trial of the Century*, awaiting the jury's determination, an electric shock hit when a note was passed from the jury room to the judges.

The attorneys returned, but bin Laden did not. The jury remained sequestered.

"The jury has informed us that they are at an impasse on three of the ten listed charges. I will inform them to continue deliberations and see if they can reach a decision."

The court recessed. The attorneys departed, Booker and Harriet, to confer with their client, to give him no opinion as to the news being good or bad.

Callie, who had a career in law enforcement, and had testified in criminal trials, saw things differently and was not pleased. She, from the start, wanted bin Laden strung up. Crime was crime.

To Samantha, she bristled, "I hate to say it, but somehow there might be a Pyrrhic victory here in play. Someone on the jury has balked for whatever reason. If it holds, Cotton Matther would have a face-saving win but will have lost the moral high ground, for whatever advantage I can't see unless it makes Booker and Harriet able attorneys at defending the damned."

At 4. p.m, while the Stadium crowd was listening to a local bluegrass band playing on the infield, the alert went out: A verdict was in. The rush was on. Media to their phones. Attorneys to their places. The restive audience to their seats and channel and cable stations with 'breaking news' as the world-watching population gathered before their television sets. Osama bin Laden was led to his position in the dock, unruffled, nonplussed as usual.

The jury returned, and to the media, there was a mix of facial tics. Stern yet unsettling.

"Has the jury reached a verdict in this matter?" inquired the judge.

"Yes, we have, Your Honor." Then, the jury judgment papers were passed to the judge, who read them, read them again, and passed them over to his fellow judges.

The bailiff read the summary. Guilty is what everyone heard, but it was more than that. Guilty on two counts, with the jury unable to reach a decision on six other charges. Not so! This was a massive verdict yet an upset in the conclusion, unexpected, a vile injustice, but to what true meaning?

The public reaction was total stupefaction, outright disapproval, and universal outrage of jury malfeasance, which must be corruption or fraud. As quasi-riots began across the world, two related observations ought to be noted at this juncture.

Associate Justice Ruth Bader Ginsburg, currently on the Supreme Court, had recently stated in another legal issue: "The Sixth Amendment secures to persons charged with a crime the right to be tried by an impartial jury reflecting a fair cross-section of the community."

But at this moment, the better interpretation by the mob: 'A jury is composed of citizens of average ignorance.'

It would come much later, as the media was willing to harass and pay jurors for interviews and flash books were published, that it came to be seen that Osama bin Laden had been

464 S.P. Grogan

convicted of terrorism and conspiracy. Still, two separate jurors (one being Juror # 55 on four charges, the other Juror # 22 on two parts of the indictment, who had been 17 years old on 9/11) believed, even with the *9/11 Commission Report* in evidence as Exhibit #1, that the prosecution had not provided enough evidence to convict bin Laden of being the 'prime instigator and manager' of the crimes. That others more directly had been the actual cause. It was perhaps nitpicking, splitting hairs, but the accusations and the conspiracy theories of *The Trial* this day began to fester with years of debate into the future, but this was for later analysis.

The judge turned to the defendant.

"You have been found guilty on three charges. Do you have any statement to make?"

Bin Laden rose, half the Stadium crowd booed, while the other half was yelling for silence to hear what might be said. With all the noise, the subtitles on the screen were now most important.

In Arabic, he gave not a long speech, not a rant but a recapitulation of his 1996 *Declaration of Jihad Against Americans Occupying the Land of the Two Holiest Sites*, which he had modernized fifteen years forward, minimizing his attack on Saudi Arabia, blasting the present American-led coalition for killing his brothers in Afghanistan, and touching on all the catch-phrases of a religious fatwa: "The people of Islam have suffered from aggression, iniquity, and injustice imposed on them by the Jewish-Christian alliance and their collaborators."

Nine hundred years later, it was still "The Faithful against the Crusaders."

Bin Laden ended with this warning:

"From the beginning, I have dismissed this exercise of so-called American justice as being unsanctioned and illegal, and my being detained by rogue outlaws a violation of my human rights as well against a country's sovereignty. I do not accept this court's right to judge, nor accept these verdicts. But I do accept that I am now a martyr for my beliefs, for I believe this Government will destroy my body; and the world will not know when and how, but I shall be gone. Not so my vision, nor my defense of my people and my Faith, to take my cause against my enemies.

"Praise be to Allah; we seek His help and ask for His pardon. We take refuge in Allah from our wrongs and bad deeds. Whomever Allah has guided will not be misled, and whoever has been misled will never be guided. I bear witness that there is no God but Allah. Praise be to Allah who said: I only desire your betterment to the best of my power and my success in my task."

"Let it be written: My ghost shall rise and raise the holy banner and carry forth the *Crimson Scimitar,* and all not yet converted shall follow or shall fall."

Osama stared directly at the camera, then sat, satisfied in his mind that his remarks would be heard by his followers and his form of jihad would live on.

After the jury had been excused, he was led away to await the journey to his unknown fate.

The Trial of the Century ended; few were satisfied. The Stadium slowly emptied, angry attendees littered the field with their thrown trash, and several tried vandalism but were stopped cold. Media cameras rushed to gain man-on-the-street verdict reactions, encouraging curses to rage around the microphones. Although the international press reported riots, they were not large more angry attendees in agreement of an unjust verdict. In many Middle East cities, the reaction seemed mild, less than 25 deaths reported, which was interpreted as either a good sign that tempers were not so agitated towards self-sacrifice or, in another sense, that al-Qaeda was not as organized to stage demonstrations worthy of media notice. Whether related or not, the news did cover two minor bombings in Israel and one market bombing in Kabul that killed 11 shoppers.

Callie stood at the back of the VIP suite. All had departed, some to call home, others to start packing. Transportation for the 'in' group would be late the following evening, allowing any rowdy hanger-on audience members to disperse.

In the suite, only she and Hugh Fox remained, she quietly watching as Hugh Fox stood front and center at the first row of seating, his head close to the glass, looking out, gazing at the exiting crowds, people shaking their fists at the outcome, even up to where the elites supposedly took advantage of their priority seating privilege. Callie wondered what was going through Hugh's mind. Was his whole effort successful in the goals he set? Or was he in an ultimate decompression? She wanted to give him support but had not the words to fit his mood. She turned and left. Tomorrow night when they all departed back to more staid lives, she would have to take stock of where she, and if he, fit in the greater scheme of things to come.

Now, alone, by himself, Hugh Fox spoke aloud, seeking an answer out of his grasp.

"This can't be over. This creation cannot just fade away."

REEL EIGHT — Their World Upside Down

EPISODE TWENTY-EIGHT — Ambush at Skilleo Stadium

Scene 1: al-Qaeda Attacks
Setting: Colorado

The aftermath of closing the event did not go as expected. The first phase went well. The producers of *The Trial* allowed a full 24 hours to pass to give the milling, grumbling, and disappointed crowds to disperse, retrieve their cars, pile into busses, and fold up their tents and pack up RVs. The press, for the most part, stuffed laptops into travel bags to return to studios and newsrooms, preparing their notes, enhancing their stories before the world, puffery of color background filler of their on-the-scene experiences. Their frame of mind that this 'show trial' was over became substantiated when three helicopters made quite the spectacle with their arrival, flew in, landed away from the stadium, picked up various groups of VIPs, and quickly departed. The assumption was that this exodus included the leading players, probably undercover agents posing as ticket holders and perhaps even bin Laden being hustled from the scene. In truth, to avoid backlash, the players were deftly and safely removed, including Judge Sanborn, the jurors, and the witnesses. The fake bin Laden likewise made a visible departure, speculating rumors that 'the terrorist had left the building.'

The next phase, the handover, did not go so well.

"It's time," from Wendell, at the door.

"I will miss my television shows," responded bin Laden, picking up a small suitcase, a valise of basic toiletries, several new medicines, vitamin supplements, a few of his favorite movie videos, and an unfinished novel. He was close to finishing an advanced reader's copy of Alā Aswāni's *On the State of Egypt: what made the revolution inevitable*. Bin Laden, as others, wondered why the Muslim Brotherhood jihad had not gained control over the government.

Both Wendell and Osama accepted the government would seize the suitcase, but the gesture had been made as a final farewell, with no meaning or emotions attached.

Outside bin Laden's detention apartment, he was met by Hugh Fox, his defense team of Langston and Eberhardt (to whom he offered a nod of recognition), and two armed guards. CAMERA ONE was present, as was one still camera person, clicking away, less for a future show, more for legal documentation regarding the assumed contractual understandings and the hand-over.

1:30 a.m. At the exit of the tunnel, rising into a ramp, the future backstage — marshaling yard, a grouping of official vehicles awaited. Two lead cars, to be followed by a military vehicle, more like an armored bank truck, a limousine, and finally, a Colorado State patrol car. Those associated with *King's Retribution*, who had been in close proximity to him since his capture, watched the dark-suited government protection team lead Osama bin Laden to the back of the armored truck. He had one last look at his captors, at Wendell, his nemesis of years back and the past few days, and by chance, his eyes caught the side wall of the loading ramp and saw the graffiti. Not the cursed scribbling: "Trial fixed. Osama Guilty." But it was the seemingly random red slash, the curving arc, that was the sign that he must prepare himself for eventuality…soon. To this, he smiled, and the watchers of the exchange tried to interpret his expression when he was unceremoniously handcuffed, a black bag placed over his head, and assisted into the truck, the door bolted behind him; the solitary occupant alone with his thoughts. As expected, the valise had been taken from him and thrown into the truck's front seat.

Booker and Harriet were directed to the limousine, where they discovered Cotton Matther seated, anxious to depart. The official truck convoy would travel with them as far as the Air Force Academy, where a government black ops plane awaited to ferry bin Laden and his guards to who knew where. The three attorneys would follow on the I-25 highway as far as the AFA turn-off, then head south to the Colorado Springs airport and return flights to their separate lives. Cotton Matther, smug in the limousine, was the only one pleased, for it was determined he would receive the cash bonus as the declared trial victor.

As part of the escort parade, a military helicopter suddenly appeared out of the night sky and hovered as a protective umbrella. Wendell noted the rotor noise was muffled, identical to the crashed one he had once photographed on a night like this.

One dark-suited official, who seemed to be in charge, approached Hugh Fox and handed over a large envelope. In order to be heard, his voice was almost a shout and not friendly.

"Per the U.S. Government's agreement with you and your various associates, here are the signed documents requested and approved by the U.S. Attorney General. Included are the signed acceptance of the prisoner from your custody, release of liability statement, and receipt of reward funds disbursed per your instructions."

Fox took the envelope, accepted that the contents were accurate, and turned them over to his attorney, Lisa Goss-Scott. She, in turn, handed the Government representative a legal document dismissing the lawsuit to all issues of Federal Agents appropriating the business property and assets of Skilleo Games Technology, with the caveat that such property would be returned within a reasonable period of time. Goss-Scott went off to inspect all legal wording, seeking out any buried loopholes. But Hugh had to surmise, with silent humor, *'If you can't trust the U.S. Government, then — never mind'* and left the thought hanging.

The official, not wanting to make any declaration beyond his instructions, could not hold back his contempt.

"What you did here was a total farce, just a publicity-seeking game; you realize that, don't you?"

Better than any televised interview before or since, Hugh Fox, in a loud declaration, summed up his intentions succinctly, "We captured alive a wanted fugitive, presented the facts for and against him, and returned him alive to the government's control. The world now has the opportunity to see how the U.S. Government acts to its own laws." There, he said it just right.

With that, Fox turned away, and those of his posse who watched from afar followed him while other late night residual gawkers began to disperse.

Not totally satisfied with what might come next, yet at this moment, in his mind, Hugh Fox could find great satisfaction in an endeavor he wished to see launched and was indeed completed. Justice served as it might, never straightforward, always a little messy, yet fair and balanced righting of wrongs. For his part, nothing to be ashamed of, and in his mind, he dismissed and proverbially washed his hands of the notion that Osama bin Laden was being escorted away to his probable execution. He had created *'The Trial of the Century,'* yes, to be criticized by many as being this 'farce,' but a judicial variation of the *Most Dangerous Game*. A game, perhaps, but an extraordinary one, played by the best gamer.

1:37 a.m. Wendell Holmes remained a few moments longer and watched as the caravan departed, flashing red-blue lights dancing macabre streaks across the landscape, while the guardian helicopter above displayed a spotlight tracking the road ahead. Wendell had mixed thoughts. He had gone along with the bumpy ride of last week's show-and-tell with nothing better to do with his life. And except for the mystery of *Crimson Scimitar* yet to solve (or debunk), all of his personal activity seemed to be winding down. But then, he mused, there was the Samantha Carlisle problem, or was it a problem or a new door opening? Was he a sparkly ornament on a holiday tree to be plucked for momentary enjoyment and then discarded? Or was he the tree, a place to shelter from the storm? Bad analogies. He did not know. Tonight, this moment seemed to be a descending curtain. Was it the finale or merely the Second Act completed, or to his generational nostalgia, perhaps another reel of an old classic film to be changed out?

Crimson Scimitar

1:40 a.m. The zipping fiery trail that exploded the helicopter answered many of his issues. The caravan had made it only two miles from the Stadium when the sky lit up, and the attack launched with the twenty-year-old version of the Stinger shoulder-launched anti-aircraft missile, this particular weapon transported up from the Southern border through a smuggler's tunnel, only weeks before.

The explosion started a rain of flaming debris down on the road ahead, blocking it. A moment of confusion granted them no time when two clunker cars raced from side roads. One smashed into the leading government vehicle, and another weaponized car into the trailing state patrol car, generating large fueled explosions as both attacking cars and their drivers were sacrificed in napalm-type infernos, destroying their targets and incinerating all occupants. Then, rising from under night camouflage tarps, two dune buggy racers sped around the surviving vehicles spraying automatic fire, taking out first the surviving drivers, especially the cab of the armored truck. Tonight, there would be no escape, except...

Razzor, intense and methodical, alighting from one of the off-road buggies, went to the back of the armored truck, put on the explosive charge, moved to the side of the truck, pounded on the side door, and counted to four seconds before the detonation blew off the back door. Then, in the billowing smoke, he helped Osma bin Laden, removed his head covering, and assisted him down from his brief mobile prison, the truck now a hulk, starting to burn, adding to the conflagration.

One of the attackers, Maj, appeared with bolt cutters, severing the leg chains and handcuffs, the residual parts of the wrist and ankle bracelets remained for later removal.

"Are you alright, my lord?" asked Razzor. He had only met bin Laden once, years earlier, but mythology among fanatics breeds blind reverence.

"Shoulder separation. I am fine."

"We will kill them all," said his rescuer.

"No. In the limousine. A black man and a woman. Secure them. Hostages."

Razzor did not like the idea of mercy but would obey.

As the scene was lit with fire, the renewed and re-established Emir also gave direction. "I believe they may have put my small suitcase in the truck cab. Can someone bring that with us?"

It must be something important, Razzor thought and wondered. He directed his leader to stand and hide in the brush on the side of the road as he began to finish the killing, retrieve prisoners, and grab an overnight bag filled with toiletries and swag.

The first explosion, as viewed from the limousine's interior, provided quick brilliance. Booker instinctively grabbed Harriet and pulled her to him, protective. The limousine lurched

470   S.P. Grogan

to a halt, trapped; the front windshield shattered as automatic fire laced the front seat, killing the driver. A few seconds outside of explosions and gunfire built indecision of anguished turmoil. Matther, no longer a defiant prosecutor, finally panicked, and flung himself to the side, grabbed a door handle, threw it open, and made it to his feet ready to run, confused on which direction, when he was slain, punched off his feet to the ground by rapid bullets striking.

Harriet, scared to the core, feared the worst, appreciated Booker's macho first instinct, yet didn't they need to do something, take any action, but what?

"Can we run?"

"Matther didn't make it." Langston had no ready solution when the smoking barrel of what looked to be a machine gun [Russian PP-2000] pushed into the open door, a scowl behind it.

Accented anger. "He wants you. I don't. Come quietly. He is waiting."

Expecting what he heard was a lie and that they were to be executed, Booker reluctantly, slowly helped Harriet out of the limousine, the hood and engine now afire. She glanced at Matther's body. She had spent a lifetime voicing the mitigation of violent acts, on her part, displaying gruesome evidence photos. She now lived her advocacy. Numbly, she stumbled forward, held up by Langston.

Gunfire had ceased; the noise of secondary vehicle explosions, crackling, hissing flames kept the night flickering day-glow.

Razzor, shouldering his weapon, forcing the black man to carry the small luggage, directed the three survivors — Booker, Harriet, and Osama to hurry off the road, and soon they were walking, tripping over uneven ground through sagebrush, between scattered pines to a black Range Rover, Sport version. Langston noted another 'attacker' exit from the driver's side, and both Booker and Harriet stopped, gaping. A bin Laden look-alike, beard, narrow face, but Harriet saw in the scattered light that greasepaint make-up had been added to exaggerate and age the double's face. Booker noticed the man's eyes were distant, non-focused. He knew the symptoms: drug inducement for courage.

"Be strong with Allah, my son," said bin Laden, laying a hand on the man's shoulder, which seemed to awaken his stupor, and enforce the look-alike's resolve to his task.

"That way," Qurbān," pointed Razzor, "towards the fires. "And remember, be seen." As the man turned towards his fate, as an afterthought, Razzor said, "Allahu Akbar."

Bin Laden turned to his captives, "My people never thought of a double until the suggestion was produced at the trial. By me. 'Crayfish.' We shall see if the improvisation works."

Shahin's man Maj came to quickly zip tie their hands, rope for their feet, before shoving Booker and Harriet into the back of the Range Rover, pushing them together and covering them with a tarp that had covered the weapons and smelled as such. Harriet heard laughing anger, "A rough road ahead," leaving her to wonder about several interpretations of what that sentence meant. But then, with headlights off, dim lights only, the cross-country bouncing and shaking began.

With the helicopter's destruction, Wendell turned to find a ride, to only see a small freight tug hauler at hand, keys in place, cursing when the speed would only hit 40 mph before oscillating vibration began. He braked sharply. Standing near one of the outside gates Samantha had seen him, seen the explosions, and had chased after him. She had flung herself at him, hands waving, to force him to stop. The hauler screeched across the gravel, and she jumped in.

"Sam, you can't come with me; that's a goddam ambush out there." He started up to regain turtle speed. He knew he wouldn't win any argument with her.

Getting aboard, she said casually, would you believe it, like they were on a 'date,' "You carrying? I've got my present from a special man. Locked and loaded. What do you think is happening?"

"No friendlies. Either they're trying to kill our recent prisoner or facilitating his escape. And please, Sam," he said with as much care and sincerity that was within his soul. "Please take my lead. You can cover me. Stay with the vehicle, but I'm not rushing you into a firefight."

In the midst of danger, she had her answer.

"You *do* like me, don't you, Wendell?" Not a question, mere verification.

"Yes, but will I regret it?" He concentrated on the road ahead.

"Not with my passion, honey." She put her left hand on his knee, her right hand holding her shiny new pistol.

"Damn it, woman, not the right time!"

They came to the tragedy too late. Several bodies on the ground, Samantha recognized Cotton Matther, his shirt front blood-dark in the night, eyes still open, set by fatal surprise. Around the destruction, a distinct odor of burned flesh sickened the nostrils.

Sirens were heard in the distance from the west, the police manning the traffic roadblocks at the highway were responding. Then, finally, a string of lights announced 'rescuers' racing from the Stadium. Not the smartest idea, Wendell considered, like moths to the flame.

Among the first of the curious onlookers to show up, oblivious to the stupidity in showing up to the carnage still smoldering, were Callie and Hugh. Callie, weapon ready.

472 S.P. Grogan

Soon, a small crowd gathered to gaze at the macabre massacre scene; Samantha gave up obeying safety caution and walked to Wendell. No active shooters. On the other side of the burning caravan wreckage, the police jumped out, likewise ready for anything. And then he appeared.

From around the melting pyre of the armored truck stepped...

"Bin Laden!" someone in the crowd shouted, and the bomb vest detonated body parts and gore upon the stunned.

Scene 2: Escape and Blowback
Setting: Colorado

2 a.m.

Bin Laden was exhausted, speaking little as they drove the backroads going northeast. The driver was the bug-eyed Spanish-North African named Majnoon, called 'Maj' concentrating on navigating open desert to a dark dirt road, slightly high on Adderall-derivatives, uppers. Bin Laden, with eyes closed, listened to Razzor talking low from the front seat passenger side as he relayed his story of watching the courtroom charade. "Blasphemous," he called it. He explained that his plan to launch this attack was spur-of-the-moment, the need to rouse the sacrificial spirit of his three other team members. All fated to Allah's wishes. Maj mumbled, "Sólo podrá ocurrirnos lo que Alá nos haya predestinado." [*Nothing will happen to us except what Allah has decreed.*]

Razzor said they were merely looking for opportunities to launch a rescue attempt, but if the Emir were too well guarded, they would have to back down and return to Los Angeles.

"Commander Shahin has informed me that courier Khalaf is in New York. He had to take the place of the London agent and is now in America, ready to strike. He has informed us he is in place to launch the Pelham part of *Crimson Scimitar*. For security measures, he has not been informed of your escape. Like others, we hope, he will believe you are dead."

"That is terrible. What happened to the London banker and the stockbroker?" Razzor said he did not know but planted the seed that Shahin did not believe Khalaf could perform his tasks well. That thought simmered with the escapee, bin Laden, resting, regaining his will and strength. "But if he now believes I have been killed, perhaps he will concentrate on avenging me; perhaps he will concentrate more on his tasks. I will only arise when all succeeds. And do so from Mexico with my manifesto that will bring America to its knees. And force them out of the Mideast." His old goals were revived, believing the coming attacks were at hand.

"We shall discover if this Khalaf succeeds. As Shahin tells me Khalaf wants to join us for the attack. Shahin tried to dissuade him, but we were not expecting that gaining your freedom would cost losing three men, affecting our main attack. So, yes, he might be helpful. He will join us near Denver."

"Denver? Isn't that the wrong direction?"

"Plans like these must have flexibility. Having you with us may launch the shutdown of all highways, and vehicles will be searched. I put the Professor on notice two days ago, just in case. He has secured a warehouse that is remote from the city, where you can rest, and we can prepare and modify plans at the last minute. We are to wait here in this Aurora suburb for about three weeks, prepare, and then follow the convoy. As we have been told, it comes through this Aurora city going south. And by then, as we travel on I-25, the infidel press will have gone elsewhere, on to other headlines."

"Yes, I see your thoughts. Thank you, Brother Razzor, for being a true leader in our Cause."

The two prisoners, manhandled by Maj with a fist to the stomach for Booker and a squeezed bottom for Harry, found themselves shoved into the tight back cargo space, knees bent. They could hear acceleration but none of the front-seat conversations. Instead, their talk was of comfort, the search thereof.

"I'm going from Jell-o to whipped pudding,' grimaced Harriet, whispering, her face mere inches from Bookers.

He could feel her heated breath against his face. His reply: "At least we are alive, shaken, not stirred. Since I'm black, being black and blue seems redundant."

"Not to discuss outcomes, but for how long are we safe?"

"I believe our longevity is a direct order from our 'client.' Instead of famous attorneys a day ago, we are trussed-up pawns in some greater game plan either as hostage or witness to bin Laden's new transgressions."

They could have edged themselves farther apart, but closeness meant comfort, which both of them needed.

"Where do you think they — we — are heading?" She leaned into him when the Range Rover took a sharp curve across a washboard road.

"Only a guess, but we've been on back roads. When we bounce, and I can look out, seeing the horizon going grey, I'm guessing we are heading north, maybe a little east. Not sure." Just then, all of a sudden, the road went from heavy rough road vibration to grating smooth, and they felt a turn to a new direction. "Now, we are on maybe an access road, maybe to a highway shortly. Civilization." And there it was; first, they felt a cattle guard, the Rover's speed

474 S.P. Grogan

increasing, the noise of a semi-truck hurtling past. He told her he thought they were going towards the end of the night on the highway going west.

Harriet re-adjusted herself to her back, still up against him.

"Any chance there will be roadblocks and a rescue?" She had to ask.

His lips were against her ear, quietly soothing, trying to alleviate her mind of worry, but it came out wrong.

"Harry, consider what we saw in the bloody attack. Chances are they all think we were shot and then burned up."

"Great. Just great. So, you're saying, '*King's Retribution*' won't save us?"

"Sorry, that's a scripted television show. No real cavalry. Besides, I never watched one of their programs, so not a fan."

She turned her head to him.

"God, what's that?" Booker pulled his head back.

"I stuck my tongue out at you. Can't help it if I licked your face."

Scene 3: Investigation
Setting: Outside the Stadium, morning

The Federal Bureau of Investigation took jurisdiction away from the Colorado State Patrol, even though one of their own had died, and since the attack was just outside the entrance to reservation land, came not one peep from tribal police, satisfied and thankful the mayhem was not their case, though they guarded their entrance with extreme diligence, waving off the curious. The Stadium access was barred and locked down, excepting Hugh Fox's select few.

As dawn broke, two major investigation tents had been put in place, one for crime scene evidence gathering, the other to interview those first on the scene. Crime scene forensics would take a day or two, then to Washington, D.C. and Quantico for myriad lab results before an official declaration. The de-briefing and taking eyewitness statements resulted in that parable of seven blind Buddhist monks touching an elephant for the first time: different observations of the same happening. The majority leaned in their recollections of having seen Osama bin Laden blow himself up (the story the national press ran with). Others were not so sure, specifically Hugh, Wendell, Samantha, and Callie, who looked to each other, then told the investigators they weren't sure what they saw — which was true, reserving any formal statement, skeptical of their skepticism. They offered very little and kept any questionable narrative to themselves.

The media these days receive all news story leads from wire services, telephoned tips and rumors, and monitoring the internet chat rooms. Grainy photos were posted on Facebook and conspiracy threads on a new platform founded last October 2010 called Instagram. The Associated Press got the jump with the bold headline *Terrorist Slain by Terrorists*, the sub-lede: *White Supremacists Ambush al Qaeda terrorist in Colorado — Osama bin Laden killed in suicide explosion.* Supposed journalists made the leap by viewing a posted iPhone photo showing the crowd of onlookers, washed out by poor camera resolution, weak flash red-eye, and lingering fire backlighting. All in the crowd looked 'white.' The story was never revised by subsequent events and remains online to this day.

The next investigative coup would come from CNN, which had covered last week's *Trial of the Century*, and still hovered around, trying to push King's Retribution to do an in-depth television interview. When the field reporter could not locate all the key trial players, further digging at the surface resulted in *Breaking News*: "Our associate in Colorado Springs has just learned from the El Paso County coroner (who never saw a body, let alone the collected disassembled body parts) that among the government officials slain, also killed were the legal teams involved in *The Trial of the Century*. Assumed victims beyond government agents are New York District Attorney Cotton Matter V, Defense Attorneys Booker Langston and Harriet Eberhardt. More details are forthcoming as we await a press conference from the FBI (delayed, citing 'ongoing investigations')." It would not be until two days later that one reporter who had been at the Skilleo Stadium called his fellow media buddy with this confusing question: "Didn't we see bin Laden board a helicopter the day before the night attack?" Another public round of fomented speculation ensued, wasting two days to gain the truth when the bin Laden actor showed up at a highly publicized press conference to set the record straight and pass out his publicity headshots.

Meanwhile, the *King's Retribution* team, after that violent night, with little or no sleep and a morning of intense FBI questioning, were able to engineer a retreat to their temporary War Room at the Stadium by 2 pm. The Executive Committee members were exhausted and collapsed into chairs as the other crew and cast arrived. The first statement as they all crowded in, "No, I don't know if they are dead," Wendell said firmly. "The fires were too intense. I saw burned bodies in the vehicles, and I thought the form of one body in the limousine where the driver sat. Beyond that, I can offer nothing positive, only assumptions, and I won't." He let others hold out hope. Over the length of this bin Laden courtroom drama, Booker and Harriet had become adopted cohorts of the Discovery, Hunt, and Capture Teams.

Bennie was exasperated, wanting facts. "Cotton Matther was shot at the limousine outside; then why not the others?"

Storm King, on a speaker phone from the rehabilitation hospital, sounded raspy, a little drugged up from the pain, and still had not modified his stilted opinion.

"Morning news said some American heroes offed Osama, but it's a weird killing. I don't see a sanctioned military team for this. Too messy. The coward took the easy way out pushed his own trigger. Kerplooie."

"Maybe the news services are wrong," was Samantha's flat, embittered response, sad that friends may have died horribly.

"Before we all get morbid or think the worst," said Fox, showing some mild excitement on purpose. "I suggest we continue our work, which I think may be more important than ever, and do so based on three facts from my own view, on what I think I actually saw. One, I will go forward on the assumption that Booker and Harriet are alive somewhere, probably kidnapped, now prisoners, and hopefully not abused. Do I know? No, but until shown evidence otherwise, to me, they survived. Two, Osama bin Laden is alive and well and somewhere else. No, I can't be certain of that either. Going on: and three, if number Two is correct, his plan, this *Crimson Scimitar* he mentioned several times, may officially be in full action mode, and still not knowing what we face, there is a countdown ticking. Bin Laden overseeing his own plan is more dangerous than ever."

Storm was doubtful over the phone. "Why do you think our boy didn't turn himself into mincemeat? Everyone else saw him do it."

Wendell weighed in. "People in extreme situations see the large picture in a visual flash, not trying to focus on small details. I was looking for a gun in his hand, only saw the detonator, but what I didn't see were tensile steel restraints."

"Restraints?" from Gizmo, who had missed all the excitement, playing a Skilleo game at the Stadium's Game Center.

"Handcuffs and bin Laden's leg shackles." Callie began to nod, understanding. "We saw him placed in the armored truck restrained," she said, "but less than 15 minutes later, he's free as a bird, with an explosive vest strapped on. I just don't see bin Laden as the self-martyr type; why not walk into the crowd and detonate? Why not try to escape into the desert? And above all, in this fuck-up, if the people showing up wanted to kill him, they didn't; and if they were rescuers, why didn't they spirit him away? Something's fishy, I agree. But what?"

"We are all on the same page," said Wendell, dismissing Storm's views. "And it will take the Fibbies about four days to realize they may have the Main Terrorist back on the loose. And knowing them, they may just not want to tear this country apart, looking for a terrorist who escaped them more than once. If we accept Hugh's logic, Booker and Harry are prisoners of bin Laden and/or with the terrorist strike force which freed him. Yes, finding and freeing our friends is now our prime focus, perfect for *King's Retribution*, but so is investigating *Crimson Scimitar*. I say you all take the public position that Booker and Harry have been kidnapped, and we use that as cover to pursue *Crimson Scimitar*. I'm sorry I'm talking so much, but don't you see that when we find the attorneys, we locate *Crimson Scimitar*?"

That juxtaposition, the correlation where two separate acts would meet at the same point, had never really struck them. So the Ali Baba Library came back to the forefront.

Samantha had been silent. She was impressed by Wendell's 'outburst,' if you would call it that. That man is not only a doer; he is a leader, quiet, unassuming, but a natural. She could work with that.

In the course of the conversations, another idea was generated, a material one not yet broached.

"Hey, the reward money was paid out," Bennie had been keeping score. "Does that mean if we find bin Laden again, we could get another reward?"

"Reward money?" Storm King, over the phone, cured out of his haze with this new revelation. "We did get the reward money. How's that going to be divvied up?"

"Your altruism is *so* appreciated," a nasty smirk from Callie; she had her former lover pegged as the prick he had always been. Life-threatening accident or no accident.

Hugh Fox overlooked the co-star's dig and played Fox the Benevolent, with co-owner Samantha's blessing.

"Half of the funds will go to the established foundation for disbursement to the 9/11 victims' families and the families of the police and firemen who lost their lives. The remainder of the funds will be distributed as year-end bonuses to all employees of *King's Retribution*, including those Skilleo techies on internet research. Hugh gave an evil-eye stare at the phone wherein was the show's star: "Contributing to those impacted by 9/11 meets with your approval, Storm?" Hugh could be as catty as the next.

"Yeah, I guess," feigning sincerity, King slunk back to silence.

"Oh," said Fox, "Again, small details. The reward offered by the U.S. Government may be taxable. You may need to do tax planning to protect your net payment. My accountants will call your accountants." There was some snickering. The *KR* people knew their series star was a lousy financial record keeper and had been audited by the IRS several times.

"Meanwhile," continued Fox, "Let's get back to the business at hand. *Crimson Scimitar*. Let's adjourn for today, get packed up, and an early bedtime to recharge batteries. Tomorrow we will be shutting down our workplace here and returning to California. I will find a schedule where all of us can meet as soon as possible.

"But knowing what we are doing is a priority. This morning I rented a sound stage near Five Aces Studioz, where we should keep out of the radar from the press, paparazzi, and deranged fans. Please, let's try to maintain a low profile. Everyone has had enough visibility, and publicity, good and bad, to last a lifetime. Our next phase, I pray, may be critical to help Booker and Harriet. Keep that in mind." With the phone as a barrier, the group still wanted to stare dagger eyes at *you-know-who-never-keeps-his-damn-mouth-shut*. Low-key, when it was about Storm King, did not compute.

"You mentioned 'everyone,' Bennie asked, looking around. "Where is our new fire-power team member, Pacheco? I didn't see him the last several days."

Fox deflected. "Oh, he's on special project assignment. He will join us when we get to our new digs."

With that, the meeting broke up, all curious, no one satisfied, about anything. What would happen next? That's what bothered them — those who had been at *The Trial* sincerely worried about the lawyers gone missing.

For the public's perception, *The Trial of the Century* had met audience penetration expectations, breaking all records. The surprise verdict was not the desired outcome to an overwhelming majority of the attending and world viewers, but guaranteed weeks of public debate sustained the buzz. The attempted assassination by a religious zealot and his ilk became only the prelude to the rushed announcement of bin Laden's death and soon thereafter came the press release announcement of *Ambush at Skilleo Stadium*, a *telenovela*, going into fast-track production for the small screen by a Spanish-speaking soap opera television studio. Hugh Fox wondered why he hadn't thought of the idea but was going to push his writer to finish the narrative of *The Trial* for book publication, and he would put in a call prepping Five Aces Studioz to issue a press release announcing a movie based on the trial — mainly to forestall other production companies. He was back in his element, a young man who thrived in creative crises.

Scene 4: Departing Events
Setting: Skilleo Stadium

#1

The Skilleo attorney, Lisa Scott-Goss, ran into Gizmo as he left the Game Center. They had a friendly exchange of 'how's it going?' talk when Gizmo took the leap out of his league and stuttered out,

"Last night here, we are back at it for Mr. Fox. Back in L.A. I'm on a special project for him while at the same time trying to read an Ali Baba Library book and watch a movie that Storm King doesn't want to view."

"Yeah," attorney Goss offered friendly understanding. "While here, I read a book myself, Alex Berenson, *The Faithful Spy.* Fittingly, an al Qaeda biological plague attack. Doesn't fit though with Mr. Holme's theory on something nuclear. I think I heard he and Miss Carlisle are going to watch *The Peacemaker.* Bosnian Serbs and a dirty bomb."

"I guess what I'm babbling about is that I have this old VCR movie that was sent to us called *Villains,* starring Richard Burton, and I have jerry-rigged a digital cross-face system so I can play it. And there is a coach's screening room for future soccer strategy films, and I'm just wondering if you'd like to watch it tonight, with me. It's all private and such, so we won't be bothered, and they got theater-type seating, some of it at least built out, a lot of cushions in plastic lying around the floor. Just wondering if you'd be interested?"

For the first time, Attorney Goss examined the nerd, and separated her study of him from her past impression of Gizmo, lost in the miasma that made up all the Skilleo tech grunts and day workers those she paid no attention to on a daily basis at the Headquarters campus. All were certainly creative and bright; among them, Hugh Fox had himself selected Gizmo for some clandestine research project she knew no details about. So he must be a 'somebody.'

"Yeah, it could be a fun break."

Later, in the evening, just before their private tête-a-tête showing of *Villain* began, she asked him, "What is your real name?"

"Andrew," he replied, uncomfortable in the confession.

"I like Gizmo better; it suits you." Her smile was infectious.

The next morning, Attorney Goss walked into an impromptu meeting of the Executive Committee and announced:

"I can prove that Osama bin Laden is alive."

They were dumbfounded, with a few 'What?'

"I watched a movie last night called *Villain,* starring Richard Burton. 1971. Very graphic. Bad reviews."

"One of Ali Baba's collection," interjected Wendell, wondering who he had originally assigned that to; he thought it was to Storm King, to watch. "Go on, please."

"After the movie, I Googled background information on it and found that the basis of the film was a story about two London gangsters who actually existed, active in the 1950s to about 1967. In prison by 1969, various appeals processes over the next several years Organized crime leaders in the East End of London. They were semi-famous. Get this. The two gangsters were not only brothers, they were twins, and their last names were 'Kray' with a 'K.'

"Los hijo de puta!" exclaimed Callie. "The bastard bin Laden was telling his people, 'twins,' that was those two identical letters, II, meaning two alike. Create a double of me if it helps in your plans. You got to hand it to him. And Ali Baba knew the answer. Both deserve credit. Dios Malditos sean al infierno!" ('Damn them to hell!')

Attorney Goss jumped back in. "And I researched further, bin Laden as a teenager was in London, maybe around the time, 1970-1971, when they were still in the news. He's there at the same time the film is released. I would guess he's got some sort of sick fascination with infamous bad people, and later, grown up, went looking for a copy of that movie. It's a very psycho-violent movie, like *Clockwork Orange*."

"Excellent work, Linda," beamed Hugh. "If bin Laden is alive, chances are he has Bookie and Harry, for what purpose I don't know, maybe a bargaining chip if they are cornered."

Linda saw the Executive Committee animated, exchanging theories, and made a quiet exit; it was for the best.

This morning she was walking a little funny and hoped no one noticed. The cream lotion on the inside of her thighs still stung from the facial beard burns.

#2

11 pm His not-much stuff to pack was already finished for the next morning's departure. Still restless, he settled on the top of his bed covers with one of his reading list books, Brad Thor's *The Path of the Assassin*; a quiet knock came on his door.

Samantha in her silk robe. She walked past him into his room. He shut the door. Internal, suppressed anguish gushed to the surface: "I'm a wreck. Explosions in the night, gunfire, and you go charging towards whatever danger might get you killed. And then, I go with you, not to be some Calamity Jane to your Wild Bill Hickock, but I go because I am worried about you. I want to protect you. I don't want anything to happen to you. I was not thinking straight about what I wanted or how stupid my actions were. I can take care of myself. Always have. I have never pursued a man until last night. I don't know what this all means. But Wendell, tonight, will you just hold me? Nothing more. Let me spend the night trying to define my feelings, figure out if I'm in a new world out of my depth, or sinking in an emotion, wanting to be saved…by you."

To that soliloquy, Wendell could not equal a response. He opened his arms, and she came to him, and he wrapped her in an embrace, not of passion but of concern, tenderness. He took her to his bed, removed her robe to view a transparent negligee that defined a toned lovely woman, age irrelevant to the depth he saw in her. He set his book aside as he removed his clothes to his underwear. As she requested, they lay next to each other, holding, feeling warmth. A tear from businesswoman Samantha Carlisle graced his shoulder. She leaned on him, sensing the hardness of his excitement. She moved her own desire to safer ground and asked simply, still an invitation, "Tomorrow, let's start watching movies together."

Lights off, they talked half the night with intermittent quality hours of light touching, shoulder-rubbing out aches, face caressing, sensitive fingers roaming, teasing wetness, but went no further; a postponement of pleasure explosions to future anticipation. This, as a beginning, could be enough until the next moment. Finally, they fell asleep in an embrace and, by morning though they had not eternally or physically coupled, had, with silent smiles and a mouth-wash gargled morning kiss, become more than casual friends.

Scene 5: Temporary Destination
Setting: Early morning, Aurora, Colorado

6 a.m. Both Razzor and bin Laden, for the first time, heard a voice from the back. Booker half-shouting, "I have a request for a bathroom stop."

Razzor's response back. "20 minutes, and you can shit all you want."

"I don't know if I can hold it even that long," Harriet's low wail.

Booker offered her weak empathy. "No worries. It'd be no worse than Riker's Island cells."

"Gee, so considerate." This time her lips to his cheek brought a swift peck.

He went serious. "I'll get you through this, Harry." She knew immediately he reverted to a distant failure, a deep nightmare when he hadn't saved his fiancée. Hopeless then, did he feel hopeless again? Even ten years later, was it *her* face he envisioned before him in the darkness of the hard cargo space? By the morning graying, could he not see the real person who lay next to him? He must see her, see that she too could provide strength to their unknowns.

"We will get through this… together…Bookie."

"Yes," acknowledging her with his chin touching the top of her head.

Good, she thought, get to know me, feel the press of my body.

"Oh, dear God." Facing mortal danger or not, she pissed herself. *Not helping, Harry.*

By the time semi-darkness became morning light, the leader of al-Qaeda had become invigorated, so reaffirmed with confidence from a daring escape that he could believe success was so close. Driver Maj turned down an aisle of warehouses and drove the SUV into an open warehouse, the door closing behind them. Soon, Osama bin Laden, to his surprise and self-gratification of his worth, was surrounded by his *Crimson Scimitar* attack team, receiving

482   S.P. Grogan

adulation, tears, men on their knees, his soldiers of Allah, kissing the hem of his robe, kissing his feet, even Shahin kissing the hand of the future Emir of the Caliphate, the dream reborn.

Later, when the leader, bin Laden, met privately with his mission commander, Shahin, they discussed their part of the *Crimson Scimitar* attack and agreed they might have two obstacles to face; what to do with their prisoners from *King's Retribution* and what would be the role for their super courier Khalaf, and after the attack what would be his role in the New Order. Bin Laden was now having doubts about promoting the boy as a peace conference attendee, even as a delegate secretary, wondering if better-qualified jihadists would now join or that he, the supreme leader of his organization, who always was the best to espouse al-Qaeda's position in any negotiations with the U.S.-led coalition.

"From the limited discussions I had with my captors," said bin Laden, processing all he recalled from capture to escape. "Though I constantly teased them about *Crimson Scimitar,* they pretended they knew about our attack, just not place and time. Frankly, I don't think they have a clue, but it was unfortunate that Khalaf allowed his resource documents to be compromised."

"I do not think Khalaf is worthy of any higher appointment in your administration, as I have heard from discussions I had with leaders in Wana before the missile attack on our brothers. May Allah embrace them," said Shahin.

"I am having second thoughts myself. But at this time, it is critical that he successfully launch the First Phase. Al-Qaeda needs the financial funds from the attacks he is overseeing."

"And his coming here before we launch the final attack at the Bridge?"

"Let him come, and I will judge the circumstances."

"And as to your concern about this TV show of fake soldiers, I think you can be assured they have been castrated and become eunuchs. Their main star is severely injured; sadly, he survived."

"Yes, very bold action. I am pleased this Razzor Hassim, one of us, took such initiative. That should set them back. And the morning newspaper that you have shown me has the enemies of *King's Retribution* saying it is their fault you escaped and then were killed. They will lose public favor, and they will stay home to tend their wounds."

"But, my Sheik, I have to ask, what are your plans for these two prisoners? They could also become a handicap to our planned operation."

"Skillful strategies must allow for flexibility and contingencies. It was a spontaneous decision to bring them with us, but I have ideas about their usefulness."

"And if they do not prove valuable to the attack plan we are now ready to strike?"

Crimson Scimitar

483

"We can discard them when we leave for Mexico and home." Bin Laden said this to salve Shahin's militant attitude towards anti-Moslem detainees. He had a history of taking no prisoners, yet one of the reasons he was chosen to lead this operation.

And bin Laden knew he only needed one of his ex-attorneys to advance his message.

Scene 6: The Jihadist Bends
Setting: New York City, July 22-25, 2022

Sabz had never heard of the ancient Greek comedy *Lysistrata* by Aristophanes, where women withhold their sexual favors to stop a war between the men of two city-states. To that long ago era, it was not feminist doctrine, just plain bawdy humor.

Sabz, more rascal than vixen, had come to believe in a variation of such policy — ask favors thought important, and when denied, pout and close her legs to Khalaf's eagerness to bed her.

She knew her mind. She would not be stuck as a virtual prisoner in their hotel room while Khalaf sat glued to the television to watch *The Trial*. Politics bored her. As she saw the world beyond her hotel window, it offered a vibrant and exciting life, beyond her daily devouring of newspapers or watching American sitcoms where she could not easily follow the jokes. Why not more? Sabz wanted to immerse herself into the life of New York City, even with the stifling hot summer heat melting the air and scorching the sidewalks which then drove the wealthy capitalists to summer cottages in guarded enclaves on secret islands to the northeast, places like Long Island and Cape Cod, and a sought paradise called Connecticut.

She beamed with the requests granted, showing him the two-hour time difference from the East Coast to Colorado, where they could go out for quality dinners after the *Trial* court adjourned for the day. In this subtle push, she was able to explore restaurants like Mario Batali's Eataly Marketplace and a Nuevo Latin menu at Nuela. Khalaf, at first, hesitated, not yet comfortable in his pretend role at night as a Emirates diplomat or, during the day, a London market investor. Finally, curiosity got the best of him, but at all times, out of the hotel, he carried his burner phone that could instantly put him in contact with the other mission members.

During the five-day period of *The Trial*, and thereafter for nearly a month, without him knowing it, his character began changing, mellowing, accepting the urban environment around him, noticing the variety of citizens scurrying past, and not being so disgusted because that's the way he had been taught, a required hating of all things not pure to the dogma he grew up in.

During these dinners, walks around neighborhoods, or visits to tourist areas like museums, their conversations were not small talk between lovers; they still did not yet define their relationship, nor was there any talk about back home. Khalaf's paranoia and furtive glances around as he walked showed his penchant for secrecy still paramount. In their conversations, with the boundaries of subject matter, he was not going to encourage her to speak constantly of clothing fashions, nor would she let him convert her to his strict fundamentalism, fending off his arguments with an avalanche of 'why?' At an impasse in the beginning of this New York sojourn, it came to be that the only common ground where they found intelligence and mutual excitement was the stock market and the corporations that made up the daily rise and fall of share pricing. In their downtime, they were reading stock market investment guides, scouring through the *Wall Street Journal* and *Barron's,* seeking an understanding of economic trends. They were compulsive; he for the cause, she for her love of mathematics and its harmony tracking underlying valuations.

He asked one evening while they were glowing, lounging post-coitus, "What would you invest in today if you had, say, $10,000 U.S. dollars?" He continued the thought, "By my study, one should look around and decide what interests them, what product is new and innovative, that might have a future to be profitable."

Sabz gave the question serious thought. "Fashion is growing, and good companies follow the trend of what women buy, so yes, they should be considered."

"Any company in mind?" He knew she adored the flashy clothing magazines.

"I read the fashion house Michael Kors is considering, how do they say, going public, selling ownership, later this year. They are popular and what they call themselves is 'affordable luxury.' You bought me one of their purses last week." He had started buying her gifts that made her happy. He enjoyed seeing her child-like joy for such a simple present. "It was very gracious of you since it cost $175 U.S."

"$175!" That had been two months of his courier salary. He was going to lash out at her extravagance, but then he would have to make her crawl off him. Something struck him; when he had asked the store clerk to help them choose the right purse, and Sabz selected this Michael Kors brand, the saleswoman said something like that was the last one they had in stock, and they were selling like, what was it, 'like hot bread' or was it 'hot cakes' like atayef?"

"And dear Khalaf, what of you?" She propped herself up and looked into his eyes; he saw it, genuine interest in what he now thought. Very comforting. He gave his wisdom so that she might learn from him.

"Yes, I have been reading, and I like technology, but more analyzing what events on a grand scale might impact a company and its stock price. He was thinking in terms of *Crimson Scimitar* strategies.

"Let me give you an example of my thinking. Just saying, and this is hypothetical, but what if the world's fleet of oil tankers, say 20%, would not be able to carry crude from Saudi Arabia? What do you think would happen to oil prices?"

She was pleased he asked her opinion.

"Oil prices would go very high, and people could not afford to drive their cars. Economies might suffer"

"Yes, and they would be forced to turn from fuel consumption to either taking buses or perhaps try out automobiles with these new electric batteries. There is a company that sold its stock last year called Tesla — named after a man Tesla who designed alternating current electricity. One must think long term and believe there may be many crises to disrupt Americans' love of their big cars. I am watching Tesla stock (as well as stocks of amusement parks, he did not tell her).

"Another company I had considered was Apple Computers."

"Yes, you bought me that small portable, a laptop."

"Their sales have been strong, but recently their founder, Jobs is his name, has taken a medical leave, and I think the loss of leadership can cause investor doubt as to the future."

She kissed him lightly. She saw a new opportunity but said her words sweetly.

"Dear Khalaf, that is a brilliant thought. But, like your al-Qaeda plans, you must not take personal risks to achieve such goals." (Within their faith, one of the Pillars of Islam is in giving wealth to zakat, charity — *'O you who have believed, do not consume one another's wealth unjustly but only business by mutual consent.'*) She encouraged him gently, "Wealth is a gift of Allah; profit is allowed but not greed."

That night and for days thereafter, they discussed how the business world worked and how one played the market…for wealth.

Sabz's insular world, like Khalaf's, came undone with the guilty verdict from *The Trial*. It was anticipated, but not the split verdict. Khalaf still agonized over his leader being publicly executed or locked away for life. Then, the next day came the national news that Osama bin Laden had been murdered by American nationalist vigilantes. Sabz had to deal with him for six hours in distraught melancholy, the loss of what was the true path if his spiritual leader had been slain, or later as the news stations reported, he had taken his own life by suicide vest. Khalaf, in this depression, became confused. He knew, personally more than others, that bin Laden never spoke of that ending; he had pills to consume if cornered. Khalaf now wondered why did he not take them when he was captured in Abbottabad? Did he not have time?

His worry ended. At 8 pm, his secreted cell phone buzzed. Khalaf left the television show he and Sabz were watching, to take the call in another room. Shahin's message was short.

"Your actions shall proceed, perhaps in four weeks. Be prepared to act in mid-September."

The line went dead. Khalaf gained purpose and direction once more. He would act and achieve revenge for the killing of his emir.

486   S.P. Grogan

She saw his flushed face, his tensing. "In a month or two, I shall do my duty and then leave to meet with my brothers." Then, he said something a jihadist warrior would not normally say at the door's threshold as one left for battle. "You can stay here until my return."

Sabz hugged him. He accepted her tears as her sincere caring, her thankfulness that he would be her protector, but it was more than that. Sabz knew she had only this limited time to persuade him that staying with her, both of them in a life together, without political turmoil, would be the far better decision.

EPISODE TWENTY-NINE — New Investigations

Scene 1: The Meeting Never Held
Setting: Somewhere in Washington, D.C.

The Month of August, Week 1-7th

A meeting was held by top representatives of the government's intelligence agencies on the 4th of August 2011. No records were taken. Months later, national investigative reporters writing in *The Washington Post* alluded to it from a 'reliable source' when they were trying to wrap their hands around the events in a two-series article entitled: "*Did the Crimson Scimitar Plot Ever Happen?*"

Their vague hypothesis in their writing, with no affirmed evidence, was that the government sought to put a lid on terrorist activities in the United States to protect and prevent the American people from inevitable panic around the 10th anniversary. Partially true, but not the entire story.

Another decade would pass before certain private hand-written notes of an official in attendance at this 'non-meeting' found the light of day and are mentioned herein, the summary of which, by the first week in August, the U.S. Government (again consisting of certain alphabet agencies with the White House ad-hoc 'being brought up to speed,' that by their findings: (a) Osama bin Laden was not killed by detonation at the Skilleo ambush (DNA confirmed such), and remained at large; (b) The two defense attorneys of this *Trial of the Century* had not been slain as was the prosecutor, their whereabouts unknown, the prevailing theory that they were captured as human shields, later killed, their bodies disposed of (as an expected reaction by terrorists); and (c) the final consensus was that the related events during these times required stealth P.R. management 'to lessen the public awareness of non-verified threats.'

By this directive, the powers of the government decided their response to the continual inquisitive media would be to 'suggest' that with the arrest of Pastor Tate and his co-defendants, presently charged with attempted murder, they were part of a larger white nationalist supremacist cabal. By association, similar like-minded criminals, in most likelihood, are suspects behind the attempted kidnapping of Osama bin Laden, forcing his suicide by vest bomb, the murder of government officials, the targeted killing of prosecutor Cotton Matther (for failing to convict the terrorist on *all* charges), and the kidnapping of attorneys Booker Langston and Harriet Eberhardt (for failing to attempt, by legal subterfuge, to set free the terrorist bin Laden). The FBI announced with fanfare that they had launched a nationwide search for these white nationalists.

This became the messaging that the national media ran with. Both government and the 'legacy' media had an unspoken agreement that they had been raked over the coals publicly for massive Islamophobia in Bush's administration, both the 9/11 attack and the manipulation with misleading intelligence that the Iraq war was justified to combat the War on Terrorism. White supremacists in 2011 were the better choice and the more politically correct boogeymen.

With this news fodder, *The Trial* and bin Laden's 'suicide' remained at the public's forefront, as was the acceptance that the FBI would diligently search for the kidnappers and the kidnapped victims. The underlying strategy was that this stated public reasoning would mask the search for their, once again, misplaced terrorist, Osama bin Laden, who was free to do untold damage.

Ironically, *King's Retribution* would likewise use the hunt for their kidnapped friends as a facade to launch their own search (validating that bin Laden still lived would create a tsunami shitstorm of false leads and unwanted publicity.).

Finally, the CIA, also represented at this meeting, had to admit that there had been increased chatter in the ether of intelligence collection on jihadist's doublespeak but nothing definite. However, they agreed that the term *Crimson Scimitar* mentioned by bin Laden in court and by other clandestine collection methods had been logged as a repetitive coincidence, but nothing more of substance and discounted to be the usual propaganda ploy of continued attacks-to-come bragging, as had been used in the past, with no actual incidents to follow.

What the CIA did not feel germane to the current discussion was that going back to the Abbottabad attack, they had confirmed that a 'mystery resident' not yet identified had been living at the compound. The filtering process of achieving an accurate identification was within the purview of Matthew Brady's section, and when accomplished, the al-Qaeda presumed sub-leader would be rewarded with an arrest warrant, superfluous since a cash reward bounty attached to a kill-on-sight order was the preferred outcome.

488   S.P. Grogan

In the final note-taking, all agreed that there should be heightened vigilance by the law enforcement community, again closer to the September 11th tenth anniversary. As for Osama bin Laden, a majority in the meeting assumed he had already fled the United States via the cartel smuggling routes; his goal, desperately seeking to reach a secure hideout in the Mideast and resources in those regions should be called in, put on standby, and prepared when he would next appear internationally.

How wrong they were in this appraisal on the 4th of August, yet in the days following, how effective as the U.S. Government continued with its conspiracy of fact suppression and manipulation of what the public viewed as truth.

Scene 2: Pacheco's War Wagon
Setting: Somewhere in Los Angeles, August 8th

Unavoidable scheduling conflicts did not bring them to this location until nearly ten days later. The new War Room: a small open sound stage, folding tables became a conference table, with about five computer stations for the Skilleo nerds to the side on smaller card-like tables. Coaxial cables taped to the floor. The latest laptops awaited the *KR* stars and the Skilleo supporting cast. A minimalist warehouse décor like a newsroom without the news.

Shawn Pacheco had rejoined the group. He could sense the palpable anxiety and concern about their legal friends, missing, going into the second week, and no new information. Too much speculation, all false leads.

In joining in, Pacheco's military sense felt the strange vibrations in the air at the makeshift conference table. Obvious, a depressed feeling that no one held anything concrete, no skywriting in the sky pointing to lurking terrorists, who would be quickly identified and dispatched to their ancestors.

The star personnel aspects within the room could not hide emotions when viewed through Pacheco's dispassionate skills of observation. Hugh Fox and Callie Cardoza exchanged quick, furtive glances, taking seats close to each other. The same could be said, as Shawn noticed, of Wendell Holmes and Samantha Carlisle; they ignored each other even when one might be talking to the group, but their silent nods and facials tics, let him know somehow, somewhere, the two had developed a relationship. Pure Hollywood, he surmised, recreational bed hopping must be the norm around the elites, and such mental voyeurism brought him to be faithful to his estranged fiancée Janet and seek some action to win her back.

Here, as he viewed the scene, if Pacheco were the team leader, he would have delivered a harsh scolding to all four of them, 'think only of the mission' and shut away the personal issues in the farthest recess of your brain until all is over, retrieval the foremost, save our friends, then it would be over, and all so enamored could fuck like rabbits.

When 'what' was all over? That was the central question as various team members gave verbal reports. Storm King on a remote television conference feed, sat in a wheelchair, drinking certainly non-alcoholic juice from a sippy cup. He played his usual role as the devil's advocate, and Shawn found the star egotistically brusque and offensive, yet he was scoring points. The entire hypothesis of a terrorist attack by al-Qaeda could be distilled down to only gut feelings, those of Wendell Holmes and Shawn Pacheco, both with less than transparent credentials. Besides, if the 'assumptions' from the 'Ambush at Skilleo Stadium' brought no new hard information, then the interest would invariably die off, and old lives would be resumed.

Hugh Fox had the antidote for the doldrums: introduce a new toy gadget.

Pacheco pushed a garage door opener for the back of the building, and *KR* driver Bennie drove the surprise inside.

"What is it?" asked one of the geeks, the ever-quiet and withdrawn Brigit.

"From our gameplay, it looks like a souped-up SWAT truck," said the ever-knowing Gizmo.

"No, better than that," answered SEAL Pacheco. "This is the 'Storm Wagon.' He and a beaming Fox noted the demeanor change on the screen from *KR* star King and could see him pleasantly mouth, 'Storm Wagon.' Pandering once again essential to coincide with the star's physical therapy regimen.

Pacheco launched into his project, boasting, and should be proud to do so — it had the best features.

"This is a tricked-out beauty, double the size of the standard city SWAT; the front module, a Desert Storm Humvee styling, is a reinforced cab for the driver and guard; behind them is the Attack Team. The back detachable Iron Maiden trailer configuration is the command tech center with full 360-degree camera capabilities. Extra plating, highway certified to 100 mph, one hiddenM60D vehicle-mounted machine gun on a top turret pop-up, and an entire blast-proof closet for your every weapon desire, from high-capacity ordinance, riot shotguns to a miniature bazooka, explosives big and small, like multiple grenade choices. For Abbas, a cubicle station to perform special effects magic. Even glide parachutes for stealth soaring. This is a SWAT Beast on steroids." Like a Detroit car show, a thirty-minute under-the-hood and inside module inspection tour ensued, Q & A, and a fair question near the end of the presentation.

"Hell, I love it for riots and urban war, but what does one do with this testosterone monstrosity?" Callie's insight, her tease with a misandrist grin.

"Rapid Response," explained Hugh; after all, he paid for the 'toy.' "One here for the West Coast; I am preparing another to be stationed on the East Coast, maybe in Florida. A 'just-in-case' geographical placement with quick deployment to whatever challenge. If nothing pans out, we can strip it down to a mobile production studio and the exterior design an 'A-Team' prop feature in Season Three. That's what the stage I rented is for; to build out an interior replica for close-ups." Hugh Fox had been a fast learner to show business. His remarks brought genuine smiles to those of *King's Retribution*. There was still a future out there, as plastic as it now seemed to the reality of death and destruction outside the Skilleo Stadium.

"Shall we return to our agenda," pushed Samantha. "So we can hear all your best deductive guesswork. Booker and Harry are counting on us." All, like Storm King, were again sober.

Scene 3: Captivity
Setting: Warehouse in Aurora, Colorado

The prisoners spent the first week of captivity trying to make the best of their warehouse cell. To Harriet's appraisal, it was tolerable, considering other possibilities, including torture. They were housed in a small office that, fortunately for her, had a bathroom. Unfortunately, their interior location precluded windows to judge day and night or possible escape routes. Booker, she was pleased to see, had spent serious time investigating all nooks and crannies for possibilities but came up empty. After the first day, where they thought there would be some freedom of movement, the meanest of them all (they kept hearing his name, a word sounding like 'Maj') brought them long chains attached to handcuffs, and they were secured to a steel post, and had about ten feet of reach, enough to make the bathroom toilet, not enough to share their mattress beds at either end of the room. Bin Laden informed them, 'Wendell had given me this idea, movement but not freedom.' The harsh quarters meant Booker and Harriet learned more about their personal sanitary habits and idiosyncrasies while seeking ways to keep busy and not go stir-crazy.

The office did have one small window that looked into the warehouse, and by this method, they could take stock of their captors, give them nicknames, and, in the form of entertainment, define the hierarchy. Bin Laden, of course, at the top, then two sub-lieutenants, one thin-faced with a noticeable part of his ear missing. He seemed to be a loner and, by his feral smile at them, was probably the most dangerous. The other, Booker called him an operations officer, and he seemed to be the leader of what looked to be the rest of the 'troops' or 'squad.' There were six of them, including this 'Maj' character — a jihadist with a look of evil combined with stupidity, and as Booker defined him, always seemed a strung-out druggie.

Then there was this other fellow, out of place, more 'Westernized,' well groomed, and not happy to see that his 'brothers' had hostages. They did not know at the time that this was the Professor, who acted as their contact to the outside world and 'Costco' quartermaster to stock them with supplies. He always looked uneasy about being in the mix. He came and went at odd times.

Since they had not been immediately garroted in their sleep or paraded before some mini-cam to be beheaded for media blood-lust, they sustained themselves with hope to get them through these stressful days. At the end of the first week, Booker told Harriet not to dwell on the length of passing time or how this predicament would eventually end. For better or worse, they kept telling the other, 'no, you are the true rock of courage.'

Bin Laden finally came to speak to them, with the Operations Officer, introduced as the one called 'Shahin.'

"My plans, our *Crimson Scimitar*, as you know the name, depend on certain other events. If all goes according to plan, you will accompany us on our travels, and at our destination, you will be chained together and left behind as we depart. Somebody I presume will find and will free you. Your sole purpose with us is to bear witness to our actions, where we humble the great United States. You all don't understand our tenacity. This is a war of 200 years. We will continue to exhaust and deplete America until you become so weak you can't overthrow the caliphate in any state where we establish it. Heed me. I will be giving you a manifesto that I am writing that you can give to the press. Our releasing you will show we can be benevolent and merciful. But the world also shall see our wrath."

As he was leaving, Harriet asked for female toiletries so she could be clean. Booker spoke up for some reading materials; hell, even a 1,000-piece puzzle would pass the time. He noted Shahin's facial expression showed he had a different opinion of what should be done to them. Strangely, Booker prayed that bin Laden stayed in control over his people.

Bin Laden at the door made them understand how al-Qaeda planned for the long view.

"You will be here with us until early October, so be comfortable, do not be nuisances. Any mischief, well, I only need one of you to deliver my political missive.

"And, oh, you should know, I thought your defense of me was as good as one could have expected; if I felt otherwise, you would be dead by my hand. Extending your lives is my payment for legal services rendered."

Scene 4: First Clue
Setting: L.A.-Miami telephone call, August 10th

Holmes left another meeting deep in analysis to take the incoming call from FBI Agent Curtis from Florida, a telephone conversation that would set a tone of urgency for subsequent *King's Retribution* meetings. Things were real, and time was of the essence.

"Shit, Holmes, you are not going to believe this!"

"Try me."

"An Arab-looking 'gentleman' just visited Gator Donaldson's repair shop."

492 S.P. Grogan

Silence from Holmes, so Curtis added.

"And he didn't ride in on a Harley."

"Do you have wires or surveillance inside?"

"No, we thought they were paranoid enough. Where we are now, I have to think they electronically sweep the place daily."

"Probably a good call. These type assholes are getting wiser these days."

"Well, Holmes, you know what this fuckin' means, is that something big is coming down, just like you thought. My local bosses already want to pull the plug, bring this jerk in. I told them 'no'; we have nothing."

"Keep that thought, Curtis. You got squat right now. He's an appendage, one leg of a poisonous spider. We need the body, or at least pull all the legs, make the spider immobile and dead. Track the guy, bury him in surveillance."

"We're on that. The Middle Easterner is staying in a grungy motel over off the I-95. And he has a friend of similar looks staying with him."

"Above all, you need to get an idea of their target. You guys rush in on him, and my past employers will want to step in and water board them; by then, it will be too late. We think these guys are part of a bigger bin Laden cell, devout sons of 9/11. I'm certain they were hand-picked by the Supreme Council, they're top of the al-Qaeda class and not going to crack for a month, and by that time, you will have a nuclear incident spreading across the Okeechobee."

"We've already put the nuclear plants on high alert. And the call went out to our D.C. office, but nothing came back; they don't seem excited, except for us to keep them in the info loop. They call it an 'interesting development.'"

Holmes felt derision at the incompetency of a bureaucracy that was suffocating on itself.

"Homeland Security is the culprit, with too much layering like the old Soviet apparatchiks. And I am guessing the CIA is not waving red flags to the public; think if there is fire where there's smoke to them, it's a small blip on the radar, not worth their time; so, they think you guys can handle it. And Curtis, you J. Edgar boys have the cojones, but our team is getting to a scary conclusion this might be a national op, bigger than we ever could conceive. Think 9/11 to the tenth power. We need to discover Mr. Evil and where the Big Show will be playing."

"If so, you better hustle. The hammer is going to drop on these al-Qaeda dipshits sooner than later, regardless of where they are going to take their pretty pink bombs."

"Hey, I want to be there. Give me a heads up."

"You brought the party; you're on the list."

At the CIA, at Langley, a staff meeting was going through the bullshit process of tossing out ideas to their long-listed agenda items, when one of the agents said, matter-of-factly, "What about *King's Retribution?*"

"What about them?" from another spook executive. "They had their week of televised fame." This agent paused, comprehending. "Are they a problem?"

Participating in the casual chat, Matthew Brady spoke up. "Not really for us, but for the bad guys, I would say, yes. Their 'employees,' the lawyers, were kidnapped. I can tell you, and I know one of them, who used to be one of ours, now an ex, they will marshal all their efforts to find their compatriots."

Another question: "What if they do locate these 'white supremacists (laughter around the table knowing the public scam)? Seriously, what if they do recapture bin Laden?"

One of two field agents in the room was suddenly, within their mind, creating plans that were against the laws of their own country, if not moralistically corrupt, but kept quiet.

"Any suggestions? At the least, the FBI should have them under surveillance."

"I will make that call," said the one who had a West Coast contact.

"You know," said Brady, giving a face of serious contemplation to emphasize something he had been going to do anyway, "I think we should quid pro quo them. Let's find some middle ground accommodation. If they are going to use their millions of dollars and this *KR* team, maybe what they find benefits us. We need to be in the know, and if we find, we share. Of course, we won't share all of our stuff. But they did get him once. Maybe an off-the-books secret pact?"

"Think you can coerce them to cooperate?"

"Worth a shot. And that's not a pun."

Others not so willing. "We don't need a bunch of yahoos to screw it up." The talk soon shifted to other agenda items.

Brady thought differently and wanted to say, 'Yeah, that's what we told ourselves the last time, and so who captured the bad guy? Not us.' But, he stayed silent and listened to responsibilities being divided up, trying to tame the internal chaos out there in the world arena. He would make the call. As he said, quid pro quo them. Who knows? That's what counts.

Scene 5: The Warehouse
Setting: Aurora, Colorado, August 20th

The bane of the U.S. Government and, again, the world's most wanted man, Osama bin Laden, was in his cubicle office/sleeping quarters in the warehouse, trying to find a program on television to watch. He had been working on his 'Attack on America' Manifesto, beginning with an outline as far back as March as the *Crimson Scimitar* plan coalesced. He bemoaned that he did not have Suyiama and Mariam by his side to collect his scribbled notes, give him their fervent opinions, more al-Qaeda theology than many of his followers who only gave lip service. Now, his ideas were in outline form, ready to be set to pages. His Manifesto would be an entirely new approach, but though aimed at America, because of the damage from the pending attack, his greater audience was to gather new converts to his banner.

His mood was not euphoric. There might be three or four weeks more of waiting in this one location. He had no room for movement except to walk the warehouse floor and stare in at his prisoners, chained in another office, playing a board game. His fellow battle-born travelers were not great conversationalists, still in such awe of his on-site presence; hence a television was provided with antennae to bring in limited channels. He had moved from a new show called *Game of Thrones* as being a too fantastical drama, too violent, even for him, and as a series, he would not be around to follow the multiple plots. The same for the teasers on a CIA-Terrorist series called 'Homeland' but not to be released until October. Again, he planned to be gone.

He tried to find a *King's Retribution* show but guessed they were waiting for the new fall season lineup, where he would be featured. He had his opinion of American television, and it was not kind. He knew they did not know how to write true-to-life Arabic experiences, only cut-out caricatures. Beards, turbans, and dark skins were evil. How one dimensional. He watched a movie called *Vegas Die* on mobster killings found on the History Channel, and that seemed interesting to best highlight cultural decadence. He did favor *American Idol* though it concluded in May, and he would have watched only because it resembled the Arabic version, *SuperStar*, where contestants were of the Mideast, not Westerners.

He found old movies and summer re-runs to keep his mind off of what was coming, and afterward, his return to a new home, and not in Pakistan. That bridge burned. He would reunite his family under more tightened security, under his control. At least his bodyguard problem had been solved in the SEAL Team raid. Shahin would lead him home and would be rewarded. It suddenly came to him, what should be done with Khalaf? Would he perform his part?

Scene 6: Shaking Things Up
Setting: CIA Headquarters, Langley, Virginia, August 23rd, 1:15 p.m.

Deputy Director Givens fell out of his chair, literally, on his ass on the floor of his office.

"What the ...?" What was going on? Did he misjudge? Had they attacked? Had a plane hit his building? How could they? The military maintained an anti-missile rocket battery on the roof for just such a threat.

His secretary rushed in, holding the door frame, swaying. She yelled at him; her face flushed.

"Earthquake, sir. The alarms are going off; everyone's evacuating." She rushed away without waiting for him.

Earthquake, of course it is. He considered himself a brave man, but to go up against the power of Mother Nature, he quickly deferred and found himself scurrying out onto Langley's manicured grounds. By the time he exited the front door with the rushing crowd, the ground's vibration had subsided. He milled around with other CIA employees; most he had never seen before; such was the place. They were all in the same wonderment. An earthquake on the East Coast was a rarity. And to think, he thought it was a terrorist attack when all his daily briefings spoke of the quiet out on the grid. Well, except, if you consider the blip down in Florida that the FBI had their eyes on. It's just speculation, he told everyone who would listen; a single sighting of an unconfirmed olive-skinned person does not constitute an assault by foreign elements. Hard facts, he said, would receive a hard response.

Within half an hour, along with the others, they returned to the building, everyone chatty over the excitement of the ground shaking beneath them. Instead of going back to the drudge of his office, paper shuffling, he walked down the corridor to a section of intelligence gathering which they classified as 'loose chatter.' He saw Matthew Brady standing at a desk, reading over the shoulder of an analyst who specialized in the National Desk, and both were reading the incoming wire reports. Brady walked over and handed Givens a printout.

It read the earthquake measured a magnitude of 5.8 and lasted only 30 seconds. The epicenter, and this was a surprise to Givens, was centered in Mineral, Virginia, only 84 miles southwest of Washington.

"What are the incoming damage reports?" He questioned Brady in a snappy, bossy tone.

"So far, very little, dishes rattled off shelves sort of thing, though no one is taking chances. Amtrak stopped its trains, and several airports have diverted planes or put those flying into holding patterns. Homeland Security, through FEMA, asked the public to refrain from using text messaging and cell phones to clear up congestion on the networks. Negligible aftershocks; one was magnitude 2.8 about three minutes ago, but no one felt it."

Givens turned to go, considering, nothing much at all in the scheme of things, yet a needed break for him.

"Did you get my memo?" asked Brady, "On that explosives tie-in between a bomb explosion that killed a man in Florida and similar bomb-making materials over in Pakistan?"

496

"Yeah, I glanced at it," Givens spoke dismissively. "But thought it was a reach. The only tie-in seemed to be similar wrapping paper which probably is a common manufacturing style and widely sold. Need harder evidence to make a case for me. Besides, the FBI has jurisdiction, and I hear they're on it."

The man at the desk handed another printout to Brady.

"Anything else?" Givens stopped at the door.

"Reports that a tourist saw a crack in the Washington Monument. And Dominion Virginia Power shut down its North Anna nuclear-generating station, located only 20 miles from the epicenter. Said their units tripped offline automatically as planned and no damage to the plant reported."

"The Washington Monument damaged?" Givens reacted as if in alarm. "Now that is quite serious. What if it toppled over; what about our national pride?" And he exited with a flourish, already formulating in his mind a plan to insert himself into assessing damage to the monument, suggesting whatever repairs, and in doing so, he would, from behind the scenes, orchestrate the creation of a V.I.P. committee of Senators and Congressmen, movers and shakers. He laughed at his own wit.

Sadly, Givens had given his attention to the wrong part of that news report.

The North Anna Nuclear Plant had been impacted by the earthquake and the undulating roll of the land, which was close to the epicenter. But why alarm the public? There had been structural damage, not severe, and the report about the power generators being undamaged stood correct, but unreported was the critical damage to the waste storage facility, which remained shut, and was already at full capacity. Several storage containers, when tested for stress signs of vibration metal fatigue, showed leakage. Indeed, there were critical concerns in the findings and a disaster in the making unless something wasn't done immediately.

Scene 7: Keep on Truckin'
Setting: New York Indian Points Nuclear Generating Plant, New York State, August 24th,

"They want us to do what?"

"There has been an emergency at the North Anna plant in Virginia. NRC (Nuclear Regulatory Commission) has asked us to add another truck to our convoy and move up the transportation date from mid-October to depart in a week. They will have several other trips required in the foreseeable future but want to get this over and done with, so they can review the trip data and comfort the locals."

Crimson Scimitar

"Impossible timing." Brahma Singh's negative reply might have been him speaking out as the Assistant Operations Manager of the Indian Points facility, but his thoughts were tied to the timetable dictated by the al-Qaeda plans for *Crimson Scimitar*.

"Inconvenient, but not impossible," said the plant manager. "You've had plans for a hurry-up transfer out of here in place for months. Okay, activate it. You will be getting their truck here in three days; plan to leave the day after, say, on the 29th. When would the transport trucks arrive in Nevada?"

Singh, the 'Scientist' in the *Crimson Scimitar* plan, found his mind reeling. *Are the other members of this operation in-country? Can they be in place in time when the trucks reach the targeted ambush spot?* He calculated quickly for his supervisor's question.

"The trip will be taken at a slow speed with several stops to check the loads, three days, with coordinated overnight secured breaks at military bases along the way. If everything goes to schedule, we should be at the Yucca Mountain storage terminal on the late afternoon of September 3rd" *But not if Crimson Scimitar is successful*, he thought. The attack would now occur sometime in the morning or by noon on the 3rd of September, four hours before their expected arrival at Yucca Mountain.

"Remember, in all our communication we must use the wording, 'temporary holding at the in-transit terminal.'"

"Yes, of course, our trucks are merely stopping on their way to their final destination."

"And such a halt at Yucca Mountain might turn into years." And they both laughed though Singh felt his heightened nerves beginning to fray.

"Will you need to add any additional personnel to the transit team?" asked the manager.

To the Scientist, this meant more security.

"No, there's our truck, this newly-added truck from the North Anna generating station, and the Fort Calhoun truck that will drive down from Nebraska to meet us on I-70 near Fort Leavenworth, Kansas. Maybe I will put a mechanic into one of the truck cabs for any emergency repairs, but no, I think the less we look like a military convoy and more like three trailer trucks perceived as general carriers, the better." Singh asked about cargo. "By the way, will their manifest likewise be spent fuel rods?"

The manager hesitated, not anxious to complicate matters with details they could do nothing about.

"No, much worse, I presume. Barrels of highly concentrated tritium, the highest I have ever heard. Five million picocuries per liter."

498   S.P. Grogan

"You're kidding," said the Scientist with a shocked expression, but to himself, *This is excellent news, a blessing from Allah. This is the first truck that must be targeted, the highest priority.* "What radioactive isotopes are in this batch?"

"High readings of Cesium-137. They've used the new magnetic concentrator on the tritium, so we can expect more requests to ship after this first test run."

"Wow, I remember when we had our own tritium leakage readings here at Indian Point. That was Strontium-90, but the releases were at such low levels."

"That's why we have been asked to expedite this specific transfer. Not only put it in a safe place for a thousand years, but the Virginia Power people say they have ten more truckloads of this stuff that need to be taken away and safeguarded. They've found stress corrosion in the metal holding containers, and if there's one major spill, it will set our industry back a hundred years, let alone most of Western Virginia evacuated. The sooner, the better."

He gave the mantra his boss wanted to hear. "It is sad because nuclear energy is the most efficient and with the best industry safety record." He felt more confident, "And yes, sir, I will start hustling." Singh turned back to his work desk and made the necessary calls to activate his transportation plans. It could be done, both the transit of the radioactive waste and the hurry-up of *Crimson Scimitar*. He was still amazed that lethal dosages of tritium would be given to him as a bonus. Beyond merely causing radioactive damage with his original truck shipment of spent fuel rods, he now had two additional truck trailers, and the havoc would multiply exponentially. If *Crimson Scimitar* now succeeded and all three trucks compromised, then millions of people would be unable to drink their water or eat their produce, and if they did eat or drink, most certainly, the incidences of cancer would spike beyond reason, and as a result, the U.S. medical and insurance industries would be overwhelmed and collapse. Governmental anarchy and dying and death for countless nonbelievers, a proud moment for al-Qaeda and proper revenge for their leader's recent death (he, like most Americans, believed bin Laden had blown himself up to escape re-capture), and the Scientist smiled and thought, *the sooner, the better.*

That evening, the Scientist, went on a rental computer at the office store and sent a bubbly email about his cousin's triplets' arrival earlier than expected, so a revised baptism was now scheduled for the 3rd of September. Like the earthquake which triggered the advance in the schedule, this simple notice of multiple births would stir up aftershocks. Being focused on transportation as his only task meant that *Crimson Scimitar* operations were highly compartmentalized. The Scientist had no knowledge that the first part of the plan would actually happen two days before Shahin launched his team for the attack on the bridge. *Crimson Scimitar* would launch on August 29th. Five days from now.

EPISODE THIRTY — CRIMSON SCIMITAR

Scene 1: The Attack Begins
Setting: The Warehouse, city of Aurora, Thursday, August 25th

"Curse the Infidels and our own incompetents!"

"What is it?" Razzor asked of Shahin as they sat in the kitchen of the warehouse while the rest of his attack brigade watched senseless television. Bin Laden was napping.

"They are sending the shipment out a month early. Not October 4th. It will arrive at the bridge sometime on the 3rd of September."

"Your men seem prepared. Waiting until October is a long time and could make them lazy and tempted by American filth."

"Yes, but the strategy was to attack when everyone was complacent after the 9/11 anniversary. They would have said, 'See, nothing happened, so we are all safe,' and they would be made foolish."

Shahin looked back to the email he was writing to Khalaf, and Razzor could see the disgust.

"I thought such news would please you."

"It is the add-ons to the message from the Scientist which disturb me. There are now three trucks, three babies born, instead of just one, and we are told to target all three, but most specifically, one particular truck (baby), one truck with two container configuration, which is to have a red 'birthmark' on its rear end. That seems strange. All three must be destroyed, but the message must imply we have to prioritize that particular one. And then, there is the final part, our temporary new leader, Doctor al-Zawahiri has approved sending Khalaf as a representative to be part of our attack team. I don't like it. I know this man. He is neither a soldier nor a leader, merely a messenger boy. Most assuredly, he will think highly of himself and do no good in our plans. We are a tight team. We don't need outsiders who could wreck the mission."

"Do you wish me to 'babysit' him? Keep him out of your way."

"If he were to stumble in front of a stray bullet, I do not feel the cause would shed a tear."

"And we would gain another martyr."

"True enough."

Both men rose from the table. Shahin walked to the TV and shut it off. The lazy men of the attack brigade, bored from inaction, looked to their mission commander.

"The schedule has changed. The time is at hand. The first phase begins tomorrow. I will alert the Professor to launch his people. You all know your assignments. Let us rehearse again to execute them. I will inform our leader. Let us clean this place up and destroy our papers. Allah be with you all. We shall next meet at the bridge."

Those in the warehouse knew exactly what they must do over the next two days. With three teams of two men each, their jobs were specific. One team would drive east, seeking to meet up with the government truck convoy coming their way. Presumably, there was a low-watt tracking device on one of the trucks which could be picked up within a thirty-mile radius. If they missed the convoy, the second group of two men was stationed at Trinidad, Colorado, as a backup spotters. When the convoy was located, it would be tailed by one group while the other rushed to be in front. The third team would have departed earlier to Kingman, Arizona, along Interstate Highway 40, and on the day of the truck arrival, they would position themselves as one of the two traffic-blocking elements. All would be in radio communication and coincide their movements, timed to the minute, to achieve a pincer trap at the bridge. There be one last stop of all together before they split and took positions on the day of the attack.

Shahin turned to Razzor with a questioning expression. The man had never said what his role was to be, and Shahin never pressed. Over the last several weeks, they had become close companions with the same sort of radicalism in their blood, understanding brothers to the cause, that Islam should rule the world, and that all others, the unbelievers, must convert or be exterminated.

"I have places to go," said Razzor, heading to the door. "May the wisdom of Allah be with you."

"And with you."

"But I will be back soon enough to stand with you on the bridge."

"Do not forget our discussion of the courier who will be here in a few days."

"I accept your wishes. Our leader will have his mind full of success and not miss a minor functionary, unimportant to his future leadership."

The next morning, in another part of the warehouse, Booker called to Harriet, who was sleeping on the mattress provided for her on the floor. She started, eyes flashing, her ended dream met reality in blended fear, "What?"

"Something's happening. That outsider (the Professor) just drove in with a motor home, a recreational vehicle type. And our captors are a lot more active, prepping their equipment. I'm guessing, but we may be moved."

They met, chains rattling, in the middle of the room. She held his hand; with the one question she dared not ask earlier. "Do you think they really are going to take us with them?

Aren't we a burden to them?" She had become fatalistic in the last several days. Hope had kept her spirits up, but she, with a linear mind, saw few scenarios of their survival.

"As long as bin Laden is running the show, he sees a purpose for us. So, yes, we will be going with them. Let's just not piss off any of them."

To his own thinking, he was not that assured. He must find a way to escape, for both of them. And soon.

Scene 2: The Pelham 123 Plan
Setting: The Waldorf Hotel, New York City, Sunday, August 28th

Khalaf read the obscure text message from Shahin, which in turn had come from the Scientist, its coded meaning clear. *Now it begins*, he considered. His life would turn on these momentous events. He picked up the phone and called his contact, Nidal.

"Tomorrow, when the market opens (9:30 a.m.) you may begin our short sale strategy. I will email over the exact list of stocks I wish to short."

"Yes, of course." Commissions for the stockbrokers with increased fee remuneration for himself, thus Nidal would follow these orders to the letter.

"I will also send over additional instructions but remember, specifically, put a cover order on these stocks, to buy back in if any of the stock prices drop 12% by the end of the day. I may call to tell you to liquidate our entire position at that time, or the next morning, depending on how the news in the marketplace is."

"I see, not trying to make a stunning success if trading is halted at a 20% drop."

"One must be watchful not to become too greedy." He *had* been listening to Sabz.

What Nidal and Khalaf were discussing was that under SEC rules, certain high-end stocks were required to undergo a trading pause if the stock made significant gyrating swings, up or down outside the price band (those levels arbitrarily set at 5%, 10%, or 20%). These halts, usually 15 minutes, and called 'Circuit Breakers,' allowed the market to adjust to a new base level, balancing between buyers and sellers to avoid major gains or losses. Usually, such events also drew the eyes of the SEC Enforcement Division against market manipulation.

Khalaf expected bad news Monday afternoon. How bad would be determined by news reports, impacting stock market jitters at unforeseen calamities (the comedy movie *Trading Places*, 1983, demonstrated the similar news effect in the Chicago commodities trading markets). Khalaf would not hold out to squeeze the last dollar profit from the scheme. He had respect when it came to using OPM (Other People's Money).

Nidal knew what was happening and, in fact, might quietly parallel Khalaf's action, believing the young man held inside information. Khalaf educated him to the point he added in his verbal instructions. "And you will have a second list from me to turn and buy back in on the lowest stocks that dropped on Wednesday if the prices are still down at the same level. And I will have future sell-stop ceilings put on these. And I want my instructions followed even if I am unreachable, as I might be traveling. Sometime during my trip, I will contact you to liquidate all my holdings in the special account I set up and transfer the funds to my bank accounts. When I return, I will re-enter the market with new trades."

"Yes, Mr. Rasil."

Khalaf had no intention of coming back to use Nidal. He would, as he planned, take his money and run, transferring from his trading accounts to his 'cleansing account', eventually to al-Qaeda's offshore accounts. He ended the call pleased with himself, feeling the power of leadership, and all things considered, indeed, it was he who was in charge of this phase of *Crimson Scimitar*. He felt elated.

He looked over to Sabz, watching him, a fashion magazine she had been reading in her lap.

"I will be leaving town Tuesday and should be gone only a few days."

"So soon?" She had been prepared to argue, throw a tantrum, but accepted it would be to no avail. Her own needs, even his affection for her, could not yet breach his intractable political beliefs. She prayed to Heaven for his conversion to see the light in rejecting violence against innocents but saw no miracle in the making.

He went over to a dresser and pulled out a large envelope, which he handed to her. She put down her magazine, took the package, and gave him a quizzical look.

"My gift to you. I have set up a trading account for you in your name, where we have our main brokerage accounts. There is also $10,000 U.S. in cash. I have prepaid the hotel for another week. It is quite expensive, you know."

Confident, no longer hesitant, he gave her a committed pledge. "I will return to you, and then we will discuss our future…together." She did not happily kiss him; he knew her opposing feelings about his plans. Satisfied with his generosity, he turned and went to the bedroom to pack a small travel bag. He would miss her a lot, and his heart was heavy. But duty was duty.

Her eyes did mist. She opened the package and looked within. There was another envelope, sealed, with the notation, '*Return to me unopened on my return.*' Within the package was the paperwork on her account, and he had included a list of stocks she should consider buying. There were several surprises. Khalaf did not direct her to buy those stocks recommended, but 'suggested,' meaning use your own research conclusions. He thought well of her analysis — another surprise. The account had been funded with $150,000 U.S., unrestricted, to do with as she wanted. There was a tied packet with $10,000 U.S. in ready cash. She knew; it pained

Crimson Scimitar 503

her. All this was his 'farewell' gift to her, a nest egg for her survival. A tear edged her eye for his concern. But the real shock was that the funds he had provided had to have come from certain trading accounts; those funds specifically to be used for the al-Qaeda strategy he spoke of so strongly. Khalaf, her lover, had taken money under his fiduciary control to provide for her. She smiled at the implications. He had, for her, made an amendment to his beliefs, a crack in his ideological façade. There was hope for her, for them.

Scene 3: A New Hunt Launched
Setting: War Room Reconfigured — Los Angeles, Friday, August 29th

In the new War Room, all the attendees stared at several walls of postings — lists of all books and movies from the Ali Baba library posted in columns of subject matter, then description, and ranking on realistic possibilities. For example, *The Hunt for Red October* (1990) and though not from the Abbottabad compound, other similar entertainment they might have missed, or bin Laden had viewed in earlier times, had now been included, like the movie *True Lies* (1994), those were at the bottom of nuclear incidents, while at the top, *The Peacemaker* (1997) and *The Sum of all Fears* (2002). In viewing the list under 'mass poisoning,' the list caught many off-guard because there were many choices, including *Executive Decision* (1996) and Frederick Forsyth's novel, *The Afghan* (2006). There were subgroup roundtable discussions where they would mix and match ideas into possible simulation of attack scenarios and then turn over their findings to the three remaining Nerd Crew members (Gizmo was up at Skilleo HQ on a special hush-hush project), who would then put in real asset 'ingredients; to see if an actual plot could be launched.

From all this work, the newly-configured Hunt Team was not having good luck. What kicked out many possible threats were usually the high expenses of such undertakings and the logistic requirements being the main impediments. Meanwhile, at a bank of two computers, two *KR* employees were scanning all news sources, compiling and filtering possible leads to the kidnappers and their victims. Again, nothing of merit.

Holmes found himself being the coordinator in these meetings, trying to keep the importance of what was facing their missing friends. King was still absent in physical rehab, so most were trying to be optimistic in the difficult task of pure guessing, staring them in the face.

"We finally figured out that Hawk title," said Lars, a Skilleo Nerd, the very laid-back, mellowed by recreational chemicals, sort of young man. "It turns out it is an obscure eco-thriller going back to 1969 — man, that is so prehistoric. Called *Wellspring* by Edward Hawkins.

504   S.P. Grogan

"And I presume there is a loose nuclear bomb in the plot?" Holmes expected that thread of plotting, very popular in the early Vietnam war days.

"No, Mr. Holmes, just water pollution stuff in the Colorado Rockies, I think. Teaser says, 'toxins in the nine major rivers of the West.' None of us have had a chance to read it; we can't find a copy. Brigit is out now rummaging through all the used bookstores. There's one copy on the internet we sent away for. Should be here today or tomorrow."

"Water pollution of sorts was in Tom Clancy's *Dead or Alive*," recalled Holmes, "an attempt of nuclear pollution at a place called Yucca Mountain, and by someone called the 'Emir.'"

"Well," Holmes studied the various grids on the wall. "Put it under both 'poisoning' and 'nuclear.' Seems like my friend Mr. Bin Laden or our mysterious Ali Baba were Tom Clancy fans."

"If any of these plots were in play, it still doesn't give us a place or time," said Callie, feeling everyone's dejected spirit. "Near hopeless." She knew the longer a kidnapping remained unresolved, the less chance of the victim's survival.

And on that note, they broke for a working lunch, deli sandwiches ordered in, and tried to move off into social chatter of no significance.

In one exchange, Bennie jokingly asked Pacheco, "Well, now that we're armed to the teeth, thanks to you, but nothing to shoot at, what are you going to do in your spare time?"

"Oh, nothing much. When there's the chance, I have been going around to the amusement parks doing the extreme rides." That started an animated discussion.

"What's your fave?"

"Last weekend, I rode the 'Silver Bullet,' the longest inversion ride at 3,000 feet."

Callie, walking past, added, "Space Mountain is still the all-time classic."

"That's on my list," said Shawn, "But if nothing is going on tomorrow, I am going to take on twelve of them at one park."

"What are you clowns talking about?" Samantha questioned, moving in their direction, nibbling on cheese and crackers, self-consciously realizing Wendell was walking right behind her.

Shawn laughed.

"Why, 'The Riddler', the tallest and fastest stand-up; 'Superman' that goes from 0 to 100 in seven seconds; twelve varieties of rollercoasters are out there waiting for me. I get the same rush like during Jump Week, where we made five parachute jumps at 1,250 feet from the back of a C-130 to get a Silver Wing badge."

Crimson Scimitar

"Rollercoasters?" As if struck by a freight train, Wendell understood with clarity. He spoke to Samantha, "The movie, *Rollercoaster*. Ali Baba's movie." His paper plate of food was tossed unceremoniously to the table, and he rushed back to the conference room. Everyone had stopped mid-bite.

"*Rollercoaster*," said Samantha, as she followed him and waved the others to follow.

Wendell was punching in numbers on the conference desk telephone, putting it on speaker as everyone crowded in.

"Agent Curtis, Holmes here. I am with a bunch of my investigative cohorts talking to you, and we think it may or may not be nuclear, but we now have a lead that the attack might be aimed at…amusement parks."

"Amusement parks, Holmes? You gotta be kidding? What proof do you have?"

"Let me ask it this way: have your suspects under surveillance taken any road trips in the last two weeks?"

Dead air in the conversation.

"Yeah, I have a general report our suspects took two long drives with Gator Donaldson, the repair shop owner, but the agents said it seemed fairly aimless, like the biker was giving his buddies a day out, but mostly, I recall, it was just a drive, nothing that seemed like they were casing any specific target."

"Where did these trips take them?"

"Hold on, let me read the field reports." Silence hung in the room as they all waited, listening to shuffling papers over long distance; even Fox wanted an answer. They could hear Agent Curtis returning to the phone.

"Shit, Orlando, two trips. Drove right past the major amusement parks but didn't stop, not even slowing, so it wasn't logged as 'of interest.' Damn. Why would that be the target?"

Callie Cardoza spoke up and introduced herself as an ex-San Diego police to give herself better creds to the FBI agent.

"We're dealing with terror to generate mob hysteria. Like the two Washington, D.C. snipers that paralyzed that whole region until they were caught. Think of it; amusement parks are part of the psyche of fun-loving Americans. Make them afraid to go out and enjoy themselves and you do mental damage as much as physical, let alone the catastrophic hit to the economy when free-spenders stay home."

"You all may have something. I never did see this 'nuclear' angle. The al-Qaeda bunch are not smart enough to go out and find a nuclear weapon, even a dirty bomb; we've never heard of them having that sort of expertise for constructing any radioactive device."

Several heard one of the nerds mutter under his breath, '9/11 was a pretty brilliant plan.'

"You may need to bring the Arab jokers in and see if you can sweat it out of him and his newfound biker buds."

"I'm starting to agree."

"I want to be there, Curtis, when it goes down."

"Fine, but there is something else that might be an expedient factor; yesterday, our Arab visitors to Florida received a twenty-second phone call to their motel room. Not enough time for a trace, but we gained point of origin. You ready?"

"Let me guess," scoffed Abbas, "a pay phone in Abbottabad?"

"How about the call coming from California, the Los Angeles area?"

"Rollercoasters," said Pacheco.

"There are two groups, two attacks, maybe more," said Samantha, shocked at her own conclusion.

"And the Florida cell yesterday must have got the launch code date," Holmes with his serious assessment. "Curtis, can you notify your California office, inform them of our thinking?"

"I will do so and put them in contact with you."

"Tell them to check out their local skinhead covens and see if any had any foreign-looking guests visit recently. Put area amusement parks on alert but don't panic them. Have your counterparts out here contact Mr. Hugh Fox. I will be with you by tomorrow."

The conversation ended with a disconnect, and all in the room chewed over in their minds trying to guess the sick strategy of unknown killers.

Samantha stood beside Holmes, ready to let her emotions take a back seat.

"I think I have another thought on *Rollercoaster*, she said. "We need to stand back and look, not at just one Ali Baba book or movie, but to see if various plots might have been spliced together."

"Like what?"

"*The Taking of Pelham One Two Three*, the latest version, 2009, the one you did not see, but I did. I think...."

Scene 4: Debating the Priority
Setting: Anaheim, California, August 29th, Sunday, late afternoon

He had come to the location to gain perspective, perhaps to have a vision. He stared to the heights, at the ribbed edifice, and heard the screams of the people high above, screams where fear and joy mixed with the rush of air as bodies were thrown towards death and then pulled back, only to repeat.

"I don't want you to leave," a voice from behind him. Samantha Carlisle.

He turned to face her as the rollercoaster made another pass, his voice muffled against the mechanical grating swoosh.

"A personal request, or otherwise?"

"Perhaps both, but I think we are all on our own emotional rollercoaster, some of us even more so, rushing beyond the tracks."

"You mean me?"

"I don't know you all that well, Wendell, …yet…those genetics, as you told me, which make up your drive to save the world…so now rushing off to Florida to do battle might not be the best use of your talents. Besides, personally, I don't want you anywhere near a terrorist cell, especially after what happened to King."

"We at least know where two of the sons of bitches are, and I am going to make them regret the day. Hey, wait a minute, how did you get here? How did you find me?"

They were standing in the parking lot of the amusement park, against the fence, below the rollercoaster structure. Holmes had sought out a place to think by himself, to try and separate the events of yesterday; the King attack, the latest War Room data that moved them away from a nuclear plot to something to do with targeting public gathering spots like Florida amusement parks. He had told no one of his destination, but here she was. What did he feel about that?

Samantha replied, "After last night and waiting for King's latest surgery to be completed, Hugh said we were at war, or at least someone had declared war on us, so he activated the first operating 'Storm Wagon.'

"Activated?"

"Abbas had installed a bunch of monitoring electronics into the van, so he went around making sure all of us were GPS connected."

"GPS? Like planting bugs? Why, that sneak."

"In your car and on your person. Don't ask how he did it. You can compliment him personally or beat him up." She pointed past several lines of parked vehicles, and Holmes could see Bennie and Abbas sitting in the Storm Wagon, waving back at him.

Holmes turned to Samantha, actually glad to see her but still set on his mission.

"I have to fly out tomorrow morning."

"Your Agent Curtis and his troops can handle the Florida show. Go interrogate the creeps when they're in custody. Yesterday, I didn't even have a chance to advance my theory; you were in such a tizzy to organize amusement park surveillance. God, I am surprised I didn't see you wearing an 'S' on your chest and flying around with a cape."

"Samantha, please, you are trying to tell me something."

"If you recall, in the original movie *Rollercoaster*, the bomber was extorting money from the amusement park owners."

"Right, and that's been checked out. These owners are multi-national conglomerates, publicly traded companies, who would have been required to report such threats to the police and the FBI."

"Exactly. But what if our Ali Baba took plot A and added a little from plot B?"

"Okay, I can accept the possibility, but we saw so many, the variations might run to a hundred."

"Yeah, but going back and removing all the nuclear threat books and movies limits us significantly. Personally, I can see only one working that fits with your guess that Florida might be a target for amusement parks."

"And that is?" They began walking towards the Storm Wagon.

"*Pelham One Two Three*. This actually fits with the extortion of *Rollercoaster* but modernized. At the end of the 2009 version of *Pelham*, the bad guy, played by John Travolta, uses fear of subway killings to cause panic in the stock market, thus making a financial killing, so to speak, and does a stock transaction called 'selling short' to make millions."

"You think al-Qaeda terrorists are trying to steal rather than kill?"

"Maybe both. Dual objectives. Think on this, their main money source from the wealth of the bin Laden family is probably on hiatus. Bin Laden's on the run and does not, I am guessing, have easy access to his checkbook; many al-Qaeda leaders have been killed, so their rogue state sponsors like Iran or Syria don't know who the new checks are to be sent to. I could see very easily that bin Laden himself, in his last act, unknowingly, of course, wanted to hurt America as well as rob a capitalistic system, the height of radical Islamic arrogance. But now, the terrorists, post-bin Laden (I believe he will be caught), need cash, and his final plan will create a tidy nest egg for them. Pay the creditors to keep the jihad humming."

Holmes started thinking. Samantha had made millions herself, she knew Wall Street, and with her smarts, she certainly oversees her own investment portfolio, and thus is looking at the scene in the larger landscape versus his narrow view, that an evil plan usually functions under the simplest of conditions. Holmes sought to see the diabolical and never thought of bombs exploding being 'investment-related.' His own financial advisor overseeing his CIA retirement pay-out had him conservative in mutual funds, while the rainy-day fund under the mattress was actually in an unreported offshore banking account stuffed to seven zero figures, earning little interest. So, he gave her thinking the credit it was due.

He mapped out the strategy. "So, they will attack the amusement park? In doing so, adverse publicity drives the parent company's stock down; yes, that would happen. And the bad guys know the news beforehand, so they basically have insider information? The market is rigged."

"Correct. There could, however, be a twist to that plot, and going back to my original statement, that is why 'we' want you here."

"And that is?"

"Let your mind wander on this one. What if merely attacking one company in the East doesn't do the trick? The entire stock market would not necessarily drop even if they attacked one public company in only Florida, and the amusement park in Orlando is tied to the largest entertainment company in the world. A bomb exploding on the East Coast doesn't make it as visible as al-Qaeda might desire but making the impact 'national,' putting fear into everyone across America, will also strike the West Coast at the same time. Think back, to three planes crashing, not just one. And basically simultaneously."

"So, you believe one attack will take place in Orlando, and the other…?

"Here, in L.A. You need to run *King's Retribution* here."

Adding that scenario into his mulling equation, he pulled out his cell phone and put in a call to the Florida FBI. Instinctively, so she could hear the conversation, as it was her hypothesis, he pulled Samantha close to him.

"Agent Curtis, I won't be able to make it. Something came up. You have to follow your perps all the way to the gate of the amusement park before rushing them." Samantha, at this point, leaned into his embrace. "…and your people here need to go on alert that at the same time, it is now our guess, the terrorists will be targeting an amusement park in the Los Angeles basin."

They could hear the agent yelling his own stress, warning of the risks to civilians, questioning where Holmes got his information, begrudgingly agreeing finally, when Holmes simply said, "Trust us." The call ended.

"What about the economic aspect, this stock market play? What do we do there?" Wendell asked his new New York girlfriend of sorts.

"I can call a few of the head broker honchos I know. But what can they do? The SEC simply can't act fast enough on a rumor that causes a stock price to fall. They usually act after the fact and sanction the offending party with fines or a lawsuit. Since it is non-life threatening,

I say that is the lesser priority. Let the smart securities authorities handle it if we are right about amusement parks.

"But you're right, Sam," said Holmes. "Looks like I will be staying here. When the Florida attack is in motion, we will know the L.A. parks will be hit simultaneously. We are the only boots on the ground who believe what is coming is an actual terrorist attack."

She enjoyed seeing his calculation. Perhaps not as brainy smart as Hugh Fox, but methodical plodding still reaches the goal line. She kissed him lightly on the cheek.

"Why does having you here in the middle of all this not make me feel any better?"

Scene 5: Poignant Good-bye
Setting: The Waldorf Hotel, New York City, Sunday evening, August 28th

Khalaf clicked off the computer. All was in place. The short sale orders would be placed in the morning into the marketplace, transactions into several entertainment companies, masking any chance of a computer program spitting out anomalies. The first phase attacks were to begin mid-morning after the parks opened on Monday, early enough to allow the news to have an impact across the stock wires and the time coordinating with Los Angeles amusement parks first opening their gates.

On the other fronts of the *Crimson Scimitar* operation, he had been informed that two trucks would depart tomorrow on schedule, with one more truck joining up along the way. This would be fortuitous for Shahin's assault team.

On Tuesday, if his goals were achieved, Khalaf decided he would fly to Denver to join the attack team. There could no longer be any doubt of attaining success, for if they missed on one truck, there were two other windows of opportunity. If they destroyed all three, the Southwestern United States would become a wasteland and uninhabited. Khalaf would share in this glory, his name etched in history books.

He watched the news eagerly. He knew the press was demanding more facts, whether or not bin Laden was really dead. The airwaves were filled with conspiracy theories. Somehow, he held a lingering doubt, an itch he could not reach. If they had really killed bin Laden, the President of the United States would be touting the success for political gain. But the White House was not taking a victory lap for bin Laden's suicide; at least, they were downplaying the outcome. Was it possible the story was not truthful? To find the answer, to be part of the glory, Khalaf *had* to join the attack at the bridge.

He turned to see Sabz coming out from the bedroom; she was holding a newspaper in her hands. She was the newspaper reader, he the television. She muted the show he was watching.

"Come sit with me on the couch, my husband." To him, it was an odd command. Indeed, he was exhausted; it was late, and tomorrow there would be anxiety in the waiting during the stock transactions. Over the last several weeks he had become used to being called 'her husband' in public, less the teasing lie, more recently spoken as an endearment he silently enjoyed.

He sat on the couch, and in another oddity, she sat right next to him, a show of closeness she never gave easily. He tried to make light of it.

"You found another clothing sale in the newspaper?"

She leaned over him to turn on a side lamp next to the divan and handed him a section of the Sunday *New York Times*.

"My Sheik," her voice was breaking. "I have bad news. Your friend, your comrade, the Libyan, Atiyah Abd al-Rahman, has been killed."

His eyes blurred, trying to read the headline. He knew immediately — predator drone strike.

Of the story he read, certain parts stood out. '*Thousands of electronic files recovered at Bin Laden's compound in Abbottabad, Pakistan, revealed that Bin Laden communicated frequently with Mr. Rahman.*' Many of those messages Khalaf had couriered between them. The article continued, '*They also showed that Bin Laden relied on Mr. Rahman to get messages to their Qaeda leaders and to ensure that Bin Laden's recorded communications were broadcast widely.*' Again, the inference to Khalaf's role in being the go-between. He might soon be targeted himself.

At this moment, he did not curse the Americans for their death from the sky; such lethal happenings were becoming commonplace within the tribal lands. He did mourn for the soldier al-Rahman, but was more numb for himself, having no idea where his standing was. Would he report directly to al-Zawahiri, or would another take Rahman's place, and would he be pushed aside? Khalaf wondered what was not said in the story, for he heard if the *Times* got any leak on a good story, they would run with it, regardless of consequences to American security. He did a mental check. First, he was convinced the treasure trove of gathered documents bin Laden had in his personal possession most likely led to Rahman's hide-out and his horrific death. Second, in reading between the lines of the *Times* story, Khalaf found no suggestion that *Crimson Scimitar* had been compromised; the national terrorist warning level had not been summarily raised. If otherwise, it did not matter; they all must go forward. Did this mean martyrdom would await and he would die at the bridge? Finally, in the previous weeks, he had read no news article suggesting there had been a third courier at the compound, himself thankfully undiscovered, and he could somehow find ease that as others died, he had no bounty on his head nor believed he was in the cross-hairs of a missile strike.

512   S.P. Grogan

A soul-searing truth came to him: he did not want to die a martyr. His life, in this present time with Sabz, was the peace he truly sought. But he was trapped in his mind, warring conflicts; he could not turn back. But he must return to her and decide where his life would go from there.

Nevertheless, he mused, if he were in charge, going outside on a clear day should be taboo for all al-Qaeda leaders. His prayers henceforth would be for overcast weather.

Sabz sat listening to Khalaf's heavy breathing and believed it to show the extreme grief he held within. She felt a pang of tenderness and set aside her own selfish financial motives for a higher cause of her own self-preservation, turning instead to comfort a sad man, but she could not do that so easily without speaking her troubled thoughts she had previously suppressed.

"I don't want you to go. Don't you see; *you* are the only one left? They are killing all the others. You must stay here where they cannot find you."

Khalaf did not see this, himself as the rare breed, one of the few surviving members of the al-Qaeda echelon. He again saw himself as having no future, unable to reach and embrace his personal goals. This conjured up the specter of fatalism, as if he were being drawn to Allah's command, not his, to an unknown destiny in the Nevada-Arizona desert.

"We have been over this before. I must leave on Tuesday. I believe it is written and out of my hands."

She leaned over him, turned off the light, and eased onto his lap, whispering, "Nothing is written that you cannot erase. But if that is your decision, then I wish you to have me. If you are so determined to leave, then do so with my body smells on you. Let that be the perfume to remind you to return safely to my arms."

She pulled her robe apart; she was naked beneath.

In the early morning hours, as he had done on so many occasions in the last several weeks, he opened his hotel room door and hung out the sign reading 'Do Not Disturb.' He had three more hours of bliss before all hell broke loose.

Scene 6: Enlightenment to a Plot
Setting: CIA Headquarters, Langley, Virginia, 29th August, Monday, Washington, D.C.

Matthew Brady and his entire section were swamped, for once, with too much Class A prime intelligence. The plastic bags that Pacheco had seen his SEAL team cart from the Abbottabad compound were now giving up their secrets with positive results. A bomb-making cell in Germany had been broken apart with the radicals detained. A stockbroker in London had been arrested nearly a month back with damning Islamic manifesto treatises in his possession, while last week, one of his associates, a banker, committed suicide rather than face interrogation.

Brady's desk was cluttered with leads to assign to his analysts; this was going to be his excuse for not taking former CIA agent Wendell Holmes's telephone call, except he did need to ask him one question, clarify a point on the hidden alcove with the mattress and bookshelves found empty.

Something the SEALS uncovered in bin Laden's bedroom, a name that meant very little in the data searches, was bothersome to him.

"This is my obligatory call," said Holmes, and Brady made a light comment that it must be important since the call was at 5:30 am West Coast time. "A day of stake-out," Holmes gave his quip back, and he went on to explain how the shift was being made from fear of a nuclear plot to that of the minor, if one dare call it that, bombing of amusement parks and the somewhat good news that the FBI had Arabic-looking suspects under close surveillance in Florida. Holmes had to ask, "To be sure, you've heard nothing about the Russians losing a nuclear bomb or the Iranians or North Koreans selling fissionable materials to Mideast terror groups?"

"Not a peep. And stolen nuclear bombs are no longer your prime scenario? Amusement parks the real plot?" Holmes could visualize the CIA analyst smiling in debunking mirth.

"Not that you guys don't run the real Google Search of the War on Terror, but our preliminary research…."

"Meaning your bin Laden empty closet analysis?"

"Okay, don't shoot the amateurs. But, yes, we had the itchy feeling something was leaning towards a nuclear-type incident. Even more so recently, the imaginary plot got a lot more farfetched.

"How's that?"

"Open a weird file and call it 'Wellspring,' from an old novel I finished reading last night. Here's where al-Qaeda would have to be ultra-genius types. Somehow, they take a nuclear bomb, or perhaps radioactive chemicals, make some sort of poisonous brew, and dump them into the streams at the Continental Divide in the Rockies."

"Continental Divide?"

"Mountain waters from snow melt run to the east and west; we're talking about al-Qaeda trying to poison the Western United States. The same plot with a nuclear variation in a Tom Clancy novel. But, Wellspring breaks down into pure fiction; you would need to haul in a lot of radioactive junk to the top of the mountain, locate the right streams into which to dump it, but even a handmade dirty bomb would consist of solid components, not liquid-based. And

514   S.P. Grogan

beyond that, dilution would cause the poison to go inert. So, the author just created a 'mystery environmental poison' to dump. As I said, that was our latest stab at guessing. Attempting to blow up amusement park roller coasters with C-4 seems to be where we are heading." Holmes didn't try to complicate the conversation by throwing in a short-sale stock conspiracy.

Brady felt the conversation had lasted too long as it was. "Sorry, I can't give you a roadmap leading from bin Laden to his American target, if one really exists. Nothing you have is solid. Stick with the FBI; I have been told several times already; it's their jurisdiction anyway. Oh, by the way, Holmes, did you ever see or hear the Arabic phrase, *Crimson Scimitar*?"

Two seconds of consideration from Holmes. "Have heard it twice, both from Bin Laden. He used it in his closing statement at the trial. We are trying to follow that thread but have found little to define an active plot."

"Are we being confidential here?"

"Oh, come on, Brady, I have been the saint of cooperation. Plus, you are taping."

"Well, not much to show for you, just rattling our chains. The name *Crimson Scimitar* popped up a couple of times on our radar, but nothing definite. Our people do feel like it could be the name of an operational plan that was being considered but never went anywhere, except...."

"Except...don't torture us retirees."

"*Crimson Scimitar* was by itself scratched on a crumbled piece of trash paper in bin Laden's compound, found in fact, in his bedroom, and the name was found again only a few days ago in the study of a banker who committed suicide in London. The local constabulary was looking into fraud among some Islamic benevolent charities the man ran. Seemed like he absconded with their funds and then killed himself when the Bobbies closed in. We did get some scuttlebutt that he might have been a front, channeling funds to Middle Eastern terrorist groups. But we are only in the preliminary investigation. Coincidently, from what the Brits have been uncovering from the SEAL raid, MI-6 had earlier picked up a stockbroker associate friend of this banker, who did have radical Islamic literature in his flat. They think it could be a sleeper cell put in place years ago. And the stockbroker did have a flight ticket to New York."

"Stockbroker, you say? That is interesting."

"And, why so?"

"Let me get back to you on that. I need to dig, but now that I put aside all these hare-brained schemes, I see a strange linkage of sorts."

"What sort?"

Crimson Scimitar

"In our secret hideaway in Abbottabad, if you go back to the photos we and you probably took, among the graffiti on the wall, there was a sword-like drawing; and if it weren't so dark, I would now surmise it was drawn in red, maybe even in dried blood."

"Damn. The London banker, the report I read with crime scene photos, showed a sword doodling on a message pad on the man's desk, where they found his body, his brains blown out first obscured it. Isn't a scimitar an Arab sword? What's this all mean, Holmes? Give me your on-the-spot field op opinion."

"I think our Ali Baba, the mystery man of the compound, he with American-British best-selling books and movies at his disposal which we found, is a close associate of bin Laden, is maybe a co-creator of this *Crimson Scimitar*, and it is an active plan poised to strike, I am guessing soon, around the 9/11 anniversary. And what's worse, Osama bin Laden is going to be leading it himself.

"Bin Laden is dead."

"Yeah, right. Who you going to believe these days, White House press releases or the talent at *King's Retribution*?"

Even if they had a secure line, and it wasn't, Brady would not offer public comment.

Holmes continued." I am going to take a wild guess I don't believe Al-Qaeda is going to launch it on the anniversary of 9/11. That's when Homeland Security will issue its standard warning around the 9/11 anniversary. Al-Qaeda will launch it before or after that date. And you have interconnected plots, as in plural: Florida and California with amusement parks and something to do with money and a London connection. The stockbroker."

"Keep me apprised." The call ended with each analyzing what they had heard and spoken of, trying to connect the disconnections. *Thank God,* thought Brady, *if King's Retribution is half correct, at least it's not going to be a dirty bomb in Times Square or what did they call it, a 'Wellspring' nuclear poisoning at the Continental Divide.*"

Later, as he pondered, Brady could have filed his conversation with Holmes away in a dusty drawer and gone back to the euphoria permeating the intelligence section of the Mideast Department. After all, the military had just erased Atiyah Abed al-Rahman from the ledger of killers.

If only bin Laden's intel could lead them back to Anwar al-Awlaki and Doctor al-Zawahiri, then the troubled ghosts of 9/11 might be somewhat appeased. And, of course, as Holmes knew the facts, eliminate once and for all the mastermind, Osama bin Laden.

He could not dismiss so easily Holmes and his TV cowboys. Sure, they were prospecting leads, and some sounded promising, especially since it seemed someone was trying to kill off the show's stars like Storm King. Most likely local police would check out the car bombing

516   S.P. Grogan

and discover a disgruntled fan. And this hype of a Florida attack being imminent had his interest, but if home-grown terrorists were around, the FBI wouldn't want the Agency sticking their nose into their domestic shit.

Crimson Scimitar, whatever it might be, rankled his mindset requiring systematic order to all things unknown. It was Matthew Brady's job and obligation to make sure a 'what if' did not turn into his greatest fear of 'why did we miss it?' as the intelligence community itself had allowed to occur in missing signals that might have prevented 9/11. So, it would only take a few telephone calls to dismiss this line of reasoning as a false alarm.

His first call went internally to the National desk with the question: "Any problems at the nuclear plants?" The reply, after scanning the data links: outside a few short-term closures from the earthquake in Virginia, nothing out of the ordinary. "How is security at the plants?" and he heard as he expected planned security reviews in preparation for the 9/11 anniversary.

He did not relish his next call and expected the result. NORAD, buried under Cheyenne Mountain, Colorado, held tracking control of American missiles and the running inventory of nuclear weapons locations. He made it sound routine, but the question tumbled out all wrong,

"May sound strange but is all your ordinance accounted for?" He got the expected dismissive laugh, then a few moments of silence, and he knew that call would come back on him. Most certainly, he just initiated a massive double-check accounting of their entire nuclear inventory.

Damn you, Holmes.

His last call was to the National Regulatory Commission, the government's nuclear industry oversight organization. Brady found himself passed off to a sub-manager, where he shot the breeze for a moment, then, following an earlier cue, asked how their protective preparation was going regarding the upcoming 9/11 anniversary. As expected, he received a lecture on the security systems in place for the country's highly secret enrichment program, the stuff big bang bombs were made of. Just as he was ready to sign off, he asked, "So, sounds like everything is secure?"

"Yes, everything will be on lockdown," came the official reply, "a week before and a week after the anniversary. Taking no chances. Of course, the stuff in motion, that's under a separate NRC division."

Brady's mind blinked. "*In motion?* What do you mean?"

"Nuclear waste by-products. There's always some disposed centrifuge or spent fuel rods off to secure locations. They have their own security detail."

"How is this 'waste' taken to these locations?"

"Depending on size, shipment either by train or truck."

Brady made a redial to NRC and asked for the Chairman's office. Acting as if he was merely verifying what he already knew, he asked if any transit shipments were 'in motion' this week or next, part of the required check-up on 9/11 anniversary preparedness.

The response was not the answer he wanted to hear, ever.

"Yes, we have a transit shipment going out by truck. Destination unknown, highly classified, but then you people know about it."

That news surprised him, so he played along. "Oh, yes, we do. Just doing, as I said, this protocol verification. If I send a form around, again, who is the person in our shop that's on your need-to-know list?"

He heard, "Your Deputy Director, Ronald Givens; why, he even sits on our ad-hoc task force committee on nuclear waste with our Chairman, the Homeland Security people, FBI representative, you know, all the oversight agencies."

"When does the next shipment get dispatched?"

"Oh, I believe from what I understand, it's already on the road."

Even though he had only assumptions, a dire premonition sent a cold chill down Matthew Brady's spine. He buzzed the duty officer at the CIA's central input-output desk on his intercom. "Get me anything on the world net dealing with the word *Wellspring*."

Scene 7: In High Gear
Setting: Indian Point Nuclear Power Plant, New York State, early evening, August 29th, Monday

The Scientist was quite pleased with how the day had gone. All the overtime effort resulted in his crew seeing the two trailer trucks leave the Indian Point station. They were nondescript-looking freight carrier trucks, one a truck with two containers, the other two of one container, the two marked with logo signs stating, *Eagle Freight*, a design of a screaming, plunging eagle with a captured trout in its talons — but no warning signs affixed reading 'Dangerous Chemicals.' The Anna Generating Station's truckload containing the concentrated trillium bore two additional eagle design tags. Singh then had simply taken a spray paint can and placed a slash of red against the back of the prime double carrier, odd-looking, like graffiti, but nothing to draw anyone's attention, and that was the point. A red slash, but to his conspirators, the suggestion of a curved red sword, a guide to the promised land of the coming emirate. When unnoticed, he affixed a GPS tracking beacon with limited range on the undercarriage. The metal-looking device looked scuffed and worn like an ordinary truck component.

518   S.P. Grogan

As to the truck convoy details, in front of the three-truck caravan would be a black Hummer, setting the lead truck's pace, a half a mile ahead. Within the lead vehicle were two armed guards, not military, but private hire under government contract, each one with a concealed sidearm and one automatic rifle in the vehicle and, as Singh noted, not really in a place where the rapid-fire weapons could easily be reached, but they were not expecting emergency usage as this would be a long, grueling but otherwise routine trip. An identical guard-Hummer configuration would travel behind the tractor-trailers, again far back so as not to draw attention — four guards only, three drivers, with one relief-mechanic driver to rotate between trucks. The whole plan was to make the trucks look invisible to the whizzing traffic along the interstate roads they would travel.

Singh, the employee at Indian Point, was heading home for the evening, relieved his part of the operation had gone off without a hitch. No longer the 'Scientist.' He knew nothing more of the *Crimson Scimitar* operation but was smart enough to want to be glued to the television, knowing the attack on the trucks would garner major media coverage. He was not worried at all that his cover might be blown when the trucks were destroyed and the government would come looking for the leak, on who might have told of the truck's planned cross-country trip route and its eventual transit across the bridge. Singh felt an inner strength that he could weather any sort of interrogation. They would have to kill him first before he would betray his fundamentalist brothers.

With deepening shadows and clouds bringing on early dusk, Singh's car rounded a curve on the country road a mile from his home, and in a sudden response, he was alert, his car's brakes screeching to a stop in front of the auto accident, a car halfway off the road, at an awkward angle on the graveled shoulder strip. Singh shook his head knowingly. This curve had seen many such accidents, usually when the roads were wet with rain. This evening at dusk, the road was dry but still dangerous as the accident bore witness. He could see a man slumped over the wheel, probably unconscious. Singh pulled in behind the car, put on his emergency blinkers, and got out to offer assistance.

The car did not look damaged. He reached into the open window and gently shook the injured man's shoulder, "Mister, are you alright? Where do you hurt?" Only then did the Scientist note the oddity; the driver's ear was missing.

EPISODE THIRTY-ONE — ACTORS, HIT YOUR MARKS

Scene 1: Khalaf and Sabz's last day
Setting: New York City, August 29th, Monday

Idyllic was not a word that Khalaf would usually bring to mind to describe his feelings.

Nidal had coordinated the short-sale orders this morning, the trucks from Indian Point had departed on their journey, and the attacks on the amusement parks, the first phase of *Crimson Scimitar*, would be in less than two hours, West Coast timed to be at 11:30 am, while the East Coast amusement park opened at 8:30 a.m. Those thoughts gave him mixed emotions. He was a man committed to the Islamic cause, but he did not want to leave Sabz. His mind bore a question he dared not dwell on. Were his goals the same as al-Qaeda's? Self-happiness against the harsh dogma of constant war, to believe the world of such diversity in modern thinking could be conquered from harsh tribal lands espousing extreme conservative dogma. He shook his head to think such irresponsible nihilistic thoughts.

Yet, here he was, Monday morning, finishing a pleasant stroll in Central Park, Sabz by his side, exiting close to the entrance near the Plaza Hotel. And though a romantic outing was not sex, and though most of his efforts over the last evening bore animalistic ardor, he currently sensed the rising urge to be such a romantic, to hire one of the horse and buggy rides through the park to extend the idyllic peace of the moment. No, that would be for his return visit. Tasks were at hand.

During their walk, did she read his mind when she asked, "You are happy? Your telephone calls this morning and the emails today will bring your cause success?"

"It seems so."

You are happy with me?"

"Yes."

"Then we should marry when you return."

At that, he coughed, and his pace stumbled, surprised, but he did not want to cloud his future.

"We shall see."

"Are you going to take other women for your wives?" She said this with a childish possessive pout.

"Only if you bother me too much." He smiled at her. Allah protect me against two women such as her.

520 S.P. Grogan

"I saw on the television that they have, what do you say, a porn-o-graphic channel. You have to pay for it to watch. I hope I have pleased you, but I am not experienced. Can tonight we watch how other women perform so that I might learn to do these strange things that make men crazy with desire? And be so willing when you return?" She had not stopped her plotting to change him.

Khalaf recalled the few tattered adult sleaze magazines circulated among the couriers in the Abbottabad compound. Watching western women naked and cavorting could be interesting, and if it were to give Sabz ideas for physical exploration, that might be an acceptable benefit.

"We shall see." The statement not being negative was taken as an affirmative by Sabz, and she grabbed onto his arm in a joyful hug, then skipped over to watch squirrels chasing each other around the base of a large tree.

For the first time, Khalaf was going off to do battle and would leave someone behind whom he now understood he cared about.

But these inner debates were troublesome. This world of comfort was enticing, for around him, instead of the whipping hellish desert wind, he had started to relish the sounds of the city, men and women of all looks and faiths, temperaments tested daily, yet moving on. They all had political opinions, but he saw no one caning a person in public because they did not follow another's religious scriptures. How strange it had all seemed to him on his arrival, and today, civilization teeming around him and having an attractive woman beside him gave him a new perspective, like a new blasphemy, that perhaps people living together in toleration was a religion unto itself, greater than those from holy books. Such a thought he again quickly shook from his mind, mad at himself for even conjuring up such speculative temptation.

"Let us return to our hotel room," he said. Sabz smiled back, for she knew someday, if he survived, she would have Khalaf as her champion, and someday, by her wits, she would gain control over her own future. Maybe she would leave him then, but then maybe not. She enjoyed his touch, recognizing in that first passionate embrace that he was as much the novice as she was.

"Yes, my Sheik, and I shall endeavor to figure out how the television pay system works."

Scene2: Amusement Park Stake-out
Setting: Florida and California, August 30th, Tuesday

"They're on the move," said Curtis in his hurried phone call. "We are mobilizing. Chopper is in the air. And they are heading north, and as you guessed, one utility-type van. We can't see what's inside. But four men inside, two of them our foreign suspects.

"We have about two hours before they reach Orlando. They should be in the area around noontime."

Holmes glanced at his watch. "That will make it at 9 a.m. here, just when the parks open. I bet they will coordinate strikes, just like 9/11. Please keep me informed of any breaking news. We'll get going on this end."

"I have put our L.A. office on alert. There will be an undercover presence at all the amusement parks."

"Yes, but, and I don't know; if they get the publicity for the East Coast, they only need one to confirm the nation has been attacked. We have two groups of our people at the two main parks here. And we have lost anyway if they have another team at any other parks across the country. Too many to cover in one day, and panic if you notify all jurisdictions. And they win on that", noted Holmes.

"I know you all helped, but please keep your people out of the way. This is our job," Curtis told him.

"Another couple of eyes won't hurt. I will coordinate with your office; we have two parks in stake-out mode only."

"You do that."

The *King's Retribution* Team did their own form of mobilizing. They had the one Storm Wagon truck available and were using Storm's new replacement SUV, which was no longer his as he could not drive except as a 'handicap' vehicle with special equipment required, not yet installed for his useless legs.

So, the two vehicles were off. They were in radio contact to position one at each amusement park that Holmes felt would most likely be attacked, one in Burbank, the other in Anaheim. And, he thought ruefully, he could be totally wrong, but that's not what made Holmes Holmes. To survive, you had to work off a few facts and inbred instinct, and there still could be a total error in judgment. So, with Samantha's information, he had asked himself: which corporate publicly traded company with amusement parks was most likely to be visible, where an attack would garner the most publicity and drive their stock spiraling downward? He had asked her, 'was there any one company whose trading stocks usually were more volatile?' He would follow a gut filled with guesswork. Right ideas and the wrong location would mean failure — with catastrophic results.

Before they headed out, Holmes sought to dissuade everyone from going, as did the hesitant Fox. Let law enforcement handle the operation, they said. When all the key players said no, they all wanted to tag along, Holmes tried to get the most professional to be assigned to each vehicle. Cardoza, Fox, Holmes, and Samantha in the SUV. Cardoza even emphasized the need for CAM ONE and CAM TWO to be present, to record all the events so Storm,

522   S.P. Grogan

back in the hospital for another reconstructive surgery, could see the results of *his* Teams. Pacheco (armed), Abbas, and Bennie were taking the Storm Wagon on its first combat test drive application.

Holmes, in resignation, only shook his head; he was in a damn reality show, after all!

They were all crazy, believed Pacheco. Why weren't the police and National Guard brought in? This called for military intervention. But he knew the answer: they were operating on hunches, and putting fear into the public would only set off mob panic. What he found not so much humorous but a sign of the times was when Holmes said, "It would be easy to do racial profiling and believe every Arab-looking person was a terrorist, but keep in mind the Florida suspects are skinheads traveling with Middle-Eastern 'friends', so you have to believe we are probably going to see a mutt-jeff mixture of bad guys. Keep your mind on looking for a facial tic of nervousness or people wearing long jackets in this heat. If you see something out of place, you will have the correct radio frequency to notify your nearest FBI agent. Don't be the hero."

Curtis's call came close to noon. He named the amusement park where the van was headed. The dice had been thrown, and the SUV (Holmes, Cardoza, Fox, Carlisle with CAM ONE) and the Storm Wagon (Pacheco, Bennie, Abbas with CAM TWO) went to their designated amusement park that they expected to be targeted. Arriving at both locations, they could see the rollercoaster above the park's landscaping.

Holmes directed. "We should probably join the FBI at the entry gates and start eyeing those coming in."

Callie and Samantha filtered through the crowd on the inside. Fox stood near the ticketing office while Holmes took up a position at one of the gates, which required personal bag checks, as it was his opinion that if there were any hardware to be smuggled in, then this would be the most likely port of entry. He spotted the supposedly discreet FBI agents too easily, talking to no one yet mumbling into their hands. Likewise, the Hunt Teams had their own earbuds and hidden mike coms, but it was the cell phone which vibrated, and Wendell answered. The number reflected it was FBI, Curtis.

"Damn mess here."

"Say again," Holmes was watching a Mexican family group entering the park for some birthday occasion; three men carrying balloons, wrapped presents, and a large flat box with the cake (he could see the white icing as the gate guard inspected the pastry box). Within the group must be the lucky birthday recipient; he saw a woman carrying a small boy and a man with a ball cap and jacket dragging along a crying boy. How could that little boy being forced along be unhappy to have a whole day of frivolity, plus cake and gift unwrapping?

He turned back to Curtis's out-of-breath shouting.

Crimson Scimitar

"We were set up to nab them at the parking lot entry, but they ID'd us and rammed their way through, trying to crash in the main entrance. We blocked them, surrounded them, and the bastards blew themselves up. Took out about a dozen cars, injured about five of our guys, no tourists, no one critical. Confirms all you said. My bosses said to put a lid on the whole thing, to maybe force the California people to call off their attack. Better to avoid a panic. We're calling the explosion a propane tank on a camper. I've notified our people out there to call in reinforcements. If anyone confirms a suspect near or within the park, call it in, and we will evacuate the whole damn place and only then approach with caution. We have locked the park down here, keeping everyone inside so we can do a safety sweep."

Samantha walked over to him.

"I see nothing standing out. Just looks like happy families ready to enjoy all the rides."

The FBI agent in northern Florida at Orlando, frazzled in his situation mode, hung up.

"Agent Curtis said the Florida creeps blew themselves up."

"Hell, you say."

"That's where they went, hell. So long, Gator. I have a feeling the surrounded al Qaeda goons did the self-detonation, and the skinheads were as surprised as the FBI."

"We have to be very cautious, Wendell."

"Yes. If cornered, it's a one-way ride; they will detonate their explosives, become suicide bombers. Could be much worse than just destroying one rollercoaster to make news."

Holmes's eyes were still scanning the crowd. He watched the birthday mother children walk by, exiting the park at a fast pace, the smaller child in her mother's arms, pulling along the still bawling boy. That was unusual. Skin color and texture, he recalled of the supposed 'father,' a baseball cap hiding eyes and features. Spanish-looking and Arab-looking could be misidentified, especially if the Arab were tugging along a screaming brat. Everyone would look at the unruly child. And the birthday presents, even with colorful ribbons, were wrapped in varieties of pink paper. That was weird. Both children were boys. Wasn't pink for girls? And some of the smaller pink packages, the design....

"They're already in the park!" Holmes began squawking into his microphone, gathering his forces, speed dialing his FBI counterpart. "There are four of them. Brought in explosives, probably guns, hidden in presents and a cake box. We're heading to the rollercoaster." He heard the FBI agent yelling at him to stay where he was. Sure thing, amigo. He ignored the advice.

Holmes had told Fox and Samantha that when the terrorists were spotted, their job would be to help coordinate the evacuation of the park safely and without scaring anyone. The al-

Qaeda terrorist would definitely blow himself up and try to take a large number of innocents with him.

No heroes, please.

Callie Cardoza merely gave him her patented, 'Oh, yeah,' and her hand moved into her purse, no doubt her finger firm on a trigger housing.

The park would be crowded, parents grabbing at wayward children, dabbing on sunblock, hydrating them with bottled water, and letting them scurry in front to jump into the ride lines. The rollercoaster was in the process of making practice runs, but the line of families anticipating entrance to the ride extended into several rope turns. Holmes scanned the crowd. He did not see anyone, and then he did. Three of them bunched together off to the side, near the barricade, over which someone might be able to scramble and climb up the siding to set an explosive charge. Three Hispanic men, tattooed and gang-looking, were providing security. The ball cap guy nowhere to be seen.

The FBI agents found the birthday party gangbangers at the same time the trio spotted them — two seconds of staring back, weapons pulled out, and a firefight exploded. The crowds screamed and fell to the ground while others scrambled, sprinting away. Pandemonium.

Holmes needed to find the bomber. If he drew his firearm, he would probably be picked off by friendly fire from over-eager Fibbers who did not receive the memo on who were the good guys. So, he moved around to the side, keeping his eyes on the structure, feeling Callie Cardoza near his side, Hugh Fox reluctantly trailing behind.

"There!" She pointed.

Ballcap guy had climbed the barrier, wearing a backpack and a heavy zipped-up leather jacket; he was working his way into the center of the ride's structural latticework. The first ride of the day was in motion, with less than a minute to retrace its run above the bomber.

Holmes motioned to Callie.

"Go around, don't let him out that side, and if his hand goes into that jacket, duck. I'm betting he's not only carrying explosives; he's wired with a vest." Callie darted away. He did not look back, knowing Samantha would curse him for going into danger, like usual.

The gunfire around them had trailed off to an occasional ping of single fire, and Holmes glanced back to see a prone body not moving, one of the Hispanic attackers. Feeling a little old,

Holmes grabbed the top railing of the fence, pulled himself over, and plopped down on the other side. As he climbed, the bomber was using the structure of the rollercoaster to conceal himself.

Holmes guessed the explosive charge had to be fitted with a timer, and knowing the troops were closing in on him, he would set it for a quick sequence, so Holmes had to reach him before he set off the device and made his getaway, which meant he would run to another spot in the park, one with crowds, and blow up himself and those around him.

Holmes could not take that chance and pulled his Glock and, through the steelwork, spotting the moving ball cap, fired and expectedly missed. Make the man jumpy; if he could not stop him, then get him to blow himself up away from the people. By the shot's miss, the bomber now knew it was all over except for him to meet his perverted version of a Supreme Being. In a blind craze, the bomber pulled a revolver and let off a blast of gunfire back at Holmes, forcing him to duck behind a thin beam that offered little protection. The bomber threw his gun away, shifted his stance, stepped up and onto another steel girder, and wrapped one arm around a central leg to the rollercoaster's famous upside-down hairpin turn, seeing the onrushing coaster riders, happy and screaming in fearful joy. The bomber knew his time had come and what most probably was a cry of 'Allahu Akbar!' reached into his jacket — only to stop and look up, startled. Holmes saw the hole materialize in the man's forehead, a red mist floating in the air behind him, no sound heard beyond the rollercoaster's noisy tumult as the hurtling cars rocketed past. The man toppled from his perch but, in his fall, jammed in the cross-beams and lodged there, upside down, a Daliesque crucifixion.

Hugh Fox ran up to Holmes, panting.

"I didn't mean to hit him. I wasn't trying, I swear. I was just trying to give you more covering fire. Unfortunately, I am not that good a shot."

"Good enough," said Callie, arriving and removing the fired weapon from Fox's shaking hand.

Holmes took in the scene with swarming FBI agents in clean-up mode kicking weapons away from the dead, one agent being tended to with an arm wound. "Best we all get out of here without fanfare; it's better we not get caught up in this; there are ramifications." Holmes looked around as the Team re-assembled, with Samantha joining as they blended into the fleeing throng of park visitors. Then, over his shoulder, Holmes added, "And Callie, tell CAM ONE to shut off the damn camera. You don't want the world to know that your billionaire boyfriend just killed someone."

"What?" Callie and Hugh looked at each other, reacting simultaneously in embarrassed denial.

526 S.P. Grogan

Scene 3: Judging the Results
Setting: New York City, 1 p.m. East Coast Time

Khalaf followed the Associated Press stories as they came across the newswire on his computer trading program in real time.

12:30 p.m. — *Explosion reported at amusement park, Orlando, Florida*

The stock of this entertainment company dropped two points on the NYSE. *Very good, just as planned,* thought Khalaf, but minutes later, a different story started to materialize.

12:45 p.m. — *Propane explosion in motor home forces park shutdown. Five people injured, three fatalities reported. Fire Marshall promises full investigation of park safety.*

What's going on? An anonymous text message should now have been received by the media outlets announcing al-Qaeda's revenge attack. The stock dropped another three points, a slight shift downward across most other entertainment securities. The 5% threshold, a short period trading freeze, hit several entertainment companies with amusement parks, even a few listed without parks.

10:30 am West Coast — *Gunfire reported at amusement park.*

11 am West Coast — *Gang warfare breaks out at amusement park, first of its kind. Two dead. Park closed as police investigate.*

A coincidence? East and West Coasts. Amusement parks. The news junkies started the sell-off. The funds, with their computer programs of formula decline analysis, added to the sell, and the entire entertainment segment, movie companies, and amusement parks took a hit: 10% loss, another circuit breaker stoppage. After those entertainment companies who owned their respective amusement parks, though a small part of their overall revenues, saw losses when trading resumed and a move downward at 12 % loss in the day's value. "A major one-day hit to entertainment stocks caused by on-site incidents, not from any earnings report", said one cable channel trading analyst. "This sector should rebound tomorrow."

At 2:15 pm, Congressman L.D. Sheftel of Missouri makes a public call in Washington for an industry-wide review of safety procedures at all entertainment park facilities. The two companies directly affected by their park shutdowns and loss of substantial revenues issued separate press releases stating 'that the incidents in question had nothing to do with park operations and were occurrences not controlled by us. Therefore, with police approval, the park will be open for business tomorrow as usual, and all customers inconvenienced by the day's event can either gain a full refund or be issued a free ticket for another day, provided they have previous proof of purchase.'

At 2:45 pm, Congresswoman Polly Hicks, representing the hardworking entertainment workers in her Florida constituency, spoke to a reporter from CNN, saying, "It is sad that tourists lost their lives when their motor home caught fire, but such a tragedy should not undermine or call into question the exemplary record of safety by all businesses in Florida."

When the New York exchanges closed for the day, Khalaf heard from a pleased Nidal.

"Congratulations, Mr. Rasil. Though those stocks dropped to 15% before rebounding with a 9% loss for the day we, I mean you, covered at 12% and so did extremely well. Are we buyers tomorrow?" He did not question the bad news which caused the trading profit gain.

"I expect another day of concern, but no, no buys for tomorrow, but let's put in some buy orders for Wednesday if there seems to be a low floor to those companies we shorted (Khalaf now had mastery over the lingo). As I told you, I will be leaving town for a few days. My wife has further written and notarized instructions if you require further direction. Understood?"

"Yes, of course, Mr. Rasil." Nidal knew him only as Rasil, not knowing he stayed at his hotel under his UAE alias. Khalaf felt insulated by these false identities, but today he was not a happy person.

Apparently, this phase of the *Crimson Scimitar* operation had been outfoxed.

Law enforcement was in a conspiracy to expunge all attempts to paint this with a terrorist brand.

He knew why — the 9/11 anniversary. As al-Qaeda wished to demonstrate its omnipotence to strike anywhere, anytime, with no opposition, the American Government had to show that al-Qaeda was not a threat, that the obese and lazy population could go about their lives and enjoy their sense of complacency.

He saw this quite clearly when someone unknown (the *Crimson Scimitar* plotters outside his scope] emailed the Los Angeles *Times,* informing them that the California attack at the amusement park was the work of al-Qaeda. Most probably sent by Shahin himself, upset at whatever occurred at the park. Undoubtedly, Khalaf mused, it wasn't a major news story of a rollercoaster exploding and riders falling to their deaths. The newspapers downplayed the terrorist claim, calling it a hoax.

By early evening, in L.A., a brief news release was issued by the FBI, 'preliminary investigation by local police reports that a turf battle between local gangs resulted in three deaths. We have no indication that such shootings were in any way related to a terrorist act; however, we do ask citizens to be mindful and alert as the 9/11 Anniversary approaches and to report anything unusual.'

Khalaf looked at the big picture. The first phase of *Crimson Scimitar* had achieved half of its objectives: al-Qaeda received no credit, and the American people were not again in fear for their lives, but on the positive side, the plot from that subway movie did actually result in a gain of several millions of dollars in Khalaf's trading accounts. This part of the *Crimson*

Scimitar plan was over. He was tempted to take some of the profit and play the futures of stock market gyrations, especially on the approaching news of the destruction of the trucks at the bridge and the devastating implications to millions of Americans. He felt a growing knowledge of how to play the market, but now he hesitated in giving Nidal the direction to make untried investments. In the back of his mind, there was a shuddered tinge of worry: what if Shahin's attack failed and the shorting strategy on American stock exchanges would not react? He might lose all he had gained. No, he would wait, play it safe; rather be the wise investor than an uncertain speculator.

He made up his mind. On Wednesday, when he arrived in Denver, if the market had rebounded, he would move a minimum amount of liquid assets into the al-Qaeda blind accounts he was told must be set up to transfer funds back to the organization's coffers. A majority of funds he would move into other more conservative growth stocks and liquidate sufficient funds to cash for bank accounts he individually controlled, which he would disperse later *under his direction as he felt could be best used.* Another departure from his mandate, but one based both on caution and self-preservation. He would leverage this money for recognition and a voice at the table. The worst sin against orthodoxy he had committed was that on a thumb drive in the package, the letter not to open, he had given Sabz instructions to give half to al-Qaeda and half to various charitable groups for wounded Islamic warriors and their families. Of course, there was to be a fee for Sabz to handle such transactions. Would she realize those instructions were his last will and testament? It meant he would not return, ever.

His mind turned to more pleasing matters. 'Tonight, I will take Sabz to an expensive restaurant. I would like to show her off in these new garments she buys. Besides, tonight is my last night before I travel.' A long night of television experimentation in the bedroom would be his reward for today's partial success.

Scene 4: Blame Game
Setting: West Wing, The White House, August 30th, Tuesday, 5 p.m.

In the hastily called meeting, the main players of American intelligence were there: the heads of Homeland Security, the FBI, CIA, with the meeting run by the President's National Security Advisor. Several supporting-sub directors were in attendance, including Ronald Givens and, unexpectedly invited, Matthew Brady, who felt he might be the sacrificial lamb to be thrown to the lions.

"And, in fact, this was an al-Qaeda operation, not some homegrown loony?" The President's Advisor looked around the room, settling on Givens, who in turn looked to Brady for help, so he responded.

"We had no intel from our own Mid-East sources; the FBI Florida office gained information on a totally unrelated case they were working on."

The FBI director spoke up, unsure whether he should take the credit or if his Agency would be a scapegoat, so he did a little blame-spreading. "Our local office actually got a lead from one of your former employees." He glanced at the Acting CIA Director and at Givens, then at a paper he held. "Former CIA Agent Wendell Holmes."

"Holmes!" cried out Givens in surprise. *So, this is where the trouble is coming from;* "The guy is a rogue, totally not a team player."

"And yet," said the President's Advisor, "He uncovered a plot to attack our institutions, even if they were amusement parks."

"It is imperative that we maintain the charade," offered Homeland Security, who earlier had developed the strategy to present at this anticipated meeting. "Downplay these incidents as being totally unrelated and having nothing to do with terrorists, especially al-Qaeda."

"I am in agreement," concurred FBI, "There could be other attacks in the making, and we need time to search them out, perhaps meanwhile cause division in their ranks to where they might make a mistake. If we let the press know, the public would inundate us with thousands of false leads. Racial profiling would be an unimaginable witch hunt. A behind-the-scenes investigation is our best hope at uncovering any other planned cell attacks."

"Are we expecting more?" The top leaders of the nation's Intelligence community looked at each other and gave hesitant nods of 'I don't know.'

"Should we bring in this Holmes fellow, as Mr. Givens characterizes him, a 'loose cannon'?

"I have no problem if you arrest him," Givens smiled that such a chance was possible.

"It may be best if we let him operate outside the box, develop his own independent research. He did uncover the amusement park attacks." Brady did not mean to step up to the defense of Holmes as much as he did not want Givens to gain his way. He accepted the glare from Givens.

"And what makes you think this former agent, out there by himself, can develop better leads than all of our departments combined?" Homeland Security knew he was on the top of the heap, as most others in the room reported to him.

"Because he sent a photo showing himself on a private tour of bin Laden's home the night after his death. Isn't that correct, Director Givens? He sent the photo to you directly."

Givens found himself in a corner, cleared his throat, and squeaked out, "Yes, that's right. To me and others."

"And, Mr. Holmes," continued Brady, "uncovered intelligence that we missed when the SEALS swept through the Compound, no fault of their own, as it was secreted away in a wall."

"What intelligence?" The Acting Director of the CIA was not in the loop.

"We aren't really sure. Holmes has not revealed much. Seems he has a bitter taste in his mouth over how he was dismissed from the agency." Brady did not make eye contact with Givens.

"So how did he end up believing the amusement parks would be attacked?" asked the FBI Director, who needed the information to develop his own background story if the press ever put two and two together.

"Books and movie DVDs he found in Abbottabad that were later destroyed by the enemy. From what he saw, I believe he notified the FBI of his finding, his guess, and we should be thankful the guess was the correct one."

"Al-Qaeda books and movies? Sounds ridiculous," Givens was not giving Holmes any credit if he could help it. "Plus, you should all know he's running around with those TV people of *King's Retribution*. No creditability at all, if you ask me."

The President's National Security Advisor briefly recalled the pain *King's Retribution* had caused in the White House from the trial of bin Laden. He had to agree with Givens that they had no need of further interference from bounty hunter TV show personalities.

"Let's hear no more of Holmes. Well, where do we go from here?" The FBI discussed for a few minutes the ongoing kidnapping of the attorneys. After several minutes, they all came to the consensus that the announcement of a warning to the public in the approach of the 9/11 anniversary should be issued forthwith and that all the intelligence agencies would go onto quiet alert and sift through past data to glean if any other plots were being fomented. The 9/11 timeframe seemed to be in all their minds when another attack might be scheduled.

In concert with concern, the decision was made to put additional assets on the larger amusement parks around the country for a few days until past September 11th, a just-in-case alert.

The White House very, very subtly said if any 'incidents' could be categorized as non-terrorist events, that would be for the best of all parties. The unsaid meaning was that a political year was approaching, and they needed to be strong on foreign policy and the continuation of a successful War on Terror, but not fought on U.S. soil, which might suggest dereliction of their duty to protect U.S citizens at home.

Ronald Givens, not to miss an advantage, and having received an earlier call from U.S. Senator Crandall of California, offered the suggestion, "If the President or the First Lady or their children could be scheduled to visit an amusement park, shake hands, and take a ride, that would make a favorable and subtle impression on the public's confidence." They all thought the idea a sound political move.

Outside the meeting, Givens braced Brady, angered.

"You certainly didn't help me in there."

"Actually, Director Givens, I thought I did. Holmes's latest brainstorm is that some al-Qaeda plot is aimed at attacking nuclear plants or nuclear waste shipments."

Givens was visibly shocked.

Brady said, "If I had brought that up, you would have laughed at it, and if it turned out to be true, you might have been caught up in the blame game. You are overseeing a truckload of waste byproducts delivered to an undisclosed location?"

"Yes, but it is totally secure."

Playing the detective, Brady had confirmed that a truckload was 'in motion.' He hoped Givens would give up more information.

"Holmes made up some story that the nuclear waste would be hijacked and dumped into streams at the Continental Divide in the Rockies."

"Absurd. Wherever he's getting his ideas, they are off the wall. Our truck group won't be going anywhere close to the Colorado mountains; they will swing south in Denver and go through New Mexico. And besides, the NRC and all the other agencies approved the route. My signature is required only for the formality. I think Holmes should be arrested for fear-mongering."

Brady, without launching clandestine spying within his own agency, which was tantamount to getting himself prosecuted, had gleaned enough information from the Deputy Director. But what to do with it? Who within the American government would believe him? They would only say he was crying 'Wolf,' the same accusation he warned Holmes about. But what if Holmes was one hundred percent correct in his assessment? As farfetched as the whole plot sounded, such an eventuality meant a nuclear environmental catastrophe.

Matthew Brady, a good man, not a great man, still a Company man, vacillated between self-courage and self-preservation of his future Washington employment.

He returned to his office, closed the door, and quickly wrote another one of his cover-your-ass memos, which he was becoming proficient at, basically laying all future blame at the feet of Ronald Givens for being biased against giving credence to a possible threat. Then, with the memo completed and placed in his personal and secure safe, he picked up the phone. Maybe Holmes and *King's Retribution* could save America from al-Qaeda and itself.

532 S.P. Grogan

Scene 5: Nightmare
Setting: The Warehouse, Colorado. Middle of the night, August 31st

Booker was unsure of what sound brought him semi-conscious, perhaps the dream of what their last journey might be. This morning they were to be on the next stage of their captivity, and now he found himself suddenly awake, staring at the ceiling.

He rolled over to look at Harriet and saw something strange in the darkness. Where she lay on her mattress, a mound was moving, no, two bodies moving, one writhing.

What the — ?

"Hey, hey!" He jumped up and rushed towards her, only to be yanked to a halt by the length of his chain manacles. "Get off her!" Their chains had been lengthened only so far, probably because of some ideology or torture, that neither one could join the other on their separate mattresses. He did not know and did not care at the moment. Just yelling loudly was his only hope of protecting her.

Harriet was fighting, trying to bite the attacker's hand, but that was not working, with her mouth clamped shut. She felt the fumbling at her clothes with his other hand as his body draped on top of hers, grinding. Booker's shouts had the effect of interruption, and the brute, it was Maj, rose from his groping and staggered quickly to Booker to hit him hard and hit him again. Booker, chained with his attempt at fighting at a disadvantage, was knocked to his knees, enduring another fist, this to his jaw; laid out prone on the floor, struggling, determined to rise to help Harriet.

His hope to help and the distraction seemed to work even if he was beaten senseless for his effort. This gave Harriet a few moments of respite to catch her breath and allow a sufficient intake of air to emit blood-curdling screams that surely would have woken the dead.

Maj gave off a feral snarl and turned to continue his assault on Harriet as if she should be awaiting and accepting his advances. There was no escape for her, but she had crawled to the bathroom and was hunched down in a corner.

Maj, at the bathroom door, went no further and crumpled when the butt of the automatic rifle slammed into the back of his head.

"Get him out of here," bin Laden commanded to the curious onlookers who came to stare but saw no reason to interfere in one of their own mishandling the infidels. "Tie him up, and throw him in the back of the car. The first hundred miles on our drive should bring him alert. And find out where these drugs are he keeps taking and throw them away."

Bin Laden went over and stared down at Booker, who was on his knees again, weaving, shaking off the bell ringing inside his head. The al-Qaeda leader then peered in at Harriet, quaking in the bathroom corner. Seeing her clothes were not ripped or torn off, he accepted that her honor had remained intact. However, when her eyes went to him, they were not forgiving, no 'thanks for saving me.' Instead, her expression was anger at all that had befallen them, this last indecency par for the course. She was giving him the evil eye bestowing a curse of damnation, and sensing her mental intent, he quickly turned away.

His own anger was more for a soldier who did not obey commands. Bin Laden perhaps realized he could not depend on Razzor or Shahin to maintain discipline. They had to see him as a leader of determination, and he had to establish for them all to obey his decisions without hesitation or questions. The rape of a captive was not the message he wanted al Qaeda to convey to the world. Nor any execution of one of them for jihadist publicity. Not at this time.

To the two victims, he only said, "We will leave in two hours…to meet our destiny." And he left.

Booker crawled to Harriet, and she crawled to Booker. In the middle of the office, they held each other for long moments. He did not know how to ask the obvious and personal question of whether the bastard had hurt her or gained the advantage over her. She sensed that.

"I'm okay. Just not how I wanted to wake up, looking into the face of a total evil bastard."

"Don't worry. It'll be payback time. I'll find a way."

"You're bleeding." His injured mouth smiled at the fact they were still alive, which gave them a reason to replace fear with hope again.

She held him tighter, his blood dripping onto her cheek.

Scene 6: Wellspring
Setting: New War Room, Los Angele, August 31st, Wednesday

So much for the privacy using the hidden new War Room location.

Shawn Pacheco waded through a mini media circus in front of the office soundstage they were using, dodging questions asking who he was and what did he know about the gang shootings at the amusement park. Two burly guards at the door checked his driver's license, checked him off the list, and let him pass into the building. Here, he met Callie Cardoza with a fresh cup of coffee in her hand.

"What's going on out there?" He pointed to the hungry press.

She gave him a wry grin. "A tourist said they thought they saw TV star Callie Cardoza, gee, that's me, running through the park with a drawn pistol. At today's meeting, I guess, we'll be told how to spin this whole episode."

"Well, I certainly wasn't there." Pacheco's response reflected his frustrated demeanor.

534   S.P. Grogan

He had been in the *King's Retribution* Storm Wagon at the *other* amusement park, missing all the action, a downer for any battle-honed SEAL. They were giving him a consolation prize of sorts. Holmes said he would try to get a breakdown on the timer elements found on the bomber's body and the recovered IED strapped to the rollercoaster base structure. Pacheco would then be able to make a comparison to see if there was any uniqueness in the bomb's creation, which would be disturbing if so. On the other hand, if there were similarities to what the Taliban or al-Qaeda used on the Afghan battlefield, then law enforcement bomb squads could react with more confidence on how to diffuse a future explosive threat. The Team at least gave Pacheco his due, accepting him into their ranks as the expert in explosives, now requiring his active presence.

In the large workroom, Callie and Shawn found the Team gathered. As Fox spoke, the mood of chattering gossip quickly descended into gloom.

"It is my opinion that we should shut down our offices," said Fox, grimacing, his voice strained, his eyes showing a lack of sleep. "We rose to the occasion, you all gave 150%, and I believe we made a difference." They all knew he was still reeling from killing a man, even if the dead man carried a death-maiming bomb..

"I don't know why the government is keeping a lid on this," said Bennie, "Calling it a gang turf war. That doesn't help us using it in *King's Retribution* and telling the whole story."

Abbas added, "We would lose creditability going up against their present storyline."

Callie said nothing. She knew something they did not. The others thought the FBI had killed the bomber under the roller coaster. Not Hugh Fox, games inventor and nice guy.

"They can't admit the general citizenry got wind of a terrorist plot," surmised Samantha, "and their billions spent on intelligence gathering missed all the road signs of clues."

Fox agreed. "They have egg on their face and are pissed, but they have the power to react and cause us all misery. The Studioz office has already been put on notice that the FBI (and probably the CIA) want formal sit-downs with all the principal stars and management."

"Speaking of which," Samantha turned to Callie, asking gently, "How is Storm doing today?"

"Much improved, though the doctors think he will be crippled in his legs. Rehab will tell. He's a fighter."

That brought silence to the hybrid conference room. Beyond the genuine concern for Storm's recovery, the underlying message was clear: a bounty hunter who could not chase the bad guys signaled the death knell to *King's Retribution*. Fox looked with empathy to Callie, seeing that she might face the hard facts of life: possible unemployment. But, as she had told him, she wished Storm a speedy recovery and emphasized that any continued cruise of romantic interest with the show's star had sailed away months earlier.

Fox brought them back on track; after all, he was co-funding this strange, now deadly, adventure.

"We set out to capture bin Laden, and we succeeded. He escaped, and the entire law enforcement of this country is on alert and out searching for bad guys, and one of them is bin Laden. We have become superfluous, if not, by their threats, interlopers if not interfering, and all of us subject to arrest. I can't put any of you through that wringer.

"We gained access to his house but had one of our own killed, murdered before our eyes. We played this game of clues and stopped irrational killers from hurting others, American citizens. I don't care if all we did ever becomes a television exclusive. To hell with pandering to a fickle public audience; real life is sometimes not in our destiny to create it as we see fit. Now, we just need to pack it in and resume our day jobs."

"What about Booker and Harriet? Just asking." The question from attorney Linda Scott-Goss. She was sitting to the side, not in the Executive Committee but with a bunch of the Nerd Crew, Gizmo next to her, waiting for new instructions. Shutting down was not what they had come to hear. Depression descended within the room at the thought of breaking up the Team's camaraderie.

Fox continued, as serious as anyone had ever seen him, "Like you, I am concerned. But we are nowhere close to finding them or bin Laden along with them. I am willing to keep funding our group of computer jockeys here to keep information flowing on possible clues and leads to find the kidnappers, which we'll then turn over to the authorities."

"What do you think, Wen?" asked Samantha. Everyone turned to Holmes. In the midst of everyone's genius, skills, and talent, this mysterious, silent man had become their solid anchor, centered stability.

His cell phone buzzed. He answered, listened, then put the phone down on the table and pushed the 'Speakerphone' button.

"Please repeat," said Holmes, "And do not identify yourself; you are in a large room with those who were in Abbottabad. Please speak very succinctly."

The voice on the other end, a rasping voice, definitely employing a voice changer modulation device, spoke slowly, enunciating with clarity, as if to convey the import.

"Three tractor-trailer trucks are heading west, in your direction. Each is carrying nuclear waste by-products. I know they are going to Denver, then south to New Mexico, and then west from there along I-40. They are not crossing the Rocky Mountains. I do not know their destination. I don't know how potent their cargoes are but I've been told they have adequate security. If you react, you will have no support until there is viability that the convoy is at risk. The cavalry cannot ride to the rescue." The mysterious call ended.

"*Wellspring*," said Samantha, knowing and fearful.

"I expected," said Gizmo, "that the phone would hiss out smoke, like on *Mission Impossible*." All smiled, and attorney Goss patted his knee as approval of his nerdiness.

Holmes scoffed but made sure he had disconnected the speaker phone...carefully.

"*Crimson Scimitar*. It was apparent from the beginning it would be a multi-attack operation," affirmed Holmes. "Small feints at amusement parks to create national panic, but what else did they accomplish: the entire force of police and Federal agents are running around, swarming amusement parks across the country — How many are there?" He looked to Gizmo and the Nerds. "425," said Gizmo. Holmes continued. "Federal resources are spread too thin, going in the wrong direction, while others are spinning their wheels chasing thousands of false leads. Al-Qaeda is ready to deliver the knock-out punch. Yes, *Wellspring*."

"And I bet you if we can find the next choke point of the attack, guess who we will find there, gloating?"

"Osama bin Laden," almost a chorus spoke, now animated.

"And," Fox had to join in, seeing what might be occurring and not having the will to prevent it. "Where bin Laden is will be the answer to Booker and Harry. God, I hope they're safe. So, when are these trucks leaving?"

All thoughts of dismantling the Team were no longer a subject of discussion.

Looking at his phone, Holmes answered. "According to a cryptic text I received a minute ago, they left the nuclear generating station back East on Monday, the 29th. A day ago."

"Ay, Dios mio!" exclaimed Callie. "Wherever they're going, they're almost there."

Scene: 7: Good Intent Slammed
Setting: The Warehouse, Aurora, Colorado, September 1st, Thursday,

Khalaf received two shocks that went to his core. His leader, his hero, Osama bin Laden was alive! And he was yelling vitriol at Khalaf in berating screams.

"Where is my money? Why did you think you should step into our stock market plan...You are just a...courier! And look what all your books and movies have caused! They were discovered by the CIA! They have figured out *Crimson Scimitar*. Will they be waiting for us? I don't know. You failed. And what of my money?"

Bin Laden paused for breath. They were behind the closed door in bin Laden's living quarters, yet everyone with ears would have heard the cursed chastisement.

Khalaf, reeling from the exploded temper, processed that he had been verbally struck with false charges from his mentor, who he would willingly die for. What was this?

He rushed out his defense. "My leader, we did make money in the stock market, but not as much as you hoped. I brought $100,000 U.S. cash for what I thought might be needed by the attack team."

"Where are the rest of the funds?"

"There is a process; the transactions have just occurred, and the funds require a week to transfer to your accounts. There should be over $8 million available to al-Qaeda. We doubled the money we invested."

Khalaf could see bin Laden partially calming, hopefully mollified by the new funds that would give financial strength to the organization's depleted coffers.

"I do not see why you were put in charge of this Pelham Plan. There are others more capable." Bin Laden did not wait for any excuse. His mind was set. "Give the money you brought to Shahin. Now that you are here, we will be leaving. You are to wait for the Professor. You two will follow in his car and be auxiliaries at the bridge, called on if required. After our success I will ask the Professor to put you on a plane back to New York to speed along the funds' disbursement. That is your only task." Bin Laden paused as if thinking, for the first time, considering what was beyond *Crimson Scimitar*. "I instruct you to come to our new base in Yemen. I will give you orders then. Khalaf, you have disappointed me. We will discuss your future on our return."

The head of al-Qaeda's departure signaled his brusque rejection. As the unsung co-developer of the plan in motion today, Khalaf stood traumatized, absorbing his feelings — dejected? — emasculated?

It got worse. Shahin and Razzor entered the room, stern men of anger matching their leader.

"He said you brought money for us." Not a question, a command. Shahin extended his hand, waiting. Khalaf, in slow numbness, removed a money belt from under his shirt and passed it over.

Shahin pointed to the door. "We are going over the attack sequences for the last time. Since you decided to impose yourself into our 'venture,' you should listen to your responsibilities. We want you to understand where *you should not be*." Shahin left, and Khalaf followed, noting that this man called Razzor followed them. Khalaf sensed he was not considered one of them but under their watchful eyes, as a guard might treat a duplicitous prisoner.

538   S.P. Grogan

He saw bin Laden pick up a travel valise and enter a waiting motor home. Behind him came a man and a woman, the 'prisoners.' These, Khalaf surmised, were the kidnapped attorneys. They were shuffled aboard, guarded, and secured by handcuffs. The motor home door closed.

Khalaf found himself directed to a large table with diagrams laid out, including the design of a bridge. Khalaf, tired and worn from his cross-country flight, knew he should make no small talk. He would say nothing about the failed amusement park attacks. He knew Shahin's temperament would be explosive, for he had lost three of his men with no publicity gain for al-Qaeda. In the compartmentalization of *Crimson Scimitar* to protect each element from discovery, he assumed Shahin was unaware of the stock market manipulations tied to the bombings, and to learn that Khalaf held a role in that part of the operation would only foment the man's jealous wrath. To them, to all that were there, he was just the courier, the interloper into their own mission, unwanted. He asked himself, another reflective truism, 'Did my purpose in coming have any real value...to them ...to me?' His mind was confused, he standing there numbed, from finding himself demeaned by his Leader's wrath. 'What did I do wrong? Where did I fail?'

Khalaf looked around the table, noting the other men standing represented the Attack force. Shahin did not make introductions. Names did not matter. The layout on the table said it all. The attack would be located 30 miles northeast of Las Vegas. Not at Yucca Mountain. Any stranger looking at this model landscape and the miniature layout would recognize Hoover Dam and a bridge arching the surrounding canyons. A bridge over the Colorado River.

"To you all, our current update is that we expect the trucks to cross the bridge sometime tomorrow afternoon. As we will, if on schedule, they will be spending the night in Albuquerque, New Mexico. Probably secure on a military base."

Shahin, using a laser pointer, let the beam hit the bridge. "There are two blind spots on either side of the bridge. Force One [the Professor's own student cell], on the Arizona and Nevada side will be ready and we will drop off one of our team to each location where posted construction barricade signs a mile back will be put in place to slow the the trucks and reduce their separation. By the time they reach the bridge, we want them close together. After the last truck passes, Force One will close the road for a construction delay, hopefully blocking out the last escort vehicle. They, and any other auto traffic, will be told it will be a twenty-minute delay. That is when our time clock will begin. Twenty minutes to hijack the trucks."

Khalaf found Shahin's explanation interesting. He knew the truth, knowing the scope of the entire operation from bin Laden's computer thumb drive. They were to destroy the trucks on the bridge, not steal them. Khalaf guessed the reason for such subterfuge. The Professor's cell, those who were going to block either end of the bridge to keep traffic away, were not privy to the entire plan. Younger and without battlefield experience, they were merely programmed robots, blinded by enthusiasm for whatever private motivation, just like most of the 9/11 hijackers, who were not all informed about the plan. They carried out a hijacking, not realizing Atta and the selected al-Qaeda pilots were on a suicide mission. Khalaf had no reason to say anything. The plan was to destroy and escape. Shahin would not kill himself, believed Khalaf, knowing the man's ambition, equal to his own, the reason for their competitiveness among al-Qaeda. He must have a good tactical reason for this lie.

Force Two, as the attack groups were named, would block traffic with similar construction delays on the Nevada side of the bridge.

Shahin looked at Khalaf.

"You and the Professor will be on the bridge on the Nevada side, but not near and not where we attack the trucks. You and the Professor are to grab any of our wounded. The Professor has a medical clinic prepared for private treatment. Razzor, you will help if required."

Khalaf noted that this man, the one looking intent, even malevolent, about his assignment, merely nodded, then exchanged eye contact with him. *I do not like this man*, thought Khalaf. Then, it came to him just where he thought Shahin might have put him, as a 'lowly courier' in a rearguard position, reacting to bin Laden's yelling, he found Shahin had placed him on the bridge. Yes, he was reduced to a minor role, but still, he would be part of the battle.

His mind came back to Shahin, who was quietly laughing.

"As of yesterday, the Americans are ignorant of what is about to be brought upon their heads. The old road across the dam is now a dead-end turnaround. Police, one patrol car, will be at the wrong location with a checkpoint, believing someone like us would drive onto the dam and blow up such a formidable place with nearly 7 million tons of poured concrete. And yet, there is no slowdown or police surveillance on this bridge, their weakest point."

According to the plan's scenario, the road was blocked at this point. After that, any stray auto traffic would be allowed to proceed by one of Shahin's personal teams, the Attack group, Force Three, dressed in fake Nevada State Highway Patrol uniforms. Only the trucks, with both convoy escorts, would remain, blocked to either side of the bridge, out of sight. Their fate would be left to Force Three, the professionals from Yemen.

Khalaf began to regain his internal composure. He would be in the honored position with Force Three and partner with this man who had not yet arrived, the 'Professor,' both overseen by Razzor, who would instruct them on their positioning. That was it, the stand-by medical transport unit. It seemed Force Three, as Khalaf himself had seen in Southwestern Pakistan where they practiced on an abandoned bridge, were prepared and confident, and did not need a refresher. Was that overconfidence or again hiding their plan from others? Or was this last briefing just for him?

With the final instructions reiterated, the last planning session ended, the table and terrain map were broken apart and sent to a dumpster, and the departures began. Two black SUVs with shaded windows left, followed by the motor home. Khalaf was left alone, waiting for his ride, this Professor, the sleeper agent, who Khalaf knew very little about. He had time to think, and the more he did, the more he became angry, but at Osama bin Laden. 'I have been unfairly treated. I was not wrong to use my own initiative.' He knew one thing bin Laden did not, the stock market funds would be allocated to bank accounts he had control over. It would be his decision when those funds were to be transferred to the off-shore al Qaeda accounts. He fumed. By my actions, bin Laden will receive his loot. He will thank me then for the role I played.

Khalaf should have perhaps concentrated on other subtle worries — they did not give him a firearm to protect himself from harm. And why did this Razzor, a significant participant, have to oversee a medical transport car?

One clue might have been the words of Razzor spoken as he entered the vehicle with Shahin.

"This Khalaf, is he one of al-Zawahiri's people?"

"He is merely a messenger boy. Leave him as a martyr on the bridge."

"His martyrdom is assured," said Razzor. As was the Professor's. Those were his instructions from on high. No blabbing confessions under the infidel's torture.

Razzor's function in *Crimson Scimitar* was clean-up.

The Bridge — Photo by Mariordo (Mario Roberto Durán Ortiz)

REEL NINE — The Attack

EPISODE THIRTY-TWO — To the Bridge

Scene 1: Burying his worry
Setting: Washington, D.C., September 1st, Thursday

Deputy Director Ronald Givens initiated the call to the head of the National Regulatory Commission, who served with him on the nuclear waste task force committee. "I have been giving some thought to the convoy on the road. With 9/11 approaching, Homeland Security has issued the appropriate 'Alert' warning. So perhaps it might be a good idea to beef up security along the route."

"You have heard something?"

"No, nothing at all." Meaning he had no verifiable evidence, only rumors as he saw them.

"Well, that's good. We can't turn the trucks around. We have no place to put them. It would be a logistical nightmare, especially with the death at Indian Point of their main transit manager a couple of days ago."

"Death?"

"Auto accident. Ran off the road and broke his neck. We're kinda in a fix; we have to finish this one trip since Singh put it in motion and prepared all the routing.

"Too bad. Well, yes, I agree, it must be completed. Forget my request."

"Well, we don't want to draw attention to our cargo; that's the way it was planned."

"You said the man who died, his name was 'Singh'? Is that a…" Givens wanted to say, 'was the man a Moslem; was Singh a Muslim name?'

"Singh is Sikh, immigrated from India. His family is back there," said the plant manager, "but they can't seem to find any of them to let them know of his passing. Probably will have to do the funeral in New York and send his ashes back to be poured into the Ganges."

Givens ended the conversation somewhat relieved. He felt his call had been ill-advised, that he was only on edge from his White House meeting and what Brady had said of Holmes's wild theories. He needed to think of a solution to put the ex-CIA agent out of everyone's reach. Too bad he had no say-so over the Black Ops division. Like the dead Hindi, a simple car accident would rid him of an intrusive thorn.

542 S.P. Grogan

How true to the times; religious ignorance had pervaded the conversation. Singh was not

Hindu. Hindus cremated their dead and placed their ashes in the Ganges River, home of the Ganga maa (the goddess who removes sins). What Singh had purported to be was of the Sikh faith, a monotheistic religion of 30 million followers, the fifth largest religion in the world. It did not matter. Singh, in truth, had been a secret Islamic radical, murdered as part of a greater scheme. His body lay in a funeral home, against all tenets of his hidden faith, awaiting instructions as to his final place of burial, wherever, and under whatever religious mantra, the final choice would essentially be wrong, all except the 'ashes to ashes, dust to dust' part.

Scene 2: Mounting Up
Setting: Los Angeles, Friday, September 2nd

Wednesday into Thursday saw a frenzied rush, each hustling to their assignments, all without a clue of where the ending might lead.

Bennie serviced both the TV show's film equipment van and the lethally armored Storm Wagon. Pacheco worked with Abbas inventorying the various equipment and moving duplication of weapons from the Wagon to a smaller van. Pacheco, not used to an unlimited budget from a for-profit corporation, made the point to add gas masks, even a couple of glide parachutes to both vehicles to the humor of both Abbas and Bennie until they wondered if they were expected to be the jumpers if the circumstances presented themselves.

At 10 a.m. on Thursday, the *King's Retribution* van with Bennie and Abbas departed, along with CAM TWO, with the strange directions to take I-15 east to Las Vegas and then continue on Highway 95 into Arizona. First, they were to keep their eyes open for three trucks escorted by either military or unmarked vehicles in convoy fashion. Then, they were to drive into New Mexico until these trucks were located.

Later in the afternoon, Pacheco would follow in the Storm Wagon with CAM ONE. He was to meet in Las Vegas with Callie, Fox, Samantha, and Holmes, who would fly in. Callie and Holmes would join Pacheco and then proceed east, following the route of the *King's Retribution's* S/FX van.

Meanwhile, Fox and Samantha planned to take a private helicopter and fly from Vegas along Highway 95 to act as spotters, looking for anything unusual.

They had taken a circuitous journey to these decisions, and the dialogue between the principals revealed their struggle.

"So, we are in agreement that another attack will occur, and against this truck shipment?" Fox again found himself as the designated chairperson.

"Yes." A collective consensus.

"Beyond Holmes's contact at his old place of work, we have no more information," said Callie. "And it seems we can't go out and scream warnings. What if we got it all wrong?"

"Let alone looking like fools to a predatory press," agreed Samantha, "I think there must be a dozen Federal laws we would break interfering with a government shipment."

"If my contact is correct," began Holmes, his mind juggling, "then the assumption doesn't jibe with the trucks being driven over the Rockies up I-70 and their radioactive cargo dumped into streams on the Continental Divide. And I just don't see that as the flash and flamboyance that al-Qaeda uses as its signature attack. However, if they go south to New Mexico and then west, I see too many opportunities."

"Like what?" Fox could wonder, but he preferred to have a visual reference.

"Let's say the trucks reach Las Vegas. They can go north into Utah, west to L.A., or south to San Diego. If I felt those trucks carried a 'dirty bomb' that al-Qaeda could detonate, we might presume they would try to explode it in Las Vegas, courtesy of Stephen King."

"The author?"

"Ali Baba may have picked up a copy of *The Stand* by Stephen King. In the end, the bad guys explode a nuclear bomb and destroy Las Vegas."

"That's what they call an oxymoron, isn't it?" Weak smiles at Fox's humor.

"I don't see wasting a nuclear incident on Sin City," said Holmes, dismissive of the possibility, "Even though a million people live in the metropolitan area. L.A. would be a more dramatic target. But if they have the makings of a bomb, their targets should be New York or Washington, D.C. Seats of power."

"Well, let's revisit Ali Baba's books and movies. He mixed the disaster themes of a roller coaster and a subway high jacking. What if..." said Callie, looking at the board list of all they had seen in Abbottabad. "How about Clancy's *Dead or Alive* and that old copy of *Wellspring*.? Both have water elements, one a poison dumped into Rocky Mountain rivers at the Continental Divide, the other, a nuclear incident at Yucca Mountain that impacts groundwater."

Callie weighed with each hand, "Nuclear waste products and water pollution." They watched as she clasped her hands as in a fisted prayer, her elbows on the table. "You bridge these together, and what have we got?"

Holmes stared at her gripped hands and heard her last words.

"That's it. *Bridge.* A bridge, not just any bridge. That new bridge that spans the Colorado River at the Hoover Dam."

544 S.P. Grogan

Fox quickly Googled on his laptop. "The Mike O'Callaghan-Pat Tillman Memorial Bridge, the second highest in the U.S. after the Royal Gorge Bridge. It carries Route 93 over the Colorado River between Arizona and Nevada. Opened just last year in October 2010."

"Plenty of time to be developed into this *Crimson Scimitar* plan," said Samantha, starting to understand what might be the target. "Look up The Colorado River."

Fox did so, and read, skimming, "The principal river of the southwestern United States and northwest Mexico...The Colorado's steep drop through its gorges is utilized for the generation of significant hydroelectric power, and its major dams regulate peaking power demands in much of the Intermountain West...The river is a vital source of water for agricultural and urban areas. It furnishes water for irrigation and municipal supplies of almost 40 million people both inside and outside the watershed."

Holmes summed up the growing truth. "Blow up one truck or all three and drop the contents off the bridge. Poison the river with radioactive pollution. Destroy crops, make tap water undrinkable. Perhaps not instant death but the panic, a massive population fleeing eastward would overwhelm all services and collapse our entire economy. It's diabolical, and all out of the creative minds of our own best writers/directors, instigated by crazed zealots." He concluded somberly. "The attack will happen on the bridge."

The rest looked stunned.

Finally, Samantha asked the all-important question: "But when will they strike?"

Fox called in Gizmo, the computer nerd of the War Room.

"What is your estimation of arrival? We think the attack will come at the Nevada-Arizona Border."

Gizmo pulled out his hand-held P.A. and reconfigured all the assumptions he had been given; departure time he knew; speed of trucks to stay near the speed limit; definite stops for tired drivers, anticipating they were union drivers with required breaks.

"Best guess; sometime on the third, barring unforeseen delays."

"Shit," said Fox. "That's tomorrow."

"We should notify somebody, the authorities, everybody," suggested the practical Samantha.

"Full circle to our earlier conversation: who's going to believe us?"

Holmes offered the compromise.

"I will let all the authorities know what we believe will happen. I will make it from me and assume all the blame. Gitmo is probably lovely this time of year. But until we identify an Arab-looking terror group heading toward government trucks carrying radioactive materials, I also believe we will not be taken seriously."

Fox put forth a reality check. "And if we're wrong and it's not at the bridge, but they strike somewhere else, as bad?"

"America is in for a nuclear winter or rather a nuclear flood," said Holmes. No one was smiling as the ramifications sank in.

Scene 3: East Bound. Last minute conversations
Setting: Los Angeles September 2nd

By the end of the day, the *King's Retribution's* two 'war' vehicles were on the road towards I-15, heading east to Vegas and points beyond. The TV-Special Effects production van, leaving first, had to locate the convoy somewhere on I-40 coming from Albuquerque. When discovered, Abbas and Bennie were to give the trucks an unobserved escort. The Storm Wagon driven by Pacheco with Gizmo a last-minute addition for computer logistical command, would see the larger picture and could direct forces, would meet in Las Vegas Saturday morning with Holmes and Cardoza. This group planned on being situated near the bridge's Nevada crossing. Non-combatants Hugh and Samantha, with would seek out the convoy from the Arizona side from a leased helicopter and pilot from a Vegas sight-seeing tourist company.

In anticipation of how events might unfold the next day, September 3rd, 2011, there was a gravitational pull between the main players into a new coupled grouping — unexpected but perhaps not.

Hugh gave Callie a lift to the hospital to check on Storm, but he was unavailable for visitors. Hugh felt somewhat relieved that the recovering star would not receive an up-to-date on his show's latest involvement. Unfortunately, the prognosis for Storm's recovery still remained guarded, with the doctor surprising them with a new setback. *Delirium tremens.*

"Did you know he was alcoholic?" the doctor asked, light in condemnation, knowing those closest usually never comprehend the signs.

"I knew he drank a lot and was a sloppy drunk," answered Callie.

"He must have hidden the fact he was constantly ingesting alcohol. With his injuries, we can't put him into cold-turkey withdrawal. The sudden changes in his system could lead to a heart attack. We will need to keep him longer and try weaning him off his addiction. But to accomplish that, he will need a network of support. It is always a battle to walk away from the bottle."

Callie nodded, accepting that Storm King had a disease that she had only responded to with anger.

Fox tried to offer her comfort, to say Storm's actions were of his doing.

546   S.P. Grogan

This did not help, and Callie felt the guilt, which put her in a piss-poor mood, and they said very little as he drove them back to her condo.

"We will meet at private aviation. My plane will get us to Vegas early."

"Yes," she said, exiting his car, somewhat numb to her emotions. Then, she stopped and turned to him. "Hugh, you have been absolutely the best in what you have done. Without your drive and goals, these assholes would have hurt a lot of people. Whatever happens tomorrow…."

She let the words hang, turned, and headed off to try to find some form of sleep.

Hugh Fox, even with his mental brilliance, could not, in time, splice together the proper response to his emotions. He liked Callie but saying that aloud required the effort from his heart to his mind to his mouth.

Samantha Carlisle and Wendell Holmes had an entertaining dinner at a French restaurant on the 3rd Avenue Mall in Santa Monica, as if the weight of 'whatever happens tomorrow' was indeed tomorrow, and those problems would be dealt with at that time.

Their conversation consisted of small talk, each exploring the other's history and listening to stories of how they became who they were. Samantha pestering him to hear some of the agency secrets. Holmes gently declined, talking more about what he should do in retirement, which brought a scoff from his dinner companion.

"Retire? You're too young. Why should you? Look at the troops you have mobilized, the confidence you have given all of us. I can now fire an Uzi without messing up my makeup."

They both laughed.

He heard her rags-to-couture biography, of her interest in the *Save the Animals Foundation* and inquired when 'tomorrow' was over would she be less eager to find a new thrill?

She asked him how his religious writing was going; was that going to be his retirement hobby?

"No, a mere exercise in applying my thoughts to solve a problem, creating a basis for tolerance among medieval dogma. I have been a traveler in that world where violence has become a faith, and I feel I could create a better utopia, one where we could actually live comfortably and safely."

"Again, I am impressed in seeing the deeper man."

He laughed at himself.

"Well, it helps soothe my spirits, a release of sorts. Probably will go nowhere, but I will have two professor friends give me critique, offer suggestions, and actually turn my prose, not into Western propaganda, but written from the eyes of someone, you know, like a person preaching in the wilderness. It will allow me perspective."

"I assume you will let me read it?"

"I would be honored."

The meal was excellent, and they talked on like a couple who were coming to realize it was a very pleasant experience. They tried to ignore their barrier, Samantha of society, the constant pursuer of rainbows, seeking her true life's purpose, and Holmes, as described by others, the cowboy, un-tethered, now unsure in a world he had avoided. Not opposites attracting more two travelers on the same wave length meeting, seeking cohesion together.

The first sex they enjoyed, the act of making love, had been gentle, tender, and endearing. Perhaps they were more compatible because of their incompleteness than they had realized.

Finally, as dinner ended and over brandy, they returned to what had been avoided during the evening and on the mind of all the Team members. The next day.

"Do you really think the terrorists will be at the bridge?"

"I wouldn't bet the farm, but if we believe the Ali Baba plots come out of American books and movies, and pray they have no access to their own nuclear weapons, then, yes, dumping the trucks into the Colorado River will be the last component of *Crimson Scimitar*, and we must stop them."

They sat in silence, understanding the daunting task before them, seeing this craziness as being Citizen Soldiers, as Minutemen rushing to, so to speak, the Concord Bridge. The answer they saw before them on the street — other couples, shoppers, families out for an evening stroll, listening to the street musicians — with all urban freedoms, avoiding the beggars or in kindness proffering a token dollar to the less fortunate for solace in food, shelter, even cheap wine escapism. All they asked for was peace and happiness, and some cretins wished the worst on them.

"Let me ask you something," said Holmes, "about the first part of the *Crimson Scimitar* operation."

"Yes?"

"Do you have good contacts in the New York financial industry? I mean, like owners of stock brokerage houses, even officials on the stock exchanges?"

"Why, yes, of course. I have been a major charity maven." She didn't want to tell him the president of the largest investment bank in the country personally handled her portfolio. "Why do you ask?"

548 S.P. Grogan

"I think we might have been remiss in not using our talents, your talents most particularly, in this situation, in tracking down who might have been selling those entertainment stocks short against the amusement park attacks."

"Wendell, you're right. I forgot about that direction. I think we might be able to do that. As they say, 'Let's follow the money.'"

They were both silent for a moment. "Going back to my al-Qaeda spider analogy," Holmes spoke, with deep-voiced determination, "If we are lucky, the authorities, or us, are going to locate the spider's legs and chop them off, but in the end, we need to sever the head." He paused in his thoughts. "Or graft on a new head."

Where the Team had all interpreted the character of Wendell Holmes as being a governmental action-hero spook, Samantha knew it was only a part of the whole. She had come to discover a man introspective about life, methodical in his observations, and all-consuming when participating. Tonight, he had opened himself up just enough for her to look in, and she liked what she saw. In that revelation, within her core, she gained new insight, a feeling of deep attraction towards Wendell Holmes; a desire to be with someone, not for the credentials, required dress code of labels, nor a large bank account but for the individual's inner worth, a valuation unique in her world. Samantha dared not define her feelings, for if tomorrow would bring disaster, losing him would hurt deeply, and if they survived, then it could probably become the worst of all passions, *unrequited love*.

A man of hidden surprises, he surprised her.

"Let's go walk on the beach and then find a warm bed."

Scene 4: Road Trip of the Awakening
Setting: Between Albuquerque and the Bridge, September 2nd-3rd, 2011

The leader of al Qaeda, Osama bin Laden, made a grievous error in judgment. He had paired his courier-turned-market-player, Khalaf, with Professor James Rogers.

Both men said little for the first hour after leaving the suburbs of Denver and heading south, the destination an overnight stay in Albuquerque, New Mexico, before the final ride to the attack zone at the midpoint on the Arizona-Nevada border, at the center of the bridge.

Their conversation edged slowly from silence to basic inquiries of background, and in doing so, discovered that James Rogers was indeed a professor of political science and international affairs at the University of Nevada, Las Vegas, while the Professor learned that Khalaf was a serious student, had graduated from Cairo University with a degree from the Faculty of Economics and Political Science, before being radicalized into the jihad. He had hoped to secure another degree in religious studies at the highly prestigious and only six years new *Future University in Egypt.*

During this light banter revealing their curriculum vitae, casual chit-chat revealed a mutual craving for topical American and English fiction, those political thriller plots full of danger and adventure. Escapism for the studious.

Khalaf mentioned he had read *Protect and Defend* by Vince Flynn and found it mesmerizing. What he did not allude to, and did not detail to the Professor, was the plot that caught his fancy. Israel stops an Iranian nuclear development program with sabotage, creating a radioactive tomb and environmental disaster in the middle of Iran's second-largest city. Flynn's hero, Mitch Rapp, faces off against a Hezbollah master terrorist. Rapp has twenty-four hours to 'avert an unthinkable catastrophe.'

Professor Rogers countered the young man's enthusiasm, keeping his eyes on the road ahead, saying he was a fan of the writing of British novelist Robert Harris and his political thriller *The Ghost*, with its shock revelation ending. The Professor encouraged Khalaf to watch the film, *The Ghost Writer,* released just last year, if he had the time and opportunity. After he explained the book's plot, with the main character being thinly based on former British Prime Minister Tony Blair, the Professor added as an afterthought, "Did you know that in 1982 while a BBC journalist, Robert Harris co-wrote a study on chemical and biological warfare, entitled *A Higher Form of Killing* which offered very perceptive modern possibilities of usage?"

"I did not know that," responded Khalaf, wondering; did the British have better ideas than those he cobbled together? For a while, both remained silent, understanding they were treading on sensitive issues of mission planning that neither wanted to really talk about. And it was during this quiet period a sense of nervousness pervaded the car as the Professor purposefully drove the speed limit. They were half an hour from Colorado Springs, now passing the off-ramp to the Arapahoe Reservation and the Skilleo Stadium, back under construction. A police presence could be seen on both sides of the overpass as they sped by, believing their car was inconspicuous among the thousand vehicles passing by hourly. The truck convoy would pass the same intersection later in the day.

Khalaf mulled over what that publicized episode had meant. Was it only a little more than two months ago that my leader was on trial for his life? What had changed bin Laden's demeanor to go against me? Such bewildering thoughts as this gave him pause, that there might be two worlds, two separate interpretations of the insular world he lived in, and the outside, the greater sphere, he had not fully grasped. To that quandary, and spoken carefully, he asked of the Professor, "And what of your family? Tell me about them."

The dialogue became pleasant once more with funny tales of children behaving mischievously and then Khalaf's turn, trying to explain the antics of Sabz. That got them to their motel room in Albuquerque for the night, where a new conversation on the eve of battle had them both animated until it was near midnight, and with bodies and minds exhausted, they slept. Still, both determined to renew the scholastic-theological debate of their cause.

In the morning, their dissection of philosophies, tearing down, then building, more re-configuration, offering salient points to question, to debate with each other's intellectual intelligence adding to ideas yet secured.

Their car whizzed past Native American tribal reservations, seeing bronze-skinned Indians in drab outdoor work clothes, in decades-old pickup trucks eking out a harsh living in an unforgiving sandstone, red dirt land. So, they debated, did these indigenous people of the land have any stake in the battle these new foreigners (themselves) were bringing from distant causes?

On this journey, drawing closer to its destination, the Professor and Khalaf noted rainbow colors mixed with advertising slogans as they viewed the rising of a local hot-air balloon festival. Were these monstrously designed lanterns which floated, invoking participant and onlooker pleasure alike, with no evil visible, were they only demonstrating an unthreatening peace against a wispy ocean-blue sky of aerial grandeur. Sightseeing vistas brought thought. What was their true goal beyond presumed violence which probably would not truly gain their sectarian goals, half a world away? If we believe as we were taught but are smart enough to know there may be other options, are there any ways better than this?

The Professor, seeking clarity in his perspective after ten years of being in obscurity, holding a hidden yet fading grudge against his current adopted homeland, said, "'Now I am become Death, the destroyer of worlds.' This is from physics professor J. Robert Oppenheimer, the 'father of the atomic bomb.' He quotes from a religious sacred text of the Hindus, their Bhagavad-Gita. Are we two, such people, 'destroyers of worlds?'"

As they caught up to the caravan of the motor home followed by the attack team's SUV, both Professor Rogers, the family man, and Khalaf, the student still learning, could admit aloud, between only themselves, without fear of repercussion: they saw the world through a myopic spectrum of political ideology, not theological absolutism. Their daily lives of love and hope bore witness that the world at large, its entire people of a hundreds of nationalities, was not in lock-step to the sacrosanct. To each other, they confessed: 'I do not want to become a martyr at the bridge; my life has value and purpose of continuing.'

Sometimes, unfortunately, such heartfelt confessions must be tested.

Crimson Scimitar

Scene 5: With a little bit of luck
Setting: Albuquerque layover

The three-truck caravan bedded down for the night secured within Kirtland Air Force Base in Albuquerque, New Mexico. Under the protection of Air Force MPs, the night went peacefully. The convoy's crew of drivers and four guards enjoyed a well-deserved steak dinner, no alcohol allowed.

Prey and hunters were currently in the same city. The feelings among the al-Qaeda stalkers showed heightened anticipation. They found a cheap motel, definitely in need of business, not asking questions, even perhaps a way station of coyote smugglers. Very seedy.

Staying in the motor home, bin Laden retired early after dinner had been brought to him. He wanted to be alone. He was sick and tired of the two prisoners that had bothered him for the duration of the seven-hour trip. If he had not already decided to use them as his chroniclers, they would have found a mutual bed of silence in a roadside ditch.

Yes, they were bored. Who would not be? But to overcome it for this leg of the trip, they were allowed to sit in the front of the motor home. They verbally argued past cases, switching sides, offering arguments, and critiquing how they would have handled cases. And drove bin Laden to distraction.

This night they were placed in a motel room, the phone removed, and the television cord ripped apart. The guards outside would be interchanged every three hours, who otherwise sat in the SUV facing the motel room at the back of the building.

Run, and they knew they would die horribly, was their warning from Razzor, and they knew he meant it. Not a chance to take.

Harriet and Booker each remained handcuffed, hands in front. Harriet asked that the handcuffs be removed for a bathroom stop for personal hygiene. The motorhome driver, their guard of the past day, received permission and stood outside the door as she performed her ablutions. Booker found her insistence on hygiene her own form of standing up to the goons, but they could not have another smelly SUV as on the first night of their capture. Still, he noted she stared hard at the guard uncuffing her and repeated the process when she exited the bathroom.

"Shall we just go to sleep?" queried Booker, pointing to the two single beds.

"I've got a better use of our time." Harriet went to the side table between the two beds, opened the drawer, moved aside both the Gideon Holy Bible and the Mormon Bible, and found a small pencil and a pad of paper. As best she could, she scribbled out a small sketch. Then, she went around the room, searching.

552   S.P. Grogan

First, with the long chain attached to the bed, she stretched to reach a wire hanger in the closet.

"Can you see if you can bend off any wire from the ripped television cord?"

"What's up, Harry?" He pointed at her pencil doodle.

"That's what a handcuff key looks like, the key that unlocks these cuffs, and we are going to try to fashion two crude knock-offs. Just might give us an edge."

Booker reappraised his associate, fellow prisoner, now close acquaintance.

"You just come up with this brilliant thought of Girl Scout grifting."

"Not really. I recall one of my earlier public defender cases, a meth head I was representing. He got hold of a paperclip from my file, fashioned something similar to what we are going to try to manufacture, and made it down the hall before the sheriff's deputies tackled him."

"Ah, I see where your legal vocation has benefits. Hope we can figure out if it might work."

"Booker, I think we need an edge, and you — we — need a game plan. I've been thinking, why does he need live hostages to present his manifesto against the United States for all of our perceived ills? He can just stuff the document into our dead mouths, which would be a much more brutal attention-grabbing form of sending his message."

"Yes, I can see that. Keep us misled that we are worth something to him. When in the end...."

Harriet interrupted. "Two keys. By that, I mean if one key opens, but we can't open the other handcuffs, one of us must flee, run."

"I am not leaving anyone behind, never again."

I'm not her, Bookie, she thought, the old ghosts of abandonment still ever-present. "You don't need to save me or the world. And in the same situation, I might have to make the hard choice, too. Survival, not self-sacrifice. One of us must carry on, run for help, get even, all that shit. That's what I expect from you."

"Let's beat the odds; that's our mutual goal."

"Agreed. Let's get to work before there is a bed check."

Scene 6: The Attack Team's Last Prep
Setting: Arizona — On the Road — Close to the Bridge, September 3rd, 2022

They met 45 minutes from the bridge at a pull-off rest area, ahead of the NRC convoy by a good 25 minutes. The pit stop had four vehicles, including the advance rent-a-car driven by two attackers. Their task had been to locate the convoy driving from Colorado and tag along at a safe distance to see that it was keeping to schedule. This vehicle then raced ahead for this meeting and again would lag behind and follow the convoy to add support at the first roadblock.

Shahin left the SUV and walked over to join bin Laden in the motor home. He would change into a rough facsimile of an Arizona State Trooper uniform. Six of the attack squad donned highway maintenance Day-Glo vests.

Razzor, looking awkward as a state trooper, walked over to the Professor's car and handed Khalaf something wrapped in a motel towel.

"Put this under your car seat. Use if only necessary."

He asked the Professor, "Are your schoolboy jihadists in place as we instructed?"

The Professor had bad vibes about Razzor, did not like his mindset, and saw in him the violent zealot, so with that intimidation, both hands clenched on the steering wheel, he responded with chosen words, "Yes, and will act when you arrive. One of my people on the Arizona side, two on the Nevada side, about a quarter mile each from the bridge." Razzor nodded and walked back to the SUV.

The al-Qaeda vehicles back on the road, the SUV speeding up to rush ahead, the motor home and Professor's car in tandem at the speed limit, and the fallback vehicle waiting on the approaching convoy.

Driving off, Khalaf glanced down at the 'gift' he had received; two pistols, both Beretta M9 semiautomatic 9 mm, weighed heavy in his hand. He quickly stuffed the package under his seat. He was shocked. Did Shahin, did bin Laden, arm him to fight? Had their confidence in him been restored? He had mixed feelings between confusion and elation. Finally, settling on what he really felt, he said in a dazed, distracted voice, almost a whisper, "I'm really not ready for any of this." Though speaking aloud more to himself than to the Professor, he looked over to see a nod of understanding from the scholar.

Scene 7: King's Retribution Makes an Appearance
Setting: Nevada — On the Road approaching the Bridge

Still known as the 'Hunt Team,' they had used Las Vegas as their coordination point and were heading to the bridge from three angles. Abbas and Bennie had gone ahead in their modified S/FX van, bringing along CAMERA TWO. Pacheco had armed the van with left-over weaponry he had scrounged though the emphasis was on them to be reconnaissance only, with no military involvement. To which Abbas had sourly commented, "And you can see how that's kept us out of trouble."

Abbas and Bennie radioed in. They were pretty certain they had located the convoy on the west side of Kingman, Arizona. In the early hours, they had neck strain from jerking around, checking all the different tractor-trailers traveling on State Highway 93. What decided the final acquisition of their target was the observation that these trucks had minimal signage, *Eagle Freight,* with a design of an attacking eagle, while all other tractor-trailers were plastered with brand advertising and, most lacking were gasoline tax stamps or multi-state license tags. Also noted were the two ink-black Hummers with darkened windows, one in front, one trailing the three trucks, both going right at the speed limit, letting those tourists getting close to the neon destination of Las Vegas zip past.

"The three trucks are strung out with a quarter mile of separation on each," said Bennie. "Two tractor-trailers, the cabs both silver, and a tandem double cargo truck in the center. They look too pristine; we're pretty sure we got the right ones."

The Storm Wagon, where Gizmo maintained the electronics and communication grid between team members, texted the message to Samantha in the helicopter. She responded that they would be on top of them in half an hour. The helicopter had been rented at a hefty price from a Grand Canyon tour company based in Vegas, so she and Hugh could make the pilot do a wide turn over the Hoover Dam and gain an open view of the O'Callaghan-Tillman Bridge.

Fox called into the two Teams motoring along the highway. The aerial reception was bad static.

"Looks like a desolate desert, and I see nothing unusual. Some construction crews working on the road. On both sides and near the bridge. Don't we find that odd?"

The helicopter pilot, oblivious that he was in the midst of a thrown-together citizen op, was ready to show them the sites, with the special tip on the side he was promised, blithely added his tour director comment.

"The bridge is the first concrete-steel composite arch built in the United States, and it incorporates the widest concrete span in the Western Hemisphere. It is 840 feet above the Colorado River."

"Good to know," Samantha shouted back through the headphones. The pilot might be getting the surprise of his life, not to be found in the tour guidebook.

EPISODE THIRTY-THREE — The Bridge Attack

Scene 1: Roadblocks Come First
Setting: O'Callaghan-Tillman Bridge — Nevada/Arizona border, September 3rd

"Looks like a goose egg trip," said Hugh as he directed the helicopter pilot to go east, saying he wanted to follow the highway but actually to catch sight of the three trucks approaching the bridge.

"We're five miles from the bridge," Holmes, through Gizmo, sent a text to the group, "Nothing on our side."

Fifteen seconds of static silence, all processing that they were on a false trail.

"Wait a minute!" exclaimed Bennie from Arizona. "Traffic slowing down. The road crew just threw out traffic barriers after the third truck passed by. We're stopped. The last security cops also stopped."

On the Nevada side, Pacheco himself was slowing the Storm Wagon.

"They've thrown up a roadblock on the eastbound traffic in front of me. Three of them waving signs."

"It's at the bridge; it's begun." Holmes took control. Earlier, they all had agreed a coordinator leader would be required; even Callie understood who might have the best tactical insight.

Quick commands by intra-radio communication and repeated texts.

"Gizmo, launch request for help messages!"

In the Storm Wagon, Gizmo jumped into his role.

"Repel boarders command, aye-aye Admiral."

Holmes: "Hugh, try to stop truck #3, the last one, before it reaches the bridge. Imperative the bad guys have one less weapon." Catching the mood, Holmes directed his driver, Pacheco, "Ram the blockade, damn the torpedoes, full speed ahead and expect incoming."

Callie pulled an AR-15 automatic rifle off a wall side mount, preparing for the worse.

Holmes had pre-programmed and prepared three calls, just in case, and Gizmo simultaneously had the messages relayed, a scrambled unidentifiable voice speaking.

— To: Matthew Brady [1 pm in Washington, D.C.], the 'informant' voice explained what he believed was about to occur. 'It's the bridge over the Colorado.' If and when he received the message, Brady would make his calls but still expected a disbelieving response. The disguised voice also asked for tow trucks and major 'truck-lifting' crane and helicopter lifting equipment. If Brady understood who might be calling, beyond an expected call to local law enforcement and the regional FBI office that immediate help was essential — expedite — for an expected weapons stash bust at the bridge, hopefully, he would also place a call to Nellis Airbase in northeast Las Vegas, speak to the commander, and put him on notice that specialized equipment was required. National security was at stake.

— An anonymous call to the Las Vegas Metropolitan Police Department, a tourist passing by who thought he saw two suspicious people, Middle Eastern, near Hoover Dam on that 'new bridge.' Holmes did not expect a SWAT team to show up, but he was hoping that some police witness would be sent to the bridge and in position to call for backup. No big deal if nothing materialized.

— Finally, in his own form of Holmes's Retribution, a voice message was left with CIA senior executive Ronald Givens:

"Hi, Mr. Givens. Since you did not deem our previous call (a lie) about the attacks on the amusement parks as serious, we wanted to give you a heads-up that terrorists will soon attack a government shipment of nuclear waste. You know all about it (another lie). Have a nice day."

If what might occur occurred, that recorded call ought to do the trick for his own personal zinger… if Holmes was correct. If not, what could they do to him?

For everything else, almost simultaneously, attack and response impacted all present.

Scene 2: The Attackers
Setting: The Bridge

From both sides, Arizona and Nevada, the four-lane highway(State highway 93, Interstate 11) came up hills and rounded curves before, if driving, a quick rush from one side to the other side, no time for sightseeing of the dam, far below. The bridge span had a slight arch to it in the middle. Along the dam side, there was a walkway for tourists who would take steps up from a parking lot and who had the best view of the Hoover (Boulder) Dam and Lake Mead beyond the spectacular and historically important dam. Like a bathtub ring of white coloring against a red rock background, the lake water diminished by low snowfall run-off was being depleted by downstream farms and metropolitan consumer cities.

Bearing names such as the Great Basin Highway and Hoover Dam Bypass, as the highway approached the bridge, there were two exit roads; from east to west, the Kingman Wash Access Road and west to east, Hoover Dam Access Road. The roadblocks were to be placed right after these exits but around a curve out of sight. Considering mid-day traffic volume, even for the short duration of the planned attack, miles of traffic back-up would impede any emergency response, while the attackers would find no traffic reaching the exit roads making their escape.

On the bridge road, two lanes ran in both directions, east and west, separated by a concrete abutment the length of the bridge and beyond about 5 feet high, maybe 8 inches thick, top to bottom. On the tourist walkway, another concrete barrier separating traffic and walkers, and there was an iron railing with various plaques to read about the building of the bridge, but on the downstream side, the two-lane part of the highway going into Arizona had no walkway, just the concrete barrier.

They realized that two timed explosions were required to be orchestrated by one of the attackers, who had been trained as a 'sapper,' an elite combat engineer, whose job was: (a) after the westbound trucks were halted, an opening consisting of about five sections of the concrete barrier would need to be created by explosive charges, so that the trucks could be driven over onto the eastbound highway. Then (b) a similar-sized length of sections of the bridge on the river side would be blown. (c) The sapper then had to affix mini bomblets to the undercarriage of the three trucks (only two would be stopped on the bridge). The bombs would be set off by a timer as they were jettisoned off the bridge into the Colorado River. The attackers, with their CS Plan, not created by stupid men, were to explode the trucks as they were jettisoned off the bridge, minimizing fatal radioactive poisoning to themselves.

The entire attack had been pre-timed to be only 20 minutes in duration, and all participants had been told to then head towards Las Vegas and coordinate to flee to the Southern border, escape into Mexico, and return home to fame and glory. So, they were told.

The attack began. Razzor, in the SUV, had dropped off one of the attackers at the west side bridge roadblock and then returned to cross the bridge and stop in the middle on the eastbound side. As planned, two of his attackers, one as an armed guard, the other as the sapper with a satchel of explosives, ran to the center concrete barrier and affixed a string of small packages at the base, a width of 30ft. Running back, he pushed the handheld detonator, and a chain reaction explosion left a gap in the middle of the roadway wide enough for a truck to be driven through.

The second act of destruction was repeated on the downriver concrete barrier, so the trucks could be pushed through, right above the Colorado River, 890 feet (270m) below. (With the tourist walkway and the steel guard rail, going towards the dam would have been more time-consuming, and bent steel could have caused a possible blockage, plus the river flowing at the point below was narrow, and a truck might hit the rocks, and not totally disintegrate. However, a directed explosion would accomplish this.)

The RV drove onto the bridge on the dam side bridge lane, not far, carefully, not near the first explosion, yet turned sideways as another blocking element. The driver took his weapon and sprayed the cab of the first truck as it came onto the bridge, killing the driver immediately. The truck rolled slowly ahead, bumping into the RV and coming to a stop. Another attacker, the guard to the bomber, walked past the first truck and sprayed the second truck. Not according to plan, the second driver of the double tandem, with the most poisonous contents, had become alerted by the attack on the first truck.

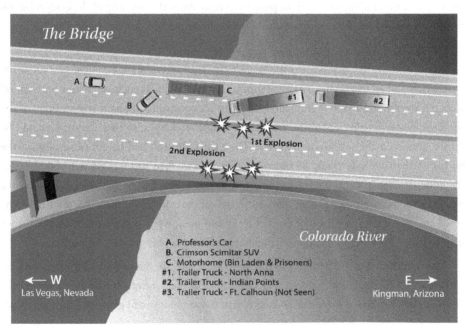

With seconds to spare, he slammed on the brakes, put the tractor-trailer in park, and, like a bat out of hell, jumped out, running behind the truck to the east side, flinging himself over the concrete barrier onto the tourist walk, running through startled tourists. Overlooking his basic training in his panic, he had forgotten to turn the engine off.

The trucks were stopped by the gunfire, and immediate explosions on the concrete barrier set the few tourists on the walkway into panic, running back the way they had come to the lower parking lots. Some, more terrified, cowered in place, ducking, hiding as best they could. Terror had come to America and threatened those innocents who just wanted to take in the marvel of a 1930s engineering feat to harness a river for electrical power. Instead, infamy was on the roadway.

Shahin saw the truck driver of the most essential Truck Two escaping and, grabbing a pistol, left the RV to stop the escapee. Bin Laden moved into the driver's seat to watch Shahin's action and follow the next step of destruction, those trucks taking a high dive.

Bin Laden, as their captor, glanced back at Booker and Harriet, saw them handcuffed securely to cabinet handles, gave them a smile, and waved his Manifesto at them as if to say, 'Your time is coming to deliver my message.' And then smiled; his years of planning had come to fruition.

The Professor, before the explosions, had driven past the RV and Razzor to park on the other side of the SUV, his car pointed towards a fast exit, prepared to accept any wounded for a quick drive to a private clinic. The exit road led to Boulder City, then to Las Vegas. He and Khalaf were stunned by the quick ferocity of the mini-explosions and could only stare until Khalaf saw what Shahin was up to and then noted some innocents at the far end of the bridge within Shahin's line of fire. He reacted. The wrong action for all the right reasons. Khalaf grabbed one of the pistols from under his seat and took off after Shahin. Professor Rogers stared, aghast at what might happen.

The attack bomber/sapper, having accomplished his first two tasks, leaving concrete dust swirling in the air, hurried to the first tanker to rig the explosives, set the timer for ten minutes, and move on to the second truck. He, for an instant, wondered where the third truck was. But he was not concerned; two explosions would have the desired effect, tear apart the cargo carriers of expended fuel rods and the tanker of concentrated radioactive sludge, letting the contents 'sprinkle' into the river below.

Scene 3: The First Responders
Setting: On the Arizona side

"I want you to head back along the highway, now, please," Fox gave directions to the pilot who, following his client's wishes, swung the helicopter around.

"Now, and listen carefully. I want you to go ahead of that truck down there and land in front of it."

"What? I can't do that! We have a specific FAA license, tourism only. No side trips." He thought he had made his point until Samantha pulled her pistol from her large carry bag and put it on her lap. "Please," she said, "It is a matter of life and death." She did not elaborate on whose death her statement might have referred to. The pilot grumbled but accepted this was an out-and-out highjacking.

Bennie decided he likewise had to take action. He swung the van onto the highway shoulder, kicking up dust as he passed cars and trucks with drivers and families upset at the delay. Only as he started coming up to the front of the roadblock, with the government vehicle stopped, with one of the government guards yelling at the 'highway maintenance' crew about priority, was he able to catch up to the truck disappearing down the highway.

The *KR* van's approach caused one of the attackers, one of Shahin's men, to drop all pretense and reveal his automatic rifle, which he unloaded at the government guard near the barricade, and accidentally fired at one of the Professor's student jihadists, killing him. The government for-hire guard took a round to his shoulder, knocking him over, at which time his partner went searching for his own weapon. A few seconds of ducking gave him a chance to fall away from the shattering windshield glass and fall outside the vehicle that was starting to disintegrate, including radio communication to call for help. Not bulletproofed as advertised.

Abbas jumped out to help the wounded guard; big mistake. An unidentified man, Arab-looking in features, showing up behind the bullet-riddled government car, had Abbas retreating under a fusillade of panic shots aimed at him. He tried shouting. "We are on your side! We are here to help! We are not the bad guys!" The convoy security guard was listening to his moaning wounded partner and scared to death in an actual life-and-death situation; the guard's bravado had long since disappeared. He was shooting at any sudden movement, regardless of friend or foe, not knowing who was who.

Now, the rent-a-car came along the side of the road, passing cars to take up a position, and the attacker jumped out and started spraying the cars ahead, with drivers ducking, and bringing fire to the back side of the government car and the S/FX Van, both now at risk, caught in a cross-fire. The government survivor realized maybe two of the guys were trying to help, and began firing to both the front of him, letting Abbas get off potshots at the bad guys.

Meanwhile, down the road from the roadblock, the tourist helicopter landed a good way off in front of the truck in the middle of the highway, causing cars leaving the bridge not knowing what was behind them and the oncoming truck to slow down, its warning horn blaring, amazed to see a helicopter land on the highway.

The driver in Truck Three, the one from Nebraska, and the ride-along mechanic stared as an attractive woman came running towards them. In these circumstances, even with a load they knew to be classified, the driver rolled down the window as she approached.

"There is an incident on the road. Your trip has been compromised. The other two trucks have been stopped on the bridge in some sort of attack. We just saw it from the air and came to warn you. I think it best you back up, turn around using that side road, and head back towards Kingman."

The mechanic, who had gotten on the radio to verify with anyone in their convoy but could not reach anyone, looked to the driver, "She's right. Something is terribly off. Let's head back to meet security behind us." The driver looked at her, "Thanks, lady."

"We'll use the helicopter radio to have the Arizona State Patrol meet you."

Neither driver nor truck mechanic, in their own frantic concern, asked the simple question: 'What was that fashionable lady doing out here in the middle of nowhere?'

When Samantha returned to the helicopter, Hugh, who was keeping the pilot in line with a shaking hand holding a pistol, said to her, "Gizmo texted. Abbas and Bennie are under fire at the roadblock. Need help. He said, 'Plan B.'"

"You're kidding. Turn a helicopter into a dive bomber?" The pilot looked aghast.

"You sit in back; I'll handle this."

Accepting that the crazy landing episode was over, the pilot tolerated the request for high hovering over the roadblock — until Hugh produced a hand grenade and dropped it out of the helicopter side window. Yes, he pulled the pin. The hand grenade landed right next to the attacker who was firing from the rear, ending that threat. Hugh Fox had overcome his tribulations about blowing away bad guys to save others.

The attacker at the roadblock realized what might happen to him from above, and took off to the pick-up truck for a race to the bridge, and presumed safety. One of the student jihadists-in-training beat him to it and started the engine, taking off. The Yemeni attacker jumped into the truck bed. The other young jihadist saw he was being abandoned and started chasing after his disappearing ride, when the wounded agent finally retrieved his pistol and shot the young man dead. A wasted life.

The fleeing al-Qaeda attacker from the pickup truck bed started spraying machine gun fire at the helicopter, which swiftly banked away before returning to land after the attackers fled, the pickup heading towards the bridge.

As soon as Hugh Fox and Samantha Carlisle ran from the helicopter, the pilot took off, abandoning his paid client.

562 S.P. Grogan

"How rude. Remind me to buy that tourist company, and fire that guy. Just because of a little firefight."

When the traffic congestion stopped by the roadblock, and the curious travelers, realized all the gunplay and explosions were not an extemporaneous movie production, the rush to turn around and flee eastward became a road rage epidemic. This left the S/FX van with Bennie, , Abbas, and the two government security guards, Bennie tending to the wounded and, in the distance, approaching Truck Three, seeking rescue. And Samantha and Hugh stranded momentarily.

Scene 4: Metro Police Respond
Setting: On the Nevada Side

Detective Chase Taggart of the Las Vegas Metropolitan Police Department, motoring slowly in her unmarked patrol car, headed from the dam towards an early lunch break when she received an in-car computer message: Please check and advise on report of suspicious behavior on 93 bridge. *Shit, as if it couldn't get any worse,* she thought. *Please, not a jumper.* The bridge highway traffic had been opened less than a year, and with a scenic walkway on the eastern side with a spectacular view of Hoover Dam, the bets were on when the first suicide would take the plunge.

She rolled down her window and shouted to the two U.S. Bureau of Reclamation police officers manning the tourist checkpoint access road leading to the dam.

"Everything okay here?" When she got the thumbs up, she replied, "Making a run on the bridge, will be back." *After a long lunch* was her follow-up thought.

The Metropolitan Police Department covered all of Clark County, which included Las Vegas, Lake Mead, and Hoover Dam. Within the Federal boundaries of the Hoover Dam, usually, Nevada State Patrol and Metro Police steered clear of overlapping jurisdictions with the Reclamation's Security Response Force, but in this case, Detective Taggart had been assigned to a solitary outpost as part of her trip in purgatory. Three months earlier, she had been caught up in an officer-involved shooting; she being the shooter stopping the perp and his life. Although cleared by Internal Affairs, Chase had been thrust into the middle of a tug-of-war between Internal Affairs bureaucracy and the Sheriff's political fortunes. While not calling it a suspension, since to some she was still the department's first female heroine (another story), to others, her exile to the boonies seemed justified for her supposed grandstanding.

Bored with inaction and perspiring from a straining air conditioner spitting at her, she turned her car up the dam access road towards its junction with Highway 93 and the O'Callaghan-Tillman Memorial Bridge, going east.

Then, the next radio call came in, from 911 calls, more urgent. "Shots fired. O'Callaghan-Tillman Bridge." She radioed her response and floored her patrol car. Was this a suicide by gun or jumping or both? Detective Taggart's wild guess was way off, but her day was no longer boring.

She had just pulled onto Highway 93 when she saw the eastward bound line of cars, backed up, bottlenecked.

Shit, she sighed. It was a jumper. Just then, a large black-silver truck raced past her speeding car. To her, it looked like SWAT. Instinctively, she put the mobile light on her departmental unmarked car's roof, flashing and turned on the siren. Quickly, racing to catch up, she saw an unprecedented action; the truck blew through a construction barricade, smashing it to bits and sending a worker jumping to the side. *What the...?*

She could only follow, but her real shit shock came when once she was past the destroyed barricade, her back window blew out. *Holy...!* A quick glance saw a construction worker in a yellow vest and hard hat firing an automatic weapon at her.

Trying to keep her head low beneath the dash, avoiding a bullet to the head, she grabbed at her radio and shouted out in a quick hurried breath. "11-99 (*Officer Needs Help* code]. Shots fired at the Tillman Bridge! Deranged construction worker armed and shooting. Approach with extreme caution."

She gave one second to consider if she should stop and deal with the armed man, but something was not right. This was not about a jumper. Whatever was happening, the answer was with the speeding SWAT-like truck. Detective Taggart cursed to herself. Violent action and bad karma seemed to dog her career.

Scene 5 Turning On Each Other
Setting: On the Bridge

Shahin had a clear shot at the fleeing truck driver when a movement to his left caught his attention. At the far end of the bridge's east side was a walkway, and on it, a group of Asian tourists was staring back at him. He could care less about collateral damage. Distracted, he turned back to the driver. He fired, missing him. The driver took the opportunity to throw himself over the railing into the tourists and scramble through them, bowling over several in a mad attempt at escape. Shahin leveled his gun, ready to take out all witnesses and leave his calling card when he was again distracted. Shots were fired behind him.

Near the back of the RV, Khalaf was shooting his gun into the air, yelling, "No, no!"

564   S.P. Grogan

Shahin could only smile his grin of death. This would be his bonus kill. Trying to avoid hitting the motor van, he fired two well-aimed shots, but they hit close on either side of Khalaf, sending him cowering.

But from the ground, Khalaf was dazed and angry, and his aim was directly at Shahin's body mass. His next two rapid shots missed. How could that be? A feeling of mad panic hit him, realization of his bad decision. Quickly, he turned his Beretta to the tires of one of the stopped trucks, a shot impossible to miss. But he did — but he didn't. 'I am firing a gun with blanks!' was his first reaction. Next moment: 'I am unarmed.' Khalaf scurried around the RV and started running back to the Professor's car, still carrying his useless pistol, shouting as the Professor sought to hear, "Our guns are empty! They are going to kill us!"

Razzor, who had been overseeing the fixing of the bomb to the underside carriage of the first truck, looked up to see Shahin firing away at fleeing tourists and Khalaf fleeing with a gun in his hand.

Not guessing what Khalaf was doing or shouting, he came to the same conclusion as Shahin, this would be the best time to remove this thorn from al Qaeda's purity. He started walking towards the Professor's car when he heard the siren and saw a large black truck rush forward and crash into the SUV, their escape vehicle.

Their expressions said it all. Shahin turned from his indiscriminate firing, perhaps wounding a few tourists, and saw the black truck, definitely military, followed by a police car. Razzor stood in the middle of the bridge; bin Laden gripped the RV's steering wheel and cursed: "*Crimson Scimitar* is betrayed!" The Professor realized he was about to die and reacted characteristically. He stepped on the accelerator and sped his car past the Storm Wagon and Detective Taggart, who was trying to process the ongoing crime scene, and a running Khalaf, who, failing to catch his fleeing ride, was left breathless, standing alone in the middle of the bridge. Then, looking to the other side, he saw the sneer on Razzor's face as his pistol was raised for the coup de grace.

Callie put a bullet through Razzor's wrist. It was not the shot she was seeking, more a throwaway round as she leaped from the back of the Storm Wagon. And what the hell? One terrorist trying to kill another terrorist? Holmes saw the interaction as did Pacheco; was there a 'good terrorist' in the middle of all this? And which was which?

Khalaf ran for new cover, seeking protection behind the stalled second trailer truck.

Two blunt truths came to Shahin, Razzor, and bin Laden. Where was the third tractor-trailer? And *whatever the cost, the two remaining trucks carrying prolonged death must be destroyed. The plan still could succeed.*

Crimson Scimitar

Scene 6: The Prisoners
Setting: On the Bridge

Click. With all the rifle and pistol clattering exchanges and the earlier small bomb explosions, the opening of both of the handcuffs by Harriet's ingenuity was a mere whisper to the outside furor. Booker and Harriet, now freed, hoped to be ignored as they realized they required a plan of escape past the world's most wanted terrorist sitting in the driver's seat who was becoming more agitated by the moment at the intensified battlefield outside the motor home. [again, the RV with the three of them is on the dam side of the middle barricade, normal traffic would be going east to west.]

"Okay, Harriet," his low voice to her ear. "You must listen. We can't wait. Only one way out. I will distract him; you run past and run like hell towards those two police cars. I don't know what that black truck is, but I'm guessing the police were called. If you stay low and run against the walkway on the dam side, your sudden appearance will catch them off-guard. Then run across the road and jump the barrier. " He rushed his words; she had to listen, *Don't think of me, please*, he thought. But she did.

"I won't leave without you", she answered with conviction." Booker Langston finally got it. She had feelings for him. What a doofus he was. What a time to realize that!

"I will be right behind you, but please, a crouching run."

They looked deeply into each other's eyes.

Booker walked quickly to the front, Harriet behind him, ready to dart away from the RV. But plans invariably change.

Scene 7: Storm Wagon
Setting: On the bridge

Immediately after the Storm Wagon had crushed the SUV and ground it into incapacity, Pacheco jumped from the driver's side, Holmes from the passenger side, and Callie went out the back. She and Holmes laid down covering fire as each took a defensive position One shot had hit the hand of an attacker. She had not meant to deflect Razzor's aim. To her, terrorists could kill terrorists. They were vermin.

Just then, a car, a drab grey-green nondescript sedan, hurtled past them. Holmes accepted it must have been a trapped tourist seizing an opportunity to escape. He turned his priority attention to the incoming fire but felt it haphazard, and surprisingly, the Storm Wagon, though receiving dings, its engine block with extra plating avoided being riddled. Thank you, Skilleo technology.

Before them, they could see the field of fire, the layout of the attack. Holmes saw the government waste carriers, a bloody unmoving form in the first truck. Damn, if he could only have known with more certainty the bridge was the target, they could have stopped all three trucks earlier. His millisecond reverie was broken as Shawn Pacheco rose from a crouch and, with a tight formation of concentrated shots, killed a man who tried running from the front of the second truck, his AR-15 firing at them.

"Was that a construction worker you killed?" yelled Holmes.

"He was shooting at us. Ours or theirs, we'll sort it out later," said Pacheco. "But two of the bad dudes trying to kill us are dressed like State Patrol, but their ethnicity gives them away." Pacheco fired again.

Callie fired at a State Patrolman trying to shoot what seemed to be the same terrorist the other State Patrol jock was trying to kill. What gives?

"Oops. Hope you're right. It's a bad disguise. He doesn't look official. And what is this? Bad guys shooting good-bad guys?"

"Please aim at men, not at the two trucks." Holmes admonished, knowing the silent radiating killer which could be unleashed with an errant bullet or explosion.

Though keeping their focus ahead, they heard the approaching siren. Then they saw the uncontrollable braking skid as a presumed police car became an attracting pegboard of automatic fire, its front end going from smoke into a burst of flames under the hood. Scrambling from behind the driver's side fell out a woman, assumed to be a police officer, a regulation firearm in her hand. Behind her destroyed car, she caught her breath, then ran to the Storm Wagon, crouching behind Callie.

"What the fuck is going on?"

"I believe terrorists are attempting to outdo 9/11," said Callie casually as if they were girlfriends at cocktails, still sighting her aim down the roadway. "And you are who, that's joined our *bridge* game?"

"Detective Taggart, Metro Police. Stay where you are. We should have backup in about thirty minutes."

"Afraid not, ma'am!" Holmes shouted from the other side of the van. "We are dealing with bombs and timers. They're trying to blow up the trucks, toxic chemicals we don't want to see go into the river."

Detective Taggart moved to the man behind the voice.

"And who the fuck are you people anyway? You don't look like law enforcement."

"Wendell Holmes, ex-CIA, at your service."

Callie called out, "Carlita Cardoza, ex-San Diego police. Got your back, Detective."

A third voice of the posse. "Shawn Pacheco, SEAL Team Six, on medical leave. I am spotting a string of IEDs tied to the first truck."

Damn, must be insubordinate misfits like her, and hunkering down, Detective Taggart smiled. "Okay, what's the plan?"

Could be no plainer to Holmes, "Shawn, I need to get you to those bombs ASAP."

"Aye, aye, sir. But wait a second." He ran back into the back of the Storm Wagon.

"Time's a-wasting, said Holmes. "I will clear a path from around all those trucks. You ladies keep your heads down."

Callie spoke to the policewoman. "Holmes here is a very, very old-school gentleman." She turned to Holmes. "We, ladies, will give *you* covering fire."

Shawn returned. He had retrieved two nylon bags with straps and four flat vests.

"Body armor. This automatic fire is still penetrating, but this might slow down anything bad." Giving a scrunched nose put-down to Holmes, Callie said with sweet sarcasm.

"Now, *that* is a thoughtful young man."

Detective Taggart, who was wearing a thin Kevlar vest anyway, took the added tensile-mesh density, hefted it on, and fastened it, as did Callie with her vest.

The detective looked at the young man who was putting on a different style, the nylon 'backpack' over his shoulders.

"What?"

"Parachute, ma'am. I don't like heights," Holmes, taking one offered, shrugged, then strapped on the pack handed to him. He mused, *if I get shot in the back, I'm protected.*

Scene 8: Attacker's Desperation
Setting: On the Bridge

To the surprise of the al-Qaeda team, the pickup from the Arizona side roadblock rushed onto the bridge, adding two more supposed fighters to the bullet-flying scrum. However, rather than an al-Qaeda fighter, the young student jihadist demonstrated his worthless courage by sitting in the truck, sobbing; his cause was slogans and protest; he was not prepared for an ideological baptism by bloodshed. Shahin ran to use the pickup as cover.

That movement gave Callie an idea, and she lunged back into the Storm Wagon while Detective Taggart gave covering fire. Seconds later, a small turret rose from the top of the Wagon, and Callie sent tracer fire from the mounted machine gun into the newly-arrived pickup and the terrorist dressed like highway road crew, who had just arrived. And in exiting the pickup truck, he was blown off his feet, part of his head missing. Before the pickup was

568   S.P. Grogan

reduced to scrap metal, Shahin grabbed the Professor's whimpering man-child, threw him out of the pickup's cab, and, seizing the wheel, wrenched the vehicle behind the second truck. Standing confused, not knowing what to do, he turned to run, before Callie ended his life. To Callie, he was not a forced martyr but a terrorist impediment.

Razzor, in pain from a shattered wrist, gained a shield behind Truck Two, wrapping his hand with a torn shirt from one of Shahin's team, dead on the roadway. He noted the flying ordinance was not coming his way and reasoned the government agents and police firing on him knew what the cargo was! For a moment, he felt safe, then painfully and awkwardly, he picked up a fallen assault rifle, looking for a target.

The al-Qaeda bomber had been excellent at roadside bombs and had practiced for *Crimson Scimitar* with smaller explosive charges under far quieter circumstances. Flustered and excited, he affixed the bombs to the first truck and ran, with terrorist Maj's covering protective fire, to the second truck and began arming the underside of Truck Two, the most important tandem, with all the radioactive stew in sealed canisters. This time he was rattled and shaken by the constant gunfire around and above him, even chipping at the concrete with ricochets. Still, he went forward with arming the tandem cargo to blow it to hell. Holmes, acting as covering fire for SEAL Pacheco, who was carefully undoing the bomber's nasty work on Truck One, looked under the tanker, took careful aim, and put a bullet through the bomber's skull, but not before he had set the timer to explode in ten minutes.

A stand-off was in place, and the gunfire tapered off. Callie had the field of fire covered with the turret machine gun while Detective Taggart looked for random headshot possibilities.

Holmes stopped firing with quick glances at Pacheco, the SEAL in his element, calmly dismantling the charges, his final focus on the small timer clock. He started to say 'piece of cake' to Holmes when he heard one of the terrorists yelling a taunt, "Khalaf"…then something in Arabic, another 'Khalaf,' some more gibberish. A distant memory, never forgotten — the stable area at Abbottabad, when he yelled for the dog, the jihadist who had hit him yelled, 'Caliph,' or was it 'Khalaf?' A man's name. Pacheco turned to Holmes, "Ali Baba is on the bridge."

Khalaf heard his name, followed by a curse. Behind the pickup truck, Shahin had decided to use this moment of quiet to place a text message back home while at the same time berating the courier who had taken a position behind the RV.

Khalaf knew he was to going to die.

Although unarmed and frightened, he had done a stupid noble act of trying to save strangers. Somehow it made him feel good. Stopping a vicious man from killing. When Shahin, still texting, yelled at him that Khalaf was a coward and traitor. Khalaf responded, first with a short sentence in Arabic saying he was not such a man, and then to his future killers, he spoke loudly in English. He realized he needed a final audience, attesting in his last few moments of life to a new testament forming in his mind, now seeking the right words into sentences.

"I am still true to a cause where one country stays out of another's internal affairs. Where my faith is my own and not beaten into others. But this attack, I see, is not the way. I want a peaceful resolution, a change of hearts. I shall die believing I could accomplish more and not by your brutality."

There he had said enough; he was prepared to go to Allah.

In the lull of the moment, those trying to listen to curses and confessions dropped their guard and allowed for desperate movement.

— Maj, the protector of the bomber, now dead, understood by his upbringing that honoring bin Laden's wishes meant sacrifice. He ran to Truck One, aiming to drive it off the bridge, knowing the timer had only a few minutes left, not realizing Holmes and Pacheco were still working on defusing the timer and the multiple bombs under the cargo carrier.

— The *KR* S/FX van drove onto the far end of the east side, westbound traffic lane, just off the bridge, honking its horn, attracting attention.

— And Harriet, taking full advantage of others' movements, jumped from the RV steps, took off running, scrambling, ducking, leaning over, fast-paced, so surprising the al-Qaeda killers that no shot was fired at her. She fell over the center concrete wall barrier and saw a policewoman behind the SWAT (Storm Wagon) truck and fell down next to her.

"Thank God, we made it!"

"We?" asked the policewoman.

Harriet turned; Booker was not behind her. Then she heard the motor start, and the RV hurled itself across the roadway and slammed through the exploded concrete center and crashed into Truck One, knocking it parallel to the bridge's guard rail, not completely blocking it, but making it impossible for Truck One to make the turnover and off the bridge.

EPISODE THIRTY-FOUR — Momentum Shift

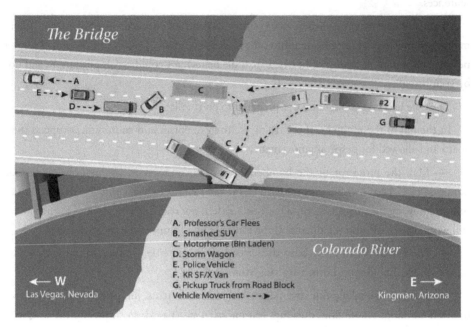

Kelly Kure sketch requested by FBI

Scene 1: The Prisoner Remains Behind
Setting: Michael O'Callaghan-Pat Tillman Memorial Bridge, Arizona-Nevada Border, September 3rd, 2011

"How's my client doing?" Booker questioned. At the same time, he leaned over, slapped the handcuffs on the al Qaeda leader's hands, and fastened them to the steering wheel of the RV. Harriet did not see this move as she rushed past, jumped out, and sprinted for safety. Booker sat down in the passenger front seat.

"Well, it looks like we'll just sit here until the cavalry arrives."

Osama bin Laden finally had a shocked look of fear on his face, shaking his new bracelets in an attempt to free himself.

"Let me go, and I will spare your life. My people will be right back when the trucks explode."

"Can't do that." He was eyeing Harriet in her run for life, seeing her reach and take cover behind the Storm Wagon.

"You were going to release my Manifesto. You would be famous, the messenger of my words."

"From the silence outside, I think we all are at a stalemate." He looked out and, to his amazement, saw Wendell Holmes peek from around Truck One; Callie Cardoza stared through her gunsights on top of the Storm Wagon and saw the attorney. Langston waved at her. She waved back.

Booker realized who his rescuers were. "Well, I'll be. You'll never in a million years guess who came to our rescue!"

Before he could supply an answer to tease 'his client,' he saw the deviant druggie, Maj, run to Truck One and jump in the cab.

"Oh shit, that can't be good."

Before bin Laden could understand that he could have stopped Booker by jamming his foot on the brake pedal, Langston had turned the key in the ignition, yanked the steering wheel to the left, and pulled bin Laden's hands with the action. At the same time, he floored the RV, bouncing over the concrete to the other lanes, using the RV as a battering ram as it struck Truck One, pushing it sideways before it had run off the bridge side. Booker hit the windshield and was thrown back to the RV floor, dazed.

Holmes saw the motor home's acceleration, and with no time to yell, he grabbed and pushed Pacheco out from under the carrier and back against the railing as the force of the motor home hitting the tractor truck turned it before hitting rubble that stopped the momentum. Holmes and Pacheco, squished with a thin amount of movement, but not pinned, exhaled slow breaths. What they saw caused their hearts to miss a beat.

The cab of the trailer truck was dangling at a skewed angle off the bridge. The motor home itself leaned precariously over the edge, even wavering, a balancing children's teeter-totter.

Harriet knew Booker was in the RV and screamed. Detective Taggart made a grab for her to keep her from running. Razzor saw his opportunity and shot the policewoman in the side, the bullet knifing the outside of her rib cage. Harriet saw what had occurred, what she had precipitated, and dragged the police officer back behind the Storm Wagon.

At the same time, Bennie took the new distraction to race the *KR* van next to the Storm Wagon. Callie handed the machine gun chores over to Abbas while Samantha and Fox crowded around the fallen officer.

"It hurts," said Detective Taggart, through gritted teeth, "But it didn't go deep, sliced my side, the vest saved my life. Your buddy saved my life. Is he single?" Like the brave woman she was, she tried to make light of a near-death experience.

"Sorry, I hear he's engaged," said the newcomer, Samantha.

572   S.P. Grogan

"Pity, I seem to miss finding my hero."

Always the business operative, Fox had to ask, "What can we do now?"

Just then, they heard distant gunfire out of sight on the Nevada side.

Taggart, grimacing in pain, said, "Those are my people neutralizing that roadblock. Rescue shortly. Just stay put. Don't become me."

Fox had to then ask the wrong question, "Where's Bookie?"

Just regaining consciousness would be the answer. Booker could look out to the horizon, but when he tried to regain his feet, the motor home dipped so he could see the river below. Not a good view. Bin Laden was now conscious, with blood streaming from his forehead.

Rattling his handcuffs, he shouted, more in hysteria. "Get me out of this!" Then, understanding his position, he added, "Please."

Booker staggered towards the door. "Sorry, your other attorney took the handcuff keys with her. And one rescue at a time. Me first. I will get help and have them pull this back. If I don't get shot by one of your goons."

Bin Laden looked out, saw the danger, and then glanced up to the side and out the passenger side window to the tractor-trailer cab they had struck. Someone was crawling across the truck's hood, peering in at a seeming unconscious Maj, looking over to the damaged weapon that was the RV. Wendell Holmes smiled devilishly at Osama bin Laden.

"Ya Kalb!" cursed bin Laden.

Booker, ready to escape, went to open the RV door only to find it bent and stuck tight. Trapped. He and bin Laden were in the same fine mess. He began throwing his weight against the door. The RV began tilting back and forth.

Scene 2: Flight and Fight
Setting: The Bridge

At the bridge, there seemed to be only two mobile active attackers left: Shahin and Razzor, and both made separate decisions, one of sacrifice, the other of survival.

Razzor's mind processed that *Crimson Scimitar* was going to, in some fashion, fail. He had seen the S/FX van rush onto the bridge, realizing the opposite side had reinforcements. He heard the distant shooting at the western bridge access and accepted that there would be a delay, but overwhelming force would bring more support against al Qaeda. The Cause, his religious beliefs were important, but they fit better with self-preservation. Revenge and other attacks of magnitude could come later. And there was only one viable means of escape — the bullet-riddled pickup truck with its engine still running, two dead bodies on either side.

Razzor sprayed his automatic weapon in the air and in an arc at the two trucks of the enemy, forcing heads down. He made a dash for the pickup, slammed it in reverse, and zigzagged, out of control, backing up off the bridge before he spun the truck around, with wheels burning rubber, and sped off. He knew there were side roads back toward Kingman and felt his best goal was to become invisible, quickly abandon the truck and look for an alternative ride. Angered at his own retreat, he swore there was one final stop he wanted to make before he fled into Mexico.

He took the Kingman Wash exit to safety and disappeared.

Shahin, on the other hand, more zealot than pragmatist, had sent his text message, his last words of explanation, encouragement to continue the path, extolling prayers for jihadist victory. He saw that *Crimson Scimitar* had been compromised, but it was not defeated. His mind did not focus as much as it snapped. Listening to Razzor suddenly let off a stream of rounds, he believed he had support and likewise filled the air with an automatic rifle spray, flung down his weapon, and sprinted to Truck Two. He was determined to take both trucks over the roadway precipice into the canyon below and into the river, which would distribute their contents.

He revved the engine and put it in gear. Then the passenger door opened.

Khalaf.

It was not an easy decision to make. Khalaf had been hiding behind the RV when it took off. He tried to run and catch up but was too slow, and when he found himself in the open, he quickly ran under Truck Two to hide behind the front wheels of the attached tractor truck when he heard the cab door open. If this truck moved, he would be an open target. Perhaps he could wrest control and drive away, away to safety. However, he was not thinking rationally.

He saw Shahin was the driver. The tractor truck with its cargo of poison was aimed at Truck One, and a hard crash would push it over the side of the bridge. Khalaf grabbed for the wheel.

Scene 3: King's Retribution in Action
Setting: On the Bridge

"Shit!" Shawn Pacheco had a problem. The timing detonator for the bombs was more sophisticated than he thought. He was not sure, but it might just have a backup hidden internal wire to detonate if he snipped the wires between the bombs and the detonator. And the timer itself was secured to another explosive package he was unfamiliar with, a secondary explosion, a fail-safe that would go off if tampered with or perhaps if the timer stopped. That explosion would set off the other bombs, regardless. *Two minutes* until detonation, read the timer. He did have a simple alternative bomb makers don't usually think of. *Just take the ticking damn thing with you.* Yanking the bombs off the undercarriage and ripping off the masking tape, he peeled away the string of bomblets. But where to take it? Decision: just throw it off the bridge. Neat solution.

Holmes saw that man in the truck (Maj) was not moving. He edged his way over to the RV, where he saw an incredible sight; bin Laden handcuffed to the steering wheel. Someone was beating against the motor home door, but with each slam, the RV teetered on the edge.

Sequences occurred in flash seconds.

Pacheco crawled up on the hood next to Holmes. "I got the bombs."

"Great," said Holmes, not looking.

"No, *here are* the bombs. One minute to countdown. Going to throw them off the bridge."

Holmes heard Truck Two fire up its engine's RPMs.

Booker pounded his shoulder on the door, and it popped open.

Realizing who it was, Holmes yelled, "Jump!"

Booker leaped to the side of the truck cab, holding on to the mirror.

Truck Two lurched forward; Khalaf, grabbing the wheel, turned it left instead of right, away from Truck One but on a direct impact with the RV.

Holmes grabbed the string of explosives from Pacheco and hurled it into the motor home's open door.

The RV, hit by Truck Two, went over the edge.

Booker, clinging on, barely missed being sideswiped and catching his breath, said nothing aloud of historical importance, but to himself, he muttered, "*9/11 says goodbye.*"

What Osama bin Laden's last words for posterity might have been were lost. His last manifesto to the world, the loose pages, floated in the air within the RV as it plunged. The explosion came next, too quickly.

The shock wave shook the bridge.

Holmes, who had shielded his eyes from the blast, opened them. He was falling.

Scene 4: The Last Throes
Setting: On the Bridge

Those at the Storm Wagon reacted when Truck Two lumbered hard into the RV, sending it sailing through the air. The gunfire had ended. They were all armed and wary. But Truck One was still in gear, slowly grinding, inching forward, towards going over.

Fox saw what might happen.

"Bennie, move the Wagon over this way. Abbas, help me with the winch." They took action, oblivious to any remaining danger. Quickly, Fox grabbed the lead cable, ran to the back of Truck One, and fastened it to the Mansfield bar of the truck's last cargo carrier. Abbas tried reeling the cable back, but the truck barely moved while its continuing acceleration moved it forward over the rubble.

Fox had to get to the driver and turn the engine off.

Pacheco came from around Truck Two, a little disoriented from the explosion.

Two questions were rapid-fired at him.

"Where's Wendell?" asked Samantha, her concern showing.

"Who was driving this truck?" Callie saw the cab door open on Truck One.

Maj came around the truck corner, weaving, raising his rifle.

"Hey, asshole!" He turned toward the shout, and Harriet shot him with Detective Taggart's service revolver.

"And where's Bookie?" Harriet's near screaming wail.

Pacheco remembered and blurted out, not meaning to be so truthful. "They went over the bridge."

Harriet and Samantha, panicked, ran to the side, looking over. Holmes was nowhere to be seen, but Booker Langston held on for dear life to the half-disconnected front bumper of Truck One. Nothing but air under him.

Hugh Fox heard fighting in the cab of Truck Two and yanked the truck door open. Two men fell out, fighting. What was going on? The smaller man was the same guy who was shot at by another terrorist and was now flaying his fists with a different one. Fox ignored them, stepping up, leaning in, and turning off the engine. Then he felt a hand grab him from behind, yank him out, and put him in a bear hug, which was more like a strangulation hold. Shahin had hold of Hugh Fox, getting a grip to snap his neck when he saw a woman pointing a gun at him. He used the man he was holding as a shield, maybe a hostage. Desperate times. Shahin backed up to the open bridge, seeking a way out. Left and right, considering choices.

"I will kill him!" shouted Shahin in broken English. Callie paused but did not lessen her aim at Hugh's head with Shahin's head directly behind it. For a quick moment, she recalled all they had gone through with *King's Retribution*, her time with Hugh; tragically, was it over? A bad idea, the only idea, came to her.

"Hugh, remember the end of the movie we watched? Bruce Willis in *Live Free or Die Hard*?

Not the time, Callie, thought Hugh, struggling against the neck pressure; then it came to him; 'No," he gurgled the word out, meaning yes, he remembered but ....

"No!" he shouted. Callie shot him through the shoulder, clean, clear through and through, but not so for Shahin, as the bullet entered his upper chest. The shock of the impact sent him reeling back...but he was still gripping Fox's shirt. Shahin slowly tumbled over the edge, Hugh following, until one of his legs was caught...by the bloodied Khalaf on the ground...Hugh dangled over the bridge, glancing down at nothingness...then Khalaf passed out and lost his grip...and Hugh slid...and Callie grabbed his other leg and held on as if his life depended upon it...which it did.

Pacheco came around the corner, followed by Harriet and Booker, the rope that had pulled him up still around his waist.

Pacheco eyed the three people on the ground, two of them almost delirious with the close call, the other unconscious.

"Oh, I see you have met our Ali Baba," said SEAL Pacheco. Callie and Hugh stared at the young man who had just saved Hugh Fox's life.

"I want to shoot him," said Callie, looking around for the gun she had discarded in grabbing for her 'boyfriend'(?). She was gripping his leg to pull him fully upward onto the roadway.

"No. No killing. I have an idea," responded Fox, the games guy. Although in pain, his mind was always working, but dealing with that feeling when a woman was pulling at his leg, his thigh, even if under such stressful circumstances. Helluva way to start a meaningful relationship.

Of course, Wendell knew to pull the parachute cord. As the wind hit his face, it was his first thought, no, his second thought; the first was remembering he was wearing the parachute Pacheco had given him. He knew this was definitely not the time to do extreme parasailing, waiting until the last minute to pull the ripcord. He pulled it immediately. The chute bloomed beautifully. *Easy-peasy*, he thought, but he knew he had to make circular swings, gliding turns, so as not to crash into the canyon cliffs on both sides. He looked up to the bridge, the sky above — and thought, *you have got to be kidding* — the parachute was logoed — *King's Retribution*.

Wendell Holmes did have one problem to face. He was going to hit the water, a raging, fast-moving tumult, though with the late fall season and dropped water level, he might hit the water and then smack into a half-hidden boulder. So, he had to concentrate, see if he could pinpoint his landing, and aim towards the narrow rock shoreline.

Then, by that damn fate, a body hit his parachute center-on, collapsing his descent into free-fall, sending him careening with a hard splash into the Colorado River, finding himself drowning in a tangled shroud. Not the career retirement he had sought.

Scene 5: PR Aftermath
Setting: Press Conference, September 4th

When Metro Police and FBI stormed the bridge, delayed twice, and according to their later filed report, here's what they discovered (released in a joint press conference, stories matched and sanitized):

"Late yesterday morning, Detective Chase Taggart of the Las Vegas Metropolitan Police Department accosted suspicious characters in two vehicles that were stopped on the O'Callaghan-Tillman bridge. At which time when she approached the vehicles, she was shot at by numerous armed suspects. She was assisted by a Mr. Shawn (sic) Pacheco, a Navy SEAL combatant on furlough and a tourist who happened to be in the area touring Hoover Dam and the Lake Mead National Park. Detective Taggart, though wounded, was able to return fire, killing three suspects; Pacheco, under fire, was able to storm the recreational vehicle and discover two kidnapped victims, Mr. Booker Langston and Harriet Eberhardt, attorneys who were involved in the Trial of the Century in Colorado Springs last July.

During this time of bringing the kidnapped victims to safety, the surviving suspects raked Detective Taggart's patrol car with heavy automatic weapons, which turned out to be covering fire as the alleged kidnappers used explosives to blow apart a section of the highway's middle barrier and part of the guard rail on the side of the bridge, the side away from the dam. Then, for whatever reason, the remaining suspects, number unknown, drove both the recreational vehicle and a pickup truck off the bridge in apparent suicides.

Mr. Langston and Ms. Eberhardt have informed us they cannot identify any of their kidnappers as they were secured with black hoods during the time of their captivity. A fisherman below the bridge on the Colorado River, a Mr. W. Holmes, was interviewed and said he saw two vehicles plunge into the river and saw no survivors. At this time, due to the current and water visibility, there will be no attempt at recovery of the vehicles.

It is our preliminary speculation, and this is still a new and an open investigation, that these suspects were probably the perpetrators of the ambush at Skilleo Stadium that resulted in the deaths of government agents and U.S. District Attorney Cotton Matther and the related suicide by vest bomb of the 'convicted' terrorist, Osama bin Laden, found guilty of being the mastermind behind the attacks on America, September 11, 2001.

We will not take questions at this time and will probably have more information as our investigation dictates. Thank you."

Scene 6: Flashback — Clean-up
Setting: On the Bridge

Of course, enough holes to be Swiss cheese could be uncovered in the later public press release version, and in a few years, drips and drabs would raise inquisitiveness. The national press in this time frame was satisfied that persons unknown, still suggestive of a supremacist faction yet unidentified, had coordinated the lethal attack at Skilleo Stadium, kidnapped the defense attorneys of the trial, and had been freed by the brave interaction of a lone policewoman (no longer in exile, hero darling again) and dedicated military in the guise of a brave and unafraid Navy SEAL (the Navy gained positive recruiting kudos by his action). And the terrorist bin Laden, as one would expect for a 'dirty little coward,' had accepted his guilt and blown himself up weeks earlier. A neatly tied story, just short of a ballad. If one gave this introspection, all news coverage saw a sad observation about American journalism. The world of investigative reporting from that point on to today has faded in the rush of television and cable clickbait, where headlines are the narrative, facts distorted by interpretation of the journalist's prejudices, and anything of opinion viewed by hastily reading through the prism of political tribes. Truth is no longer pure. But then what was the truth, if never told?

What actually transpired was this:

Hugh Fox, lying next to Detective Taggart, his shoulder throbbing with medicine dumped on the wound, hastily bandaged, found himself half-loopy on good drugs, and, with the absence of Holmes, he went into hyper-alert and took control.

Basically, though in pain, he was not ready for new national exposure…did not need the press gossiping about him being injured…especially the tabloids…when they found out he was purposefully shot…and by whom?! Hugh Fox had to dictate the script of these happenings. It was clean-up time, especially something this messy.

"Okay, people. Here's what we are doing. Shawn, you stay and tend to the detective's wounds. Bookie and Harriet, you both remain behind. You do not know who kidnapped you. You are elated, thankfully relieved to be rescued. Put that into your faces."

Abbas came running back from a head count.

"There's a group of South Korean tourists cowering at the end of the observation entrance. They have a small tour bus down at the parking lot. Their driver was with them and was wounded, and a lady tourist, nothing critical, but they're all in shock. Something about never coming back to the United States. Also, it seems the truck driver of…Truck Two, I believe, is hiding on the bus; he has shrapnel in his leg and says he won't leave."

"Bennie, you go and drive the tourists towards Boulder City; it's closest. Find a hospital for them.

"Detective, can you wait for your people? Stay here? Shawn is going to stay with you. These two friends of ours also."

"Sure, our University Hospital is the best 'knife and gun' club repair shop in the West." She turned to the SEAL. "I heard you're engaged?"

"Yes, ma'am. Hope to be married this spring if she'll have me."

"She's a loser if she doesn't sign up for the long hitch."

Jeez, thought Fox. *A little shoot-out and hormones go raging.*

"Back on script, people. Where's Samantha?"

She jumped out of the Storm Wagon with a pair of binoculars.

"I was told he had a parachute. Dumb clod probably forgot to open the damn thing. Presenility." She hid her fear as she took off to the bridge's destroyed side to see if she could spot her lost lover.

Fox turned to the other woman, his shooter.

"Callie, you drive the Storm Wagon. We'll head to Kingman. Lay low. When we hit whatever police presence at the roadblock that Abbas and Bennie drove here from, just wave and drive past. Let them be confused. Say, where's Gizmo? Gizmo!"

The tech nerd peered out from a rifle-slit window inside the Storm Wagon.

"This tank is bulletproof, impervious to direct hits. Best place to be. By the way, I hacked the police frequencies. They killed everyone at that roadblock and are about seven minutes out, by my estimation."

Okay, let's mount up. Shawn and Detective Taggart: Quick plot line, be humble. Detective Taggart, you accosted the bad guys, they opened fire on you, and you took most of them out. Shawn came to help. He rescued Booker and Harriet. Say little more; my attorney will be at your side within three hours to clean up the statements before you give them."

"What about him?" Booker asked. Everyone looked at the unconscious Khalaf, their 'Ali Baba.'

"He comes with us in the Storm Wagon. Abbas, give him another knock-out shot to keep him immobile for several more hours."

"He wasn't with the original kidnappers; he came later. He treated us as human beings," explained Harriet, her arms firmly wrapped around Booker to support both of them. Booker didn't mind.

Callie held a far different, angry opinion. "Shit, you gotta be kidding. If this guy is Ali Baba, and if this were a movie or television show, and I know them best, he would be the screenwriter, the concept man, and bin Laden only the director but maybe with a bigger screen credit."

"But he was being shot at by his own people," even Pacheco had to offer the curious facts, "and he did save your boyfriend." Pacheco smiled gleefully, putting forth the accusation.

"Aw, shit," said Callie, giving up at the craziness still to come. "Grab his legs, Pacheco."

"I see him!" yelled Samantha. "He's waving!" She gave exaggerated waves down to a pin-sized man on a narrow rocky sandbar.

"Come on, Sam!" yelled Hugh. "We'll get him rescued, but now we must make ourselves scarce."

She had run up to the Wagon but then put the binoculars back to her eyes.

"What's that?" Fox grabbed them from her and adjusted until he saw focused on what was coming.

"That's it, we're off." Everyone started loading into the vehicles, including Bennie running down the steps to the tourist bus and Abbas to the *KR*'s FX van. To Detective Taggart, SEAL Pacheco, Langston, and Eberhardt, Fox emphasized, pointing to the sky. "Whatever comes next, whatever you see happen, did not happen. This is the road to Vegas, and the real clean-up people are coming." Hugh Fox was helped by Callie into the passenger side of the Storm Wagon, and the two *KR* vehicles tore east off the bridge, out of sight.

A fleet of five helicopters arrived. Two of the smaller ones, Sikorsky UH-60 Black Hawks, landed on either side of the bridge, and new roadblocks, manned by Army Rangers, stood guard, lethal. Next came four white hazmat suits from each copter, eight altogether, who ran to the trucks, Trucks One and Two. They detached the tractor truck from the cargo carrier #1 and the tractor truck on the tandem hook-up Two. By setting the crank dollies on each tractor-trailer, and disconnecting the electrical and air suspension lines, when they pulled the pin on the 5th wheel, the torque pressure on Truck One had been so severe that the truck part dropped loose, slid down, and fell off the bridge. Truck Two was separated, put into neutral, and it too was pushed over, out of sight, to fall into the river. Two soldiers made a head count of the dead, then gathered up the deceased driver's body and put him aboard one of the waiting choppers. At the same time, in formation, came three helicopters, even larger than Pacheco had ever seen, military certainly, but without markings. If he had known, he would have been surprised to discover they were Russian-manufactured Halo MI-26s, the world's largest helicopter in production. The three behemoths were heavy twin-engine transport helicopters with a lifting capacity of 62,170 lbs., an easy hoist of a cargo container.

Crimson Scimitar

"I want to ask," said Chase to her three companions, seated with their backs against the far concrete abutment next to the walkway, looking innocent and unarmed. She emphasized with a laugh, "But I know nothing."

"You and me both," agreed Shawn, watching one soldier come over and stand by them, weapon ready, intent ready, but making no demands. Silent, waiting for others more senior to arrive.

One of the soldiers, looking at the destruction on the bridge, had happened to glance over the guardrail, a definite majestic and scary view looking down.

"Hey, there's a guy way down there waving at me."

The survivors of the 'Shootout at the Dam Bridge' as it came to be known, smiled at each other knowingly. One of the HAZMATS walked over to them, studied their faces, and without a word, stuck a radiation tracking dosimeter badge on each of them, then rejoined the others. Whoever they were ran Geiger counters along the containers, then helped attach the large cradling straps under the container of Truck One to the hovering Halo, which without effort, lifted and departed. The procedure was repeated on Truck Two on the front container, then the last heavy-lift Halo for the last container. All three, with their Eagle talons bared designed logos disappeared, heading north. The other two Black Hawks with passengers likewise departed, the roadblock was lifted, and the police arrived, followed by Federal agents.

The convoy via aerial sky lifts would finally reach their destination at the Yucca Nuclear Storage Depository Facility, even if in such an unusual form of transportation.

EPISODE THIRTY-FIVE — Revisionary History

Scene 1: Local Television News Report
Setting: Las Vegas, September 4th

Channel 8 News:

"Highway 93 is open to restricted one-lane traffic across the O'Callaghan-Tillman Bridge. State structural engineers have finished an immediate inspection and found the bridge itself has been undamaged. The explosions that occurred during the gun battle and subsequent suicide dives off the bridge by several of the kidnapping suspects caused minimal damage to the roadway and traffic barriers and did not undermine bridge integrity. The State Patrol is still at the scene directing the traffic as emergency road repair is ongoing. We will bring you updates from our Eye-in-the-Sky traffic reporter as we receive them.

582 S.P. Grogan

"In other chilling news of the day, an elderly Wisconsin couple was found slain in their travel camper off Blue Diamond Road. We will be right back with more details after these announcements."

What the police did not provide to this story nor put high on their evidence collection guesswork was that of all the travel logos of interesting sites visited glued to the camper's back side, two decals were of a visit the day earlier to the Grand Canyon, and the other of Hoover Dam.

Scene 2: Home Invasion
Setting: Henderson, Nevada. A gated community neighborhood, suburb of metro Las Vegas, September 6th

The Professor could not endure the waiting to face his killer. Two days after his escape from the bridge, he knew from the press and media reports that the attack had been a debacle. He knew this would incense Shahin, and the man would want to clean up loose ends before using the border tunnel escape route.

He had taken measures, but would they be enough? He had planted the seed with his wife Marcie that he thought some burglars might be casing the neighborhood. He called the police to express his concern; and encouraged his wife to allow her sister to take the children for a couple days of late summer fun, which she did hesitantly. To avoid being murdered in his sleep, he added a chain lock to the bedroom door. He bought a few high-tech gadgets for the rest of the house and installed them himself. Yet, if he and his family were marked for execution beyond three days, he could not maintain his vigilant paranoia, which already began to take a toll on his health.

He expected something to happen, and it did, almost on schedule, on the third night of his uneasiness.

He was working at his desk in the family den. He had the light on over his desk and the window shades open so that anyone from the street could see him sitting there. He did not expect a bullet through the window glass. If they shot him from the yard, through the sliding glass door, it would be a just punishment, Allah's will, for allowing himself to be caught up in such a scheme. No, his death, he knew, would be personal.

A small red bulb illuminated on the device on his desk. Someone had breached the security and entered the house. He did not wish to set off the home burglar alarm, which would bring the security company; little good they would do, and too late. No, it had to end now.

He pushed a button on a garage-door-type remote he held in his hand and waited.

"Professor, good to see you again." Razzor Hassim walked into the den from the kitchen. Shahin had sent him to do his dirty work.

"I guess I should have expected it would be you."

Razzor held a large, serrated knife in his hand.

"You left the attack and did not die on the bridge; that was most unfortunate."

"You mean, run like you, and I presume as Shahin did? And, of course, you helped bin Laden to escape. But like you, I plead guilty where survival wins out over martyrdom every time." He needed to stall for time.

"But I guess I have to ask: did the al-Qaeda attack succeed on the bridge? The press does not mention your glorious deeds, so I presume there was no leaked radiation. No major press release of triumph from bin Laden. He's in hiding, I presume. And the FBI today released only two wannabes killed on the bridge. They call them 'homegrown terrorists.' I do feel sad for the student cell I created, that they died. I had cutouts and secret messages between me and them, so no one knows I was ever involved. No mention of al-Qaeda in all of this."

"The American government is hiding the facts. But their press is predatory, and the truth will eventually come out." Razzor sneered.

"But why was their security response on the bridge immediate? *Crimson Scimitar* failed from the onset. I can't be blamed for that." That rattled Razzor as he went from controlled killer to defensive anger.

"We were betrayed."

"It did not come from me."

"Does it matter?"

Everything is in place, thought the Professor, and beneath the desk, he pushed the pre-dialed 911 on his cell phone. Then, giving a second for the connection, he spoke loudly in a scared voice to his attacker.

"I can pay you money, and you can leave here a wealthy man, no one knowing you entered the Anthem Highlands neighborhood. And please don't kill my wife. She's innocent."

"Once I take care of you, then it will be your wife and children. And your wife will die screaming after I pleasure myself."

The Professor gave a slight wail of anguish. Faked.

"You can't kill my children; they are not here. Don't make the Roger children orphans."

"I will hunt them down. You can count on that." And Razzor took a step forward, menacing with the knife.

584 S.P. Grogan

"I don't think so," came the voice from behind Razzor, a woman's voice, and he turned in surprise. "You will never touch my children," Marcie, the Professor's mousy gentle wife, fired the Remington 1100 shotgun, purchased only yesterday. The impact of the 12-gauge shell threw Razzor up and back through the sliding door leading to the patio, shattering the glass into body-slashing shards.

The shotgun's recoil knocked Marcie to the floor, the shotgun dropped from her grasp.

"My God!" she screamed. "What have I done, Jim? You told me the shells were loaded with rock salt. They would scare the burglar, sting him. I have killed him!" She was in hysterics.

He tried a calming voice, "The sporting goods store must have given me the wrong shells. But don't worry, dear, please; you saved us all. You heard him. This was a home invasion, and he meant to rob and kill us. And most certainly, he would have raped and tortured you. Don't worry; everything will be all right."

Under Nevada's laws of self-defense and the right to protect one's home, the Professor knew his wife would have no fear of prosecution. The 911 call recorded Razzor's lethal threats, and there was his knife lying on the floor. All would be right again; he would collect his children tomorrow and call the family doctor for advice. Of course, his wife Marcie would need psychiatric help for some time.

Tomorrow, or the next day, he would return to UNLV to prepare for fall classes. All that had happened, his dialogue with the young Khalaf, had cured him of future misadventures. From this point on, he would seek to become a model of this American community committed to the love and protection of his family. The past was truly the past.

A week later, the San Diego *Union-Tribune* reported the discovery of a major tunnel under the U.S.-Mexico border when an undetermined explosion collapsed it. One of the most professional and modern tunnels yet uncovered, officials reported. U.S. Border Patrol and Mexican Federal Agents recovered quantities of drugs, including cocaine and small amounts of a new drug in pill form, 4-anilino-N-phenethyl-4-piperidine (ANNP), also known as a fentanyl precursor. In addition, a weapons cache and C-4 explosives were uncovered. One of the four men killed in the explosion was the paid tunnel builder, Alvarez.

When Alvarez had not heard from Shahin on the scheduled rendezvous date, he claimed default ownership and possession of the tunnel, abrogated any verbal contract he held with the foreigners, and began opening boxes of his newly purloined boxes of treasure. One of the attackers, the bomber, had left a gift for those who opened Shahin's property without permission.

The U.S. Border Patrol, in its inventory, drew attention to the fact that much of the C-4 explosives were wrapped in pink paper and manufactured in France. This tidbit made it to the

FBI and the CIA, who concluded that this tunnel, as good as any place, was how Osama bin Laden escaped into Mexico, heading back to a new home, somewhere yet unidentified.

Scene 3: Treaty Negotiations
Setting: Fraunces Tavern, New York City, September 10th

Wendell Holmes thought of the location, Samantha endorsed the idea, and Hugh Fox relished the ironic symbolism. Perfect for privacy and negotiations. The Washington Room at Fraunces Tavern on 54 Pearl Street. Established in 1762, the tavern was New York's oldest and most historic bar and restaurant. More dramatically and historically, in 1783, when the last British troops had left American soil, General George Washington met with his senior officers here before retiring from military service and returning to Mount Vernon. He gave a heart-felt emotional farewell speech to his officers and aides that left all attending in tears.

What Hugh Fox enjoyed was that most forgot that George Washington ran a pretty effective spy system that helped the Colonial cause and led to Yorktown and the Treaty of Paris, creating the fledgling United States. He was also an innovative farmer, an idea man.

This day the formal dining room held two sides in parley. For the government were representatives of the FBI, DOJ, CIA, and the White House. On the other side, Hugh Fox and Samantha Carlisle representing Five Aces Studioz, owner of the *King's Retribution* television show, and attorneys Booker Langston and Lisa Scott Goss, representing all parties of interest not present but feeling representation essential to protect their rights (to keep them from government harassment and out of jail).

The luncheon was quite cordial. Each side knew what the other side had done, repressed, or accomplished, and none need repeat it aloud to make their case any stronger. Most of the negotiated points were verbal and not meant to be reduced to writing.

Points of record:

All those involved with King's Retribution, Five Aces Studios, employees, and contract consultants (this last included Holmes, Langston, and Eberhardt) would be released of any and all legal issues in regard to the hunt, capture, trial, and ending of Osama bin Laden, or other terrorist activities during the year of 2011.

These stated groups would pledge by agreement not to mention anything in public or private concerning the events in question and would remain silent for a period of 20 years (2031) and not contradict any statement issued by the government concerning such events. (The government asked for silence in perpetuity, but that was rejected, and it was accepted that the current administration knew they would be long gone from political ramifications and certainly not further involved in what might eventually be released in future best-seller untold-story publications].

586   S.P. Grogan

Points off the record:

Navy SEAL Shawn Pacheco deserved special commendation for his gallantry. The story would stand that on the 3rd of September, he and Detective Taggart were the only heroes to be so recognized. The government had no problem with that view of events as it fit within an acceptable narrative.

On behalf of Skilleo Games Technology, Hugh Fox asked a special favor of the U.S. Military (to be conveyed later in a private conversation); he had a product in the prototype stage, which, if successful, might have military applications. It required field testing. Cautious and wary, the White House representative present at the luncheon agreed to give his support to the proper channels within the designated Department of Defense agency this request might apply to.

They all thought, with good humor on both sides, that the so-called *Treaty of Fraunces Tavern* agreed to this day was memorable, not realizing that certain historical aspects would later arise.

The luncheon consisted of pear and arugula salad, pan-seared salmon, and dessert being a banana caramel cheesecake roll and vanilla bean whipped cream. No alcohol was served (a silent nod to the absent Colonel Storm, who those at the table gave credit for such a successful television show that was the talk of the nation. He was toasted with iced tea and mineral water.).

At the luncheon's conclusion, the DOJ representative asked Hugh Fox what would be the best game of the 2011 holiday season that Skilleo Games planned to release, and all listened intently to the answer.

Scene 4: Hotel Visitors
Setting: New York City, September 11th, 2011

Sabz, agitated and fretful, knew today would not bring good news. The telephone call had come two days ago to the hotel suite. She was asked if Mr. Rasil lived at this residence. No, she said, this suite was registered under the name of Sheik Khalaf bin Zayed from the United Arab Emirates. Did she know a Mr. Rasil? She clutched. Yes, she lied; he was an associate of her husband, knowing full well Rasil was one of Khalaf's several passport aliases. Someone would be coming by at 10 a.m. on the 11th to visit with her and her husband on a matter of Mr. Rasil's stock brokerage accounts.

She did not know what to do. There had been no word from Khalaf since his departure.

She knew some operation of al-Qaeda was in play, but every day she watched the television news, and there was no alert of al-Qaeda presence in the United States. She still viewed plenty of American violence — from domestic dispute shootings to robberies that went wrong to gang warfare. Through her constant watching, she found herself caught up in the movie star drama and politician indiscretions and sought out those television shows where they talked about such events in empty chatter.

The only news item close to an attack was the freeing of two attorneys involved in defending Osama bin Laden, and those kidnappers had all been killed or committed suicide. In the back of her mind, she saw the connection to bin Laden and worried that the connection included *her* Khalaf. Afraid and apprehensive, she was approaching the decision on whether or not to open the sealed envelope he left her, afraid he would be mad that she had done so if indeed he returned.

She fretted and worried and kept her eye on the television shows and nightly news. On the international front, governments, especially in the Middle East, continued to crash inward under the rhetoric of seeking democracy, finding anarchy instead, what American officials labeled in blind optimism, 'Arab Spring.' Sabz had seen firsthand such futile violence but cared little for radical politicians as they never seemed to make life easier. Iraq and Syria were falling back into anarchy, with religion and tribes at each other's throats. Seeking peace and comfort had become her only priority. It had pushed her decision-making in that direction, and this discovered fortuitous happiness she shared with Khalaf, as much the naïve child he acted. Could he not see that his jihad beliefs outside tribal borders were irrelevant to the daily lives of billions of people? As much as she subtly tried, he did not see the better world surrounding him, the freedom to act as one pleased.

This particular morning, the 11th, she was watching distracting television when the doorbell to the suite rang. She was sure they were here to announce Rasil's (Khalaf's) death, then to arrest and deport her. Her dream had ended.

When she opened the door, an Arab, an American Arab, asked to see her passport. He sounded official, and she complied. He studied her face against the counterfeit English passport she held.

"You live in London?"

"Yes. My husband travels a lot, but we are temporarily staying here."

"And you will be returning to Great Britain soon?"

"As soon as my husband returns."

"Oh, he is not here?"

"He has been traveling. I really don't know his itinerary." She paused. He had made no police-like threats, and young as she was, she overcame nervousness to regain her strength. "And this questioning is in regard to what?"

"There has been an accident."

"Oh, no." The blessings on her life and Khalaf's were dashed. She caught herself before her tears began. "My husband, he's dead?"

"No, no. It is his friend, Mr. Rasil. He was in a serious auto accident, but he shall recover. He just needs a place to regain his strength, and it was thought your husband and you might help nurse him back to health."

"Rasil?" She was confused.

"Excuse me, one moment." And the man stepped into the hall, returning with a wheeled stretcher and another man pushing one end.

Khalaf lay unconscious on the stretcher, covered in a sheet, one side of his head and jaw bandaged.

The joy in her expression, tears welling, brought a humpf grunt of displeasure from the other man.

"Where do we put him, Abbas?"

"The bedroom, of course, Bennie."

Once they had eased Rasil/Khalaf on top of the bedcovers, they departed, but not before the man that had identified as Abbas, spoke seriously to Sabz.

"A doctor will drop by daily to check his injuries. It is our recommendation that as soon as he is able to walk, you both return to London."

"Who are you?" Her suspicions rose.

"His new friends. We have left a packet for him to open and read when he is feeling better." Abbas stepped to the wide window overlooking the balcony. Later today, rain was in the forecast. He turned to the small Middle Eastern woman. She was quite attractive though her face bore signs of exhaustion.

"Do you know what this month signifies? What September 11th, 2001, meant? No, probably not. Ten years ago, on this day, 3,000 people were murdered in this city and elsewhere in the country, a tragedy to make us all realize how lives can be controlled by evil people. It will not happen again. We have made an investment in Mr. Rasil, and we expect our due return. So please take care of him. He is destined to become an important man."

Abbas and Bennie left, closing the door behind them.

Sabz ran to the bed and stared down at the bandaged Khalaf. Tears flowed between tiny sobs. She lay next to him, held his hand, and watched the rise and fall of his chest. When this Abbas man appeared, she had been watching the television in the living room, and the set remained on; now, she was too tired to turn it off. She tried not to hear the programming, but it was so repetitive, like Khalaf's steady breathing: a name spoken, a different name stated, a new name, another. Even after Sabz closed her eyes to sleep, the names continued. A bell rang with each name called until 2,983 names were read and marked, a somber repetition of warning, containing the same message Abbas had repeated in Wendell Holmes's speech to be told to the terrorist's bride. A theme: *We will not forget. We will act proactively. And your man shall play an important part.*

On the street outside the hotel, Hugh Fox and Wendell Holmes waited.

"How did it go?" Abbas and Bennie were asked.

"Seldom do you see a woman glad to see her man return," responded Bennie. "He must be something."

"Let us hope so," agreed Holmes. "This will be a historic journey for all of us."

"Let's get our Ali Baba healthy and back home and see what happens next," said Hugh Fox, ready to reprise his role as the manipulative puppeteer, the mystery man behind the curtain, a co-creator of scenes to follow with his fellow traveler, Holmes; and as Samantha continues reminding us all, this quiet fellow of surprises.

Scene 5: The White House Ceremony
Setting: Washington, D.C., September 15, 2011

"I don't want to know, do I?" An entirely rhetorical question as the President of the United States indeed did not want to know. If the entire story became public, exposing the failure of the government's intelligence community to ferret out threats within the U.S., heads would roll, and with the election next year, his up-poll numbers rising might suffer a setback. He could find his political neck on the electoral chopping block. At least with this 'understanding' reached, this *Treaty of Fraunces Tavern*, any heads rolling in the future would be further down the chain of command, damage control could be initiated, and what had transpired at the amusement parks and on the Arizona-Nevada bridge would be seen as a long-ago event, befuddled in a mix of storytelling, diffused and mitigated. To be recalled in the distant future as epic legend more than annotated history.

"No, sir, it is better this way. We have reached an accommodation with all parties," explained the head of Homeland Security. "And nothing was put into writing."

"Actually, we have had to give up very little," said the new CIA director (there had been a shake-up within the Agency), "mostly future accommodations which we can live with."

"No money exchanged hands," said one of the officials as an afterthought, as if to imply money might have been required to buy silence.

590   S.P. Grogan

"Well, if you all are comfortable, then I will accept your direction and wisdom," said the President, ready to move on. "We shall look at these events as having been concluded in a positive light. A national disaster was averted. You have told me, in not so many words, that proper punishments have been meted out and deserved rewards tendered. Gentleman, I do not want this possibility to ever happen again, not only on my watch but in years beyond my Administration."

Around the room, there were nods of concurrence from the four individuals in the Oval Office who would be in that tight circle of knowing the truth and taking it to their graves: the Head of Homeland Security, the Director of the FBI, the Director of the CIA, and the President's National Security Advisor.

To these four powerful government leaders, he said, putting a newly manufactured smile on his face, "Now, ladies and gentlemen, let us set aside our country's close call and bestow a just reward to the truly courageous." And the President rose, as did the others, and as if on cue, the visitors were ushered in.

Recently promoted to E-9 Rating, Shawn Pacheco came first in full-dress Navy uniform, followed by his fiancée Janet, and her father, former Army Captain Russell Mosswood (retired), definitely awestruck at the majesty of this well-known odd circular office. Pacheco saluted the

President and the President extended his hand. The grip between them was solid. The President made small talk, emphasizing to his fiancée, "You should be very proud of him." "Yes, I am," replied Janet, feeling more confident than ever in her life, ready to be a SEAL's wife.

In the short formal ceremony and among the remarks made by the President of the United States, Janet remembered the President's words in a blur.

"The United States is in a continuing battle to protect our citizens from those who have no morality and desire only the total extermination of our way of life. Many in uniform rise to the occasion when there are times of crises. Because of issues concerning National Security and recent events that have transpired, the actions of Ensign SO Pacheco may never be known to the public, but I can tell you both that since he wanted you to share this historic and special occasion with him, he exemplifies the best in our men and women of the Armed Forces."

With that, the President opened the small case and placed the Congressional Medal of Honor around Pacheco's neck.

"Navy SEAL Shawn Pacheco, the United States and all its citizens owe you a debt of gratitude that can never be repaid. I proudly award you this decoration, the highest in the land for our military heroes, for exemplary courage and decisive action in facing extreme danger in saving countless innocent lives." Brief, vague, and well said.

Again, sailor and Commander-in-Chief shook hands. Shawn turned to Janet and gave her a kiss, and she tingled in the excitement that there would be many more. Even Janet's father knew this was more than a momentous occasion. There were no cameras, no press in the room, and the four witnesses to the ceremony were among the top officials of the Administration. What his future son-in-law must have been involved in had to be so dangerous and so critical to the security of the country that total secrecy had to be invoked. Obeying orders and duty, he understood; it was part of his own fabric of past military service. He was so proud and, at the same time, so ashamed he ever doubted the young man's character, and he knew he would spend years in atonement and pledged to himself, hopefully in the not-so-distant future, to be the best grandfather ever.

As the ceremony ended and the good-byes were being said, the President casually asked

Pacheco, what were his plans, was he going back to his SEAL unit for reassignment?

"No, my Commander gave me an open-ended extended leave and has approved my being assigned as a military technical liaison to the television show *King's Retribution*."

As they say, the surprise on the face of the President of the United States: 'priceless.'

Scene 6: Diplomatic Reunion
Setting: The U.S. Embassy, Islamabad, Pakistan, September 18th

He signed his name to the two documents.

"Here you are, folks. Temporary passport replacements. Please remember, next time, do not leave your travel documents lying around in your room. The hotel safe would be more secure."

The tourists departed, grateful for the embassy's quick response to their travel distress.

Governmental Affairs Director and Senior Attaché Ronald Givens looked up from his desk in the U.S. Embassy and saw the man approaching him, the military bearing obvious, the dress coat in this Fall weather a poor attempt at being discreet.

"Mr. Givens, I heard you were back. Welcome."

"General Khan. How unexpected."

"I presume your new posting was for great service rendered back home."

Givens sought to put his demotion, the 'take this exile position or leave' offer, in the best possible light.

"Yes, it was decided to put me back into the field. They call it a 'refresher course' in preparation for future advancement." Not true. He knew his career had stalled for good. He would now only hang on, do the required, and wait out his pension.

590

S.P. Grogan

"Well, then, allow me to extend once again my friendship. Let's do lunch next week at my club. Perhaps, if you will allow, let me help you integrate yourself back into our country's wonderful society."

Givens' face brightened.

"Yes, that is very kind." Perhaps this place might have diversions to keep him from utter melancholy.

"Good then, my secretary will call you for our luncheon date. And again, welcome."

As General Khan walked out of the U.S. Embassy, he could only laugh and wonder.

'How did this perfectly plump pigeon get placed on my table for carving? It will be only a matter of weeks,' he bet himself, 'before I start extracting all the gossip and news from the goings on in the Embassy. Why did they send such an ineffectual louse? Or did they? No, it couldn't be. He shouldn't have such clout; he's retired. But if he was behind this man's arrival, he must know the incompetence that has been unleashed. Such a contrived gesture is certainly tit-for-tat. As I gain access to U.S. State Department secrets and CIA loose chatter, the same will be expected of me. Well, such are the games we must play.'

Outside, the general eased himself into the passenger side of the shiny new convertible roadster.

"Like your car?"

"Of course, haven't I shown you my appreciation many times over?"

Yes, you have, smiled the general to himself, and will again and again, accepting the odd irony that all his intertwined benefits were due to the unfortunate Sheik. bin Laden. Such was the way in this shadow world.

Scene 7: Claridge's Hotel
Setting: London, September 20th

He was a wealthy yet a very disturbed man. Daily, he tried to sum up and recount what he knew and guess at what he did not.

He knew he first awoke in his suite at the Waldorf in Sabz's arms, warmth and tenderness. A specialist doctor soon showed up at the hotel and removed stitches from the top of his head and jaw from his 'auto accident,' as he was told, giving him a bottle of pills and offering to prescribe more pain medication if required. He spent a week after that recovering in complete confusion. When he was lucid and voiced his curiosity, Sabz recounted as best she could his arrival on the stretcher and her conversation with the American Arab (Persian) called Abbas. Whether by Khalaf's suggestion or their mutual fear of imminent arrest, they decided to leave for London when he felt he could make the trip and did so shortly thereafter. Ensconced back in their Claridge suite, he again masked as an Emirate diplomat.

Before their departure, he received back the letter that Sabz kept in safekeeping, unopened. Not so much a test of loyalty as it was his last will and testament, giving her everything he owned, and the documents allowing her access to all his accounts.

In a quandary and angry, he did his first 'treasonable' act, both in distrust and towards self-preservation. He liquidated nearly all his investment portfolio through his middleman Nidal in New York, who as always eager for more fees. However, with these funds secured he wired only a small amount of investment capital back into the al-Qaeda laundering accounts, mostly to grease palms of the new jihadist leaders to suggest there had been some success to *Crimson Scimitar*. The remaining funds found a safe haven in Switzerland and the Grand Caymans, with a token management account in London. To anyone asking, and they would, he could rationalize that with the failure of *Crimson Scimitar* without any market-shattering news, the short sales were a loss when he had to cover the stock positions and only a pittance remained, since rightfully returned.

His investment program in the American stock market indeed made a sizable profit. First, the short sale was effective when entertainment stocks dipped slightly on the amusement park news; second, covered on that, he repurchased into a small portfolio that did well on the short-term market correction, and though prepared to go short on the bridge attack, he held back; a wise decision as no particular American company would reel and falter from the bridge attack. The stocks he left in place were unaffected because there was no crash from the bad news of a national disaster, and within a week, the stock market ticked upward on reports of strong quarterly earnings of major bellwether stock indicators. In short, Khalaf, the stock market-playing novice, made a quick killing that would have brought envy from the likes of Jay Gould and the robber barons.

Ultimately, $US 7 million fell into Khalaf's personal ownership. Totally mercenary, he believed his and bin Laden's *Crimson Scimitar* had value, assured of success, and when this was undone by Shahin's bungling, Khalaf deserved to exact a penalty against a failure to perform. Trying to kill him to shut up such failure made any niggling guilt at perceived thievery negligible.

He was not totally unscrupulous. Over $1 million was returned anonymously to the London-based Islamic Benevolent Association, in memory of Taher Abboud, the banker. And he did leave one trading account open in New York for several miscellaneous stock holdings Sabz had found interest in. While waiting for his return, she had begun to delve into internet communities where she could learn more about America and the world without revealing herself.

594   S.P. Grogan

When he had sufficiently recovered, she told Khalaf that many people in the chat rooms she visited were upbeat on what was called 'social media'; so, to appease her, to let her know he did appreciate that she had waited for him, that she wanted him, and to extend his faith in her he had his stockbroker invest in a few of these internet companies where masses of people, without prejudices, interacted. One of them, in particular, he bought in a private market sale, a 'restricted' stock where insider talk was about launching an IPO in the middle of next year. Though satisfying to continue to play in the investment world, his mind floated in limbo at the unknowns.

The rest he kept, not out of greed, but for the unknown future, seeking to define a purpose, to understand why he had been saved, by whom, and as Sabz related, the veiled threat of a debt now owed that would be collected.

In the London hotel suite, he stayed in seclusion, regaining his strength, making love, and working out thoughts he was too afraid to speak aloud. He remembered little of the bridge battle, except that Shahin desired his death by Razzor's hand. *Crimson Scimitar* had been a failure, as no announcement of a radiation cataclysm appeared in the press, and if the disaster had occurred, everyone would know. He accepted the certainty that bin Laden was dead and even wondered if it was indirectly by his hand? But there was no lasting guilt if that were so. What had really happened? He had little memory of or rightly suppressed his haphazard choices. What he came to accept, as his past reading of spy thrillers suggested, was that the Americans had 'sanitized' the attack site.

What started growing in his consciousness was the shock that al-Qaeda, specifically the Supreme Council, must have sanctioned bin Laden with the command to Shahin to kill all participants in the attack. Killing true Muslim patriots seemed a damnable sin and tainted the cause. These thoughts added to those doubts about his base beliefs from his road trip discussions with Professor Rogers.

His greatest agony was in not deciphering who his unknown 'angels' were. He concluded they could not be the CIA, or he would be in Guantanamo at this moment, being tortured with sleep deprivation or near-drowned by water boarding. Sabz suggested that this Abbas might be part of an Arabic crime syndicate like she saw on TV, like the Russian mobsters who shared control of any number of lucrative criminal enterprises in New York with the Zionists.

Most bewildering was the packet that they had left for him. It contained two cellular phones, which he assumed allowed international use anywhere. And, mystery of all mysteries, also included in the packet, a five-page document, an essay, written in Arabic, and a note attached with two parts. He had read the transcript over twenty times, amazed at its premise. He was afraid to follow the instructions in the note's demands, though they seemed minor.

Now, safe, he hoped, as a hermit in his hotel suite in London, he faced hard choices.

When he re-established his presence in a certain Islamic chat room, he received a coded back-door communication from Doctor al-Zawahiri: *What happened to your sword? What happened to your allowance?*

Khalaf responded warily, no longer assured of who his friends were, even at the top.

Sword broke in desert. Our banker died. His crimson investments failed without sword; remaining money returned.

After a day where the recipient of this response probably was engaged in high-level discussions, Khalaf received a message he was not expecting.

With sword broken, must concentrate our strength at home. Our uncle, al-Shari, fell and died. You are one of my few loyal friends. I am choosing you to join our business. Proceed to visit our friends in Yemen to confirm and receive instructions.

It was powerful news in its interpretation.

Bin Laden's schemes of attacking the United States were to be shelved. From now on, the Doctor and al-Qaeda would focus on weak governments where their attacks might sway control into their hands. The uncle in the code who had been killed was Abu Hafs al-Shari, chief of al-Qaeda operations in Pakistan, and as Khalaf believed, al-Shari would have been the logical choice to take over the Number Two role left by the death of al-Rahman. He could now see why Doctor al Zawahiri, officially the heir after bin Laden's accepted suicide (the escaped bin Laden himself had forbidden communication with the Council until his victorious return), was consolidating his forces to only mount attacks in Pakistan, Afghanistan, and Yemen. Sabz was right; he was among the last in the old organization's hierarchy.

Osama bin Laden's ideal for the caliphate was no more; al-Qaeda operated numbly under siege, its leadership decimated, its power ebbing. Soon, al-Qaeda would be made up of only impressionable suicide bombers, and such fanatics don't conquer governments. Khalaf noticed he did not think in terms of 'we' of al-Qaeda. Although a position in the Supreme Council would have been his goal achieved, that ambition had been muted against harsh reality. He had new thoughts; perhaps the way of jihad and fatwa was not the stepping stone to victory; perhaps other, less violent ways might pave the way for the goals modern Islam required. In fleshing out his innermost thoughts, using Sabz as a sounding board, he found, not so surprising, she offered support for his ideas of a new direction to his life struggle.

Her open frank comments tipped the scale to his decision.

Sabz agreed that he must find his true path. "If you go to Yemen, then you go. I will not try to stop you. And yes, I will wait for you, for you say we are to be married before Allah. But I will not sit in this room and do nothing. I am going to work, to find employment."

"What?" He now had money; she could do anything, within reason.

596   S.P. Grogan

"It will be for our benefit. While I was shopping the other day, I met another Arab woman, from Tunisia, but a British citizen, who said she was working at a bank, and they were looking to hire Arab-speaking employees for their local and international business. I am smart with math. I could learn and help you with your investments. Would you rather trust me or some stranger?"

He had grown to trust her. She had her own interests, but at this time, they seemed to be coinciding with his, and she enjoyed the trappings of success, a role he also had easily found to his liking.

"And what should I do with these writings and this note left with me?" He asked of Sabz, ready to consider her opinion.

"Did not this Abbas and his companion, the short man called Bennie, did they not save you from death?"

"That is so."

"And if you do what they ask, how can it harm you? I would rather you do it than find them at our door, threatening or worse."

"It all seems innocent enough, but they are using me."

"I do not see how. In truth, it all seems to your advantage. Let's look again at what they ask and take one step at a time." She picked up the note and read: *Sign this writing and mail to the following address*. The address seemed to be a postal box in Mayfair. Sabz considered. "The essay is positive, asking for a consolidation of Sunni and Shi'ite beliefs into one Islamic voice. To me, it is merely an opinion without teeth."

"I do not want to put my name to any such paper." Khalaf was not so eager to become complicit in who knew what might be the outcome.

"Well, then sign with a different name. Did you not say we need to re-invent ourselves? Neither the name you use as the courier nor from the Emirates or the investor Rasil. Tell me, what shall my married name be, my future husband?" She gave him a light laugh which in turn gave him the strength for his first decision. He took a long moment. "Yusuf ibn Ayyub ibn Shadi."

Sabz gave him a loving smile.

"The Unifier. Yes, that would work with such a document. We are nomads ourselves between the Western and Eastern worlds. Saladin is the name they called him in the West."

"It is only for this one document. I shall sign it *Yusuf Sala ad-Din*, and be done with them."

"Yes. Yes. Consider it for all time. I would be married to Sheik Yusuf Saladin, and people will know me as Sabz Saladin." She handed him a pen. "Sign it and throw this back in their faces."

She looked at the note again.

Turn on the red cell phone. "I would not think this is a bomb." But she was not sure.

Khalaf...Saladin, with his future wife's help, had regained his courage and agreed to what the Abbas fellow had told Sabz, that someday he would be a man of distinction. With his wealth, he was halfway there, now for the recognition of his peers, to rise above the status of messenger. New strength to again seek recognition had returned.

He stared at the two silent phones.

"The Israeli Mossad might make this phone a bomb, but who am I? Do you see a reward upon my head? Not yet, at least. No, these are Americans; they like to talk, to play silly games." Holding his breath, Khalaf turned the red phone on and let it power up. Both he and Sabz stared. Nothing happened.

He laughed and put it down on the table. The phone buzzed a silent vibration. A text message in Arabic. He read it and, with wide eyes, said aloud in alarm, "By the beard of the Prophet." Sabz took the phone, read the message, and agreed: "I am now in fear for you, my Sheik." They both looked at the text again, understanding that he was no longer in control of his destiny. And worse yet, his 'angels' were everywhere, all-knowing.

Yusuf Saladin. Go to Yemen. Take these phones with you. Follow instructions. May Allah bless your journey.

Scene 8: Showtime
Setting: Internet Communication and Satellite Feeds, September 27th, 2011

In a posh, leased London penthouse condominium, Samantha and Wendell had set up their own mini-War Room in one of the extra bedrooms. Against one wall, four large television screens were mounted and tied into his and her computer systems.

Holmes looked at all the electronic bells and whistles and said, "Time to boot up the show; where's the on-off switch."

"Such a caveman." Samantha worked the keyboard, and within a few minutes, four wall screens were illuminated in real-time, and Sam and Wendell said their hellos.

"Hugh and Callie, are we ready?" The back-forth viewing was like a Pentagon version of Skype. The pixel faces of Hugh and Callie smiled back from California. Samantha noted Callie's hair looked out of place and wondered if their tele-cam system, like hers, was set up in Fox's boudoir versus the Skilleo offices.

"Yes," said Fox, "Gizmo is going to walk us through as it goes down." Gizmo, sitting in the Santa Monica War Room offices, seemed to have several worker bees punching away on cameras, and in turn, they had a large wall-mounted screen full of words and oscillating swirls.

To the other face staring back at them on the fourth screen, Holmes gave a welcome,

"Deputy Director Brady, glad you could join us. Are your people in place?"

"Considering how you saved our bacon in Nevada, you have gained carte-blanche to call us up anytime and use our resources — of course, it would be helpful if we knew what was going on today."

"And Matthew," said Holmes, "Congratulations on your new position with the agency. I heard the former agent who occupied the office of Deputy Director is brushing up on his Pashtu."

"Enough of the feel-good moments," said Brady in a heavy voice, everyone accepting they were being recorded. "You have the best of our Joint Special Operations Command. I have that 'special' satellite in place, my military field counterpart standing by and an eye-in-the-sky communications bird circling above Yemen. An armed drone has just taken off from one of our ally's military bases that no one knows about."

"Works for us," agreed Fox, moving his eyes to a screen on his end. "Gizmo, the clock is ticking. Might as well bring all our new-found friends up to speed, and please observe the little secrets we must omit."

Showtime.

"Ladies and Gentlemen and Spooks," Gizmo enjoyed his role as the ringmaster.

"We have in place a gentleman of al-Qaeda persuasion who at this moment is meeting with the Supreme Council of al-Qaeda on the Arabian Peninsula and…" All watching could see the tech nerd puffed up his chest.

"Let me combine a few viewing channels to his location." On a split screen with the CIA feed, a grainy overhead live shot of a small village, closing up to a nondescript house, with cars and jeeps parked outside."

"How in the hell did that just happen?" A voice behind Brady expressed surprise with a follow-up comment. "Our satellite positioning has been hacked."

Gizmo said nothing. "You are viewing where our 'friend' is. We have this guy wired for sound and with an embedded GPS tracker. We know right where he is. We can hear him speak, listen to who he listens to, and a few other choice tech apps."

"Good God," came another unseen voice on the CIA side.

"No, Good going, Skilleo," said Gizmo proudly, "and our tech is not for sale, nor can we be coerced. However, for any torture, contact the Skilleo front office for an appointment."

"Gizmo," admonished Fox.

Crimson Scimitar

"Ok. Listen in. The gentleman in question, and we are listening in now (Arabic background voices were heard), is having his clock reamed by several speakers. We have two Arabic translators who know multiple dialects doing real-time translation. Care to listen in?"

Voices came in, fast and definitely furious. On the screen, which everyone could see from Gizmo's input, were the subtitle written words of the conversation. No actual visuals of the room interiors. Everyone who heard the dialogue could read the moving translation. The man called Khalaf was seeking to defend his conduct about an operation called *Crimson Scimitar*.

"Did he say *Crimson Scimitar?*" asked Brady. "Isn't that bin Laden's last messenger? He's a high-value target."

"Off limits," said Holmes. "Part of our treaty agreement. We've turned him...in a way."

"You've turned him? He works for us?"

"Not quite, but I'm working on it."

Another Arabic voice came into the conversation, and when it could be heard and read on the screen, the CIA team listening in on the feed showed noticeable excitement.

"What's up, Mr. Brady?" asked Samantha.

"We've just identified the voice belonging to al-Qaeda's most dangerous recruiter and mouthpiece, Anwar al-Awlaki. American-born, Yemen ethnicity, ties with the powerful Al-Awlik tribe that gives sanctuary to al-Qaeda fighters. I'm sorry, Wendell, but al-Awlaki trumps all. We're going to drop a big one on that gathering."

"Matthew, you gave your word that I would have operational control."

"I would be derelict in my duty, brought up on insubordination charges, if I did not stop the greatest threat next to Zawahiri."

"It doesn't matter," interrupted Gizmo. "They're on the move, meeting over; probably have to stay one jump ahead of your spy cams."

"Can you track al-Awlaki? We need the GPS coordinates for our eye-sky surveillance."

"I will have to ask Mr. Holmes. He's in charge on our end."

"Wendell, give us a hand here. For old-time's sake. For the Agency."

"Don't press my good side. If I can, I will get you a bead on al-Awlaki, but on my terms. Let me put you on hold and get back to you in one minute." The CIA screen went dark.

Holmes turned his attention to the Hugh/Callie and the Skilleo/War Room screens.

"Okay, we don't have much time. Callie, you heard the conversation with our Ali Baba, I mean, his new moniker, Yusuf Saladin, not a bad choice, by the way — but what is your investigative read in the tone?"

"Definitely, that was a kangaroo court. One guy there accused our buddy of al-Qaeda treason, blamed him for every mistake of *Crimson Scimitar*, even said he had abandoned the al-Qaeda attack team and ran like a dog at the bridge."

"Hey," said Gizmo. "We have a problem. They just searched him and took the two phones we gave him."

"Damn it," said Samantha. "We can't contact him; put him on notice he's in danger."

"Not so fast," said Fox. "We have a Skilleo backup system."

"Another hey," Gizmo working his systems. "They don't know the phones confiscated are still hot for listening, even if our Khalaf-Yusuf-Ali guy has left the room. Here's the translation coming in."

Voices were heard, angry. A young voice speaking. The translation script came over their computers. Holmes got the gist. "One of Yusuf's accusers is a boy, the son of one of the bridge attackers, somebody named Shahin or something like that. Says he received a text from his father that this Khalaf, a courier for bin Laden had turned against the *Crimson Scimitar* plan and was trying to stop it. The other leaders in the room have just verbally convicted our guy. Al-Awlaki's bodyguards say they are leaving with their boss and will take the 'traitor' with them and dispose of him in the desert. The phones are going with them. We can let the CIA track the phones."

"Shit," Callie's read of the situation. "This guy on the bridge that I was going to blow away might actually be a good bad person? I don't want these animals to kill our new prime contact."

"Boiling it down, Ali Baba-Yusuf walked into a trap; they're looking for a fall guy for *Crimson Scimitar*, and if they're on the move, it's certain Ali Baba is getting a one-way ride."

"Gizmo," Fox pushed. "What do you have for us?"

"Secure satellite feed says they left in two cars. Our own GPS headset says our man Khalaf is in one, with a driver and a guard, no doubt. The other vehicle, a matter of deduction, contains al-Awlaki and three men. Not sure if they are VIPs. The phones are in that car."

"Okay, going back on screen."

Samantha put the CIA back into visual.

"And?" queried Brady, somewhat miffed in being held off.

"I need fifteen minutes. Here's the GPS of their location in motion. Let us in on your visual."

Thirty seconds later.

"We have them," said one of the CIA intel techs, and the satellite on the split screen showed a high-level grainy view of two cars on a dirt road, dust trails billowing.

"Need fifteen minutes."

"I can't lose the chance, Holmes."

"They're going to execute my man. I need fifteen minutes. And if you target, target the second car. That's al-Awlaki's ride."

"We're taking out both vehicles. You can't save your man from London."

"I need to make a telephone call."

"He's not going to get a signal from California or London to Yemen."

"I can if you patch me through your flying com control center."

Stare down. Brady between Holmes

"*King's Retribution* can accomplish anything," added Hugh Fox and put his arm around Callie. Samantha squeezed Holmes's hand. *There is more at stake*, prayed Holmes, *than just the body count*. It reminded him of the assignment a long time ago, in the darkened Khartoum streets in Sudan, knowing the cruise missile was incoming, that the innocent watchman had run back into the warehouse and died; Holmes could not save the man then. Was this Khartoum all over again? Was he helpless?

"Our drone is ten minutes out," said Brady. "Make your damn call. You are all delusional; there's no chance you can save him."

Fox pushed a private com to Gizmo, and the visual of Fox went dark to the CIA while he made 'his call.'

Predator drone

602   S.P. Grogan

Scene 9: Angels on High Descend
Setting: Small village, the deserts of Yemen, September 30th

With the Jirga of top regional al-Qaeda leaders in full swing, he felt elation. He had presented his credentials that Doctor al-Zawahiri had requested his presence at the regional Council meeting. He offered that from his past experience, he could help bridge the divergent philosophies of the wisdom of Yemen leaders and those in South Waziristan within Zawahiri's circle. He even assumed, for a few minutes, that he might be elevated to a sub-leader within al-Qaeda and be able to help direct the future of the organization, perhaps even in negotiations with the West. But, in his ongoing inner debate, he was uncertain that such elevation was what he now sought; that he did not yet see the end plan of what he might become. Amidst the desert world of men sitting on carpets discussing the next bombing, he longed for the optimistic advice of Sabz. How could it be jihad blasphemy, wishing peace for all and reconciliation or tolerance of faiths?

As if his hesitation signaled his weakness, the world of his expectations came crashing down. A young boy entered accompanied by two rough-cut men, slinging rifles, appearing to be his bodyguards, as if the boy was some sort of revered leader, and they seemed, by their clothing, to be from al-Awlaki's tribe. Both Khalaf and the boy exchanged hard looks. Khalaf recognized him; this was Shahin's son, whom he had seen witnessing the execution ordered by his father. It was not only for Shahin's soldiers, but Khalaf realized, also a learning lesson for a future jihadist. What was the boy's name?

Khalaf realized he had come to his own trial, definitely pre-staged. Even Dr. Zahwari had played a role, providing encouragement to attend and assuring him he might be rewarded. The tribunal told him to stay silent. He would not be allowed to tell of the amusement park stock market play nor what he saw at the bridge. All he might say would point to the deceased Shahin's incompetency, that bin Laden's plan was flawed.

The jihad's top recruiter, al-Awlaki, spoke as his prosecutor. His speech was one of angered accusation against the failure of *Crimson Scimitar*, not because of how it had failed to be carried out, but because the whole battle plan had been flawed, created by those who knew nothing of true holy war. The last indictment was pointed at Khalaf and indirectly cast aspersions on bin Laden's wisdom. A deceased martyr cannot defend himself.

Khalaf thought of the Jewish biblical expression, that he saw the handwriting on the wall, the changing sand of power politics, an adept art he still was not proficient in. Murdered Osama bin Laden would remain the poster martyr to the masses, but his policies must be rewritten to give new and tight control to the next regime. Instead of the caliphate or any confederacy, those remaining in al-Qaeda were dividing up the spoils. Anwar al-Awlaki, a man Khalaf had never trusted as to his ambition believing he sought to gain equal ranking to bin

Laden, dominated this meeting. Indeed, others spoke, jockeying to be his right-hand hatchet man.

Khalaf understood. In this new order, al-Awlaki would have the fiefdom of Yemen; Doctor Zawahiri would become the dominant dictator of Pakistan's tribal regions and master over an infiltrated conservative Islamic Pakistan. In the course of the conversation, new men he had never met before stood and asked for their piece of the basboosa cake. Iraq and Syria were divided and given to the New Jihadists, who promised the current governments would be attacked and undermined. Through fomenting rebellion in each state, al-Qaeda would gain renewed strength. Local first, then global.

The underlying conclusion of the Jirga was this: the ghost of bin Laden must be purged, and to Khalaf, this meant him, the only reminder of their failed quest for Islamic world domination. He felt what it must be to suffer like the prophet Abraham of making hard choices or the prophet Jesus, his own people casting stones against him, and Khalaf among those two spirtual leaders being condemned for his cowardice, believing he ran from bin Laden's compound and pushed an inept plan which could not possibly work against the formidable Americans. At this moment, faced with such denunciation, Khalaf lost all faith in the cause he had embraced and to which he swore fealty. It seemed too late.

"Enough," said al-Awlaki. "We will take all this into consideration. It is time we moved on to Ma'rib." He looked at Khalaf. "We must seek a solution to end this disharmony." The meeting ended, and Khalaf felt himself being herded to one of the cars by al-Awlaki's men and shoved inside. Al-Awlaki's main bodyguard sat in the front with the driver, Khalaf, in the back with another of the bodyguards. Traveling in the second following car was al-Awlaki, another bodyguard, and an American born in Saudi Arabia, Samir Khan, editor of al-Qaeda's English-written web magazine, *Inspire*.

As they drove the desert dirt roadway, the bodyguard leaned over the front seat toward him and spoke in a false sympathetic voice.

"Perhaps my Sheik's words were too strong. You should be able to convince al-Awlaki to place you in a position of importance. It has always been your wish, is that not so?"

Hearing such blatant pandering, Khalaf realized he would be executed before they reached the Ma'rib Governorate meeting. This would not be a public spectacle to reveal the rifts within al-Qaeda ranks; instead, a bullet in the head and abandoned as a white-ribbed skeleton in the wasteland. He would never see his true future, as he believed Allah wished. He would never see Sabz again.

A few minutes later, as he contemplated his impending death, there came to him a voice. He looked around to see if the driver had spoken. He had not, and neither had the guard. In wonder, Khalaf heard the voice again... in his head!

604   S.P. Grogan

A voice in Arabic, then English.

"Yusuf, move away from the car — NOW!"

The shock of this was almost too much, the warning so specific, not from heaven, but from his 'angels.' And for a second, then, *Yes, 'Yusuf is my name.*

"Please stop. I am going to be sick," groaned Khalaf. "The food today must have been spoiled."

"You can wait," growled the bodyguard.

"If you want diarrhea smells all over the car for the next hour…."

The bodyguard and driver exchanged a knowing look at the thought of such unpleasantness. The guard stared at Khalaf, despising such weakness, then motioned the driver to stop. Behind them, al-Awlaki's car came to a halt.

Khalaf-Yusuf bending over, and hugging his stomach, groaned and walked from the car. The message had given him a command but had not specified what would happen next. He began to have an idea; a searing memory of that night in the village near Wana came back to him. He must get as far away from the two cars as possible. He started to walk towards a car-sized boulder.

"Do not go far," said the driver, obviously knowing his passenger was a 'prisoner.'

"I feel diarrhea coming on. I must hide my embarrassment."

The driver walked back to tell the others in the second car of Khalaf's sudden illness. He was laughing to the others, probably telling them how a condemned man wanted to cleanse his bowels when death would easily release them.

Standing next to the boulder, having no idea what might come next, Khalaf pretended to vomit, then made a show of squatting down next to the rock, his robe pulled up, actually relieving himself, taking advantage of his nervousness. Peering around the rock, he took in the two cars, the impatience of the passengers in the second car, and looked to the bodyguard of his car, seeing him checking the slide arm of his automatic. Whatever was to happen would come too late for him.

The bodyguard, with a nod from the VIPs in the second car, had decided this was as good a place as any to hold an execution and dump a body. A laugh of conspiracy between them and the bodyguard, with the pistol to his side, a menacing sneer on his face, as he turned towards Khalaf and took two steps to become the executioner, and an odd thing happened. In al-Awlaki's car, a phone rang. They all looked at each other, then sought the ringing phone. Certainly, one could not get reception in this part of the country through the hills that blocked signals.

It was Khalaf's phone, and all within the car wondered if they should answer the phone of the condemned. That thinking allowed the homing signal to continue to emit its broadcast.

The bodyguard looked to Khalaf, also wondering but now noticing — Why was this man about ready to die looking to the heavens? For forgiveness? Vain prayers to Allah. A momentary thought came to the guard. A glance to his right and left, then back to Khalaf. The phone kept ringing. The editor of *Inspire*, as a reporter, upset at the bother, grabbed at the phone to answer. He, too, saw Khalaf look upward. The editor knew. And turned to warn the pretender to the al-Qaeda throne in Yemen. Too late. The executioner saw it for two seconds: a microscopic reflection of sun against metal. Surprised panic and his last word: "Predator!"

A second later came obliteration.

When the noise and falling stray shrapnel had subsided, Khalaf picked himself up off the ground and looked at the two destroyed vehicles, smoldering wreckage, metal, and body parts.

Khalaf grimly recalled the code of the Al-Awaliki tribe: "We are the sparks of Hell; whomever interferes with us will be burned." Such irony.

He looked around, having no idea what he should do next. No, he should depart the scene as quickly as possible. And an idea came to him. Everyone around him, all that knew him as 'bin Laden's lowly messenger' were no more: Osama Bin Laden, those at the compound, al-Ramen, Shahin. Yes, Doctor al-Zawahiri knew him but not well and not with the intimacy of friendship. He would believe Khalaf had been killed along with the Council leaders and al-Awlaki. And the Doctor could never leave his hideout to discover the truth. As Sabz faked her own death in Wana to avoid a bad marriage, so too would he reinvent himself, and al-Qaeda would not be part of his future. But what future?

The Voice came to him. *Are you alive, Yusuf Saladin?*

He screamed out a relief of salvation. Allah would see him through this new danger. He laughed at hearing the Voice, finding strange comfort.

"Yes, I am," Yusuf Saladin shouted aloud, "Thanks to angels."

The Voice came again. *Yes, and they will help you on your journey.*

They were angels. They heard him when he spoke. He must listen to them.

His spirits lifted, his courage building from escaping death three times, twice from the skies and from the bridge. Allah and the angels favored him. He started laughing uncontrollably.

He heard a noise, a bell, and turned to see a lone villager coming over the hill, curious about the rising smoke, the smell of burned flesh in the air — to witness the yelling and joyous dancing of a strange man. The villager walked a path toward him, holding a rope to a beast of burden, the bell around the animal's neck.

The born-again new man, Yusuf, sighed through teary laughter, 'what does fate hold for me if I must enter a new life on the back of this donkey?'

FINAL REEL — Time for the Denouement

EPISODE THIRTY-SIX — The Angels and the Mujaddid

Scene 1: Non-spontaneous Press Conference
Setting: Gatwick Airport, Great Britain, October 1st, 2011

The disembarking passengers clearing customs surged around them. There were hugs of solid friendships among the four alumni of *King's Retribution,* those heroes of sung and unsung adventures.

"Good to see you both, and arriving with the common people versus your jet, how did you manage?" Holmes gave Fox a pat on the back.

"First class helps."

"Well, it is a business deduction," added Callie. "I went the length of the plane and counted three children and two different adults playing Skilleo Games."

"Well, welcome to London," Samantha locked arms between Callie and Hugh. "Wen wants to show you our little experiment. It should be happening soon."

"You are staging a flash mob for our benefit."

"No, but a surprise nevertheless, and then we will wine and dine you both and spend the next several days discussing Five Aces Studioz and the future of *King's Retribution.*"

Callie's response was sad.

"With King making slow therapy progress, I don't see much good for the show's continuance."

"Well, I have a few ideas to bounce off you both."

Wendell halted them off to the side, next to a boisterous group of anxious members of the Fourth Estate, a small gaggle of British and international press.

"I tried to coordinate this all for your benefit, but it's hard to initiate delays and extra baggage checks to have one airline a little late to match your arrival."

"Isn't he just the best 'fixer' you've ever met?" beamed Samantha, "And he's all mine."

They could see the press gain excitement and crowd around one of the exiting passengers. The journalistic interrogatories began.

"Mr. Saladin, are you aware of the amount of interest your essays are having within the Muslim communities?"

The target of the cameras and reporters' microphones, thrust in his face, seemed surprised.

"Essays?"

"Your third essay was published yesterday by *The Sun-Times*. 'Islamic Faith in the 22nd Century.'"

"I have just arrived and certainly will pick up a copy." Several of the media people laughed.

Another question: "In your first essay, you say that Sunni and Shi'ite should put aside differences and join in a new Islamic union. Do you feel that's possible?"

"Yes, that was written…by me." He paused. "Yes, I believe peace among our brothers and sisters should be the highest priority. A combined society of faiths is possible."

A few more questions were lobbed at him, and he answered cautiously and awkwardly.

Another reporter had her opportunity. "Can we look forward to seeing your thoughts in a book soon?"

A young woman garbed in Muslim dress of modest decorum pushed her way through the throng.

"Yes, he is working on a book," said Sabz, demurely, with lowered eyes, respectful of her husband-to-be in public, "but please give him a chance to recover from his trip. Contact us through the new Madrasah school he will be opening. His press secretary will be happy to set up interviews with you all."

The working press never accepts an ending dictated by others.

"A final question. Al Jazerra Television, here. Do you consider yourself *The Mujaddid* for this century?"

Yusuf Saladin reacted, taken off guard, but seeing a potential road map of the direction he must follow, the first, understanding the pitfalls of grabbing too quickly at the prize.

"I am a simple man, a messenger, you might say, neither *rasul* [direct messenger of Allah] or *nabi* [prophet] who hopes his words will bring all my Muslim brothers and sisters into a new Islamic harmony." He used his hand in a traditional thank you and farewell that some took as a blessing for all those present and those who saw it again when the interview was played over and over on televisions in Muslim populated countries and revisited many times on YouTube. Many thought highly of his modesty and sought to find and read his other writings.

Sabz led him by the arm towards the exit and an awaiting limousine. Holmes noted the newly patented celebrity pulled a cell phone from his jacket, looked at it, reacted disappointed at seeing no message, and put the phone away. He then turned to hug his wife-to-be with the ardor one sees in a soldier returning from war, to ask many questions of his absence, and to tell none himself.

Fox turned to Holmes showing his surprise.

"That's our Ali Baba? You stage-managed this whole affair with the reporters."

"Can never dismiss good press and yes, indeed our Ali Baba, reborn as Sheik Yusuf Saladin, to be a philosopher and teacher in Islam on how the modern Moslem should exist within modern society."

"Who or what is a Mujaddid?" Callie asked.

"A planted question, well placed," smiled Samantha.

"A Mujaddid is a person who comes once a century to revive Islam, bringing it back to its purity; such could be a prominent individual, a teacher, scholar, and yes, a caliph. I think Sheik Saladin's brain is churning right now on the ramifications of such possibilities."

"Of course, our Sheik doesn't have the full story," explained Samantha. "Wendell still hasn't completed the working script."

"And you expect him to do exactly what you say?" Callie was a little more skeptical.

"No, at a point he will become his own man, perhaps more the pragmatic politician, at which point he will hopefully have the savvy to compromise with liberals, moderates, and conservatives in all Islamic beliefs, hopefully finding common ground...."

"Which, by the way," Samantha interjected, "will be based on love for the fellow man, peace among your neighbors, and stop killing each other."

"That's a big order," whistled Fox.

"The big order is to give him support to find his own courage."

"The Voice." Fox was happy that his experimental tech was proving out.

"But someday the Voice he hears must end, his own voice to rise to speak to the masses."

"And that is?" From Callie, always the cautious skeptic.

Fox understood some products have limited usefulness. "The Skilleo jaw implant inserted during his 'auto accident' must be put into hiatus."

Holmes concurred. "When he makes his move from teacher to prophet to leader. We know what his ambition is; he has mentioned it before to Sabz in pillow talk. It will be up to us to help him achieve his goal if it restores peace and stability among nations."

"And what is our goal?"

610   S.P. Grogan

Holmes began leading the delegation of 'angels,' the team of *King's Retribution*, out the airport doors. As one might expect, the British day was filled with a light rain. Each couple drew close to their mate, heartfelt smiles all around.

"We are going to take the Arab Spring and mold it into the Pan-Arab Caliphate ruled by Sheik Yusuf Saladin."

Scene 2: Stormin' Back
Setting: Southeastern Kenya, One Year Later, 2012

The poachers, three of them carrying automatic rifles brought over from Somalia, walked in silence along the brush path, many miles within the boundaries of the Tsavo Conservation Area near the Galana River. For the last half hour, they had been listening to the trumpeting of the bull elephant and guessed he was in the stand of acacia trees just ahead. There, they spotted the largest land mammal in the world, its gigantic head swinging back and forth, displaying enormous tusks worth a fortune on the Asian markets. Running forward, the lead man dropped to a knee, took careful aim, and spit out a burst of rifle fire. The poacher's expression was puzzled as his compatriots, laughing at his apparent miss, unloaded their weapons, each knowing they had struck the beast. However, the animal did not collapse but continued its trumpeting calling, shaking its head, again and again, the same movement, over and over.

Sirens screamed, and from hidden blinds, Park Rangers, with their own firepower, stepped into view, the barrels of their rifles aimed at the three men. A loudspeaker blared out in English: "Throw down your weapons and put your hands in the air." Another voice made the same command in the local dialect. A jeep bowled through the underbrush and pulled within feet of the criminals as they complied and surrendered to the overwhelming force.

From the Jeep, leaning heavily on a lavishly ornate and decorated cane sculpted in African mahogany stepped Colonel David 'Storm' King (ret.). "I arrest you in the name of decency to protect our wildlife heritage. You will now face *King's Justice*." He paused for a moment, his face a malevolent grin, sweat leaking from under his pith helmet. He then yelled, "Cut!"

A small bus came up to him, and the mini production crew alighted.

"Abbas, sorry, old fellow, but it looks like they peppered up Jumbo, full of holes." They both looked at the animatronic creature still doing its routine. Abbas pushed a remote button, and the fake elephant went into stasis.

"I'll get on it. We have a pacing lion ready for the next episode."

"Good." Storm wiped his brow with a wet towel handed to him by a staff member, a cute young thing. Storm's eyes lingered on her for a second too long, but obvious to all.

Storm being Storm.

"This heat is getting to me. A gin and tonic would do the trick right about now."

"Here's a cold ice tea," replied Bennie, handing over a thermos. "Remember your contract."

"Yes, yes, I do, but considering everything, a little libation might add some edge to my character."

"Storm, you are the top show on Animal Planet. *King's Justice — The African Campaign* is renewed for another year. And you don't have to worry about playing up to advertisers. SammyC Wildlife Foundation underwrites the program costs. This is your cash cow. Treat it gently."

Storm's eyes followed the attractive young intern snapping background publicity stills.

"And," added Bennie, pulling King back into his reality check. "You are a father figure to all nature-loving children around the world; *National Geographic* wants to do a documentary on your saving African wildlife from extinction. Remember the image; remember the large paycheck that comes with the image. A soldier's duty, Colonel."

Storm affirmed his mission. "That's right, duty. And the fact that we are one of the top shows on cable." Then, he returned to business, always the main man on battlefield logistics. "CAM TWO, get a close-up of them carting off our suspects. The viewing audience must be made aware that our planet and its creatures must be protected."

Bennie and Abbas rolled their eyes behind Storm's back but accepted their duty as glorified babysitters, stipulated in their contracts, with a generous bonus by Five Aces Studioz. 'Combat pay' as they reminded each other many times during the Kenyan production season.

Scene 3: Game Play
Setting: Silicon Valley, south of San Francisco, One year later, 2012

"Can I read you this article out of the *Hollywood Reporter*?"

Callie put down the book that Holmes and Samantha had mailed to them, the one just published and released by their friendly terrorist from the bridge, Ali Baba, though the author's name on the book's cover read Sheik Yusuf Saladin.

"Sure. Feel-good philosophy with a dash of world politics was about to put me to sleep. Where's a good wordsmith like Elmore Leonard, even Michael Connelly, for some hard-boiled Bosch dialogue? So, what do you have?" She curled her legs under herself on the couch. They were at 'their' place, once Hugh's, now her things were slowly appearing in the closets. Still, the décor remained minimalist and not frou-frou. Callie never was a *House Beautiful* sort of girl.

Hugh read:

"'Reviews are positive over ABC's debut show, *Queen's Revenge*, put out by the Five Aces Studioz and starring Carlita 'Callie' Cardoza, the former co-star of *King's Retribution*. The show also features former SEAL Shawn Pacheco who some are calling the Young Stallone.

'The premise of *Queen's Revenge* is similar to the bounty hunters of *King's Retribution*, but with a new twist, *cybercrime*. As you have heard, *King's Retribution* will be released next year as a full-on action film starring the original television cast. Independent testing on *Queen's Revenge* scored high among three strong demographics; Cardoza, a steaming bombshell ex-cop, pulling in the male audience; women drawn to ex-SEAL Shawn Pacheco, especially when he takes off his shirt, reminiscent of Storm King's antics (sorry girls, Shawn's married); and finally, the plot line, creating top suspense in the cyber hunt for white collar criminals which seems to have attracted the geeks away from their Xboxes and PlayStations. Congrats to *Queen's Revenge* on your upcoming second season.'" Hugh gave her the once-over.

"'Steaming bombshell,' is that my soulmate?"

"You want me to show you my interpretation of 'steamy' as an adjective?"

"Yes, but later." He handed her a small oblong box, the cardboard sleeve a familiar design of pink paper with 'C-4 Explosive' markings.

She looked at it warily but saw his smile. "When they called me a bombshell, you shouldn't take it literally. Besides, I don't need any more gifts from you; the necklace expresses what you sometimes can't." She toyed with the diamonds, extravagant, suggestive to the message given, the emotional turf staked.

Fox spoke with excitement, something Callie relished as a good trait in him. "Holmes suggested the paper, for old time's sake. We will test market it, but I think the buyer will understand the significance of packaging once they're into the game."

"A new game?" Out of the covering sleeve, she looked at the cover, like a classic motion picture poster of the 1940s, all action, depicting four people running towards the camera, their guns blazing, explosions surrounding them, a truck tipping over a bridge.

Terror on Demon Bridge read the game title.

"Hugh, you can't be serious?"

"The understanding agreed to by *King's Retribution* and by each of us, and the U.S. government is never to speak of what happened in Abbottabad, at the amusement parks or the bridge; or how American thriller authors were used in bits and pieces to foment one of the most diabolical terrorist plots ever unleashed on our soil. I have said nothing, only a game plot that tells an interesting story about trying to stop a terrorist plot.

"Greenscreen characters, some animation. With Level Six, some of the terrorists melt into zombies. Of course, the government won't believe a VR game could create real threat circumstances." He gave a sarcastic laugh at the implied irony.

Callie frowned. "One of the women on this cover looks a lot like me."

"Who, you? *The steaming bombshell?* I find you more the firecracker type." She gave him a disbelieving look. He continued, shrugging his shoulders, in an effort to extract himself, "In the game, there are standardized characters if you don't want to build your own avatar."

"The others on the cover look a lot like Wen, Sam, and you. Let me ask, what's the name of my 'standardized' character?"

He gave an impish grin. "'Viper.' The one that might look like me is 'Woolf.'"

"Okay, Wolfie, come over here and let's play this game and see who can kill off the most terrorists and save America. But let's do it differently: 'Strip Video Game,' the loser will end up naked."

"No fair. I tested the prototype against our female engineers and won every game."

"Sexist, chauvinistic deviant." Slugging him in the shoulder brought her within arm's reach. And he reached.

"And the point of your game, Wolfie, is what? As I see it, lose or win, I still win."

"Oh, yeah," Hugh Fox, president of Skilleo Games Technology, finally caught on.

Callie smiled as a devilish Viper might; sometimes, with geniuses, you got to lead them by....

Scene 4: Making Deposits
Setting: London Financial District, 2012

The banker held out her hand, and the other woman shook it and sat down.

"And you want to open an account, Miss...."

"Carlisle. Samantha Carlisle."

"You wouldn't happen to be, and pardon me for being rude, 'SammyC.'"

"The same."

The young girl flushed.

"Oh, I am a big fan of your fashion. I have several outfits and wear them when I can."

Samantha regarded the nameplate on the banker's desk, which read, "Sabz S."

"Nice to find someone who appreciates quality design. Do I call you Sabz, or what is your last name if we are going to be banker and customer?

"Saladin. Sabz… Saladin, Head of New Accounts."

"Saladin? You aren't related to that famous author, are you?"

Embarrassment from Sabz.

"Yes, he is my husband."

"Why, my dear, you should be so proud. An immediate best-seller throughout the world everyone is talking about '*A Modern Moslem Life.*' For a non-Islamic person, it opened such a new world of possibilities between world religions, and that one part of bringing all Muslim countries into their own style of a United Nations, very progressive intellect."

"I am impressed you read it. There have been critics, those I know who have not read the book, and said it was trash, like that German book by Hitler."

"Oh, you mean, 'My Struggle.' In German, '*Mein Kampf.*' Rubbish. Nothing like it at all, I'm sure. Any public figure will have envious naysayers," and Samantha paused with a little of her own inside humor, 'until all truths are self-evident.'"

"Yes, the Sheik, my husband, in many countries, is being recognized for his wisdom."

"To imagine he wrote with such insight. He did not have help in writing this book, did he? Such a gifted work."

Sabz stumbled. "No, he worked very hard; it is all his own words."

"Well, many congratulations to you both."

Sabz picked up the bank account forms. "What sort of account do you want to be opening?"

"I should ask you. On the one hand, I am considering opening a small boutique where I can create new designs under another brand. My non-compete clause runs out this year, so I will start over, but just for the fun of it. So, a business account. And then, I want an account where I can draw on funds for some speculation in the stock market."

"Stock market? I should not talk personally, but I do the same thing. My husband has been generous and allows me a small account to pursue growth companies, mostly American high tech."

"Really? That's exactly what I do. In fact, my stockbroker put me into a new fast-growth company called Facebook before it went public."

"That is a remarkable coincidence. I was able to talk my husband into making a similar purchase. We are quite fortunate and look forward to holding the company long term."

"I agree. I think social media tech companies might hold promise. You know, we should talk sometime soon, maybe over morning coffee. I would be interested in your opinion on some of my other investments."

"I would like that very much. I don't believe it would be against bank policy."

"No, of course not, I'm sure. And perhaps, you and your husband might wish to join me, my boyfriend, and a few friends for a small social gathering next week."

"Oh, I'm sorry; although I would be honored, my husband is spending a lot of time working on his presentation when he goes on his book tour."

"A book tour? How exciting. I am sure the crowds will be thick; he will be mobbed with fans."

"That is what I am afraid of. More so of the religious zealots who cannot consider the suggestion of change as positive for all."

"My exact sentiments. Yes, you do have reason to worry. Fame brings out the unhinged. There are even crazies in the fashion world. My friends, Gianni Versace and Maurizio Gucci, were both murdered. I should give you my boyfriend's business card; he is in the security business. He provides bodyguards and security systems for some of the top celebrities in the U.K, movie stars, even soccer stars."

"Soccer stars?"

"Oh, yes, your European football. We get free tickets all the time to the major matches. You seem interested? Let me know, and I will arrange some tickets. Here is his card; please call him, or have your husband or his publisher call Wendell's office. One can't be too careful in this turbulent world, especially when it comes to someone who has become as famous as your husband."

"Oh, yes," agreed Sabz, eager to place the business card of *Sherlock Holmes Security* where she would not lose it.

"Shall we start doing the paperwork? I have been so lucky to meet you, Mrs. Saladin."

Outside the bank, after her account was opened and an invitation firmed up to have coffee with Sabz in two days, Samantha met up with Wendell, sitting on a park bench, scanning his copy of "*A Modern Moslem Life.*" He was inspecting how the writing from his clandestine cabal of professors, with him as executive editor, had been translated into print by author Sheik Yusuf Saladin.

"A very nice girl," said Samantha. "I truly believe we will become close friends. And you did overhear correctly; on her advice, her husband made several million dollars in an early buy into this Facebook and, in their culture of gratitude, gave her some pin money of half a mil to play the market. I may have met my analytic match."

"What of Sherlock Holmes Security?"

"The bait is dangling, and they should take it. She is afraid for him, and he knows his old comrades might want to set an example against his polemic on 'modernizing moderation.'"

616 S.P. Grogan

"I will take very good care of him. Keep him alive and hope he amounts to something positive for us all."

"Well, if he doesn't prove out, don't have him assassinated. You are definitely retired."

"You mean, have Brady fly a drone over him. No, we are setting this plan in motion, planting the seeds of what we believe is the right course. The war I now fight is on the battlefield of publishing marketing. Winning reader eyeballs. Saladin must grow himself, nourish, find wisdom; then, the harvest, good or bad, will be the fruit of his conviction. We can only pray that his ambition is refocused on this better path. Here is where we must have faith in a higher authority, whether God, Allah, or Zeus." Holmes put his arm around Samantha, happy to be with her. They should go home, make love, and then he would go back to his writing. He knew that churning out good writing was now his challenge to meet. Life adventures and love appreciated must be written perfectly. All great writing must evolve from personal experience.

Samantha had a thought.

"Saladin writing bestsellers and proselytizing to small groups is one thing, but multi-media marketing would reach a wider audience. Let's film a documentary about him."

"Good idea, reach out to the less literate masses, those who can handle a commercial or two as we change the world." Holmes caught a glimpse of the person following them. Over his shoulder, not missing a step, he shouted,

"Did you get the bank meeting with Sam and Sabz and what we just said; all of that?"

CAM ONE nodded and spoke, "Yes, a good beginning."

Scene 5: Traffic Jam
Setting: Los Angeles, California, One year later, 2013

The limousine broke down with a flat tire on the highway, on the worst highway system in the United States, the East Los Angeles Interchange, 2.5 miles from downtown Los Angeles. Harriet worried they would be late for their first child's baptism at the Cathedral of Our Lady of the Angels.

"No, we are going to make it," assured Booker Langston. "I gave us extra time for such an event." That extra time had really been allotted to quick visits with old friends. Now it would be a close call. A church with 500,000 parishioners was not tolerant of their slotted schedules out of whack.

"Here comes Roadside Assistance," he told his wife, motioning to the hired driver, who went over to ask Freeway Service Patrol for help changing the tire. Their limo guy had balked at mussing his uniform, and Booker did not think it proper on this special day to sue the guy

Crimson Scimitar   617

for stupidity or pop him a fist to the nose. Harriet would frown on such an outburst. They were a team. She had become Harriet Eberhardt-Langston, the name looking special beside her husband's name in the law office they had established in Century City. Fame from terrorist defense and terrorist kidnapping had brought in paying clients. Close proximity law work had brought marriage and the baby in that order.

From inside the air-conditioned limo, Harry E-L asked, "Did Sam and Wen make their flight in on time?" She felt the jack begin lifting the car with her and their nursing baby inside.

"Yesterday. Wen wanted to scope out where he was doing his book signing on Saturday to launch the West Coast tour." Wendell Holmes, the international security expert, had written a spy-kidnap thriller, *Mountebank Dies First,* under the pseudonym Stephen Hero.

Harry, in her mind, was checking off the guest list. Sam and Hugh were the godparents-designate. She had read the tabloids but had to ask her husband.

"Will Hugh and Callie arrive together or separately?"

"Who knows?" As sometimes happens, with the pressure cookers of fame and fortune, the 'A-list' personalities with scheduling conflicts, arguing over emotional prioritizing needs, within the last year pushed Hugh Fox and Callie Cardoza into 'a California type estrangement,' perfect fodder for the paparazzi, though not for being loveless or having torrid affairs, but more separate career path demands. Callie juggled her steady television series stardom with recent highly-selected roles in major motion pictures. Latino power was on the rise, and she was there to grab it. Hugh, comfortable as the inventor brainiac, now billionaire twice over, gained satisfaction building better tech mousetraps, a bona fide eccentric recluse known to disappear for weeks on end, hiding in some secret workshop with another odd fellow named Gizmo. The tabloids had a rumor that even Booker accepted, that the 'Hugh-Callie couple,' met once a month to satisfy urges, then went their separate ways, were given the sobriquet of the ones who popularized the modern yet awkward open relationship of 'friends with benefits,' outdoing, they said, the plot of the 2011 movie of the same name. With such unwanted publicity, of course, a spec script for a reality show of coupled friends based on the 'fad' was heading to a private home to produce a pilot.

The tire was being changed. They would be on their way shortly. Back on schedule, Booker could easily smile at the mother in the back seat nursing her child, ready for innocence to be protected by the splashing of holy water.

Booker gazed at his side of the road, watching the rat-race traffic patterns surrounding them. Whizzing and zipping. Highways I-5, I-10, Route 101, and State Route 60, all freeways crisscrossing, colliding in shifting alignments confusing all with thousands of directional signage. Going everywhere. They were parked right at what many called 'Malfunction Junction' or 'The Beast' interchange, or the 'East Delay Interchange.'

618   S.P. Grogan

At this moment, for Booker, it started as a curious glance as he looked across the highway and viewed two carrier freight trucks in their own tailgate crawl going in the opposite direction. He turned and looked at the overpass they had recently driven under before stopping. Then he saw a truck motoring down the highway similar to the others; they all had the same markings. His worried expression said it all.

Booker Langston whirled again and viewed another carrier truck as it moved slowly past the limousine in the outside lane, on their side, going their way, a lot of dents on its side and a red graffiti slash on the back of the cargo container.

Booker had not participated in the 'reading club' of trying to decipher best-selling novels and movies, but he had watched one movie years earlier and definitely recalled the ending of *Raiders of the Lost Ark* (1981). The federal government had secured the most dangerous of holy weapons in an innocuous bureaucratic location where it would be forgotten by all, still capable of annihilation.

He saw the reality of such thinking as each truck (and he saw several of them) all going somewhere…in different directions… all boldly labeled *Eagle Freight*, each bearing the colorful logo of the majestic national bird, as prey, swooping down, talons outstretched, to grasp the helpless trout.

Scene 6: Shopping List
Setting: Bookstore, Berlin, Germany, The Year 2020

Hans Luber ('Lubbie') hated everything and everybody, and if they had tested him, he would have been found certifiable and mentally incompetent, but he hid it well.

The bookstore salesclerk only saw a customer.

"Can I help you?"

"I have a reading list of books." He handed it over. "Do you have these?"

"Why, yes, I think we do have most. A few are now out in paperback, less expensive. Two of your titles are actually movies."

"Yes, I know."

"We should have those in our DVD and Audio section." The bookstore salesclerk again scanned the list. "You seem to be a fan of action thrillers. You like those cliffhangers — the world about ready to be blown up, where the good guys come to the rescue at the last minute?"

Lubbie replied, "I like to wonder what would happen if the good guys did not show up in time."

The salesclerk had no witty response but noticed the young man was carrying a dog-eared copy of a book filled with yellow Post-It notes for marking the pages important to him. With friendly customer service in mind, he asked,

"That must be a great story. Is that a book like these on your list?"

"Yes," said Lubbie, his face showing what could be a tight smile — or not. "It is my Bible. One must learn from mistakes and make improvements." He showed the clerk the title: *Crimson Scimitar.*

Scene 7: Prophetic Arrival
Setting: Eagle Pass, Texas — The U.S-Mexico Border, The Year 2023

He was one of 300 people who waded across the Rio Grande that day. The group at this particular crossing at Eagle Pass, Texas, was made up of every type of individual — families, small children on their own who would be called 'unaccompanied minors,' pregnant women who had started out their journey not pregnant, young men who banded together for protection, or a few like him, 'loners.' They represented a United Nations of ethnicities, some following dreams, some desiring easy greed, all hearing the politicians who were safe behind guarded gates, say, 'Come, our border is open to you.' He did not come impoverished. He had money; he had purpose. He had paid for his way here, knowing he could not come through customs and obey the laws of the land, and would not lower himself to pay the coyotes operated by the cartels who held control over the human smuggling routes. He could have made money with them as a drug mule. No, he had purpose.

When he was processed, he told them in broken English he was from Syria, fleeing genocide in the war between factions supported by changing interests of world powers. He was not from Syria but from Yemen. They could not tell the difference. He had discarded his passport in the desert brush.

The politicians and the NCOs, who said they cared but who did not really care but sent the undocumented on to an uncertain and dangerous future to hide in this large wealthy country. So, he was given papers that said he would have to report back to be adjudicated to see if America would let him in, but they already had. He would never come back to enter their nightmare system. He had contacts, people already here, who would help him find a job at this particular company. Acclimate. He had a purpose. He had a plan. It had been approved. Seem innocuous. It would take two years, he believed, 2025, before he could initiate his plan, their plan.

When one of the officials, who really did not care, who was not planning on helping him, asked what he intended to do now that he was in this society, the 'freest' on earth, he thought, and had been thinking, where he could do the most damage, he replied, "I want to work in the television industry in California." He was smiled at as if they knew he would end up picking tomatoes in Tulare County. No, he had purpose. When another official, the paperwork clerk, asked for his name, he gave it to them and was questioned, 'How do you spell it? That's Arabic, an odd name. Does your name have meaning?' he looked at them and proudly said, "It means 'Son of Shahin.'"

اذهب بسلام

RELATED READING

Bergen, Peter, *The Rise and Fall of Osama bin Laden,* Simon & Schuster (2021)

bin Laden, Najwa; bin Laden Omar; Sasson, Jean, *Growing Up bin Laden*, St.Martin's Griffin Edition (2010)

Hawkins, Edward H., *Wellspring*, Echo House (1969)

Keegan, John, *Intelligence in War*, Alfred A. Knopf (2003)

Lahoud, Nelly, *The Bin Laden Papers*, Yale University Press (2022)

Lawrence, Bruce (Editor), *Messages to the World, The Statements of Osama bin Laden*, Verso (2005)

Owen, Mark, *No Easy Day,* Dutton (2012)

Sun Tzu, *The Art of War,* Denma Translation Group, Shambhala Publications. (2002)

Takacs, Stacy, *Terrorism TV, Popular Entertainment in Post-9/11 America,* University of Kansas Press (2012)

Whitcomb, Christopher, *Inside FBI Hostage Rescue Team, Cold Zero*, Little Brown & Co. (2001)

Author's Notes

Special thanks to Histria Books for giving me the opportunity to re-imagine this ranging near-true historical epic. Of course, a thousand thanks to my wife, Pamela Kure Grogan, who has supported me in my desire to be a storyteller. Thanks to supporters who read and gave constructive improvement towards the manuscript's improvement. And, to Kona the cat, who sleeps on a cardboard box on my writing desk and reminds me to take breaks and pamper her.

I hope you enjoyed this fresh new perspective of *what-if* fiction.

In writing a contemporary international political action docu-thriller, the issue sometimes arises: at what point must the story's timeline be set firm and the writing finished? An almost-true thriller becomes at risk against whatever occurs in the future; current events might impact your plotting, either successful as a prophecy come true or anachronistic improbabilities relegated to a dusty bookshelf.

Over a decade ago, in writing my then-earlier plotline, I had him captured and tried in a U.S. Court (and acquitted!). Halfway through my first draft manuscript, Osama bin Laden was killed by U.S. Navy SEALS. So, off and on over ten years, I reworked my manuscript, cleaning up and adding an entire section creating *The Trial of the Century*. I welcome friendly banter from trial attorneys who feel they could have presented better prosecution/defense arguments. If you know my past works with a Quest Mystery theme you might discover at www.CrimsonScimitar.com a contest challenging participants to write a better: 'how I would defend Osama bin Laden'.

Then, to those thriller authors whose works I imagined within this story, there is no apology as I am actually applauding their success in bringing to life realistic probabilities in their own novels, par excellence of masters in plotting the *what-if* genre.

Special attribution and thanks to editor Sheila Grimes, who cleaned up and tightened the ramblings; to book cover designer Silvio Sequera; to photo magic from barrettadamsfineart.com and outstanding bridge photo by Mariordo (Mario Roberto Durán Ortiz) Own work, CC BY-SA 4.0, https://commons.wikimedia.org/w/index.php?curid=63285153

Finally, the result I hoped to convey is an entirely new envisioned story with parables and life experiences valuable today. And though we may believe we are safe and comfortable in our insulated world, there are those out there who still wish to do harm to our democratic ideals of freedom for all citizens. My point: enjoy life, but support vigilance against future Crimson Scimitar plots.

Also, by S.P. Grogan

Lafayette: *Courtier to Crown Fugitive*

Atomic Dreams at the Red Tiki Lounge

Vegas Die, *a Quest Murder Mystery*

Captain Cooked: *Hawaiian Mystery of Romance, Revenge and Recipes*
[2022 'Best Food Novel' from Gourmand International Cookbook Awards]

Cookbook Passion (Editor)